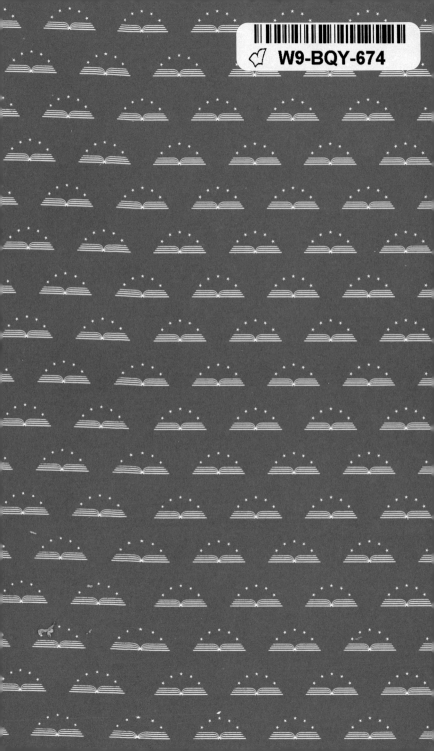

WOMEN CRIME WRITERS

FOUR SUSPENSE
NOVELS OF THE 1950s

WOMEN CRIME WRITERS

FOUR SUSPENSE NOVELS OF THE 1950s

Mischief • Charlotte Armstrong
The Blunderer • Patricia Highsmith
Beast in View • Margaret Millar
Fools' Gold • Dolores Hitchens

Sarah Weinman, *editor*

THE LIBRARY OF AMERICA

Contents

For an online companion to this volume visit womencrime.loa.org.

MISCHIEF

Charlotte Armstrong

Chapter 1

A MR. PETER O. JONES, the editor and publisher of the Brennerton *Star-Gazette*, was standing in a bathroom in a hotel in New York City, scrubbing his nails. Through the open door, his wife, Ruth, saw his naked neck stiffen, saw him fix his image with his eye, heard him declaim over the rush of running water, "Ladies and gentlemen . . ." She winked at Bunny.

Ruth in her long petticoat was sitting at the dressing table, having resolved to be as perfectly, as exquisitely groomed as ever a woman was in the world, this night. She was very gently powdering her thin bare shoulders. Every fair hair on her head was already in shining order. Her carefully reddened lips kept smiling because she knew this long-drawn-out ritual, this polishing of every tooth and every toenail, was only to heighten the wonderful fun.

It was The Night. Ruth sighed, from a complexity of emotions.

What a formula, she thought, is a hotel room. Everything one needs. And every detail pursued with such heavy-handed comfort, such gloomy good taste, it becomes a formula for luxury. The twin beds, severely clean, austerely spread. The lamp and the telephone between. Dresser, dressing table. Desk and desk chair (if the human unit needs to take his pen in hand). Bank of windows, on a court, with the big steam radiator across below them, metal topped. Curtains in hotel-ecru. Draperies in hotel-brocade. Easy chair in hotel-maroon. The standing lamp. The standing ash tray, that hideous useful thing. The vast empty closet. And the bath. The tiles. The big towels. The small soap. The very hot water.

Over this basic formula they had spread the froth of their preparations, in that jolly disorder that a hotel room permits. Her rose-colored evening dress swung with the hook of its hanger over the closet door. Peter's rummaged suitcase stood open on the luggage bench and his things were strewn on his bed. The dresser top was piled with stuff that at home would have been hidden in the drawers. Powder and ashes had spilled gloriously on the carpet. All the lights were blazing.

All the lights were blazing in Bunny's room, too, the adjoining room that was exactly like this one, except that left was right and maroon was blue.

Peter turned the water off, reached for a towel, stood in the bathroom door in singlet and his dress trousers with his suspenders hanging down over his rump. Turning out his patent-leather toes, he bowed. "Ladies and gentlemen . . ." He began to pantomime, clowning for Bunny. Ruth thought, fondly, How clever he is! She turned to watch what she loved to see, the smooth skin of Bunny's face ripple and twinkle as it always did before the giggle came out.

Bunny was nine. Her dark brows went up at the outside just like Peter's. In her blue wooley robe, Bunny hunched on the foot of Ruth's bed, her arms around her ankles, and one bunny-slipper stepping on the toe of the other. Her dark hair went smoothly back into the fat braids, so often living and warm in Ruth's hands. Ruth's heart felt as if something squeezed it, quickly, and as quickly let it go.

Peter, with a fine-flung gesture, called down fire from heaven to be witness to his wordless passion, and bowed to make-believe applause. Bunny took her cue, let go her ankles, clapped once, lost her balance and toppled over, giggling. "You see!" said Peter, poking the blue bundle on the bed in a ticklish spot. "Going to mow 'em down!"

"Peter," said Ruth in fright and curiosity, "do you know what you're going to say?"

"Well, I know what I'm going to *do*. I'm going to rise up and take a good grip on the rug with my toes and open my mouth. Oh, sure, I know what I'm going to say, in a way. I don't know how I'm going to put it, if that's what you mean."

"Oh, Peter!" She sucked in breath. She didn't understand how anyone could do such a thing as make a speech. Something made her heart jump at the mere thought of it.

"Don't get me wrong," said Peter. "I'm terrified." She knew he was. She knew he'd make the speech, nevertheless, and do it well. She knew, too, that her own tense partisanship was helpful to him, and even her fright was a channel that drew off some of his.

". . . time is it, honey?"

"Quarter after six." Their eyes met, briefly. Hers with a flick of worry. His with that quick dark reassurance.

He picked his dress shirt with the studs all in place off his bed. "Which one of you two dames wants to button me up?"

"Me!" squealed Bunny. So Peter sat on the hard rim of the footboard. "Daddy, why does your shirt pretend it buttons in the front when it buttons in the back?"

"Civilization. Tradition in the front. Business in the back. How you doing?"

"O.K.," said Bunny with a puff of effort. She never questioned Peter's polysyllables.

Business, thought Ruth darkly. "Peter," she said, "I hope you know what I think of your sister, Betty!"

"I couldn't print it," he answered promptly.

"Business," said Ruth as darkly as she felt. "Her and her business appointment! On a Saturday night! *I* think she's got a heavy date."

"Can't tell," said Peter lightly, cautiously.

"I don't see *how* she could break her date with us! Do you? Really?"

Ruth heard again Betty's high and somewhat affected voice on the phone. ". . . Terribly sorry, darling. Of course, if you simply can't get anyone, I'll cut this thing and I *will* come. . . . But I thought perhaps, if you *could* . . . ?" and Ruth stiffened once more with that shock and the anger.

Important! What kind of business appointment could be so important for Betty Jones—the silly little chit! Here in New York six months, with her job that paid what? fifty dollars a week? What on earth could Betty Jones do on a Saturday night that could be Important Business?

For years, now, Ruth had resented but been unable to combat, her sister-in-law's manner that assumed, so ignorantly and unjustly, that Ruth was done for. Ruth's goose was cooked. Oh, Ruth was buried with the rank and file, and the drab stones all said Housewife, that drab and piteous label. There was no use. One could only wait and someday . . .

"We'll try, Betty," Ruth had said, very coldly, and hung up and turned an anguished face to Peter. What if she had to plead and beg? Or not go to the ball?

But Peter had fixed it. By some hocus-pocus, he had fared forth into the halls and passages of the hotel, and he had fixed it. And Ruth had called Betty back and said, coolly, "Don't bother . . ."

"But how could she welsh like that," murmured Ruth, "when she knows . . ."

"Hold still, Daddy."

"Excuse it, pet. Look, Ruthie. Sis takes herself awful hard as the career girl. You know that. Someday . . ." Their eyes met and the gleam in Peter's was satisfactory. "Besides," he went on, "I don't suppose she thinks this convention amounts to much. Corn-fed gathering of country editors. Provincial, hm?"

"There you are!" said Ruth indignantly. "There *you* sit, seeing *her* point of view. But can she see ours? Night of the banquet, and your speech, and it was all arranged weeks ago. What if we couldn't have gotten anybody?"

"She did say she'd come if she must. No use to be bitter."

Ruth bit her lip.

"Don't fret, Cinderella," grinned Peter. "You shall go to the ball."

Ruth blinked, because he was right . . . no use to be bitter. She kicked off her mules and bent to reach for her evening shoes, feeling the soft brush of her own hair on her bare shoulders. "Oh, dem golden slippers . . ." whistled Peter, and Ruth saw Bunny's solemn eyes peek around his shoulder. For the audience, Ruth fell back into the rhythm. She arched her pretty feet and put them slowly, ceremoniously into her golden slippers.

"Someday," said Peter, with his dark eyes glowing, "do you know, girls, who's going to be putting on her golden slippers to go to the ball?"

"Bunny O. Jones," said Ruth at once.

"And who's going to be sitting with their bedroom slippers on, watching her?"

"You and me," Ruth said. Their eyes met, smiled. We'll grow old. It won't matter.

Bunny said, in a practical voice, "Is my sitter coming pretty soon?"

Peter pinched the toes in the furry slippers. "Pretty soon. And you're going to go to sleep in your room with two beds, one for each pigtail. And what are you going to do in the morning?"

"Telephone," said Bunny.

"And say?"

"Room service."

"And then?"

"This is Miss Bunny O. Jones. I want my breakfast, please."

"In room?"

"Room 809." Bunny flushed and started over again. "'This is Miss Bunny O. Jones in room 809. I want my breakfast, please.' And if they don't know what I'm talking about, I'll say, 'My Daddy, Mr. Peter O. Jones, ordered it last night.'"

"And when the man knocks on the door?"

"I'll unlock the door and run quick back in my bed."

"That's right. The key's in your door. And then they'll bring in the wagon."

"Daddy, it isn't a real wagon."

"No horses, I'll admit. A mere pushing type of wagon. And on it's going to be a whole bunch of silver dishes and your orange juice sitting in the biggest mess of cracked ice you ever saw, enough to make about four snowballs. And you'll eat your breakfast, putting on as much sugar and cream as you want, and after a while Daddy will groan and wake up."

"And tomorrow's the day," Ruth said, "you're going to the magic eating store."

"I don't bleeve it!" said Bunny, but her face was rippling.

"Oh, you don't, Miss Bunny O. Jones? Well, you'll see!"

They all three had the middle initial O. Ruth's name had been Olsen, and Peter was delighted with the coincidence. People named Jones, claimed he, had to do something. Peter O. Jones, he always was. And Bunny ran it together so that, more than once, school records had used the apostrophe.

"Quite a lot like a zoo," Peter was explaining. "A whole bunch of little glass cages and in one there's a hot meat pie, and in another there's a big fat salad, and all you do is put in your nickels and presto chango."

"But you have to have nickels," said Bunny shrewdly.

"Well, yes," said her daddy. "In the olden days, a magic wand was the thing. Now, of course, it's nickels." He grinned. He had begun the struggle with his collar.

"Peter," said Ruth suddenly, "do you believe in the elevator boy? Do you believe in his niece? Is she coming?"

"Certainly," said Peter, with his brows winging. "Why would he say so?"

"I don't know—" For Ruth, the room was rocking. The bright box it was had become dreamlike. And the city over which it hung was fabulous and all its denizens were phantoms.

"Said she'd be glad to," Peter was saying. "First, I spoke to that colored woman, that awfully nice-looking woman, the one who was so friendly? But she's—uh—dated up. So this Eddie overheard us and he offered. Glad to earn the money, he said."

"It takes nickels . . . ?" murmured Ruth.

"Papa's wand. Imagine, hon. This Eddie's been running the same elevator for fourteen years. You know which one he is, don't you?"

"I guess . . ."

"Lives up in the Bronx. No children, he told me. He'll tell you, at the drop of a hat. Speaks fondly of his wife. Must be a nice woman. This girl, now . . . they seem to have taken her in out of the goodness of their hearts since his brother died." Peter sucked his cheek. "Fourteen years, up and down. And he still runs that elevator as if his heart was in it to do it perfectly. I've seen 'em so blasé—make your hair curl. Wonder what he gets a week?"

Ruth sighed. Her momentary feeling that it was all myth was blown away. The little man who ran the elevator was real, of course . . . a human being, with a life, a wife, a budget . . . with brothers and sisters like everybody else and a niece to oblige. It was just like home, after all. You needed somebody. You asked around. It was just like asking the Johnstones who might say all their sitters were busy but they knew someone who knew somebody. You set up a kind of chain of inquiry and after a while it dredged up what you wanted. People were people and they passed the word and obliged each other and that was the way it went all over the world, truly.

"The niece comes from the Middle West someplace," Peter was saying. "Experienced, he says. I suppose a little extra means something in a setup like that."

Ruth thought, all at once, that it was better to be paying

someone, hiring someone, having the leverage of that power, than taking such a one as Betty's time for free. She smiled and reached out her hand.

"Oh boy," said her husband, "comes the twelve-dollar smell!"

"Twelve dollars and fifty cents, don't forget!" Ruth took the tiny stopper out, touched her shoulders with the precious stuff.

Peter bent over and sniffed violently. He said in her ear, "Would a couple of symmetrical toothmarks look good?" She saw herself laughing, in the glass, and Peter's dark keen face against her yellow hair.

". . . me smell," demanded Bunny.

So Ruth crossed with her pretty petticoat swirling, turned the plump little paw, touched the back of it with the perfume. "Deelicious!" said Bunny, sniffing violently as her daddy had done.

Ruth looked down at the white clean part in the dark hair. All of a sudden, she saw their two connecting rooms, the two bright boxes on the inner rim of the doughnut of this eighth floor, suspended above the boiling city. And the rising noise surrounded them like smoke . . . the honks, clangs, shouts and murmurs, the sound and fury . . . and her heart was squeezed again. And she thought, We couldn't have left her two thousand miles away . . . but we shouldn't have brought her . . . but we couldn't have left her. . . .

The Hotel Majestic was neither large nor small, neither cheap nor costly. Not the last word, it wasn't dowdy, either. It was conservative. It tried to be smart about it, in a modest way. It took the middle road. Even the elevators, although they ran smoothly, did so with a modest speed.

Eddie Munro stopped for a light at the eighth floor. A young man got on, turned at once to face the door. They sank downward in silence.

Out of the corners of their eyes, they typed each other, quickly. Eddie saw the easy grace of a tall body, the arrogant carriage of the high head, the crew cut that was somehow arrogant, too. The sharp cut of the good-looking face, the long nose with the faint flare at the nostrils, the cool gray eyes, long lashed, and almost beautiful in that hard-boned young face, but very cool and asking for nothing. A type. One of those young men who had come out of the late war with that drive, that cutting quality, as if they had shucked off human uncertainties and were aimed and hurtling toward something in the future about which they seemed very sure.

His name was Jed Towers. It was his last night in New York. He had a dinner date.

If he saw the little man out of the corner of his cool eye, it was just a little man, with his shoulders pulled back from his narrow chest in a frozen strut. With a gray face. With pale hair that never had any color to lose, lying long and lank over the bald part. Pale eyes that blinked often, as if Eddie Munro were never quite sure of anything.

The car stopped smoothly at the main floor. Jed put his key on the desk without interrupting the long fluid strides that were taking him to the outside, to the city, to the evening.

Eddie ran a nervous glance around the quiet lobby. He said to the next boy, "Gotta make a phone call. Watch it, will you?" He scuttled around a bend of wall with his nickel in his hand already.

"Marie?"

"Yeah, Eddie?" said his wife's placid voice.

"She leave?"

"She went, yeah, sure."

"How long ago?"

"In plenty of time," his wife said. Everything she said carried the overtone, Don't worry, Eddie.

"Take the subway?"

"Of course."

"Listen, Marie, I think maybe I oughta stay around after I'm off. Folks might be late. Some kind of big shindig, the man said. O.K.?"

"O.K."

"I think I oughta stay and bring her home, don't you?"

"Good idea, Eddie."

"You do think the whole idea's a good idea, Marie? She can earn a little money? You know? Get started?"

"Sure it is, Eddie."

"She—uh—liked the idea, didn't she?"

"Sure she did."

"Well . . . uh . . ." He didn't want to let go of the wire, leading to Marie and her voice saying, Sure.

"Say, Eddie . . ."

"Yeah?"

"I think maybe I'll go to the show. Miz Martin said she'd go with me." Eddie squirmed in the booth, blinking rapidly. His wife's voice went on. "That picture we didn't think we'd better take *her*? You know?"

"Yeah."

"So I thought I'd go—got the chance."

"Oh. Well. Yeah. Sure."

"Don't worry, Eddie," Marie soothed. "I'll be home long before you and Nell, probably."

"Sure. Sure," he said. He heard his wife's tiny sigh whispering on the wire. "Go ahead," he said, vigorously. "Have a good time."

"It'll be O.K.," she told him. (Don't worry, Eddie.)

He went around the wall to his car. His eyes searched toward the revolving door, across the depth of the lobby. He threw back his shoulders, trying to stand erect, to look as if he were perfectly sure.

In 807, Ruth slipped the rose-colored frivolity off its hanger and expertly lowered it past her shining hair. Peter's strong fingers zipped her up the back. She made her curtsy to the audience.

"Something like a princess," said Peter judiciously, "don't you think?"

"Zactly," said the audience solemnly.

Ruth kissed the back of the audience's neck. "And now!" she cried. Oh, they were clowning for the audience, and if the audience was having fun, so were they!

"Ah *ha*!" Peter made fending, clear-the-decks motions with both hands. He took up his ridiculous garment. Ruth skipped to hold it for him. Peter wiggled in and patted the flying front sections.

"You said it was *tails*!" said the audience in high sweet scorn.

"You don't think so?" said Peter. He put both hands under

the coat at the back and suddenly he was marching up and down with a Groucho Marx kind of crouch in his knees and his tails were flapping.

The audience was convulsed. It rolled over in a helpless giggling heap. Bunny wasn't (zactly) thought Ruth a pretty little girl, but how beautiful she was, laughing! How irresistible!

And she herself gasped, "Peter, oh stop!"

"O. Jones."

"Oh, stop! I'll ruin my mascara. Oh *my*!"

The whole long, sweet, slow, mock-solemn ceremony of dressing for The Night crescendoed in hilarity.

Somebody knocked gently on the door.

Something squeezed Ruth's heart, quickly, and as quickly let it go, so that it staggered.

Chapter 2

"MR. JONES, here we are, sir." Eddie's bright blinking eye, the thrust of his neck, were as of a mouse at the door.

"Oh, yes, Eddie. Right on time. How de do. Come in."

"This here's my niece, Nell Munro. Nell?" Eddie came in, too.

"How de do, Nell." Peter's tails were a graceful appendage to the Speaker of the Evening. Ruth, herself, moved toward them, the gracious young matron. All the fizz had gone out of the room.

"Good evening, Nell," she said. "It was nice of you to come on such short notice. Had you very far?"

"Don't take long on the subway," Eddie said. His adam's apple jumped. He stood with his skinny shoulders thrust well back. "Really don't take long at all. She came right straight down." He seemed proud of this.

The girl, Nell, said nothing. She looked to be nineteen or twenty. She stood demurely with her ankles tight together. Her shoes were shabby black pumps with medium heels. Her head was bent, her lashes lowered. Her hair was the color of a lion's hide, cut short, not very curly. She wore no hat, a navy blue coat of a conservative cut and a little too big for her. Her hands were folded on a black handbag and Ruth was pleased to see that the nails were bare. Then she hooted at herself for so quaint a connecting of character with nail polish, for, after all, her own nails were a glossy rose, the shade of her frock. Still . . .

"Won't you take your coat off, Nell?"

Eddie said, "Take your coat off, Nell. Go ahead." The girl wore a neat dark silk dress. She held the coat on her arm as if she didn't know what to do with it.

"Just put it here, won't you?" purred Ruth. "And your bag, too? I suppose you've sat with children before, Nell?"

"She did, back in Indiana," said Eddie. "Did it a lot. Not around here, so much. She only came east about six months ago."

"Is that so?"

"She's living with me and my wife, now. My brother's girl . . ."

"And do you like it here, Nell?"

"She likes it fine," said Eddie. "We've got room in the apartment, plenty of room for her. My wife's real glad to have her."

Is the girl mute? Ruth wondered. Eddie's interposing chatter was nervous, as if it covered something lumpish and obstinate in the girl, who was not helping. As one ought to chatter, and push time past this kind of stoppage in its current.

Eddie said, "What I wannida say, I'll *be* here in the hotel. I mean, I'm going to be around, see? So if you folks are going to be late, you don't need to worry."

"We may not be so very late," said Peter smoothly. The effect was as if he said, What are you talking about? He had a towel in one hand and was swiping it recklessly across the shining toes of his evening shoes.

"What I mean," Eddie blinked, "I can take Nell home, see?"

Peter looked up, drawled, "That's nice of you." Ruth heard his surprised pleasure. The job of taking the sitter home is one of the meanest chores that falls to the lot of the married male. "But I'd have seen her home, of course," said Peter virtuously.

Ruth was, at the moment, turning. She thought the pupils moved under the lowered lashes in that bent face. She said, pushing brightly at the sluggishness of things, "Bunny, dear. Nell, this is Bunny and Bunny, this is Nell."

"Hello," said Bunny.

"Hello," the girl said. Her voice was low and colorless, but at least it worked. She spoke.

"My wife, see," Eddie was saying, "took a notion to go to the show so I might's well wait around." Swallowing made a commotion in his skinny neck. "We was thinking it might be a real nice idea for Nell. There's a lot of guests bring their children. And me being right here, why, it ought to work out good."

He showed no sign of going back to his elevator. An anxious little man, the kind who keeps explaining himself, although nobody cares. Terribly concerned to do the right thing. The conscientious kind.

"Suppose we show Nell your room, Bun?" Ruth led them. "You see, this door can be left a little bit ajar because Bunny does like to go to sleep in the dark. I thought *you* could sit in here, Nell, in our room, where you can be more comfortable."

Bunny had marched ahead of them into 809. Now she threw one leg possessively over the edge of one of the beds, the one on which her stuffed dog from home was already established.

"Perhaps she ought to turn in quite soon now," Ruth said gently. "She's had a pretty exciting day, and tomorrow we have all sorts of plans. Perhaps you'd read her a story? If you don't mind?"

"No, ma'am," said Nell passively.

"That'll be nice, won't it, Bun?" It *was* like pushing, pushing something heavy. Ruth said with a bright smile, "Suppose you see if Nell would like some candy."

Bunny got the box, offered it, as Ruth had taught her, with a gracious little bend of her small body. Nell said, "Thanks a lot." And snatched. Ruth felt her heart lighten. Surely that was nice of her. That held some understanding. No grown person could care that much for candy. That greedy quickness must have been exaggerated for the child's sake.

"You're welcome." Bunny dipped in herself, companionably.

Ruth felt easier. "Bunny's such a big girl," she went on, "there really won't be anything to *do*." She realized that Eddie's voice and Peter's monosyllables were still going on behind her. "Bunny's bathroom is over there, of course." Ruth stepped to dim down the lights, leaving the lamp between the beds. "And this door," she waved at the exit from 809 to the corridor, "is locked, of course. Now, Bunny's to have one more piece of candy and then she's to brush her teeth and have her story and by that time I expect she'll be pretty sleepy." She touched the little girl's munching cheek. She looked back through the connecting door.

Eddie's high voice said clearly, "Well—uh—probably I'll look in on Nell, once in a while, if that's all right with you folks."

"Surely." Peter picked up his wallet. Ruth could tell from his back that he was both annoyed and resigned. "Well—uh—thanks very much."

"No, sir." Eddie backed away from the dollar bill. "No, I'm glad to do it, sir. It's such a good idea for Nell. You just pay her what she earns. Fifty cents an hour. And that'll be fine. That's the arrangement. Nell's mighty glad to have a chance to earn a little something. It's going to work out real nice for her. So—uh—" he looked rather defiantly past Peter. "You folks go on out and have a good evening, now."

Ruth guessed he was speaking to her. "Thanks very much, Mr. Munro. Good night."

"Good night. Uh—good night. Have a good time now, Mr. and Mrs. Jones." His hand hovered in a kind of admonishing gesture. It fell. At last, he was gone.

"O.K., Ruth?" said Peter with a touch of impatience.

"In a minute. Nell?" Summoned, the girl moved. Ruth could hear Bunny making a great splutter, brushing her teeth. "Peter, do you mind looking up the number, where we are going to be? Where we can be reached? We'll just leave it by the phone in here, Nell, and if there is anything at all, why, you *can* call us. You must remember to ask for Peter O. Jones. Don't forget the O. It takes so long to comb out the Joneses otherwise." She laughed.

Nell said without humor, "Yes, ma'am."

Ruth began to turn off lights in 807, leaving only the standing lamp over the big maroon chair and the little lamp between the beds. "That's enough, Nell?" The girl nodded. "And if you'd like something to read, there are all these magazines. And please help yourself to the candy. And if you get drowsy, you must lie down in here. I'm sure that will be all right. And," she lowered her voice discreetly, "perhaps you had better use this bathroom. Now, is there anything I've forgotten?"

She stood in all her finery, her brow creased just a little, feeling unsatisfied. The girl had said so little. Yet, what was there for her to say? Something, thought Ruth impatiently, some little thing volunteered . . . *anything* to show she's taking hold! "Can *you* think of anything else?" she prodded.

The girl's head was not so bent, any more. Her face was wide at the eyes with high cheek bones, and the eyes were large and a trifle aslant. Her chin was small and pointed and her mouth was tiny. The face was not made up, and the skin had a creamy yellow-or-peach undertone.

She wasn't bad looking, Ruth thought with surprise. In fact, she might have been stunning, in an odd provocative way.

Even her figure was good under that ill-fitting dress, now that she was standing more erect, not so meekly bent. The eyes were blue. There was too much blue in them, as if the seeing center were too small, the band of color wider than it needed to be. The tawny hair straggled over her ears, but Ruth noticed that they were tiny and tight to the head.

"I guess you've thought of everything," Nell said. The tiny mouth seemed to let itself go into a reluctant, a grudging smile. Her teeth were fine.

Ruth watched her. For just a flash, she wondered if, in that perfectly flat sentence, there had been some mischief lying low, a trace of teasing, a breath of sarcasm.

"Better get going," Peter moved, full of energy. "There's the number, Nell, on this paper. Ask them to page us. Doubt if you'll need it. *We* may call up, so if the phone rings . . ." He tapped the slip of paper on the phone table. He started briskly for the closet. The whole world, for Ruth, seemed to take up where it had left off.

Bunny was curled around the jamb of the connecting door, toothpaste lingering on her lips. "Pop into bed, baby," Ruth said. "And Nell will read to you a while."

Herself in shadow, she watched them obey . . . Bunny peel out of her robe, climb in and pull the covers up, toss her pigtails behind . . . watched the girl move nearer and seat herself tentatively, rather uncertainly, on the edge of the bed, where the light haloed her hair.

Suddenly, Bunny took charge. "Read me about Jenny and the Twins." She pitched her book at the girl.

"O.K.," said Nell, meekly.

Ruth turned away. She bustled, putting things into her evening bag, her wrist watch, her compact, handkerchief, hairpins, lipstick. Her heart was beating a little fast.

Peter was standing silently, with his overcoat on, with her velvet wrap over his arm. She went over and he held it. She looked up at him, wordlessly asked, Is it all right? Wordlessly, he answered, Sure. What can happen? The wrap was soft and cool on her bare arms.

"Eddie's got his eye on," said Peter in her ear. And she saw, at once, that this was true. Eddie was responsible. Eddie had worked here fourteen years. He couldn't risk losing that record. No. And Eddie was conscientious to a fault. He'd be fussy and watchful. It was Eddie they were hiring, really. He'd have his anxious eye on.

"Take us a while to get across town," said Peter aloud. Together, they went into the other room. The girl was reading. Her voice was low and monotonous. One word followed another without phrasing. She read like a child.

"All cozy?" said Ruth lightly. "Night, Bunny." Her light kiss skidded on the warm little brow.

Peter said, "Don't forget about your breakfast. So long, honey bun."

"So long, Daddy. Make a good speech."

Oh, bless her heart! thought her mother. Oh bless her!

"I'll see what I can do about that, sweetheart," said Peter tenderly, as touched as she.

The girl sat on the edge of the bed with her finger on her place in the storybook. She watched them go. As they crossed room 807, Ruth heard her voice begin again, ploddingly.

Not all of Ruth went through the door to the corridor. Part remained and tasted the flat, the dim, the silent place from which she had gone. After all the lights and the love and the laughter, how was it for Bunny? Hadn't all the fun too abruptly departed? A part of Ruth lay, in advance of time, in the strange dark. Heard the strange city snarling below. Knew only a stranger's hired meekness was near when something in the night should cry. . . .

Peter put his finger on her velvet shoulder. An elevator was coming. (Not Eddie's, and Ruth was glad. Not again did she wish to hear, "Have a good time, you folks. Have a good time.")

She shook at her thoughts. She knew what Peter wanted. By her will, she pulled herself together. (Bunny was nine. Bunny would sleep.) She drew the tardy part of herself in toward her body until she was all there, standing by the elevators, dressed to the eyes. She looked up at Peter and showed him she was whole.

It was The Night. At last, it was!

Chapter 3

J ED TOWERS picked up his date at her family's apartment on East Thirty-sixth Street. Her name was Lyn Lesley and she was more than just a date. She had achieved a certain ascendancy on Jed's list. In fact, she was right up there on top. Lyn was slim, dark, with a cute nose and a way of looking out of the corners of her eyes that was neither sly nor flirtatious but simply merry.

He'd known her a year or more, but not until these two weeks, all free time, between jobs, had he seen her so constantly. This had happened easily. A kind of rollicking slide to it. Very smooth and easy to slide from "see you tomorrow, question mark" to "see you tomorrow, period" to "what shall we do tomorrow?" They had fun. Why not? But this next morrow, Jed was off for the West, all the way to the coast, in fact, where he'd be pinned down a while, in the new job. Tonight, their last night, had accumulated without any deliberation on Jed's part the feel of being decisive.

Maybe it wasn't their last night together—but their last night apart. He didn't know. He wasn't stalling. He just didn't know.

They were not in evening clothes. Lyn wore a fuzzy blue coat with big pockets and big buttons and a little blue cap on the back of her head. They decided to walk. They didn't know where they were going, anyway. The mood was tentative and merry . . . no tinge of farewell in it, yet. Lyn hopped and skipped until Jed shortened his stride. They drifted toward the deepest glow in the sky. They might go to a show, might not. It depended.

On Thirty-ninth Street, the block west of Fifth, a beggar accosted them, whining to the girl, "Help an old man, missus?"

"Oh . . . Jed?" She stood still, impelled to compassion, her face turned up confidently.

Jed's fingers bit her arm. "Sorry . . ." He dragged her along. "Just a racket," he said in her ear. The man's muttering faded in their wake, audible in the shadowy quiet, for the city's noise was, like fog, thicker afar, never very thick near around you.

She was really dragging her feet. "How do you know?" she said.

"Know what?" He was surprised. "Oh, for Lord's sake, Lyn, grow up! That old beetle probably's got more in the bank than we'll ever see."

"You can't know that," she said stubbornly.

He stopped walking, astonished. Vaguely, he realized that his brusque decision, back there, may have broken something in her mood, some enchantment maybe. He had no patience with it. He said, "Now, look. Of course I can't know it, but the chances are, I'm right. You know that. And I don't like being taken for a sucker, Lyn. Now, skip it, shall we?"

She walked along only somewhat more willingly. He said teasingly, "But you'd have fallen for it, eh? Softie!"

"On the chance he really needed help," she said in a low voice, "I'd have risked a quarter."

"Don't be like that." Jed laughed at her. "Sentimental Sue!" He wheeled her into a restaurant. "This all right?" Jed had been there before. The food was good. He wasn't guessing. He was sorry the mood had been broken. It was his instinct to change the setting, and use the difference and food and drink to bring back whatever it was between them.

They took their table and Jed ordered dinner. Lyn had her lower lip in her teeth, kept her eyes down. When their cocktails came and he lifted his glass to her, she smiled. She said, "I'm not sentimental, Jed. It isn't that."

"No?" He wished she'd skip it. He, himself, was finished with that trivial moment. "Drink your drink, honey." He smiled at her. When the cool beauty of his face broke, in his smile, to affectionate attention, it pulled on the heart of the beholder. Jed did not know that, in such terms. But he knew, of course, statistically, that what he offered was not often rejected.

But Lyn said, wanly, "You have an awfully quick way of mistrusting people." Her voice was gentle but he thought there were stormy signs in her eyes and anger stirred in Jed's own.

He said, evenly, gently, "I didn't think you were that childish, Lyn. I really didn't."

"I can't see," she said, holding scorn out of the voice carefully, "how it would have hurt. Two bits. Or even a dime."

"Spare a dime," he mocked. "For Lord's sake, Lyn, let's not fight about it."

"No." She pushed her glass to and fro on the cloth and she smiled. "But you do expect the worst of people, don't you, Jed? I've . . . noticed."

"Certainly," he grinned. "You damn well better, as far as I can see." He offered her his certainty with careless cheer.

She took a deep swallow of her drink, set down the glass, and looked across the room. "I don't think I care for cheap cynicism," she said.

"Cheap!" he exploded. Women were the limit! What a thing to come out with, just like that! He realized he must have hurt her, somehow. But he also knew he hadn't meant to. "For Lord's sake!" he said, "that's about the most expensive piece of education I ever got myself. I'd hate to tell you what I had to pay for it." He was still genuinely astonished.

"You don't believe . . ." she began and her lips were trembling.

"Don't believe!" he scoffed. "Listen—aw, you baby! What I believe or what you believe makes no particular difference to the way things are. Lyn, honey, sooner or later you get to know that. All the difference it makes is whether you're comfortable or not. Well, it just happens I don't like to be fooled and I've got to the point where I don't even enjoy fooling myself." She flicked her lashes. "This," he said soberly, "is a pretty stinking lousy world."

"Is it?" said Lyn.

He was annoyed. "If you haven't noticed that you're unintelligent," he said crisply.

"And what do you do about it?"

"Mind your own business. Take care of yourself, because you can be damn sure nobody else will. Lyn, for the love of Mike, let it go, will you? Anybody thinks *he* can save the world isn't weaned yet. You're old enough to know that much."

"If everybody figured the way you do . . ." she began, looking unhappy.

"You like the boy-scout type?" he challenged. "The sunshine kids?"

"No."

"The dreamy boys? The old stars in the eyes?"

"Stop it!"

"O.K.," he said. "So I'm not going to water myself down and play pat-a-cake with you." He canceled his anger. He offered, again, his smile and himself.

"I don't want you to," she said. "I'm interested in what you think about things." Her voice was low again.

"But you don't think much of my way of thinking?" he said, more challenging than he had intended to be. "Is that it?"

She turned her hand.

"Well . . ." he shrugged. "I'm sorry, honey, but one thing that stinks high in this lousy world is the lip service to sweetness and light. Everybody's for it. But does their left hand know what their lip is saying?" At least, I'm honest, his eyes were saying. I'm telling you. "Look, I didn't expect an inquiry into my philosophy of life. I thought this was a date . . . you know, for fun?"

Her lips parted. He read in her look that they both knew it wasn't just a date . . . for fun. But she didn't speak.

"Show?" he said lightly. If they went to a show, it would deny, somehow, their ability to be together. He felt that, suddenly.

She said, "In such a stinking lousy world, what do you expect?"

"Oh, say, the love of a good woman," he answered lightly, because he *didn't* want to discuss this kind of thing seriously any more. And then he was sorry. He saw her lips whiten. He'd hurt her, again, when all he wanted was to get lightly off the subject. "Aw, Lyn, please . . . What are we yapping about? How'd we get off?"

"Coffee now?" inquired the waiter.

"Coffee, honey?" Jed put his hand on hers.

"Please," she said, not smiling. But it seemed to him that her hand was on his and he thought if he could kiss her, hard, right now, it would be a fine thing.

Bunny listened politely to the story. When Mommy read, the story seemed more interesting. When Daddy read to her, it was interesting, too, although Daddy never did finish a story.

He always got off to explaining something, and the explaining turned out to be *another* story. She sat quietly against her pillow, her stuffed dog under her arm, until the voice stopped. Nell looked at her, then. "I better go to sleep, now," said Bunny, "I guess."

"O.K." The mattress moved, the spring changed shape, as Nell stood up.

"I can turn off my light," said Bunny kindly.

"O.K. then," Nell said. She put the book down on the other bed. She walked away. She picked up the candy box, looked once over her shoulder, and went through the door.

Bunny snapped off the light, watched the pattern of shadows establish itself. She wondered if the window was open. Nell hadn't looked to see. The room felt stuffy and dusty hot. Bunny wasn't quite sure she knew how to work the Venetian blind. She lay still quite a long time, but it didn't feel right to go to sleep, not knowing whether the window was open. She sneaked her feet out and felt the bristles of the carpet. She fumbled with the thin ropes and after a while there was a soft rattle and the slats changed. Now, she could see. The window *was* open. It was all right, then. Bunny crept back under the blankets. The air smelled dusty, just the same, and the pillow didn't smell like her pillow at home, either. Bunny pushed her nose into it and lay still.

Nell set the communicating door at an angle that almost closed it. Then she stood absolutely still, tipping her head as if to listen. Room 809 was quiet, behind her. Room 807 was a pool of silence. Her eyes shifted. The big lamp flooded the spot near the windows where the big chair stood. The small lamp touched the upper ends of the twin beds. Elsewhere, there were shadows.

Nell put the candy box down on a bed and walked back with a silent gliding step to the windows and tripped the blind. The court was too narrow to see very far up or down. Across, there was only one lighted window. The blind, there, was up a third of the way, and she could see the middle section of a woman, seated at the desk. A black and white belt marked a thick waist on a black dress. There was nothing else to see. Not many spent their evenings in, at the Hotel Majestic.

Nell pivoted, glided in that same step to the middle of room 807 and stood still. She did not stand still long. Although her feet remained in the same flower of the carpet pattern, they began to dance. The heels lifted and fell fractions of an inch, only, as her weight shifted. Her hips rolled softly, and her shoulders and her forearms. Her fingers were the most active part of her body in this dance. They made noiseless snaps and quick restless writhings of their own. Her chin was high and her head, swaying with the tiny movements of her body, wove the pattern of a wreath in the silent air.

Meantime, Nell's eyes, wide open, darted as she danced. Very alive and alert, they were. Her whole face was vivid, more sly than shy, not in the least demure.

In a little while, the feet danced daintily, in the tiniest of steps, off the one flower. Nell swooped over Peter's suitcase. Her hand, impiously, not tentatively at all, scooped through its contents. Handkerchiefs and ties flew like sand from a beach castle. There were some letters and a manila folder flat on the bottom. The girl snatched them out, opened the folder awkwardly, and all the paper slid out in a limp curve. She stood with the empty folder in her hands and looked down at the spilled papers in the suitcase. Then she yanked the letters from the clip that held them to the folder. They didn't interest her for long. She dropped all the paper out of her hands, as if it were merely paper, with no other meaning. She flipped the lid of the suitcase with one finger and it fell.

She made three long steps and pivoted with one leg out like a dancer's, pulling it slowly around. She sat down, with an effect of landing there by sheer accident, on the bench in front of the dressing table. Ruth had turned the two little lamps out. It did not seem to occur to Nell to switch them on. She rummaged in Ruth's box of jewelry. There were three bracelets and Nell clasped them all on her left arm. There were two brooches and she pinned one above the other on the left lapel of her dress. There were a string of coral colored beads, and Ruth's three-strand pearls, and a silver locket on a silver chain. All these Nell took up and fastened around her neck. A pair of tiny turquoise and silver earrings that matched one of the pins, she put at her ears. She looked at herself in the shadowy glass, solemnly, lumpishly. She smiled. Slowly, she began to take everything off again. As she removed each piece she did not return it to its place in the box. When the table top was scattered with most of the things, Nell seemed to lose interest. She still wore the earrings.

She turned, very slowly, sliding around, moving her legs as if they were in one piece. She kicked off her black pumps. Ruth's aquamarine mules with the maribou cuffs were standing neatly under the dressing table. Nell put her feet into them. She rose and walked up and down in them, watching her feet, acquiring more and more skill and arrogance in the ankles and the arches. At last, she seemed almost strutting. Then, she seemed to forget, and moved about as easily as if the mules had long been her own.

She ate three pieces of candy, slowly.

Then she sat down on the bench again and picked up Ruth's perfume. The tiny glass stick, attached to the stopper, she discarded. She tipped the bottle on her forefinger and dabbed the forefinger behind her ears. She held the forefinger under her nostrils and inhaled dreamily, swaying to and fro as if she tantalized her own senses in a dreamy rhythm. The little bottle dropped out of her left hand, cracked on the table top, lay on its side. The liquid began to seep out among the jewelry. (The twelve dollars that had been Peter's, the fifty cents that had been Bunny's, last Mother's Day.)

Nell noticed it, finally. Her face did not change. She picked up Ruth's hairbrush, dipped it, making a smearing motion, in the spilled perfume, and began to brush her tawny hair. She brushed it sharply back from her ears. Now her face took on another look. Now the shape of it, the sharp taper to the chin, the subtle slant of the eye sockets, became older, more sleek, reptilian.

She drew the hairbrush once around her throat.

She rose and walked between the beds, turned, and let herself fall supine on the one to the left of the telephone. After a little while she lifted her right arm, languidly, letting her hand dangle from the wrist, looking up at her fingers that hung limp off the palm.

Then she sat up, propped her back with pillows, and opened the fat phone book. She opened it almost at the center and looked at the pages with unfocused eyes. She lifted her left hand and dropped it on the fine print. Where her left forefinger nail fell she gouged a nick in the paper.

She picked up the phone with her right hand, asked sweetly for the number.

"Yes?" A man's voice came out of the city, somewhere, hooked and caught at the end of the wire.

"Guess who?" Nell said in a soft high soprano.

"Margaret, where are—"

"Oh-ho no! Not Margaret!"

"Who is this?" said the voice irritably. "I'm not in the mood—"

"By the way, who *is* Margaret? Hmmmmmmmmm?"

"Margaret is my wife," said the voice stiffly. "What's the idea?"

"Ha!"

"Who is this?"

"Virginia," crooned Nell. "Don't you remember me?"

"I think you have the wrong number," the voice said, sounding very old and tired, and he hung up.

Nell sucked her cheeks in, turned pages, gave another number.

"Hello?" A woman this time.

"Hello. Oh, hello. Is Mr. Bennet there?"

"No, he's not. I'm sorry." Brightly, "This is *Mrs.* Bennet."

"Oh," said Nell without alarm. With nothing. Flatly. Her head tilted, listening.

"Can I take a message?" the woman said, somewhat less cordially.

"Oh, dear," simpered Nell. "You see, this is Mr. Bennet's secretary . . ."

"Mr. Bennet has no secretary that I know of."

"Oh," said Nell. "Oh dear me! Are you sure?"

"Who is this?" The voice began to sound as if the face were red.

"Just a friend. You know?"

"Will you give me your name, please?"

"Why, no," said Nell flatly and then she giggled.

The phone slammed shut at the other end. On Nell's face danced a look of delighted malice.

She stretched. She called the girl downstairs again. "Long distance."

"One moment, please!"

Rochelle Parker, at the switchboard, was efficient and indifferent. She dealt with the barrage of calls from 807 for a long time without much comment, even to herself. She got in on part of a wrangle between the long-distance operator and whoever was calling, up there, over the existence of an exchange in Chicago. The person upstairs used language, softly. It was as bad as Rochelle had ever heard over the wires and she'd heard some. And this was worse, sounding so hushed-like.

"Jeepers," said Rochelle to herself. The eyebrows that Rochelle, herself, had remodeled from nature's first idea went up to her bangs. It crossed her mind that she might say a word to Pat Perrin, the house detective. Probably, she thought, they were drinking, up there. People had a few, and went on telephone jags, sometimes.

She decided it was none of her business. What went over the wire wasn't disturbing the sacred peace of the Hotel Majestic. If 807 began to do that, somebody else would catch on.

And the telephone bill would be part of the hangover. "Oh, boy," she thought and grinned. Then 807 suddenly quit calling.

The phone book had fallen off the bed. Nell rolled over on her stomach and looked at it, lying on the carpet.

She sat up, curling her legs under her. She yawned. She listened. Her rambling glance passed the half-open closet door and returned. . . .

Chapter 4

A TALL man looks best in tails, they say. Ruth thought that, although Peter O. Jones was not too terribly tall, he looked wonderful. She saw no man there who looked more distinguished than he. Erect, compact, controlled, he walked beside her. And if the bold lines of his face were not handsome, they were better than that. People remembered Peter.

She saw herself, too, in the mirror walls of the passage to the ballroom and she began to walk as if she were beautiful. For the frock was becoming and in the soft light, she even liked her nose. Maybe it did turn up, as Peter insisted, against all evidence, that it did. At least it had, as he said, the air of being *about* to turn up, any minute.

Her hand with the rosy nails pressed the black cloth of his left sleeve and Peter crossed his right arm over and touched her hand. Here they stood, at the portal. Black and white men, multicolored ladies, flowers, table-and-chairs like polka dots over the floor, but the long white bar of the speakers' table dominated.

"Peter O. Jones," said her husband very quietly to somebody. A black back bent. They followed toward the speakers' table and Ruth could see their path, opening, and the turning faces marked it as if flowers were being thrown under their feet.

Somebody stepped into their way, holding out his hand. "Peter O. Jones?" he said joyfully. "Want you to meet . . ." "Beg pardon, sir, but this is . . ." "How do you do?" "*Mrs.* Jones, ah . . ." They were in a cluster. Yet they were moving slowly, surely, toward the speakers' table. Peter had the nicest *way* about him. So many people knew who he *was*. Ruth struggled to remain balanced, to lock names to faces. It was confusing! It was glorious!

Jed and Lyn were still sitting in the restaurant. Coffee, brandy, more coffee, and many cigarettes had gone by. They'd had no ambition to stir themselves, to go to a show. They were caught in the need to settle something. Maybe it was never to be settled. This was what they needed to know. Jed shared, now, Lyn's feeling that it was important. They were hanging onto their tempers, both of them.

They'd about finished, speaking awkwardly, obliquely for the most part, with God.

"What I know," he said, "the Lord ain't Santa Claus. You got them mixed, honey. Santa Claus, sure, *he'll* open his pack if you been a good girl. I don't think it's the same." His brows made angles.

"You don't believe in it at all," she said wearily.

"I don't nag myself about it." He shrugged.

"All I'm trying to say, Jed," she was making an effort to be sweet, "is just this. I'd like . . . all right, call it soft . . . call it anything you want . . . I'd have *liked* it, if you had given that old man a coin. What would it matter if he really needed it or not? It would have been good for *us*."

"Aw, that's junk, Lyn. Pure junk."

"It isn't junk!"

His voice slipped. Dammed-up irritation slipped out. "It's ridiculous!"

Her eyes flashed. They had worked to smile, too long. "I'm glad to know you think I'm ridiculous."

"Maybe it's a good idea to know these things," he agreed coldly. "You called me a cheap cynic, remember?"

"And perhaps you are," she said shortly, "just that."

"It's no chore of mine, Lyn," he fought to sound reasonable, "to contribute to the income of a perfect stranger who's done nothing for me."

"It's not a question of your responsibility. It's your charity."

"Nuts to that kind of charity. I intend to earn what I get. . . ."

"People can't, always. There's such a thing as being helpless . . . through no fault . . ."

"The rule is, you get what you pay for, pay for what you get. You grow up, you know that."

"Suppose *you* needed food . . . or a place to . . ."

"Then, I go beg from organized charities who recognize that so-called helplessness and, incidentally, check up on it to see if it is real. *I'll* never expect a stranger on the street to shell out for me. Why should he? Why should he believe me? It works both ways. You look out for yourself in this world, that's all I . . ."

"It's not true! People have to believe . . ."

"Why?"

"Why, anything, then?" she blazed. "What are you living for?"

"How do I know? I didn't put me here. Of all the idiotic—"

"I think you'd better take me home."

Their voices came to a dead stop.

"Why?" he said finally, his eyes glittering.

"Because this isn't fun."

"Why should I take you home?" he said, smoldering. "Ask some kind stranger."

She stared. She said, "You're quite right. I do nothing for you. Or your ego. Do I? I'll be leaving now."

"Lyn . . ."

"Yes?" she said icily, half up, her coat on her shoulders.

"If you go . . ."

"Why should I not? You're not entertaining me. Nothing's for free, you say."

"If you go . . ."

"I know. We'll never meet again. Is that it?"

"That's it, I'm afraid."

"Jed, I don't want to . . ." She was more limp, more yielding.

"Then for Lord's sake," he said irritably, assuming it was all over, "sit down and quit talking like a little jackass."

Her sidewise glance was not merry at all. "Good night," she said quietly.

He settled in the chair, took a cigarette out of the package. "Got your mad money? Here." He threw a five-dollar bill on the tablecloth.

Lyn's lips drew back from her teeth. He could feel, like a strong sudden gust, her impulse to hit him. Then he thought she'd cry.

But she walked away.

He sat, staring at the messy table. Of all the stinking lousy dates he ever had in his life! Protectively, he thought of it as just a date. He was furious. He advanced to being outraged. His last night in this town! Last night in the East! Last date! And she walked out on him.

For what? He oversimplified. Because he didn't give that

mangy old deadbeat a quarter. Of all the . . . ! He sat there and let anger become a solid lump. After a while, he paid the check and put his coat on. Outside, he looked east, then west. Lyn was nowhere about.

He began to walk, fast, hands dug in his coat pockets. He supposed gloomily it was a good thing he'd found out what kind of stuff passed for thought in her head. (Lyn, with the dark head, his shoulder high.) So . . . cross *her* off the list. Yeah. Couldn't she see he hadn't tried to hurt her? Couldn't she concede he'd learned a few things, formed some opinions, had to have a core of conviction that was, at least, honestly come by? No, she couldn't. So, she walked away.

But Towers would have a date tonight, just the same. His little book (with the list) was at the hotel, damn it. He swung north. Hadn't thought he'd need it. But he *had* it. He could put his hand on it. His pride, his proof, his very honor began to get involved here. Towers would have a date his last night. Wouldn't be stood up, not he!

Jed slammed through the revolving door. It stuttered, not moving as fast as he. He stood, towering, teetering, smoldering, at the desk, crisply after his key. He went up to the eighth floor, unlocked his door, put on his light, flung off his coat, in one swift surge of entering.

He visited the bathroom.

He came out with the bathroom glass in his hand and stared around him. He dipped into his bag for that bottle of rye. He could think of nobody on his list who'd do him good. And the preliminaries. He was in no mood for them. Call any girl, this time of night, and you could hear her little brain buzzing. Oh, will I look unpopular if I admit I'm not busy? They all wondered, the nit-wits. So she'd say she had a date. And he'd say, "Break it for me?" Knowing damn well she probably was just about to wash her hair or something. So, she'd "break it." Phony. Everything was pretty phony.

(Not Lyn. She was just too naïve to live.)

He looked at the telephone. Call her and apologize? But what was there, honestly, to apologize for? He'd only said things he believed. He couldn't change his spots. They'd only start over again. They didn't think the same. And nobody walked out on Towers twice! This, she'd find out.

Aw, quit stewing.

The blind across his bank of windows was not drawn. He realized that he stood as one on a lighted stage. It felt, too, as if eyes were upon him. Somebody was watching him.

He moved toward the windows that looked out on a court.

He was looking directly across the narrow dark deep well into another lighted bank of windows. The other room hung there in the night like a lighted stage. The scene had no depth. It was lit by a lamp near the windows. The light fell on a female figure. There was a girl or a woman over there. She was dressed in some kind of flowing bluish or greenish thing. She seemed to be sitting *in* the window, probably on the flat top of the long radiator cover. Her neck was arched. She had short yellowish hair. She seemed to be looking down at a point on her right leg just above the knee. A garter or something? Her right foot rested on the radiator top. The nicely shaped leg was bent there, framed and exhibited, with the bluish-green fabric flowing away from it.

She was not looking out, not looking at him. He was absolutely certain that she had been. He knew he must be silhouetted in the frame of his own windows. He stood still, watching her, making no further move to pull his blind down. He was absolutely certain that she knew he was there.

She moved her right palm slowly down the curve of her calf. Her head turned. She looked across at him. He did not move.

Neither did she.

Her hand rested on her ankle. Her garment remained as it was, flowing away from the pretty knee. Her head was flung up from the neck. She looked at him.

There was something so perfectly blunt about the two of them, posed as they were, each in his bright box, suspended, aware . . . It was as if a shouted *Well?* crossed the court between them.

Jed felt himself grin. The anger that hummed in his veins changed pitch, went a fraction higher. What was this? and why not? he thought, pricked and interested.

Chapter 5

THE GIRL took her hand from her ankle, put both hands on the radiator top behind her, bent her body to lean back on the stiff support of both her arms, kept looking out at him. There was something direct about it that fitted with his mood.

Jed was reading the floor plan of the hotel that lay in his head. He was counting off numbers, calculating. He had the kind of mind that carried maps and floor plans with him always. He felt pretty sure he knew what the number of that room must be. He put his bottle of rye down and raised both hands where the shape of them would be silhouetted for her to see. He signaled with eight fingers, with both hands bent in an O, and then with seven fingers.

She sat up, suddenly, wrapped both arms around her middle, and turned so that the knee slid down. She was facing him, her head tilted as if to say, What do you mean?

He took up the bottle in his left hand, pointed at it, at her, at himself.

Her chin went high, as if her head fell back in laughter.

He put down the bottle, pantomimed himself at a telephone. She understood because her head turned and she looked behind her toward where the phone in that room must be.

She made the sign of seven.

Jed backed away from the window. He knew he was still perfectly visible, perhaps even plainer to her sight now, in the glare of the overhead light. He picked up his phone. He said to the girl, "807, please."

Downstairs, as Rochelle made the connection, a thought no clearer than the word "huh?" crossed her mind fleetingly. Pursuing it, she remembered. Oh yeah, 807 was the whispering foul-mouth. What now? Probably, she surmised 821 was going to complain. She was tempted. She heard a man's voice say, "Well?" It was blunt and a trifle mocking. It wasn't going to complain. Rochelle's interest, faint in the first place, faded. The muscles of her mouth made a quick cynical comment, soon forgotten.

Jed could still see the girl, in the little puddle of light by the

33

beds in there, answering her phone. He waved. "Hi," he said, over the wire.

She made a soft sound, like a chuckle. "Hello."

"*Would* you like a drink?"

"I might," she said.

"Alone?"

She knew what he was asking. "You can see, can't you?" she said and the hint of laughter came again.

"If I walk around, will you open the door?"

"I might."

"It's a long walk," he said.

He had the impression that she would have teased him, but something happened. He saw her head turn. Some sound . . . that she could hear but he could not. She said, in a different mood and a different tempo, "Wait a few minutes?"

"This is an impulse," Jed said frankly. "It might not last."

"Five minutes," she said, sounding eager and conspiratorial, now. "There's somebody at the door." Then she said, "Oh, please," very softly and very softly hung up.

Jed sat on the bed in his room, and automatically put the phone down. He saw her at the window, lowering the blind, but she tripped it so that he could still see into the room. He knew when she went into the shadowy part, when she opened the door. The visitor came in the direction that, to Jed, was downstage, came in far enough so that he could identify the hotel livery.

Bellhop, or something. Oh, well . . . He went into his bathroom with a vague sense of stepping into the wings for a moment, out of the footlights. He looked at himself in the glass. His anger was no longer so solid. It had broken into a rhythmic beat. It came and went, ebbed and flowed. When it pulsed high he felt reckless and in a mood to smash. When it ebbed low he felt a little bit blank and tired. But the pulse was strong, the beat was urgent. It seemed necessary to do something.

Eddie said, "Little girl went to sleep, all right, did she? You all right. Nell?"

"Umhum," Nell murmured. She'd fallen into the maroon chair and looked relaxed there. Her lids fell as if they were heavy over her eyes. Her face was smooth and seemed sleepy.

"What you got on? Nell!" Eddie's voice was thin and careful.

"I'm not hurting anything."

Eddie's flitting eye caught the top of the dressing table and the condition it was in. His gold-flecked teeth bit over his pale lip. He moved closer to the dressing table. After a while he said, in a low voice, "You shouldn't monkey with other people's stuff, Nell. Really, you shouldn't."

"I'm not hurting anything," she repeated and her voice was more truculent than before.

Eddie gnawed his lip. He rescued the perfume bottle and replaced the stopper. Almost furtively, his fingers began to neaten the tumble of jewelry. He began to talk, softly, coaxingly.

"It's kind of an easy job, though, isn't it, Nell? Don't you think so? Just to sit for a few hours in a nice room like this. And just think, you get paid for it. Fifty cents an hour isn't bad, for nothing but being here. If you was home, you'd be sitting around with Aunt Marie, waiting for bedtime, just the same. You like it, don't you, Nell?"

"Oh, sure," she said drowsily.

"Nell, you . . . better take off that negligee . . . and the slippers. Honest. I don't think Mrs. Jones would like that."

"She won't know the difference," said Nell shortly.

"Well," said Eddie, "I hope you . . . Will you take them off, like a good girl?"

"Umhum," she murmured. "Sure I will, Uncle Eddie." She lifted her eyes and smiled at him.

He was enormously encouraged and pleased. "That's right," he cried. "That's good. Take them off, Nell, and put them where they were, so she won't know. Because you want to get paid. You want to get more jobs like this. Don't you see, Nell? It'll be a real nice kind of little work for you. So easy. And you can do what you want with the money, after. You can buy some fancy slippers like those for *yourself*, Nell. Or a pair of earrings. Wouldn't that be nice?"

She turned her cheek to the chair.

Eddie wished he knew how it was Marie talked to her, what it was she did. Because Nell was good when Marie was around, real quiet and good.

"Tell you what I'll do," he said heartily. "When I get off duty, I'll bring you up a coke. O.K.? Have a little refreshment, you and me. It won't seem so long. You'll be surprised how the time will go by."

"Sleepy," she murmured.

"Well," he said, bracing his shoulders, "nap a little bit. That's a good idea." He looked at the perfume bottle that was now nearly empty. He cleared his throat. He said in a nervous rush, "And you ought to apologize for spilling the perfume . . . right away when she comes back."

Nell's lids went up slowly until her eyes were very wide. "It was an accident," she said an octave higher than before. Her whole body had tightened.

"I know. I know," said Eddie quickly. He stepped near her and put a gentle hand on her shoulder. She twisted away from it. "Of course it was an accident. I believe you, Nell. Sure it was. The only thing I mean is, it's a good idea to say so, real soon, before she notices. Anybody can have an accident like that. She won't blame you."

Nell said nothing.

"It'll be all right," said Eddie, comfortingly. "You couldn't help it. Now, you just—just take it easy a little bit. I'll be back." He looked nervously behind him. The open elevator, standing too long on the eighth floor, was present in his consciousness. "I gotta go. But you're all right, aren't you?" He swallowed. "Please, Nell," he said in a thin pleading voice, "don't get into no more mischief with their things?"

"I'm not doing anything," she said sullenly.

But, when he sighed and paused in his progress toward the door as if he would plead some more, she said quickly, "I'm sorry, Uncle Eddie. I'll put everything back. You know I get . . . restless." Her hands moved to the earrings. "I'll take them off."

Immediately, he was pleased. "Sure, I know you get restless. I know you don't mean anything. I want you to . . . kinda get used to this idea. The thing is, to *think*, Nell. We could work up a kind of a little business, here. If you'd just . . . if you like it."

"I do like it," she said, sounding thoughtful and serious. An earring lay in her hand.

The little man's face reddened with his delight. "Good girl! That's swell! And it's a date, now. Don't forget. I'll bring the cokes." And so he withdrew, pointed little face going last, like a mouse drawing back into its hole.

Nell waited for the door to close. With no expression on her face she put the earring back on her ear lobe. She got slowly to her feet. Then they began to move on the carpet in that tiny dance. She listened. She went to the blind and it rattled up under her hands.

Jed was standing in the middle of his room, his weight even on both feet, looking rather belligerently across at her.

She flung up both hands in a beckoning gesture, let them go on, until her arms were in a dancer's high curve, and she whirled backward from the window. Jed stood still. And the girl stood still, posed with her arms high, looking over her shoulder.

In a second, Jed put the bottle in his pocket, and his finger on his light switch. His light went out.

Nell pawed, disturbing the order Eddie had created, and she snatched at Ruth's spare coral lipstick.

Chapter 6

JED'S IMPULSE had been flickering like a candle in a draught. He put the bottle in his pocket for the necessary little drink that you take while you look the situation over, put his key in his pocket, too, heard the elevator gate closing. So he waited for the faint hum of its departure before he went around the corner to his right and passed the elevators and turned right again.

His mood was cautious when he tapped on the door marked 807.

She was not very tall, not very old, not bad looking, either. But he couldn't type her. No curly blonde. Not a sleek blonde. Her face, tilted to look at him, was a triangle and the eyes were set harlequinwise. Jed's nostrils moved. She reeked . . . the whole room reeked . . . of perfume. She opened the door wider, quickly. He took a step and the door closed behind him as if she had fanned him into this perfumed place. His glance went rapidly around. He looked, and knew it, as if he were ready to take the step back again, and out.

"What's in the bottle?" she asked.

He took it out of his pocket and showed her the label. He said, mechanically, "Too nice a night to drink alone." His cool gray stare examined her.

Her blue eyes examined his. For a minute, he thought there wasn't going to be any act . . . and he was fascinated by that same sense of blunt encounter that he had felt before.

This wasn't a type he knew.

She turned, tripping a little on the aquamarine hem of the negligee, so long it puddled on the floor around her. She said, "Won't you sit down?" Her voice was flat and matter-of-fact. Yet he wasn't sure whether she used a cliché or mocked one.

He set the bottle on the desk and walked past it, going warily to the big maroon chair. "Nice of you to let me come over," he said, perfunctorily. His eye caught certain signs and he was not pleased. He thought he had better get out of here as gracefully as was quick. Obviously, this room was half a man's.

She walked over a bed on her knees and then was standing

38

between the two of them with complete dignity. It was an odd effect, almost as if she didn't notice how she had got there, as if she assumed that of course she must have walked around the bed like a lady. She put her hands on the phone. "We must have some ice," she said grandly.

"Fine."

"Ginger ale?"

The name on that envelope caught in the hasp of the suit-case was Jones. "Whatever you like, Mrs. Jones," Jed said.

She was startled. Her body stiffened as she held herself high in surprise. Then her reddish lashes swept down. Into the phone she said, grandly, "Please send ice and ginger ale to Mrs. Jones in 807."

Jed guessed she was being some movie star or other. But they'd cut a line out of the picture. She forgot to ask for room service. The operator obliged. Looking over Jed's head, posed like a model for a photograph of glamour, the girl repeated her order with exactly the same inflections. It was mimicry, all right.

But when she hung up her whole face changed. "I'm not Mrs. Jones," she told him with sly delight. "Mrs. Jones went out." This wasn't mimicry. It was . . . odd.

Jed looked mildly interrogative.

"This isn't my room," she chuckled.

He thought to himself that this was no worse a dodge than any. "That's funny. The room over there isn't *my* room, either. Coincidence?" He leaned back, grinning.

"Mr. and Mrs. Jones went out," she said frowning.

"The fellow whose room I was in went out, too," said Jed, still grinning. "He's got a date." He felt anger pulse in his neck and jaw. "Lucky guy. Or is he? Or am I?"

She sat down on the bed and stuffed a pillow behind her. "I'm going to South America tomorrow," she remarked lightly.

"Oh? What part?" She didn't answer. "I'm off to Europe, myself," he lied cheerfully. He didn't believe a word she'd said, so far.

"Mr. Jones is my brother," said the girl. "I hate him. I hate all my relatives. They won't let me do anything. They don't want me to have dates." She looked both dreamy and sullen. Jed began to believe some of this. Something was real about it.

"Shall we make it a date?" he suggested. "Would you like to go dancing?"

Her head jerked. He saw her quick desire to go and her recollection of some reason why not . . . the jump of a flame and its quick quenching. "I haven't any evening clothes," she said, and he gawped at such an excuse. If excuse it was. "Mrs. Jones had a beautiful evening dress."

"Your . . . sister-in-law?"

"And a velvet wrap the color of this." She touched the negligee. "You can't buy that for fifty cents an hour."

Jed made no sense of what she was saying. A rap on the door cut into his puzzling. Boy with the ice. Jed got up and turned his back, looking out through the blind as if there was something to see. There was nothing to see but some old biddy writing letters over there. Jed hardly noticed even that. He was annoyed by the notion that he ought not let himself be seen in here.

Still, a hotel, he guessed, in its official consciousness, usually knew by some nervous sympathy what went on within its walls. It pounced or it did not pounce. But it knew. Probably he wasn't fooling anybody.

"Sign, miss?" The boy was mumbling.

The girl was at a complete loss. She had never seen this in the movies. Her grand air was punctured. She didn't know anything about signing a check.

Jed turned around. "Better let me get it, honey." He fumbled for money. "What time did your brother go out?" he asked her over his shoulder.

She said nothing.

"Do *you* know?" Jed watched the boy's worldly young eyes. "Notice a couple in evening clothes? She wore a wrap, that color."

"Mr. and Mrs. Jones?" said the boy smoothly. "Yeah, they left quite a long while ago."

"How long will they be?" Jed asked the girl.

She shrugged. "Some shindig . . ."

"Yeah? Well . . ." Jed watched the boy whose eyes were first satisfied, then veiled. The boy took his tip and departed.

The boy, whose name was Jimmy Reese, went down the corridor jauntily, his lips pursed to whistle, shaping a tune without the breath to make it audible. Eddie's elevator picked him up. They eyed each other with a kind of professional contempt. Jimmy's whistle went right on.

The guy in 807 belonged in 821. This Jimmy knew. Who that girl was, Jimmy did not know. So she was Jones's sister. For all he knew. He didn't know she had anything to do with Eddie. He looked up at the grillwork, coming to the chorus. He didn't think 821 was looking for Jones in there, though. Jimmy kept a lot of amusing things to himself.

Eddie didn't know that Jimmy had just been to 807. He'd listened hard at the eighth floor. He'd eyed the boy. All seemed quiet.

So they sank down, professionally aloof, exchanging no comments, no gossip, no information.

Jed, fixing drinks, thought it over. He hadn't been trying to set up a picture of himself, the dropper-in who had missed his host. He guessed he wasn't fooling anybody. On the other hand, he had established something. Mr. and Mrs. Jones *had* gone out. Who was this, then?

"You got a name?" he asked gently.

"Nell." She told him so absent-mindedly he believed it was true.

Nevertheless, he lied, saying, "I'm John." He handed her a glass.

She took a deep swallow, looked up, and laughed at him. "You don't know what to think about me. You're nervous. You're funny."

He let it ride. He went over and fixed the blind. Then he sat down on the bed next to her. "Where you from, Nell?"

"California."

"What part?"

"All of it."

"You can't do that. California's too big."

"It's not so big."

"San Francisco?"

"Sometimes."

"Tulsa?" he said.

"There, too," she answered serenely. She was rolling this stuff off the top of her head, not even bothering to make sense.

"Where is Tulsa?" he asked, in sudden suspicion.

"In California." She looked surprised.

"Nell," he said amiably, "you're a liar."

"Oh, well," she said, suddenly soft as a kitten, leaning against his arm, "you're lying to me, too."

"I haven't said anything."

"You're lying, just the same."

He took her chin in his left hand, turned her face and searched it and his pulse jumped, recognizing the cockeyed honesty there. You're a liar. I'm a liar. Well? No, it wasn't a look, given cynically, after long practice. There was something perfectly fresh about it.

She was not a type he knew.

"Well?" he said, aloud. He bent his mouth to kiss her.

The taste of her lips was very close when a ripple went down his spine. He turned Nell's quietly waiting face with his hand, pressing it to his shoulder. His neck worked stiffly, slowly. He looked behind.

There was a little girl with dark pigtails, barefooted, in pink pajamas. She was watching them silently.

A wild animal could have startled him no more.

Chapter 7

THE SHOCK seemed to lift him into the air. He croaked, controlling his voice better than his reflexes, "Seems to be an audience." He had pushed Nell to her balance. He had pivoted without straightening his knees. He was suddenly sitting on the other bed, facing the child . . . reaching for his glass. . . .

Jed, going about his business, brushed by the children in the world without making any contact. They didn't interest him. Like philatelists or monks or surrealist painters, they were out of his orbit. Events that had artificially aged him had also knocked awry the continuity of his own memories. It seemed a long time ago, if not in another planet, that he himself had been a child. Fathering none, and, in fact, acquainted with few young parents, Jed didn't know any children, as friends. He would have mentioned "a bunch of kids" as he would comment on a "flock of chickens" or a "hill of ants." He didn't individualize them. He simply had no truck with them.

This little girl, with her dark eyes in an angular face, wasn't a pretty little girl. Too thin. Too solemn.

Nell was in a crouch, leaning on her arms. "Get back in there," she said viciously.

"I want . . ."

Nell went across the bed on her knees. "Go on. Get back in there and go to sleep." Her fingers clawed the little shoulders.

Nobody spoke to Bunny O. Jones in such a fashion. Nobody came crawling at her like a big angry crab. Nobody handled her so cruelly. Bunny was severely startled. She began to cry.

"And shut up!" said Nell.

"Yours?" said Jed coolly.

"She's not mine," said Nell angrily. "She belongs to the Joneses."

"Oh . . . your niece?"

Nell laughed.

"You've got my mommy's things on," wailed Bunny.

"Shut—"

43

"Just a minute." Jed rose. Glass in hand, he came toward them. He was very tall next to Bunny O. Jones. He had no instinct to bend down. "What's your name?" He felt awkward, speaking to this mite, and was impelled to speak loudly as one does to a foreigner or someone who may not readily understand the language.

"I'm Bunny O. Jones." She twisted in Nell's harsh hands.

"Let go of her, Nell. Bunny *Jones*, eh? This isn't your aunt, is it?"

"What are you asking *her* for? She's not supposed to be in *here* . . ."

"Suppose you shut up a minute," Jed said.

"She's my sitter," sobbed Bunny.

"Oh, for Lord's sake." Jed put his glass down and settled his jacket around him with angry shoulder movements. Now he knew what he had got into.

Nell's hands were off the child but not far off. "I don't like you," sobbed Bunny.

"I don't like you either, you damn little snoop," Nell said.

One did *not* speak to these strange little creatures in such terms. Jed felt this much out for himself. It came slowly to him with a sense of how big he was, how big and how powerful even Nell was, and how helpless was the child.

He said, "Nobody's going to hurt you, Bunny. Don't cry."

But she kept on crying. Perhaps she didn't believe him. He couldn't blame her for that. She was shrinking away from Nell. And Nell contrived to loom closer and closer, so that the child was menaced and pursued and sought to escape, although the chase was neither swift nor far, but done in tiny pulses of the foot on the carpet.

"Why don't you ask her what she wanted?" Jed said.

"She wanted to snoop," said Nell.

But it was clear to Jed that the little girl hadn't snooped for snooping's sake. It was clear to him that she had done nothing in malice. He put his arm like a bar across Nell's path and her throat came against it. "No," he insisted. "There was something. What was it, hm? Bunny? What did you want?"

"It's too hot," wept Bunny. "I want my radiator off."

"You might have asked," Jed said scornfully to Nell. "It's simple enough. I'll take care of it."

He strode through the communicating door, which for all his caution he had not noticed to be open. The other room was stuffy. He found a valve. He thought, Towers, fold your tent. He noticed the exit to the corridor from here, from 809, and the key in the lock.

But the crying child, the girl again pursuing her in that gliding stepless way, were in the room with him.

"It's O.K. now," Jed said. "Cool off in a minute. Better get back to bed."

"*She'll* get back to bed."

Bunny broke and ran. She rolled into the bedclothes. She burrowed as if to hide. She was still crying.

Jed stalked into 807, making directly for the bottle. He had a notion to leave without breaking his stride, snatch the glass, drain it, pick up the bottle, cross the room, and fade away. But he was angry. What a stinking evening! First one thing and then another! Cutting phrases came to his mind. *Now* he understood that crack about fifty cents an hour . . . this late! . . . when it should have informed him, before, if he'd had the wits. He was furious for having been stupid. He was embarrassed and humiliated. He was even half angry with the little girl for having walked in and stared at Towers making a jackass of himself. A baby sitter!

He wanted this Nell to know he was angry. So he freshened from the bottle the drink in the glass.

As Nell, on his heels, entered 807 and closed the door firmly behind her, he snarled, "Were you going to pay me my two bits an hour? Or wasn't this a fifty-fifty proposition?"

"What?" She spoke as if she'd been preoccupied, as if she hadn't quite heard. Her face was serene. She drifted toward the mirror. She touched her hair. It was as if, now that the door was closed, it might as well never have opened.

But Bunny was crying bitterly beyond the wall.

Jed said, furiously, "Why didn't you tell me there was a kid in there?"

"I didn't know she was going to come in here," Nell said.

Jed looked at her. For the first time, something nudged him, something said the word inside his head. But he didn't believe it. The word is easy to say. It falls off the tongue. But it is not so easy to believe, soberly, in all reality.

She walked to where he stood, by the desk that had become the bar.

He'd had cats press themselves around his shoes and ankles.

Nell fitted herself into the hollow of his shoulder and turned up her blind face. She was back where she'd been when so rudely interrupted. She was waiting for them to take up where they had left off. Jed stood still, angry enough to throw her brutally away from him, but bitter enough to stand still in unresponsive contempt.

The little kid was crying, in there, a tearing, breaking—a terrible sound.

Nell's tawny head rested against him. He grabbed her shoulder. "Don't you hear that? You got something the matter with your ears?" He shook her.

"Hmmmmmmm?" She was smiling. She enjoyed being shaken. So he let her go. Her eyes opened. "I heard you. I know what you said. You're mad at me. I don't see why you're mad at me, John. Johnee! I haven't done anything."

"You haven't done anything?"

"No."

"Well," Jed said. He put the stopper in the bottle of liquor and kept it in his hand. He was ready to go. He could make no sense here, no use arguing, no point to that.

"Don't go," Nell said rather shrilly. "I haven't done anything. It's all right now, isn't it? She's gone."

"Gone!" The sound of the child, crying in the next room, was preying on Jed's nerve ends. As bad, he thought, as if a cat had been yowling under his window and he trying to sleep. It was too irregular even to be a background noise. It pierced. It carried you with it into its anguish. "Can't you hear that!"

"That? She'll go to sleep."

"She will?"

Nell shrugged. Using one hand, she lapped the long silk robe so that it didn't drag. She whirled, seeming quite gay. "Can't I have another drink?"

The sounds the kid was making were not, Jed discovered, quite like a cat crying. Either a cat shut up, or it went elsewhere, or you went elsewhere. You got away. And if the cat cried where you couldn't hear it, why, let it cry. He didn't know anything about kids. But you didn't need to know anything. Just listening told you. *This* sound of *this* crying had to stop.

"Does it bother you?" the girl said rather casually, holding out her glass.

"It bothers the hell out of me," Jed said roughly. "She's scared. And you did that. Why did you have to jump at her like a wildcat? This the way you always treat your customers?" He poured whisky into her glass, hardly aware he was doing so.

She looked sullen. "I didn't mean to scare her."

"She startled *me*. O.K. But you knew she was in there. You're supposed to be taking care of her, aren't you? Listen . . ."

He was listening, himself, all the time. The sound was intolerable. "You better get her to stop that."

"When she gets tired . . ."

"You want the whole hotel up here?" he snapped.

"No." She looked alarmed.

"Then do something. I'm telling you."

He stalked toward an ash tray, walking between the beds. "If I go in there, you'll sneak out," Nell said flatly. The thought was crossing Jed's mind as she spoke. He put the whisky down beside the phone. He took his hand off the bottle as if it were hot.

"I don't have to sneak out, you know," he said cuttingly. "I can walk out, just about any time. I won't stay here and listen to that, I'll tell you."

"If she stops crying, will you stay?"

"I doubt it."

She put her glass in her left hand and worked her right as if it were stiff and cold. Her blue eyes had too much blue.

"This is no business of mine, remember," Jed said, slashing the air with a flat hand. "Nothing to do with me. But I'm telling you . . . Why don't you try being a little bit nice?"

"Nice?"

"Don't smirk at *me*. Nice to the kid in there. Are you stupid? What am I wasting my—"

"This is a date, isn't it?" she began. "You asked me—"

But Jed was thinking how that little throat must ache. His own throat felt raw. He growled, "Get her quiet. Get her happy. Go on."

"If I do?"

"If you do," he said rather desperately, "well . . . maybe we can have a quiet little drink before I go."

The girl turned, put down her glass, went to the door and opened it quietly. She moved obediently. She vanished in the darkness.

"I'm afraid," Lyn said, "Mr. Towers must have gone out again. His room doesn't answer."

"I can only say I didn't see him, Miss." The man behind the desk at the Majestic wasn't terribly interested.

"But you did see him come in a little while ago?"

"Yes, I did." He threw her a mildly irritated glance.

"Well . . ." she turned uncertainly.

"A message?" he suggested politely. She was a cute girl, trim and cuddly in the bright blue coat with the big brass buttons. And she seemed distressed.

"Yes, I could leave a note."

He used a pencil to point the way to a writing desk in the lobby, aiming it between a pillar and a palm.

"Yes, I see. Thank you." Lyn sat down at the desk, put her purse down under her left forearm. She shifted the chair slightly so that she could keep an eye on a spot anyone entering the Hotel Majestic from the street must pass.

She thought he must have gone out again, perhaps through the bar. She hoped he wasn't, even now, upsetting her family. She herself didn't dare call home to ask. If they didn't know she was alone, so much the better. They'd have a fit, she thought. A fit. But . . . never mind. If they were anxious, too bad, but she was actually safe enough and they'd forgive and perhaps they'd even have confidence enough in her not to worry too much.

This was something she had to work out for herself. The family tended to side too blindly with her. Any man, they would assume, so benighted as to quarrel with their darling would never be worth her efforts to patch it up.

But I can be wrong, she thought, not far from tears.

No, she couldn't go home quite yet. She'd stay free for a while, even as long as a date might have lasted. Because this was important. She knew. It would be hard to explain how and why . . . embarrassing . . . maybe impossible. She had to work it out alone.

Anyhow, she didn't think Jed would go to her apartment. It would be capitulation. He wasn't that type. He was pretty proud.

Was she the type, then, to hang around? All right, she thought stubbornly, I *won't* be the huffy female type who, right or wrong, sits and waits for the male to come with his hat in his hand, like the dopey heroines of old romances who huffed and waited their lives away.

Ah, nobody was a type! This was Jed and Lyn, and this had to be worked out on the basis that they were unique and alive, and it had to be worked out *now*. Tomorrow, the plane . . .

Wherever he was, he'd come back here. He hadn't checked out. It was all so childish. . . . She could at least say that much.

"Dear Jed," she wrote. "It was all so childish . . ." She watched a man and a woman cross the lobby. "And I don't want you to go West thinking that I . . ."

Am I doing this, she wondered, because I'm vain? "Thinking that I . . ." what? How could such bitter words have been spoken between them? Because she'd been riding a high romantic crest of expectation and been dragged rudely off it? Maybe, for him, there'd never been such a crest. No, no. That was a huffy-type thought, a fear to *seem* vain. She *had* known that Jed was fond of her. She'd had *reason* to expect him to say so or say more. Never mind that inside-out kind of vanity.

She tore up the sheet and wrote again, "Dear Jed: I've been trying to find you because—" A tear fell and the ink blurred and she thought, Oh no . . . not this! Wouldn't he be amused!

Would he? Lyn sat a long time with her hands quiet on the desk. She worked it out. It was true. She was in love with Jed Towers . . . in love enough to lash out at him, to get as mad as that, to have it matter.

It was true. She had thought he might ask her to marry him tonight. They'd been together, together . . . until that old man touched this off.

And it was true. She'd have said "yes." Gladly, yes. Yes, right or wrong. Yes, just because of his mouth, maybe.

And they had quarreled.

But it was *not* true that she thought him a cheap cynic. He was . . . wary. Yes, he was. And he talked cynically. Part of it was simple reporting—what he saw around him. Part of it was defensive . . . or something like that. But it was talk. People don't always know what they are. They talk *at* themselves a lot. She thought, but I can really be tough. If I believe, then I must do . . . or all *I* said was only talk.

So Lyn worked it out, painfully. It was also true, whoever began it, whatever it amounted to, she had been the one to walk away, and cut off communication, and she didn't (she'd always *said*) believe in that.

Very well. She clasped her hands. It was important. Here was a crest from which she would coast away all her life long. And a huff wouldn't do.

But what could she put on a piece of paper? If only he'd come. People crossed the lobby, none of them he. Tomorrow, that plane . . . Maybe he'd call her. No, it went so early. She could ask in the note. All her thoughts were splintering. Dawn was such a chilly time.

She took up the pen. "Dear Jed: I can't let you go—" But you can't keep him, Lyn. He isn't that type. Maybe he was only something charming and exciting flashing through your life, and what you seemed in his, for a little while, you'll never know. Might have discovered whether there was any meaning but not now—too late. "Misunderstanding," she wrote desperately. It was too late. She ought to go home.

What can I say? she wondered. What can I do? How can I go home?

Get out of here, Towers. Get out, quick. And forget it. Skip it. Jed paid his inner talk to himself no heed. He sat down on a bed. Under the verbalized thought ran uneasy pictures. What if the child were to cry a long time, and he, in his own room, could hear? How was he in a position to be the indignant guest, to protest, to do anything about it? *He'd* been stupid. Nell, the baby sitter, had already made a complete jackass out of Towers. This rose to world level. He looked into his glass and contemplated this state of affairs.

When Nell came back carrying the child, he knew her reason. She didn't trust him not to sneak away. He remained quietly where he was. He was not entirely displeased. He wanted to watch her quiet the child.

"If you're scared, that's silly. Nothing to be scared about," Nell said impatiently. "Now don't start to cry any more. Shall I read another story?"

"No," said Bunny. She wasn't quite crying at the moment, but she was shaken by an aftermath of shuddering. It was a reaction not subject to her control.

Nell set her down on her bare feet. Three strangely assorted people looked rather helplessly at each other.

"You know, *you* nearly scared the life out of me," Jed said to the child in a friendly tone. "And Nell, too. That's why Nell was cross."

"She was . . . too . . . cross," said Bunny as well as she could.

"That she was," he agreed grimly.

Nell looked as if she would flare up defensively, but she did not. "You O.K. now?" Her voice was edgy. "You're not going to cry any more?"

Bunny wasn't sure enough to say. Her eyes turned from one to the other.

"I'm a friend of Nell's, stopped by to see her a minute," Jed said, feeling his face flush. Why he should be trying to explain himself to this half-pint creature he didn't quite know. "You ought to be asleep, I guess," he went on awkwardly. "How old are you?"

"Nine."

Nine. What was it to be nine? Jed couldn't remember. The drinks were beginning to blur his concern a little. He began to feel these events less shattering, as if his ego went somewhere and lay down.

"I'm too hot," said Bunny. "I'm all sticky."

"Come over here, then." Nell went to the windows. "We'll let some cool air blow on you. Then you'll be cooler. Then you can go back to sleep." She nodded wisely. She pulled up the blind. She pushed up the sash.

Jed jumped quickly out of the line of vision through those windows. His back felt for the head board. He poured another drink. The ice was all the way over there. So, no ice. Because he wouldn't cross in front of the windows. Place like a goldfish bowl. He knew. And that was where you made your mistake, Towers.

"See the lady, Bunny?"

Sob and shudder answered.

"I see a man, down there. He's playing cards."

Jed's warm drink was nauseating.

"I think," Nell went on, "there's a kitten under the table."

"What," sob, "table?"

"Down there. The card table."

"I don't see . . ."

"Maybe it isn't a kitten. But it looks like a kitten."

"I've got a cat," Bunny said. "Is the kitten stripe-ed?"

"No."

"Is it gray?"

"Maybe."

Miss Eva Ballew wrote, on the Hotel Majestic stationery, in her flowing script . . . "seems to be a child crying in this hotel and I am so distracted, I hope you can understand what I am writing, since I seem to have two predicates and no subject in my previous sentence! My dear, this trip has really . . ."

Her pen paused. The child had stopped crying. Thank goodness, thought Miss Ballew. But now the night seemed hollow. She ducked her head enough to glance briefly out, under her blind.

The pen resumed, "been a treat for all us teachers to have visited so many historical sites here in the East . . ." It was not a sentence.

She put down her pen suddenly and ducked again to look out, across the dark well of the inner court.

"I don't see any kitten," Bunny said, "at all." Her pigtails hung down in front, swinging.

"Well, you're not looking . . ." Nell said softly. "But you won't cry any more, will you?"

Jed glanced across at the bowl of ice. He rose. Why did she have to put the damn blind up? Dare he cross over? *Was* there anybody taking all this in? He'd just as soon get out of here without some guest having seen . . .

When he turned his head over his shoulder, the question dropped out of his mind. He stood quite still, puzzling about what was wrong. It seemed to him, definitely, that something was wrong. Bunny was kneeling on that radiator top. And Nell sat there, beside her. Nell's hand was flat on the little rump in the pink sprigged muslin—

Her hand was flat!

And there was some wild throbbing in this room.

Miss Eva Ballew, peering out, exclaimed. Nobody heard her, for she was alone. "No!" she said. Then, whimpering, "Oh, no! Please!"

The back of Jed's neck prickled. Must be his own pulse, doing that throbbing. Just the same, it was intolerable. He began to move, silently, with the speed and grace of the young and strong.

"Way down under the table?" Bunny asked.

"Way down . . ." crooned Nell. "Way, way down. Are you going to be quiet, I wonder?"

Bunny screamed.

Jed, with his fingers tight around the little brown ankle, caught her forward pitch with one arm and said, on a rush of breath, "Excuse me. Shouldn't lean out like that, for Lord's sakes. I *had* to grab."

Nell's face turned, tipped back and up. She looked drowsy and unstartled. "What?" she murmured. "What's the matter?"

Jed had the child. "Better come away," he said to her. "You'll catch cold, anyhow." He could feel little twitches the whole length of the arm that held Bunny. He squeezed her as gently as he could manage. "I'm sorry, honey, if I scared you. Trouble is, you scared *me* again. Sure did. Awful long ways down—kind of tough landing."

Bunny, having screamed once in her surprise, did not begin to cry. Her face was pale. Her big dark eyes seemed to turn and keep some wisdom of her own.

Jed said, "You're chilly. You're shivering. Aren't you sleepy now?"

Bunny nodded. She wiggled out of his arm. Her feet hit the carpet. She looked at him gravely. "I can go to bed myself," said Bunny O. Jones.

———

Miss Ballew straightened her cramped body. Her heart still lurched with that old devil of hers, that hair-trigger onset of the physical sickness of fear. She felt her throbbing throat. But what was going *on*, over there? Her pale lips tightened. She'd heard the man say, "Put that blind down!"

So, it was to be secret, and it was male, and it was, perhaps, evil? She focused on her letter. "And even in this wicked city," her pen wrote, at last, too shakily.

"Put that blind down!"

Nell was still sitting by the window, still looking dreamy. She stretched to obey and Jed thought there was something snake-like in the smooth uncoiling of her arching back and her reaching arm.

He stood at the door of 809, through which Bunny had marched herself. 809 was quiet . . . dim and quiet in there. So he closed the door, gently.

Bunny's rigid neck muscles let go a little. The head began to dent the pillow. The eyes were wide open. The hand reached for the little stuffed dog and tucked it under the stiff chin. The throat moved, against the fluffy toy, in a great and difficult swallow.

Jed swung around. You're nuts, Towers, he said to himself, angrily, using the words, in his mind, to knock out the pictures. You must be nuts. Where'd you get such a nutty idea? Nobody shoves kids out of eighth-story windows, so they won't cry any more! Made his hair curl, the mere idea, even now. Where had he got it?

He began to fish ice out of the bowl.

It crossed the level of his mind where slang was not the language that there is something wild about total immersion in the present tense. What if the restraint of the future didn't exist? What if you never said to yourself, "I'd better not. I'll be in trouble if I do"? You'd be wild, all right. Capricious, unpredictable . . . absolutely wild.

He looked at the girl. She was leaning beside him, watching

the ice chunk into her glass, with a look of placid pleasure. She glanced up. "You've had more than me," she stated.

"That's right," Jed said. He felt perfectly sober. The slight buzz was gone. He didn't bother to put ice into his own glass, after all. He wasn't going to have any more liquor, not for a while.

He gave her the drink. He sat down, nursing his warm glass.

He couldn't get rid of the shimmer on his nerves of narrowly missed horror. Nuts, Towers. Forget it. She was careless. Nobody's going to have an idea like that one. She just wasn't thinking what she was doing.

"I guess I wasn't thinking," Nell said, with a delicate shrug.

"Are you a mind reader?" He sagged back on his elbow. "That's a couple of times you've said what I had in my mouth, practically."

She didn't answer.

"But you sure should have put a good hitch on the seat of her pants or something. Don't you know that's dangerous?" If the future didn't operate in your thinking, you wouldn't even know that word, he thought. Danger wouldn't have a meaning. Would it? He shivered. His mind veered.

If there *was* such a thing as telepathy, why, it would work both ways. If she could catch an idea out of his mind, then he might catch one of hers. Couldn't he? *Hadn't he?* Listen, Towers, don't be any nuttier than you have to be! Mind reading, yet! Fold your tent . . . fade away.

But he was hunting for comfort. He remembered something. He said, "So you couldn't go dancing with me on account of the kid?" (So, you did feel responsible?)

"Uncle Eddie's on the elevator."

"Huh?"

"He'd have caught me, going out," she said placidly. "He never lets me."

"Your Uncle? Uncle Eddie runs an elevator? In this hotel?"

"Yes."

"Oh." Jed turned this information over. "Maybe he got you the job, eh?"

"Yeah," she said with weary scorn, "my wonderful job."

"You don't like it?"

"What's there to like?" she said. And he saw the answer come into her head. He saw it! He *read* it! "There's you, though," Nell was thinking.

He closed his eyes and shook his own head. None of that. But he considered, and on the whole he thought he felt relieved. The future tense had operated. Hadn't it? If she thought ahead of her, to Eddie on the elevator?

His mind skipped to his own future. Tomorrow morning on the airplane. By tomorrow night, a continent away, looking back on a weird evening, which was about over, he judged. Time to go.

His anger was gone. *He* was operating in the future tense, looking back, saying to somebody, "And *what* a sitter! What a dame she turned out to be! Nutty as a fruitcake!" he would say. If he ever said anything.

"Well," he spoke. "Nell, I'll tell you. It might have been fun. We'll never know. So here's to the evening. Bottoms up and then good-by. See you in South America, sometime?"

He grinned. Her eyes were too blue, not in the quality of the blue, but in the quantity. Strange eyes . . .

"You're not going," she said, with no rising inflection at all. It wasn't even a protest. She just said this, as if it were so.

Chapter 8

THE UNWRITTEN law that links green peas to roast chicken had not been flouted tonight. Peter pointed with his fork and winked. He wasn't really eating.

Ruth could eat no more than he. They picked and pretended. But nobody, she thought, was there for the sake of nourishment. The food marched by, as it were, in a sedate order, perfectly conventional, with no surprises, so that nothing about it should interrupt the real business of the banquet. Be seen, buzz, bow . . . Preen yourself, flatter your neighbor. Oh, it *was* fun!

But now they were nearly past the ice cream. They were at the coffee . . . the end of the line. Peter's conversation with his neighbors had been slowly lessening. Fewer and fewer words came out of him.

Ruth's nerves tightened right along with his. She let a little ice cream melt in her dry mouth. Peter was taking tiny sips of water, oftener now.

Every once in a while, the buzzing and the bending-to-chat got a little unreal for Ruth—whenever Bunny came into her mind. It was a little distressing that her vision of Bunny in her bed was shaky and unreal, too. Bunny, she told herself, making words, as if the words had power, was sound asleep. As sound asleep as if she were in her bed at home. Oh, Bunny was real! Warm and beloved, Bunny was there. But those hotel rooms, those formulas, did not wrap her around with the safe sense of being home.

But *of course not*! Ruth said to herself.

Still, it was a great city, vast and unknown, and the West Side seemed divorced from the East Side, where they were . . . seemed far.

"I'd like to call back to the hotel pretty soon," she murmured to Peter. "Where are the phones?"

"Saw them as we came through," Peter said. "Around the corner, past those mirrors . . ." He dabbled in his ice cream. The toastmaster was still chatting peacefully.

"Have I time, do you think?" breathed Ruth. They, at the

57

speaker's table, were as far as it was possible to be, away from the double doors to the mirrored place beyond which were the telephones. Parade, in my pink, thought Ruth. Conspicuous. Peter could not go, *now*.

The toastmaster shifted in his chair. He sipped his coffee. Ruth felt all Peter's muscles wince. For the toastmaster glanced their way and made a tiny nod. His eyes nodded deeper than his head did.

Imperceptibly, Peter responded. The toastmaster shoved with his hips and his chair began to move backward.

Not now! No time, now! Ruth would call, afterward. After the man had said whatever he was going to say. Later than that, for without intermission, it would then be Peter's turn!

It would be good to call, later, with this tension gone. And all clear. Oh yes, it would be much better.

There was no doubt that Bunny was sound asleep, anyway. Ruth must now lift her chin and turn her head and listen sweetly to the Speaker of the Evening. (Oh, what was he going to say! Oh, *Peter*!)

Bunny was nine and surely had fallen sound asleep by this time.

The toastmaster rose like Fate. Ruth released her glass and patted her cold hands together in tune with the crowd. "I am happy," the man said, "to be here . . ." Who cares how happy they are? Always so *happy*! She could hear every tiny wheeze of the toastmaster's breathing. Peter had turned slightly in his chair, as if this were fascinating, but no concern of his, of course. . . .

"And I am particularly glad," the man said, "to have this opportunity . . ." They were always so *glad*!

Ruth smiled faintly and let her fingers play with her water glass. She must display the perfect confidence she felt, that under her pounding heart lay so truly sure. . . .

Jed fended her off and it was balm to do so. It was sweet revenge on the whole female race who had loused up his evening. He laughed at her. He had her by the elbows, at arm's length. "It's not that automatic, toots," he said. "I know. There's a school of thought that says it is. But make a note, why don't you? There is such a thing as being choosy."

Her rage made him laugh and he let himself go back against the headboard. "The time, the place, and the girl," he mocked. "*I'll* choose them all, and this ain't *any* of them, sweetheart."

She looked ready to screech. But then her face closed down, took on that sleepy look. She leaned heavily on his grasp, limply, now, with nothing but her weight.

"So I'll say so long, Nell," he snapped, watching her suspiciously. "Understand?"

The wild thing about her which, he knew now, had attracted him in the first place, and then made him uneasy, was getting entangled with her will. She wasn't sleepy. Oh, no! Now, he knew that the dreamy look was, on her, a dangerous sign. Maybe a part of her did go to sleep. Maybe it was the part that took into account the future.

He sat up, thrusting her with stiff forearms. He was a little bit sorry for having indulged himself in that laughter. He wondered just how he was going to get out of here without a row, without, say, too much racket. He said, quietly, "I'm really sorry, but I've got to go. Some other time, Nell."

She didn't seem to hear. Then, she did seem to hear, not his voice, but something less loud and less near. Her pupils traveled to the right corners of her eyes.

He heard it, too. There came a discreet tapping on the door of Room 807.

Oh-oh! Exit Towers! Jed muttered under his breath, "I'll get out the other way, through the kid's room."

"No." She spoke no louder than he, not a whisper, only a movement of the lips that was nearly mute. "You won't." The words were clear and stubborn on her small mouth.

". . . find me," he said in the same fashion, "you'll lose your job."

The tapping was gently repeated. It would persist, insist. It was patient.

Nell's face lit in malice and delight. "No, no. I'll say . . . you pushed in here. Say you're . . . after me."

Jed's eyes flickered. She would, too. She damn well would! He was quite sure she would. For the hell of it! For the sheer wild mischief of it! And, if she did, the benefit of the doubt rests with the female.

"You wait," she said. "I know who it is."

Their almost soundless conversation was taking place in a depth of silence that was uncanny. The room pressed silence around them. The city bayed at the feet of the building, but here, high, they spoke without voices in a soundless place. Although someone kept tapping in gentle hope upon the door.

"Who?" Jed was rigid in alarm. How in hell was he going to get off this spot? What to do?

"It's Uncle Eddie. I can get rid of him."

"I can get out," Jed gestured. His eyes were somber.

"No." She knew her wild will held him.

"What, then?" He ground his teeth.

"In there. Be quiet." She intended him to hide in the bathroom!

He rose, slowly, letting her go. He could knock her aside. He could get swiftly into the kid's room.

And she could yell.

And she was opening her mouth.

Jed stalled, by picking up the bottle and hiding it in his pocket. Quickly, she put his glass into his hand. And then she had him by the elbow. She was pushing, guiding.

The tapping faltered. "Nell?" someone said softly and a trifle anxiously. "Nell?"

Nell said, "Who's there?" Her very voice seemed to stretch and yawn. But her eye was watching Jed and her face rippled. She would just as leave cause trouble . . . just as leave as not!

"It's Uncle Ed. You all right?"

Nell's brows spoke to Jed. Twitted him with it. *Well?* they asked. *Am I?*

He growled, voice muted in the bottom of his throat. "O.K. Make it snappy." He went into the bathroom and pushed the door back behind him, not quite tight.

"Gee, I'm sorry, Uncle Eddie. I guess I must have been asleep," he heard her saying . . . heard her yawning it.

Towers stood in the bathroom and cursed Towers in his mind. What'd she have, a hex on him? Of all the damned lousy situations. He looked at his watch. He said to himself, Let Uncle Eddie get away and I am gone. Brother, will I be gone. I really fade. Without a word, he'd go. Without a waste motion.

You picked up dames, sure. Every once in a while. On a train. Maybe in a bar. Sometimes a thing like that turned out not bad. If it was sour, you blew. In cold blood. You got out, fast.

How come Towers was hiding behind a door?

He sat on the edge of the tub, to wait, reciting curses, rehearsing in his mind his swift passage out and away.

Lyn turned away from the phones. No answer.

I will smoke another cigarette, one more. I will wait until ten more people come in from the street, ten more. I can write a better letter. I know I can. I can try.

Chapter 9

EDDIE LOOKED at his niece in the negligee and his eyes were disappointed. He said, "I brought the cokes." Disappointment made his voice bleak. He had the bottles in his hands and he went toward the desk and stood there looking down at the tray, the bowl of melting ice, and Nell's glass. "What's this?" An inch and a half of rye and ginger ale remained in the glass.

Nell said, "You were a long time, Uncle Eddie. I got thirsty. Let me wash that out." She took the glass out of his meek hand. "I ordered ginger ale," she said defiantly to his troubled eyes. "Mrs. Jones said I could."

"That was nice of her," said Eddie.

"Want a piece of candy?" Nell said brightly over her shoulder. "She said I could help myself."

"I don't believe I care for any," Eddie said. "Thanks." His bleak stare went around the room.

Nell pushed in the bathroom door. She went to the wash basin and rinsed the glass.

Not even in the mirror did her eye meet Jed's. There was not a gesture, not a wink, not a sign that she even knew he was there. Jed felt his blood rage. It was an abuse of power. A little grin, a tiny glance, a hint that they conspired to fool this Eddie, would have eased the thing, somehow. But, oh, no! She'd forced him into this ignominy and now she let him stew in it. He could have beaten her. He ground his teeth. Some baby sitter!

Eddie said, "Little girl sleeping? I see you closed her door."

Nell left the bathroom, pulling its door behind her. She would have closed that, but Jed threw his strength on the inner knob and they tugged secretly, silently, and she lost.

"Could you hear if she cried or anything?" Eddie was saying in worried tones.

"The light bothered her," Nell lied calmly.

"Now she's sleeping, though, it won't bother her." Eddie, gentle on the knob, released the catch. "I think Mrs. Jones would rather it was a little bit open, Nell."

"O.K." she said indifferently. She waited for the coke.

"And it's getting later. It would be better if you took Mrs. Jones's clothes off, Nell. Honest, I thought . . ." Eddie's adam's apple betrayed his hurt, although his voice was careful.

"Gee, I meant to." Nell's fine teeth bit her lip. "I was so kinda comfortable . . . I just didn't hurry . . ."

At once, Eddie brightened. "Sure you meant to, Nell. I know that. Uh—" he fiddled with an opener. "Why don't you do it now, though?"

"All right, Uncle Eddie." She sat docilely down on the little bench and slipped her feet out of the mules. Eddie scrambled for her own black pumps and she put them on. Then she took the earrings off, slowly. She put them into the jewel box. Her fingers began to pick up other things, tidying them, putting them away.

Eddie brightened with his lightening heart. "That's right! Good girl!"

She turned her bent head, smiled at him. She rose and her hands worked at the sash of Ruth's gown. Eddie's eyes turned primly down. Nell said, sounding modest and shy, "I'll just step into the closet."

Her Uncle Eddie took a long relieved pull on his coke bottle.

She came out of the closet in her own rumpled dark dress. It had been a heap on the closet floor for some time. But now Nell made elaborate motions of finicky care as she hung the negligee on a hanger and arranged its folds. "There," she said, "that's just the way it was. Is that O.K., Uncle Eddie?"

He beamed on her. "That's fine, Nell. Now!" He sighed. "Mightn't be so very long before they get back, you know. But you're all set."

"We'd better drink our cokes," she said mildly. "It might look better if I was alone in here. Do you think?"

"You're right," he said. "Yes, you're right. I told them I was going to drop in, but it *would* be better if they find everything quiet and you on the job, eh? Well, here you are. You know," he blurted, "I want to do everything *for* you, don't you, Nell? You know why I want you to take a nice little job like this. I want you to get started."

"I know, Uncle Eddie." She was all meekness. Her lashes were lowered. She showed no sign of impatience at all.

He took a swig. "Well, it's because I believe in you, Nell. And Aunt Marie does, too." His blink was contradicting the courage in his voice. "I think you'd rather be here with us than back in Indiana."

"Oh, I would," she murmured.

"If the insurance company would have paid on the house and furniture—but as it is, there's nothing left. You know that. So you'd be on some kind of charity, till you got a job, and I wouldn't like that for Denny's girl."

"No," she said.

"You know I haven't got much money," he went on. "I got a steady job. But you can see why it's a good thing if you can . . . kinda get over this trouble pretty soon."

"I'm O.K.," she said without force.

"You're *better*. That's sure. You certainly are a lot better."

She was looking at him with that blind blue abstraction she sometimes had. "But they ought to pay," she said. "Why can't we make them pay?"

"I don't know how we can," said Eddie uneasily. "I don't know if we can ever *make* them. You see, they claim, because the fire was *set* . . ."

"It was an accident." Her voice went higher. And he cleared his throat nervously. "*Wasn't* it?"

"It was. It was. That's what they said in the court, yes. It was an accident."

Suddenly her face was calm, her glance cold. "So why don't they pay?"

"Well, the insurance company, they figure—I tell you, Nell. I think it's best to kinda forget about that. Might take a lawyer and quite a lot of money and you wouldn't be sure you could win, you see? I think the best thing is, forget about that and try and get started . . . There wasn't so much insurance. How's the coke?"

"It's good," she said meekly. "Is yours?"

"Fine." He took another swig. It might have been wine, for he seemed to mellow. "You just needed somebody to stand back of you," he said. "Me and Marie knew that, Nell, at the time. And we do stand back of you. We really do. *I* can understand just why it is you get kinda restless streaks. *I* don't blame you."

"You've been good, Uncle Eddie." Her lips barely moved.

But he looked very happy. "It's just that I can see how it is," he said eagerly. "After such a terrible experience, a lot of little things seem pretty *little*. Don't matter much, eh? That's the way it is, isn't it, Nell?" The little man seemed to hold his breath. Every fiber of his worried little being was yearning to make contact, to understand and be understood.

The girl didn't look up, but she nodded.

He swallowed and leaned closer. He said softly, "You want to remember, Nell, your father and mother don't blame you. You mustn't ever think that they would. They know you wouldn't ever have done anything bad, Nell . . . not to them. You see, wherever they are, *they* must know that even better than we do. And if they could talk to you . . ."

"I don't want to think about them," she said in a perfect monotone. "I don't want to think about them."

"No, no," said Eddie quickly. "Nobody wants to make you think . . . about that. But I been trying to tell you one thing, Nell. The doctor said it would be good if you'd know . . . and here we're so quiet and all, maybe I can say it. Me and your Aunt Marie, we stand back of you. We believe in you. We don't doubt, for one minute, you set the fire walking in your sleep that night . . ."

He watched her face. Her lashes flickered. "That's what the court said," she remarked lightly.

"But—but—don't cry," he whispered to the tearless blue of her eyes.

"I'm not going to cry, Uncle Eddie." She turned her empty glass in her fingers. She put it down.

Eddie blinked the tears out of his own eyes. He swallowed the sick flutter of his heart. That Julia his brother married, something about her he never had liked. But surely she'd never been mean to Nell. Denny wouldn't have stood for it. Denny wouldn't be mean to anybody. No, no. There could be *no reason*. She was still shocked, poor Nell. She *couldn't* cry. She *loved* them. She'd meant no harm. She'd cry, someday. *Sure*, she'd cry.

"Tasted pretty good, didn't it?" he said cheerily.

Jed controlled his rage almost immediately. He'd got into this jam by getting senselessly angry and it was about time, he told himself, that Towers used the brains he was born with. He settled coldly to wait this out. He could hear their voices and a part of his brain recorded the words.

But, in part and at the same time, he was reviewing the way he had come. It had come back to him, the year he was nine. Not the events of that year, so much, as the feel of it. By then, he mused, the boy was all adjusted to the family. He had been trained. He knew what the rules of conduct were in so far as his mother and father had taught them. All that was smooth, so smooth he couldn't remember much about it.

But he was also stepping out, newly bold, into the world his parents did not know. He was beginning to test himself more daringly with his contemporaries. School, the gang, society and his personal meeting with it had been the part of life that was filled with interest. Warm security at home and one toe in the cold waters of the outer world, testing to take his weight.

Pretty soon, he remembered, the boy began to pick up the stuff that isn't down in the home rules. The ways and the means, the maneuverings, the politics, the exchanges of influences, the worming one's way, the self-interest of everybody and how to use *this* for himself. Through high school and a part of college, and then the war, and the final bitter tutoring of the peace. Sharper lessons, all the time. Trial and error. What worked and what didn't. Lessons in the possible. Knocking home what's possible and what is not, and what is only a fool's goal.

So now, here's Towers. A young man, out to "make his fortune" as they used to say in the old stories when he was nine. Out to make his fortune without a dream in his eye. Wangled himself a damn good job on the coast. Pulled strings to get it. Young man on the way up, and gangway for him! Old enough to begin to think, if only obliquely, that he might take a wife.

So Lyn was on his mind, eh? A dream, there? He pushed her image away.

So, here was Towers, skipping the whole middle of the country, tomorrow, letting it flow under his plane, not planning to stop and see the family. Why? Oh, business, he'd said. They understood. Not wishing to stop and hear the blind love speaking, pretending he was nine?

Well, he thought, people probably settled on a pattern that worked, for them, and there they stayed. And if his pattern was shaping up a little differently, why, no use arguing. Dad talked service. Lived it, too, as far as anyone could see. And it worked, for him. Or anyhow, it worked pretty well. It made a kind of guide, a touchstone . . . Jed could see. And mother talked love—*was* love, dammit. He wished, a little wistfully, that the world really was what they seemed, incomprehensibly, able to assume it was. How come they could hang onto that kind of peace, whatever it was, and make it a shell around them?

Or did they? Were they besieged by disappointments? Were they only huddled in their shell, like people in a fort? He didn't see much of them, these days. It was the family tradition to exchange only cheerful news, as far as one could. Did their hearts despair?

He didn't want to think so. He supposed you battled through, sooner or later, and came out on the other side of struggle, when you accepted something or other and put the blinders on and just kept them on and didn't look, any more.

But when you're young and scrambling in the market place, you have to watch out. Yeah, out. Not in. That is, take a hard look at the way the world operates. You didn't want to be pushed around.

Oh, Towers was a wise one, all right, sitting on the bathtub, behind the door. He knew the score.

His jaw was tight. Definitely, a detour, this little expedition. Get on your way, Towers!

Still talking, this Uncle Eddie? Still yammering in there?

"And so, I thought," Eddie was saying, "the best idea is for you to start out easy. Take a little job once in a while. The thing is, Nell," he was expounding his creed, "you do something for somebody else and you do a good job. So they're glad to pay you for it. Then you're earning. You're being useful. You got to get into the idea. After a while, you'll get so you can do a bigger job or a better job. You'll get into the idea. You'll get over being so restless."

"You told me all this," she said. Her ankle was swinging.

Eddie saw it and silenced himself.

"Going?" she murmured. Her head fell against the chair. She turned her cheek. Her eyes closed.

"I'll take the coke bottles. I don't think the Joneses are going to be so long, now. Couple of hours, maybe. Tired?"

She didn't answer. Eddie rose and the bottles clinked together as he gathered them. She was breathing slowly. "I'll be
in the building," he murmured. His eye checked over the
room. Everything was in pretty good order. Looked all right.
He took up the glass from which Nell had sipped her coke.

Absorbed in his own thoughts, his anxieties, his endeavors,
his gains and his losses, Eddie went mechanically toward the
running water, which was in the bathroom.

Chapter 10

EVEN BEFORE he met, in the mirror, the little man's shocked and unbelieving eyes, an appraisal of this new situation flooded clearly through Jed's thoughts. The jig was up, all right. O.K. He rose smoothly. The frightened eyes followed him up, still by way of the glass. But Jed was smiling.

This could be handled.

The mind has an odd ability to play back, like a tape recorder, things heard and yet not quite attended to at the time. Jed knew, immediately, that Eddie could be handled. And that it was a way out for Towers, too.

He knew from what he had overheard that Eddie was by no means sure of his little niece Nell. Eddie had stuck his neck out, getting her this job. Eddie knew she was unreliable, to put it mildly, although he tried, he struggled, to make himself believe everything was going to be all right. All that pitch about his belief and understanding, all that stuff, was a hope and a prayer, not any conviction. Oh yes. Eddie had taken an awful chance here and Eddie was liable.

All Jed needed to do was use Eddie's self-interest. Very simple. Jed would apologize. Nothing happened, really. Had a couple of drinks, very sorry, sir, he'd say. I'll be leaving now. No harm done and enough said. Nobody need say anything more about it?

Jed would make it easy for the other fellow. He'd ask silence as a favor to himself. Eddie could escape by magnanimity the consequences of his own folly. Eddie would be glad to say "good-by" and only good-by.

So long, Nell, Jed would say, quietly. And he'd be out of it.

So Jed rose, smiling, knowing he had the power of charm and attractive friendliness when he chose to use it. In the time it took him to rise and open his mouth, the little man had jerked with a mouse-squeak and backed toward the door, keeping a frightened face toward Jed's tall figure in the tile-lined gloom. Jed not to alarm him, stood quietly where he was.

But Nell, like a cat, was lithe lightning across room 807. She had the standing ash tray, the heavy thing, in her wild hands.

She swung it up. Jed's lunge and Jed's upraised arm missed the downswing. The thing cracked on Eddie's skull. The detachable portion of heavy glass clanged and boomed and echoed on the tile. And Jed said something hoarse and furious and snatched the thing out of her hands cruelly, and Nell jabbered some shrill syllables.

All at once, the noise was frightful.

Only Eddie made no noise. He sank down, very quietly.

There was an instant when everything was suspended. Then the phone began to ring, in 807, and at the same time Bunny's voice screamed terror, in 809. And the glass part of the ash tray, rolling off a brief balance, rumbled and at last stopped rolling, unbroken.

"Now!" said Jed thickly. "Now, you . . ." He squatted beside the crumpled little body.

Nell turned and walked over to the telephone, which in some freak of time had rung four times already.

"Hello?" Her voice was fuzzy and foggy.

Jed touched Eddie's temple and then his throat.

"Oh yes, Mrs. Jones," Nell said. "I guess I must have been dozing."

There was a pulse under Jed's fingers and he stopped holding his breath.

"She's fast asleep," Nell said, blithely. (And Bunny kept screaming.) "Oh no, no trouble at all. Everything's just fine."

Jed, crouching, found himself listening to that voice. It was pretty cool. Just the faintest undertone of excitement. It could pass for enthusiasm. He could feel the child's cries pierce him, and he shuddered. He looked down at Eddie, feeling a blank dismay.

"Yes, she did. Went right to sleep after her story, Mrs. Jones. I hope you are having a nice time."

Phone to ear, Nell pivoted to see what Jed was doing and one stare was as blank as another. Her hand rose to hover over the mouthpiece.

The kid was frantic in there! Frantic!

"Please don't feel you need to hurry, Mrs. Jones," purred Nell, "because I don't mind— What?"

Her eyes widened as her voice acted surprise. "Noise? Oh, I guess you can hear the sirens down in the street." Her hand clamped on the mouthpiece. She said, through careful fingers, "They're just going by. There isn't any fire near here." She laughed. "Oh no. You just have a real good time," she advised gaily. She hung up the phone.

Her face set.

"It's a wonder he's not dead," Jed growled. "You little fool!"

"Isn't he?" said Nell absent-mindedly.

She walked into 809.

Jed's hand, going about the business with no conscious command from his numb brain, felt carefully of Eddie's head. The dry hair crisped on his finger tips. He left the dismayed welter of his thoughts to pay attention, here. Couldn't tell what the damage was, but there was, at least, no bleeding. Gently, he straightened the body. He lifted it, shifting it all the way over the threshold within the bathroom and, reaching for the thick bath mat, he slid it gently between the hard tile floor and the head. He took a towel and wet it. He washed the forehead gently, the eyes, and the cheeks.

Eddie's breathing seemed all right . . . a little difficult, not very. Jed thought the pulse was fairly steady. Knocked out, of course, but perhaps . . .

He lifted his own head suddenly.

Bunny was not screaming. The empty air pulsed in the sudden absence of that terrible sound.

Jed sat motionless on his heels. A trickle of sweat cut a cold thread of sensation down his neck and blurred in the fabric of his collar.

Ruth stepped with slow grace out of the phone booth. "Have a real good time." The phrase rang in her ears. Not the *mot juste* for such a night as this! This Night of Triumph! A time to keep in the mind for reference, forever. Even now, so soon afterward, it was an hour to live over again, and feel the heart stop, when Peter got up from his chair, and lurch, when he began, so nervously. And pound proudly, because she soon knew that all these politely listening people were warming to the man, who began a little bit nervously and shyly, as if to say, "Gosh, who am I?"

And then, Peter getting interested, himself, in what he was saying. Everybody feeling that. First, the words, coming out grammatically, properly placed, in full sentences. Then, the thought transcending, and driving the grammar into vivid astonishing phrases that rang just right. And finally Peter in the full power of his gift, taking directly from his mind and heart the things he knew and believed. The heads turning because they could not help it. They must hear this.

He was still excited (oh, bless Peter!) and he was reaping his reward. Now that his speech was over, now that they were pushing the tables out of the middle of the floor, and music was playing, and people stood in little groups, and he in the middle of the largest group of all.

Peter was reaping an evening's worth of praise and glory. But maybe even more. Maybe even the real thing! Was it possible, the Joneses wondered, that some might remember, might retain and refer to some small part, at least, of what he had told them?

A victory! But the rehashing, the reaping, the wonderful fun of this, might go on for hours.

Ruth turned her bright nails into her palms. Bunny was fast asleep. The girl had told her so. Everything was fine. The girl had said so.

But Ruth stood, trembling, in the hall of mirrors, and she knew in her bones that everything was *not* fine.

"Don't be silly!" she gasped to her own image. "Don't be such a *mother*! Don't spoil it, now!"

Peter's head craned toward her out of the group, and she gave him a gay little signal of the hand that meant "all's well."

For it must be so.

But that hadn't sounded like the same girl. Oh, it was the same voice. But it was not the same manner. The girl on the phone, just now, was neither dull nor passive. *She wasn't stupid enough*! No, she'd been too decisive. Too . . . too darned *gay*! Too patronizing . . . "Run along, little Mrs. Jones, and have your real good time. Don't bother me."

"Don't you be so *silly*!" Ruth told herself once more. "Are you going to be mean and spoil Peter's wonderful night, being such a hick and such a female? What's *wrong* with you?"

She shook herself and walked forward.

"What's wrong, oh, what's wrong where Bunny is?" her bones kept asking.

Peter was in full flight, amplifying something he hadn't touched on quite enough in the speech. Men, standing around him, were smoking with very deliberate and judicious gestures, and nodding, and breaking in to quote themselves. "As I said at lunch the other day . . ." "I was saying to Joe . . ." It seemed as if only last week or the other day they'd been thinking the same things Peter thought. They'd been telling somebody, in some fumbling fashion, that which Peter has just told them so well. (Ah, sweet praise!)

"O.K., hon?" Peter was tuned in on the wave length of Ruth's bones. Often and often he'd heard what they were muttering. But now, when she answered, smiling, "All quiet. Everything fine, Nell says." Peter didn't hear her bones proclaim, "But I don't believe it."

"Good." He squeezed her, swung her, "Ruth, this is Mr. Evans, and Mr. Childs, and Mr. Cunningham."

"How de do . . . how de do . . ."

"Husband of yours has a head on his shoulders and a tongue in his head, Mrs. O.—uh—Mrs. Jones. Fine talk. Fine."

"I thought so, too," said Ruth in sweet accord.

"Isabel, come here. Turn around, want you to meet . . ." The women murmured.

Peter said, "So, a man says to you, 'Honesty is the best policy.' You don't need to look up his antecedents, and if you find his great uncle stole fifty cents thirty years ago, figure what he *says* must therefore be suspect. What he *says* you can agree to or *not* agree to. However, if he claims he is prohonesty, but expects you to rob a bank with him, you can see the difference, I hope. In fact, you had better learn the difference."

"Right," said a cigar.

"I claim the truth can come out of a rascal's mouth, but how can a rascal fool us, if we learn to sort out words from deeds and keep our heads clear?"

"Just what I said to Isabel. I said . . ."

"And how old is your little girl, Mrs. O.—uh—Mrs. Jones?" Isabel was cooing.

"Bunny is nine."

"Ah, I remember Sue when she was nine," said the woman sentimentally. "A sweet age. A darling year."

Ruth smiled, bright eyed. She had no voice for an answer.

Chapter 11

M RS. PARTHENIA WILLIAMS said, "I can't help it."
"Aw, Ma," her son said, keeping his voice down in the evening hush of the place where they stood. "Listen to me—"

"I can't help it, Joseph, hear?"

For old Mr. and Mrs. O'Hara in the front suite, the Hotel Majestic had somehow, in the inertia of the years, acquired the attributes of home. Now, Mrs. O'Hara wasn't very well. She wasn't ill enough to warrant a nurse, yet they were unwilling to risk her being alone. So Mrs. Parthenia Williams came by day and sometimes, when Mr. O'Hara had to be away, she remained late into the evening. Whenever she did so, her son, Joseph, came to see her home.

As they stood in the hush of the eighth-floor corridor, Joseph said, "You better keep out of it, Ma. You know that. Don't you?" He was a thin nervous Negro with an acquiline face.

"I know what I know," his mother said.

Mrs. Williams's chocolate-colored face was designed for smiling, in the very architecture of her full cheeks, the curl of her generous mouth, the light of her wide-set eyes. Nothing repressed her. Nothing could stop her from saying "good morning," in the elevators in her beautiful soft voice. She seemed to acquire through her pores bits and scraps of knowledge about all these strangers, so that she would say, in the corridor, "Did you enjoy the boat trip, ma'am? Oh, that's good!" with the temerity of an unquenchable kindness. Mrs. O'Hara, who was sixty-two and so often annoyingly dizzy, felt at rest on Parthenia's bosom. She told Mr. O'Hara it was as if, after thirty orphaned years, and in her old age, she were mothered once more. (Mr. O'Hara crossed his fingers and knocked on wood.)

Joseph knew his mother's ways and adored her, but some of her ways . . . He tried to protest this time. "Some things you can't—Ma!"

"Something's scaring that baby in there nearly to death," Parthenia said. "She's just a bitty girl. She's in 809 and her folks next door. I spoke to them today. A real nice child. And I can't help it, Joseph, so don't you talk to me."

Her big feet carried her buxom body down the corridor. "If her folks ain't there, somebody ought to be comforting her. It's not good for her to be so scared."

"Ma, listen . . ."

"All right, Joseph. Her papa, he was asking about a sitter and I *know* they were planning to go out. Now, if her mama's there, that's one thing. But I got to ask. I can't help it. I don't care."

Jed got to his feet. His eyes rolled toward the frosted bathroom window. He unlocked it and pushed it up. Cold air hit him in the face.

The deep court seemed quiet. He thrust his head through to look down into the checkered hollow. He couldn't, of course, see all the way to the bottom. He couldn't see Bunny's window, either, for it came on a line with this one.

He could see that old biddy across the way and she was walking. She walked to a chair and held to the back of it with both hands and let go with a push and walked away. And back again. He could see only the middle section of her body, and those agitated hands.

The fear that hadn't been verbalized, even in his mind, seeped away, and he wondered why he was looking out of the window. He wondered if the dame over there was upset because she had been hearing things. He wondered, and in the act of wondering, he *knew* that someone must have heard all that commotion.

Get out of here, Towers, he warned himself, while you got the chance, you damn fool! Before all hell's going to break loose. This guy's not going to die. He'll be O.K. He's resting peacefully. Look out for Towers!

Jed realized that he had a perfect chance, right now. While the wildcat was in 809, Towers could fade out of 807. And Towers would run like crazy away from here.

What he heard himself growling aloud, as he stepped over Eddie's body, was, "What in hell is she *doing* in there?"

The knock made him jump. Too late? He groaned. He eyed the distance from where he stood to 809. Through there, where the key, he remembered, dangled its fiber tag on the inside of Bunny's door . . . that would have to be the way out, now that someone, and he didn't doubt it was trouble, knocked on 807. He waved. How would he get by whoever it was, once in the corridor? He would, he thought, get by and he'd better.

Then, he saw Nell standing in the way. She looked at him and moved her left hand. It said, "Be still." Jed shook his head and tightened his muscles for the dash. But Nell was too swiftly across 807 . . . so swiftly that Jed caught himself and ducked backward into concealment again, only just as she opened the door to trouble.

"Yes?" Jed could see her and he cursed, silently, her dark-clad back (she'd changed her clothes!) and the fantastically cool lift of her chin.

He expected a man's voice, an official voice, cold and final. But the voice was deep music, and not a man's. "I heard the little child crying so bad," it said. "Is there anything I can do?"

"Why, no," said Nell in chill surprise.

"You taking care of the little girl for Miz Jones, ma'am?"

"Yes."

"That's good. You know, I spoke to the little girl and her mama . . . she might know me. I wonder could I comfort her?"

"She's all right, now," Nell moved the door. But Parthenia's big foot was within the sill.

"I had so much experience with childern. I get along with childern pretty well, it always seems. She was scared, poor child? I hear that."

"Just a nightmare," said Nell indifferently. "Come on, Ma," Joseph said. "You asked. Now, come *on*."

"Who are you?" said Nell sharply, peering at him.

"This is my middle boy," Parthenia said with pride. "I've got three boys and two girls. Yes, ma'am, a big family but they raised. Hurts me to hear a baby cry so bad. Just hurts my heart like a pain. Poor little child . . . and all so strange . . ." It was like a song, a lullaby.

"It's none of your business that I can see," said Nell coldly.

"Maybe not," said Parthenia. But her big foot stayed where it was. A big foot, worn with carrying a big body, bunioned and raked over at the heel . . . a big strong stubborn foot. "Maybe not," the lovely voice said sadly, "but I got to try to stop my pain. Can't help trying, ma'am, whatever child is crying."

"She's not crying now," said Nell irritably. "And it's too bad you've got a pain. Please let me close this door, will you?"

"Ma—"

"You got a charm for the nightmare?" Parthenia asked with undefeated good will.

"If you don't get out of here, I'll call somebody."

"Ma . . . Excuse us, miss . . . Ma, come *away*."

"I can't feel happy about it," said Parthenia softly mournful. "That's the truth. It's just," her soft voice begged, "could I be sure she ain't scared any more? Little childern, being scared sometimes in the night, you got to be sure. Because it hurts their growing if they're not comforted."

"She's comforted," spat Nell. Then she changed. "But thank you for asking," she said in a sweet whine that had a threat to it, somehow. "I guess you mean well. But I really can't ask you in here. I don't know who you are or this man—"

Joseph plucked his mother from the doorway roughly.

"Good night, then," Parthenia said forlornly and, as Nell closed them out, "If I was white I wouldn't—"

"Shush!" said her son. "Hurry up. Get the elevator. Get home. She's trouble."

"Trouble," his mother murmured.

"You ought to know better, Ma. I told you. We can't fool around that white girl. Believe me, not *that* one!"

"I wasn't fooling. Something's bad wrong, Joseph. Baby's mother's not there. I can't feel happy about it."

"Listen, Ma, you better feel happy because you can't win. You know that, don't you? You can't stick your nose in that white girl's affairs, if you're right a million times over." He rang for the elevator, jittering.

"No child," said Parthenia gravely, as they waited, "no child gets off the nightmare as quick as that. No child, Joseph. Nobody's child."

"You can't do anything, Ma. Forget it, can't you?"

The elevator stopped. The door slid. Parthenia's enormous foot hesitated. But she stepped in, at last, and Joseph sighed as they sank down.

He heard her mutter, "No, I wouldn't go."

"Shall we stop for a bite?" said he in nervous animation. "You hungry, Ma?" She didn't answer. "Ma?"

"I don't believe I'll stop, tonight, boy," Parthenia said.

"Not hungry?" He grasped her arm and pushed her off the elevator, around the bend, to the back way out.

Parthenia said, looking at the stars, "No, I'd make a fuss. I wouldn't go."

Chapter 12

". . . NIGGERS!" said Nell.

All of a sudden, all Jed's cool purpose to depart was burned up in the flame of his raging need to tell her off.

"You damn wildcat! Dope! Fool! What's the idea of doing what you did? What's the idea of swatting him down like that? What in hell did you think you were doing? What kind of cockeyed dream was in your stupid brain? Answer me!"

He shook her. The dark dress was too short. Also, it was cut to fit a more matronly body. So she looked younger and less sophisticated, but also older and dowdier. Her head went back on her neck, as a snake's head poises to strike, and her tiny mouth over the sharp tiny chin looked venomous. Her face with the yellowish glow to the unlined skin was no age one could guess or imagine.

"Answer me!"

She was angry. "What's the matter with you?" she cried. "You didn't want to be seen, did you? Did you?"

He could see her pupils, pin points in the fields of blue.

"You're the one who's a dope!" cried Nell. "You didn't want him to see you? Well? He was walking right in there."

"So you'd just as leave murder the man, eh? Just for walking? So you don't care whether he lives or dies? Do you?"

"He's not going to die," she said scornfully. "I didn't hit him so hard."

"The hell you didn't! You hit him as hard as you damn well could. Just luck that you didn't . . ."

"Did you want to be seen?" she hissed.

"So you did *me* a favor? Don't do me no more." He flung her to one side of him, holding both her wrists in one hand. It crossed his mind that time was sifting by. It began to look as if no one had sounded any alarm to authority. Nothing was happening. He yanked her along as he went to peer through the window blinds.

The dame across the court was just standing there. He could see her hands on the back of that chair.

He swung Nell back into the center of the room. She stum-

79

bled, unresisting, although she looked a little sullen. She said, "I thought you didn't want to be seen in here. You acted like it."

He looked at her. "Just a point," he said dryly. "The little man had a perfect right to walk in there if he wanted to. He wasn't doing a thing he shouldn't do." Nothing happened to her face, no change of expression. He might as well have said it in Choctaw, or something. "Didn't think of that, eh? I suppose," he mocked, "you 'just weren't thinking'?"

"I thought you didn't want him to see you."

"So, you shut his eyes. That's logical. That's great!" Jed wanted to slap her, hit her, worse than he had ever wanted to hit anything smaller than he was. He took his hands off her as if she would soil them. "O.K. Where did it get you? What did it do for you?"

She didn't seem to follow.

"I was going. Remember? I'm still going. I'm going faster and farther, if that's possible. And don't think you can frame me with any lying yarn," he stormed. "I'll be gone," he snapped his fingers, "like smoke! You don't know who I am, my name, where I came from, or where I'm going to be. And you'll never see me again in this world, Nelly girl. The point I'm trying to make. You might as well . . . might a hell of a lot better . . . have let your Uncle Eddie show me out! Do you get that? Can you?"

She said nothing. But she moved a little bit, working around, he thought, to put herself between him and the door. He laughed. "Single track, your mind. One-idea-Nell. One at a time is all you can handle? Listen, you never had a chance to keep me here since I found out you were a baby sitter. Never. Not a chance. All your monkeyshines . . ."

"Why not?" she said.

"Say I'm allergic," said Jed shortly, "and skip it. I've got nothing against kids." His hand chopped the air nervously. "That's got nothing to do with it. They let me alone, I let them alone. Nothing to me." He didn't like this line. He shifted, quickly. "Start thinking about yourself, and think fast, Nell. How *you're* going to get out of the jam you got yourself into, I couldn't say."

"I'll get out of it," she murmured carelessly.

He didn't hear. He was listening for something else. "It's quiet in there," he muttered.

"She's all right," said Nell, carelessly. Her lids seemed to swell at the outsides of her eyes, puffing drowsily.

"What did you tell her?"

"I told her nothing to be scared of. Somebody just fell down." Suddenly Nell laughed, showing her teeth. "Somebody *did*," she giggled.

"How true," said Jed thoughtfully. His anger churned inside of him still, but he had the upper hand of it. He had an uneasy feeling that he had better not indulge in so simple a response. He stepped around one of the beds and looked into the bathroom. "Eddie's going to be missed, you know. Naturally, you didn't think of that."

"He won't be missed," she said indifferently. "He's off duty." She sat down and put her ankles together and looked at her feet. Her toes made a miniature sashay.

Eddie was about the same, still out, breathing better. Jed turned around.

Nell fell back on her elbows, smiling up. "Take me dancing?" she said coquettishly. "Johnee?"

"Dancing!" he exploded.

"Uncle Eddie's not on the elevator now." She seemed to think she was explaining something!

He wanted to say, I'd just as soon take a cobra dancing. But he said, "And? Who sits with the baby, in the meantime?"

"It's a dumb job," she said. "I don't like it."

His lips parted, closed, parted. He sat down, facing her. It seemed important to make plain what it was she left out of her calculations. It seemed important to try reason out against unreason. It seemed necessary to try to cut through a wall of fog, to clear things up. "You're in a mess," he said, rather patiently. "Don't you know that?"

"What mess?" She was sulky.

"You bop this guy, this Uncle Eddie. O.K. Now, what's going to happen? Look ahead a little bit. The Joneses come home from the party. There's a body in the bathroom. What are you going to say?"

"It's only Uncle Eddie," she murmured.

Jed took his head in his hands. He meant to make a semi-humorous exaggeration of the gesture, but it fooled him. He was holding his head for real.

"Now, listen carefully," he said. "What's *going* to happen? Future tense. Consequences. You ever heard of them?"

She used a word that rocked him with the unexpectedness of its vulgarity. "————, Uncle Eddie isn't going to say it was *me* who hit him."

He had to admit that he himself had reasoned along this line. For a moment, he was stopped. "O.K.," he resumed patiently. "So Eddie won't tell on you. Then, what *is* the story? Did he knock himself out? What did knock him out? Who? Don't you see, you've got to have an answer?"

"I can say you did it," she answered placidly.

"*After I'm gone*, you'll say it!" He was furious.

"Unless we're out dancing."

He stood up. This time he spit it out of his mouth. "I'd just as soon take a cobra dancing as you."

"You asked me when you first—"

"*Then*," he snapped. "That was before I knew what I was getting into. Now I see you do the way you do, I retract, believe me." He paced. "Why don't you *think*, first! That's what I can't understand. You swat him down without a brain in your head working. Can't you imagine what's *going* to happen? Doesn't that mean anything to you? Ever plan? Ever figure ahead? What's wrong with you, anyhow? How come you do the way you do?" He looked coldly down. "I think you're insane."

It's easy to say. The word falls off the tongue. This was the first time Jed had ever said it, in perfect sincerity. He did think she was insane.

She lifted her head, on the neck, slowly. It was the neck that lifted, as if it uncoiled. She said a few ugly words. Then she was screeching and clawing at him and biting his self-defending hands with savage teeth and her shrill refrain was, "No, I'm not! No, I'm not! Take it back! You take it back!"

He handled her, but it wasn't easy. He got her in a locking hold and he shut her mouth with his hand. "Cut it out! Cut it! You'll scare the kid. You'll have cops in here."

She was still screeching, as well as she could, "Take it back!"

"O.K. O.K. I take it back. If that does you any good. So you're a model of foresight and wisdom. So anything! So cut it out!"

She cut it out. She seemed satisfied. It was necessary to her that the word not be used. The word "insane." But it was a matter of words. The words "I take it back" were just as potent. Which, thought Jed grimly, is insane.

He felt chilled. He did not want this to be true. She was a crazy kid, a wild kid, in the slang sense. Only in the vernacular. She was all mixed up and she didn't know how to stop and think. He told himself that was it. But he felt sad and chilly. He didn't know what to do. She was limp in his hold. Then he knew she was not so limp, but too happy to be held so tightly.

He loosed her, warily. He said, vaguely, "Why should we fight? Makes too much noise." He listened. There was no sound from the child's room and he let out his breath. "Good thing *she* didn't begin to howl again. I can't take any more of that."

Nell said, "I know." A flicker of contempt crossed her face. "I understand about the future," she muttered.

"I talk too much, sometimes." He was trying to be careful. "What I need . . . Finish the bottle with me?" He took it out of his pocket. "Good thing this didn't get smashed in the excitement." He looked vaguely around. "Aw, what's a glass?" He tipped the bottle.

She took it from him with both hands. The notion of drinking out of the bottle seemed to tickle her.

He said, "Say, where did the Joneses go?"

"Why?" Her voice was as careless as his.

"I was wondering how late— Was it theater? Or a party someplace?" He feigned relaxing.

She still had the bottle in both hands. Carrying it, she walked between the beds and sat down near the head of one of them. "I don't know," she said vaguely.

"Shindig, eh? That sounds like a party. Somebody's apartment?"

"Your turn." She gave him the bottle. Her face was full of mischief. She said, "I understand about the future, Johnee. Everybody does."

"I guess so," Jed said.

She took a slip of paper off the table between the beds, where the phone was. She began to pleat it in her fingers. "You think I'm stupid?" she asked, looking sidewise.

"Everybody's stupid, sometimes. Looks kinda stupid of the Joneses not to say where they'd go. What if the kid got sick or something?"

"Oh?" Nell said brightly. "You mean they should have thought ahead? About the future?"

"Did I say something about the future, ever?" He grinned. He was thinking, I got under her skin, though. Must have. He felt better.

Nell tore the paper idly into fancy bits. When Jed passed over the bottle she let the bits fall on the carpet. Too late, Jed saw them fall. He received, in a telepathic flash, the news. What had been on the paper. Why she had torn it. How she had foxed him. And the news of her sly laughter.

He was chagrined. He kept himself from showing it, he hoped, and from anger. They may know at the desk downstairs, he comforted himself, where the kid's folks went. He said, and perhaps this was the result of the damped-down anger, "Say, what was this about a fire?"

"Fire?" Nell smoothed the bedspread. She cocked her head. She seemed willing to talk about fire if that's what he wanted to talk about. It didn't mean anything to her.

"I got a little bit of what your Uncle Eddie was saying."

"Oh, that."

"Was it your house, burned? Your parents? I thought he said so." She didn't answer. "Upset you, Nell?"

"That's what they say," she said demurely.

"Who?"

"Oh, doctors. Uncle Eddie. Aunt Marie." She frowned. "Aunt Marie went to the show tonight."

"Where was the fire?"

"Home."

"Some small town, was it?"

"It wasn't big." She curled up her legs.

Small, all right, Jed thought to himself, if they let this one loose. But he said to himself, quickly, No, no, there must have been some testing. Yet his thoughts went somberly on. Probably, Eddie showed up ready and willing and anxious to take her far, far away. Probably, the town would just as soon not face up to it. Nell wouldn't be any of the town's business, far, far away.

"So it was an accident," he said, making a statement. "Well, I'll tell you something. The future's one thing you got to look out for. The past is another. Because the past adds up. You know that?"

She frowned.

"This accident. Your father and mother both died in it?"

"It was an accident." He heard the jump of her voice to a higher pitch. He knew it was a threat. It warned, Look out! It reminded him of that screeching tantrum. It warned, Be careful! Danger! Touchy!

"Well, I'll tell you," he drawled, nevertheless, "and it's a funny thing. You take one accident, why, that's too bad. Everybody's sorry. Poor Nell." She was curled up as tense as a coiled spring. He tried to fix her gaze, but it was all blueness. He kept on drawling, "But you take *two* accidents, that's different. That's not the same. It's really funny how, after a second accident, right away, the first accident doesn't look so much *like* an accident, any more."

Her face went blank, either because he'd hit her with an idea, or she didn't know what he was talking about.

"Good thing to keep in mind," he said lazily.

She said, "They didn't do anything to me." Her face was sullen. But Jed felt a sick wave of absolute knowledge.

He watched her. He said, as quietly and steadily as he could, "What I'm saying . . . the first time is different. But things like that have a way of piling up. It gets harder. Because it counts. It adds. One and one make more than two. They make questions. So, maybe you better not get walking in your sleep," he finished gently.

She didn't move. He thought, *I got it over*.

And the bottle was empty. He gathered himself to get up, now, and go quietly.

Miss Eva Ballew believed in many things. One of them was duty. She walked toward the telephone. One of them was justice. She walked back to the chair.

But however strong her beliefs and her conscience, Miss

Ballew was a physical coward and knew it and all her life had fought her weakness. Now, she realized full well that she had been prodded too many times . . . three times . . . and she was taking too long . . . much, much too long . . . to make up her mind what she ought to do.

Sometimes, if you take time to decide, the need to do anything passes of itself . . . Miss Ballew reproached herself with bitter shame and she walked toward the phone.

But . . .

She walked to the chair. She banged her fist on the chair back and the pain helped her. Justice. Very well. If justice won, it was because this was going to take more physical courage, and she was a coward, and she wished to deny her cowardice.

She went to the dresser and got her purse, not to be naked without it, once away from her room. She left the room and, flogging herself, marched around the hollow square of the eighth floor.

Nell hadn't moved. Jed, all the way up, standing, said, "So long." He felt a little pulse of compassion for her, who was lost, and had no inner compass to find the way again. "Be seeing you."

Once more, and briskly, somebody's knuckles knocked on 807's door.

Nell was up, lynx eyed.

"Oh no," said Jed softly. "Oh no, my lady, not again! Not this time!"

He faded. Towers faded, the way he had to go, through the door to the kid's room, to 809 . . . and closed it behind him.

Chapter 13

M ISS BALLEW rapped again. Because she was afraid, she did her best to be angry. She knew someone was in there. Did they think they could lie low?

The door opened so swiftly it surprised her. A girl in a dark dress, not a very big girl, not very old, looked at her with blue, blue eyes and said, with an effect of stormy anger, although her voice was low, "What do you want?"

"My name is Eva Ballew. My room is across the court on this floor." Miss Ballew's words were as neat and orderly as herself. She tended to begin at the beginning.

"Yes." The girl seemed to listen, but not to hear, almost as if she were listening for something else. And it seemed to Miss Ballew that her anger was aimed elsewhere, also.

"Before I call the manager of this hotel," said Miss Ballew more boldly, to command attention, "I think it only fair to ask whether you can explain."

"Explain what?"

"What is going on in these rooms," said Miss Ballew, loudly and firmly.

"I don't know what you mean." The girl was looking at the caller, but not seeing her, almost, thought Miss Ballew, as if she were *also* looking for something else out here in this bare corridor.

"There is a child," said Miss Ballew coldly. "Is she your child?"

"I'm taking care of her."

"I see," Miss Ballew's mouth was grim. "Yes, so I imagined. Is there or was there a man in here?"

"A man?"

Miss Ballew longed to cry, Pay attention, please! "I saw the man," she announced, sharply, "so that is an unnecessary question and you need not answer it." She could see into room 807 and no one else was visible, at least. She did not feel physically afraid of rather a small girl. And if the man had gone— Miss Ballew was encouraged. She said, yielding to curiosity, "Who was the man?"

"Listen, you can't—"

"The child," cut in Miss Ballew coolly, "has been crying in a most distressing manner, twice. And I have witnessed certain rather strange scenes over here. I must ask for an explanation."

"Who are you?" began Nell.

"I am someone who will call downstairs if I do not get the explanation," said Miss Ballew dictatorily. "In the first place," she went on, beginning at the beginning in her orderly fashion, "a while ago, you were at the window with the child?"

"Yes, yes," said Nell impatiently, "what are you trying to—"

"I have already told you. I am trying to find out whether or not it is my duty to call the manager."

"But why should you?" Nell stepped closer, with the door behind her now. Her glance slipped down the corridor to the right, briefly.

"Because," snapped Miss Ballew, wishing this girl would pay attention and not carry on this duel with some invisible thing, "it seemed to me, for one thing, that the little girl very nearly fell out the window."

"Well, she didn't," said Nell carelessly. "While you were at your snooping you must have noticed that."

Miss Ballew bridled but stood her ground. "Snooping or not, I wish to see the child."

"See her?" For the first time, Miss Ballew felt that her words were heeded.

"Yes, see her for myself."

"You've got a crust!"

"Nevertheless, if I do *not* see her, I intend to call the authorities." So much for rudeness, Miss Ballew's eyebrows remarked.

"I don't know what's the *matter*!" Nell said in whining exasperation. "What do you want to see her for? She's sleeping. What are you talking about?"

"Why did she scream so dreadfully?" Miss Ballew narrowed her eyes.

"When?"

"The second time. Come now, stop evading, young woman."

"What?"

"I think you'd better let me in."

"*You* listen," Nell said. "I'm here to take care of her. You're a stranger. How can I let a stranger in? How do I know . . ."

"You don't," agreed Miss Ballew, "but unless I see her for myself, the manager or the detective here *must*."

"What business is it of yours? I don't underst—"

"Are you afraid to let me see her?"

"I'm not afraid," said Nell shrilly. "But I can't do it. I'm not supposed to. You talk about duty—"

"Now, see here. I am a schoolteacher. I'm sure I look like one. You ought to be able to tell that I am a responsible person."

"You're trying to cause trouble."

"On the contrary. I wish you would realize that I could have called downstairs directly. I felt, however, that it was not fair to cause trouble, as you say, if there is no reason. Therefore, I have taken the trouble to step around here. There may be some simple explanation and if the child is perfectly all right and asleep, then there is no occasion for any trouble at all. Now, is that clear?"

"What would her mother say if I let any old person?"

"What would her mother say about you entertaining a man?" In the same tone, Miss Ballew would have said "about your smoking opium."

"He's gone." The girl's eyes flickered toward the right again. "And she *is* perfectly all right. She *is* sleeping."

"I beg your pardon if I seem to insist in the face of your direct statements, but after what I saw—"

"Saw?"

"Perhaps you don't know that the Venetian blind was so adjusted that I *could* see."

"See where?" Nell's head went back on the neck.

"Into the child's room."

"It's dark in there," Nell said stupidly. Perhaps a little drowsily.

"Not quite. There was a very little light, perhaps through the connecting door."

"Light?"

"And the child did stop her screaming rather abruptly," said Miss Ballew.

Nell's eyes slipped sidewise. "What did you see?" asked she.

Ruth was only half listening to the women's voices. She would have preferred to be in the group of men where the talk, she was sure, must have more meat in it. It could hardly have less. These women, from far-flung spots, had no basis for gossip and, since they weren't even sure who each other's husbands were (except Ruth's, of course) they didn't even have the fun of ranking each other.

Except Ruth. She could have been preening herself, for no woman had missed her rose-colored presence at the Speaker's elbow. But her heart wasn't in it.

There was a faint superstitious element, too, a fear that if she got to thinking herself too darned smart, something bad could happen. She felt, absurdly or not, as if she rode the narrow edge of danger, as if, by standing here among these party-painted women, she was taking a risk. She said, "Yes, indeed," again, and again the sense of danger fluttered her heart.

Peter strode out of his group and snatched her out of hers. Their steps fell together to the music as if they were at home at the Saturday night Neighborly. "Smatter, hon?"

Ruth looked up with clouded eyes. "Now, I thought I had you fooled."

"Nuh-uh. Worried? About Bun?"

"I'm sure I'm silly."

"No, you're not sure," he said. "Something on that phone call bother you?"

"I don't know." She slid her hand higher on his sleeve. "Probably it's just because I'm a hick and this great big town scares me. Listen, Peter, even if I don't always act it, I am a grown woman. Let me do something. Let me take a cab over to the hotel and see. I'll be perfectly all right, and I'll come straight back and dance till dawn. And I won't *spoil* it."

"We could leave now," he said, guiding her in a turn.

"But . . . the fun!"

He grinned, admitting the fun. "Man from Chicago, I'd like to have a few words—"

"Then do. Please. If you go, I'll feel terrible. *You* can't go."

"My night to howl," he grinned. "Got cab fare?" He would let her go. Peter wouldn't *make* her spoil it.

"Not a penny," she confessed.

He danced her into the mirrored exit, squeezed her, let her go, and gave her a five-dollar bill. "Don't trust any handsome strangers with all this moolah on you, baby."

"I won't." Ruth thought, I don't trust that stranger, that girl. It's what's wrong with me.

She wouldn't let him come any farther than the cloakroom with her. He looked at her little watch from her bag and said rather seriously, "It shouldn't take you long to get across town at this hour."

Somebody said, "Oh, Jones," or was it, "O'Jones"?

Ruth smiled at him. She left the scene. She felt, at once, much better to have escaped, to be free, to be going.

A doorman found her the cab. The city thought nothing of a young woman in evening clothes taking a cab alone in the night. No look. No comment. The city minded its business.

In the outer night, in the streets, were many many people, all minding their business. Millions and millions of people, thought Ruth, not only here, but millions of other places, too, who never heard and never will hear of me. She thought, For each of us, me, and every one of them, how few are anything but strangers.

Chapter 14

JED STOOD in the dark. He heard Miss Ballew introduce herself and knew at once *this* was the old biddy from across the way. Through the slats of Bunny's blind he could see her room, still lit.

He wondered if he were going to be able to get around the two of them, out there, without an uproar. Maybe Nell would let her into 807. But if not . . . He wondered about going around the hollow square in the other direction. He had an impression that one could not. It was only a U after all. Suites across the front, perhaps. Dead ends for the corridors.

He wondered if he could take refuge by knocking at a stranger's door. God forbid, he thought piously. No more strange hotel rooms for Towers. Only God knew what's in them.

He rehearsed his exit in his mind.

And he meant exit. Total exit. There were worse things in the world than sitting the night out at the airport.

The stairs went down, he knew, just beyond the elevators. Well, he could move fast, Towers could, on his long legs. In his mind, he placed all the stuff in his room. Where to snatch up this and that. He traveled light. There was little to snatch. He could be in and out of that room, he thought, in a matter of sixty seconds, and exit, bag and baggage.

Then let her screech her lies.

He had little doubt she'd cook up some lies, all right. If necessary. Or even just if it seemed like fun at the moment. Or, if she was mad at him. And, he thought, she is!

Dancing, yet!

Unless he had knocked, with a few words in a few minutes, a totally unfamiliar idea of caution into her head. Of course, he'd been thinking of the kid. He'd been trying to get into Nell's head the danger, the undesirability, of harming the kid.

So that Towers could fade, of course.

Damn it, Towers had to get out of this! A fine mess! Assault, maybe, on account of Eddie in there, and the benefit of the doubt on Nell's side. For long enough to make it a mess, all right. And Eddie, tempted, if not almost obliged, to say something hit him but he doesn't know what. Everything just went black, and so forth. That would be the easiest thing for Eddie to say, wouldn't it? Eddie could even kid himself that it was true.

So there's Towers, in a jam. Jail, bail, telegrams. Would his high-powered new job, his big fat step in the up direction, wait quietly for some judge to let him loose? And would a judge?

Nuts! He ground his teeth. Trouble would breed trouble. He had to get out of here. Never *was* any business of his, the kid and the sitter. Not his kid, for Lord's sake. Strangers. All strangers. If the parents didn't know any better— Probably didn't give a damn what happened to the kid, he thought angrily. Off on a shindig, all dressed up. Probably drunk as skunks by now, and painting the town. Why should Towers care?

Why should he be so angry about it?

And also if Eddie, the elevator boy, stuck *his* neck out and got bashed in the head for it, what was that to Towers? He didn't feel for Eddie. Eddie had it coming.

He still stood, just inside room 809, still listening. He didn't know what he was waiting for. No question, really, but what Towers better move fast. That old biddy had her teeth in it now. Listen to her. "I wish to see the child." Icicles hanging off every word. Sounded like a pretty stubborn old dame. "And she's white," he thought, not quite letting himself know why the word came to him.

Nell was stalling, but he thought that the old biddy would walk right over her. He took a soft step. He better get going.

Have to steam himself up to some fast footwork, now. Once out, out of this hotel, he thought, let them whistle for the wind! He'd fade. He was never here. He'd be clear away, on the town, one in millions. Gone, like smoke.

And Towers right back on the track again, on his way up, as he had it figured.

No one would ever know a thing about this. How would they? Why should they?

Kid was asleep and anyhow the old dame out there was going to raise a row. She was hell-bent to do it. No need for him to figure in it. Let her do it. She was the type to do it. Let it work out that way. Why should he duplicate what she was already going to do?

He might drop a word at the desk, on his way out, though. He could have heard a commotion over here, from his own room. The old biddy had, from hers. Just as well tip the hotel. Then Nell *couldn't* stall her.

His eyes had adjusted to the dark in here. He could see the far bed was undisturbed. On the other, the little kid must be asleep.

Funny thing she didn't wake up during his late wrestling match with the wildcat. It hadn't been a silent one.

That bed was awfully flat.

His hair moved with his scalp.

He crept a few steps in room 809. Of course, she was an awfully little girl, probably wouldn't make much of a hump on a bed. He didn't know. He'd—damn it—he'd hardly ever *seen* a sleeping child. He didn't know if they made a hump or not.

There wasn't any little girl on the bed.

He looked at the windows and Towers was sick and sickness was going through him like cream swirling down through a cup of coffee and something thumped on the floor.

He knelt in the dark crevice between the beds. He felt, blindly. Something threshed. He wanted light but he didn't dare. His fingers found a thin chilly little . . . what? Shoulder? Yes, for he touched a soft braid. He felt for the face, the warm lips, and the breath, but touched, instead, fabric.

God damn her to hell, the God-damned bitch, she'd bound and gagged the little thing. Oh, damn and blast her rotten soul! Aw, the poor little . . .

"Bunny?" he whispered. "Bunny Jones? Aw, Bunny, poor kid. Listen, sweetheart, I wouldn't hurt you for a million dollars." His fingers verified. Yes, her ankles were tied together. Wrists, too. And that cruel—stocking, he guessed it was, in and over the mouth!

"You fall off the bed, honey? Aw, I'm sorry. I'm sorry about this. Mustn't make a noise, though."

Oh, Lord, how would the child *not*! if he ungagged her. It was not possible for her not to cry! He knew this. It would not be in her control. She must cry out, must make sound as soon as she was able.

But she mustn't! Or Towers would never get away.

Now, what could he do? Thoughts flashed like frightened goldfish in the bowl of his brain.

Grab her, just as she was? Take her with him? Yeah, and run past the two women at the other door, with the kid slung over his shoulder. A kidnaper, yet!

Fantastic! No, no, better not do that.

He sat on his heels. His hand tried to comfort the little girl, smoothing her hair. He thought, coldly, "So you're in a jam, Towers?"

But then his mind went all fluid again and in it those fish-flashes and in the panic he thought, Damn it, no! He thought, I've got to fix it for the kid and get out, too!

Look out for yourself, Towers! Nobody else will. It came back to him, in his own words. A guide, a touchstone.

All right! Use your head! Nothing was going to happen to the kid beyond what already had. The woman out there would keep Nell busy. And he, Jed, would tip off the hotel. So, for five minutes' difference, five minutes more . . .

Crouching near the floor in the dark he could hear the city crying, its noise tossing and falling like foam on the sea, as restless, as indifferent, as varied, and as constant. And he saw himself, a chip, thrown, blown, attracted to another chip, to swirl, to separate, to grow arms and be, not a chip, but a swimmer, and push away.

Once away, who would know? Never see these strangers again.

Mess!

He leaned over and whispered, "I'm afraid you'd cry if I undo your mouth, honey. I wouldn't blame you. I'm just afraid you can't help it. We can't make any noise, just yet. Listen, I'm going. Going to get somebody. Get your daddy." His hand felt the leap of the little heart. "Get your daddy," he promised. "Be still just a little while longer. It'll be O.K." He didn't lift her to the bed for she was more hidden where she lay. "I am a friend," he said, absurdly, out of some pale memory in a boy's book.

He got up and went softly to the door of 809.

Chapter 15

"I SAW," said Miss Ballew in her precise fashion, "the child, as I suppose, sitting up in the bed and a figure approach and appear to struggle with her. The cries then stopped, most abruptly. So you see, I require," said she hastily, "some explanation. I cannot believe," she added vehemently to cover the shake that was developing in her voice, "that any grown person would use force on a child. What, actually, were you doing?"

Nell looked sleepy.

"Answer me," said Miss Ballew angrily. "If it wasn't you, who was it?"

"You said you *saw*—" There was a hint of impudence in the girl's face, something saucy that must be crushed at once.

Miss Ballew said, coldly, "I certainly did see *someone*, doing *something*, which has very much alarmed me. I would advise you, young woman, to take me to that child at once." (But she was afraid again. She was dizzy with her fear.)

A door, to her left and the girl's right, opened and closed very fast. A man was in the corridor and had passed rapidly behind Miss Ballew almost before she could turn her head. Moving with long gliding steps, he rushed on, he vanished around the corner. Miss Ballew staggered in the wind of his passage.

It had been so swift, so startling, so furtive, and there had been a white roll of his eye.

"Who was that!" Her knees felt mushy.

The girl looked as if she could hop with rage, as if she would begin to bounce, like popcorn.

"Explain, at once!" cried Miss Ballew and reached out to shake this stupid creature.

The girl collapsed at her touch. "Oh, oh," she said. "Oh—" and bent her arm against the doorframe and buried her face in her arm. "Oh, I was so scared! Oh, miss, whatever's your name. Oh, thank you! You've saved me!"

"What!"

"That . . . man!" said Nell, muffled.

"Why, he must have come out of the next— Yes, I see he did! Out of the child's room!"

"Yes. Yes," cried Nell. "Now do you see? He was in there all the time. He said if I didn't get rid of you . . . Oh!"

"Oh, dear," said Miss Ballew faintly.

"He said he would—" Nell's body pressed on the wood as if in anguish.

Miss Ballew rocked on her feet and reached for the wall.

"He just forced himself in here. He was so wild!" Nell cried, "and strong." Her face peeped, now, from the sheltering arm. "I didn't know what to do!"

Silence beat in the corridor while Miss Ballew fought with her wish to fall down. One heard, one read, and all one's life one feared, but not often did one encounter . . . But the ruthless predatory male was, of course, axiomatic.

"There wasn't anything I could do." The girl's whine broke the spell. "I couldn't—I'm not very strong."

"But he is getting away!" moaned Miss Ballew. For she heard, in the mists of her horrors, the yawn of the door to the fire stairs and the hish-hush of its closing. This, she felt, was outrageous. Outrageous! That such things . . . in a respectable hotel . . . and go unpunished! The anger was starch to her spine. She tightened her mouth, gathered her strength, and bustled past the girl into the room. She threw her stout sturdy form on the bed and reached for the telephone.

Downstairs, Rochelle Parker shifted the lifesaver expertly into the pouch of her cheek. "Yes?"

"This is Miss Ballew," said the agitated voice. "I'm in room—what?" she cried to the girl. "What is this number?"

"Number 807," said the girl quite promptly and calmly.

"Room 807. A man has just fled from here."

"*What* did he do, madame?"

"Fled. Ran. He ran away." Miss Ballew was often forced to translate her remarks. "He was up to no good." She tried to be basic. "Get him!" cried Eva Ballew and reverted. "He must answer for it. He must face his accuser and be brought to book. This is criminal and he must be apprehended."

"Just a moment, *please*," said Rochelle. She pressed the button that would discreetly summon Pat Perrin to a phone. Almost at once, she plugged him in. "Yeah?" "807's on, Pat."

"Yeah, what is it?"

"There was a man in here," said Miss Ballew. It was as if she said "African lion." "He is trying to get away, right now."

"What did he look like?"

"What did he look like?" cried the teacher to the motionless girl.

The girl's lips opened and her tongue slipped to moisten them. "He . . . had red hair."

"Red hair!" Miss Ballew's voice both informed Perrin and doubted the information, for this had not been her own impression.

"Very dark red," said Nell, "brown eyes, freckles."

"Dark red, brown eyes, freckles, and tall. I saw that. And I think a gray suit."

"Brownish," Nell said, "and a blue shirt."

"Brownish? Well, some light color. And a blue shirt. And he took the stairs, not two minutes ago. You had best—"

"We'll see," said Perrin. "He intruded, you say?"

"He did, indeed," cried Miss Ballew in ringing tones. It was the very word.

"I'll see if we can pick him up," said Pat Perrin, sounding competent and unruffled. He hung up at once.

Miss Ballew rolled a bit and sat up. She propped herself on the headboard. She was trembling. "This really—" she gasped. "I don't know when I've been— What did happen? How did he—? Who—?"

The girl, who had closed the door, came slowly around the bed and sat down on the other one. Her eyes were a trifle aslant and an odd blue. She clasped her hands in her lap. Unpainted nails. Dark, decent dress. Modest ankles, shabby shoes.

Miss Ballew read all these signs as she was bound to do. "You poor thing," she said. "I don't know your name."

"Nell." Not Sonya. Not Toni. Plain Nell.

"I am Eva Ballew," said that lady warmly. "I suppose you were under such strain. I thought your manner was odd."

"You don't know," said Nell wanly, and Miss Ballew's heart fluttered alarmingly. "Oh Miss Ballew, I just had to tell you those lies," the poor thing said, pathetically. "I couldn't help it. He was in there, and he said he'd listen, and if I dared . . ."

"Simply terrible!" murmured the teacher. "How ever did he get in here?"

"Oh, he knocked, and of course I went to see who it was." Nell twisted her hands. "And then he just pushed me."

"Didn't you scream?" It was Miss Ballew's conviction that a woman always screamed. It did not, at this time, cross her mind that there was any other procedure whatsoever.

"But he said . . . said he was a friend of the people's," said Nell. "I didn't know."

"No, of course, you couldn't know. Tsk. Tsk. Do you think he had been drinking?"

"Oh, he was!" cried Nell. "Look!" She seemed very young and lithe as she reached for the whisky bottle. The cheap dress twisted tight to her body. Miss Ballew felt a shiver, rather a delicious one, along her nerves. She gazed, horrified, at the bottle's emptiness.

"And then," said Nell, "Bunny—that's the little girl—she . . . she woke up." Nell put her face in her hands. She dropped the bottle on the floor to do so. Miss Ballew's mind swirled. So odd. Poor thing, so upset, to do such a disorderly thing.

"Now, now," she soothed. "It's all over, now." And then, fearfully, "Isn't it? There wasn't? Nothing?"

Nell took her face out and shook her head vigorously. Her tawny yellow hair tossed.

"Well," said Miss Ballew feebly. Her heart raced. She felt unwell.

"Anyhow," said Nell moodily, "he only tried to kiss me once. He just kept on drinking and drinking."

"You should have screamed," Miss Ballew said trancelike.

"But I was so scared, I didn't dare. . . . And I thought maybe, when Bunny cried so loud, someone might notice." The girl's eyes rolled.

Miss Ballew felt herself flushing guiltily.

"And she didn't really 'almost fall,'" said Nell with sudden passionate indignation, "at all! He was mad. That's what it was. He thought I was trying to, you know, get somebody's attention out the window like that, so he dragged her away."

"Oh, dear . . ." Miss Ballew thought how wise one is never to believe too hastily in what one thinks one sees. Always, she

noted, wait for the other side of the story. "And when she began to scream so, later? Why was that, my dear?"

Nell looked wildly around her, threw herself face down, and
her shoulders heaved, and soon her sobbing shook the bed,

"Now," Miss Ballew struggled to reach over but she felt
dizzy, herself, and she couldn't make it. "Now," she said,
"don't—" She thought, Someone must soon come. She herself
was really not in any condition to deal with this any further. It
was shameful, but she felt as weak as a kitten. Just hearing
about it. The poor girl must have had a violent psychic shock.
In fact, Miss Ballew knew herself to be suffering the same
thing, vicariously.

"She got scared and began to cry," sobbed Nell. "She just
got scared. That's why she began to cry. But he was so mad. It
made him wild. He said she had to stop that noise." The head
slipped, the face turned, the wet lashes lifted.

Miss Ballew lay against the headboard and her rather long
countenance was whitening. "Then, it was *he*, in her room?"

"You saw . . ." the girl challenged.

"Yes, I saw. But it was too dark. I couldn't clearly see. Oh,
my dear, if he has harmed—"

"Oh, he didn't *hurt* her," Nell said and suddenly she sat up
again. "He just made her stop crying." A little smile—pitiful, it
might have been—worked on her face. "And there wasn't
anything I could do because he locked me in the closet . . ."

"Incredible." The teacher's lips were stiff.

Nell looked solemnly at her. The room fell . . . as if all its
emotion-laden air swirled, falling . . . to silence. "You know,"
she said, "I think he was insane."

Miss Ballew said, "Is there— Could you? A glass of water?
Or could you call, perhaps the house physician. I really am
afraid I am having rather a reaction . . ." She closed her eyes.

Insanity was obviously the explanation. For things so wild
and wanton, insanity was the definition, really.

In the dim bathroom of 807, on the cold floor, Eddie stirred.
His right arm moved as one moves in sleep. He turned a little
to his left side. Then he lay still.

Chapter 16

THE HOTEL detective, Pat Perrin, put up the phone and crossed the lobby, moving quietly. He opened the door to the base of the tall rectangular tube where the fire stairs ran. He discounted, from long practice, ninety per cent of what he had just heard. But for the sake of the other ten per cent, he stood and listened. Any sound, he knew, would come booming down to him.

And so it did. Someone was on those bare stairs. His own ears informed him. So far, so much was confirmed. He waited, quietly. He wore a gun.

Jed realized the echoing clatter of his descent in this confined space. Nimbly, he brought himself up against a door, stopped the second or two it took to rearrange his own rhythm, tugged the door in upon himself, and stepped steadily out to the sixth-floor corridor.

As he crossed the carpet toward the elevators a man—just a man—joined him. Jed took care not to be caught looking to see whether the other was looking. The man pressed the down button and, superhumanly, Jed did not. He set his suitcase down, denying the need of his nervous hand to hang onto it. It occurred to him, freakishly, that he had left a blue tie and a good pair of socks, damn it. His jaw cracked and he deliberately let tension out of it. Without fidgeting, he watched the dial, as the other man was doing, as all elevator awaiters seem compelled to do. The hand was coming down.

Disinterested, strangers, they stepped on in silent sequence as the elevator obeyed the call. And in silent sequence they stepped out, below. Jed, looking to neither side, walked to the desk. His gait deceived. His trunk and shoulders showed no effort but his long legs drove hard against the floor and bore him more swiftly than they seemed to do.

He said, crisply, "Checking out. Towers, 821."

"Certainly, Mr. Towers."

"Mind making it quick?" Friendly and crisp but not too urgent. "Just got hold of a cancellation. I can get out of here tonight if I make it down to the station." Jed looked at the clock in the woodwork back of the man's head.

"Yes, sir." The clerk did not seem to put on speed but Jed was aware that he did, in fact, waste no motion. He recognized the skill in it. He made himself stand still.

Pat Perrin knew when no feet rattled on the stairs. He caught a boy and posted him, here, near where the stairs came down, at a door to a narrow passage that was the back way out. He caught another to watch the entrance to the bar, for one could exit to the street through that dim corner room. He himself had a brief word with an elevator boy. Then his skilled eyes ran down every man in his sight. "Tall, light suit." He weaved among the chairs. He moved along the carpet.

"You figure," Jed was asking pleasantly, "about twenty-five minutes to Penn Station?"

"That's close, sir. Might do it. Here we are." The clerk turned the reckoning around. He took an envelope from a box and presented this, too. Jed saw his name before him in a script he knew. A note from Lyn. Lyn Lesley. He stuffed it into his coat pocket. (No time for her now.) He took money out.

Perrin's eye checked Jed's tall figure in the gray suit. *Dark* hair, *no* freckles, *white* shirt. He walked on by, the eye skimming.

Jed put his wallet back, picked up his bag, surveyed the way ahead, the not-very-long distance to that revolving door and out. He was the same as out, already. The clerk already counted him for gone. To turn back, to speak again was like contradicting the forward flow of time itself.

But Jed put his palm noiselessly on the blotter and the clerk looked up.

"You'd better," said Jed, speaking slowly and soberly and emphatically to be understood and heeded in this, the first and only time he would say it, "send someone to room 807, right away. Trouble. A kid's in trouble. 807 and 809. A little girl. If you know where Mr. and Mrs. Jones went, call them. It's their kid."

He turned swiftly and went, in that same smooth, deceptive,

very rapid gait, in the shortest line to the revolving door and through it without a check.

Then he stood in the air, in the open night, and he was out of it, and it was their kid, wasn't it?

Pat Perrin knew someone on those stairs had got off the stairs. So much was true. Whether he rode down or not was a question. Now, Perrin peered through to the street, saw tall, dark, and handsome, in the white shirt, harmlessly pausing to light a cigarette. He pushed through and crooked a finger to the doorman, said a word or two. He raked Jed's back with his glance, conscientiously, turned, looped on his own tracks, and went back through the lobby because the other exit would be the one a fugitive would like. He saw Milner at the desk lift a startled hand as if to beckon. He signaled with his own, Busy (no time for him now), and he walked on by.

Jed shook out his match. All right. So he'd established Towers had nerves of iron. And what now? Cab? Bus? Subway? To the airport? His thoughts were jumpy.

A cab swerved in to the curb and braked in his very face. He thought it was querying him. Then he saw that it had a fare to discharge here. He stepped aside.

As the domelight went on, he could see her. Young woman, blond, attractive, in party clothes.

He stood with his bag at his feet and blew smoke out. Here was a cab, emptying before him, becoming available, and in it he would be gone, like smoke. Smoke poured out of his mouth. He half turned his head. He looked (because he was in some way forced to look) up behind him at the checkered façade, the tall bulk, the flat and secretive face of the Hotel Majestic.

The girl from the cab, with her change, bills and all, in her bare hand, got out. She swept her long skirts, aquamarine velvet over rosy silk, up in one hand. Her golden slippers stepped quickly on the gray sidewalk. She went by Jed. Her gaze crossed over his face blankly, and he, blankly, watched her by, for they were strangers.

Jed saw the doorman prance, and the door spin. The cab door, in front of him, remained open. It hinted, tempted, invited. Finally it said to him, "Well?"

He moved nearer and put out a hand, ducked his head, brought his bag up in the other hand, and his knee up . . . Something hit him. It seemed to him that he was struck in the face by a barrier as soft, elastic, and yielding, as easy to pass through, as a cobweb. Something that was no more substantial than the air itself. Only a faint scent . . . breathing into his face from the cab's closed place. A perfume, it was, that stopped him because he knew that scent and it made his stomach turn over. Why, he reeked of it, himself! Of course. It was *on him*! It came from himself.

He barked, "Sorry," and slammed the door. He lifted his hand, giving permission and command. Go ahead. The cab's gears snarled at him. It went away in a huff, saying with a flounce of its back bumper, "Whyncha make up your mind, stupid!"

Jed trod his cigarette out. He felt rooted on the sidewalk and his feet kicked at the invisible chain. All right. He would not shut himself up with that sickening odor. That's all. He'd air himself free of it. Walk, then. Lug your damn bag. But get gone, stupid! He held hard for anger, this kind of anger. His hand came up to brush before his face.

Milner, the man at the desk, leaned over, full of summons, but Pat Perrin was out of range of a soft hail and a loud hail would never do. Milner's still-startled eyes blinked. Towers, 821. Eighth floor, sure enough. Fellow might know what he was talking about. Something wrong in 807? Peter O. Jones, 807 and 809. Mr. Milner didn't know where the Joneses were. He was annoyed as well as startled. But of course he would check. It would never do not to check up on such a warning.

He took up a phone and pivoted, looking anxiously for some reason at the hands of the clock. "Give me 807, Rochelle, will you?"

"Sure thing." Rochelle alerted. She thought, "Oh boy, something's up!" She thought, "*I* smelled a rat up there hours ago." She was rather pleased. There were long stretches on this job that were pretty dull. She hoped this was going to be interesting. Whatever it was. She said softly, "What goes on, Mr. Milner?"

Since Mr. Milner did not know, he was haughty. "If you'll ring them, please?"

"O.K., O.K." He heard Rochelle ring them. He stood, holding the phone, staring at the clock as if he could by the willful power of the human eye stay the hand, as Ruth O. Jones went rustling by behind him.

No need to stop for her key, she reflected, since of course Nell was there to open the door. Besides, it would take time. Her feel of time wasting was because she'd been wishing too long to come. Only that. Why, the lobby was just the same, just the same.

Ruthie and the jitters. How Betty would laugh! Betty the city mouse. Betty the louse, who'd begged off. Although why on earth I assume *she's* so darned reliable . . . Betty and *her* system of values . . . Betty who doesn't even know, yet, what a woman's in the world for . . . It was the blood tie, of course. It was the mere fact that Peter's sister could not be a stranger.

Now Ruth began (for everything upstairs would be just the same) to pick and choose among excuses. One could not say, I came because I don't trust you an inch, my dear. No. But one could say, I came for a clean handkerchief, which would be pretty feeble. Obviously, no shoulder straps to break. Oh, say a pill. Say some special remedy brought from home. For a headache, say. It would do.

There was a man in a brown suit talking in rather an official manner to the elevator boy. He kept on talking. "I beg your pardon," Ruth asked. "Is this car going up?"

"In a minute, ma'am."

"Thank you." She stepped by. They kept muttering together. The boy said, "Never rode with me."

Ruth's foot in the golden slipper twitched. Oh, don't be silly! Surely a minute doesn't matter! (Except on the inner clock of her apprehensive bones.)

Chapter 17

NELL LET the water run. Then she filled the glass. She stood, holding the glass, and twisted the faucet once or twice, on and off. Her face was sullen and a little bored and weary, as she looked down at the form of the little man on the bathroom floor, lying as if he were normally asleep, twisted a bit to one side, as if to be comfortable.

The skin around his eyes twitched, as if the bright light affected him. She frowned faintly, and then her whole body seemed to shrug, to lift off the problem and let it go. The hell with it.

She snapped off the light, opened the door that she had so speedily put between her and room 807, and pulled it after her quite deftly as she stepped through. "Miss Ballew?" She was all sweet service.

The schoolteacher, with her eyes closed, was silently reciting poetry. It was a trick to play on the release of the fearful substances to the blood, on the whole panicked interior chemistry. Sometimes, by taking the brain's attention elsewhere, she could wait out, slow down, and defeat the pound of the goaded heart.

"Oh, thank you, my dear. Really, this is so feeble of me." Her teeth chattered. "But I lead rather a quiet existence. I rarely . . ." The phone rang. The glass was still in Nell's hand. "I'll get it," chattered Miss Ballew and jerked around.

Nell sat down quietly. Her toes turned in, then out, almost imperceptibly. Her finger tips danced a little on the cool damp glass.

"Yes?" quavered the teacher.

"This is the desk. I've had word of some trouble. Perhaps you can tell me?"

"Trouble!" burst Miss Ballew. "Yes, *certainly*, there has been trouble. I spoke to *someone*, long ago! Now, who was that? Really, by this time you ought to have accomplished something. Do you mean to tell me! Didn't you *stop* him?"

"I beg your pardon," said the astonished voice.

"Did you or did you not stop that man! I told you— I described him."

106

"Who is this, please?"

"This is Miss Eva Ballew. I have 823 but I am now in 807 as you ought to know since you are speaking to me here. Now, I reported this trouble minutes ago—"

"Yes. Yes, I see, Miss Ballew," he broke in. "The house detective must have taken—"

"*Must* have! Are you guessing? Who are *you*, pray?"

"I'm at the desk, ma'am."

"And do you mean to tell me that you do not know! See here. Is anything at all being done?"

"The house detective evidently—"

"Evidently! Are you men or mice down there? Where is *he*?"

"He is evid— He is looking— That is, I see, now."

"You are too late and too slow," she spoke on top of him, "and it has been too long. You have irresponsibly allowed that ruffian to escape."

Milner's spine curled. "But is the child all right?" he demanded.

"The child? Why, yes, I believe—"

Milner, man, not mouse, was delighted to say, disagreeably, "*Do you mean to tell me that you do not know!*" and snap, "Someone responsible will be up there at once," and slam down the phone. But all the same, he was relieved. Pat Perrin knew about it.

Miss Ballew hung up and her eyes were pained. So often this physical weakness had betrayed her. So often it had led her to be ashamed. She knew so well what one ought to do, but the weak flesh was a drag.

"What was it?" Nell said.

"They . . . someone will be up. They seem confused." And I, thought Miss Ballew, am a pitiful despicable cowering wretch. And she tried to shift her legs.

"He got away?"

"Evidently." It was no use. Her legs were mush, still. "My dear," she said sadly, "hadn't you better see to the child?"

"Oh, yes," said Nell quickly. But she rose without haste, in fact, rather slowly and tentatively. "Don't you want the drink of water?" She didn't seem to know what to do with it.

Miss Ballew received the glass. She was not a fool. Now, as she knew her guilt, and realized that someone ought long ago to have gone in to the poor frightened child, the terrified little girl, she began to wonder why Nell had not gone. Nell, whose responsibility she was, had fetched water for a stranger instead. It didn't ring right. First things had not come first. No, it rang wrong. Echoes of their first exchange began to come to her. Nell's rudeness and the odd manner. She could no longer so glibly excuse it. And she seemed, besides, to see in her mind's eye that the man in the corridor had no freckles on that averted cheek and no blue in his clothing.

She looked at Nell. She murmured, "It's incredible, really." The girl seemed to be waiting politely for her to go on and perhaps she didn't understand. "It's hard to believe," translated Miss Ballew. "I've never heard such a wild story. There seems to be no sense . . . not even a mad method to this man's actions. Are you sure?"

"What?"

"Are you sure you didn't encourage him?"

"I haven't done anything," Nell said, looking surprised. "I don't know what you mean."

This was an echo, too, and it rang false. "Come now, of course you know what I mean." Miss Ballew looked annoyed but she checked herself. "Never mind. This is no time for debate. See to the child, my dear, and bring her in here, do. Poor, poor baby. When the detective arrives," her voice faltered from its habitual tone of instruction, "I daresay he . . ."

"He what?" Nell frowned faintly.

"I mean to say," said Miss Ballew dryly, being fair, "perhaps he's seen more of this sort of thing . . . perhaps more of it goes on than is dreamed of in my philosophy. And of course," she added thoughtfully, "the child . . . How old is the child?"

"How old?"

"She is not an infant? She is old enough to talk?"

"Of course," said Nell wonderingly. "She's nine, I think."

"Then that is fortunate," said Miss Ballew, "for of course she will be able to corroborate your story."

Nell was just standing there, looking stupid and even half falling asleep.

What a handicap to have so limited a vocabulary, thought the teacher. "Corroborate means to confirm," she explained, "to tell the same story, or enough to prove it, do you see? That's why I point out—"

"And fortunate," said Nell, "means lucky." She was smiling. Why, she was dancing! She stood on the same spot, there at the foot of the bed, but for a moment Miss Ballew had the distinct impression that she was dancing. Even her face had a twinkling, sparkling look. Impish, as if she'd thought of something, had an idea, or knew a mischievous secret. "I know more words than you think I do," said Nell. "And I understand the future." She flung up her hands . . . yes, it was a dance! (Miss Ballew looked on, bewildered.) And then the dark skirt flopped and fell out of the moving arc and reversed. . . .

And the girl was leaning on her two stiff arms, her knuckles white on the footboard, her eyes very wide, very blue. "I . . . I wonder . . ." The eyeballs turned in slow fear and the slow fear welled in Miss Ballew.

"She's awfully quiet," Nell said, softly, softly. "*Isn't* she?"

Miss Ballew clawed her own throat.

"Don't you think . . . it's funny?"

"F-fun—" Miss Ballew wafted her arm across the air.

Nell's teeth enfolded her lower lip. Now she looked very grave and thoughtful. She walked on soft toes to that inner door. Her hand was slow on the knob and nerves in the teacher's temple turned excruciatingly with it.

The latch fell out. The door yawned. No sound emerged from 809.

"Bunny?" Nell called, softly, softly.

There was no answer.

"Bunny!" The girl's back shook as if with a long shiver. Only quiet answered her. Her eyes rolled as she looked over her shoulder. "I'm afraid . . ." she whimpered.

Miss Ballew was afraid, too. She could *not* move. Her own ears knew that frightening silence was really there. "But you said— But you told me he didn't . . . hurt . . ."

"He was in there, *afterward*. After you knocked. Do you think . . ."

"Don't think! Don't even say!"

But Nell's words fell like Fate. "Maybe he remembered . . . she's old enough to talk. . . ."

"Our Father which art in heaven," mumbled Miss Ballew. "Beseech thee . . . from evil . . ."

"It would," said Nell, glassy eyed, "be so easy. She's just . . . a little thing . . ."

"Go see!" screamed Miss Eva Ballew, up on her elbow but paralyzed for all that. "For the love of heaven, girl! Go *in* there and *see*!"

Chapter 18

L YN TOUCHED his arm. He veered away from her touch as if he expected a blow to follow. (Yah! Iron nerves, Towers?)

"Lyn! Oh for—I thought . . ."

"Didn't they give you my note?"

She was there, and not an apparition, standing beside him and, in the light of the city night, her face was sweetly, soberly wondering why he was as startled as this to see her. Ah, she was sweet and sane!

"Gosh, you look . . ." He grabbed her wooley blue arm. "What are you doing here at this hour? You been rattling around this town *alone*! It's too damn late, Lyn."

"I'm not afraid. . . ."

"The street's no place . . ."

"I *haven't* been . . ."

"I don't care where you . . ."

"Nobody bothered . . ."

"You ought to know better!"

"Oh, don't be so . . ."

"Little fool . . ."

"Oh, Jed!" she wailed. They teetered back from the brink of the same quarrel. The same damn thing. Jed even stepped backward on the sidewalk.

"I guess this is where we came in," he murmured.

"Where I walked out," she laughed uncertainly. Her eyes were not merry. But they were sweet and sane.

He put his hand in his pocket. "Jed, didn't you read it?"

"No, I . . . Not yet." He fumbled for the envelope. He felt troubled . . . troubled. Not ready to meet her. She was here too soon. He held her note passively in his hand.

"It's nothing." She tried to take it, gently, but he refused to let it go. "I've been waiting and waiting," she said breathlessly. "In the lobby, Jed. It was safe enough. I was just about to give up and go home. I went into the drugstore . . . saw you . . . I've been calling your room."

He made no reply, no excuse, no explanation.

"I waited the longest time," she said.

"Why, dear?" he asked gently.

Lyn's face looked as if she were touched to tears but she did not weep and she did not turn her face away. "Because I'm sorry, Jed. That's about all there is to say about it. I'm ashamed to have been so stubborn and ornery. I'm sure you were more in the right than I was willing to admit while I was so mad."

"Never mind." He slipped his arm around her. "Never mind. Never mind." He thought, If this isn't like her! This kind of weird, high-minded, overdone fairness, this proud dragging down of her pride.

"I couldn't bear you to go all that way," she said quietly, keeping her own balance, although he embraced her, "and us mad. That's . . . all about it."

"Was I mad at you?" he said, scarcely believing it.

"Where were you going?" She put her bare fingers to her eyes.

"Oh, I . . . was more or less lighting out," he said vaguely. He felt very sad, very sad. He had a sensation in the breast as if the heart would break.

"Could we have one drink somewhere? And would you take me home? Will you make it up, Jed, and get the nasty taste out of our mouths, before you go?"

He looked down at her. "You beat all," he said gravely. "But you're sweet. How come you do the way you . . . ?" He broke off. He looked up and the stone face on the building above him had no expression, nothing to say.

"I called you things I don't believe," Lyn said in a low voice. "Is it a date?"

Something bigger than he was took him and shook him like a rat. He covered the shudder up by grabbing for his suitcase. "It's a date, Lyn." He let his mouth curve, his voice be as tender as it wished to be, and she smiled like the rainbow.

Jed looked away, off over her head. Why did he feel so troubled and sad? Here was she, stubborn little love, trying to get back where they'd been. And why not? So Towers had his date, after all. Didn't he? Right back where he'd been. Wasn't he? (Episode over. Close quotes. File and forget.) Here's Towers in the evening with his own girl under his arm and a honey she was, wearing that proud humility, *believing* (his heart sank because it was so heavy), trusting that he was going to match it.

That they'd be together again. Be that as it may, the night was young and nothing was lost. Not a thing. Was it? And he could park the suitcase somewhere and on with the dance! March on! Te dum de dee . . .

Proceed, Towers. From where you were. Advance, right out along the line, the line you cut in your time, the track you see before and leave behind, that goes, if you are smart, straight without any stupid detours. . . .

"Please, Jed, let me have my note?" she begged softly. "You don't need . . ."

He looked down. He said, "No." He put it back in his pocket. Oh-ho no! he thought. This we look into, in some dark bar. "Just a minute, honey," he went on, sounding to his surprise exactly as if this was what he'd planned to say from the moment she had touched his arm. It came out so smooth and easy. "Something I want to check, a minute. In here."

She smiled. It was all right with her. Anything he said, of course. He thought, What a reckless attitude *that* is! But he touched her and with tenderness pushed her into a slot in the door and pushed the door, following.

What the hell was he going back in for? Curiosity? One thing, he'd surely keep it from Lyn, what he was up to. It was nothing, anyhow. Take a minute. No need to invent a lie, for her . . . innocent, reckless little love! No, he'd just take a quick look around, that's all. He thought he could tell, pretty quickly, if they'd got up there to the little kid, all right. Surely repercussions would sift down to the lobby, which he would be able to feel. Maybe no other guest could notice, or catch on at all. But surely, he could tell. And rest his mind about it.

That would really close it off. Lyn would never ask. Or, she'd take it, if he gave no answer, if he never explained. There'd be nothing to mention, nothing even to think about, once he knew nothing was . . . dangling.

Towers could then proceed.

In itself, the hotel now knew something was up. The news ran on its nervous system, in the minds of its own people. The guests were unaware and might never become aware of this as the guests had been unaware of many things on many other occasions. But the hotel knew now.

Rochelle sat at her board. She knew. She prepared to be the spider in the middle of the web. All things would eventually come to her.

Milner knew, and was nervous behind his front, although his front remained as wooden and polished as the walnut around him. He was about to leave his post. He'd had a quick word with the Assistant Manager and that one agreed that Milner himself must go up there. He would emerge from his inner place and take over at the desk.

The bartender knew, in his dim barricade in the far corner of the farthest corner. The porter, emptying ash trays, had a faint knowledgeable air. The bellboys knew. "Some guy got away," they dared say to each other softly, but they veiled their watching eyes.

Perrin was almost resigned to the idea that the man had got away. If he had not, but still lurked somewhere, where was it? No redhead and so forth in the corridors, in any of the public rooms. Not in the bar's deepest recesses, not in the men's rooms. If he was registered and had a room and lurked *there*, it might take a little doing.

Perrin strode up to the desk and caught Milner. "Who we got that's tall, redheaded, freckle-faced, light suit, blue shirt?"

"Nobody," said Milner. "Say . . ."

They wiped trouble from all their faces. The Assistant Manager said, "Yes, Mr. Hodges." A guest took his key, made a firm didactic statement about the weather, went away.

"On the trouble in 807?" the manager said.

"Yeah, dame described this man . . ."

"Just what did he do?"

"Intruded," said Perrin dryly.

Milner said, "It was a man who tipped me. Is the kid all right?"

"Who?"

"Who told me? It was . . ."

"No, no. *What* kid?"

"Little girl. Jones."

"I'd better get up there," Perrin said thoughtfully. "Nobody told me about a kid."

"That's not good, having a kid in it. I was just going . . ."

The manager said, "Uh—keep it quiet."

Two of them swung off separately. Milner negotiated his way around the walnut embankments. Perrin met him again, near the elevators.

The elevators knew, although they whispered up and down without telling.

"Couldn't have hurt the kid," Perrin remarked. "All she said, he intruded."

"All she said to me, did we stop him," agreed Milner. "Ran out, did he?"

"Yeah, he's not up there now."

"Nerves?" said Milner hopefully. Perrin shrugged. Whatever it was, they assumed it was all over but, of course, the hysterics.

An elevator whispered down. "Say, that's Towers now." Milner peered. "Fellow who tipped me. Thought he—oh . . ."

"Oh, what?"

"He's got the girl. She found him." Milner relaxed.

"Eight," said Perrin quietly and stepped on. The boy moved only an eyelash. But he knew.

"Up? Up?" caroled Mrs. McMurdock. "Come, Bobo. Come, darling. Time for beddy-bye." The little dog ran into the elevator and sniffed moistly at Perrin's socks. Milner and he exchanged looks. The car started upward.

"He loooves to ride," said Mrs. McMurdock. "Doesn't he, Bobo? Doesn't he, boy? Loves to ride! Yes, he does! Just loooves to ride!"

She did not know.

Chapter 19

RUTH, AS she rode gently upward, stuffed her change into her little evening bag without looking down at her hands. She kept watching the blank metal door beyond which the floors were sliding by. She was the only passenger. The car made no stop but hers. As it sailed toward a soft landing and went into the little shuffle for the precise level of the eighth floor, she felt a perverse regret for the ending of an ordeal, a resistance to the necessity of shifting from one mood to another.

She stepped out. Behind her, the car stayed where it was a second longer than was normal while the boy listened to the quality of the silence up here. It seemed to be mere silence. Disappointed, he looked at his lights, yanked the lever, and sailed upward.

For Ruth, the corridor was just the same, just the same. She hurried to her left. She turned the corner.

The door of 807 looked just the same . . . as bland and blank as all the others. Prepare to shift. Inside, the girl would be dozing, and Bunny fast asleep, and the debris of her parents' dressing would be strewn about just as they had left it. Shift. The mood, now, is hushed. It's the mood of— All's well. Naturally. Of course it is. Ruth tapped gently.

At once, a much agitated female voice cried, "Oh, yes! Come in! Oh, come in!"

Ruth's mood leaped like lightning. Her hand leaped to the knob. She burst into the room and met the frightened eyes of a stoutish middle-aged woman she'd never seen in her life before, who was half sitting, half lying, in a strained position on Ruth's own bed. The woman's black dress was awry over her stout leg and her mouse-colored hair was awry, too. "Who are you!" cried this stranger in a voice that was also awry.

But Ruth put first things first.

Her gold bag fell out of her hand. Without a word, she flew, hands up, across 807 to 809. She batted the partially opened door and it swung wider. 809 was unlit. Ruth aimed herself like an arrow at the light switch. She flashed around.

She saw Bunny's two bare feet twitching on the bed and the girl's dark back bent. Ruth cried out, "What's the matter?" She got one glimpse of Bunny's bound mouth, and then saw the girl's face blinking at her over the shoulder, the drowsy evil in the sullen careless glance, and she knew what the wicked hands were about to do.

Making no cry, Ruth simply flew at her. Her hands bit on the shoulders, and with all her might she heaved backward, to get the evil away. Still, she did not scream. Instead, she called out in almost a cheerful voice, "It's all right, Bunny. It's me. It's Mommy."

The shoulders rolled, writhed, and slipped away from her. The girl's body turned with vicious speed. Ruth felt herself knocked backward and the small of her back was wrenched as it slammed against the other bed and she felt her neck crack with the backward weight of her head. She flipped herself quickly over and slipped downward to her knees, hearing silk rip. She fastened both hands on an ankle. She crawled backward, yanking and pulling, out from the narrow place between the beds. *Get it away from Bunny.* This was first. And Nell came, hopping, tottering, kicking . . . and her hands clawed for Ruth's face, hunting Ruth's eyes.

O.K., thought Ruth. *All right.*

Ruth had not always been a gracious young matron, a pretty wife, a gentle mother. In her day, she'd climbed many a tough tree and hung by knobby knees off ladders with pigtails dragging. And she'd chased the other kids off rafts and over rooftops. And she'd played basketball, too, on a tough team, even in so-called free style, which meant she had pulled hair and bitten and gouged with the rest. And she'd run up and down the playing fields of many schools and been banged in the shins by hockey sticks. She'd had her bruises and given them. The world of direct physical conflict, violent and painful, had not always been beyond her ken.

"So!" she hissed with her teeth closed. There was lightning on her eyeballs as she got her hands in that yellowish hair and yanked and the girl screeched and fell forward, twisting, and Ruth rolled on the hard floor to get from under her.

She felt the teeth in her forearm and pain as claws ripped at her cheek. Ruth's long rosy nails went into the other's flesh, where she could, and with the sharp spurs of her heels she slashed at the other's shins. Her own head thudded on the carpet and hands like wires sank in her throat.

She wouldn't have screamed, anyhow.

She pulled up her knee. Silk ripped, velvet tore. She put her sharp golden heel in the wildcat's stomach and straightened her leg and Nell went sprawling. Ruth walked on her knees and dove on her, got the hair, whammed the head to the floor.

But the head bounced. The body in the dark dress was taut and strong. It wasn't going to be that easy.

Ruth heard herself growl in her gullet, now it was free. Fast as the fighting went, she yet summoned with a cold brain old strengths, old tricks, and when they were not enough, she began to invent . . . She had realized, long ago, that she fought, here, something wild and vicious, that wanted to hurt, that didn't care how. Probably mad, and strong by that perfect ruthlessness.

But Ruth, too, was fortified. She was wilder than the tomboy she used to be. She was more vicious than the girl athlete. She was Bunny's mother and she was easily able to be absolutely ruthless in that holy cause.

She said to herself, *O.K. All right.* And she was not afraid.

It never crossed her mind to scream. It seemed her sole and simple duty and even her pleasure to fight with all her body's strength and her mind's cunning. (Outside of any rules, if that was the way it was, and O.K., too.) It did not cross her mind to wonder who would win, either. She sank her own strong teeth in the enemy's wrist, while she tried with her mind to think just how she was going to conquer . . . what trick would do it . . . even as she was tossed and the merciless elbow was crushing her breast.

Miss Ballew managed to get her feet to the floor but her weight would not balance over them. The column of her leg would not stand, the knee joint would not lock. She knew now she would be forever haunted by remorse and shame if she did not force herself to help in this emergency. But she was not well. Her heart hurt. There was a sharp pain in her side. Her mind knew that her body was lying, and her heart pitied the body's treasonable victory, as her lips prayed cravenly for someone else to come.

Chapter 20

THE MOMENT he was inside the lobby, Jed knew that the hotel, in itself, was aroused. The alarm was spread. He saw it in the stiff pose of a different head behind the desk. He knew, too, that there had been, and yet was, a search going on. He saw that in the veiled turn of all the eyes, in the porter's spine. Looking for someone? For whom? For *him*, no doubt.

It came to him that he was taking a certain risk in the mere act of stepping back within these walls. Sure, they were looking. Once more his mind played back its recorded impressions, a glimpse of the fellow in the brown suit weaving among the chairs, and his beckoning hand and the doorman's response, and the doorman's *belated* prance to his normal duties. The man in the brown suit had been looking for someone, all right. For whom, if not for Jed?

All the way across the lobby, he could see that very suit, the same man, over there right now, waiting for an elevator. The clerk to whom Jed had given warning was beside him, and all the way across the lobby, Jed knew when they spoke his name.

What was this?

They were *looking* for him and they, for some reason, were not looking for *him*. He saw himself split in two, the object of their search, and merely Towers who had just checked out of 821. They hadn't put it together yet. They would, sooner or later. And easily. For instance, right over there lounged the boy-who-had-brought-up-the-ice. Who was, all by himself, the missing link. When would his hunting eye catch sight of Jed and recognize?

Jed guided Lyn so that she stood with her back to the elevators and he, bent as if to listen to her, could watch them with an eyebeam over her head. Those two men were authority. Obviously. Were they *only now* going up to see what was wrong on the eighth floor? If so, they were darned late! Wires must have got crossed. It had been a long time.

(A long, long time for a helpless, frightened little girl to wait in the dark for her daddy or his equivalent.)

He ground his teeth. What was going on? Lyn stood obediently, her head thrown back to look up into his face. She didn't know why they were standing here. She trusted there was a good reason.

He said, rapidly, "Do you mind? I just want to see . . . Talk to me. Make some remarks, hm?"

"You're being mighty mysterious," Lyn said lightly. It was so plain she trusted he had good reason. "Mine not to wonder why. Me and the six hundred. Lyn, number six hundred and one."

He felt his jaw crack. "Keep talking."

The elevator took on its passengers . . . two men, one woman, and a scampering little dog.

"Nothing is quite so numbing as to be told to say something. Makes your mind a blank. Just like on long distance. Hm . . . I like raspberry pie very much but the seeds do get in my teeth. I'm very fond of cucumber sandwiches in the summertime. Is this better than the weather? Am I doing all right?"

"You're fine."

Jed was farsighted, been so all his life. He could see from here the indicator moving on the dial. He could not read the numbers but then he knew already where the eight came. He said bitterly, "Why in Christ's name didn't I lock the damn door!"

"If I ask questions," said Lyn placidly, "I won't be making remarks, will I? Cross out 'will I.'"

"The door *between*," he growled. What he was telling he didn't know.

"Oh, between. Well, that's nice. That's quite illuminating."

"If I had any brains . . ."

"Oh, you have, Jed. I think you have. Good-looking as you are, you must have a brain. I think it's very possible. Lessee, what's my favorite flower. At a time like this, I ought to know so I could tell you. But I like too many kinds, too much. But you take roses."

Although he kept his eye on that dial, he knew Lyn's face was full of peace. She had no right! His glance flicked down. She had her hands in the big pockets of her coat and her back was bent in a sweet, almost yearning arch, in order for her face to turn up to him, and her eyes were sweet and sane and full of peace because she believed . . . She was a little fool to believe in anybody!

"You look about nine years old," said Jed with a whipsnap of anger. And he sent his eyes again to the dial.

"Oh, I don't think so. I think I probably look about nineteen and just as if I've got a terrible crush on you, a bobby-socks-type crush. And you look like thunder, Jed. If I knew what the matter was I'd try to help. But you know that, of course." (I even trust you to trust me.) "Mine only to keep talking, eh? Why, then, I'll go ahead. Babble. Babble. Do you care for the chamber music? No, that's a question. Well, I always say it depends. And it does. Everything depends . . ."

The hand on the dial had stopped . . . must be at about four. It seemed to be stuck there. Was it out of order?

"Come, boy. Come, boy. Ah, naughty Bobo! (Loves to ride!) But this is home, boy. Home! Now, Bobo must be a good boy. Biscuit? Bobo want his biscuit? If Bobo wants his biscuit . . . Oh, what a naughty, bad doggy! Bobo! Listen to me! No . . . more . . . ride. Do you understand, sir? Beddy-bye, now. Come, Bobo."

Bobo retreated to the inner corner of the elevator and sat down.

Mrs. McMurdock giggled in her throat. "So ki-yute! Isn't that— Little monkey! Bobo, boy, Mama will leave you. Biscuit, biscuit?"

The hotel's people stood silent. Mrs. McMurdock was a guest. Bobo was a guest. A guest need not know all there is to know. They wore small chilly smiles, not too impatient, not too amused, either.

Bobo frisked between Milner's ankles.

"Shall I pick him up, madame?" the elevator boy said most respectfully.

"No, no. Now, he must learn," said Mrs. McMurdock. "Now, he'll mind in a minute." The trouble was, Bobo did look as if he would mind, any minute.

The hotel's people cleared their throats with professional patience. It wasn't going to be very pleasant placating that woman on the eighth floor, admitting to her that her wicked intruder had got away.

———

In the lobby, Jimmy said, "Hey, kids, sumpin's funny! See that fellow over there, one with the girl? Say, what was the room again?"

"Room 807."

"Yeah," drawled Jimmy. "Yeah . . ."

Jed's eyes flickered in his stony face.

". . . partial to rum," Lyn said, "with pink stuff in it. And you sure can get thirsty, talking so much. Filibuster is running down, Jed. Don't elect me senator, anybody. Is it all right now? Can we go?"

In Jed's head exploded the loud NO for an answer.

Her face changed. One second, sweet and pretty, and pleased with the nonsense she was able to spin. The next it had lost all that pretty animation, light, and color. Jed did it. By the look he bent on her, he wiped the pretty peace off her face.

He said, quietly, "I'm a rat, Lyn. A complete rat. Go home."

"But, Jed, I've been wait—"

"Don't wait any more. Never wait for me."

He stepped around his suitcase. His face was flinty. His muscles surged. He went across the lobby in a walk so smooth and fast that he seemed to float.

He knew that bellhop straightened with a start.

The hell with that!

He pushed on the door to the fire stairs.

Ah, God, NO!

He shouldn't have run out on that little kid! What kind of rat did such a thing? A rat like Towers. A complete, no-good . . . He was sad, he'd been sad over it a long time. So sad his heart was heavy.

Ah, NO!

A pair of socks wasn't all he had left and lost up on the eighth floor. And left, forever. Gone, like smoke! Yeah. You can't catch it back again, no more than you can a wisp of smoke. Thing like that, you can't retrieve.

And who would know? *Towers* would know.

This trip, all the way down to the lobby and out, wasn't even as good as a detour. There wasn't a way back from this side road to the main track. No way *on* again, *in* again. Rat forever, amen.

But he went up. Went up with all the great strength of his long powerful legs, three steps at once, then two, but pulling on the rail, around and around, climbing the building more like a monkey than a man going upstairs.

Passed the buck. Towers! Let the old lady take care of it. Towers! White! He sobbed breath in.

He thought, I don't know what I'm doing . . . know what I did . . . Never even thought to lock that door. Could have made sure to keep her out of there. Could have done that much. He and he *alone* (not Eddie. Eddie was out on the bathroom floor) . . . Towers *alone* knew what kind of sitter that Nell turned out to be. Knew the poor little kid was waiting. The old biddy couldn't know *that*, and where was she all this while? Arguing? No reason to think . . .

No, no. What Towers *alone* knew was that, reason or no reason, there would always and forever be some risk with that Nell around. But a risk for somebody else, of course. For somebody else's kid. A little thing who couldn't do a thing about it. So *Towers* figured the risk to his own six feet three, to his man's hide, to his . . . what?

Now, he couldn't remember any risk for Towers. For *nothing*, he ran out. For the sick shadow of nothing at all, he'd lost what he'd lost.

This complete revulsion was making him sick. O.K. Cut it out, Towers. What's done is done. Take it from here.

Eighth floor?

He must be in pretty good condition.

Yeah, condition!

There was the elevator. And there they stood, talking. Questions and answers, with the elevator boy. The hell with them. They didn't know there was a risk. Or they'd hurry. He couldn't understand why they hadn't hurried. Jed rushed past.

Aw, probably Bunny was all right. Probably. Pray so, and if so, here's Towers heading right back into the middle of this jam, for nothing. Doing no good. But maybe not for nothing. He didn't know. All he knew was, while he could still move for himself, he was going to make sure. He was going to bust in there and if the old biddy hadn't found her yet, Towers was going to untie the little kid and the hell with everything else

. . . and five seconds more, one second, one pulse beat more was too long.

Room 807's door was wide open. The old biddy, crouched on the edge of the bed, took one look at Jed's wild figure and heaved in her breath and let out a scream to wake the dead!

But Jed was in 809 before it died.

Nell, hair hanging over her eyes, had one knee on either side of the slim body of a woman, supine on the floor. Their hands were braced, hand against wrist, arms against aching arms. The woman on the floor had blood on her mouth and her cheek was torn and her breathing was shallow and difficult. But her eyes were intelligent and they yet watched for her chance.

Jed took little Nell by the short hair of her head. He ripped her away. She came up in his grasp, screeching, and hung from his hand, limp in surprise like a sawdust doll.

In the corridor, Milner and Perrin saw the racing figure and in their startled ears rang the woman's scream. Perrin got his gun in his hand as they began to run.

The door of 807 was wide.

"The man," croaked Miss Ballew, voice thick and hoarse. "That's the man!" Oh, she knew him. By the indescribable. By the habits of motion, the line of the back, the tip of the shoulder, the cock of the head.

"The *one*," she sobbed. "The man . . . the same one!"

Perrin looked toward 809.

He saw a tall man with a face of utter fury drag, by the hair of her head, a small blond girl through that door. Saw him drag her around the wooden frame as if he didn't care whether she lived or died, as if he didn't care if he broke her bones.

"Drop that girl! Let her go!"

Jed's head went back and the eyes glittered down the long straight nose. "The hell I will! You don't—"

Perrin fired.

Chapter 21

R UTH O. JONES lifted her shoulders from the carpet, and pulled her twisted rags and tatters aside to free her legs. She wiped the blood off her mouth with her arm. She combed her fingers through her hair. Some of it, torn out at the roots, came away in her broken nails.

She walked on her knees—there was no need to rise higher—over to Bunny's bed.

She paid not the slightest attention to the gunshot as it blasted off, behind her.

She said, in her firm contralto, "O.K., honey bun? For goodness' sakes, what happened to *you?*" Her cut mouth kissed the temple lightly. Her fingers were strong and sure on those wicked knots.

Jed kept standing, somehow, because he had to keep an eye steady on Nell. She fell on the floor when he had to drop her as if she had been a sack of meal. As soon as he was sure she lay as limp as she seemed to lie, he looked at his right hand. He took it away from his left side and looked at the bright blood on it.

He looked at the men, standing tense and threatening in his path, and he tried to smile. The elevator boy was behind them. Then he saw his girl, Lyn, behind *him* . . . looking, as if she peered through trees in a glade, between the men's bodies, in at the strange tableau.

Ah, the little fool! "Go home," he said.

Then he heard it. In the other room, Bunny began to cry.

Over Jed's face passed a look of peace and thanksgiving. He turned, reeling, because he was wounded and no kidding, stumbled, and made for the big maroon chair. He thought he sat down in it. Perhaps it was more like falling.

"Oh, Jed!"

"But that's Towers . . ."

"It's the same man. . . ."

Now, he was three. Or maybe only one, again. Or nothing. No matter. There was a difference in the way a kid cried. Funny . . . could you write down the difference in musical terms, he wondered. Pitch or timing or what? One kind of crying that gnawed on your nerves and pierced your head. This kind didn't do that. No, it didn't do that at all. It was a thing not unmusical to hear. . . .

Perrin, kneeling over Nell, barked, "What did you do to this girl?"

Jed didn't feel like bothering to say.

Miss Ballew let out another yelp of pure shock. Eyes starting from her head, she reacted to her sight of the little man in the hotel's livery who was standing in the bathroom door, holding his head, looking out mouselike at them all.

"Munro!" thundered Milner. "What—"

Eddie blinked. Silence rustled down, that they might hear his feeble voice. "I guess . . . Nell musta got into more mischief. Did she? My niece? Nell?"

"Who?"

Jed pulled himself from the mists. "Nell, the baby sitter. On the floor." He braced himself, watchfully. "Nutty as a fruitcake," he said.

But Nell only rolled, drowsily. Her arm fell aside in sleepy grace, revealing her face. Her eyes were closed. The blue gone, her small face was left perfectly serene. There was a long scratch from eye corner to jaw. It looked as if it had been painted there, as if she felt no pain. She seemed to be asleep.

"That's Nell. Yes, she . . ." Eddie tottered to look. "That's the way she did—before," he said in awe. "After the fire, they say, she slept . . . just like that." He swallowed and looked around at all their set faces. "How can she sleep?" he whimpered.

"Somebody," said Jed wearily, "go see. I suppose it's Mrs. Jones. This one pretty near killed her."

Perrin got off his haunches and lurched through the door. Milner's horrified eye sent fury in sudden understanding where, from his point of view, it belonged. "Munro!"

"I . . . didn't think . . ." said Eddie. "I kinda kept hoping she'd be all right. But I guess . . ."

"Next time, don't guess," said Jed. "Lyn, go home."

"Not now." She moved toward him, drawn. "I won't, Jed. I've got to know . . ."

He closed his eyes.

When a fresh scream rose up, out there in the other room in another world, Ruth's finger tips did not leave off stroking into shape the little mouth that the wicked gag had left so queer and crooked. "That's right. Just you cry. Golly, Bun, did you see me fighting! Wait till we tell Daddy . . . missed the whole thing . . ." Ruth held the little head warmly against her battered body. There was comfort soaking through from skin to skin. "Cry it all out, sweetheart. Cry."

"Mrs. Jones?" a man said to her. His hair seemed to her to be trying to stand on end.

"Go away. Hush. Please call my husband . . ."

She stroked and murmured on. Not until she heard Peter's voice did her wounds and gashes remember pain.

"We're just fine," Ruth said quickly. "Jeepers, have we had an adventure!"

Peter's face was dead white as he looked upon his wife and child.

"She was the crossest sitter I ever saw," Bunny said indignantly. Her arms went around her daddy's dark head where he had hidden his face against her. "She tied my mouth all up, Daddy, so I couldn't cry. She certainly didn't want me to cry awful bad."

Peter roused and looked at those stockings.

"Bound and gagged," Ruth said quietly. Her face said more.

"G-gosh, she must have had terrible ears." Peter's voice trembled. "I expect she's got sick ears, Bunny."

His hands curled and uncurled. Ruth's eyes said, I know. But it's over. Be careful.

For Bunny didn't realize what had almost happened to her and it was better if she didn't. You mustn't scare a little girl who's nine so that all her life she carries the scar. You must try to heal what scar there is. Ruth knew, and deeply trembled to know it, that someday she would leave Bunny again. And with a sitter, of course. She must. (Although not for a good while with a stranger. Maybe never again with a total stranger.) Still, they would go gaily as might be on in time and they would not permit themselves to be cowed, to be daunted. They dared not.

Poor Peter, shaken and suffering, right now, and fighting so hard not to betray it. Peter knew all this as well as she. They were tuned to each other. "Bunny's fine and I feel fine, too," she told him. "Really. A few scratches. Did they take her away?"

"They're coming. They'll take her to a hospital," added Peter, for Bunny's sake, "because she's sick, really. She doesn't know how to get along with people who are well."

"Will she get better," said Bunny with a huge snuffle, "from those sick ears?"

"I don't know, pudding. They won't let her be with well people any more, unless she gets all better."

Bunny's shuddering sobs were becoming like the soft far murmur of the last thunder of a departing storm. "Daddy."

"What, Bun?"

Ruth felt the head turn on her breast. "Did you have fun?"

Peter couldn't answer. But Ruth could. "Oh, Bunny, it was lots of fun. And Daddy made a good speech. I wish you'd been big enough to go." She rushed on. "Daddy stood up and all the people, everybody was dressed up . . ."

Peter looked upon the condition of his wife's clothing. "Those . . . scratches, hon," he said in a minute, sounding as if half his throat was closed. "There's a doctor out there."

So the doctor came in and looked them both over.

"You know," said Ruth when he had gone, licking the antiseptic in her mouth, "I pretty near had her licked! I think!" She laughed. "I must look terrible but I feel fine."

And she did. Ah, poor Peter with the retrospective horror and the wrath locked in and buttoned down. But Ruth had got rid of it by tooth and claw. And she remembered, now, with relish, certain digs and blows. She felt quite peaceful. Fulfilled, she thought, the tigress in me. "Hand me in some of my things, Peter. I'm going to bed in here with Bun."

"O.K., girls."

"Maybe we'll order hot chocolate! Shall we? Lets!"

"In the middle of the night!" squealed Bunny and the sweet smooth skin of her face rippled in the warning of delight to come.

Peter O. Jones, with a smile covering (from all but his wife) the tears bleeding out of his heart, went back to 807.

Chapter 22

EDDIE WAS gone, damned for a reckless fool, with all the anxious ignorant hope he'd called his caution dust in his whimpering throat. (Don't worry, Eddie, Marie would say.)

Milner was gone, to harmonize with the walnut, downstairs. (Keep it out of the papers, if we possibly can.)

Perrin was gone. ("Sorry, Towers. You can see how it was?" "Sure. That's O.K.") He went with Nell.

And Nell was gone. Still seeming asleep, looking innocent and fair. Only Jed spoke to her. Jed said (and it seemed necessary—somewhere once, this he had planned to say), "So long, Nell."

She was asleep so she didn't reply. Yet there was a lazy lift of the lashes. (They won't do anything to me.)

Nearly everyone was gone. Miss Ballew remained, sick in her soul, with the doctor's suggested sedative in her hand. Jed was in the big chair again, bloody shirt loose over the vast bandage. Lyn was still there.

The doctor warned once more that Jed must take a few days' rest before trying to travel with that wound. Then, he was gone.

"You'll stay over, Jed, won't you?" Lyn's mouth was stiff.

"A couple of days, at least. I'll see." Jed's side was stinging like the devil, now. Telegrams, he thought, but time for that later. Maybe he'd break his cross-country trip and stop to see the family. Felt like it, somehow. Worry them, though, if he turned up shot. "Lyn, will you please . . . Your family's probably . . . Why don't you go home?"

"I will, soon." She didn't look at him. She looked at her trembling hands.

Peter took Ruth's things to her, came back, flipped up his tails, sat down, put his head in his hands. "Jesus."

Lyn said, with that stiff mouth, "You're terribly upset, of course. Shouldn't we go, Jed? If I can help you to your own room . . ."

"Or I," said Miss Ballew drearily.

"Don't go. Ruth wants to say good night. A minute."

"Your little, uh, Bunny's all right?" asked Jed.

"Soon be. Kids bounce back. Thank God. Drink with me?"

Jed didn't feel sure. He felt this room rejected him. But he was *fallen* in this chair.

"I ought to go home," said Lyn whitely. "I don't mean to hang around . . . be in the way."

"I ought to go," said Miss Ballew. (To be a worthless old coward and on top of that be fooled and fail in the mind, too!) "I was of very little use."

"Take it easy," Peter said. "Better try and take it easy, all of us."

Jed shifted his stiff side, reached slowly for the pocket of his coat, for the envelope. He managed to open it with one hand. It said, "Dear Jed:" And that was all. No more.

Well. He looked back into dim reaches of time. It would have been enough. It would have been plenty. He crushed it up and put it back in his pocket. He didn't look at Lyn.

Peter passed drinks. "Nonsense, Miss Ballew. You need this. There." He sat down. His brown eyes locked with Jed's gray. "As I understand it, you left Bunny tied up? But you told them at the desk on your way out?" Peter's voice was light, tentative.

"I figured it wasn't my business," said Jed levelly. "I didn't want to get into a mess. I figured to get away."

Well, he hadn't got away. He'd got shot. And Towers was a rat. So, then, he was. The little girl was O.K. now. Mother, too. Nothing, thank God, they couldn't get over. So . . . if Towers was left in his rathood, that was not too important to them, any more.

Gray eyes locked on brown. "That's the kind of rat I am, I guess," Jed said quietly. "Later, I got a little nervous . . . a little too much later."

Miss Ballew's lips trembled. "I was so stupid," she said. "I was worse than no use. My *fault* . . ."

Jed's gray eyes met hers. They said, Don't blame yourself too much. They said, I understand. They said, Us sinners—

"Seems to me," Jed drawled, "if you're hunting for blame . . . if I hadn't come over here in the first place . . ."

"If I hadn't walked out," Lyn said bleakly.

"No. Lyn . . ."

"You think *I'm* not doing any iffing?" Peter asked. Brown eyes met gray. "If I'd even looked at the girl with half my brain on it. Me and my big important speech! I left it to Ruthie. Of course, she got it. In her bones, the way she sometimes does. If . . ."

Jed shook his head.

"Ruth knew I needed her. She chose. Even *Ruth* can if . . ." Brown eyes said to gray, *All us sinners.*

Peter got up to pace. "Ruth says she had her licked. But I don't know . . ."

"I don't know, either, sir. I couldn't say." Eyes locked again. "Now, don't kid me, sir," Jed said gently. "They weren't two steps behind me. They'd have been on time."

And then he smiled. Because it only mattered to Towers, now, and Towers could take it. "Tell you, it isn't often a man says to himself, You ought to be shot, and right away, someone obliges." He moved and made the wound hurt. It was not so bad. It was like a session with the hairbrush, or a trip to the woodshed. He didn't mind.

But then Lyn said, as if she broke, "I'm afraid." Why, she was all to pieces. She wasn't *Lyn*. She looked white and old and sick and she was shaking to pieces. "I'm scared to go home. That's the truth," she wailed. "I'm scared of the night. I'd g-go but I'm afraid. Such t-terrible things . . . I don't know anything. I'm scared of what a f-fool I've been." She wept.

Jed winced. "And you ought to be," he said grimly. But it wasn't *Lyn*. It was sick and ugly.

Ruth said, "Ssssh . . ." She stepped out of Bunny's room, leaving the door wide. She wore a man's woolen robe because she was cold, now, with shock. (And Jed was glad, remembering Nell in the long silk.) But her battered face was serene.

Lyn choked off her whimpering.

Peter held Ruth's hand to his cheek. "Asleep?" he whispered and she nodded. She looked lovely, this little blond Mrs. Jones.

"Drink, darling?"

"Not on top of the chocolate."

"Ruthie, would you be scared if I took this young lady home?"

"Why, no," Ruth said, smiling.

"Uh, you see, Towers can't do it. He ought to be in bed."

Jed said, appalled, "Yes, and I'm going there. But listen, get the hotel to send somebody. Lyn can't go alone. But you can't leave Mrs. Jones, sir." She's had enough! he thought.

Ruth smiled at them all. "Don't be afraid," she said, gently.

"Here we sit, with our hair turning white," murmured Peter, in a moment, but his eyes were shining. "'Don't be afraid,' she says."

"Well, you *dasn't*!" Ruth smiled. "Or what would become of us all?"

She wasn't long for them. She wasn't all in room 807. She kissed Peter's brow, made her good nights. She didn't say thanks. Perhaps she forgot, or she knew . . . She withdrew, went back to her sleeping baby, and the door closed behind her.

They sat, sipped quietly. Lyn's face was pink, her eyes were ashamed, her back was straighter. Jed thought, I know her. I know what she's made of. And, he realized, *she* knew more about Towers, the real Towers, than anyone else on earth. Something grew, here . . . never could have grown had they gone, say, to a show. Something known, for better, for worse. He touched her hand. She turned hers and her icy fingers clung. "Put an ending on my letter, sometime, honey?"

"How, Jed?"

"The regular ending," he said, soberly. Yours truly. That was the way to end a letter.

Lyn smiled like the rainbow.

I'll just have to take care of her, he thought. She mustn't be afraid. His finger moved, humbly, on the soft back of her hand.

Peter said, "Yep. We oughta be scared, all right. Ignorant optimism won't do it. Won't do it. But we've got *not* to be scared, just the same."

"Courage," sighed Miss Ballew. She rose to say good night.

"We are strangers," Peter said darkly. "Whom do we know? One—if you're lucky. Not many more. Looks like we've got to learn how we can trust each other. How we can tell . . . How we can dare . . . Everything rests on trust between strangers. Everything else is a house of cards."

Miss Ballew went around to her room, having been drinking at midnight with strangers! Strangers and friends! She was, and not from liquor, a little bit intoxicated. She felt warm around the heart and a bit weepy and quite brave.

Peter came back and sat down, gazed at the two of them, moving his lips. "Damn it," cried Peter O. Jones. "I wish I'd said that!"

"Said what, Mr. Jones?"

"What I just said!" Peter was cross.

Lyn's eye met Jed's and dared be a little merry. "But . . . Mr. Jones, you just *did*. Didn't you?"

"In my speech!" cried Peter. "*Now*, I have to think of a better ending." He glared at them.

THE BLUNDERER

Patricia Highsmith

For L.

C'est plus qu'un crime, c'est une faute.

I

THE MAN in dark blue slacks and a forest green sportshirt waited impatiently in the line.

The girl in the ticket booth was stupid, he thought, never had been able to make change fast. He tilted his fat bald head up at the inside of the lighted marquee, read NOW PLAYING! "MARKED WOMAN," looked without interest at the poster of a half-naked woman displaying a thigh, and looked behind him at the line to see if there was anyone in it he knew. There wasn't. But he couldn't have timed it better, he thought. Just in time for the eight o'clock show. He shoved his dollar through the scallop in the glass.

"Hello," he said to the blonde girl, smiling.

"Hello." Her empty blue eyes brightened. "How're you tonight?"

It wasn't a question she expected to be answered. He didn't.

He went into the slightly smelly theatre, and heard the nervous, martial bugle call of the newsreel that was just beginning. He passed the candy and popcorn counter, and when he reached the other side of the theatre, he turned, gracefully despite his bulk, and casually looked around him. There was Tony Ricco. He quickened his step and met Tony as they turned into the center aisle.

"Hello there, Tony!" he said in the same rather patronizing tone he used when Tony was behind the counter of his father's delicatessen.

"Hi, Mr. Kimmel!" Tony smiled. "By yourself tonight?"

"My wife's just left for Albany." He waved a hand, and began to sidle into a row of seats.

Tony went on down the aisle, closer to the screen.

The man squeezed his knees against the backs of the seats, murmuring "Excuse me" and "Thank you" as he progressed, because everyone had to stand up, or half stand up, to let him by. He kept on going and came out in the aisle along the wall. He walked down to the door with the red EXIT sign over it, pushed through two metal doors, and came out into the hot sultry air of the sidewalk. He turned in the opposite direction of the marquee and almost immediately crossed the street. He walked around a corner and got into his black two-door Chevrolet.

He drove to within a block of the Cardinal Lines Bus Terminal, and waited in his car for about ten minutes until a bus marked NEWARK–NEW YORK–ALBANY pulled out of the terminus, and then he followed it.

He followed the bus through the tedious traffic of the Holland Tunnel entrance, and then in Manhattan turned northward. He kept about two cars between himself and the bus, even after they had left the city and the traffic was thin and fast. The first rest stop, he thought, should be around Tarrytown, perhaps before. If that place wasn't propitious, he would have to go on. And if there wasn't a second rest stop—well, right in Albany, in some alley. His broad, pudgy lips pursed as he concentrated on his driving, but his tawny eyes, stretched wide behind the thick glasses, did not change.

The bus slowed in front of a cluster of lighted food stores and a café, and he drove past and stopped his car, pulling in so close to the edge of the road that the twigs of a tree scraped the side. He got out quickly and ran, slowing to a walk only when he reached the lighted area where the bus had stopped.

People were still getting off the bus. He saw her descending, caught the clumsy, sidewise jerks of her stocky body as she took the few steps. He was beside her before she had walked six feet.

"*You!*" she said.

Her gray and black hair was disheveled, her stupid brown eyes stared up at him with an animal surprise, an animal fear. It seemed to him that they were still in the kitchen in Newark, arguing. "I still have a few things to say, Helen. Let's go down here." He took her arm, turning her toward the road.

She pulled away. "They're only stopping ten minutes here. Say what you have to say now."

"They're stopping twenty minutes. I've already inquired," he said in a bored tone. "Let's go down here where we won't be overheard."

She came with him. He had already noticed that the trees and the underbrush were thick and high on the right, the side near his car. Just a few yards down the road would be—

"If you think I'll change my mind about Edward," she began tremulously and proudly, "I won't. I never will."

Edward! The proud lady in love, he thought with revulsion. "I've changed *my* mind," he said in a calm, contrite tone, but his fingers tightened involuntarily on her flabby arm. He could hardly wait. He turned her onto the highway.

"Mel, I don't want to go so far away from the—"

He lunged against her, bouncing her deep into the underbrush at the side of the road. He nearly fell himself, but he kept his grip on her wrist with his left hand. With his right, he struck the side of her head, hard enough to break her neck, he thought, yet he kept the grip on her left wrist. He had only begun. She was down on the ground, and his left hand found her throat and closed on it, crushing her scream. He banged her body with his other fist, using its side like a hammer in the hard center of her chest between the mushy, protective breasts. Then he struck her forehead, her ear, with the same regular hammerlike blows, and finally struck her under the chin with his fist as he would have hit a man. Then he reached in his pocket for his knife, opened it, and plunged its blade down—three, four, five times. He concentrated on her head because he wanted to destroy it, clouting the cheek again and again with the back of his closed fingers until his hand began to slip in blood and lose its power, though he was not aware of it. He was aware only of pure joy, of a glorious sense of justice, of injuries avenged, years of insult and injury, boredom, stupidity, most of all stupidity, paid back to her.

He stopped only when he was out of breath. He discovered himself kneeling on her thigh and took his knees from her with distaste. He could see nothing of her but the light column of her summer dress. He looked around in the dark, listening. He heard no sound except the chanting whir of insects, the quick purr of a car speeding by on the highway. He was only a few steps from the highway, he saw. He was quite sure she was dead. Positive. He wished suddenly that he could see her face, and his hand twitched toward his pocket for his pen flashlight, but he did not want to risk the light's being seen.

He leaned forward cautiously, and put out one of his huge hands with the fingers delicately extended, prepared to touch, and he felt his loathing swell as his hand went closer. As soon as his fingertips touched the slippery skin, his other fist shot out, aimed directly beneath the fingertips. Then he stood up, breathing hard for a moment and thinking of nothing at all—only listening. Then he began to walk toward the highway. In the yellowish highway light he glanced at himself for blood, and saw none except the blood on his hands. He wiped his hands together, absently, as he walked, but they became only stickier and more disgusting, and he longed to wash them. He regretted that he would have to touch his steering wheel before he washed his hands, and he imagined with a fastidious exactitude how he would wet the rag under the sink when he got home and would wipe the entire surface of the steering wheel. He would even scour it.

The bus was gone, he noticed. He had no idea how long it had taken him. He got back in his car, turned it around and headed south. It was a quarter to eleven by his wristwatch. His shirtsleeve was torn, and he would have to get rid of the shirt, he thought. He reckoned that he would be back in Newark just after one.

2

IT BEGAN to rain while Walter was waiting in the car.
He looked up from his newspaper and took his arm from
the window. There was a peppering of darker blue on the blue
linen sleeve of his jacket.

The drumming of the big summer drops grew loud on the
car roof, and in a moment the arched tar street became wet
and shining, reflecting in a long red blur the neon sign of the
drugstore a block or so ahead. Dusk was falling, and the rain
had cast a sudden deeper shadow over the town. Down the
street, the trim New England houses looked whiter than ever
in the graying light, and the low white fences around the lawns
stood out as sharply as the stitching on a sampler.

Ideal, ideal, Walter thought. The kind of village where you
marry a healthy, good-natured girl, live with her in a white
house, go fishing on Saturdays, and raise your sons to do the
same things.

Sickmaking, Clara had said this afternoon, pointing to the
miniature spinning wheel by the fireplace of the inn. She
thought Waldo Point was touristy. Walter had chosen the village after a great deal of forethought because it was the least
touristy of a long string of towns on Cape Cod. Walter remembered that she had had quite a good time in Provincetown and
she hadn't complained that Provincetown was touristy. But
that had been the first year of their marriage, and this was the
fourth. The proprietor of the Spindrift Inn had told Walter
yesterday that his grandfather had made the spinning wheel for
his little daughters to learn on. If Clara could for one minute
put herself—

It was such a little thing, Walter thought. All their arguments were. Like yesterday's—the discussion of whether a man
and woman inevitably tired of each other physically after two
years of marriage. Walter didn't think it was inevitable. Clara
was his proof, though she had argued so cynically and unat-
tractively that it *was* inevitable, Walter would have bitten his
tongue off before he told her that he loved her as much physically as he ever had. And didn't Clara know it? And hadn't that

been the very purpose of her stand in the argument—to irritate him?

Walter shifted to another position in the car, ran his fingers through his thick, blond hair, and tried to relax and read the paper. My God, he thought, this is supposed to be a vacation.

His eyes moved quickly down a column about American army conditions in France, but he was still thinking of Clara. He was thinking of Wednesday morning after the early trip out in the fishing boat (at least she had enjoyed that fishing trip with Manuel because it had been educational), when they had come home and started to take a nap. Clara had been in a rare and wonderful mood. They had laughed at something, and then her arms around his neck had slowly tightened. . . .

Only Wednesday morning, three days ago—but the very next day there had been acid in her voice, that old pattern of punishment after favors granted.

It was 8:10. Walter looked out the car window at the front of the inn that was a little behind him. No sign of her yet. He looked down at his newspaper and read: BODY OF WOMAN FOUND NEAR TARRYTOWN, N.Y.

The woman had been brutally stabbed and beaten, but she had not been robbed. The police had no clues. She had been on a bus en route to Albany from Newark, had been missed after a rest stop, and the bus had gone on without her.

Walter wondered whether there would be anything in the story for his essays; whether the murderer had had some unusual relationship to the woman? He remembered an apparently motiveless murder he had read about in a newspaper that had later been explained by a lopsided friendship between the murderer and victim, a friendship like that between Chad Overton and Mike Duveen. Walter had been able to use the murder story to bring out certain potentially dangerous elements in the Chad-Mike friendship. He tore the little item about the Newark woman out of the edge of the paper and stuck it in his pocket. It was worth keeping for a few days, anyway, to see if anything turned up about the murderer.

The essays had been Walter's pastime for the last two years. There were to be eleven of them, under the general title "Unworthy Friendships." Only one was completed, the one on Chad and Mike, but he had finished the outlines for several others—and they were all based on observation of his own friends and acquaintances. His thesis was that a majority of people maintained at least one friendship with someone inferior to themselves because of certain needs and deficiencies that were either mirrored or complemented by the inferior friend. Chad and Mike, for example: both had come from well-to-do families who had spoiled them, but Chad had chosen to work, while Mike was still a playboy who had little to play on since his family had cut off his allowance. Mike was a drunk and a ne'er-do-well, unscrupulous about taking advantage of all his friends. By now Chad was almost the only friend left. Chad apparently thought, "There but for the grace of God go I," and doled out money and put Mike up periodically. Mike wasn't worth much to anybody as a friend. Walter did not intend to submit his book for publication anywhere. The essays were purely for his own pleasure, and he didn't care when or if he ever finished them all.

Walter sank down in the car seat and closed his eyes. He was thinking of the fifty-thousand-dollar estate in Oyster Bay that Clara was trying to sell. Walter said a quiet little prayer that one of her two prospects would buy it, for Clara's sake, for his own sake. Yesterday she had sat for the better part of the afternoon, studying the layout of the house and grounds. Mapping her attack for next week, she had said. She would sail into the prospects like a fury, he knew. It was amazing that she didn't terrify them, that they ever bought anything. But they did. The Knightsbridge Brokerage considered her a topnotch saleswoman.

If he could only make her relax somehow. Give her the right kind of security—he used to think. Well, didn't he? Love, affection, and money, too. It just didn't work.

He heard her footsteps—*tok-tok-tok* on the high heels as she ran—and he sat up quickly and thought, Damn it, I should have backed the car in front of the inn because it's raining. He leaned over and opened the door for her.

"Why didn't you put the car in front of the door?" she asked.

"Sorry. I only just thought of it." He risked a smile.

"You could see it was raining, I hope," she said, shaking her small head despairingly. "Down, darling, you're wet!" She pushed Jeff, her fox terrier, down from the seat and he jumped up again. "Jeff, really!"

Jeff gave a yelp of fun, as if it were a game, and he was up like a spring for the third time. Clara let him stay, circled him affectionately with her arm.

Walter drove toward the center of town. "How about a drink at the Melville before we eat? It's our last night."

"I don't want a drink, but I'll sit with you if you've got to have one."

"Okay." Maybe he could persuade her to have a Tom Collins. Or a sweet vermouth and soda, at least. But he probably couldn't persuade her, and was it really worth it, making her sit through his drink? And generally he wanted two drinks. Walter suffered one of those ambivalent moments, a blackout of will, when he couldn't decide whether to have a drink or not. He passed the hotel without turning in.

"I thought we were going to the Melville," Clara said.

"Changed my mind. As long as you won't join me in a drink." Walter put his hand over hers and squeezed it. "We'll head for the Lobster Pot."

He made a left turn near the end of the street. The Lobster Pot was on a little promontory of the shore. The sea breeze came strong through the car window, cool and salty. Walter suddenly found himself in absolute darkness. He looked around for the Lobster Pot's string of blue lights, but he couldn't see them anywhere.

"Better go back to the main road and take it from that filling station the way I always do," Walter said.

Clara laughed. "And you've only been here five times, if not more!"

"What's the difference?" Walter asked with elaborate casualness. "We're in no hurry, are we?"

"No, but it's insane to waste time and energy when with a little intelligence you could have taken the right road from the start!"

Walter refrained from telling her she was wasting more energy than he. The tense line of her body, the face straining toward the windshield, pained him, made him feel that the week's vacation had been for nothing, the wonderful morning after the fishing trip for nothing. Forgotten the next day, like the other wonderful nights, mornings, he could count over the last year, little oases, far apart. He tried to think of something pleasant to say to her before they got out of the car.

"I like you in that shawl," he said, smiling. She wore it loose about her bare shoulders and looped through her arms. He had always appreciated the way she wore her clothes and the taste she showed in choosing them.

"It's a stole," she said.

"A stole. I love you, darling." He bent to kiss her, and she lifted her lips to him. He kissed her gently, so as not to spoil her lipstick.

Clara ordered cold lobster with mayonnaise, which she adored, and Walter ordered a broiled fish and a bottle of Riesling.

"I thought you'd have meat tonight, Walter. If you have fish again, Jeff gets *nothing* today!"

"All right," Walter said. "I'll order a steak. Jeff can have most of it."

"You say it in such a martyred tone!"

The steaks were not very good at the Lobster Pot. Walter had ordered steak the other night because of Jeff. Jeff refused to eat fish. "It's perfectly okay with me, Clara. Let's not argue about anything our last night."

"Who's arguing? You're trying to start something!"

But, after all, the steak had been ordered. Clara had had her way, and she sighed and looked off into space, apparently thinking of something else. Strange, Walter thought, that Clara's economy extended even to Jeff's food, though in every other respect Jeff was indulged. Why was that? What in Clara's background had made her into a person who turned every penny? Her family was neither poor nor wealthy. That was another mystery about Clara that he would probably never solve.

"Kits," he said affectionately. It was his pet name for her, and he used it sparingly so it would not wear out. "Let's just have fun this evening. It'll probably be a long time till we have another vacation together. How about a dance over at the Melville after dinner?"

"All right," Clara said, "but don't forget we have to be up at seven tomorrow."

"I won't forget." It was only a six-hour drive home, but

Clara wanted to be home by mid-afternoon in order to have tea with the Philpotts, her bosses at the Knightsbridge Brokerage. Walter slid his hand over hers on the table. He loved her hands. They were small but not too small, well-shaped, and rather strong. Her hand fitted his when he held it.

Clara did not look at him. She was looking into space, not dreamily but intently. She had a small, rather pretty face, though its expression was cool and withdrawn, and her mouth looked sad in repose. It was a face of subtle planes, hard for a stranger to remember.

He glanced behind him, looking for Jeff. Clara had let him off the leash, and he was trotting around the big room, sniffing at people's feet, accepting titbits from their plates. He would always eat fish from other people's plates, Walter thought. It embarrassed Walter, because the waiter had asked them the other evening to put the dog on a leash.

"The dog is all right," Clara said, anticipating him.

Walter sampled the wine and nodded to the waiter that it was satisfactory. He waited until Clara had her glass, then lifted his. "Here's to a happy rest of the summer and the Oyster Bay sale," he said, and noticed that her brown eyes brightened at the mention of the Oyster Bay sale. When Clara had drunk some of her wine, he said, "What do you say we set a date for that party?"

"What party?"

"The party we talked about before we left Benedict. You said toward the end of August."

"All right," Clara said in a small, unwilling voice, as if she had been bested in a fair contest and had to forfeit a right, much as she disliked it. "Perhaps Saturday the twenty-eighth."

They began to make up the guest list. It was not a party for any particular reason, except that they had not given a real party since the New Year's Day buffet, and they had been to about a dozen since. Their friends around Benedict gave a great many parties, and though Clara and Walter were not always invited, they were invited often enough not to feel left out. They must have the Iretons, of course, the McClintocks, the Jensens, the Philpotts, Jon Carr, and Chad Overton.

"Chad?" Clara asked.

"Yes. Why not? I think we owe him something, don't you?"

"I think he owes us an apology, if you want my opinion!"

Walter took a cigarette. Chad had come by the house one evening, just dropped in on the way back from Montauk, and somehow—Walter didn't even know how—had taken on enough martinis to pass out on their sofa, or at least to fall deeply asleep. No amount of explaining that Chad had been tired from driving all day in the heat had been of any use. Chad was on the blacklist. And yet they'd stayed at Chad's apartment several times on nights when they went in to New York to see a play, when Chad, as a favor to them, had spent the night at a friend's in order to give them his apartment.

"Can't you forget that?" Walter asked. "He's a good friend, Clara, and an intelligent guy, too."

"I'm sure he'd pass out again, if he were in sight of a liquor bottle."

No use telling her he'd never known Chad to pass out before or since. No use reminding her that he actually owed his present job to Chad. Walter had worked at Adams, Adams and Branower, Counselors at Law, as Chad's assistant the year after he graduated from law school. Walter had quit the firm and gone to San Francisco with an idea of opening his own office, but he had met Clara and married her, and Clara had wanted him to go back to New York and keep on in corporation law, which was more profitable. Chad had recommended him more highly than he deserved to a legal advisory firm known as Cross, Martinson and Buchman. Chad was a good friend of Martinson. The firm paid Walter a senior lawyer's salary, though Walter was only thirty. If not for Chad, Walter thought, they wouldn't be sitting in the Lobster Pot drinking imported Riesling at that moment. Walter supposed he would have to ask Chad to lunch some time in Manhattan. Or lie to Clara and spend an evening with him. Or maybe not lie to her, just tell her. Walter drew on his cigarette.

"Smoking in the middle of your meal?"

The food had arrived. Walter put the cigarette out, with deliberate calm, in the ashtray.

"Don't you agree he owes *us* something? A bunch of flowers, at least?"

"All right, Clara, it's all—*right*."

"But why that horrid tone?"

"Because I like Chad, and if we keep on boycotting him, the logical result is that we'll lose him as a friend. Just as we lost the Whitneys."

"We have not lost the Whitneys. You seem to think you've got to lick people's boots and take all their insults to keep them as friends. I've never seen anybody so concerned with whether every Tom, Dick and Harry likes you or not!"

"Let's not quarrel, honey." Walter put his hands over his face, but he took them down again at once. It was an old gesture he made at home, and in private. He couldn't bear to do it at the end of a vacation. He turned around to look for Jeff again. Jeff was way across the room, trying his best to embrace a woman's foot. The woman didn't seem to understand, and kept patting Jeff's head. "Maybe I ought to go and get him," Walter said.

"He's not harming anything. Calm yourself." Clara was dismembering her lobster expertly, eating quickly as she always did.

But the next instant a waiter came up and said smilingly, "Would you mind putting your dog on a leash, sir?"

Walter got up and crossed the room toward Jeff, feeling painfully conspicuous in his white trousers and bright blue jacket. Jeff was still making efforts with the woman's foot, his black-spotted face turned around and grinning as if he couldn't quite take it seriously himself, but Walter had a hard time disengaging his wiry little arms from the woman's ankle. "I'm very sorry," Walter said to her.

"Why, I think he's adorable!" the woman said.

Walter restrained an impulse to crush the dog in his hands. He carried him back in the prescribed manner, one hand under the dog's hot, panting little chest and the other steadying him on top, and he set him down very gently on the floor beside Clara and fastened the leash.

"You hate that dog, don't you?" Clara asked.

"I think he's spoiled, that's all." Walter watched Clara's face as she lifted Jeff to her lap. When she petted the dog, her face grew beautiful, soft and loving, as if she were fondling a child, her own child. Watching Clara's face when she petted Jeff was the greatest pleasure Walter got out of the dog. He did hate the dog. He hated his cocky, selfish personality, his silly expression that seemed to say whenever he looked at Walter: "*I'm living the life of Riley, and look at you!*" He hated the dog because the dog could do no wrong with Clara, and he could do no right.

"You really think he's spoiled?" Clara asked, fondling the dog's floppy black ear. "I thought he followed rather well this morning when we were on the beach."

"I only meant, you chose a fox terrier because they're more intelligent than most dogs, and you don't take the trouble to teach him the most rudimentary manners."

"I suppose you're referring to what he was doing across the room just now?"

"That's part of it. I realize he's almost two years old, but as long as he keeps on doing that, I don't think we should let him roam around dining rooms. It's not particularly pleasant to look at."

Clara arched her eyebrows. "He was having a little harmless fun. You talk as if you begrudge him it. That astounds me—coming from you," she said with cool amusement.

Walter did not smile.

They got home the following afternoon. Clara learned that the Oyster Bay sale could easily hang fire for a month, and in her state of suspense a party was out of the question until she either sold it or didn't.

During the following fortnight, Chad was rebuffed when he called and asked to come by, refused and perhaps hung up on before Walter could get to the telephone. Jon Carr, Walter's closest friend, was put off right in front of Walter one Saturday morning when he telephoned. Clara told Walter that Jon had invited them to a little dinner party he was giving the following week, but Clara hadn't thought it worth driving in to Manhattan for.

Walter had dreams sometimes that one, or several, or all of his friends had deserted him. They were desolate, heartbreaking dreams, and he would awaken with a breathless feeling in his chest.

He had already lost five friends—for all practical purposes lost them because Clara wouldn't have them in the house, though Walter still wrote to them, and when he could, he saw them. Two were in Pennsylvania, Walter's home state. One was in Chicago, and the other two in New York. And Walter, to be honest with himself, had to admit that Howard Graz in Chicago and Donald Miller in New York were so down on him he no longer cared to write them letters. Or perhaps they owed him letters.

Walter remembered Clara's smile, really a smile of triumph, when he had heard about a party at Don's in New York to which he had not been invited. It had been a stag party, too. Clara had been sure then that she had alienated him from Don, and she had been delighted.

It was really then, about two years ago, that Walter had realized for the first time that he was married to a neurotic, a woman who was actually insane in some directions, and moreover a neurotic that he was in love with. He kept remembering the wonderful first year with her, how proud he had been of her because she was more intelligent than most women (now he loathed the very word intelligence because Clara made a fetish of it), how much they had laughed together, how much fun they had had furnishing the Benedict house, and he hoped that the Clara of those days would miraculously return. She was after all the same person, the same flesh. He still loved the flesh.

Walter had hoped that when she took the Knightsbridge job eight months ago, it would be an outlet for her competitiveness, for the jealousy he saw in her, even of him, because he was making a career that was considered successful. But the job had only intensified the competitiveness and her curious dissatisfaction with herself, as if the activity of working again had unplugged the neck of a volcano that until now had only been smoldering. Walter had even suggested that she quit. Clara wouldn't hear of it. The logical thing to occupy her would have been children, and Walter wanted them, but Clara didn't, and he had never tried very hard to persuade her. Clara had no patience with small children, and Walter doubted that she would be any different with her own. And even at twenty-six, when she married, Clara had facetiously protested that she was too old. Clara was very conscious of the fact that she was two months older than Walter, and Walter had to reassure her often that she looked much younger than he did. Now she was thirty, and Walter knew the question of children would never come up again.

There were times, standing with a second highball in his hand on somebody's lawn in Benedict, when Walter asked himself what he was doing there among those pleasant, smugly well-to-do and essentially boring people, what he was doing with his whole life. He thought constantly of getting out of Cross, Martinson and Buchman, and he was planning a move with Dick Jensen, his closest colleague at the office. Dick, like himself, wanted his own law office. He and Dick had talked one night, all night, about starting a small claims office in Manhattan to handle cases that most law firms wouldn't look at. The fees would be small, but there would be many more of them. They had dragged out Blackstone and Wigmore in Dick's book-lined den, and had talked about Blackstone's almost mystical faith in the power of law to create an ideal society. For Walter, it had been a return to the enthusiasms of his law-school days, when law had been a clean instrument that he was learning to use, when he had felt himself, in his secret heart, a young knight about to set forth to succor the helpless and to uphold the righteous. He and Dick had decided that night to get out of Cross, Martinson and Buchman the first of the year. They were going to rent an office somewhere in the West Forties. Walter had talked to Clara about it, and though she was not enthusiastic, she at least hadn't tried to discourage him. Money was not a problem, because Clara was evidently going to earn at least $5,000 a year. The house was paid for: it had been a wedding present from Clara's mother.

The only thing that could give Walter a positive answer to the question, What was he doing with his life? was the law office he meant to open with Dick. He imagined the office flourishing, sending away streams of satisfied clients. But he wondered if the office would fall far short of what he expected; if Dick would lose his enthusiasm? Walter felt that perfect achievements were few. Men made laws, set goals, and then fell short of them. His marriage had fallen short of what he had hoped, Clara had fallen short, and perhaps he had not been what she expected, either. But he had tried and he was still trying. One of the few things he knew absolutely was that he loved Clara, and that pleasing her made him happy. And he had Clara, and he had pleased her by taking the job he had, and by living here among all the pleasant, dull people. And if

Clara didn't seem to enjoy her life as much as she should, she still did not want to move anywhere else or do anything else but what she was doing. Walter had asked her. At thirty, Walter had concluded that dissatisfaction was normal. He supposed life for most people was a falling slightly short of one ideal after another, salved if one was lucky by the presence of somebody one loved. But he could not put out of his mind the fact that Clara, if she kept on, could kill what was left of his hope for her.

Six months ago, in the spring, he and Clara had had their first talk about a divorce, and had later, inadequately, patched it up.

3

ON THE evening of September 18th, about fifteen cars were lined along one side of Marlborough Road, and a few more had pulled up on the Stackhouse lawn. Clara didn't like people to put their cars on the lawn: it had just undergone an invigorating treatment of superphosphate, agricultural lime and some fifty pounds of peat moss which had cost nearly two hundred dollars, including the labor. Clara told Walter to ask the people to move their cars.

"I'd do it, but I think it's a man's place to ask them," Clara said.

"If we move these, there'll only be more cars later," Walter told her. "They move up because the women don't want to walk so far in high heels on that road. You can understand that."

"I can understand that you're afraid to ask them!" Clara retorted.

Walter hoped she wouldn't ask anybody to move. Everybody put cars on lawns in Benedict.

All the guests, even the Philpotts, who were the oldest and most conservative, seemed to be in high spirits. Mr. Philpott wore a white dinner jacket and evening trousers and pumps, out of habit, Walter supposed, because Clara had made it clear that the men didn't have to dress formally and the women could if they chose. The women always wanted to dress and the men never did. Mrs. Philpott had brought a large box of candy for Clara. Walter watched her present it with a few words of praise that made Clara's face glow. Clara had sold the Oyster Bay estate to one of the Philpotts' clients about ten days ago.

Walter went over to Jon Carr, who was standing by himself in front of the dogwood-filled fireplace. Jon's face was taking on that look of imperturbable good humor that came after his fourth or fifth drink. Jon had told him he had just come from a cocktail party in Manhattan, and hadn't had dinner. "How about a sandwich?" Walter asked him. "There're stacks of them in the kitchen."

"No sandwiches," Jon said firmly. "Got to watch my waist-line and I'd rather add the inches with your scotch."

"What's new at the office?" Walter asked.

Jon told Walter about the new issue of his magazine that was to be exclusively on glass and glass building materials. Jon Carr was the editor of *Skylines*, a six-year-old architectural magazine that he had founded himself, and that was now as strong as any group-published architectural magazine on the market. To Walter, Jon represented a rare type of American, well bred and well educated, and not above working like a navvy to get what he wanted. Jon's parents had not been wealthy enough to help him in his career, and Jon had even worked the last part of his way through architectural school. Walter frankly admired Jon, and frankly was flattered that Jon liked him. Walter even put their friendship, from Jon's standpoint, in the "unworthy friendship" category.

Jon asked Walter if he could get away the following Sunday to go fishing with him and Chad in a sailboat off Montauk Point. "If Clara wants to come along, that's fine," Jon said. "Chad has a new girl friend and I thought Clara could stay with her on the beach while the rest of us go fishing. Her name is Millie. She's bright and Clara might like her. Clara likes beaches, doesn't she?"

"I'll ask her if she'll go," Walter said. "I'd certainly like to myself."

"By the way, where is Chad?"

Walter smiled a little. "Chad, I'm afraid, is *persona non grata* at the moment."

Jon made a little gesture with his hand that said, "All right, let it go."

Walter took a fresh highball from the tray Claudia was pass-ing round, and carried it over to Mrs. Philpott. She protested she didn't need a new one, but Walter insisted. Unobtrusively, as he chatted with her by the fireplace, he interrupted, with a gentle foot, Jeff's assault on a woman's leg. Jeff ran off to the door to greet some new arrivals. Jeff had the time of his life at parties. He circulated through living room, terrace, and gar-den, petted and fed canapés by everybody.

"Your wife is the most wonderful worker we've ever had,

Mr. Stackhouse," Mrs. Philpott said. "I think there's nothing she couldn't buy or sell if she put her mind to it."

"I'll tell her you said so."

"Oh, I think she knows it!" Mrs. Philpott said with a twinkle.

Walter smiled back, feeling that he exchanged with her little blue, wrinkle-shrouded eyes a profound confidence. "Just don't let her work too hard," he said.

"But that's her nature. I don't think we can do anything about it."

Walter nodded, smiling. Mrs. Philpott had said it gaily, and of course from her point of view it was fine. Walter saw Clara standing in the hall door of the living room, and he went to her.

"It's going pretty well, isn't it?" he asked her.

"Yes. Where's Joan?"

"Joan called and said she couldn't come. Her mother's sick and she's staying home with her." Joan was Walter's secretary, a bright, attractive girl of twenty-four, whom Walter thought highly of. Walter was glad Clara had never shown any jealousy of Joan.

"Her mother must be awfully sick," Clara remarked.

Clara didn't like her own mother. Walter had noticed she never approved of other people liking theirs. "You look terrific tonight, Clara, absolutely terrific!"

Clara gave him a glance and a trace of a smile. She was still looking over her guests. "And that other one—what's his name? Peter. He isn't here."

"Pete Slotnikoff! You're right." Walter smiled. "Very clever of you to notice, since you've never met him."

"But I know all the people who *are* here—obviously."

Walter had seventeen minutes past ten by his watch. "Maybe he'll turn up. He might have gotten lost."

"Was he coming in a car?"

"No, he hasn't got a car. I suppose he'll take a train." Walter wanted to offer Pete the couch in his study for the night, in case there wasn't anybody who could take him back to New York, but decided to put off mentioning it to Clara until it became necessary. "By the way, honey, Jon asked me to go fishing with him next Sunday. Out around Montauk. You're invited to come and stay on the beach, if you want to, because a girl friend of—of Jon's will be along, too."

"A girl friend of Jon's?"

"Well—a friend," Walter corrected, because Jon was notoriously shy of women since his divorce.

Clara's small face had that rather stunned look, as if she were off balance for a moment until she had surveyed the idea from all possible angles, seen its advantages and disadvantages to herself. "Who is the girl?"

"I don't even know her name. Jon says she's nice, though."

"I'm not so sure I want to spend a whole day with someone who might be a terrible bore," Clara said.

"Matter of fact, Jon said she—"

"I think your friend is arriving."

Peter Slotnikoff was coming in the front door. Walter started toward him, trying to assume the pleasant, relaxed expression of a good host.

Peter looked shy and bewildered and glad to see Walter. He was twenty-six, serious-looking and a little plump. His parents had been White-Russian refugees, and Peter had not known any English until he came to America at the age of fifteen, but he had finished brilliantly at the University of Michigan Law School, and Walter's firm considered itself lucky to have him as a junior.

"I brought a friend," Peter said after Walter had introduced him to a few people near the door. Peter indicated a girl Walter hadn't noticed. "This is Ellie Briess. This is Walter Stackhouse. Miss Elspeth Briess," Peter said more carefully.

They exchanged greetings, then Walter took them into the living room to introduce them and get them drinks. Walter hadn't thought Peter would have a girl at all. She was even rather pretty. Walter chose the darkest-looking highball from Claudia's tray and handed it to Peter.

"If you don't find anybody you want to talk to, Pete, there's television out on the terrace," Walter said to him. Walter had put the TV set on the terrace for the people who wanted to watch the ball game that night.

Walter went to the rolling bar and made Clara a drink of Italian vermouth and soda, her favorite, and took it to her. She was talking with Betty Ireton by the fireplace.

"I wish my husband took as good care of my drinks," Betty said.

"I'll get you another," Walter offered.

"Oh, I didn't mean that. I've still got plenty." Her handsome, narrow face smiled at him above the rim of her glass.

Betty Ireton loved to flirt, in a thoroughly harmless way, and she often told Walter right in front of Clara that she thought he was the best-looking man in Benedict. And Clara, knowing its harmlessness, paid it no mind at all.

"I wanted to take you over to meet Peter," Walter said to Clara.

"And I'm going to check up on my husband," Betty said. "He's disappeared in the garden."

"How about Sunday?" Walter asked Clara. "I want to give Jon an answer tonight."

"Must you choose the only day we have to spend together to go off fishing? I don't think it's very nice for *me*."

"Come on, Clara. It's been months since I've gone fishing."

"And Chad's undoubtedly going, there'll be drinking, and you'll come back reeking for hours from it."

"I don't think that's entirely warranted."

"I do. I know it too well." Clara walked away.

Walter set his teeth. Why the hell didn't he just *go*? Well, the answer to that was: the hell she would raise later just wasn't worth it. Mrs. Philpott was watching him from the sofa. Walter relaxed his expression at once. He wondered if Mrs. Philpott understood? Her face looked very old and sagacious. Practically everyone else at the party understood, everyone who'd ever spent an evening with him and Clara.

"Walter, old man, do you think I can get a refill?"

Walter smiled at the familiar, rubbery face of Dick Jensen, and felt like putting an arm around him. "You sure can, brother. I want one, too. Let's go in the kitchen."

Claudia was busy with the cold roast beef. Walter told her it was too early to start serving, and that she'd better see who needed another drink.

"Mrs. Stackhouse told me to bring the food on now, Mr. Stackhouse," Claudia said with a neutral resignation.

"There you are," Dick said. "Overruled by the court."

Walter let it go. Even Dick knew that Clara meant to prevent anybody's getting drunk tonight by serving the buffet at an early hour. Walter made Dick a whopping drink and a generous one for himself. "Where's Polly?" Walter asked.

"Out on the terrace, I think."

Walter made a drink for Polly, in case she didn't have one, and went out on the terrace. Polly was leaning against the terrace rail, watching the TV, but she smiled and beckoned to Walter when she saw him. Polly was not beautiful. Her hips spread, and she did her hair in a dull brown bun at the back of her neck, but she had the most pleasant personality in the world. For Walter simply to be near her for a few moments satisfied a deep craving, like the craving he felt sometimes to lie naked in the sun.

"How does it feel to be married to a real estate tycoon?" Polly asked with her big toothy grin.

"Great! Now I haven't a financial worry in the world. I'm thinking of retiring soon." Walter had just begun to notice his drinks. He felt a little warm in the face.

Dick came up and took his wife's arm. "Sorry, I have to borrow this. I want her to meet Pete."

"Why can't Pete come out here?" Walter asked.

"He's deep in some discussion in there." Dick took Polly off.

Walter picked up the extra highball that Polly hadn't wanted, and looked around for someone to offer it to. His eyes stopped on a girl who was looking at him from the far corner of the terrace. It was Pete's girl, all by herself. Walter went over to her.

"You don't have a drink," he said. He couldn't think of her name.

"I've had one, thanks. I just came out to enjoy your country air."

"Well, you'd better have another!" He handed it to her and she accepted it. "Are you from New York?" he asked.

"I live there. Just now I'm looking for a job there—or anywhere." Her eyes looked up at him directly, warm and friendly. "I'm a musician. I teach music."

"What do you play?"

"The violin. Piano, too, but I'm more interested in the violin. I teach music to children. Music appreciation."

"Music to children!" The idea of teaching music to children seemed suddenly enchanting to Walter. He wanted to say: what a shame we haven't any children for you to teach music to.

"I'm looking for a job in a public school, but it's tough without a lot of degrees and qualifications. I'm just about to try some private schools."

"I hope you have luck," Walter said. The girl looked about the same age as Peter. There was a simplicity about her, a peasanty robustness that Walter supposed suited Peter to a T. She was suntanned and there was a faint highlight down her nose. When she smiled, her teeth looked very white. "Have you known Pete long?"

"Just a few months. Just after he started working for you. He's very happy there."

"We like him, too."

"He started talking to me on the bus one day—because we were both carrying violin cases. Pete plays the violin, too, you know—a little."

"I didn't know," Walter said. "He's a nice boy."

"Oh, he's *such* a nice boy," she said with so much conviction, Walter felt his own remark had sounded flippant by comparison. "I'd love a little angostura in this drink—if you have any."

"Of course, we have! Give me your glass." Walter went into the living room to the rolling bar, dropped six drops in carefully, and stirred it with a muddler. When he went back on the terrace, Jon was talking with the girl. The girl put her head back and laughed at something Jon had said.

"Walter!" Jon said. "What about Sunday?"

"I'm not sure I can, Jon. It looks like Sunday we're supposed to—"

"I understand, I understand," Jon murmured.

"I'm sorry. If I'd—"

"I *understand*, Walter," Jon said impatiently.

Walter glanced at the girl, feeling embarrassed and a little sick. If the girl hadn't been there, Jon would have said, "Oh, tell Clara to go jump in the lake!" Jon had said that a couple of times in the past, though Walter hadn't gone along on those occasions, either. Jon wasn't going to bother saying it much longer, Walter thought.

"Listen to me for a minute," Jon said in the authoritative

voice of an editor-in-chief, then he stopped and let his breath out as if it were hopeless.

The girl had tactfully gone away, was walking down the steps into the garden.

"I know what you're going to say," Walter said, "but I have to live with it."

Jon smiled his easy smile. He was choosing to say nothing. "By the way, Chad told me to tell you he wants you to come to the party he's giving next Friday. Dinner at his house, then we go to the theatre. His friend Richard Bell is opening in his new play on Friday. There'll be about six of us. Get away from Clara. It'd do you good. Chad knows he's in the doghouse with Clara. He doesn't even want to telephone you out here."

"All right, I will." If Clara excluded Chad, he thought, Chad could exclude Clara.

"You'd better." Jon waved a hand at him and went down into the garden.

Nobody got drunk that night except Mrs. Philpott. She lost her balance and sat down hard in front of the radio-phonograph, but she took it very cheerfully and continued to sit there, listening to the music that Vic Rogers was playing for a small, attentive group. She was still there at 3 A.M. when all but six people had gone home. Clara got exasperated. Clara thought three in the morning was time for any party to break up, but clearly it was the Philpotts who were holding things up, and she could hardly dare drop a hint to the Philpotts.

"Let her enjoy herself," Walter said.

"I think she's *drunk*!" Clara whispered, horrified. "I can't get her off the floor. I've asked her three times."

Suddenly Clara marched over to Mrs. Philpott, and Walter watched incredulously as Clara put her hands under Mrs. Philpott's shoulders and lifted her bodily. Bill Ireton quickly pulled up a chair to catch her. For an instant, Walter saw the look that Mrs. Philpott gave Clara, a look of speechless surprise and resentment.

Mrs. Philpott shook her shoulders, as if to rid herself of Clara's touch. "Well! I never knew it was against the law to sit on the floor before!"

A terrible silence fell in the room. Bill Ireton looked suddenly sober as a trout. Walter came forward automatically to help ease the situation, and began to tell Mrs. Philpott how often he sat on the floor himself.

Bill Ireton burst out laughing. So did his wife. Everybody roared then, even Mrs. Philpott, everybody except Clara, who only smiled, nervously. Walter put his arm around Clara and squeezed her affectionately. He knew her impulse to pick Mrs. Philpott up off the floor had been absolutely irresistible.

A few minutes later, everybody had taken leave.

The bedroom window showed the milky gray of dawn. Jeff lay in the valley between the pillows of the turned-down bed, his favorite spot.

"Come on, boy," Walter said, snapping his fingers to awaken him, and the dog got up sleepily and jumped down from the bed. Walter patted the pillow in Jeff's basket bed in a corner of the room, and Jeff crawled in. "He's had a hard night," Walter said, smiling.

"I think he takes it a lot better than you do," Clara said. "You smell of liquor and your face is red with it."

"I won't smell when I brush my teeth." Walter went into the bathroom.

"Who is that girl Peter Slotnikoff brought?"

"Don't know," he called over the shower. "Ellie something, I think."

"Ellie Briess. I just wondered *who* she was."

Walter was too tired to yell that she taught music, and he didn't think Clara really cared to know. Ellie had a car, apparently, because she and Peter had driven back to New York together. Walter got into bed and put his arms gently around Clara, kissing her cheek, her ear, careful to keep even the smell of toothpaste away from her.

"Walter, I'm awfully tired."

"So'm I," he said, snuggling his head beside her on the pillow, avoiding the still warm spot where Jeff had lain. He passed his hand slowly around Clara's waist. She felt smooth and warm under the silk nightgown. He loved the rise and fall of her middle as she breathed. He pulled her toward him.

She twisted away. "Walter—"

"Just kiss me good night, Kits." He held her despite her squirming and her expression of distaste that he could see in the gray light.

She pushed him away and sat up in the bed. "I think you're a sex maniac!" she said indignantly.

Walter sat up, too. "I'm closer to a shrinking violet these days! The only thing the matter with me is that I'm in love with you!"

"You disgust me!" she said, and flung herself down on the pillow again, her back turned to him.

Walter smouldered, wanting to spring out of bed and go out, outdoors, or down in the living room to sleep, but he knew he would sleep badly in the living room, if at all, and feel worse for it tomorrow. *Lie down and let it go*, he told himself. He sank down on his pillow. Then he heard Clara make a little sound with her lips to summon Jeff, heard the *click-click* of Jeff's sleepy steps across the floor, and felt the vibration of the bed as Jeff jumped up on Clara's side.

Walter threw the sheet back and leapt out of bed.

"Oh, Walter, don't be absurd," Clara said.

"It's perfectly all right," he said with grim calm. He got his silk bathrobe from the closet, put it back, and groped on the back hooks for his flannel robe. "I just never liked sleeping in the same bed with a dog."

"How silly."

Walter went downstairs. The house was gray, the color of a dream. He sat down on the sofa. Clara had removed the ashtrays and the empty glasses, and everything was in its proper place again. Walter stared at the big Italian bottle full of philodendrons on the windowsill. He had given Clara the bottle and a gold-chain bracelet on her last birthday. The dawn light shone through the green glass of the bottle and revealed the gracefully crisscrossing stems. They were beautiful, like an abstract painting.

Ah, gracious living!

4

WALTER FELT tired and sickish the next day. He had a slight headache, though he did not know whether it was from lack of sleep or from Clara's haranguing. She had found him asleep on the living room floor, and had accused him of being so drunk he had not realized when he fell off. That morning, Walter took a long walk in the woods that began at the dead end of Marlborough Road not far from the house, then came back and tried unsuccessfully to take a nap.

Clara had bathed Jeff and was brushing him out in the sun on the upstairs terrace. Walter went into his study across the hall from the bedroom. It was a room on the north side of the house, darkened restfully in summer by the trees just beyond the window. It had two walls of books, a flat-topped desk, and it was carpeted with a worn oriental rug that had been in his room at his parents' house in Bethlehem, Pennsylvania. Clara wanted to get rid of the rug because it had a hole in it. It was one of the few things Walter took a stand about: the study was his room, and he was going to keep the rug.

Walter sat at his desk and reread a letter that had arrived last week from his brother Cliff in Bethlehem. It was a letter on several pages of a small cheap writing tablet, and it told of the everyday events around the farm that Cliff supervised for their father: the rise in the price of eggs, and the champion hen's latest record. It would have been a dull letter, except for Cliff's wry humor that came out in nearly every line. Cliff had enclosed a clipping from a Bethlehem newspaper that Walter had not yet read, with the notation: "Try this on Clara. See if it gets a laugh." It was a column called "Dear Mrs. Plainfield."

DEAR MRS. PLAINFIELD:

My wife has a way of getting under my skin like no one else I've known. She doesn't do anything but she becomes so darned expert that you can't live with her. If she follows football, well, she knows the scores all over the country, and the records of the teams better than anyone else, so it's no fun talking football with her.

Right now it is the indoor planter fad. She has spent
weeks, to say nothing of dollars, amassing her collection
of philodendron dubia, philodendron monstera, and
even a poor little philodendron Hastatum—elephant ear
to you and me.

There's a perfectly nice Fiddle Leaf plant in her collection, but let me call it Fiddle Leaf and she goes up in
smoke and snarls "Ficus pandurata!" at me. It's the same
with the rubber plant. It's not rubber plant to her, it's
"Ficus elastica."

I'm not against plants or those who plant them, but I
am against people who turn up their noses at a sweet
potato vine because it isn't a deacaena Warneckii—and
that's the way my wife is.

MR. ASPIDISTRA

Walter smiled. He doubted if it would get a laugh from
Clara. He knew what had prompted Cliff to send it: the time he
and Clara had visited his father, and Cliff had shown them
around the barns, pointing out a tractor he called "Chad,"
which was an abbreviation of its make-name. Clara had asked
Cliff very seriously what he meant by "Chad," and then had
peered at the front of the tractor and announced that it was
"Chadwick." After that, without cracking a smile, Cliff had
called every piece of machinery he pointed to by some unintel-
ligible, abbreviated name. Clara had not apparently gotten the
point. She had only looked bewildered. Clara thought Cliff was
half-cracked, and often tried to convince Walter that he was,
and that he ought to do something about him. He was grateful
to Cliff for staying on the farm, and for looking after their father. Walter's father had wanted him to be an Episcopalian
preacher, like himself, and Walter had disappointed him by
holding out for law. Cliff was two years younger than Walter,
and not as serious, and their father had never even tried to
persuade Cliff into the church. Everyone had expected Cliff to
go off after he quit college, but he had chosen to come back
and work on the farm.

Walter tossed the letter to one side of his desk, and opened
the big scrapbook that he used for his essay notes. The scrapbook was divided into eleven sections, each dealing with a pair

or group of friends. Some pages were covered with dated notes in Walter's small handwriting. Others were spotted with pasted pieces of paper on which he had written thoughts at odd moments, sometimes on his typewriter at the office. Other pages held the beginnings of outlines. He turned to the outline he had begun on Dick Jensen and Willie Cross. There were two parallel columns listing Dick's traits and their complements in Willie Cross's character.

Dick idealistic and ambitious under a bland, folksy exterior. Admires Cross and protests that he despises him.	Cross greedy and ostentatious, most of his achievements due to bluff. Afraid of Dick's potentialities if he gives him free rein.

Walter remembered another note he had written about them in his memo book, and he went into the bedroom to get it. He felt in the pockets of his jackets for other loose notes, found a piece he had torn out of a newspaper, and a folded envelope on which he had written something. He took them back to his study. The note on Dick said: "Lunch of D. and C. D.'s violent resentment of C.'s proposal to freelance for other law firm."

That was a fertile little note. Cross was also a partner in another firm of legal advisors, Walter had forgotten the precise name. Dick had told Walter all about the offer. It was tempting. Walter wasn't sure that Dick would resist.

There was a gentle knock at the door.

"Come in, Claudia," he said.

Claudia came in with a tray. She had brought him a chicken sandwich and a beer.

"Just what I need," Walter said. He uncapped the beer.

"I thought you might be getting kind of hungry. Mrs. Stackhouse said she's already eaten her lunch. Don't you want me to open these curtains, Mr. Stackhouse? There's such a bright sun today."

"Thanks. I forgot them," Walter said. "Did you have to come today, Claudia? We shouldn't need any cooking with all that food from the party."

"Mrs. Stackhouse didn't tell me not to come."

Walter watched her tall, thin figure as she opened the long curtains and fastened them back. Claudia was that rare thing, a servant who enjoyed her job and consequently did it to perfection. A lot of people around Benedict had tried to out-bid them and buy her away, but Claudia stuck with them, in spite of the exacting routine Clara laid down about the running of the house. Claudia lived in Huntington, and came by bus every morning at seven on the dot, left at eleven to baby-sit in Benedict, came back at six and stayed until nine. She couldn't sleep in, because she took care of her little grandchild, Dean, who lived at home with her in Huntington.

"I'm sorry we ruined your Sunday," Walter said.

"Why, Mr. Stackhouse, I don't mind!" Claudia stood by his desk, watching his progress on the sandwich. "Will there be anything else, Mr. Stackhouse?"

Walter stood up and reached in his pocket. "Yes. I want you to take this—and buy something for Dean." He handed her a ten-dollar bill.

"Ten dollars, Mr. Stackhouse! What can he use for ten dollars?" But Claudia was beaming with pleasure at the gift.

"Well, you think of something," Walter said.

"I sure do thank you, Mr. Stackhouse. That sure is nice of you," she said as she went out.

Walter sipped his beer and opened the newspaper clipping. It was the item he had torn out in Waldo Point.

BODY OF WOMAN FOUND NEAR TARRYTOWN, N.Y.

Tarrytown, Aug. 14—The body of a woman identified as Mrs. Helen P. Kimmel, 39, of Newark, N.J., was found in a wooded section about a mile south of Tarrytown, the police of the 3rd Precinct reported today. She died from strangulation and from dozens of savage cuts and blows on face and body. Her pocketbook was found a few yards away from her body, its contents apparently untouched. She had been travelling by bus from Newark to Albany to visit a sister, Mrs. Rose Gaines. The driver of the bus, John MacDonough of the Cardinal Bus Lines, stated that he noticed Mrs. Kimmel's absence after a 15-minute rest stop at a roadside café last night at 9:55 P.M. Mrs. Kimmel's suitcase was still aboard the bus. It is believed that she was assaulted while taking a short walk along the highway. None of the passengers questioned reported hearing an outcry.

The victim's husband, Melchior J. Kimmel, 40, a book-dealer of Newark, identified the body in Tarrytown this afternoon. Police are searching for clues.

Not of any use for the essays, Walter thought, because the attacker had probably been a maniac. But it was strange no one had seen or heard anything, unless she had been a very long way from the bus itself. Walter wondered if someone she knew could have met her there, lured her quietly away under a pretense of talking to her, and then attacked her? He hesitated, then leaned toward the wastebasket and dropped the clipping, saw it flutter down to one side of the wastebasket onto the carpet. He'd pick it up later, he thought.

He put his head down on his arms. He suddenly felt that he could sleep.

5

B Y TUESDAY, Walter was in bed with the flu.
Clara insisted on calling the doctor to find out what it
was, though Walter knew it was the flu; somebody at the
party had mentioned a couple of cases of flu around Benedict.
Still, Dr. Pietrich came, pronounced it flu, and sent Walter to
bed with pills and penicillin tablets. Clara stayed for a few
minutes and briskly assembled around him everything he
would need—cigarettes and matches, books, a glass of water,
and kleenex.

"Thanks, honey, thanks a lot," Walter said for everything she
did for him. Walter felt he was inconveniencing her, that she
was grimly doing a duty in trying to make him comfortable.
On the rare occasions when he fell ill, he felt as constrained
with her as he would have felt with a total stranger. He was
glad when she finally went off to work. He knew that she
wouldn't call all day, that she would probably even sit downstairs reading the evening paper tonight before she came up to
see how he was.

That evening he couldn't force down even the bouillon that
Claudia made for him. He had acquired a flaming soreness in
his nasal passages, and smoking was impossible. The pills made
him drowse, and in the intervals when he was awake a depression settled on his mind like a black and heavy atmosphere. He
asked himself how he had come to be where he was, waiting
for a woman he believed himself in love with to come home, a
woman who would not even lay her hand on his forehead? He
asked himself why he hadn't pushed Dick a little harder about
getting out of the firm in the fall instead of the first of the year?
He'd talked to Dick the night of the party, which had been a
bad time, but Dick was shy about discussing it in the office, as
shy as if the office were full of hidden dictaphones planted by
Cross. Walter wondered if he'd finally have to get out by himself. But even in his feverish anger, he realized that he needed
Dick's partnership. The kind of office they had in mind would
take two men to run, and Dick, as a working partner, had
some virtues that were hard to find.

When Clara came home, she said, "Are you feeling any better? What's your temperature?"

He knew his temperature, because Claudia had taken it that afternoon. It was 103 degrees. "Not bad," he said. "I'm feeling better."

"Good." Clara emptied her pocketbook methodically, put a few things on her dressing table, then went downstairs to wait for dinner.

Walter closed his eyes and tried to think of something besides Clara sitting in the living room, listening to the radio and reading the evening paper. He played a game he played sometimes on the brink of sleep at night, or on the brink of waking in the morning: he imagined a newspaper spread before him, and he let his eyes sweep rapidly over the first sentences of every story. *Today in Gibraltar, in the presence of Foreign Secretaries Hump-de-dump-de-dump, a new bilateral reciprocal agreement was signed by President Mugwump of Blotz. . . . Wife says, "He destroyed my love! I had to save my child!" . . . A grim story unfolded yesterday before District Chief of Police Ronald W. Friggarty. A young blonde woman, her blue eyes dilated with terror, told how her husband came home and beat her and her child regularly with a frying pan every evening at six. . . . Weather in South America growing ever more temperate, experts declare. A chance discovery of a tiny plastic meteorite on the left shoulder of Mt. Achinche in Bolivia has led climatologists to believe that in the next six hundred years chinchillas will be able to compute their own income taxes. . . . Radiophoto shows streams of shallumping mourners shuffling by bier of murdered Soviet explorer Tomyatkin in Moscow. . . . International Weaving Trades Fair to be inaugurated in famous Glass Receptacle at Cologne. . . .* Walter smiled. He saw the item he had torn out about the woman murdered at the bus stop. The words did not come, but he saw the picture of her. She lay in some woods, and there was a bloody gash down her cheek from her eye to the corner of her lip. She was not pretty, but she had a pleasant face, black wavy hair, a strong simple body and a trusting mouth that would have opened in horror at the first threat from her assaulter. A woman like that wouldn't have gone with a stranger any distance on a road. He imagined her accosted by someone she knew: *Helen, I've got to talk to you. Come here. . . .* She would have looked at him with surprise. *How did you get here? Never mind. I've got to talk to you. Helen, we've got to settle this!* It could have been her husband, Walter thought. He tried to remember whether the paper had said where the husband was at the time. He didn't think it had. Perhaps Helen and Melchior Kimmel had lived in a little hell together, too. Walter imagined them fighting in their home in Newark, reaching a familiar impasse, then the wife deciding to take a trip to see a relative. If the husband had wanted to kill her, he could have followed her in a car, waited until she got out at a rest stop. He could have said, *I have to talk to you*, and his wife would have gone with him, down to some dark clump of trees beside the highway. . . .

Thursday evening, Clara came in and sat for a few moments on the foot of his bed. She was afraid of catching the flu from him, and she had been sleeping on the couch in his study. Now that she had not come in contact with him for three days, Walter thought, she was positively blooming. He said very little to her, but she didn't seem to notice. She was absorbed in a new sales possibility on the North Shore.

I hate her, Walter thought. He was intensely aware of it. It gave him a kind of pleasure to think about it.

Later that evening, the sound of a car motor awakened Walter from a doze. He heard two voices on the stairs, one, a woman's voice.

Clara ushered Peter Slotnikoff and the girl called Ellie into the room. Peter apologized for not telephoning first. Ellie had brought him a large bunch of gladiolas.

"I'm not quite dead yet," Walter said, embarrassed.

Walter looked around for something to put them in. Clara had left the room—Walter knew she was annoyed because they had dropped in without calling—and there was no vase in sight. Peter got a vase from the hall and filled it in the bathroom. Walter lay back on the pillows and watched Ellie's hands as she put the flowers in the vase. Her hands were strong and square, like her face, but gentle when they touched things. Walter remembered that she played the violin.

"Would anybody like a drink?" Walter asked. "Or a beer?

There's beer in the refrigerator, Pete. Why don't you go down and fix what you want?"

They all wanted beer. Peter went out.

Ellie sat across the room in the armless chair that Clara used in front of her dressing table. She wore a white blouse with the sleeves rolled up, a tweed skirt and moccasins. "How long have you lived here?" she asked.

"About three years."

"It's a lovely house. I like the country."

"Country!" Walter laughed.

"After New York this is country to me."

"It's hard for people to get out here unless they have a car, all right."

She smiled and her bluish brown eyes lighted. "Isn't that an advantage?"

"No. I like people to drop in. I hope you'll come again— since you have a car."

"Thanks. You haven't seen my car. It's a banged-up convertible that doesn't convert very well any more, so I drive it open—unless it's really pouring rain. Then it leaks. I always had my family's car at home, and when I came to New York I had to have one, in spite of being broke, so I bought Boadicea. That's her name."

"Where's your home?"

"Upstate. Corning. It's a pretty dull town."

Walter had been through it once on a train. He remembered it as utterly gray, like a mining town. He couldn't imagine Ellie there.

Peter came back with the beer, and poured the glasses carefully.

"Does smoke bother you?" Ellie asked. "I don't have to smoke."

"Not a bit," Walter said. "I only wish I could join you."

She lighted her cigarette. "When I had the flu, my nose was so sore I could hardly get to sleep for the pain of breathing, much less smoke."

Walter smiled. It struck him as the most sympathetic thing anyone had said to him since he had been ill. "How's the office going, Pete?"

"The Parsons and Sullivan thing is giving Mr. Jensen trouble," Peter said. "There're two representatives. One is fine. The other—well, he lies, I think. He's the older one."

Walter looked at Peter's frank young face and thought: in another two or three years, Peter won't raise an eyebrow at the most blatant lies in the world. "They often lie," Walter said.

"I hope your wife isn't displeased with us for not calling first," Peter said.

"Of course not." Walter heard Clara's footsteps in the hall, coming close, going away. She had said she was going to make an inventory of the linens this evening, and Walter knew that was exactly what she was doing. He wondered what Ellie thought of Clara, of Clara's obvious indifference to her and Pete? Ellie, just beyond the circle of light thrown by his table lamp, was gazing at him steadily. Walter didn't mind. Because it was not a critical stare, he thought, not like Clara's or some other women's stares that he felt tore him slowly to pieces. "Have you had any luck about a job, Ellie?" Walter asked.

"Yes, there's a chance of something at Harridge School. They're supposed to let me know next week."

"Harridge? In Long Island?"

"Yes, in Lennert. South of here."

"That's not far away at all," Walter said.

"No, but I haven't got it yet. They don't need me there. I'm just trying to push my way in." She smiled and suddenly stood up. "We'd better be going."

Walter asked them to stay longer, but they insisted on going. Ellie held out her hand.

"Aren't you afraid you'll catch the flu?"

"No," she laughed.

He took her outstretched hand then. Her hand felt exactly as he had known it would, very solid, and with a quick, firm pressure. Her shining eyes looked wonderfully kind. He wondered if she looked at everyone the way she looked at him.

"I hope you're better soon," she said.

Then they went out, and the room was empty. Walter heard the tones of their polite exchanges with Clara downstairs, then the sound of the car motor, fading away.

Clara came into the room. "So Miss Briess is going to take a job near here?"

"She might. Did you overhear that?"

"No. I asked her. Just now." Clara laid some bathtowels in a drawer of the chest. "I wonder what she's up to, going around with that naïve Pete?"

"I suppose she likes him, that's simple."

Clara gave him a slurring look. "She likes any man around better, I can tell you that."

6

WALTER GOT up Saturday, and on Sunday they went to the Iretons' for lunch.

It was a fine sunny day, and about twenty people were drinking cocktails on the lawn when Walter and Clara arrived.

Clara stopped at a group that included Ernestine McClintock and the McClintocks' friend Greta Roda, the painter. Walter walked on. Bill Ireton was telling a joke to the men gathered around the portable bar.

"Same old dope," Bill was saying. "Always barking up the wrong girl!" The clap of laughter that followed was painful to Walter's ears. He was at that stage, after the flu, when noises were like physical blows, and it hurt even to comb his hair.

Bill Ireton squeezed Walter's hand with a hand wet and cold from ice cubes. "I'm sure glad you could make it! Feeling better?"

"Fine now," Walter said. "Thanks for all your inquiries."

Betty Ireton came up and welcomed him, too, took him over to meet a weekend guest of theirs, a woman, and from there on Walter circulated by himself, enjoying the springy grass under his feet, and the soothing effect of the alcohol that was going straight to his head.

Bill came over, took Walter's glass to replenish it, and gave Walter a sign to follow him. "What's the matter with Clara?" Bill asked as they walked. "She just took Betty's head off."

Walter tensed. "About what?"

"About the whole party, I gather. Clara said she didn't want a drink, and when Betty offered to get her a coke, she let Betty know it wasn't necessary for *her* to drink anything at all to enjoy herself perfectly well." Bill minced his voice a little and lifted his eyebrows as Clara did. "Anyway, Betty got the idea she'd have been much happier if she'd stayed at home."

Walter could imagine the scene exactly. "I'm sorry, Bill. I wouldn't take it seriously. You know, with me sick all week and Clara working the way she does, she gets edgy once in a while."

Bill looked doubtful. "If she ever doesn't want to come, fellow, we'll understand. We're always glad to see you, and don't forget it!"

Walter said nothing. He was thinking that Bill's words were actually an insult to Clara, if he chose to take them that way, and that he didn't choose to take them that way, because he understood Bill's reaction to her completely. Walter moved away across the lawn, looking over the people, the women in bright summer skirts. He realized suddenly that he was looking for Ellie, and there wasn't a chance that she would be here today. Ellie Briess. Ellie Briess. At least he could remember her name now. The name suited her perfectly, he thought, simple but not ordinary, and a little Germanic. Walter felt himself getting pleasantly high on his second drink. He ate lunch with the McClintocks and Greta Roda on one of the long gliders, assembling his meal from the trays of delicious barbecue and french fried potatoes that the Ireton maid and the two little Ireton girls passed around. When he got up to leave, he staggered, and Bill and Clara came up to walk on either side of him.

"I don't feel drunk, just awfully tired suddenly," Walter said.

"You just got out of bed, old man," Bill said. "You didn't have much to drink."

"You're a good egg," Walter told him.

But Clara was furious. Walter sat beside her in silence while she drove home—she insisted he wasn't able to drive—reviling him all the way for his stupidity, his sloth in getting drunk at noon.

"Just because the liquor's there and nobody stops you from drinking yourself into a stupor!"

He had had only two drinks, and after a cup of coffee at home, he felt thoroughly sober and he acted thoroughly sober, sitting in the big armchair in the living room, reading the Sunday paper. But Clara continued to harangue him, intermittently. She sat across the room from him, sewing buttons on a white dress.

"You're supposed to be a lawyer, an intellectual. I should think you'd find better things to do with your intellect than soak it in alcohol! A few more episodes like today and we'll be blacklisted by all our friends."

Walter looked up at that. "Clara, what *is* this?" he asked

good-naturedly. He was debating going up to his study and shutting the door, but often she followed him, accusing him of not being able to take criticism.

"I saw Betty Ireton's face when you staggered across the lawn. She was disgusted with you!"

"If you think Betty would be disgusted at seeing somebody a little high, you must be out of your mind."

"You couldn't have seen it anyway, you were drunk!"

"May I say a few words?" Walter asked, standing up. "You took the trouble to scowl disapproval on the whole gathering today, didn't you? And to your hostess at that. You're the one who's going to get us blacklisted. You're negative toward everything and everyone."

"And you're so positive. Sweetness and light!"

Walter clenched his fists in his pockets and walked a few steps in the room, conscious of a desire to strike her. "I can tell you the Iretons weren't so fond of you today, and I don't think they have been for a long time. That goes for a lot of people we know."

"What're you talking about? You're a paranoid! I think you're a psychopathic case, Walter, I really do!"

"I can enumerate them for you!" Walter said more loudly, advancing toward her. "There's Jon. You can't bear it if I go fishing with him. There's Chad who passed out once. There's the Whitneys before that. Whatever became of the Whitneys? They just drifted off, didn't they? Mysteriously. And before that Howard Graz. You certainly gave him a hell of a weekend after we invited him here!"

"All written down and labeled. You must have spent a lot of time preparing this devastating case."

"What else've I got to do at night?" Walter said quickly.

"There we go again. You can't stay off that subject five minutes, can you?"

"I think I can stay off it permanently. Wouldn't you like that? Then you can be completely independent of me. You can devote your time exclusively to maneuvering me away from my friends."

She began to sew again. "They concern you much more than I do, that's obvious."

"I mean," Walter said, his dry throat rasping, "I can't be a partner to a negative attitude that's eventually going to alienate me from every living creature in the world!"

"Oh, you're so concerned with yourself!"

"Clara, I want a divorce."

She looked up from her sewing with her lips parted. She looked very much as she did whenever he asked her if she minded if he, or they, made an appointment with one of their friends. "I don't think you mean that," she said.

"I know you don't, but I do. It's not like the time before. I'm not going to believe things can get any better, because obviously they can't."

She looked stunned, and he wondered if she were remembering the time before. They had reached the same point exactly, and Clara had threatened to take the veronal she had upstairs. Walter had made a batch of martinis, and had forced her to drink one to pull herself together. He had sat down beside her on the sofa where she sat now, and she had broken down and cried and told him that she adored him, and the evening had ended very differently from the way Walter had anticipated.

"It isn't enough any more to be in love with you— physically—because mentally I despise you," Walter said quietly. He felt that he was uttering the accumulation of the thousand days and nights when he had never dared say these things, not from lack of courage but because it was so horrible and so fatal for Clara. He watched her now as he would watch a still-alive thing to which he had just given a deathblow, because he could see that she was believing him, gradually.

"But maybe I can change," she said with a tremor of tears in her voice. "I can go to an analyst—"

"I don't think that'll change you, Clara." He knew her contempt for psychiatry. He had tried to get her to go to a psychiatrist. She never had.

Her eyes were fixed on him, wide and empty-looking and wet with tears, and it seemed to Walter that even in this breakdown she was in the grip of a fit more frenzied than the times when she had shrieked at him like a harpy. Jeff, restive at their quarreling voices, pranced about Clara, licking her hand, but Clara did not show by the movement of a finger that she knew he was there.

"It's that girl, isn't it?" Clara asked suddenly.

"What?"

"Don't pretend. I know. Why don't you admit it? You want to divorce me so you can have her. You're infatuated with her silly, cowlike smiles at you!"

Walter frowned. "*What* girl?"

"Ellie Briess!"

"Ellie Briess?" Walter repeated in an incredulous whisper. "Good God, Clara, you're out of your head!"

"Do you deny it?" Clara demanded.

"It's not worth denying!"

"It's true, isn't it? At least admit it. Tell the truth for once!"

Walter felt a shiver down his spine. His mind shifted, trying to adjust to quite a different situation, the handling of someone mentally deranged. "Clara, I've seen the girl only twice. She's got absolutely nothing to do with us."

"I don't believe you. You've been seeing her on the sly—evenings when you don't come home at six-thirty."

"What evenings? Last Monday? That's the only day I went to work since I've met her."

"Sunday!"

Walter swallowed. He remembered he had taken a long walk Sunday morning, the morning after he met the girl. "Haven't we got reason enough to end this without dragging in fantasies?"

Clara's mouth trembled. "You won't give me another chance?"

"No."

"Then I'll take that veronal tonight," Clara said in a suddenly calm voice.

"No, you won't." Walter went to the bar, poured a brandy for her and brought it to her.

She took it in her shaking fingers and drained it at once, not even looking to see what it was. "You think I'm joking, don't you, because I didn't the other time. But I will now!"

"That's a threat, darling."

"Don't call me 'darling,' you despise me." She stood up. "Leave me alone! At least give me some privacy!"

Walter felt another start of alarm. She did look insane now with her brown eyes hard and bright as stone, her figure rigid as if an epileptic seizure had caught her and left her standing, balanced like a column of rock. "Privacy for what?"

"To kill myself!"

He made an involuntary half turn to go to her dressing table upstairs where he thought the pills were, then looked back at her.

"You don't know where they are. I've hidden them."

"Clara, let's not be melodramatic."

"Then leave me alone!"

"All right, I will."

He ran upstairs to his study, closed the door, and walked around for a few moments, drawing on a cigarette. He didn't believe she would. It was partly a threat and partly her real terror of being alone with herself. But it would subside again. Tomorrow she would be as hard and self-righteous as ever. And meanwhile was he supposed to play nursemaid to her all her life, be chained to her because of a threat? He yanked the door open and ran downstairs.

She was not in the living room, and he called to her, then ran up the stairs again. He found her in the bedroom. She turned quickly to him, concealing something in the white dress she carried, or perhaps only holding the dress against her while she waited for him to leave. Then as she shook the dress out and slipped a hanger into it, he saw that she had nothing else in her hands. When she walked to the closet, Walter saw a brandy inhaler half full of brandy on the windowsill. He looked at it incredulously for a moment.

"Why don't you leave me alone?" she asked. "Why don't you go out and take a long walk?"

Jeff stopped his gay trotting around the room, sat down and looked straight at Walter as if he waited, too, for him to get out.

"All right, I just might do that," Walter said, and he let the bedroom door slam when he went out.

He went back to his study. He was not staying to protect her, he told himself, he just didn't happen to want to take a walk. He started violently as the door opened behind him.

"I thought I should remind you, to make you feel a little better, that after tonight you can be free to spend *all* your time with Ellie Briess!"

Walter had a glass paperweight in his hand, and for an instant he wanted to throw it at her. He banged the paperweight down on the desk and strode past her out of the room, angry as he had never been before, yet still able to see himself objectively—a furiously angry man, hurling shirts and a pair of trousers into a suitcase, toothbrush, washrag, and as an afterthought the brief-case he would need tomorrow. He snapped the suitcase shut.

"The house is all yours tonight," he called to her as he passed her in the hall.

Walter got into his car. He was on the North Island Parkway before he realized he did not know where he was going. To New York? He could go to Jon's. But he didn't want to spill out all his troubles to Jon. Walter took the next exit lane, and found himself in a little community that he did not recognize. He saw a movie theatre close by. Walter parked his car and went in. He sat in the balcony and stared at the screen and smoked. He was going to force himself to sit there until they got around to the animated cartoon that he had come in on. Somewhere near the end of the feature picture, Walter thought, if Clara *had* taken the sleeping pills, it was already too late for a stomach pump to be of much help. A thrust of panic caught him unawares.

He got up and went out.

7

O<small>N THE</small> bed table stood a greenish bottle that was empty and a glass with a little water in it.

"*Clara*!" He picked her up by her shoulders and shook her.

She didn't stir at all, and her mouth hung open. Walter grabbed her wrist. There was a pulse and it felt even strong and normal, he thought. He went into the bathroom and wet a bathtowel with cold water, brought it back and wiped her face with it. There was no reaction. He slapped her face.

"Clara! Wake up!"

He sat her up, but she was limp as a rag doll. Hopeless to try to get coffee down her throat, he thought. Her tongue lolled out of her mouth. He ran into the hall to the telephone.

Dr. Pietrich was not in, but his housemaid gave him the number of another doctor. The second doctor said he could be there in fifteen minutes.

Twenty-five minutes went by, and Walter was in terror that she was going to cease breathing before his eyes, but the shallow breathing went on. The doctor arrived and went briskly to work with a stomach pump. Walter poured warm water for him into the funnel at one end of the tube. Nothing came out of her but the water, colored with a little bloody mucus. The doctor gave her two injections, then tried the pump again. Walter watched her half-open eyes, the limp unnatural-looking mouth, for any signs of consciousness. He saw none at all.

"Do you think she'll live?" he asked.

"How do I know?" the doctor said irritably. "She's not waking up. She'll have to go to the hospital."

Walter disliked the doctor intensely.

A few moments later, Walter carried Clara in his arms down the stairs and out to the car.

Some of the doctors, Walter thought, acted as if it were most annoying that they had to bother with a suicide case. Or as if they assumed automatically that he was to blame.

"Ever had any trouble with her heart?" a doctor asked.

"No," Walter said. "Do you think she'll live?"

The doctor's eyebrows went up indifferently, and he continued to write in his tablet. "Depends on her heart," the doctor
said. He led the way down the corridor.

She was lying under a transparent oxygen tent. The nurse was
rubbing her arm for another injection, and Walter winced as the
big needle slid two inches up her vein. Clara didn't twitch.

"She'll just either sleep it off or not," the doctor said.

Walter leaned over and studied Clara's face intently. Her
mouth was still lifeless, misshapen, lips slightly drawn back from
her teeth. It gave her face an expression Walter had never seen
before, an expression like that of death, he thought. He believed
now that Clara didn't want to live. And instead of her unconscious will working to live as a normal person's would, he
imagined her will pulling her toward death, and he felt helpless.

By two in the morning, there was no change in her condition, and Walter went home. He called the hospital at intervals,
and the message was always "No change." At about six in the
morning, he had a cup of coffee and a brandy and drove off to
the hospital. Claudia came at seven, and he didn't want to see
her because he didn't know what to tell her.

Clara lay in exactly the same position. He thought her eyelids had swollen a little. There was something horribly fetuslike
about the swollen eyelids and the expressionless mouth. The
doctor told him that her blood pressure had decreased slightly,
which was a bad sign, but so far as her heart went, she seemed
to be holding her own.

"Do you think she'll live?"

"I just can't answer that question. She took enough to kill
her, if you hadn't brought her here. We should know in another forty-eight hours."

"Forty-eight hours!"

"The coma could last even longer, but if it does, I doubt if
she'll pull out."

Around nine o'clock Walter drove to New York. His suitcase
was still in the back of the car, and he got his briefcase out of it
before he went up to the office. It seemed to him that he had
never intended to go to a hotel with the suitcase, that it was
only a prop in his real intent to get out of the house in order to
let Clara kill herself without his interference. Walter couldn't
escape the fact that he had known she was going to take the

pills. He could tell himself that he hadn't really thought she would take them, because she hadn't the other time, but this time had been different—and he knew it. In a sense, he thought, he had killed her—if she died. And therefore he thought he must have wanted to kill her.

Walter skipped lunch and sat at his desk, trying to make sense out of Dick's notes on the Parsons and Sullivan interviews. Walter read one passage over and over, without being able to decide whether a piece was missing or whether his own mind could no longer attach a meaning to the words. Suddenly he reached for the telephone and dialed Jon's number. Walter asked if he could see him right away, in Jon's office.

"Is it about Clara?" Jon asked.

"Yes." Walter hadn't known his voice would betray him, but only Clara could put him in such a state, and Jon knew it.

Jon had whiskey in his office and offered Walter some, but Walter declined it.

"Clara's in the hospital in a coma. She may die," Walter said. "She took sleeping pills last night. Every pill in the house. She must have had about thirty." Walter told Jon about their talk of a divorce, her threatening to kill herself, and his leaving the house.

"This wasn't the first time you talked about a divorce, was it?" Jon asked.

"No." Walter had told Jon months ago that he was considering a divorce, but he hadn't told Jon that he had talked to Clara. "She threatened to kill herself the first time I asked her for a divorce. That's why I didn't believe her yesterday."

"And that's why you patched it up the first time, because she threatened?"

"I suppose so," Walter said. "One of the reasons."

"I know." Jon stood up and looked out the window. "And you reach a point finally, don't you—as you did yesterday?"

"What do you mean?"

"You reach a point where you say, 'All right, I'll damn well let her kill herself. I've had enough.'"

Walter stared at the large brass penholder on Jon's desk that he had given to Jon on the first anniversary of his magazine. "Yes. That's it." Walter put his hands over his face. "That's a kind of murder, isn't it?"

"No one would say it's murder who knows the facts. You don't have to tell anyone about it, anyone who doesn't know the facts. Stop turning it over and over in your mind, the fact that you walked out."

"All right," Walter said.

"She'll probably pull through. She's got a tough constitution, Walt."

Walter looked at his friend. Jon was smiling, and Walter gave a little smile in return. He felt suddenly better.

"The real problem is, what happens when she wakes up? Do you still want your divorce?"

Walter had to force himself to imagine Clara well again. His mind was obsessed with remorse, with pity for her. "Yes," he said.

"Then get it. There are ways. Even if you have to go to Reno. Don't let yourself be paralyzed by a pint-sized Medusa any more."

Walter felt a rise of resentment, and then he thought of Jon, paralyzed by his love for his wife when she was having the affair with the man called Brinton. Walter had sat with Jon almost every night for two months, but finally Jon had gotten over it, and gotten his divorce. "All right," Walter said.

Walter drove by the hospital on the way home that evening. Now her fingernails were bluish. Her face looked puffier. But the doctor said she was holding her own. Walter didn't believe it. He felt she was going to die.

He went home, intending to take a hot bath and shave and try to eat something. He fell asleep in the bathtub, which he had never done before in his life. He only awakened when Claudia called him to tell him his dinner was nearly ready.

"You'd better get some rest, Mr. Stackhouse, or you'll be good and sick again yourself," Claudia said to him.

Walter had told her that Clara was in the hospital with a bad case of flu.

The telephone rang while he was eating, and Walter ran for it, thinking it was the hospital.

"Hello, Mr. Stackhouse. This is Ellie Briess. Are you all over the flu?"

"Oh, yes—thanks."

"Does your wife like bulbs?"

"Bulbs?"

"Tulip bulbs. I've got two dozen of them. I just had dinner with a supervisor over at Harridge, and she insisted that I take them, but I've no place to plant them. They're very special bulbs. I thought you might be able to use them."

"Oh—thanks for thinking of us."

"I can drop them by now, if you're going to be home for the next twenty minutes."

"All right. Do that," Walter said clumsily.

He felt very strange as he turned from the telephone. He remembered Clara's accusations. He imagined her numbed lips moving as she said it again. Like a prophecy from the dying.

A few minutes later, Ellie Briess was at the door. She had a cardboard carton in her hands. "Here they are. If you're busy, I won't come in."

"I'm not busy. Do come in." He held the door for her. "Would you care for some coffee?"

"Yes. Thank you." She took a folded paper from her handbag and laid it on the coffee table. "Here're the instructions for the bulbs."

Walter looked at her. She looked older and more sophisticated, and he realized suddenly she was wearing a chic black dress and high-heeled black suede pumps that made her taller and slimmer. "Did you get the Harridge job?" he asked.

"Yes. Today. That's who I was having dinner with—my future boss."

"I hope he's nice."

"It's a woman. She's nice. She was insistent about those bulbs."

"My congratulations on the job," Walter said.

"Thanks." She smiled her broad smile at him. "I think I'll be happy there."

She looked happy. It shone from her face. He wanted to look at her, but he looked at the floor.

Claudia came in with the tray of coffee and the orange cake she had baked especially for him.

"You know Miss Briess from the party, don't you, Claudia? Ellie, this is Claudia."

They exchanged greetings and Walter noticed Claudia's

pleasure in being introduced. He didn't always introduce Claudia to people. Clara didn't like it.

"Isn't your wife here?" Ellie asked.

"No, she isn't." Walter poured the coffee carefully. It was a rich black, stronger than Claudia would have made it if Clara had been here.

He got the brandy bottle and two inhalers. Then he sat down and was conscious for an uncomfortable minute that he had nothing to say to the girl. And he was conscious of a sexual attraction for her that shamed him. Or was it sexual? He wanted to lay his head in her lap, on the thighs that curved a little under the black dress.

"Your wife works very hard, doesn't she?" Ellie asked.

"Yes. She loves to work hard or not at all." Walter glanced at Ellie's eyes. The beautiful outgoing warmth in her eyes was still there, had not changed as her hair and her clothes had changed tonight. Walter hesitated, then said, "Just now she's sick with a touch of my flu. Well, more than a touch. She's in the hospital."

"Oh. I'm very sorry," Ellie said.

Walter felt very near a cracking point, but he did not know what he would do if he cracked—faint, seize Ellie in his arms, or run out of the house forever. "Would you like some music?" he asked.

"No, thanks. You wouldn't." Ellie was sitting on the edge of the sofa. "I'll finish my brandy and go."

Walter watched helplessly as she got her bag and gloves, took a last pull on her cigarette and put it out. He followed her to the door.

"Thanks for the delicious coffee," she said.

"I hope you come back again. Where do you live?" He wanted to know where to reach her.

"I live in New York," she replied.

Walter's heart jumped as if she had given him her telephone number and asked him to call. And he already knew that she lived in New York, anyway. "You'll be commuting every day?"

"Yes. I suppose so." She smiled, suddenly looking shy. "Give my good wishes to your wife. Good night."

"Good night." He stood in the open doorway until the sound of her car had faded nearly away.

Walter went to the hospital and stayed there all night, alternately reading and dozing on a bench in the corridor.

On Tuesday afternoon, Walter got a call in his office from the hospital. The nurse's familiar mechanical voice had a happy note in it: "Mrs. Stackhouse came out of the coma about fifteen minutes ago."

"She'll be all right?"

"Oh, yes, she'll be all right."

Walter hung up without asking any more questions. He wanted to leap up to the ceiling, wanted to go running in and shout the news to Dick, but he had only told Dick that Clara had the flu. One didn't get so excited about a recovery from flu. Walter forced himself to finish up the piece of work on his desk. He did it humbly and patiently, as a grateful sinner just saved from hell would do a small chore for a redeemer.

Clara was sleeping, the nurse told Walter when he arrived, but he was allowed to go in and see her. Now her lips rested quietly together. She would be very groggy for a couple of weeks, the doctor said, but she would be able to go home in a day or so.

"I'd like to talk to you for a moment," the doctor said. "Will you come in my office?"

Walter followed him. He knew what the doctor was going to say.

"Your wife's going to need psychiatric care for a while. To take an overdose indicates a kind of insanity, you know. Besides, suicide is a crime in this state. If she hadn't had the luck to get into a private hospital, she'd have had a lot more trouble with the law than she's had."

"What do you mean, than she's had?"

"We had to report this, of course. Since I'm her private doctor, I'm responsible to a certain extent. I'd like to know that she gets psychiatric care once she leaves the hospital."

"It's going to take some persuading. She doesn't like psychiatrists."

"I don't care whether she likes them or not."

"I understand," Walter said.

That was the end of the interview. Walter called Jon to tell him the good news.

Some time after ten o'clock that evening, Walter saw Clara

stir. He had been sitting by her bedside. Walter bent over her. He expected her to show resentment because he had left her that night, and when she didn't, when she only smiled weakly at him, he thought that perhaps she was too groggy to recognize him.

"Walter." Her hand slid toward him on the sheet.

Walter touched her tenderly with both hands, sat down on the edge of the bed, and put his face down on the sheets that covered her breast. He could feel her body, warm and alive. He felt he had never loved her so much.

"Walter, don't ever leave me, don't ever leave me," she said in a quick, feathery whisper. "Don't ever leave me, ever."

"No, darling." He meant it.

Clara came home Thursday morning. Walter carried her from the car to the house, because she had grown too sleepy during the ride in the car to walk.

"It's like carrying a bride over the threshold, isn't it?" Clara said softly as they went through the front door.

"Yes." Walter had never carried her over a threshold before. Clara would have thought it too sentimental when they were first married.

Claudia had filled the bedroom with flowers from the garden and Walter had added more. Jeff was freshly washed, and greeted Clara with licks and barks, but not as enthusiastically as Walter had expected.

"How have you been getting on with Jeff?" Clara asked.

"Jeff and I have been fine. Do you want to sit up a while or go straight to bed?"

"Both," she said, laughing a little.

He got her dressing gown from the closet, removed her shoes from her brown stockingless feet, and hung up the dress she had pulled off. Then he propped the pillows behind her. She wanted lemonade, she said, with a lot of sugar in it. Walter went down to make it, because Claudia was busy making vichyssoise, which Clara loved, and the recipe was complicated.

"Who did you tell about this?" Clara asked when he came back.

"Only Jon. Nobody else."

"What did you tell my office?"

Walter barely remembered when they had called. "I said you had the flu. Don't worry, darling. Nobody has to know."

"Claudia told me Ellie Briess was here."

"She dropped in Monday night. Oh, she brought you some tulip bulbs, too. You'll have to look at them tomorrow. Very special ones, she said."

"Evidently you weren't bored while I was in the hospital."

"Oh, Clara, please—" He handed her the glass of lemonade again. "You have to drink a lot of liquids, the doctor said."

"I was right about Ellie, wasn't I?"

He shouldn't get angry, he thought. Mentally, she was still groggy, not normal yet. Then he remembered, she hadn't been normal before she took the pills, either. She had just come back to life again, and she was taking up where she had left off. "Clara, let's talk tomorrow. You're very tired."

"Why don't you admit that you're in love with her?"

"But I'm not." Leaning forward, he half embraced her. It was ironic that he had never loved her, never desired her so much as now, and that she had never mistrusted him so much. "I did tell her you were sick. She called up last night to ask how you were. I told her you were fine."

"That must have pleased her."

"I'm sleeping in my study tonight, honey." Walter pressed her arm affectionately and stood up. "I think you'll rest better if you sleep alone," he added, in case she misunderstood his reason.

But from her affronted, staring eyes, he knew she had attached another meaning to it, anyway.

8

For about a week, Clara spent most of her time in bed, taking naps every couple of hours. Walter took her for short rides in the car in the evenings, and bought her chocolate sodas at the curb-service drugstore in Benedict. Betty Ireton came to visit her twice. Everybody seemed to believe the story that Walter had given out, that Clara had had a bad case of influenza. Finally, Clara was able to go to the movies one evening, and the next day she announced that she was going back to work on Monday. It was less than two weeks since she had come from the hospital. On the same evening, a Friday, Clara's mother called from Harrisburg.

Walter heard Clara's cool, unsurprised greeting to her mother, then a long pause while her mother, he supposed, pled with Clara to come and pay a visit.

"Well, if you're *not* feeling so bad, why should I?" Clara asked. "I've got a job here, you know. I can't just come at anybody's whim."

Walter got up restlessly and turned the radio off. Her mother was not well, Walter knew. She had had two strokes. How could Clara be so merciless with somebody else's weakness, he wondered, when she had been so near death herself twelve days ago?

"Mother, I'll write to you. You're going to run up a big bill talking all this time. . . . Yes, Mother, tonight, I promise you."

Walter suddenly thought of Ellie's tulip bulbs.

Clara turned around, sighing. "She's the end, the bitter end."

"I gather you're not going."

"I certainly am not."

"You know, I think a month out there would do you good. Provided you relaxed and didn't—"

"You know I can't stand to be around my mother."

Walter let it go. He was trying to avoid subjects that irritated her, and this was certainly one of them. "Say, whatever happened to those tulip bulbs? Didn't Claudia show them to you? I told her to."

"I threw them out," Clara said, reseating herself on the sofa, taking up her book again. She looked up at Walter challengingly.

"Was that necessary?" Walter asked. "You don't have to take it out on a dozen innocent tulip bulbs."

"I didn't want her flowers gracing our garden."

His anger leapt suddenly. "Clara, that was a stupid, petty thing to do!"

"If we want tulips, we can buy our own bulbs," Clara said. "That's why you want me to go to Harrisburg, isn't it? You'd like to have me out of the way for a while."

Walter came nearer slapping her face than he ever had before. "It's disgusting, what you're saying. It's degrading."

"Go off with her. Call her up tonight and see her. You must miss her after all this time."

Walter took a step toward her and seized her wrist. "Stop it, will you? You're hysterical!"

"Let go of me!"

He let go, and she rubbed her wrist. "I'm sorry," he said. "There're times when I think a good slap in the face might bring you back to sanity."

"Shock treatment," she said scornfully. "I'm in my right mind and you know it. Why don't you tell the truth, Walter? You slept with that girl while I was in the hospital, didn't you?"

Walter started to say something, then gave it up and went out of the room. He went into the kitchen, unbuttoning his shirt. In the half-light that came from the living room, he took off his clothes and began to put on the old clothes that hung in the kitchen closet back of the brooms and the dustrags. He put on old manila trousers and the old shirt and sweater he wore when he worked around the house. Under the dustmop he found his pair of tennis shoes. Then he went out of the house and got into his car.

He drove toward Benedict. He was trembling, and most of it was exhaustion, he knew. Ever since the Sunday night she did it, he had been tense as a board, and now that she was on her feet again, it was no better. What an idiot he had been to think they could start over!

He shied away from the Three Brothers Tavern. He wanted

to go to a bar where he had never been before. He saw a place on the roadside before he got to Huntington.

Walter went up to the bar and ordered a double scotch and water. He glanced around at the people at the bar: a couple of men who looked like truck drivers, a dowdy woman reading a magazine with a repellent-looking crème de menthe in front of her, a very ordinary, middle-aged couple who were a little drunk and arguing with each other. Walter squeezed his eyes shut and listened to the inane words of the song that was playing on the juke box. He wanted to forget who he was, forget everything he had been thinking tonight. He looked down at the manila trousers as he sat at the bar, noticed there was a button unbuttoned, fastened it casually, and stood up from the stool and leaned on the bar. The quarreling voices of the man and woman grew louder, intruding on the juke box.

He was about fifty, with a skinny face that needed a shave. She was fat and untidy, and they had probably been married thirty years, Walter thought. He envied them. Their quarrels were so simple, so on the surface. Even when the man's face twisted with anger, it was a mild and superficial anger. The man lifted his forearm and swung it back playfully as if he were going to hit her, and then put his arm down again.

Walter felt it reminded him of something, though he couldn't think of what. He never had struck Clara. Walter lifted his glass and set it down empty. He remembered the murdered Kimmel woman: her husband hadn't stopped at striking her; he had murdered her. But they hadn't said at all that the husband had done it, Walter remembered. That was an idea of his own. The husband *might* have done it, however, just approached his wife at the bus stop and persuaded her to take a little walk with him. Walter wondered what had ever been discovered about the case, and if he had missed other items in the newspaper. He easily could have. It wasn't a case that the newspapers gave much space to. Walter wondered, if the murderer hadn't been found, if the husband had ever been under suspicion?

"Refill?" the barman asked, his hand on Walter's glass.

"No, thanks," Walter said. "I'll wait a minute."

Walter lighted another cigarette and continued to stare down at the bottles and glasses on the lower shelf of the bar.

Melchior Kimmel was a bookdealer, Walter remembered. Walter wondered if anyone would be able to tell if someone were a murderer just by looking at him? Not beyond a doubt, of course, but be able to tell if a person were capable of murdering or not? Suddenly he was filled with curiosity about Melchior Kimmel. He wanted to go to Newark and see if there were a bookshop owned by a Melchior Kimmel, if there were a man called Melchior Kimmel whom he could actually see.

Walter paid for his drink, left a tip, and went out.

That night, sleeping in his study, Walter dreamed that he went to visit Melchior Kimmel at a bookshop, and that Kimmel turned out to be one of the half-naked atlantes of gray stone that supported the long lintel of the store. Walter recognized him at once and began to speak to him, but Melchior Kimmel only laughed, his stone belly shaking, and refused to reply to anything Walter asked him.

9

T HE NEXT day was Saturday. Walter slept until after nine, and when he went downstairs to breakfast, Claudia told him that Clara was gone.

"She said she was going shopping in Garden City," Claudia said. "Didn't know when she'd be back."

"I see. Thanks," Walter said.

By three in the afternoon, Clara was still not home. Walter had mowed the lawn and trimmed the two thick clumps of hedges, and had finished a book that Dick Jensen had lent him on the New York penal code. He felt restless, and drank a bottle of beer, hoping it would make him sleepy enough to take a nap. It didn't. Just before four, Walter got into his car and headed for Newark.

There was no Melchior Kimmel in the telephone book, but there was a Kimmel's Bookstore at 313 South Huron Street. Walter didn't know the first thing about Newark streets. He asked directions from a clerk in the cigar store where he had used the telephone book. The man said it was about ten blocks away, and explained how to get there.

The shop was in a grimy commercial street. Walter glanced automatically for the atlantes on the front of the shop, but there were not any. He saw a couple of dusty-looking front windows full of books on both sides of a recessed door. It looked like a shop that specialized in students' texts and second-hand books. Walter put his car on the other side of the street, got out, and approached the shop slowly. He saw no one inside except a young man with glasses, reading a book as he leaned against one of the long tables. There was a pyramid of algebra texts in one window, and in the other window an assortment of popular novels spread out in radiating lines from a card that said 89¢ in red letters. Walter went in.

The place had a stale, sweetish smell. Shelves of books covered every wall from floor to ceiling. There were two long tables extending half the length of the shop, on which books were heaped in disorder. Two or three naked lightbulbs hung from the ceiling, and there was a brighter light in back. Walter walked on slowly. Under the bright hanging light that was shaded with a green glass shade, Walter saw a baldheaded man of about forty sitting at a desk. Walter felt as positive that he was Melchior Kimmel as if he had recognized him from a photograph he had seen before.

The man looked up at Walter. He had a large pinkish mouth with oversized lips that looked painfully swollen. His small eyes behind rimless glasses followed Walter's progress for a moment, then he looked down again at the papers on his desk. Passing him—the shop extended another couple of yards beyond the desk and ended in more shelves of books—Walter saw that his body was proportionally as large and heavy as his face. The curve of his back looked mountainous under the fresh white shirt. The remains of a light-brown head of hair curled a little above his ears and curved around below the rather disgusting, shiny pink back of his head.

"Are you looking for anything in particular?" the man asked Walter, pulling himself around in his chair by gripping a corner of the desk. His heavy underlip hung a little.

"No, thank you. Do you mind if I just look around?"

"Not a bit." He turned back to his papers.

It was a civilized voice, Walter thought, not at all the voice he had expected from that body. Except that the man's face was intelligent, too, despite its ugliness. Walter felt his momentum beginning to stall. He was only a man whose wife had been killed, Walter thought, a man to whom a violent tragedy had happened. It struck him as absurd now that he had ever wondered if Melchior Kimmel had actually murdered his wife. Wouldn't the police have found out by now if it were true?

Walter stood facing a shelf that was labeled POETRY-METAPHYSICAL. The books were old, most of them scholarly-looking. Walter saw the law division and went toward it. He wanted to talk to the man again. Walter stared at the row of rotting volumes of Blackstone's *Commentaries*, a hodgepodge of torts, *New Jersey Civil Courts 1938*, *New York State Bar Journal 1945*, *American Law Reports 1933*, Moore's *Weight of Evidence*. Walter strolled back toward the man under the lamp.

"I wonder if you possibly have a book called *Men Who Stretch the Law*?" Walter asked. "I'm pretty sure of the title, but I'm not sure of the author. I think it's by Robert Miles."

"*Men Who Stretch the Law*?" the man repeated, getting up. "About how old is it?"

"About fifteen years, I think."

The man stopped at the law shelves and pointed a pen flashlight at the titles, went over them rapidly, then pulled the front row of books down with his forearm and looked at the books behind. The shelf was lighted, and there had been no need of the flash for the front row. Walter supposed that his sight was bad. The light over the desk was extremely strong.

"That wouldn't be by Marvin Cudahy, would it?"

Walter knew the name, but he was surprised that Kimmel knew it—a retired Chicago judge who had written a couple of obscure books on legal ethics. "I'm pretty sure it isn't Cudahy's," Walter said. "I don't know the author. I only know the title."

The man looked Walter over from his superior height, and Walter sensed or imagined a personal element in the inspection that rattled him a little, made him glance from the man's tiny pale brown eyes down to the front of the clean white shirt. "I can probably get it for you," Kimmel said. "A matter of a few weeks at most. Do you want to leave your name so I can notify you?"

"Thanks." He followed the man back to his desk. He felt suddenly shy about revealing his name, but when Kimmel waited with his pencil poised over the tablet, Walter said, "Stackhouse," and spelled it out as he always did. "Forty-nine Marlborough Road, Benedict, Long Island."

"Long Island," Kimmel murmured, writing quickly.

"You're Melchior Kimmel, aren't you?" Walter asked.

"Yes." The tawny eyes, reduced to absurd smallness by the thick glasses, looked straight at Walter.

"I seem to remember—your wife was killed not so long ago, wasn't she?"

"She was murdered, yes."

Walter nodded. "I don't remember reading anywhere that the murderer was ever found."

"No. They're still looking."

Walter thought he heard annoyance in Kimmel's tone. He imagined that Kimmel's body had stiffened, ever so slightly. Walter didn't know where to go from there. He wrung his driving gloves between his hands, and sought for a phrase to take leave on.

"Why? Did you know my wife?" Kimmel asked.

"Oh, no, I simply remembered the name—by accident."

"I see," he said in his precise, pleasant voice. His eyes did not leave Walter's face.

Walter looked at the broad, plump back of Kimmel's right hand. The light from over the desk fell on it, and Walter could see a spattering of freckles and no hair at all. Suddenly Walter felt sure that Kimmel knew he had come to the shop only to look at him, to assuage some sordid curiosity. Kimmel knew now that he lived in Long Island. Kimmel was standing very close to him. A sudden fear came over Walter that Kimmel might lift his thick slab of a hand and knock his head off his neck. "I hope they find the man who's guilty."

"Thank you," Kimmel said.

"I'm sorry I've intruded like this," Walter said awkwardly.

"But you haven't intruded!" Kimmel said with sudden heartiness. The bulging lips, shaped somewhat like an obese, horizontally divided heart, worked nervously. "Thank you for your good wishes."

Walter walked toward the front door, and Kimmel followed him closely, courteously. Walter felt suddenly easier, and yet in the last few seconds, actually at the moment Kimmel had protested that he had not intruded, Walter had felt that it was possible Kimmel could have killed his wife. It was not his physical brutishness, not the wariness in his eyes; it was the sudden overfriendliness. It even occurred to Walter that Kimmel had been relieved to know that he was only wishing him well, and that he was not a police detective. Walter turned at the door and without thinking held out his hand.

Kimmel took the hand, shook it with a surprisingly soft grip, and bowed a little.

"Good-bye," Walter said. "Thank you."

"Good-bye."

Walter crossed the street to his car. He looked back at the shop from the car, and saw Melchior Kimmel standing behind the glass of the front door, saw him raise his arm and pass his hand slowly over the naked top of his head, the gesture of one who relaxes after a period of tension. Walter saw him walk serenely back into the depths of his shop, bald head high and the long arms standing a little out from his huge body.

Melchior Kimmel sat down at his desk and stared into the cluttered cubbyholes. Another snooper, he thought. Only a more intelligent and better dressed one than most. Or had he *possibly* been a detective? Melchior Kimmel's tiny eyes nearly closed as he went over their conversation cautiously. No, the man had been too genuinely ill at ease, and besides, what had he tried to find out? Nothing. He'd had the feeling the man really was a lawyer—though he hadn't said he was. Kimmel reached for the tablet on which he had written the man's name and the book he wanted, tore off the yellow page and stuck it into the cubbyhole where he kept his outgoing matters. The gesture, as if it had started a machinery of habitual gestures, was followed by more picking up and putting away of papers, letters, various notebooks of all sizes into various cubbyholes of the desk in front of him that looked as complicated as some kind of switchboard. His heavy body rolled with his movements, and for a few moments his brain seemed to be concentrated in his fat arms and hands. Before he deposited one little brown notebook in its proper cubbyhole, he opened it to a page near the back and drew a short vertical line followed by the date and "see B-2489," which was the number on the next order page minus one. There were seven vertical lines now with dates beside them on the page, and three asterisks with dates. The three asterisks stood for police detectives, men whom he had been able to recognize as police detectives and who probably thought they had not been recognized. The rest were merely visitors. And Kimmel did not think the whole list of much importance.

He yawned, stretching his fat fists up, arching his strong back sensuously. Then he relaxed and leaned back in the armless, leather padded chair. He closed his eyes and let his head hang, supported a little on the fat below his jaw. But he did not doze. He was savoring the delicious sensations of his relaxing muscles, the laziness that flowed softly through his body and down his arms to his limp, bulbous finger ends. It had been a busy Saturday.

IO

IT WAS around nine when Walter got home. He had brought a dozen white chrysanthemums for Clara. She was sitting in the living room, going over some office papers that she had spread out on the sofa.

"Hello," he said. "Sorry I was late for dinner. I didn't even know whether you'd be here or not."

"Oh, that's quite all right."

"These are for you." He handed her the box.

She looked at the box, then up at him.

Walter's smile went away. "Do you want me to put them in a vase for you?" His voice was suddenly tense.

"Please do," she said coolly, as if the flowers had nothing to do with her.

Walter opened the box in the kitchen and filled a vase with water. He had even written a little card: "To my own Clara." He tore it up and dropped it in the empty flower box.

"How was Ellie?" Clara asked when he brought the flowers into the living room.

Walter did not answer. He put the vase on the coffee table, and took a cigarette from the box and lighted it.

"Why don't you spend the rest of the evening with her?"

That's a fine idea, Walter thought, but he kept his mouth closed and his teeth set. He went into the kitchen, washed his hands and face with soap at the sink, and dried them on a paper towel. Then he went down the hall to the front door. Clara was saying something else as he went out.

He looked around in the Three Brothers Tavern to see if Bill or Joel was there. He would have liked to have a drink with them. There was no one he knew. He waved hello to the barman, Ben, then went to the Manhattan telephone directory and looked for Ellie Briess' number. He saw an Ellen Briess and an Elspeth Briess. The Elspeth Briess address seemed more likely. Walter called it. The operator told him that the number had been changed. She gave him a number in Lennert, Long Island.

Ellie answered. She said she had just moved that day.

"What are you doing?" he asked. "Have you had dinner yet?"

"I haven't even thought about it. I had to stay at school to-day till four, and the moving men just dumped everything in the middle of the floor. Sorry, I don't think I can get away for dinner."

She sounded so pleasant, though, that Walter smiled. "Maybe I can help you," he said. "Can I come over? I'm not far away."

"Well—if you can stand a mess."

"What's the address?"

"Brookline Street, one eighty-seven. The bell's under Mays. M-a-y-s."

He rang the bell under Mays. When the release buzzer sounded, he thrust the door open and climbed the stairs two at a time, clutching the champagne bottle under his arm like a football. In his other arm he carried a bag from the delicatessen.

Ellie stood in an open door on the second floor. "Hello," she said. "Welcome."

Walter came to a nervous stop in front of her. He held out the paper bag. "I brought a few sandwiches."

"Thank you! Come on in—but I doubt if you'll find a place to sit down."

He came in. It was a single large room with two windows on the street side, and in back a hall that led to kitchen and bath. He glanced around at the clutter of suitcases and cardboard cartons. There were two violin cases, one battered and one new-looking. He followed her into the kitchen.

"And this," he said, handing her the champagne bottle. "It isn't cold. The refrigerator just happened to be broken in the Benedict liquor store tonight."

"Champagne? What's this in honor of?"

"The new apartment."

She held the champagne bottle as if she appreciated champagne. There was nothing that would serve as an ice bucket. Ellie got a bathtowel from one of the cartons in the living room and wrapped the bottle and two trays of ice cubes in the towel.

"Would you like a scotch while we wait for this?" she asked.
"Fine."

"And a sandwich? You've brought such nice things. Turkey sandwiches—and what's this?"

"Truffles."

"Truffles," she repeated.

"Do you like them?"

"I adore them." She took some plates out of newspaper wrapping. She was in moccasins and a blouse and skirt and she wore no make-up. "I'm very glad to have company. I don't like to pack or unpack unless I have a drink and it depresses me to drink alone."

"I'll help you drink and unpack, too. Want me to help you with any of this?"

"I want to forget it for a while." She offered him a plate and he took a sandwich from it.

They took their drinks and the plates into the living room, and, because there was no table, set the plates on the floor.

Ellie looked down at a stack of her music books. "Do you like Scarlatti?"

"Yes. On the piano. I have some—"

"That's fine, I play him on the violin."

Walter smiled a little. He set the suitcases down on the floor and they sat down on the sofa. He had the feeling he had been here many times before, and that in a few minutes, after they finished their drinks, they would start to make love, as they had done many times before. Ellie was telling him about a woman in New York named Irma Gartner, who was going to miss her because, Ellie said, she depended on her to change her music books at the library every two weeks. Irma Gartner was a cripple, about sixty-five years old, and she played the violin.

"She still plays well," Ellie said. "If she weren't a woman, she'd certainly be able to get a job in some string orchestra playing in a restaurant or somewhere, but no one would hire a woman at her age. It's too bad, isn't it?"

Walter tried to imagine Clara caring enough about someone to visit him or her out of friendship or pity; it was impossible. Ellie's shoulders looked soft under the white shirt, and he longed to put his arms around her. What if he did? Either she would respond or she wouldn't. Either she would respond or she would be very cool and it would be the last time he would see her. Walter thought: if he couldn't put his arm around her, he didn't want to torture himself by seeing her again, anyway. He put his arm on the back of the sofa, then lowered it around her shoulders. She glanced up at him, then laid her head against him. His desire crept, vinelike, down his body. She turned her head as he did and they kissed. It was a long kiss, but suddenly she twisted away from him and stood up.

She turned and looked at him from the middle of the room, smiling a wide, embarrassed smile at him. "How much farther is this going?"

He came toward her, but she looked a little frightened, or annoyed, and he stopped.

She walked slowly into the kitchen. Her body in the skirt and blouse looked very young to him, young in its pretense of indifference. She felt the champagne bottle.

"With ice in the glass, this should be all right," she said. "Do you mind ice in the glass?"

"No."

She looked at him with the shy, excited eyes again. "I'm not dressed for champagne. Can you wait ten minutes? Here're the glasses. I don't have anything but old-fashioned glasses." She handed them to him, then went into the living room and got something white out of the suitcases. Then she disappeared in the bathroom.

Walter heard the shower running. He put ice in the glasses and set them with the champagne bottle on a suitcase lid. The shower ran a long time, and he started to fix himself another scotch and then didn't.

Ellie came out in a thick white bathrobe, barefoot. "I ought to put on my best suit," she said, looking into a suitcase.

"Don't put on anything." The bathrobe was of terry cloth, and Walter thought suddenly, Clara hates terry cloth. "I wish you'd take that off," he said.

She ignored the remark completely, which for Walter was the most exciting reaction she could have had. "Open the bottle." She sat down on the floor beside the suitcase and leaned against the sofa.

Walter worked the cork out and poured it. They tasted it in silence. He had turned off the main light, and there was only a light from the kitchen. She had lovely feet, smooth and narrow and brown as her legs. They did not look as if they went with her hands. He poured more champagne. "Not bad, is it?"

"Not bad," she echoed. She leaned her head back against the sofa. "It's wonderful. There are times when I like disorder. Tonight's one of them."

He got up and spread a green blanket on the floor. "Isn't the floor getting hard?" he asked.

She lay on her stomach on the blanket, with her cheek down on her arm, looking up at him. He sat beside her on the blanket. The champagne seemed to go on forever, like the pitcher in the myth.

"Why don't you take off your clothes?" she asked.

He did, and then he untied the terry-cloth belt. She felt wonderfully soft, her breast against his hand as soft as milk. He was very slow and very careful not to hurt her on the floor that was still hard in spite of the blanket, but Ellie didn't seem to feel it, and then he forgot the floor. But he had a cool, rational moment when he wondered if anyone had ever made love to her as well as he. He felt they had been together many times before, and that for them it would never diminish, as long as they lived. And that Clara was a pale thing, compared to this.

He wanted to say, I love you. He said nothing.

She opened her eyes and looked at him.

He poured the last of the champagne, then lighted a cigarette to share with her.

"Do you know the time?" she asked.

He hated the fact that he was still wearing his wrist watch. "It's only five to two."

"Only!" She got up and went to the radio and turned it on, low. Then she came back and kneeled down in front of him. She kissed his forehead.

He watched her put her robe on. Then he put on his own clothes quickly. He didn't want to stay the night, yet he felt that she wanted him to. "When will I see you?" he asked.

She looked up at him, and he knew from her eyes that she was disappointed because he wanted to leave. "I don't want to plan anything."

"Can I do anything for you?"

"What do you mean?"

"Errands. For the new apartment."

Ellie laughed. She was leaning against the empty bookcase. He could see her brownish blue eyes in the dim light: they were smiling as if she adored him. "Maybe I'll never get it straight. I told you I liked disorder."

He walked slowly toward her. "I'll call you."

"Nice of you," she said.

Smiling, he took her by the wrist and pulled her toward him. They kissed, and he could have started all over again, but he opened the door. "Good night," he said, and went out. Going down the stairs, his body felt loose-jointed and young, as if every cell in it had somehow changed. He was smiling.

He woke Clara up as he went into the bedroom.

"Where've you been?" she asked sleepily.

"Drinking. With Bill Ireton." He didn't care if she found out he hadn't been with Bill. He didn't care if she found out he had been with Ellie.

Clara evidently went back to sleep, because she did not say anything more.

Walter called Ellie on Monday morning and asked if she could have dinner with him. He was going to tell Clara that he had a date with Jon in New York. He was not going to go home after work. But Ellie said that she had to practice her violin all that evening, absolutely had to, because of a new group of music appreciation selections for her class. Walter thought she sounded very cool. He felt that she had decided to break it off, and perhaps would never agree to see him again at all.

During his lunch hour Monday, Walter went into the Public Library and looked up the Kimmel story in the Newark newspapers for August. There was a picture of the body on the scene. The woman looked stocky and dark, but the face was averted and he could see very little except a bloodstained light dress, half covered with a blanket. He was most curious as to Kimmel's alibi. He found only one statement, repeated in various ways: "Melchior Kimmel stated that he was in Newark on the night of the crime, and had attended a movie from 8 to 10 P.M." Walter assumed that he had a witness to substantiate it, and that it had never been challenged.

But neither had the murderer ever been found. Walter looked over the Newark papers for several days following the murder. There were no further clues. Walter left the library feeling frustrated and rather angry.

II

"I'VE GOT to see you," Walter said. "Even if it's just a few minutes."

Ellie finally agreed.

Walter hurried to Lennert. It was only seven o'clock. Clara was out for dinner with the Philpotts, Claudia had told him. He hoped Ellie was free the whole evening. He heard her violin from the sidewalk below the house. He waited until she had played a phrase over three times, rang the bell, and heard her strike a loud chord. The release bell buzzed.

She was standing in the doorway of her apartment again. He started to kiss her, but she said: "Do you mind if we go out?"

"Of course not."

The apartment had completely changed: there was a rose-colored rug on the floor, some pictures were up, and the books were in the bookshelf. Only the stack of music books, still topped by Scarlatti, remained to remind him of the other evening. She came back from the closet with her coat.

He decided to take her to the Old Millhouse Inn near Huntington, because he was not likely to see anyone he knew there. In the car, she talked about her school. Walter felt she was worlds away from him, that she had not missed him at all.

They ordered martinis at their table. Walter would have preferred to drink in the more secluded bar, but the bar was taken over by a noisy group of men, either a club meeting or a stag party, carousing so loudly they could hear them from where they sat. Ellie had stopped talking. She seemed shy with him.

"I love you, Ellie," he said.

"No, you don't. I love you."

It hit him right in the heart, a sweet pain like an adolescent's. "Why do you say I don't?"

"Because I know. I'll never do again what I did the other night until you do love me. Maybe I only did it the other night to prove how strong I am."

"Oh, Ellie!" He frowned. "That's all very complicated. And very Russian."

"Well, I am half Russian." She smiled. "Shall I be very straightforward? You don't love me, but you're attracted to me because I'm different from your wife. You have troubles with your wife, so you come to me—don't you?" She spoke so softly he had to strain to hear her. "But I'm not so unwise as to have an affair with a married man—even if I am in love with him."

"Ellie, I could love you more than any woman on earth. I do love you!"

"But what are you going to do about it, I wonder? I don't think anything." There was no resentment in her tone. She said it like a simple statement of fact.

"How do you know?"

"Well, I don't. Perhaps I'm wrong."

It was her seriousness that stymied him, he realized. He realized that he didn't match it with any plans, any solution of his own, and perhaps not with any emotion, either. He suddenly saw himself objectively, as she must see him, and he felt ashamed.

"I don't know you and yet I think I know you—enough to love you," Ellie said. "I think you're basically decent. I think you're strong. And I think I fell in love with you the first time I saw you."

Walter wondered if he could say the same thing? That night of the party—

"I haven't had a very merry life," she went on. "My father drank. He died when I was sixteen. I had to support my mother, because my brother is about as useless as my father was. My mother named me Elspeth, because she thought it was a pretty name. It's the only thing I can think of that she ever got her way about—with my father. The only sure thing I ever found was music. I had two loves before—little ones, not like you." She smiled and she looked very young, younger than her voice. "I like sure things. I want a home. I want children."

"So do I," Walter said.

"And with a man I can look up to. I want something definite. It's just my luck I had to fall for you, isn't it?"

"I know exactly. I know all you're saying." Walter stared down at the brown wood of the table. "I never told you that I intend to get a divorce from my wife very soon. Of course I'm not getting on with her. That's obvious to everyone who comes in the house. I want to get a divorce as soon as it can be arranged." He did, but did he want to marry Ellie? He felt he couldn't definitely answer that yet, and it was that, he thought, that kept any more words from coming.

"When?" she asked.

"It's a question of a few weeks only. Then if we still like each other—still love each other—"

"I'll still love you in a few weeks. You see, it's you who're in doubt." She lighted a cigarette. "I don't think you'd better see me again until you know for sure."

"That I love you?"

"About the divorce."

"All right," Walter said.

"I love you too much—do you understand? I shouldn't even tell you that, should I? I love even being near you— geographically. And that's all I am now. But you'll never find me hanging around Marlborough Road."

He stared down at his lighter.

"Do you mind if I go home now? I can't talk any more— about anything else."

"All right," Walter said. He looked around for the waiter to get the check.

The men were still whooping it up in the bar as they went out.

It was only 9:15 when Walter got home, but Clara was in bed, reading. Walter asked her how the evening at the Philpotts' had been.

"I didn't see them," Clara said in the toneless voice she used at the start of a quarrel.

Walter looked at her. "You didn't go?"

"I saw your car in front of Ellie Briess' apartment tonight," she said.

"So you even know where she lives now," he said.

"I made it my business to find out."

Walter knew she must have kept a patient watch, because he hadn't stayed more than five minutes at Ellie's apartment, either time tonight. "What are you going to do about it? Why don't you divorce me for adultery?" Slowly he opened a fresh pack of cigarettes, but his heart was pounding with a kind of terror, because for the first time he was actually guilty of what she had accused him of.

"Because I think you'll get over it," she said. She was lying back on the pillow, but her head and shoulders had that rigid look, and her mouth was drawn in a straight line. She looked suddenly years older to Walter. She lifted her arm to him. "Darling—come here," she said in a voice made hideous to him by its pretense of affection.

He knew she wanted him to kiss her, to go even further. It had happened a couple of times before, since the hospital: cursing and accusing him by day, and at night trying to make it up, trying to bind him to her by making love to him. The one time Walter had responded, he had felt a horrible compulsion in her lovemaking that revolted him.

"Shall we have this out now? I want to. I can't wait."

"Have what out?"

"I'm getting a divorce, Clara. I'm not asking you this time, I'm telling you. And it's not because of Ellie, I'll tell you that, too."

"Six weeks ago you said you loved me."

"That was an error on my part."

"Do you want another corpse on your hands?"

"I am not playing nursemaid to you for the rest of your life—or mine. If you won't agree to a divorce, I'll go to Reno and get it."

"Reno!" she scoffed.

Walter stared at her. She probably didn't believe him, he thought. That was too bad.

12

Somewhere behind him, Ellie had aided and abetted him in it. Ellie was waiting not far away. The bus was lighted, and he could see the people getting off one by one, and there was Clara with something like a laprug over her arm, descending the steps. Walter approached her quickly.

"Clara?"

She did not look particularly surprised to see him.

"I have to talk to you," he said. "We left the bedroom in such a mess."

She murmured something that sounded reluctant, but she came with him.

He led her along the road. "Just a little farther, where we can talk in privacy," he said.

They approached the dense thicket he had chosen.

"We shouldn't go too far away. The bus leaves in ten minutes," Clara said, though not at all anxiously.

Walter sprang at her. He had both hands around her neck. He dragged her into the underbrush, but he had to exert all his strength because she had become strangely heavy, heavier even than a man, and she was clinging hard to the bushes with her hands. Walter tugged at her. He kept his hands on her throat so she could not cry out. Her throat began to feel hard and twisted, like a thick rope. He began to fear that he couldn't kill her. And then he realized she had stopped struggling. She was dead. He took his hands away from her ropy neck. He stood up and covered her with the laprug she had been carrying. Jeff was there, barking and prancing as merrily as ever, and when Walter stepped out of the woods, Jeff followed him.

And there was Ellie, waiting for him on the road exactly where she had said she would be. Walter nodded to her as a sign it was all over, and Ellie smiled with relief. Ellie took his arm and looked up at him with admiration. Ellie was just about to say something to him, when there was an explosion right in front of them, like a bomb or a car wreck, and a cloud of gray smoke blotted out everything.

"The bridge is out!" Walter said. "We can't go any farther!"

But Ellie kept on going. He tried to hold her back. She went on without him.

Walter found himself face downward, trying to push himself up with his arms. He turned his groggy, ringing head. Was that Ellie lying there? He stared until Clara's dark head and small face came dimly into focus. She was lying with her face toward him.

"What were you dreaming?" she asked in a calm, alert voice, as if she had been awake for minutes.

Walter felt transparent. "Nothing. A bad dream."

"About what?"

"About—I don't remember." He sank down on the bed again, and turned his head from her. Had he talked out loud? He lay rigid, waiting for her to say something else, and when she didn't, listened for the faint sound of her breathing that would mean she was asleep. He didn't hear that, either. He felt a drop of sweat run down the groove in the small of his back. He gripped the cool wood of the bedstead and twisted it in his sweaty hands.

13

HE CALLED Ellie from the Three Brothers Tavern.

"Are you alone?" he asked. She didn't sound as if she were alone.

"No, I've got a friend here," she said softly.

"Pete?"

"No, a girl."

Walter imagined her standing at the telephone in the hall, her back turned to the doorless living room. "I wanted to tell you that I'm going to Reno next Saturday. I'll be gone six weeks. It's the only way I can get it." He waited, but she said nothing at all. Walter smiled. "How are you, darling?"

"I'm all right."

"Do you ever think of me?"

"Yes."

"I love you," Walter said.

They listened to each other's silence.

"If you still feel that way in a couple of months, I'll be here."

"I will," he said, and hung up.

Clara met him at the front door. "Did you hear what happened? I've had a wreck. My car is ruined!"

Walter dropped his briefcase on the hall table. He looked at her trembling body. He saw no sign of any injury. He put his arm around her shoulder and guided her toward the sofa in the living room. It was the first time he had touched her in days.

She told him a truck had hit her, backing out of a side road in some woods near Oyster Bay. She hadn't been going more than twenty-five miles an hour, but she hadn't seen the truck for the trees, and the truck hadn't made a sound because it had been coasting backward down a slope.

"The car's insured," Walter said. He was pouring a drink for her. "Just how bad is it?"

"The whole front end is smashed. It nearly turned me over!" She jerked her hand away from Jeff's solicitous kisses, then reached down and patted him nervously.

Walter handed her the brandy. "Drink this. It'll calm you down."

"I don't want to be calmed down!" she cried and got up. She ran upstairs, holding a kleenex to her nose.

Walter fixed an iceless scotch and soda for himself. His own hand was shaking as he lifted it. He could imagine the impact on Clara. She had always prided herself on never having had an accident. Walter carried his drink upstairs. Clara was in the bedroom, half-reclining on the bed, still weeping.

"Everybody runs into an accident once," he said. "You shouldn't let it throw you. The Philpotts can let you have a car with a driver, can't they? You probably shouldn't drive for a few days."

"You don't have to pretend you care how I feel! Why don't you just stay out this evening and go to see Ellie? You don't have to come home to a woman you hate!"

Walter set his teeth and went out again, downstairs. He knew Clara thought he was with Ellie every evening he spent away from the house. He ought to move now, he thought. But the real truth was, he was afraid Clara would do something like set the house on fire and burn herself up in it. He wouldn't put that past her at all. So he was guarding her, he supposed. And becoming as jittery as she in the process.

Claudia came into the room. "Are you and Mrs. Stackhouse ready for your dinner, Mr. Stackhouse?"

That wasn't the way she usually announced dinner. Walter knew she had heard Clara shouting upstairs. "Yes, Claudia. I'll go and call her."

14

THE FRONT door chime sounded while they were at breakfast. Claudia was in the kitchen. Walter got up. It was a telegram for Clara. He had a feeling it was from her mother.

Clara read it quickly. "My mother's dying," she said. "This is from the doctor."

Walter picked up the telegram. Her mother had had another stroke and was not expected to live more than thirty-six hours. "You'd better catch a plane," he said.

Clara pushed her chair back and stood up. "You know I won't fly."

Walter knew. Clara was afraid of flying. "But you're going, at least." Walter followed her into the hall. She had to leave the house very early that morning in order to be somewhere by nine o'clock.

"Of course. I've got to settle some financial matters that she's been neglecting all these years," Clara said in an annoyed voice. She collected some papers from the hall table and put them into the cardboard folder she always carried.

"Too bad your car's laid up," Walter said.

"Yes. It makes the whole thing more expensive."

Walter smiled a little. "Do you want to take my car?"

"You'll need it."

"Only today and tomorrow. By Saturday I won't need it." Walter was flying to Nevada on Saturday morning.

"You keep your car," she said.

Walter drew on his cigarette. "What time do you think you'll leave?"

"Late this afternoon. There's some business in the office I have to take care of, mother or not."

"I'll try to call you," Walter said. "What time can I get you in?"

"What for?"

"To find out when you're leaving! Maybe I can help you in some way!" he said impatiently. He was vexed with himself. Why in hell should he help her?

"Well, if you must, call me around twelve." She glanced out

the window as the big black Packard of the Philpotts came into view. "There's Roger. I've got to go. Claudia! Would you lay out some things on the bed for me to pack? My gray dress and the green suit. I'll be back around three or four." Then she was gone.

Walter called Clara at twelve in her office. Clara said she had decided to go by bus, and that she would be leaving from the 34th Street terminal at 5:30.

"*Bus*!" Walter said. "You'll get there exhausted, Clara. It'll take you hours."

"It's only five hours to Harrisburg. The trains don't fit my schedule. I've got to go, Walter. I have a lunch in Locust Valley at twelve-thirty. Good-bye."

Walter put the telephone down angrily. He loosened his collar and heard the button give and hop twice on the cork floor. He'd be there to see her off, he supposed, but he rebelled against doing her that courtesy. He really wanted to find out some things that he had planned to ask her before Saturday. What she was going to do with the house, for instance. The house was hers, of course. And why should he care what she did, anyway? Was there ever a woman better able to take care of herself?

He slid his tie up to close his collar, and dragged a comb through his hair. Then he rang for Joan. He had some letters to send out. Joan didn't answer, and Walter realized suddenly that it was her lunch hour. He started to do the letters himself, and then Joan came in, carrying two paper bags.

"I brought you some lunch," she said, "because I don't think you'd eat anything if I didn't. It's my good deed for to-day."

"Well, thanks," Walter said, surprised. It wasn't like Joan to do anything as personal as this for him. He reached in his pocket. "Let me pay you for it."

"No, it's my treat." She pulled out a sandwich and a container of coffee and put them on his desk. "Mr. Stackhouse, I don't know what's happening around here—between you and Mr. Cross, but I just wanted to say, if you're thinking of leaving or going into another office, I hope you can arrange for me to stay on with you. The salary wouldn't matter."

It touched Walter to the point of self-consciousness. The

office had agreed too readily to his taking a six-week leave. Walter imagined that Cross was going to inform him sometime during those six weeks that he needn't come back at all. Cross had implied that he knew that he and Jensen planned to leave the firm, and Cross had also told him, yesterday, that he was not satisfied with his work. "There might be a change," Walter said. "In fact I hope there is. If I don't come back, Joan, I'll keep in touch with you."

"Fine." Joan's round face smiled.

"But don't say a word around the office, please."

"Oh, I won't. And I hope you take care of yourself, Mr. Stackhouse."

Walter smiled. "Thanks."

As soon as Dick got back from his lunch hour, Walter went in to ask him how much he thought Cross knew about their plans. Dick said only that Cross had told him that he wasn't satisfied with Walter's work, that he thought he lacked enthusiasm. Dick told Walter to pull himself together and work for the remainder of the time they would be with the firm.

"I don't care if I never see it again after tomorrow," Walter said.

Dick frowned at him.

Walter went out and closed the door.

He was at the bus terminal at 5:15. He spotted Clara at once, bustling around the newsstand. She was in her new closely fitting green tweed suit.

"One thing more," she said as soon as he came up. "The car's ready tomorrow, and *don't* pay them extra for the re-chroming job on the front bumper. That was included in the first estimate. The foreman there's trying to say it wasn't."

Walter picked up her blue suitcase. She had to go to a window to ask something. Walter waited, staring at her. "How long do you think you'll be in Harrisburg?" he asked when she came back.

"Oh, I should be back Saturday. Or tomorrow evening." She looked up at him. Her face was animated and smiling, but there was a shine of tears in her eyes that startled Walter.

"And if she dies?" Walter asked. "Aren't you going to stay for the funeral?"

"No." Clara bent over, balancing herself on one small high-heeled shoe, and removed a tiny piece of paper that had stuck to the bottom of the other heel. She put out her hand automatically for Walter to support her, and he took it.

A strange sensation went through him at the touch of her fingers, a start of pleasure, of hatred, of a kind of hopeless tenderness that Walter crushed as soon as his mind recognized it. He had a sudden desire to embrace her hard at this last minute, then to fling her away from him.

"And this," she said, handing him a folded piece of paper from her jacket pocket. "Two people I'm supposed to call tomorrow. Just call Mrs. Philpott and tell her the numbers. She'll know what to do." She looked down as she drew one of her black kid gloves on, and Walter saw a tear drop on the glove.

He watched her anxiously, wondering if she were really this upset about her mother, or if it were something else. "Call me when you get there. Call me any time."

"Aren't you looking forward to an extra forty-eight hours without me? What are you gritting your teeth about? Why don't you take Ellie with you to Reno?" She looked at him sharply, with the evil, forced smile, as if her witch's mind had it all planned, as if she knew he would never be with Ellie, that there would never be happiness for him on earth.

Walter followed her with her suitcase as she walked away toward the buses. He squeezed the handle of the suitcase and wished he had the nerve to crash it over her head. He set the suitcase down beside the other luggage that was going aboard the New York–Pittsburgh bus.

"You don't look at all happy," she told him brightly.

Walter looked down at her with a faint smile on his lips, letting it seep into him. If he hated her enough, he thought— "Where does your bus stop?" he asked suddenly.

"Stop? I don't know. Probably only at Allentown." She glanced around her, still with the crazy, fixed smile. "I think I can get on now."

She climbed the steps of the bus. Walter watched her move down the aisle, looking for her seat, and take a seat toward the back that was not beside a window. She looked out, smiling, and waved to him. Walter lifted his hand a little. He looked at his watch. Five minutes yet before the bus was to leave. He turned abruptly and walked back into the waiting room. He suddenly wanted a drink, but he kept on going past the bar and out.

He had put his car in a parking lot a couple of blocks west of the terminal. He drove out and turned east. The street was jammed with cars. A bus turned into the avenue, going south. He could not see if it was Clara's bus or not. Calmly he inched forward in the heavy traffic, got stuck again, and lighted a cigarette. The New York–Pittsburgh bus turned into Tenth Avenue right in front of him, and he even saw Clara for an instant.

When the light changed, Walter turned right and followed the bus. He kept going downtown, toward the Holland Tunnel. Then he followed it through the tunnel.

I'll stop in Newark and drive around and come back, he thought. He thought of Melchior Kimmel in Newark. Perhaps he would drive once past the store. It might still be open. His book might have arrived.

But he kept on following the loaf-shaped gray body of the bus through Newark. He was frantic once when he was caught by a red light and the bus disappeared for a few moments around a corner.

I'll light a cigarette, and when it's finished, I'll turn around, Walter thought.

Finally the bus took one of the long commercial streets out of town, and Walter stayed behind it.

What was Clara thinking about, he wondered. Money? She was going to inherit about fifty thousand dollars, after taxes, if her mother died. That should put her in a better humor. Himself and Ellie? Was Clara possibly weeping? Or was she reading the *World-Telegram* and thinking of none of these things? He imagined her putting her newspaper down, leaning her head back as she sometimes did for a minute to rest her eyes. He imagined his hands closing around her small throat.

What kind of courage did it take to commit a murder? What degree of hatred? Did he have enough? Not simply hatred, he knew, but a particular tangle of forces of which hatred was only one. And a kind of madness. He thought he was entirely too rational. At least at this moment. If it had been a moment like some, when he had wanted to strike her. But he had never struck her. He was always too rational. Even now when he was following her on a bus, and the conditions were ideal. It was like the dream he had had.

He'd go no farther than the first rest stop, he thought. He would go up to Clara and say what he had said in the dream. What Melchior Kimmel might have said. *Clara, I have to talk to you. Come with me.* Then he would only walk with her a few yards, and the bitter words spoken at the bus terminal would repeat themselves; she would make a taunt about Ellie, call him a fool for driving all this distance out of his way, and he would walk back to the bus with her, with his nerves at the cracking point. Walter's foot kicked out involuntarily, and the car shot forward. He pressed the gas pedal down to the floor, and eased up only when he came very close to a car in front of him.

He tried to imagine what would happen if he did do it. First, he would have no alibi. And there was the danger that he would be seen by somebody at the bus stop, that Clara's "Walter!" would be heard the instant she saw him, that people would remember both of them, walking off on the highway.

And Ellie would despise him.

He kept on, speeding after the fleeing bus.

He thought of the first day he had met Clara, the day of the lunch in San Francisco with his old college friend, Hal Schepps. Hal had brought Clara along. By accident, Hal had said later, and it was true, but Walter hadn't known it then. Walter could still remember the lift in his chest the instant he had seen Clara. Like love at first sight. Later, Clara had said the same thing about herself. Walter could still remember his anxiety when he had called up Hal that afternoon. He had been afraid that Clara and Hal were engaged, or in love. Hal had assured him they weren't. *But be careful*, Hal had said, *she's got a mind of her own. She's a Jonah—for loving and leaving.* But Walter remembered how pleasant she had been, how irresistible those first weeks. She had told Walter about two men who had been in love with her before. She had had an affair with each of them for about a year, and they had wanted to marry her, but she had refused. Walter was sure, from what Clara had told him, that both men had been on the weak side. Clara liked weak men, she told him, but she didn't want to marry them. Walter suspected that Clara considered him the weakest of all, and that was why she had married him. It was not a pleasant suspicion.

Railroad tracks hit the bottom of his car like a series of explosions, and Walter's head bobbed as the car leveled off. The bus was fast. His watch said twenty of six. Walter put it to his ear. It had stopped. He gripped the wheel with his left hand and set the watch at his best guess, 7:05, and wound it. There should be a rest stop in about half an hour, he thought.

The road climbed and curved. Walter had to slow down as the bus shifted gears for the hill. Far away on the left, Walter saw the lights of a town. He did not know where he was.

Then the bus slowed on the crest of a hill, and Walter slowed. He saw the bus turn abruptly left, and Walter tensed anxiously because the bus looked as if it were going to keep on rolling and go off a cliff. The long body of the bus disappeared behind a thick blackness.

Walter drove on up the hill. He saw that the blackness was a clump of trees, and that the bus had pulled into a crescent-shaped area in front of a roadhouse. Walter drove several yards past the roadhouse, and pulled over at the edge of the highway and cut out his lights. He got out and started walking back toward the roadhouse. The crescent area was lighted by a neon sign over the restaurant that flashed alternately red and lavender. He looked for Clara's small quick figure among the people who straggled from the bus. He didn't see her. He looked into the bus as he walked closer. She was already off it.

Walter opened the glass door of the restaurant and went in, glancing around at the counter and the tables. He didn't see her anywhere. He had the feeling that he was playing a part on a stage, and playing it convincingly—an anxious husband, searching for his wife whom he had been following in order to murder her. His hands would close around her throat in a few minutes, but he would not kill her because it was only a play. He'd pretend. A mock murder.

Walter watched the door of the ladies' room. He only took his eyes from it in order to look at the glass door where a few people were still coming in. Walter looked down the long counter again and then over the tables, more carefully.

He went out and circled the bus, then came back and stood near the end of the counter, only a couple of yards from the ladies' room. By the clock over the door, he set his watch at 7:29. He had not been far off.

"How much time have we at this stop?" Walter asked a man sitting at the counter.

"Fifteen minutes," the man said.

Walter walked a few tense steps toward the door, then turned back. He estimated that about seven minutes had passed. The ladies' room was the most likely place. On the other hand, Clara didn't use public toilets unless she absolutely had to. She hated them. Walter turned abruptly and looked straight into the face of the man whom he had questioned before. The man looked away before Walter did. Walter kept going slowly toward the front door. There was a mirror along one entire wall, but Walter did not dare look at himself. He only relaxed deliberately the frown that he knew put a heavy crease between his eyebrows, the frown that often made strangers stare at him.

Walter walked quickly toward the people standing around the bus. Clara was not there. He stood on tiptoe and looked into the bus. It was about a third full. Could it be the wrong bus? But there was the NEW YORK–PITTSBURGH sign on the front. Would there be two buses on the same schedule?

Walter's fingers worked in the pockets of his jacket. He had shredded a book of matches, and he flung the frazzled mess out of his pocket onto the ground. He waited, circling the bus slowly. The fifteen minutes should be about up. He turned and collided with someone.

"Sorry!"

"Sorry!" the woman's parrotlike voice said, and she went on.

Walter felt sweat break out suddenly all over his body. Now he saw the bus driver coming out of the restaurant. The bus was nearly full. Walter strained to see into the darkness of the highway at both sides of the crescent. But it wasn't like Clara to take a walk. He looked back at the lighted doorway of the restaurant. It was empty. Above it, the script-written *Harry's Rainbow Grill* flashed lavender, then red.

The bus started its motor. Walter watched the driver walk down the aisle, his hand moving as he counted passengers. Then the driver went to the front again and stooped, looking out the door.

"We're waiting for a passenger," Walter heard the driver say.

Walter was sure it was Clara. He clenched his hands in his

pockets. He saw the driver walk into the restaurant, yell something he couldn't hear, then come out again.

The driver helped a small plump woman up the steps of the bus. "Do you know if anybody else's still in the ladies' room?" the driver asked her.

"Didn't see anybody," the woman said.

Walter stood where he could see the dark edges of the highway, the restaurant door, and the bus door. The motor of the bus roared louder, shaking the ground under Walter. Then it rolled backward, forward, and curved toward the highway. Walter set his teeth to keep from yelling. He went into the restaurant, walked to the door of the ladies' room, and started to yank it open and shout her name. But he didn't. He walked out of the restaurant again, frowning.

The only explanation he could think of was that she had gotten out in Newark at one of the red lights. But she wouldn't have been able to get her suitcase off at a red light. And hadn't the bus driver been looking for her just now? Who else could have been missing but Clara? On the highway, Walter looked in both directions and saw no one. Then he ran down the highway toward his car. It felt good to run, though he skidded on gravel and fell when he tried to stop. It scratched his palm, but he did not think it had torn his trousers. He still looked for her, insanely, on the highway as he drove back. Then he stopped looking and he began to drive fast.

15

WALTER GOT home a little after eleven. The house had no light. He went upstairs and found the bedroom empty. He went downstairs, still half expecting to see Clara's suitcase, or some sign of her in the living room. He lighted a cigarette and forced himself to stay seated on the sofa for a few moments, while he waited for the telephone call that would explain where she was. The telephone was silent.

He dialed Ellie's number. There was no answer.

Walter got into his car and headed for Lennert. He should have had a brandy, he thought. He felt jumpy, on guard, against what he didn't know. He felt guilty, as if he had killed her, and his tired mind traced back to the moments of waiting around the bus. He saw himself walking with Clara by some thick trees at the side of the road. Walter moved his head from side to side, involuntarily, as if he were dodging something. It hadn't happened. He was positive. But just then the road began to wobble before his eyes, and he gripped the wheel hard. Lights skidded and blurred on the black road. Then he realized that it was raining.

Ellie's windows were dark. He did not see her car in the street or in the vacant lot by her building. He rang the bell hopefully. No answer.

Walter drove to a bar a few streets away and ordered a Martell. He spent as much time as he could drinking it, then he went back to Ellie's house. It was still dark, and still the bell did not answer. He went back to the bar.

"What's the matter?" the barman asked him. "Got somebody in the hospital?"

"What?"

"Thought you might have somebody in the hospital." The barman grabbed a glass and began polishing it. "You know—hospital down the street here."

"I didn't know," Walter said. "No, nobody in the hospital." He felt his teeth were about to start chattering, despite the soothing brandies.

Walter tried Ellie's doorbell again at 12:30. Just as he was walking away, her car turned into the street and his heart jumped high in his chest. Ellie was not driving. Walter saw Pete Slotnikoff behind the wheel.

"Hello, Mr. Stackhouse!" Peter said with a happy smile.

"Hello!" Walter called back.

"We've just come from Gordon's," Ellie said as she got out. "We were expecting you all evening."

Walter remembered: Gordon had called a few days ago and invited him and Clara to a cocktail party. "I couldn't make it."

"I'd better take off, Ellie. I've only got about seven minutes," Peter said. "I'll put the car right at the right of the news kiosk."

"Right," Ellie said. "It was nice seeing you, Pete." She gave his hand a pat on the windowsill of the car, a nice platonic pat, Walter thought. "Good night."

Peter drove off.

Walter wondered suddenly if Pete suspected he was having an affair with Ellie, if that was why he had driven off so soon, or if he really did have a train to catch? Walter and Ellie looked at each other. He had not seen her in nearly two weeks.

"Anything the matter?" she asked.

"I just wanted to see you before I leave. Can we go upstairs?"

Her eyes were smiling, but he could feel the distance she kept from him. "All right." She turned and went directly to the door with her key.

They climbed the stairs quietly, and went into her apartment.

"A pity you didn't come to Gordon's," Ellie said. "Jon was there, too."

"I really forgot all about it."

"Don't you want to sit down?"

Walter sat down uneasily. "Clara left for Harrisburg tonight to see her mother. Her mother's very ill. I think she may die."

"Oh. That's bad news," Ellie said.

"It doesn't change my plans, of course. I'll still be leaving Saturday."

Ellie sat down in the armchair. "You're worried about Clara?"

"No. Actually she isn't upset about her mother at all. She's not very close to her mother." Walter rubbed his ankle between his hands. "Could I have a drink, Ellie?"

"Of course!" She got up to make it. "Water or soda?"

"A little water, please, and no ice." He got up and picked up her violin from the long end-table at the foot of the sofa. It felt absolutely weightless in his hand. He held it to the light and read, written inside below the strings: *Raffaele Gagliano, Napoli 1821.* He put the violin down and went into the kitchen, corked the scotch bottle that was standing on the drainboard. Ellie turned to him with his drink. He took it and caught her to him with his other arm, and kissed her, a long desperate kiss, but it did not make him feel what he had felt before with her. Even with her arms tight about his neck. He thought suddenly: suppose he was not in love with her and never could be? Suppose in another month he would be as repelled by the forthrightness, the shiny nose, the terry cloth as he had been attracted by them a month ago? But Ellie wasn't the main reason for the divorce, he reminded himself. If he had to tell Ellie that he would never marry her, he would only feel asinine because he had said he would. He released her and turned into the living room with his drink. He felt that Ellie was thinking he could spend the night. He felt she expected him to ask to.

"Is something the matter?" Ellie asked. "What's worrying you?"

He had thought, waiting for Ellie tonight, that he might tell her about following the bus. Now he felt afraid to. "Nothing really."

"Is everything all right at the office? They don't mind your going away for six weeks?"

"They mind, but I don't care. Dick Jensen and I might be out by the middle of December. Dick and I are planning to start an office of our own. A small claims office. So if the office decides to fire me, I wouldn't mind at all. As it is, they've just given me a leave without pay."

"What kind of a small claims office?"

"Just for individuals. No corporation law at all. Drunken driving, dispossessed tenants and all that." It surprised Walter that he hadn't told her about it before this.

"That's a big change," Ellie said.

"Yes."

"I've got to make a phone call before it gets any later."

Walter listened to her talking to the woman named Virginia, a woman who also taught at the school, Walter remembered. Ellie arranged a time for Virginia to pick her up tomorrow morning, because her car was parked at the railroad station.

"Do you see Pete very often?" Walter asked when she was through talking.

"No, I don't. He can't come out so easily without a car." Ellie sat down again and looked at him. "I don't think he has any serious interest in me at all, if you're thinking of that."

Walter smiled at her honesty. She was sitting half turned in the chair, her arm along its back, and her figure looked long and graceful and full of repose. He remembered he had loved her repose and her silences that were so different from Clara. Now he felt uneasy. He went to her and knelt down, and circled her body with his arm. He kissed her skin in the V of her dress, her throat, then her lips. He felt her body relax under his arm.

"Do you want to stay tonight?" she asked.

He stood up slowly, touched her forehead with his palm, and the crisp brown hair above it. "I'd rather wait."

She looked up at him, but she did not look disappointed or annoyed, he thought.

"I may not see you again until I get back, Ellie. Clara might be back tomorrow night, just might."

She stood up, too. "All right. And now you're off?"

"Yes." He went to the door, but he turned and embraced her again and kissed her hard on the lips.

"I love you, Walter."

"I love you," he said.

"I SURE hope it isn't one of them *agony* deaths," Claudia said. "Whether you likes your mother or not, it isn't nice to see anybody in agony, and whatever Mrs. Stackhouse acts like, she's not prepared to watch something like that."

"No, she's not." Walter watched Claudia's slim brown hands clearing away his breakfast dishes. "I'm going to call her this morning," he said. He got up from the table. He wanted to call Harrisburg now, but he didn't want to talk in front of Claudia.

"May I ask if you're in for dinner tonight, Mr. Stackhouse?"

"I don't know. There's a chance Mrs. Stackhouse may be back. But it's not worth your coming. Take the evening off again." He picked up his jacket from a chair. Claudia was looking at him. He knew she was about to say something about his not eating if she weren't here to cook. He hurried to the front door. "See you in the morning, Claudia. I'm here until eleven tomorrow morning."

Walter put in a call to Harrisburg as soon as he got to the office. A woman answered and said she was Mrs. Haveman's nurse.

"Is Mrs. Stackhouse there?" Walter asked.

"No, she's not. We expected her last night. Who is this?"

"This is Walter Stackhouse."

"Where's Clara?"

"I don't know," Walter said desperately. "I put her on the bus yesterday at five-thirty. She should have got there last night. You haven't heard a word?"

"No, we haven't, and the doctor doesn't think Mrs. Haveman is going to live more than a few hours."

"Will you take my number? Montague five, seven nine three eight. Have Mrs. Stackhouse call me as soon as she arrives, will you?"

Walter called up the Knightsbridge Brokerage. He spoke to Mrs. Philpott and asked if she had had any messages from Clara since the day before, at 5:30.

"No. I wasn't expecting any. Have you heard how her mother is?"

"I don't know where *Clara* is," Walter said. "I've called Harrisburg and she hasn't arrived yet. She should have been there around eleven last night."

"Good gracious! Do you suppose the bus had an accident?"

"I'd have been notified by now."

"Well, if you don't hear anything this morning, I'd suggest you tell the police."

Mrs. Philpott's thin but very wise voice had a calming effect. "I think I will. Thanks, Mrs. Philpott."

Walter had a conference at ten, and it was twelve when the conference adjourned. He went directly to his office to telephone the police, but Joan called to him from her office next door and said that the Philadelphia Police Department had telephoned fifteen minutes ago. They had left a number for him to call.

"Call it now," Walter said. He felt suddenly that Clara was dead, that her body had been picked up, bruised and knifed, in some woods.

"Mr. Stackhouse?" said a drawling voice. "This is Captain Millard, Twelfth Precinct, Philadelphia. The body of a woman tentatively identified as Clara Stackhouse was found this morning at the bottom of a cliff near Allentown. We'd like you to come to the Allentown morgue as soon as possible to confirm the identity."

THERE WAS no doubt in the world. Walter had only to see the left foot in the tattered stocking to know. The officer pulled the sheet back as far as her hips. The torn skirt was half black with blood.

"Can you tell?"

"Let me see the rest."

The officer pulled the sheet all the way back.

Walter shut his eyes at the sight of her crushed head, opened his eyes and looked at the arm that lay across her body in a semblance of naturalness but which looked shattered and limp.

"Her suitcase is in here," the officer said. "It was found aboard the bus. Will you come in here? We'd like you to answer some questions."

Walter took a grip on the door jamb as he went through and held to it a minute. He had seen dead bodies before, bombed bodies in the Pacific, and they had made him vomit. This was worse. Dimly, he saw the dark figure of the police officer rounding his desk, solid as a bull. Walter plunged his head down to keep from fainting. There was a nauseating smell of disinfectant. He raised up again, rather than be sick. He saw the officer motion to a chair, and Walter walked obediently to it and sat down.

"Her full name, please?" the man at the desk asked.

"Clara Haveman Stackhouse." Walter spelled the names.

"Age?"

"Thirty."

"Birthplace?"

"Harrisburg, Pennsylvania."

"Any children?"

"No."

"Nearest relative?"

Walter gave her mother's name and address in Harrisburg. He watched the man calmly putting checks here and there on a form as if he did this every day. "Have you got the man?" Walter asked.

"The man?" The officer looked up.

"The man who did it," Walter said.

The officer rubbed his nose. "The cause of the death is presumed suicide, Mr. Stackhouse, unless otherwise proven. Her body was found at the bottom of a cliff."

It hadn't occurred to Walter. He didn't believe it. "How do you know she wasn't pushed off?"

"That isn't the concern of this department. There'll be an official autopsy, of course."

Walter stood up. "I think somebody ought to show some interest in whether she jumped or was pushed. I want to know!"

"All right, you can talk to him," the man replied, nodding at the corner behind Walter.

Walter looked around and saw a man he had not noticed before, a young man in civilian clothes who pulled himself up from a chair and came toward Walter with a faint smile on his face.

"How do you do?" he said. "I'm Lieutenant Lawrence Corby of the Philadelphia Homicide Squad."

"How do you do?" Walter murmured.

"When did you see your wife last, Mr. Stackhouse?"

"Yesterday. Five-thirty at the bus terminal in New York."

"Did you have any reason to think your wife would commit suicide?"

"No, she—" Walter stopped. He remembered her tears at the bus terminal. "It might be possible," he said quickly. "Barely, I suppose. She was upset."

"I saw the cliff today," the young man said. "It's not likely that she fell off. The cliff isn't easy to get at and it slopes at the top for about thirty feet, and then drops." He illustrated with a movement of his hand. "Nobody's going to keep walking down there by accident. The cliff's by a roadhouse restaurant, and nothing very violent could have gone on there without somebody hearing it."

Walter hadn't thought until now that the cliff had been right *there*. Now he remembered the high land the restaurant had sat on, the blackness all around that suggested a steep drop beyond. He tried to imagine Clara rushing straight from the bus around the side of the restaurant, plunging down. He really couldn't. And when could she have done it? "But I doubt very much if she'd have taken this method of killing herself. It isn't like her. But she did try to kill herself with sleeping pills about a month ago. I think suicide was on her mind." He realized he was talking in circles. He looked at the stranger in front of him. The incongruity of the faint, polite-looking smile on his face held Walter's eyes. "But I'm not at all sure of suicide," Walter said. "I hope somebody's going to make some investigations."

"We will," Corby said.

The man at the desk said, "Here's her jewelry. Will you sign for it? One earring's missing." He pushed the heavy gold chain bracelet, the two rings, a pearl earring toward him in a heap, as Walter had often seen them lying on the dressing table at home.

Walter scrawled his name on the line. Then he put the jewelry in his overcoat pocket.

"Before you go, I'd like to ask you the usual question." The young lieutenant's small, eager blue eyes had been watching him. "Did she have any enemies that you know of?"

"No," Walter said. Then his mind flitted over the people who didn't like her, the people she had antagonized since she had begun working. "Certainly no one who would have killed her." Walter looked at the young man with more interest. At least he was going to ask a few questions, make some kind of an effort. He was no more than twenty-five or twenty-six, Walter thought, but he looked intelligent and efficient.

Lieutenant Corby sat down on a corner of the police officer's desk and folded his arms. "You went home after you left your wife at the terminal?"

Walter hesitated just a moment. "Yes. Not directly home. I was trying to reach a friend. In Long Island. I drove around for quite a while."

"Did you reach the friend?"

"Yes."

"Who was the friend?"

Walter hesitated again. "Ellie Briess. A woman who lives in Lennert. You can—" Walter stopped.

Lieutenant Corby nodded. "I might take her address."

Walter gave it, and her telephone number. He watched the lieutenant write it in a limp brown-covered tablet that he had taken from his pocket.

"Would you like to see the cliff yourself?" Lieutenant Corby asked.

Walter saw the big restaurant again, the garish lights. He thought suddenly, Clara knew the road: she had driven it often from Long Island to Harrisburg and back. She probably knew the cliff. "No, I don't think I want to see it."

"I just thought you might."

"No," Walter said, shaking his head. He watched the lieutenant's pencil moving again on the tablet. Walter saw himself seizing Clara by the throat, pulling her down the cliff, saw both of them plunging off, down to the sharp pointed rocks and brush below. He closed his eyes and when he opened them the young lieutenant was looking at him.

"Let's wait and see what the autopsy reveals," Corby said casually. "You don't entirely rule out the possibility of suicide, do you?"

The question sounded very unprofessional to Walter. "No, I don't suppose I do. I just don't know."

"Of course. Well, we'll have the autopsy report by tonight, and we'll call you about the results." Corby held out his hand, and for a moment, as Walter shook it, his face became politely grave. Then he turned and walked quickly out the door of the room.

"Can you tell us where the body is to be sent tomorrow?" the officer at the desk asked.

Walter thought of the funeral home he drove by every day on the cut-off from the highway into Benedict. "I'm not sure yet. Can I call you later today?"

"We're open day and night."

So was the funeral home. It said so in neon lights. "Is that all?" Walter asked.

"That's all."

Walter went out into the sunless afternoon. He had to think for a moment where he had put his car, and then walking toward it, he remembered Clara's suitcase. He turned back.

The police officer told him that the suitcase had not yet been examined and that it would be sent tomorrow with the body. Walter felt the man was being deliberately stubborn and indifferent. The blue canvas suitcase, bulging with Clara's belongings, stood against the wall only two yards from him.

"But there aren't any papers in it, there's only clothes," he said.

"Regulations are regulations," the officer said without looking up.

Walter gave him a glowering look, then turned and went out of the office.

He had started his car, when it occurred to him to warn Ellie. It was nearly four. She'd just be home. He opened the car door to get out, then closed it again. He realized he didn't want the lieutenant to see him telephoning, though the lieutenant wasn't in sight now. Walter drove a few blocks, and telephoned from a drugstore.

He told Ellie that Clara was dead, and that the police thought it was a suicide. He cut through her questions and said, "I'm in Allentown now. I told the police I saw you last night. They may call you to check on it."

"All right, Walter."

"I didn't tell them yet *when* I saw you. Of course we'll have to say it was after twelve."

"Does that matter?"

He set his teeth, cursing his nervousness. Pete had seen him there after twelve anyway. "No," Walter said. "It doesn't matter."

"I'll tell them that you came here around twelve-thirty," Ellie said as if she expected him to contradict her. "Isn't that right?"

"Yes, of course."

"Are you free now? Do you want to come here?"

"Yes. I'll come straight out."

"Can you leave your car and take a train?"

"Leave it?"

"You sound too upset to drive."

"I'll be there. It'll take me a couple of hours. Wait for me."

18

"I CAN'T just say blithely that it's not my fault," Walter said, throwing his hands out. "I should have forced her to go to a psychiatrist. I should have insisted on going with her on this trip. I didn't."

"Are you positive it was suicide?" Ellie asked.

"Not positive. But it's the most likely. And I should have expected it." He sat down suddenly in the armchair.

"From what you've said, everything in her life just now contributed to a suicide, even the car accident just a few days ago."

"Yes." Walter had just told Ellie about the sleeping pills, too. Ellie had not seemed very surprised. Ellie seemed to know a lot about his relationship with Clara, either by intuition or by guessing. "But *I'm* not positive it was suicide. I just can't imagine her jumping off a cliff. She'd do it an easier way."

"The police are going to investigate, aren't they?"

Walter shrugged. "Yes. As far as they're able to."

"But you really can't say it was your fault, Walter. You can't force somebody to an analyst who doesn't want to go."

Walter knew Jon would say the same thing.

"Did she know anything about us?" Ellie asked.

Walter nodded. "She suspected. Weeks ago, before I even noticed you. Accused me of being with you every time I spent an evening out."

Ellie frowned. "Why didn't you tell me that?"

Walter didn't answer for a moment. "She had a pathological jealousy, even of my men friends," he said quietly.

"I'm sorry she suspected. It was one more thing to make her do it. Then the divorce—"

"She never really believed I cared about you." Walter got up to walk again. "She had to have someone or something to be jealous of. In this case, she just happened to be right."

"Where did you tell the police you were last night?" Ellie asked.

Walter hesitated. He wanted to tell Ellie. But he remembered Corby: his answers were all down in Corby's tablet. "I told them first—I think I said I drove around for quite a while, trying to find you and waiting for you. Then I went home for a while. I went out again and spent most of the evening out."

Ellie brought a sandwich in on a plate and set it on the coffee table. She looked at him and said carefully, "I was thinking, if they—if they're not sure it was a suicide, it could look as if you had a motive in killing her."

"Why do you say that?"

"I mean—coming to see me. The whole picture."

"They're not going to ask questions like that," Walter said, frowning. "Corby hasn't even called you."

"They said it happened around seven-thirty, didn't they?"

"Yes."

"Where were you then?"

Walter's frown deepened. "I think I was home. I drove home after I put Clara on the bus."

"Gordon called you around seven-thirty. Nobody answered."

"Maybe I'd already gone out."

"He called you again at eight-thirty, too. I know because I was sitting by the phone then."

"Well, I certainly wasn't home then." Walter felt that his face had gone white. And Ellie was looking at him as if she saw it.

"I just thought, in case they do ask, you'd better be able to say exactly where you were. Do you know exactly where you were at seven-thirty?"

"No," he said in a protesting tone. "Maybe I was in Huntington then. I had a bite to eat there. I wasn't noticing the time. They're not going to ask all that, Ellie."

"All right. Maybe they won't." She sat down on the sofa, but she still looked tense. She sat upright, with one leg bent under her. "Why don't you have your sandwich?"

Did she also suspect him, Walter wondered, by intuition?

The telephone rang again. Ellie answered it.

"Oh, yes, Jon!" Ellie turned and looked at Walter. "Good lord! . . . No, I don't, I'm afraid . . . You're right, he shouldn't be."

Walter walked with stiff steps around the coffee table, watching Ellie. It was in the evening papers, Walter supposed. Walter thought Ellie looked at him with amazing calmness.

He'd expected more concern from her. And he hadn't believed her capable of pretending so well as she was pretending
to Jon now.

"I'm sure with one of his friends," Ellie said. "Yes, maybe
the Iretons . . . I hope you do. Thanks *very* much for calling
me, Jon." Ellie put the telephone down. "I didn't think I
should tell Jon you were here."

Walter shrugged. "I wouldn't have minded. Jon said it was
in the papers?"

"Yes, but he said Dick Jensen had called him up and told
him this afternoon. Why don't you call up the Iretons and ask
if you can stay with them tonight? I don't think you should go
back to the house."

He would have liked to stay with her. He felt she didn't
want him here. "I don't want to. I don't want to go over it
again with anybody. I'll go home."

"Do you think you can sleep there?"

"Yes. And I'll be going now."

Her hand was firm on the back of his neck. She kissed his
cheek. "Call me whenever you want to. Call me tonight if you
want to."

"Thanks, Ellie." He did not touch her. Suddenly he remembered he was supposed to call Allentown tonight and tell them
where to send Clara's body. "Thanks," he said again, and went
out.

19

THERE WAS a telegram at home addressed to Clara from Dr. Meacham, her mother's doctor, saying that her mother had died at 3:25 P.M. Walter put it down on the hall table.

It was midnight. He thought of calling Jon. But he didn't want to.

Betty Ireton telephoned. Walter spoke mechanically to her, thanked her for her invitation to come over and stay with them. Bill talked with him, too, and offered to come and fetch him, but Walter declined with thanks.

Then he called the Wilson-Hall Funeral Home in Benedict. Walter said he wanted a cremation. Afterwards, he called the Allentown morgue and asked about the autopsy report: no internal causes of death had been discovered, no causes other than injuries that would have been inflicted by her fall down the cliff. He told them where the Wilson-Hall Funeral Home was.

That night, Walter lay in his study listening to the silence in the house and thinking that it would never be broken again by Clara's quick, angry footsteps in the hall, that she would never again invade the privacy of his study, and he felt strangely unmoved. He realized he had not shed a single tear yet. Because she had not been human herself, he thought. His tired mind saw her as a storm of violent and whirling movement, which she had shut off with a last violent act—*bang*! Like her mother's lonely, dreary death, Clara's seemed exactly fitting for her. The storm of Clara rose in his mind, swirling around a core of doubt and ambiguity, ambiguous as his own feelings about her. Somewhere in it he fell asleep.

Walter awakened with a start at the sound of a door closing. Then he realized it was Claudia, faithfully arriving at seven. Walter pulled on a robe and went downstairs.

Claudia was standing with the morning paper in the kitchen. "Mr. Stackhouse, I saw it last night—but I just can't believe it!"

Walter took the paper from her. It was the local Long Island paper and it was on the front page. There was even a picture, the smiling picture that Clara had given the newspaper a long time ago when she had been elected chairwoman of some Long Island club.

BODY OF BENEDICT WOMAN FOUND IN PENNSYLVANIA

He glanced through the story. Presumed a suicide, it said. There was a sentence about her suitcase being found aboard the bus, and about his having identified her.

"You *saw* her, Mr. Stackhouse?" Claudia stood there as if paralyzed, her wide brown eyes oozing tears.

"Yes," Walter said. He thought the sentence about the suitcase was worded exactly the same way as the sentence in the Kimmel story. He hadn't bought any newspapers last night. He had been too tired. Now it shocked him that he hadn't. He put his hand on Claudia's shoulder and pressed it. He did not know what to say. "Could you make me some coffee, Claudia? Nothing else."

"Yes, Mr. Stackhouse."

Dick Jensen, Ernestine McClintock and some of the other neighbors called him that morning. They were all sympathetic and offered their help, but Walter had nothing that he needed done. Then Jon called, and for the first time Walter broke down and wept. Jon offered to come out and stay with him. Walter wouldn't accept it, even though it was Saturday and Jon was free. But he agreed for Jon to come out that evening at six to have dinner with him.

Just after two that afternoon, Walter got a call from Lieutenant Corby in Philadelphia. Corby asked if Walter would be good enough to come to the Philadelphia Central Police Station that evening at seven.

"What's the matter?" Walter asked.

"I can't explain now. I'm sorry to bother you, but it would help us enormously if you'd come," Corby's polite voice said.

"I'll be there," Walter said.

He wondered if Corby had picked up a suspect, had found a man who had confessed. Walter found himself unable to imagine, really, almost unable to think. He had been jumpy yesterday, and today he felt everything he did was in slow motion.

Walter called Jon and told him that he had to go to

Philadelphia, and wouldn't be able to see him until late. Jon offered to drive him there, or ride with him.

"Thanks," Walter said gratefully. "Can I pick you up around five at your apartment?"

Jon agreed.

Jon drove Walter's car from New York onward. To Jon, Walter told the same story he had told Ellie. And Jon replied much the same as Ellie had, as Walter had known he would. But there was something more in Jon: an obvious relief, that showed under his seriousness as he talked to Walter in the car, that Clara was totally out of Walter's life and by her own actions.

"Don't feel guilty!" Jon kept saying. "I understand this better than you can right now. You'll understand it, too, in another six months."

J ON WAITED at the car, and Walter went into the building by himself. He asked a policeman at a desk where Lieutenant Corby was.

"Room one seventeen down the hall."

Walter went to it and knocked.

"Good evening." Lieutenant Corby greeted him with a nod and a smile.

"Good evening." Walter saw a husky-looking man of about fifty, sitting on a straight chair, leaning forward, elbows on his knees. Walter wondered if he was the man.

"Mr. Stackhouse, this is Mr. De Vries," Corby said.

They nodded to each other.

"Have you ever seen Mr. De Vries before?"

He looked like a laborer, Walter thought. A brown leather jacket, brown and gray hair, a roundish, not very intelligent face, though there was a brightness in his eyes now, of interest or amusement. "I don't think so," Walter said.

Corby turned to the man in the chair. "What do you think?"

The grayish head between the hunched shoulders nodded.

Lieutenant Corby leaned comfortably against a desk. His boyish smile had grown wider, though there was something ungenerous about his small mouth and his small regular teeth. Walter didn't like the smile. "Mr. De Vries thinks you were the man who asked him how long the bus stop was in Harry's Rainbow Grill the night your wife was killed."

Walter looked at De Vries again. It was the man. Walter remembered that round, nondescript face turning to him above the coffee cup. Walter wet his lips. He realized that Corby must have taken the trouble to describe him to De Vries because Corby suspected him.

"You see, this is all by the merest accident," Corby said with a laugh of pleasure that actually made Walter jump. "Mr. De Vries is a truck driver for a Pittsburgh company. Occasionally he makes the run back to Pittsburgh by bus. We know him. I was only asking him if he remembered seeing any suspicious-looking characters around the bus stop that night."

Walter wondered if that was how it had been. He remembered Corby yesterday: Did you reach the friend? Who was the friend? "Yes," Walter said. "I was there. I followed the bus. I wanted to talk to my wife."

"And did you?"

"No, I couldn't find her. I looked everywhere." Walter swallowed. "Finally, I asked this man how long the bus was stopping."

"Don't you want to sit down, Mr. Stackhouse?"

"No."

"Why didn't you tell us this?"

"I thought there was a possibility I'd followed the wrong bus."

"Why didn't you tell us after you found out your wife was dead? Your story of driving around Long Island then is a lie," Corby said in his polite tone.

"Yes," Walter said. "It was very stupid of me. I was frightened."

Lieutenant Corby unbuttoned his jacket and slipped his hands into his trouser pockets. A university key dangled from a chain across his narrow vest. "Mr. De Vries tells me that the driver waited several minutes because your wife was missing, and that he remembers you standing near the bus until it left."

"Yes, I did," Walter said.

"What did you think had happened to her?"

"I didn't know. I thought it was possible she'd gotten out in Newark—changed her mind about taking the bus. I'd tried to dissuade her about taking the bus."

Corby was sitting on the corner of the desk, lifting and setting down various objects on it—the stapler, the ink bottle, a pen—with a possessive and satisfied air. A big name plate on the desk said CAPT. J. P. MAC GREGOR.

"I suppose you can go now, Mr. De Vries," Lieutenant Corby said, smiling at him. "Thank you very much."

De Vries stood up and gave Walter a final lively glance as he walked to the door. "Good night," he said to both of them.

"Good night," Corby replied. He folded his arms. "Now tell me exactly what happened. You followed the bus from New York?"

"Yes." Walter shook his head at Corby's offer of a cigarette, and reached for his own pack.

"What were you so eager to talk to your wife about?"

"I felt—I felt we hadn't concluded something we were talking about at the bus terminal, so I—"

"Were you arguing?"

"No, not arguing." Walter looked straight at the young man. "We'd better take this step by step. I saw the bus pull into the space in front of the restaurant for a stop. I stopped my car on the highway and walked back—"

"On the highway? Why didn't you pull up by the bus stop?"

All the questions were loaded. Walter answered slowly. "I shot past. I stopped as soon as I could and got out." He waited, expecting to be challenged again. He wasn't. "I don't know how I could have missed her. I hurried up, but I didn't see her in the bus or in the restaurant."

"It's several yards from the highway to the restaurant. Why didn't you back your car and drive up?"

"I don't know," Walter said hollowly.

"If she went straight from the bus to the cliff, she could have jumped off within thirty seconds. *Could* have," Corby repeated.

"She knew the road," Walter said. "She'd often made it by car. She may very well have known about the cliff."

"Had the bus stopped yet when you were walking toward it?"

"Yes. People were getting off."

"And you saw no sign of her?"

"No." Walter watched him taking notes in the limp brown tablet. His bony hand moved quickly and with a heavy pressure. It was over in a few seconds, as if he used shorthand.

Corby put the tablet away. "You found no suicide notes at home, I suppose?"

"No."

"No," Corby repeated. He looked up at a corner of the room, then at Walter. "May I ask what was your relationship to your wife?"

"My relationship?"

"Were you both happy?"

"No, we were getting a divorce, in fact. We would have been divorced in another few weeks."

"Who wanted the divorce, both of you?"

"Yes," Walter said matter of factly.

"May I ask why?"

"You may ask why. She was a very neurotic woman, hard to get along with. We clashed—everywhere. We simply didn't get along."

"You both agreed on that?"

"Emphatically."

Corby was watching him, his hands delicately poised on his hips as he sat on the desk. The little mustache made him look absurdly young instead of older. To Walter he looked like an obnoxious young fop playing at being Sherlock Holmes. "Do you think the prospect of the divorce depressed her?"

"I've no doubt it did."

"Was that what you wanted to talk to your wife about, the divorce? Is that why you followed the bus?"

"No, the divorce was all settled," Walter said tiredly.

"A New York divorce? Adultery?"

Walter frowned. "No. I was going to Reno. Today." He took out his billfold. "There's my plane ticket," he said, tossing it down on the desk.

Corby turned his head to look at it, but he did not pick it up. "You didn't cancel it?"

"No," Walter said.

"Why Reno? Were you in such a hurry, or wasn't your wife willing?"

Walter had braced himself for that. "No," he said easily, "she didn't want a divorce. I did. But she also knew there was nothing she could do to stop me from getting one—except kill herself."

Corby's mouth went up at one corner, mirthlessly. "Wasn't that pretty inconvenient for you, six weeks in Reno?"

"No," he said in the same tone, "my office had given me a six weeks' leave."

"What was your wife going to do afterward?"

"Afterward? I presume keep the house, which is hers, and keep her job." Walter waited. Corby was waiting. "It's a peculiar situation, I suppose, from your view, both of us living there together until the last minute. I was afraid to leave my wife alone, afraid of just this—suicide or something violent." Walter had a sudden optimistic feeling that his story was beginning to make sense. But Corby was still looking at him with the widened eyes,

as if the circumstances of the divorce had opened a new path for
his suspicions.

"Did you have any specific reason for wanting a divorce just
now? Are you in love with somebody else?"

"No," Walter answered firmly.

"I ask that, because the kind of situation you describe between you and your wife is the kind that can go on a long time
without anybody doing anything about it." Corby smiled.
"Probably," he added.

"That's very true. We've been married four years and it's—
the last year that we began to talk about a divorce."

"You can't remember what you wanted to finish talking
about Thursday night?"

"I honestly can't."

"Then you must have been angry."

"I was not. I simply felt it hadn't been concluded, whatever
it was." He felt violently bored and annoyed suddenly, the way
he had felt in the Navy a couple of times when he had had to
wait too long, naked, for a doctor to come and make a routine
examination. He also felt tired, so tired that it seemed even his
nerves were spent and no longer kept him twitching, and he
might have dropped on the floor and slept, except that he
wanted to get out of the building.

"Another question," the lieutenant said. "I'd like to ask if
you saw any odd-looking characters while you were looking for
your wife?"

Walter was sick of the young man's smile. "I think my wife
was a suicide. No, I did not see any odd-looking characters."

"You were not so sure yesterday that your wife was a suicide."

Walter said nothing.

Lieutenant Corby got off the desk. "You're unusual. Most
people are never convinced their wives or husbands or relatives
are suicides. They always demand that the police search for a
murderer."

"So would I, under different circumstances," Walter said. "I
don't suppose cases like this can ever be really proven suicides,
can they?"

"No. But we can eliminate the other possibilities." Corby

smiled and walked toward the door as if the interview were at an end, but he stopped short of the door and turned to Walter.

Walter wanted to ask him if the fact that he had been at the bus stop was going to be put into the papers. But he didn't want Corby to think he was afraid of it. "Is this the last of these interviews?" Walter asked.

"I hope so. Just one thing more." Corby strolled back across the room. "Did you happen to hear of another death like this a few months ago? A woman who was found dead, beaten, and knifed to death near her bus stop at Tarrytown?"

Walter was sure his face did not change. "No. I didn't."

"A woman by the name of Kimmel? Helen Kimmel?"

"No," Walter said.

"The murderer hasn't been found yet. *She* was very definitely murdered," he added with the pleasant smile. "But the similarity of the two cases struck me—that interval at the bus stop."

Walter said nothing. He looked straight into Corby's blue eyes. Corby was smiling at him, in the friendliest way his anemic-looking, overbright schoolboyish face was able to smile, Walter supposed. It was not at all friendly. "Is that why," Walter asked, "you take such an interest in this case?"

Corby opened his hands. "Oh, I don't take such an interest in this case." He looked self-conscious suddenly. "This one happened in my state. I remembered the other case because it hasn't been solved. It's pretty recent, too. August." Corby swung the door open. "Thank you very much for coming in."

Walter waited. "Have you come to a conclusion? Are you convinced my wife was a suicide?"

"It's not for me to come to a conclusion!" Corby said with another laugh. "I don't know if we've got all the facts yet."

"I see."

"Good night," Corby said with a deep nod.

"Good night," Walter said.

It was going to be in the papers, anyway, Walter thought. He had the feeling Corby was going to put it in all the papers. Walter told Jon what had happened. The only thing he lied about was his reason for following the bus: Walter said he had wanted to finish something he and Clara had been talking about.

"It's a piece of real bad luck," Jon's deep voice said. "Is it going to get in the papers?"

"I don't know. I didn't ask."

"You should have."

"I should have done a lot of things."

"Are they convinced it was suicide?"

"I don't think so. I think it's still open. Open to some doubt." He didn't want to tell Jon just how openly suspicious Corby had been. Walter realized that Jon could be just as suspicious as Corby—if he chose to be suspicious. Walter looked at Jon, wondering what he was thinking. He saw only Jon's familiar profile, a little frowning, the underlip pushed out.

"It might not get in the papers, even if you're possibly under suspicion," Jon said. "In a few days, something conclusive might turn up, proving it a murder or a suicide. Personally, I believe it's suicide. I wouldn't worry about the papers."

"Oh, it's not that that I'm worried about!"

"What is it then?"

"The shame, I suppose. Being caught in a lie."

"Take a nap. It's a long way to New York."

Walter didn't want to sleep, but he put his head back, and a few minutes later he did doze off. He woke up when the car made a swerve. They were driving through a gray section of warehouses—watertanks on stilts, a gin factory that looked like a glass-fronted hospital. It struck Walter that he had made a very stupid mistake in being obviously resentful of Corby's questions. Corby after all was only doing his job. If he met Corby again, he thought, he'd behave very differently.

"Where'll it be?" Jon asked. "My house or yours? Or do you want to be alone tonight?"

"I don't want to be alone. My house, if you don't mind. I wish you'd spend the night."

Jon drove to his garage in Manhattan to pick up his own car. Before he got out of Walter's car, he said, "I think you'd better be prepared that this *can* get into the papers, Walt. If there's anybody you want to tell it to before it does, maybe you ought to, tonight."

"Yes," Walter said. He would tell Ellie tonight, he thought.

IT WAS nearly 11 P.M. when they got to Benedict, but Claudia was still there. She had stayed to take the telephone messages, she said. She had a handful for him. Ellie had called twice.

Walter told Jon to see what he could find to eat in the refrigerator, then he drove Claudia into Benedict so she could get the eleven o'clock bus for Huntington. On the way back, he stopped at the Three Brothers Tavern and called Ellie.

"Claudia didn't know where you were," Ellie said. "Why didn't you call me all day?"

"I'll have to explain when I see you. Is it too late for you to come over to the house? Jon's here and I can't come to you."

Ellie said she would come.

Walter drove home and told Jon that Ellie was on her way over.

"Have you been seeing much of Ellie?" Jon asked him.

"Yes," Walter said stiffly. "Now and then I see her." He made himself a drink, and picked up one of the roast beef slices that Jon had put out on a plate. He was conscious of Jon's silence. Walter didn't want the roast beef. He gave it to Jeff, who was prancing nervously around the room, then went to the telephone to call Mrs. Philpott, whose message had an underlined *Please call* on it.

Ellie arrived while he was talking to Mrs. Philpott, and Jon opened the door for her. Mrs. Philpott had nothing of any importance to say, and after a moment Walter realized she was drunk. She was praising Clara extravagantly. She commiserated with him. He had lost the most brilliant, the most charming, attractive, *liveliest* creature in the world. Walter wanted to crush the phone in his hand. He tried several times to get away, and kept interrupting her with thanks for her call. Finally, it was over.

Jon and Ellie stopped talking as he came back into the living room. Ellie looked up at him anxiously.

"Had you rather be alone, Walt?" Jon asked.

"No, thanks," Walter said. "Ellie, I have to tell you something I've already told Jon. Last night—Thursday night—I followed Clara's bus. I followed it to the place where she was killed, where she jumped off the cliff. I was looking for her and I never found her. It must have happened just before I got there. I waited and looked all around for her until the bus left, and finally I came back."

"She was missing and you knew it?" Ellie asked incredulously.

"I wasn't absolutely sure. I thought she might have gotten off the bus somewhere else without my seeing her. Or I thought I might have been following the wrong bus."

"And you didn't tell anybody?" she asked.

"I wasn't absolutely sure that it was *Clara* who was missing," Walter said impatiently. "I was about to report it to the police yesterday morning after I called Harrisburg and found she hadn't arrived, but the police notified me first—that they'd found her body." Walter looked at Ellie's puzzled face. He knew there was no explanation but the real one: that he'd felt guilty even as he had waited around the bus, that he had even had some crazy hallucination afterward, driving back to New York, that he had taken her into the woods and killed her. He picked up a glass from the coffee table and drank. "Well—this evening I went to the police in Philadelphia. I was seen around the bus stop. I was identified. It'll probably be out in the papers. I don't think I'm suspected of murder. It's still considered a suicide. But if they *do* want to make anything of it in the papers—well, they could, that's all."

Jon sat with his head tipped back against the sofa pillow, quietly listening, but Walter had the feeling Jon didn't like his story, was beginning to doubt it.

"Who identified you?" Ellie asked.

"A man named De Vries. Corby— Either the man remembered me because I looked strange, walking up and down the restaurant looking for Clara, or Corby really suspects me and took the trouble to describe me to this fellow. De Vries was one of the passengers on the bus."

"Who is Corby?"

"A detective. From Philadelphia. The one I talked to when I identified Clara." Walter managed to keep his voice steady. He lighted a cigarette. "According to him—at least what he said at first—Clara was a suicide."

"If the man saw you the whole time—"

"He didn't," Walter interrupted her. "He didn't see me when I first arrived, when Clara must have jumped off the cliff. He saw me waiting in the restaurant afterward."

"But if you'd done it—killed her—you wouldn't have waited around the restaurant looking for her for fifteen minutes!"

"Exactly," Jon said.

"That's right." Walter sat down on the sofa. Ellie took his hand and held it between them on the sofa.

"You're afraid, aren't you?" Ellie asked him.

"No!" Walter said. He saw that Jon saw their hands, and he pulled his hand away. "But it couldn't look worse, could it? A thing like this never can be proven one way or the other, can it?"

"Oh, yes," Jon drawled impatiently. "They'll hammer at you for a while, they'll get more facts, then they'll decide that it's a suicide, that it couldn't have been anything else."

Walter looked at Jeff, curled up asleep in the armchair. Whenever a car rolled up, Jeff was at the door, looking for her. Walter jumped up to get another drink. *He* had loved Clara once, too, he thought. Nobody seemed to remember that he had loved Clara except old Mrs. Philpott. He smiled a little bitterly as he shot the soda into his glass. When he turned around, Ellie was looking at him.

Ellie stood up. "I've got to be going. I have to get up early tomorrow."

"Tomorrow?" Walter asked.

"To see Irma—my friend in New York. I'm going to drive her out to East Hampton. She has some friends there and we're invited for lunch."

Walter wanted to beg Ellie to stay a little longer, and he didn't dare in front of Jon, didn't even have the courage for that. "Will you call me tomorrow?" he asked. "I'll be home all day—except between three and five." Between three and five was the funeral ceremony at the church in Benedict.

"I'll call you," Ellie said.

He walked with her out to her car. He sensed a coolness in

her that he felt helpless to do anything about. Then she said through her car window: "Try not to worry, Walter. We'll come through all right." She leaned toward him, and he kissed her.

Walter smiled. "Good night, Ellie."

She drove off. Walter whistled to Jeff, who had come out with them, and they went back into the house. Neither he nor Jon said anything for several minutes.

"I like Ellie," Jon said finally.

Walter only nodded. There was another silence. Walter could imagine exactly what Jon was imagining about Ellie. Walter pressed his hands together tensely. His hands were sweating.

"But until this blows over," Jon said, "I'd keep Ellie strictly out of the picture."

"Yes," Walter said.

They did not speak of Ellie again.

The next morning, Jon came into Walter's study with the paper in his hand.

"It's in," Jon said, and tossed the paper down on Walter's couch.

22

IN THE roomy square kitchen of his two-story house in Newark, Melchior Kimmel sat breakfasting on rye bread with cream cheese and a mug of rich black coffee with sugar. The Newark *Daily News* was propped up in front of him against the sugar bowl, and he was staring at the lower corner of the front page. His left hand had stopped in midair with the half-eaten piece of bread in it. His mouth stayed open and his heavy lips grew limp.

Stackhouse. He remembered the name, and the photograph clinched it. *Stackhouse*. He was positive.

Kimmel read the two short columns shrewdly. He had followed her and had been identified, though there still seemed to be some doubt as to whether he had killed her. "Murder or Suicide?" was the heading of one paragraph.

> . . . Stackhouse stated that he did not see his wife at all at the bus stop. He waited about 15 minutes, he reported, then drove back to Long Island after the bus departed. He claimed that it was not until the next day, when he was asked by the Allentown police to identify his wife's body, that he knew that any harm had come to her. Official autopsy indicated no injuries other than those which would have been inflicted by her fall down the cliff. . . .

Kimmel's bald head bent forward intently.

"Why Didn't He Report Wife's Absence?" was the heading of the last paragraph. Why indeed, thought Kimmel. That was exactly his question.

But the last paragraph stated only that Stackhouse was a lawyer with the firm of Cross, Martinson and Buchman, and that Stackhouse and his wife had been about to be divorced. The last was an interesting point.

A chill went over Kimmel, a kind of panic. Why had Stackhouse come all the way from Long Island to see him? Kimmel stood up slowly from the table and glanced around him at the chaos of beer bottles under the sink, at the electric clock over the stove, at the worn oilcloth on the drainboard, patterned with tiny pink and green apples that always reminded him of Helen. Stackhouse must have done it. There was no explaining away a lot of funny coincidences like this! And Stackhouse was going to be nailed. He would probably break down and admit it after two hours' pressure. And suppose that would give the police ideas about himself?

Well, he *wasn't* the kind of man who would break down. And what kind of proof could they ever get on him? Especially after more than two months? Kimmel calculated carefully just when Stackhouse had come to his shop. About three weeks ago, he thought, early in October. He still had the order slip for the book, because it hadn't come in yet. He wondered if he should destroy the order slip? If the book arrived, Kimmel thought, he wasn't going to notify Stackhouse. By then, Stackhouse might be in prison, anyway.

Kimmel began to tidy up his kitchen. He wiped the white enamel table with a moist dishcloth. There was always Tony, he thought. Tony had seen him in the movie, and that story of his having spent the evening at the movie was so entrenched in Tony's mind by now that Tony believed he had looked at the back of his neck all evening. But Tony had spent only five minutes here and there with the police. What if they questioned him for several hours?

But it hadn't happened yet, Kimmel thought.

He began to gather up beer bottles by their necks, the oldest bottles first. The beer bottles extended along the wall from under the sink all the way to the kitchen door. He looked around, saw an empty cardboard carton by the stove, and kicked it clumsily over near the bottles. He loaded the carton and took it out the back door to his dark Chevrolet sedan that stood in the yard. He came back with the carton empty and he filled it up again. Then he washed his hands with soap and water, because the bottles had been dusty, and went upstairs to his bedroom to get a clean white shirt. He was still in his underwear and trousers.

He took the bottles to Ricco's Delicatessen on the way to his shop. Tony was back of the counter.

"How're you today, Mr. Kimmel?" Tony asked. "What's amatter? Cleaning house?"

"A wee bit," Kimmel said lightly. "How's the liverwurst to-day?"

"Oh, fine as usual, Mr. Kimmel."

Kimmel ordered a liverwurst sandwich and one of herring-in-cream with onions. While Tony made them, Kimmel drifted along the stands of cellophane-wrapped foods, and came back with a package of mixed nuts, peanut-butter crackers, and a little bag of chocolate marshmallow cookies, which he spilled out on the counter.

Tony still owed him money when he figured the deposits on the bottles. Kimmel bought two bottles of beer: it was too early for beer to be sold, but Tony always made an exception for him.

Kimmel got into his car and drove at a leisurely speed toward his shop. He loved Sunday mornings, and he generally spent Sunday morning and part of the afternoon in his shop. His shop was not open for business on Sundays, but it gave Kimmel a greater sense of leisure and freedom to pass his only free day in the same place in which he worked all week. Besides, he loved his shop better than his house, and here on Sundays he could browse among his own books undisturbed, eat his lunch, doze, and answer at length some of the correspondence, erudite and whimsical, he received from people he had never seen but whom he felt he knew well. Booklovers: if you knew the kind of books a man wanted, you knew the man.

Kimmel's car was a black 1941 Chevrolet, its upholstery spotted and badly worn, though its outside looked almost as good as when it had been new. Kimmel would have liked a new car, because Nathan and a few others and even Tony joshed him about the 1941 model, but since he hadn't the money for a brand-new car, Kimmel preferred to keep his ancient one rather than acquire something slightly newer on a trade-in. Kimmel drove his car with dignity. He detested speeding. He had told all his friends that the 1941 model suited him perfectly, and Kimmel had come to believe it himself.

His fat lips pursed, and he began to whistle *Reich' Mir die Hand, Mein Leben*. He gazed up at the sky and at the buildings he passed, as if the ugly section of Newark through which he happened to be driving were actually beautiful. It was a fine autumnal morning, just crisp enough to feel bracing. Kimmel looked up at the black stone eagle on the pediment of a building across the street, its reared-back head silhouetted against the sky, one taloned claw outstretched. He was always reminded of a certain building in Breslau when he looked at the eagle, though he never actually thought of Breslau: he thought rather of how peaceful Newark was, how comfortable his routine of bookshop and home, his friends and his wood carving and his reading, how calm and happy he was since Helen no longer lived in the house. He would remember that he had killed her, and it seemed a quiet but meritorious achievement on his part, an achievement endorsed by the rest of the world, too, because no one had ever called him to account for it. The world simply rolled on, as if nothing had happened. Kimmel liked to imagine that everyone in the neighborhood—Tony, Nathan, Miss Brown the librarian, Tom Bradley, and the Campbells next door—knew that he had killed Helen and didn't care at all, actually looked up to him for it, and considered him above the laws that governed other men's behavior. Certainly his status in the community had risen since Helen was no longer with him. Tom Bradley invited him to meet important people at his home, and Tom had never invited him when Helen was his wife. And there was also the fact that there had never been the least suspicion against him. He was on excellent terms with the Newark police, and in fact with everyone who had ever interviewed him.

It was 9:55 when Kimmel opened his door. He never opened shop before 9:30, even on weekdays, because he loathed getting up early, though he supposed he missed some student trade occasionally because a lot of students passed in the morning on their way to the high school three blocks away. Kimmel had had a girl, Edith, to open shop for him and work mornings until a couple of months ago. She'd gotten nervous, and Kimmel had thought she might be pregnant. Finally, she had quit. Now and then, Kimmel wondered if she had quit because she suspected him of having killed his wife. Edith had witnessed a lot: that fight that had broken his glass lampshade, and all the times Helen had come in to ask him for bits of money and a quarrel had started and he had had to twist Helen's wrists a couple of times, because that had been the only way to shut her up.

Kimmel shuddered. It was all over.

He was thinking of Stackhouse's order slip in the cubbyhole as he walked toward his desk, but when he sat down he took out the letters that he meant to answer from another cubbyhole, and dropped them in the middle of his desk. There were also some publishers' catalogues and brochures that he had not finished reading. Kimmel loved publishers' catalogues, and he read them thoroughly, whether he ordered the books or not, with the delight that a gourmet might show in perusing a well-varied menu. Here was a letter from old Clifford Wrexall in South Carolina to be answered. He wanted another esoteric book of pornography. Pornography was Kimmel's main source of profit. He was known—among serious collectors of such books—as a dealer who could be relied on to get a book if it existed at all. Kimmel hunted down books in England, France, the Isle of Man, Germany, and in the library of an American eccentric in Turkey, a retired oilman of Texas and Persia, who meted out his valuable titbits to Kimmel only after months of elaborate and tantalizing exchanges of letters. When Kimmel wrested a book of pornography from Dillard in Turkey, he made the client pay for it.

Kimmel lighted his gas stove, a necessary supplement to the feeble heat that came up through the two radiators behind the front windows, sat down again and reached into the cubbyhole where he kept his orders. He picked Stackhouse's out from among about a dozen others and looked at it. Stackhouse. And the Long Island address. Kimmel refolded the paper and folded it once more. Stackhouse's book hadn't come in yet. There was no real reason why he had to destroy the paper, Kimmel thought. That might look more suspicious than ever. But he still had an impulse to hide the order slip in the secret compartment under the lowest little drawer on the left, or at the bottom of the cigar box that was filled with pencil stubs and rubber stamps. Kimmel held the folded paper between his thumb and forefinger, debating.

The front door opened and a man came in.

Kimmel stood up. "I'm sorry," he said. "The store isn't open today."

The man kept walking toward him, smiling. "How do you do? You're Melchior Kimmel?"

"Yes. Can I help you?" Kimmel asked, though rather breath-lessly, because he had not realized until the man asked his name that he was a police detective—and Kimmel was usually faster.

"I'm Lieutenant Corby, Philadelphia Police. Do you have a few minutes to spare?"

"Of course. What is it?" He slipped the hand with the paper into his trouser pocket, slipped the other hand into the other pocket, too.

"A coincidence of circumstances." The young lieutenant leaned an elbow on Kimmel's high desk and pushed his hat back. "Did you happen to see the story of the woman who was killed near a bus stop the other day?"

"Yes, I saw it just this morning." Kimmel was affecting his earnest, straightforward and, as he thought, American manner. "Naturally, I read it."

"I wonder if you've thought of the possibility of a common killer, or if you've found out anything since your wife's death that leads you to suspect a particular person?"

Kimmel smiled a little. "If I had, I'd certainly have reported it. I'm in touch with the Newark police."

"Yes, and I'm from Philadelphia," Corby said, smiling. "But this death the other day happened in my state."

"I thought the paper said it was suicide," Kimmel remarked. "Is the husband guilty?"

Lieutenant Corby smiled again. "He's not entirely clear, let's put it that way. We don't know yet. He *acts* guilty." He got out a cigarette, lighted it, took a few steps away from the desk and turned back.

Kimmel watched him with annoyance. His expression looked silly and prankish. Kimmel could not yet tell how intelligent he was.

"It's such a convenient way to do a murder, after all," Corby said, "follow the bus, wait until it stops." Corby's blue eyes lingered on Kimmel. "He could hardly fail, because the wife's going to come with him to some secluded place. . . ."

Kimmel fairly sneered at his naïve approach, and to cover it blinked his little eyes, readjusted his glasses, then removed his glasses entirely and blew on them and wiped them slowly with a clean handkerchief. Kimmel was trying to think of something withering to say, or at least deflating.

"Only Stackhouse hasn't even got an alibi," Corby said.

"Perhaps he isn't guilty."

"Did the possibility occur to you that Stackhouse could have killed his wife like that?"

What a question, Kimmel thought. The paper had actually stated that he might have killed his wife like that. Kimmel looked at Corby with hauteur. "The subject of murder depresses me—naturally, I think. I only glanced over the story this morning. I'll read it again. I have it at home." Mr. Stackhouse, lying on the kitchen table. Kimmel liked Corby even less than Stackhouse. Stackhouse may have had his reasons. Kimmel folded his arms. "What specifically did you want to ask me about?"

"Well, I've asked it really," Corby said more modestly. He moved restlessly about in the little clear space between Kimmel's desk and one of the long tables of books. "I've just been going over the police file on your wife's murder this morning. You were at the movie that evening, weren't you?"

"Yes." Kimmel's hands played with the closed knife in his left pocket and with the folded paper in the other.

"Alibi supported by Anthony Ricco."

"Yes, that's correct."

"And your wife also had no enemies who might have killed her?"

"I think she had." Kimmel lifted his eyebrows almost humorously and looked down at the brightly lighted desk in front of him. "She was not a pleasant character, my wife. Not to everyone. But at the same time, I know of no one who would have killed her. I have never named a single name that I suspected."

Corby nodded. "Were you never suspected?"

Kimmel lifted his eyebrows even higher. If Corby wanted to antagonize him, he would be unantagonizable. "Not that I know of. I wasn't told about it, if I was." He posed, tall, erect and completely in command of himself, while Corby studied him.

"I wish you would read over this Stackhouse case carefully. If you'd like, I'll send you the police records—those we're able to release."

"But it really doesn't interest me that much," Kimmel said.

"I suppose I should thank you for thinking it would. If there's anything I can do to help you—but actually I don't see that there is." He was the earnest American again, his head tilted attentively.

"Probably there's not." Corby's lips smiled again below the small brown mustache. "But don't forget—I'm sure you haven't forgotten that your wife's murderer was never found. The most amazing connections can turn up."

Kimmel let his mouth open a little. Then he asked brightly, "Are you looking for a man who preys on women at bus stops?"

"Yes. One man, at least." Corby stepped back, taking his leave. "That's about all. Thank you very much, Mr. Kimmel."

"You're very welcome." Kimmel watched him go, watched the inscrutable angular back of his rust-colored topcoat until it moved beyond the range of his nearsighted eyes, and he heard the door close.

He took the order slip from his pocket and put it back where it had been among the other orders. If Stackhouse's book came in, he thought, he would let it lie around without notifying Stackhouse. If they found Stackhouse's order in his desk, he would say he didn't remember the name on the order. It was safer than destroying the order, if they should ever possibly make such a thorough search of his papers that they would notice a missing order.

He was getting too anxious, too angry, he thought. That was not the way. But still, no one until now had actually guessed how he had done it. And suddenly Stackhouse had, apparently, and now Corby. Kimmel sat down and made himself read through Wrexall's letter again, carefully, in preparation for answering it. Wrexall wanted a book called *Famous Dogs in 19th Century Brothels*.

About an hour later, Kimmel had a telephone call from Tony. Tony said that a man had come to his store to ask about that night, and to go over all the facts Tony had given the police. Kimmel made light of it. He did not tell Tony that the man had been to see him. Tony did not sound very excited about it, Kimmel thought. The first few times, Tony had come running over in person to tell him all about an interview with the police.

23

WALTER STAYED at home on Monday, the day after the funeral, though there was nothing for him to do at home, and it seemed he only waited like a willing victim for the polite callers, most of whom he didn't know at all. It was amazing how many people who had been Clara's real estate clients came to tell him how sorry they were to learn of her death.

Nobody seemed to suspect him, Walter thought, nobody at all. The story in the newspapers—though the more sensational newspapers had made all they could out of it—had blown over with amazingly little comment, at least to his face. Two or three people, practically total strangers, had sympathized with him for his ironic bad luck at having been there almost in time to save her—and some assumed that to have been the motive for his following her—but no one seemed to doubt his innocence, not even so much as Walter had felt Jon doubted it the night he had gone with Walter to Philadelphia. Walter suspected that Jon doubted his motive in following the bus, and he had reason to, Walter thought. Jon knew more about his and Clara's relationship than anyone else, much more than the Iretons, for instance. Walter hadn't told Jon until after Clara's funeral about his plans to go to Reno and get his divorce; Jon had thought that very strange. And Walter had been acting strange for the last several weeks, not calling Jon, not seeing anybody. Walter sensed Jon's suspicions more than saw them. He had an impulse to have it out with Jon, make a clean breast of the whole story, including Kimmel, including his own muddled intentions the night he followed the bus. But Walter didn't.

Jon, who knew the most, was still the best friend he had. Jon was there when he needed him, and gone when Walter preferred to be alone. Jon was at the house on Wednesday night when Ellie called.

Ellie only wanted to know if the police had said anything more. Walter told her that the New York police had questioned him in his office that morning.

"They weren't hostile," Walter said. "Just questioned me again about the story I'd told." The plain-clothes man had stayed only a few minutes to talk with him, and Walter thought it couldn't have been very important, or the police would have spoken to him a couple of days earlier.

Ellie didn't ask when they would see each other. Walter knew she realized they shouldn't be seeing each other after the story in the newspaper Sunday. It would add another sensational motive. But Walter's eagerness to see her got the better of him, and he blurted out: "Can I see you tomorrow night, Ellie? Can you come for dinner here?"

"If you think it's all right—of course I can."

When Walter went back into the living room, Jon was stooped in the corner, looking through some record albums.

"Just how much does Ellie mean to you, Walt?" Jon asked.

"I think quite a lot," Walter answered.

"How long's this been going on?"

"Nothing's going on," Walter said with a little annoyance.

"Are you in love with her?"

Walter hesitated. "I don't know."

"She obviously is with you."

Walter looked down at the floor and felt as embarrassed as a boy. "I like her. I may be in love with her. I don't even know."

"Did Clara know about her?"

"Yes. Before there was anything to know about."

"You must have seen Ellie a *few* times," Jon said, looking up.

"Only twice." Walter walked slowly up and down the room. He was thinking of the trouble Clara had taken in choosing this carpet, going to every store in Manhattan before she was satisfied.

"You must have made a big impression on her then," Jon said, with his good-natured chuckle.

"That may not last. I don't know her very well."

"Oh, come on, you don't believe that." Jon's voice sounded like the growl of an amiable bear.

"I've no plans at all about Ellie," Walter said, embarrassed. He and Jon had never talked very much about women—only about being married to them. If Jon had had any affairs since divorcing Stella, he hadn't talked about them. Walter had never had any, until Ellie.

Jon stood up with a load of records. "By the way, I'd like to repeat that I like Ellie. If you two like each other, I think that's fine."

Jon's smile made Walter smile back. "Let me get you a drink."

"No, thanks. Got to watch my waistline."

"You'll never make thirty-four! Let's have a drink to Ellie."

Walter fixed two generous scotch highballs and brought them to the coffee table. They sat down and lifted their glasses, then suddenly Walter crumpled. His smile had become a bitter grimace. There were tears in his eyes.

"Walter—take it easy." Jon was sitting beside him, his arm around his shoulders.

Walter was thinking of Clara, dissolved, a few ounces of ashes in an ugly gray pot. Clara who had been so beautiful, whose body he had held in his arms. He felt Jon pulling at the glass in his hand, but Walter held on. "You think I'm a dog, don't you?" Walter asked. "You think I'm a dog for sitting here and drinking to another woman when my wife's hardly buried, don't you?"

"Snap out of it, Walter. *No!*"

"And for sitting here telling you all about it tonight, don't you?" Walter went on, talking with his head down. "But I have to tell you that I adored Clara. I loved her more than any other woman in the world!"

"Walt, I know it."

"You don't—know it enough. Nobody does." Walter felt the glass snap in his hand. He looked at his own hand, holding a curved shard between bleeding fingertips, and he dropped the fragment on the floor, too. "You don't know," Walter said. "You don't know what it is." He was thinking of the empty stairway, the empty bed upstairs, and Clara's bright scarves still in the closet on the top shelf. He was thinking of Jeff, waiting all day for her, all night. He was thinking even of her voice—

Walter felt himself yanked to his feet. He realized Jon wanted him to go wash his hand, and he began to apologize. "I'm sorry, Jon, I'm very sorry. It's not the drink—"

"You haven't had a drink!" Jon was pulling him up the stairs. "Now you wash your hands and face and forget it."

24

THERE WAS very little work for Walter in the office that week, because Dick Jensen had already taken over Walter's tasks in anticipation of his six weeks' leave. Walter took advantage of it and left earlier in the afternoons. The office depressed him even more than the house in Benedict. He went in to see Dick around three in the afternoon on Thursday.

"Dick, let's get out of here next month," Walter said. "Let's call up Sherman and tell him we'll sign the lease for December first or the middle of November, if we can get the office then." Sherman was the rental agent for the 44th Street building they had chosen as an office location.

Dick Jensen looked at him solemnly for a minute, and Walter realized he had sounded a little hysterical, that Dick probably thought he was a little hysterical because of Clara.

"Maybe we ought to let things cool down for a while," Dick said. "It goes without saying that I—I know you had nothing to do with it, Walt, but it's a bad thing to try to get a new law office launched on."

"The people we're going to have as clients won't care a hang about that," Walter said.

Dick shook his head. He was standing behind his desk. There was a worried expression on his face. "I don't think it's fatal to us, Walt. But I think you're more upset by all this than you know. I'm just trying to keep us both from doing anything too hastily."

He could only mean, Walter thought, that he didn't want to be a partner in a new office that had a good chance of failing because of the other partner's bad name. And yet Dick had made such a fine speech Tuesday about his confidence in him, how sure he was of his integrity. "You said you had no doubt it'd blow over. By December first, it certainly will have blown over. I only meant we'd better give Cross notice, a month if you like, and get our publicity started. If we wait till December first for all that, it'll be the middle of January before we see our first client."

"I still think we'd better wait, Walt."

Walter looked at Dick's soft body in the conservatively cut suit, the vest slightly bulging over hundreds of bacon-and-egg breakfasts, leisurely three-course lunches. Dick had a cheerful, easy-going wife at home, alive and breathing. He could afford to be calm and wait. Walter tossed his briefcase down and put on his topcoat.

"Taking off?" Dick asked.

"Yes. This place depresses me. I can just as well read this stuff at home." Walter walked to the door.

"Walt—"

He turned around.

"I don't suppose it's too soon to give Cross notice. I didn't mean that. I think we ought to give him a month. So next Monday—that'll be the first of November, I suppose we could."

"All right," Walter said. "I've got my letter written. I only have to put a date on it."

But as he went out to the elevator, it occurred to Walter that Dick had agreed to the notice only because he could still get his job back if he changed his mind. What Dick was still hedging about was signing the lease for the new office.

On the way to his parking lot, Walter saw a store window full of glassware, and he went in and bought a heavy Swedish glass vase for Ellie. He was not positive she would like it, but it would look all right in her apartment, he thought. Her apartment was in no particular style. Ellie furnished it with pieces that she liked, whatever they happened to be.

He stopped at two or three stores in Benedict and bought steak, mushrooms, salad essentials and a bottle of Médoc. He had given Claudia the evening off, the last three evenings off, because he and Jon had preferred to cook for themselves. He spent the rest of the afternoon reading his work from the office, and around 6:30 started organizing the dinner in the kitchen. Then he built a fire in the living room fireplace.

Ellie rang the doorbell at two past seven. He had been so sure she would be punctual, he had started making the martinis at seven sharp.

"This is for you," Ellie said, handing him a bouquet under wax paper.

Walter took it, smiling. "You're a funny girl."

"Why?"

"Always bringing a man flowers."

"They're only weeds out of my parking lot."

Walter unwrapped the glass vase in the kitchen, and put the flowers in it. The short-stemmed clover and daisies nearly sank in the vase, but he carried them quickly in to her. "This is for you," he said.

"Oh, Walter! The vase? It's beautiful!"

"Good," he said, pleased that she really liked it.

Ellie got something else to put the flowers in, and brought the vase back and set it on the end table where she could admire it as they drank their cocktails. She was wearing a dark gray silk suit he had not seen before, earrings, and the black suède pumps that he preferred. He knew she had made a special effort to look well tonight.

"When are you getting out of this house?" she asked.

"I hadn't thought. Do you think I should?"

"I know you should," she said.

"I'll talk to somebody soon about it. The Knightsbridge people have already offered to handle it in case I want to get rid of it." There was also Clara's mother's property in Harrisburg, Walter remembered suddenly. In spite of Clara's prior death half of it was to go to him by the terms of the mother's will, but Mrs. Haveman had a sister somewhere in Pennsylvania. Walter was going to give the property and the inheritance over to her.

"Are you sleeping?" Ellie asked.

"Enough." He wanted to go and kiss her, but he waited. "All right, I'll change my house and my job next month. Dick agreed to send in his resignation next Monday. We should be in the new office by December first, at least."

"I'm glad. Dick isn't worried then about the story in the paper?"

"No," Walter said. "It'll have blown over by then." He felt optimistic and confident. The martini tasted perfect. It was doing just what a martini ought to do. He got up and sat down by Ellie, and put his arms around her.

She kissed him slowly, on the lips. Then she got up and walked away. Walter looked at her with surprise.

"Is this the wrong place to ask where I fit in?" she asked, smiling.

"I love you, Ellie. That's where you fit in." He waited. He knew she didn't expect him to propose a time when they might get married, not this soon. She only wanted reassurance that he loved her. That at least he could give her, he thought. Tonight he felt sure of it.

They finished the pitcher of martinis and made half a pitcher more, then went into the kitchen to start the dinner. The potatoes were already in the oven. Ellie talked about Dwight, her wonder child at school, while she fixed the mushrooms. Dwight was starting to play Mozart sonatas after less than two months of instruction. Walter wondered if he and Ellie would ever have a child who was gifted in music. He was imagining being married to Ellie, imagining her sunning her long smooth legs on the upstairs terrace, or some terrace, in summer, and imagining her head swathed in a woolen scarf when they took walks in the snow in winter. He was imagining introducing her to Chad. She and Chad should like each other.

"You're not listening," Ellie said, annoyed.

"Yes, I am. About Dwight playing Mozart."

"That was at least five minutes ago. I think it's time to put the steak on, isn't it?"

The telephone rang as Walter was carrying the steak to the oven. They glanced at each other, then Walter put the steak down and went to answer it.

"Hello. Is this Mr. Stackhouse?"

"Yes."

"Lieutenant Corby. I wonder if I could see you for a few minutes? It's rather important. It won't take long," the young affable voice said in a tone so confident that Walter floundered as to how to refuse him.

"You can't talk to me over the phone? Right now I'm—"

"It'll only take a few minutes. I'm right in Benedict."

"All right," Walter said.

He went into the kitchen cursing, yanking the dishtowel apron out of his belt.

"Corby," Walter said. "He's coming over. He said he'd just be a few minutes, but I think it's better if you aren't here, Ellie."

She pressed her lips together. "All right," she said.

She hurried, and Walter did not tell her not to. She and Corby could still run into each other at the door, and Walter didn't want that.

"Why don't you go to the Three Brothers and have another drink, and I'll call you there when he's gone."

"I don't want another drink," she said, "but I'll be there."

He held her coat. "I'm sorry, Ellie."

"Well—what can you do?" Then she went out the door.

Walter looked around the living room. He picked up Ellie's martini glass. His glass was in the kitchen. At least the table was not yet set. The telephone rang again, and Walter turned and set the martini glass in back of the ivy on the mantelpiece.

It was Bill Ireton on the telephone. He told Walter that he had just had a visit from a Lieutenant Corby of the Philadelphia police force. He said that Corby had questioned him about Walter's personal life, his friends around Benedict, and his relations with Clara.

"You know, Walter, I've known you a long time, nearly three years. I haven't got a damn thing to say against you, and I didn't. You understand, don't you?" Bill asked.

"Yes. Thanks, Bill." Walter heard Corby's car.

"I told him you and Clara weren't the happiest people on earth, I couldn't very well deny that, but I said I'd go down the line that you hadn't a thing to do with her death. He asked me if I'd ever known you and Clara to have any violent fights. I said you were the mildest guy I ever knew."

Fatal, Walter thought. Bill's voice went on and on in his ear. He wanted to go and empty the ashtray in the living room.

"He asked me if I knew about the divorce coming up. I told him I did."

"That's okay. Thanks for telling me. I appreciate it."

"Is there anything we can do for you, Walter?"

"I don't think so." The doorbell rang. Walter kept his voice low and unhurried. "I'll call you soon, Bill. Give my best to Betty." He hung up and went to the door.

"Good evening," Corby said, taking off his hat. "I'm sorry to intrude like this."

"Perfectly all right," Walter said.

Corby looked all around him as they went into the living

room. He laid his coat and hat down across a chair, and strolled on toward the fireplace. He stopped, and Walter saw that he was looking straight down at the ashtray on the end table that held a couple of lipstick-stained cigarettes.

"I've interrupted you," Corby said. "I'm awfully sorry."

"Not at all." Walter put his hands in his jacket pockets. "What did you want to talk about?"

"Oh—routine questions." Corby dropped to the sofa and crossed his thin legs. "I've been talking to some of your friends in the neighborhood, so you may hear about that. We always do that." He smiled. "But I've also spoken to this man Kimmel."

"Kimmel?" Walter tensed, expecting Corby to say that Kimmel had told him he had come into his shop.

"You know, the one I mentioned whose wife was murdered in the woods near Tarrytown—also on a bus trip."

"Oh, yes," Walter said.

Corby took one of his filter-tipped cigarettes. "I'm so convinced this man is guilty—"

Walter took a cigarette, too. "You're working on the Kimmel case?"

"As of this week, yes. Of course I've been interested in the Kimmel case since August. I'm interested in any case that hasn't been solved. Maybe I can solve it," he said explanatorily with his boyish smile. "After meeting Kimmel and learning a little of the circumstances, I'm very interested in Kimmel as a suspect."

Walter said nothing.

"We haven't the right evidence yet about Kimmel. *I* haven't," he added with an unconvincing modesty, "and I don't think the Newark police have been working on it very hard. You don't remember the Kimmel case, do you?"

"Only what you told me. Kimmel's wife was murdered, you said."

"Yes. I don't think Kimmel has so much to do with you, but you may have a lot to do with Kimmel."

"I don't understand that."

Corby leaned his head back against the sofa pillow and rubbed his forehead tiredly. There was a pink crease across his forehead from his hatband, and faint sinks under his blue eyes.

"I mean, Kimmel is very upset by the Stackhouse case, more upset than he shows. The more he's upset, the more he'll betray himself—I hope." Corby gave a laugh. "He's not the kind to betray himself very easily, though."

And meanwhile, Walter thought, I'm the tortured guinea pig. Corby was going to magnify the Stackhouse case and make a Kimmel case out of it. Walter waited attentively, unmoving. He was trying to be cooperative this time.

"Kimmel's a big fat fellow with a pretty well-functioning brain, though it's got a touch of megalomania. He likes to make toadies of people around him, his inferiors. Worked his way up from the slums, fancies himself an intellectual—which he is, in fact."

The smile irritated Walter. It's all a jolly game, Walter thought. Cops and robbers. It must take a mind that's nasty or twisted somewhere, he thought, to devote itself exclusively to homicide, especially with the gleeful zest that Corby showed. "What do you expect Kimmel to do?" Walter asked.

"Confess, finally. That's what I'll make him do. I've found out quite a lot about his wife, enough to tell me that Kimmel loathed her with a passion that probably wouldn't be satisfied with—well, only a divorce. All this ties up with Kimmel's character, which can't be appreciated until one sees the man." He looked at Walter, then stabbed his cigarette out in the ashtray and said, "Would you mind if I look around the house?"

Guests had asked it in the same way, Walter thought. "Not at all."

Walter was going to lead him to the stairs, but Corby stopped in front of the fireplace. He reached out and picked up the glass in back of the ivy, turned its stem between his fingers. Walter knew there was lipstick on the rim. And still a few drops in the glass.

"Care for a drink?" Walter asked.

"No, thanks." Corby set the glass back and gave Walter a smiling, understanding glance. "You were seeing Miss Briess this evening?"

"Yes," Walter said expressionlessly. He led the way up the stairs. Corby hadn't even called Ellie yet. Corby gave her a categorical name, Walter supposed: girl friend. Or mistress. The details didn't matter.

Corby went into the bedroom, strolled up and down the room with his hands in his pockets and made no comment. Then he strolled out, and Walter showed him the smaller room in the other front corner, which was supposed to be a maid's room, though there was no bed in it, only a short sofa. Walter explained that their maid did not sleep in.

"Who is your maid?" he asked.

"Claudia Jackson. She lives in Huntington. She comes twice a day, morning and evening."

"Can I have her address?" Corby took out his tablet.

"Seven seventeen Spring Street, Huntington."

Corby wrote. "She's not here this evening?"

"No, not this evening," Walter answered, frowning.

"Guest room?" Corby asked as they went into the hall.

"My wife never wanted one. There's a room over here, a kind of sitting room."

Corby looked into it without interest. They had never used the room, though Claudia kept it in order. It looked dead and horrible to Walter now, like a model room in a department store.

"Are you going to keep the house?" Corby asked.

"I haven't decided." Walter opened another door. "This is my study."

"This is nice," Corby said appreciatively. He went to the bookshelves and stood with his palms against the small of his back, holding back his jacket. "Lots of law books. Do you do a lot of work at home?"

"No, I don't."

Corby looked down at the desk. Walter's big dark-blue scrapbook lay at one corner. "Photograph album?" Corby asked, reaching for it.

"No, it's a kind of notebook."

"May I see it?"

Walter gestured with a hand, though he disliked Corby's touching it, disliked watching him. Walter felt for cigarettes, found he hadn't any, and folded his arms. He walked to a window. He could see Corby in the glass of the window, bent over the notebook, turning the pages slowly.

"What is it?" Corby asked.

Walter turned. "It's a kind of pastime of mine. Notes on

people for some essays I have in mind to write." Walter's frown bit deeper. He came back toward Corby, searching for some phrase that would get him away from the notebook, from the finely written lines that Corby was making an effort to read. Walter watched him turn another page. There was a newspaper clipping lying loose. Walter looked at it. The size, the heavy print at the top was familiar. He couldn't believe it.

Corby picked it up. "This is about Kimmel!" Corby said incredulously.

"Is it?" Walter asked in the same tone.

"Why, yes!" Corby said, turning his amazed smile to Walter. "You tore it out?"

"I must have, but I don't remember it." Walter looked at Corby and in that instant something terrible happened between them: Corby's face held simply a natural surprise, and in the surprise was discovery, the discovery of Walter's deceit. For an instant, they looked at each other like ordinary human beings, and Walter felt the effect on him was devastating.

"You don't remember it?" Corby asked.

"No. I never used it. I cut out a great many things from the paper." He made a gesture toward the scrapbook. There were ten or twelve other newspaper items scattered through the book. But Walter was sure he had thrown the Kimmel clipping away.

Corby glanced at the item again, dropped it where it had been, then bent over the book once more, reading the blocks of Walter's handwriting, the typed and pasted-in paragraphs on the same page. Walter saw that they were the pages about Jensen and Cross. Nothing to do with Kimmel. Better if it had had to do with Kimmel, Walter thought.

"It's a bunch of notes about—unworthy friends," Walter explained. "Something like that. I probably tore that out thinking the murderer might be discovered later. And then I forgot the name. I was interested in the tie-up between the murderer and the victim. Nothing ever came out, though, and I suppose that's why I forgot it. It is an amazing coincidence. If I'd—" Walter's mind went blank suddenly.

Corby was looking at him shrewdly, though some of the surprise was still left in his face, watching him as if he were only waiting, only had to wait, for Walter to say something that would clinch his guilt. Corby smiled a little. "I'd like to know just what did go through your mind when you tore the piece out."

"I told you. I was interested in who the murderer would be—eventually. Just as—" Walter had been about to mention that he used a clipping about a murder in his essay on Mike and Chad, a murder resulting from such a friendship, but the clipping had long ago been thrown away. "I was interested in the connection between Helen Kimmel and the murderer." Walter saw that Corby had picked up the *Helen*.

"Go on," Corby said.

"There's nothing more to say." Part of Walter's mind was playing with the possibility that someone had planted the Kimmel piece in the scrapbook. But it was the very piece he had torn out. He recognized even its outline. Then suddenly he remembered: the piece of paper had fallen on the floor that day he threw it away. He'd been too lazy to pick it up, and then Claudia had found it. "Actually, you know, I threw—" He stopped as suddenly as he had started.

"What?"

Walter did not want to confess that he remembered that much about it. Damn Claudia, he thought. Damn her efficiency! Clara had put that into her. "Nothing. It doesn't matter."

"But it might," Corby said persuasively.

"It doesn't."

"Have you ever seen Kimmel, talked to him?"

"No," Walter said, and in the next second wanted to change his answer. His mind seesawed horribly between telling the whole story now, and concealing as much about Kimmel as he could. But what if Kimmel told it all tomorrow? Walter felt he was the victim of some complicated game, a slow gathering of nets that had suddenly dropped on him and drawn tight.

Corby put a hand in his trousers pocket and strolled toward Walter, circling him, keeping a certain distance, as if to see him better in this new light.

"You're really obsessed with this Kimmel case, aren't you?" Walter asked.

"Obsessed?" Corby gave a deprecatory laugh. "I'm working on a half-dozen homicide cases at least!"

"But where I'm concerned, you seem to be hipped on the Kimmel case," Walter blurted out.

"Yes. It's the similarity of the cases that has reopened the Kimmel case, you might say. The Newark police had put it down as person or persons unknown, a maniac's attack—hopeless. But you've shown us the way it *might* have happened." Corby waited, letting it sink in. "Kimmel's alibi isn't the strongest in the world. Nobody actually saw him at the moment it happened. Did it occur to you that Kimmel might have killed his wife—either when you tore the story out or afterward?"

"No, I don't think it did. They said he—" He stopped. There was no mention of Kimmel's alibi in the story Corby had looked at.

"It's just a coincidence, isn't it?"

Walter kept a sullen silence. It annoyed him that he couldn't always tell when Corby chose to be sarcastic or not.

"Do you mind if I take this?" Corby asked, picking up the newspaper piece from the scrapbook.

"Not at all."

Corby laid the piece inside his wallet, fastened the wallet snap and put it back in his inside pocket. Walter wondered what Corby was going to do now—show it to Kimmel?

"You may find some other interesting items in the papers about Melchior Kimmel before long," Corby said with a smile, "but I sincerely hope I don't have to bother you again—like this."

Walter didn't believe a word of it. He had no doubt the story of his having the Kimmel clipping would go into the newspapers now, too. He followed Corby out of the room.

Corby went to his coat and hat on the chair. He lifted his narrow head. "Something burning?"

Walter hadn't noticed it. He went into the kitchen and turned the oven off. It was the potatoes. He opened a kitchen window.

"Sorry to spoil your evening," Corby said when Walter came back.

"Not at all." He walked with Corby to the door.

"Good night," Corby said.

"Good night."

Walter turned from the door and stared at the telephone,

listening to Corby's car start, wondering how he could explain it to Ellie. Or to anybody. He couldn't. Walter frowned, trying to imagine the story of tonight in the newspapers. They couldn't convict a man just because he had a newspaper clipping! They hadn't indicted Kimmel yet, either. Maybe Kimmel wasn't guilty. So far only Corby seemed to think he was. And himself.

Walter ran upstairs quickly. He had remembered something else. From the back of his desk drawer he took a flat ledger book in which he sporadically kept a diary. He hadn't written in it for weeks, but he had written something, he remembered, in the days just after Clara's recovery from the sleeping pills. There it was, the last entry:

It is curious that in the most important periods of one's life, one never keeps up a diary. There are some things that even a habitual diary-keeper shrinks from putting down in words—at the time, at least. And what a loss, if one intends to keep an honest history at all. The main value of diaries is their recording of difficult periods, and this is just the time when one is too cowardly to put down the weaknesses, the vagaries, the shameful hatreds, the little lies, the selfish intentions, carried out or not, which form one's true character.

It was preceded by a gap of over a month, a month of strife with Clara and then her suicide attempt. Walter tore out the page. If Corby ever found this, Walter supposed, this would absolutely finish him. Walter started to burn the page with his cigarette lighter, then picked up the diary and took it downstairs. The fire was full of hot embers. He ripped the whole book apart in three sections, laid them on the embers and put on more wood.

Then he went to the telephone and called Ellie at the Three Brothers. He apologized for the length of time Corby had taken.

"What's happened now?" There was boredom and irritation in Ellie's voice.

"Nothing," Walter said. "Nothing except that the potatoes burned."

25

"I WAS just about to go out," Kimmel said. "If you—"

"This is extremely important. It won't take long."

"I'm leaving the house now!"

"I'll be right over," Corby said, and hung up.

Should he face it now or tomorrow? Kimmel wondered. He took off his overcoat, started mechanically to hang it up, then thrust it from him with a petulant gesture into the corner of the red plush sofa. He looked around thoughtfully at the upright piano and for a moment saw a ghostly form of Helen sitting there, drearily fingering "The Tennessee Waltz." He wondered what Corby had to talk about, or was it nothing, like yesterday, was he just coming over to be irritating? He wondered if Corby had made enough inquiries in the neighborhood to find out about Kinnaird, that lout of an insurance salesman Helen had been fornicating with. Nathan, his friend who taught history in the local high school, knew about Kinnaird. Nathan had come in the shop that morning to tell him that Corby had been asking him questions. But Ed Kinnaird's name had not been mentioned. Kimmel scratched under his armpit. He had just come in from dinner at the Oyster House, and had intended to settle himself with a beer and his wood carving and listen to the radio for an hour or so before he went to bed with a book.

He'd get the beer anyway, he thought, and he went down the hall to the kitchen. The floor of the frame house squeaked with his weight. The doorbell rang as he came back up the hall. Kimmel let Corby in.

"Sorry to bother you at this time of night," Corby said, looking not at all sorry. "My daytime's taken up with other work these days."

Kimmel said nothing. Corby was looking over the living room, bending for a close look at the dark-stained wooden objects, all intricately carved and joined together like sausage links, that stood on top of the long white bookcase. Kimmel had an obscene answer, if Corby should ask him what they were.

"I've been to see Stackhouse again," Corby said, straightening up, "and I found something very interesting."

"I told you I'm not at all interested in the Stackhouse case, or in anything else you have to say."

"You're in no position to say that," Corby replied, seating himself on Kimmel's sofa. "I happen to think you're guilty, Kimmel."

"You told me that yesterday."

"Did I?"

"You asked me if I had anyone else besides Tony Ricco to substantiate my alibi. You implied that I was guilty."

"I think Stackhouse is guilty," Corby said. "I'm sure you are."

Kimmel wondered suddenly if he carried a gun under that unbuttoned jacket. Probably. He picked up his beer from the low table in front of Corby, poured the rest of the bottle into the glass and set the bottle down. "I intend to report this to the Newark police tomorrow. I am not suspected or doubted by the Newark police. I am in very good standing in Newark."

Corby nodded, smiling. "I spoke to the Newark police before I came to see you the other day. Naturally I'd ask their permission to work on the Kimmel case, since it's not in my territory. The police don't mind at all if I work on it."

"I mind. I mind the privacy of my house being invaded."

"I'm afraid there's nothing you can do about it, Kimmel."

"You'd better get out of this house, unless you'd rather be thrown out. I've some important work to do."

"What's more important, Kimmel? My work or yours? What are you doing tonight—reading the Marquis de Sade's Memoirs?"

Kimmel looked Corby's reedy body up and down. What could Corby know of such a book? A familiar confidence surged through Kimmel, a sense of immunity, powerful and impregnable as a myth. He was a giant compared to Corby. Corby would find no hold on him.

"Remember, Kimmel, I told you I thought Stackhouse did it by following the bus, persuading his wife to go to the cliff and pushing her over?"

Finally Kimmel said, "Yes."

"I think you did something like that, too."

Kimmel said nothing.

"And the very interesting thing is that Stackhouse guessed it," Corby went on. "I visited Stackhouse last night in Long Island, and what do you think I found? The story of Helen Kimmel's murder, dated August fourteenth." Corby opened his wallet. He held the piece of newspaper up, smiling.

Corby was holding the paper out to him. Kimmel took it and held it close to his eyes. He recognized it as one of the earliest reports of the murder. "Am I supposed to believe that? I don't believe you." But he did believe him. It was the stupidity of Stackhouse he couldn't believe.

"Ask Stackhouse, if you don't believe me," Corby said, replacing the paper in his wallet. "Wouldn't you like to meet him?"

"I have no interest *whatsoever* in meeting him."

"However, I think I'm going to arrange it."

It hit Kimmel like the dull blow of a hammer over his heart, and from then on he began to feel his heartbeats thudding in his thick chest. Kimmel opened his arms in a gesture that said he was quite willing to meet Stackhouse, but that he saw no purpose in it. Kimmel was thinking that Stackhouse might crack up right in his shop, or wherever it was. Stackhouse would say that he had come to see him before, might even accuse him of having confessed to him how he killed Helen, of having explained to him how to do it. Kimmel could not predict Stackhouse at all. Kimmel felt himself trembling from head to foot, and he shifted and turned nearly around, staring sightlessly in front of him.

"I know a little about Stackhouse's private life. He had sufficient motive to kill his wife, just as you did—once you got mad enough. But some of your motivation was pleasure, wasn't it? In a way?"

Kimmel played with the knife in his left-hand pocket. He could still feel his heartbeats. A lie detector, he thought— He had been sure he could weather a lie detector, if they ever subjected him to one. Perhaps he couldn't. Stackhouse had guessed it, Kimmel thought, not Corby. Stackhouse had had the appalling stupidity to leave his trail everywhere, bring it right to his door! "You have all the proof you need about Stackhouse?" Kimmel asked.

"Are you getting frightened, Kimmel? I have only circum-stantial evidence, but he'll confess the rest. Not you, though. I'll have to get more proof about you and break down your alibi. Your friend Tony means well, and he thinks you were in that movie all evening, but he could just as easily be persuaded to think differently, if I talk to him enough. He's just a—"

Suddenly Kimmel flung his glass at Corby's head, grabbed Corby by the shirtfront and pulled him up over the table. Kimmel drew his right hand back for a neck-breaking blow, and then he felt what he thought was a bullet in his diaphragm. Kimmel lunged out with his right hand and missed. Then his arm was jerked down with a sharp pain; his feet left the ground. At the sickening heave in his stomach, he closed his eyes and felt himself sailing in the air. He landed on one hip with an impact that rattled the windows. Kimmel was sitting on the floor. He looked at Corby's fuzzy, elongated figure standing above him. Kimmel's fat left arm rose up independent of his will, like a floating balloon. He touched it and found it had no sensation.

"My arm's broken!" he said.

Corby snorted and shot his cuffs.

Kimmel turned his head in both directions, looking around the floor. He got onto his knees. "Do you see my glasses?"

"Here."

Kimmel felt the glasses being poked into the fingers of his left hand that was still poised in the air, and he closed his fin-gers on the thin gold earpiece, then felt it slipping, heard it fall and he knew from the sound that the glasses had broken. "Son of a bitch!" he shouted, standing up. He swayed toward Corby.

Corby stepped sideways, casually. "Don't start it again. The same thing'll happen, only worse."

"Get out!" Kimmel roared. "Get out of here, you stinking— You cockroach! You fairy!" Kimmel went on into the sexual and the anatomical, and Corby stepped quickly toward him, raising a hand. Kimmel stopped talking and dodged.

"You're a coward," Corby said.

Kimmel repeated what he thought Corby was.

Corby picked up his overcoat and put it on. "I give you warning, Kimmel, I'm not leaving you alone. And everyone in this town is going to know it, all your little friends. And one of these days I'll come walking into your shop with Stackhouse. You two have a lot in common." Corby went out and banged the door.

Kimmel stood where he was for several moments, his flabby body as taut as it could be, his unfocused eyes staring before him. He imagined Corby going to the librarian Miss Brown, going to Tom Bailey, the ex-alderman who was the most intelligent man Kimmel knew in the neighborhood, whose friendship Kimmel had striven hardest for and rated highest. Tom Bailey knew nothing about Helen's affair with Ed Kinnaird, but Kimmel had no doubt that Corby would tell everyone about it once he found out, give every sordid, repellent detail of it, of her picking him up on the street like a common prostitute, because Lena, Helen's best friend, knew that. Helen had boasted of it! Corby would put doubt in all their minds.

Kimmel suddenly began to walk, a matter of toppling forward and catching himself, feeling his way down the hall walls to the kitchen, where he washed his face with cold water under the tap. Then he felt his way back to the telephone in the living room. It took him a long while to dial the number, and then it was wrong the first time. He dialed it again.

"Hello, Tony old boy," Kimmel said cheerfully. "What are you doing? . . . Good, because the most terrible thing has just happened to me. I broke my glasses, tripped over the rug and probably broke some other things, but the glasses are in smithereens. Come over and see me for a while. I can't read or do anything tonight." Kimmel listened to Tony's voice saying he would, in just a few minutes, when he finished doing something else that he had to do, listened patiently to the dreary, modest voice while he reviewed with pleasure the services he had done for Tony, the time three years ago when Tony had got a girl pregnant and had been desperate for an abortionist. Kimmel had found one for her in a matter of minutes, safe and not too expensive. Tony had been on his knees with gratitude, because he had been terrified that his very religious family, not to mention the girl's family, might have found out.

After Kimmel hung up, he picked up the table which had been knocked over, set up the bridge lamp and removed the broken bulb from its socket. There was a limit to how much damage a man's fall could make in a room. Then he stood by the bookcase, playing with his carvings, moving their parts at various angles and observing the composition. He could see them fuzzily against the light-colored bookcase, and the effect was rather interesting. They were cigar-shaped pieces, fastened invisibly together, end to end, with wire. Some looked like animals on four legs; others, of ten pieces or more, defied any description. Kimmel himself had no definite name for them. To himself, sometimes, he called them his puppies. Each piece was differently carved with designs of his own invention, designs somewhat Persian in their motifs, their brown-stained surfaces so smoothed with fine sandpaper they felt almost soft to the touch. Kimmel loved to run his fingertips over them. He was still fondling them when the doorbell rang.

Tony came in with his hat in his hand, and awkwardly plunged himself in a chair before Kimmel could ask him to remove his overcoat. Tony was always flattered to be asked to Kimmel's house in the evening. It had not happened more than three or four times before. Tony sprang up to help Kimmel find a hanger in the closet for his coat.

"Would you like a beer?" Kimmel asked.

"Yeah, I'd like one," Tony said.

Kimmel went with dignity, half sightless, down the hall and felt for the kitchen light. Tony was too ill at ease, he supposed, to volunteer to get the beer. Tony's stupidity disgusted Kimmel, but Tony's awe of his erudition and his manners, plus his beer-drinking good fellowship, which Kimmel knew to Tony was an unusual combination, flattered Kimmel, too.

"Tony, I'd be much obliged if you can manage to come over tomorrow morning and drive my car for me to the opticians," Kimmel said as he set the beer and the glasses down.

"Sure, Mr. Kimmel. What time?"

"Oh, about nine."

"Sure," Tony said, recrossing his legs nervously.

Amazing, Kimmel thought, that this insignificant wretch of a boy, pockmarked and devoid of any character in his face, could actually get a girl pregnant. Tony had never given the matter a thought, Kimmel felt sure, didn't have the faintest idea of the processes involved. Which was why it was so easy for him. Kimmel supposed that Tony had a girl every week or so. Tony had a regular girl friend, but he knew she was not one of the girls the neighborhood boys slept with. Kimmel often eavesdropped on their conversation from a window of his shop which gave on an alley. A girl named Connie was the neighborhood favorite. But Tony's girl Franca had never even been mentioned, though Kimmel always listened for her name. "What have you been doing lately, Tony?"

"Oh, same old thing, working the store, bowling a little."

It was always the same answer. But Kimmel always asked out of politeness that he knew was unappreciated. "Oh, Tony, by the way, there may be some more questioning by the police in the next few days—or weeks. Don't let it rattle you. Tell them—"

"Oh, no," Tony said, though a little frightened.

"Tell them exactly what happened, exactly what you saw," Kimmel said in a light, precise voice. "You saw me at eight o'clock taking my seat in the movie theatre."

"Oh, sure, Mr. Kimmel."

26

"LIEUTENANT CORBY to see you, Mr. Stackhouse," Joan's voice said over the speaker on his desk. "Shall I tell him to wait or will you see him now?"

Walter glanced at Dick Jensen, who was standing beside him. They were busy with a tax case brief that had to be ready by five o'clock. "Tell him to wait just a minute," Walter said.

"Shall I leave?" Dick asked.

Dick probably knew who Corby was, Walter thought. Dick and Polly must have had a visit from Corby—the Iretons had had two—but Dick had said nothing about it. "I suppose I'd better see him alone, yes," Walter said.

Dick picked up his unlighted pipe from Walter's desk and walked to the door without a word or a glance.

Walter told Joan he was ready, and Corby came in at once, brisk and smiling.

"I know you're busy," Corby said, "so I'll get to the point. I'd like you to come over to Newark with me this afternoon to meet Kimmel."

Walter stood up slowly. "I don't care to meet Kimmel. I've got work that has to be—"

"But I want Kimmel to meet you," Corby said with his mechanical smile. "Kimmel is guilty, and we're winding up his case. I want Kimmel to see you. He thinks you're guilty, too, and it's got him scared."

Walter frowned. "And you think I'm guilty, too?" he asked quietly.

"No, I don't think you are. I'm after Kimmel." Corby's smile brightened his blue eyes with a completely false cheer. "Of course, you can refuse to go—"

"I think I do."

"—but I can make your own situation several times as unpleasant as it is for you now."

Walter's thumbs gripped the edge of his desk. He had been congratulating himself that Corby hadn't released the story of the Kimmel clipping to the newspapers yet, had even entertained some hope that Corby had realized it might all be a series of coincidences and that he could be innocent. Now Walter realized that Corby meant to hold the Kimmel clipping over him. "What's your objective in all this?" Walter asked.

"My objective is to get the truth out," Corby said, smiling self-consciously. He lighted a cigarette.

Suddenly Walter thought: his objective was to advance himself, to trap two men instead of one if he could, to win commendation or a promotion for himself. Suddenly Corby's ruthless ambition struck Walter as so patent, he was amazed he hadn't realized before that it was Corby's only motivation. "If you're talking about publicizing the Kimmel clipping episode," Walter said, "go ahead, but I don't care to meet Kimmel."

Corby looked at him sharply. "It's more than just a story, just an episode. It could ruin your whole life."

"I fail to see the picture as clearly as you do. You haven't yet proven Kimmel guilty, much less guilty of the particular actions that you seem to think both of us—"

"You don't know what I've proven," Corby said confidently. "I'm reconstructing exactly what happened between Kimmel and his wife just around the time she was killed. When that's spread out in front of Kimmel, he's going to break down and confess exactly what I'm accusing him of."

Exactly what *I'm* accusing him of. His arrogance stunned Walter to silence for a moment. The implication was that Kimmel's confession—or Kimmel's retaliatory statement that he had visited him in his shop last month, which Kimmel might already have made—would drag himself down in the same guilt, make him confess, too.

"Do you agree to come? I'm asking a favor of you. I can promise you, if you do, that nothing of it will get in the newspapers." Corby's voice was eager, supremely confident, and to Walter appalling.

After he saw Kimmel, it wouldn't need to get in the papers, Walter thought. Maybe Kimmel had already told Corby that he had been to his shop. Why *wouldn't* Kimmel have told him? Corby looked as if he knew, as if he were waiting for him to admit it now. If he refused to go, Corby would bring Kimmel to the office, Walter supposed. Corby would force the meeting in one way or another. "All right," Walter said. "I'll go."

"Fine," Corby smiled. "I'll be back around five. I've got a

car. We'll drive over." Corby waved a hand and turned to the door.

Walter kept on gripping the desk after Corby was gone. What terrified him was the fact that Corby believed him guilty now, too. Until five minutes ago, Walter had dared to believe that Corby didn't, or at least that Corby was willing to hold his attack in abeyance until he was sure. Walter felt he had just agreed to walk straight into hell.

"Walter!" Dick snapped his fingers. "What's the matter? In a trance?"

Walter glanced at Dick, then looked down at the stapled papers on his desk that were labeled "Burden of Proof."

"Listen, Walter, what goes on with this?" Dick nodded toward the door. "The police still questioning you?"

"One man," Walter said. "Not the police."

"I don't think I told you," Dick said, "Corby came around to see Polly and me one night at the apartment. He asked me questions about you—and Clara, of course."

"When?"

"About a week ago. A little longer."

It was before Corby found the Kimmel clipping, Walter thought. The questions must have been mild. "Asked you what?"

"Asked me frankly if I thought you were capable of it. He doesn't mince words, apparently. I told him emphatically no. I told him how you reacted when Clara came out of the coma. A man doesn't react the way you did if he wants to kill his wife."

"Thanks," Walter said weakly.

"I didn't know Clara tried to kill herself, Walter. Corby told me that. I can understand the whole thing a lot better, knowing that. I can understand that Clara—well, that she killed herself the way she did."

Walter nodded. "Yes. You'd think everybody would be able to understand it."

Dick asked in a lower voice, "You're not in any particular trouble, are you, Walt—with this detective Corby?"

Walter hesitated, then shook his head. "No, no particular trouble."

"*Any* kind of trouble?"

"No," Walter said. "Shall we get back to work?" Walter

wanted to get the job done so he could be downstairs to meet Corby at five.

At five o'clock, Corby repeated his offer to drive Walter to Newark and back in his car, and Walter accepted it. They rode in silence to the Holland Tunnel. In the middle of the tunnel, Corby said: "I realize you're going out of your way to help me, Mr. Stackhouse. I appreciate it." Corby's voice had a vibrant, buried sound in the tunnel. "I expect this to have some results, though they may not show up right away."

Corby drove the intricate way to the bookshop as if he had driven it many times. Walter had slipped unconsciously into a role of pretending he had never seen the place before, though he asked no questions. The smell of the shop—stagnant, dusty, permeated with the sweetness of dry-rotting pages and bindings—seemed intensely and terrifyingly familiar to Walter. There was nobody else but Kimmel in the shop. Walter saw Kimmel get slowly to his feet behind his desk, like an elephant rising, on guard.

"Kimmel," Corby said familiarly as they approached him, "I'd like you to meet Mr. Stackhouse."

Kimmel's huge face looked blank. "How do you do?" Kimmel said first.

"How do you do?" Walter waited tensely. Kimmel's face was still expressionless. Walter could not decide if Kimmel had already betrayed him to Corby, or if he was going to, in a cold quiet way, as soon as Corby asked the proper questions.

"Mr. Stackhouse has also had the misfortune of losing his wife recently," Corby said, tossing his hat onto a table of books, "and by a catastrophe at a bus stop."

"I think I read of it," Kimmel said.

"I think you did," Corby said, smiling.

Walter shifted, and glanced at Corby. Corby's manner was an unpleasant, unbelievable combination of professional bluntness and social decorum.

"I think I also told you," Corby went on placidly, "that Mr. Stackhouse was also acquainted with the story of your wife's murder. I found an August clipping about her murder in Mr. Stackhouse's scrapbook."

"Yes," Kimmel said solemnly, nodding his bald head a little.

Walter's lips twitched in an involuntary, nervous smile,

though he felt panicked. Kimmel's tiny eyes looked completely cold, indifferent as a murderer's eyes.

"Does Mr. Stackhouse look like a murderer to you?" Corby asked Kimmel.

"Isn't that for you to find out?" Kimmel asked, placing the tips of his fat, flexible fingers on the green blotter of his desk. "I don't understand the purpose of this visit."

Corby was silent a moment. An annoyed frown was settling in his eyes. "The purpose of this visit will come out very soon," he said.

Kimmel and Walter looked at each other. Kimmel's expression had changed. There was something like curiosity in the little eyes now, and as Walter watched, one side of the heart-shaped mouth moved in a faint smile that seemed to say: We are both victims of this absurd young man.

"Mr. Stackhouse," Corby said, "you don't deny that Kimmel's actions were in your mind when you followed the bus your wife was on, do you?"

"When you say Kimmel's actions—"

"We've discussed that," Corby said sharply.

"Yes," Walter said, "I do deny that." In the last seconds a sympathy for Kimmel had sprung up in Walter so strong it embarrassed him, and he felt he should try to conceal it. He was positive now that Kimmel had never told Corby about his visit to the shop, and that he was not going to.

Corby turned to Kimmel. "And I suppose you deny that it crossed your mind Stackhouse killed his wife the same way *you* did when you read about Stackhouse's being at the bus stop?"

"It could hardly have failed to cross my mind, since the newspapers either implied it or stated it," Kimmel answered calmly. "But I did not kill my wife."

"Kimmel, you're a liar!" Corby shouted. "You know that Stackhouse's behavior has betrayed *you*. And yet you stand there acting blank about the whole thing!"

With magnificent indifference, Kimmel shrugged.

Walter felt a new strength flow into him. He took a deeper breath. It occurred to him now that Kimmel had been afraid he would betray the visit, practically as afraid as he had been that Kimmel would betray it. Kimmel evidently intended to reveal as little as he could to Corby. Suddenly it seemed so heroic and generous on Kimmel's part that Kimmel appeared a shining angel in contrast to a diabolic Corby.

Corby was moving about restlessly. He had lost the well-bred schoolboy look. He was like a long, limber wrestler maneuvering, ready to take an unfair grip. "You don't think it's the least bit unusual that Stackhouse had torn the story of your wife's murder out of the papers and then followed the bus with his own wife on it the night she was killed?"

"You told me Stackhouse's wife was a suicide," Kimmel said with surprise.

"That has not been proven." Corby drew on his cigarette and paced up and down between Walter and Kimmel.

"Just what are you trying to prove?" Kimmel folded his arms in the white shirtsleeves and leaned against the wall. His glasses were empty white circles, reflecting the light over his desk.

"I wonder," Corby sneered.

Kimmel shrugged again.

Walter could not tell if Kimmel was looking at him or not. He looked down at the book spread open on Kimmel's desk. The back of his neck ached as he moved. It was a very large old book with double columns on each page, like a Bible.

"Mr. Stackhouse," Corby said, "didn't you think when you read the newspaper story of the Kimmel murder that Kimmel might have murdered his wife?"

"You asked me that," Walter said. "I didn't think that."

Kimmel slowly reached for a leather humidor on the top of his desk. He removed its top, offered the humidor to Walter who shook his head, then to Corby, who did not look at him. Kimmel took a cigar.

Corby dropped his cigarette butt on the floor and ground it under his toe. "Another time," he said bitterly. "Some other time."

Kimmel pushed away from the wall, and looked from Corby to Walter and back again. "We are finished?"

"For today, yes." Corby picked up his hat. Then he walked toward the door.

Kimmel bent to pick up the cigarette butt that Corby had dropped, and for a moment he blocked Walter's passage. He dropped the butt into the wastebasket by his desk. Then he stepped smartly aside for Walter to pass him, and followed them both to the front door. His huge figure had an elephantine dignity. He swept the door open for them.

Corby went out without a word.

Walter turned. "Good night," he said to Kimmel.

Kimmel's eyes surveyed him coldly through the glasses. "Good night."

At the car, Walter said, "You don't have to drive me back. I can take a taxi from here." His throat was tight, as if all his tenseness had suddenly gathered there.

Corby held the door open. "It'll be hard getting a taxi to New York tonight. I'm going back to New York anyway."

To call on some more of my friends, Walter thought. It had started to rain in thin drizzling drops. The dark street looked like a tunnel in hell. Walter had a wild desire to rush back into the bookstore and talk to Kimmel, tell him exactly why he had torn the story out of the paper, tell him everything he had done and why. "All right," Walter said. He dived quickly into the car and struck his head so hard on the door frame, he felt dizzy for a few seconds.

They said nothing to each other. Corby seemed to be fuming inwardly at the failure of his afternoon. They were back in Manhattan before Walter remembered that he had an appointment with Ellie. He looked frantically at his wristwatch and saw that he was an hour and forty minutes late.

"What's the matter?" Corby asked.

"Nothing."

"You had a date?"

"Oh, no."

When Walter got out at the Third Avenue parking lot where he kept his car, he said, "I hope this interview accomplishes what you expect it to."

Corby's narrow face lowered in a deep, absent-minded nod of acknowledgment. "Thanks," he said sourly.

Walter slammed his door. He waited until Corby was out of sight, then he began to walk quickly. He tried again, now that he was free of Corby's presence, to analyze Kimmel's behavior. It wouldn't have done Kimmel any good to betray him. But Kimmel hadn't any reason on earth to protect him. Except blackmail. Walter frowned, conjuring up Kimmel's strange face, trying to interpret it. The face was coarse, but there was a great deal of pride in it. Was he the type to try blackmail? Or was he only trying to keep his nose as clean as possible by telling as little as possible? That made better sense.

Walter went into the bar of the Hotel Commodore. He didn't see Ellie at any of the tables, and started to ask the headwaiter if there was any message for him, but he gave the idea up. He walked up to the lobby, looking for her. He had given her up and was going out the front door, when he saw her coming in from the sidewalk.

"Ellie, I'm terribly sorry," he said. "I wasn't able to reach you—stuck in a conference for three hours."

"I called your office," she said.

"We weren't there. Did you have anything to eat?"

"No."

"We can get something here, if you'd like."

"I'm out of the mood," she said, but she went with him down to the bar.

They sat down at a table and ordered drinks. Walter wanted a double scotch.

"I don't believe you were in a conference," Ellie said. "You were with Corby, weren't you?"

Walter started, looked from her face to the silver pin in the form of a flaming sun on her shoulder. "Yes," he said.

"Well, what's he saying now?"

"More questions. The same questions. I wish you wouldn't ask me, Ellie. It'll blow over finally. There's no use going over and over it." He looked around for the waiter with his drink.

"I saw him, too."

"Corby?"

"He came to the school at one o'clock today. He told me about the clipping he found in your house."

Walter felt the blood drain out of his face. Corby hadn't even bothered telephoning Ellie before. He had waited, to be able to tell her something like this.

"It's true, isn't it?" Ellie asked.

"Yes, it's true."

"How did you happen to have it?"

Walter picked up his drink. "I tore the piece out the way I tear a lot of newspaper items out. It was among some notes I had for the essays I'm writing. I have them in a scrapbook at home."

"That was the night I waited in the Three Brothers?"

"Yes."

"Why didn't you tell me about it?"

"Because the story Corby was making out of it was fantastic! It still is."

"Corby told me he thinks Kimmel killed his wife. He thinks he followed the bus—and that you did the same thing."

Walter felt the same resentful self-defense, the anger that he felt against Corby, rising in him now against Ellie. "Well, do you believe him?"

Ellie sat there as tense as he, over the drink she had not touched. "I don't quite understand why you had that story. What essays are you writing?"

Walter explained it, and explained that he had thrown the piece away, and that Claudia must have found it and put it back in his scrapbook. "Good God, there was nothing in the newspaper about Kimmel following the bus! Corby hasn't proved that Kimmel followed the bus. Corby's got an obsession. I've explained the damned clipping to Corby, and if people don't believe me, to hell with them all!" He lighted a cigarette, then saw that he had a cigarette burning in the ashtray. "I suppose Corby tried to convince you that I killed my wife and that you were one of my main motives, didn't he?"

"Oh, yes, but I can handle that all right because I expected it," Ellie said.

It was the clipping she couldn't handle, Walter thought. He looked at Ellie's intent, still-questioning eyes, and it astounded Walter that she doubted him, that Corby with his wild illogical argument could have put doubt even in Ellie. "Ellie, his whole theory doesn't make sense. Look—"

"Walter, will you swear to me that you didn't kill her?"

"What do you mean? You don't believe me when I *tell* you I didn't?"

"I want you to swear it," Ellie said.

"Do I have to take an oath to you? I've been over every step of that night with you, you know every move I made as well as the police."

"All right. I asked you to swear it."

"It's the principle of the thing, that you even have to *ask* me!" he said vehemently.

"It's so simple, though, isn't it?"

"You don't believe me either!" he said.

"I do. I want to. It's—"

"You don't, or you wouldn't ask that!"

"All right, let's stop it." She glanced to one side. "Let's not talk so loud."

"Does that matter? I'm not guilty of anything. But you don't believe me, that's obvious. You choose to doubt me like all the others!"

"Walter, stop it," Ellie whispered.

"You suspect me, don't you?"

She looked back at him just as fiercely. "Walter, I'll excuse this—put it down to nerves, but not if you keep on with it!"

"Oh, you'll excuse it!" he mocked.

Ellie jumped up suddenly and slid out from the table. Walter had a glimpse of her flying coat hem disappearing around the door. He stood up, fumbled for his billfold, threw down a five-dollar bill and ran out.

"Ellie!" he called. He looked into the jumble of lights and traffic of 42nd Street, across the street to the corners. She'd go to Penn Station to catch a train home, probably, since she hadn't brought her car. Or would she? Where did Pete Slotnikoff live? Somewhere on the West Side. To hell with it, Walter thought. To hell with her.

He walked back to the Third Avenue parking lot. He headed into the old homeward groove of the East River Drive.

The willow trees that overhung Marlborough Road near the house depressed him, made him think of the dreary winged figures that hover over tombstones and deathbeds in Blake engravings. He put the car in the garage. The sound of a twig breaking under his own foot made him jump. He picked up the loose bottom rail of the gate carefully, instead of kicking it aside as he usually did, and propped it up on the crosspiece.

Walter awakened the next morning at six, from nerves and the pangs of hunger. He dressed in old manila pants and a shirt and the flannel lumberjacket he wore on fishing trips. He got a piece of bread and cheese as he passed through the kitchen, then went out to the toolshed next to the garage. He was going to fix the gate.

He had to saw a piece of firewood as a brace to go under the broken rail, but the firewood was the same kind of wood as the gate rail, and he was satisfied with the job when it was done. It was patched, not perfect, but it wouldn't drag the ground any more. It was still only twenty to seven, when he usually arose, so he got some white paint and a brush from the garage and gave the kitchen steps a few strokes where the paint had begun to wear. He was just finishing up when he heard a step on the dirt road. It was Claudia, coming from the bus stop at the end of Marlborough Road. She gave him a smile that he could see from where he was, and called out: "Morning, Mr. Stackhouse!"

"Morning, Claudia!" he called back. The author of all his troubles, Walter thought. At least, of the worst of them. She was carrying a bag of groceries, for him.

"You're up early this morning," Claudia said. She looked happy to see him pottering around in old clothes.

"I thought it was high time I fixed that gate. Watch the bottom step here. It's wet."

"Isn't that fine!" Claudia said cheerfully. She stepped over the step and went into the kitchen.

Walter took the paint back to the garage, cleaned the brush with turpentine, and went back to the house. He went to the telephone in the upstairs hall and called Ellie. He wasn't entirely sure she would be home. The telephone rang about five times before she answered it. Ellie said she had been taking a bath.

"I'm sorry about last night, Ellie," Walter said. "I was very rude. I want to say that I do swear it—what you asked me last night. I swear it, Ellie."

There was a long pause. "All right." Her voice sounded very low and very serious. "It's impossible to talk to you when you're like that. You make everything look much worse for you than it is. You give the impression of fighting against something that's got you completely terrified."

It sounded as if she were waiting for him to protest some more that he was innocent, waiting for him to prove it all over again for her. He still heard a lurking doubt in her voice. "Ellie, I'm sorry about last night," he said quietly. "It's never going to happen again. Good lord!"

Another silence.

"Can I see you tonight, Ellie? Can you have dinner with me over here?"

"I have to be at rehearsals until eight."

They were starting the Thanksgiving Day play rehearsals at her school, Walter remembered. "Afterwards then. I'll pick you up at school at eight."

"All right," she said, not at all enthusiastically.

"Ellie, what's the matter?"

"I think you're acting very strangely, I suppose."

"I think you're making something out of this that isn't there!" Walter replied.

"There you go again. Walter, you can't blame me for asking the simple questions I do when I'm confronted with someone like Corby yesterday—"

"Corby's off his head," Walter interrupted her.

"If Corby does question you, I don't see why you have to lie about it. You'd make anyone think there really is something you're trying to conceal. You can't blame me for asking simple questions when a man like Corby confronts me with a story he seems to believe and that is possibly—just possibly possible as far as the facts go," she finished in an arguing tone.

Walter crushed down what he wanted to reply to that. And in the next moment he was frantic to think of something to say to allay her suspicions, to hold on to her because he felt she was slipping away. "Corby's story is not possible," he began calmly, "because I *couldn't* have done what Corby says I did and then hang around the bus stop for fifteen minutes, asking every Tom, Dick and Harry where the woman I murdered is!"

She was silent. He knew she was thinking: he's up in the air again, and what's the use?

"I'll see you tonight," she said. "Eight o'clock."

He wanted to go on with it. He didn't know how. "All right," he said. Then they hung up.

27

WALTER LINGERED at the corner and looked around him, looking for Corby.

An old man, holding a small child by the hand, crossed the street. The cobbled pavement of the street looked filthy with grit and time and sin, like the soiled buildings that surrounded him. Walter started into the block and stopped, staring at a swaybacked horse pulling a wagon full of empty crates. He could still telephone, he thought. His first idea had been to telephone, but he was afraid Kimmel would refuse to see him, or hang up as soon as he heard his voice. Walter went on. The bookshop was on this side of the street. Walter passed a small shop with upholstery materials in the window, then a dingy jewelry repair shop. He saw Kimmel's projecting front window.

The shop was better lighted now than the other times Walter had seen it. Two or three people were looking at books at the tables, and as Walter watched through the window, he saw Kimmel come forward and speak to a woman who was handing him some money. He could still leave, Walter thought. It was a reckless, stupid idea. He had left work undone at the office. Dick had been annoyed with him. He could start back and be at the office by 4:15. Walter looked into the shop, wondering. *Leave*, he told himself. But he knew he would go back to work, back home, and the same arguments and urges would torment him again. Walter thrust the door open and went in.

He saw Kimmel glance at him, look away, and then back again suddenly. Kimmel adjusted his glasses with his fat fingers and peered at him. Walter approached him. "Can I see you for a few minutes?" he asked Kimmel.

"Are you by yourself?" Kimmel asked.

"Yes."

The woman from whom Kimmel had taken the book looked at Walter but without interest, and turned to the table again.

Kimmel went to the back of the store with the book and the woman's money.

Walter waited. He waited very patiently by another table, and picked up a book and looked at its cover. Finally Kimmel

came up to him. "Do you want to come back here?" he asked,
looking down at Walter with his cold, nearly expressionless tan
eyes.

Walter came with him. He took off his hat.

"Keep that on," Kimmel said.

Walter put his hat on again.

Kimmel stood behind his desk, huge and hostile, waiting.

"I'd like you to know that I'm not guilty," Walter said
quickly.

"That's of great interest to me, isn't it?" Kimmel asked.

Walter thought he had prepared himself for Kimmel's hostility, but face to face with it, it flustered him. "I should think it
would be of *some* interest. Eventually it will be proven that I'm
not guilty. I realize that I've brought the police down on your
head."

"Oh, do you!"

"I also know that whatever I say is inadequate—and ridiculous," Walter went on determinedly. "I'm in a very bad position
myself."

"*You* are in!" Kimmel said more loudly, though he still, like
Walter, did not raise his voice enough to attract the attention
of the people in the shop. "Yes, you are," Kimmel said in a
different tone, and there was a note of satisfaction in it. "You
are far worse off than I am."

"But I'm not guilty," Walter said.

"I don't care. I don't care what you've done or haven't
done." Kimmel leaned forward with his hands on his desk.

Kimmel's fat mouth with the heavy seam along the heart-
shaped upper lip seemed to Walter the most vulgar thing he
had ever looked at. "I realize you don't care. I realize all you
wish is that you'll never see me again. I came here only to—"
Walter stopped as a young man came close to the desk and
asked: "Do you have anything on outboard motorboat machinery?"

Kimmel stepped around his desk.

It was going wrong. Walter had thought out a long dialogue
between himself and Kimmel that even allowed for Kimmel's
resentment, but which let him say the things he wanted to say.
Now he couldn't get them out. He began again when Kimmel
came back.

"Neither do I care whether you are guilty or not," Walter said very quietly.

Kimmel, who was leaning over his desk where he had just written something in a notebook, turned his head toward Walter. "And what do you *think*?" he asked.

Walter thought he was guilty. Corby thought so. But did he act guilty? He didn't, Walter thought.

"*What*?" Kimmel asked boldly, straightening up, recapping his fountain pen. "That's of prime importance, your opinion, isn't it?"

"I think you are guilty," Walter said, "and it doesn't matter to me."

Kimmel only looked confused for a moment. "What do you mean it doesn't matter to you?"

"That's the whole thing. I have intruded on your life. People think I am guilty, too. At least the police are investigating me as if they believed I was guilty. We're in the same position." Walter stopped, but that was not all he had to say. He waited for Kimmel to reply.

"Why do you think I should care if you are innocent?" Kimmel asked.

Walter abandoned it. Something more important pressed at him to be said. "I want to thank you for something you had no need to do. That's not telling Corby that I'd come to see you before."

"Don't mention it," Kimmel snapped.

"It wouldn't have injured you to say so. It would have injured me—maybe fatally."

"I can still tell him, of course," Kimmel said coldly.

Walter blinked. It was as if Kimmel had spat in his face. "Are you going to?"

"Have I any reason to protect you?" Kimmel asked, his low voice shaking. "Do you realize what you have done to me?"

"Yes."

"Do you realize that this will go on and on indefinitely, for me and probably for you, too?"

"Yes," Walter said. Only he didn't really think so. Not for himself. He was answering Kimmel like a child who was being reprimanded, catechized. He ground his teeth against any further answers to Kimmel, but Kimmel asked no more questions.

"Did you kill your wife?" Walter asked. Walter could see very distinctly Kimmel's ugly mouth, one round corner trembling upward in an incredulous smile.

"Do you possibly think I would tell you, you prying idiot?"

"I want to know," Walter said, leaning forward. "I meant I didn't care from the point of view of whether you are proven guilty by the police. I don't. I only want to *know*." Walter waited, watching Kimmel. He felt that Kimmel was going to answer, and that everything—his life, his fate—was poised like a great rock on the edge of a precipice, and that Kimmel's answer would decide whether it fell or not.

"You don't care whether I'm proven guilty or not," Kimmel said in an angry whisper, "yet every move you've made, including being here now, is a move to incriminate me!"

"You've protected me. I'm not going to betray you."

"I would never tell you. Do you think you're to be trusted with anything? Even a man's innocence?"

"Yes. With this." Walter looked Kimmel in the eyes.

"I am not guilty," Kimmel said.

Walter did not believe him, but he felt that Kimmel had reached a condition of believing himself not guilty. Walter could see it in the arrogant way Kimmel straightened up, in the injured, defiant glance he threw at him. It fascinated Walter. He suddenly realized that he wanted to believe Kimmel guilty—and that logically there was still a possibility that Kimmel was not guilty at all. That possibility terrified Walter. "It never crossed your mind to do it?" Walter asked.

"To kill my wife?" Kimmel snorted astonishment. "No, but it obviously crossed yours!"

"Not when I tore the story out of the paper. I tore it out for another reason. It did cross my mind that you'd killed your wife. I admit it. I admit that I thought of killing my own wife that way. But I didn't do it. You'll have to believe me." Walter leaned on a corner of the desk.

"Why do I have to believe anything you tell me?"

Walter didn't answer.

"And do you blame me for your troubles?" Kimmel asked impatiently.

"Of course not. If I was guilty—guilty in my thoughts—"

"Oh, just a minute!" Kimmel called out over his desk.

"That's from Wainwright's?" Kimmel walked away toward the front of the store, where Walter saw a man with a crate of books on his shoulder.

Walter looked at the floor and shifted, feeling hopelessly incapable of saying what he wanted to say, feeling his whole mission was useless, would be useless. He was sticking it out, like a bad performer on a stage who has been hooted at and told to go off, but who was still sticking, in spite of mortification and shame. Walter gathered himself for another attempt as Kimmel came back.

Kimmel had receipts in his hand. He signed one, stamped the other, and gave the signed one to the delivery man. He turned to Walter. "You'd better get out of here. You can never tell when Lieutenant Corby is going to walk in. You wouldn't like that."

"I've one thing more to say."

"What is it?"

"I feel—I feel we are both guilty in a sense."

"I've told you I am not guilty."

Their bitter dialogue in subdued tones went on. "I happen to think you are," Walter said. Then he burst out, "I've told you that I *thought* about it, that I might have done it that night if I had seen my wife. I didn't see her. I couldn't find her." He leaned close to Kimmel. "I have to tell you that, and I don't care what you make of it, or if you tell the police what they'll make of it. Do you understand? We are both guilty, and in a sense I share in your guilt." But Walter realized it made sense only to him, that it was only his own belief in Kimmel's guilt that evened the scales, not Kimmel's guilt, because that wasn't proven. Now Kimmel was listening to him, he could see, but as soon as he realized this, his words were shut off with shyness. "You're my guilt!" Walter said.

Kimmel's hands fluttered. "Shut up!"

Walter had not realized how loudly he spoke. There was still a man in the shop. "I'm sorry," he said contritely. "I'm very sorry."

Kimmel's annoyed frown stayed. He leaned his heavy thighs against the edge of his desk and picked up some notebooks, threw them down one by one on the desk again, petulantly. Walter had the feeling he had seen him making the same gestures

before. Kimmel glanced, with an apprehensive lift of his eyebrows, toward the front of the store, and then he turned to
Walter.

"I understand you," he said. "That doesn't make me like you
any better. I dislike you intensely." Kimmel paused. He looked
as if he were waiting for his anger to mount. "I wish you had
never set foot in this shop! Do you understand that?"

"Of course I understand," Walter said. He felt curiously relieved suddenly.

"And now I wish you would go!"

"I will." Walter smiled a little. He took a last look at him—
massive, the glasses empty circles of light again, the mouth
precise and lewd yet intelligent. Walter turned and walked
quickly to the front of the store.

He kept walking quickly until he came to the corner where
he had hesitated. He stopped again, and surveyed the slightly
darker scene with a feeling of pleasure and relief. He put a
cigarette between his lips and lighted it. The smoke was fra-
grant and delicious, as if he had not smoked in days. He put
the cigarette in his mouth and walked on toward his car.

He felt more strongly than ever that Kimmel was guilty,
though he could not remember any specific thing that had
happened today that should make him think so. *I've told you I
am not guilty*, Kimmel's voice repeated in his ear, with the vibrance of truth in it. *I understand you. That doesn't make me
like you any better. I dislike you intensely. . . .* Walter walked
with a spring in his step. He felt relieved of a terrible strain,
though just what the strain had been he did not precisely
know. Kimmel hadn't cared if he was innocent or not! Walter
felt so much better, he could not believe that the only reason
for it was that he had disburdened himself of a statement that
Kimmel had not even been interested in hearing. Why in hell
had he thought that Kimmel *would* be? What kind of a confession was a confession of innocence? *It's equally damning, if you
only thought of killing Clara*, Walter thought, as he had often
thought before. *It's just as ruinous if you only intended to kill
her without ever having laid a hand on her.* Walter felt his
thoughts were spilling over, running nowhere, running dan-
gerously. He had just thought of telling Ellie about the conversation with Kimmel! Because it had been a good thing, a

felicitous thing, this interview with Kimmel, and he wanted to share it with her because he loved her. Only perhaps he didn't: he remembered last week, Ellie wanting him to stay the night at her apartment, and he had insisted on going home. Not that his staying or going proved or disproved anything, but the way he had refused to stay struck him now as selfish and callous. He was ashamed of that, and ashamed also of that first night in Ellie's apartment when Clara was still alive. For a moment, to justify himself, Walter tried to recreate the ugly atmosphere of those days—Clara's maddening accusations, that had driven him to Ellie. He could not make it as ugly as the present, or as maddening, or as wrong. Clara at least had been alive then.

Walter stood with his hand on his car door, trying to collect himself. He felt shaky again, off his course, off the course he should be taking. Had he done the wrong thing again in talking to Kimmel? The obvious peril of it struck him now, and he looked all around him for Corby, for a plain-clothes spy. It's a little late to be thinking of spies, Walter thought. He ducked into his car and drove off. It was only 4:10, but he didn't want to go back to the office. Nearly four hours till he had to pick up Ellie. Suppose Ellie had called him in the office this afternoon? She seldom did, but she might have. He hadn't even made up an excuse for the office. He had only told Dick that he was going out for an hour or so and that it was possible he wouldn't be back at all. If Ellie had called, she would suspect he had been with Corby again. She probably wouldn't believe him tonight when he told her he hadn't been.

28

WALTER WAITED in his car on the curving road that went from the school gates to the auditorium building. There were four or five other cars on the driveway, all of them empty. And one was Boadicea, hulking, canvas-topped, homely as a wooden shoe. Walter was conscious of a faint shame as he sat there, a dread that someone he knew—the Iretons or the Rogerses—would see him and know that he was waiting for Ellie. But the rehearsals had been over at six, he knew, and only the instructors were left now, discussing costumes. And he had threshed this out with himself weeks ago, he remembered. If he was going to see Ellie at all, he'd do it with his head up.

He got out of the car and went to meet her when he saw her come out the door. Walter wanted her to drop her car in Lennert and come in his, but Ellie insisted on taking hers. She wanted to save him the trip to Lennert and back tonight.

They drove to Walter's house and started the dinner right away because they were both hungry. Walter had a drink in the kitchen. Ellie said she was too tired for a drink. But she kept talking to him, entertaining him with a story about the stinginess of Mrs. Pierson, the school treasurer, in providing costumes for the *Hansel and Gretel* show. The witches had gone through their rehearsal that afternoon in skirts and no tops. "I had to *show* her those half-naked kids on the stage before she'd believe me!" Ellie said with a big laugh. "Finally, I got it. Fifty-five more bucks."

He loved to hear Ellie laugh. It was loud and unrepressed, filling a room with its vibrance, like the vigorous chord she struck when she finished a session on her violin.

They put up a bridge table in the living room. Just as they were sitting down to eat, the doorbell rang. Walter went to answer it. It was the Iretons, bubbling over with apologies for crashing in just when they were about to have dinner, but after a few moments, they were both sitting down, content to stay while Walter and Ellie ate. Walter couldn't figure out whether they were slightly high, or covering up the fact that they wanted to snoop a little bit—and had struck it rich tonight—with a lot of animation.

"I hear you're playing the piano for the Thanksgiving show at Harridge," Betty Ireton said to Ellie. "I'm going with Mrs. Agnew. You know, Florence's mother?"

"Oh, yes," Ellie said with recognition, smiling. "Flo's in the cuckoo chorus."

"Mine're too young for school yet. . . ."

Betty was being much more amiable than necessary. Walter wiped his lips carefully. Ellie had almost no lipstick on.

"How's business, Walt?" Bill leaned forward on his knees, thrusting his pleasant, ruddy face toward Walter.

"The same old grind," Walter said.

"Seen Joel and Ernestine lately?"

"No. I couldn't make it last week to something they invited me to. I forgot what."

"A Boston tea party," Bill said. It was local slang for a cocktail party that got started at four on a weekend afternoon.

At least he had been invited, Walter thought. But it suddenly occurred to him that he hadn't heard anything about any Thanksgiving or Christmas parties yet. Ordinarily, at this time of year, there was talk of eggnog parties, costume parties, and even sleigh-ride parties if it snowed. Walter was sure there had been talk. It just hadn't been addressed to him. Walter had been eating slowly and uncomfortably. He laid his knife and fork down. Betty and Ellie were talking in polite platitudes about the benefits of seeing people and possibly even a change of scene for Walter. Walter felt the silence between him and Bill was full of words: Clara had been dead only a month, and here was Ellie, sitting in the house having dinner. There had been one afternoon, about a fortnight ago, when the Iretons had seen him and Ellie buying groceries in the supermarket in Benedict. Walter still remembered how Bill had only waved to him, and had not come over to talk.

"Had any more unpleasant interviews with the police?" Bill asked Walter.

"No," Walter said. "I haven't. Have you?"

"No—but I thought you might be interested to know that Corby's been talking to people at the club," Bill said in a low tone that did not interfere with Ellie's and Betty's conversation.

"Sonny Cole told me. He talked to Sonny and Marvin Hays, I think it was. And also Ralph." Bill smiled a little.

Walter barely remembered that Ralph was the name of the club barman. "That's annoying," Walter said calmly. "What do they know about me? I haven't been to the club in months."

"Oh, it's not about you—I don't suppose. They were asking—that is, this fellow Corby— Well, after all, Walter, I suppose what they're trying to prove is whether she was a suicide or whether somebody killed her, aren't they? I suppose they're sounding around for possible enemies." Bill looked down at his clasped hands. He was pressing their palms together and making sucking noises with them.

Walter knew Corby had been asking questions about him, not about possible enemies. He saw that Betty and Ellie were listening now, too. And *he* had been there, right at the bus stop. They all knew it. Walter felt they were all waiting for him to make the statement, for the ten thousandth time, that he didn't do it. They were waiting to hear just how it would sound this time, to take it home and test it, taste it, turn it over and smell it, and decide if it were true or not. Or rather, not *quite* decide. Even Ellie, Walter thought. Walter kept a stubborn silence.

"Corby was around to our house again, too," Bill went on in the same impassive voice that was a lot different from the friendly, excited voice he had used the night he had telephoned about Corby. "Told me some story of how he'd found a newspaper clipping in your house about the Kimmel case."

Bill rolled it off as if he knew all about the Kimmel case. Walter glanced at Ellie, and in that split second saw the same look of waiting to hear what he would answer, a look that was almost as bad as the Iretons' blatant curiosity.

"Seems Corby thinks there's a similarity," Bill said. He shook his head, embarrassed. "I sure wouldn't like to be—I mean—"

"What do you mean?" Walter asked.

"I mean, I guess it looks bad, Walter, doesn't it?" Now there was a sneaking fear in Bill's face, as if he were afraid Walter were going to jump up and hit him.

It was worse than if Corby had put it in the newspapers, Walter thought. Now he was telling everybody about it, giving everybody the idea it was a vital piece of evidence in the proof he was collecting, still too secret and explosive to be put into print. "I explained that newspaper story to Corby. My explanation was satisfactory," Walter said, reaching for his cigarettes. "It looks bad if Corby chooses to make it look bad. He's trying to imply that Kimmel and I could both be murderers. Kimmel hasn't been proven guilty. He hasn't even been indicted. I certainly haven't been."

Betty Ireton was sitting bolt upright, listening with eyes and ears.

"He seems to think Kimmel also followed his wife," Bill began tentatively, "and killed her that night at the—"

"That hasn't been proven at all!" Walter said.

"Do you want a cigarette?" Ellie asked.

Walter hadn't found his cigarettes. He took the one Ellie gave him. "I don't see any similarity in my case to Kimmel's except that both our wives died while they were on bus trips."

"Oh, they're not suspecting *you*, Walter," Betty said reassuringly. "Good heavens!"

Walter looked at her. "Aren't they? What are they doing? Can you imagine how it is when you've told the same story over and over, every inch, every move you made, and they still don't believe you? As a matter of fact the police do believe me. It's Corby who doesn't—or pretends he doesn't. What I should do is appeal to the police for protection against Corby!" But he had already tried that. There was absolutely no way of stopping a detective on a police force from investigating a man he thought ought to be investigated.

"Walter-r," Ellie said deprecatingly, trying to quiet him.

Walter looked down at his napkin. His shaking hands embarrassed him. The sudden waiting silence of everybody embarrassed him. He wanted to blurt out that if you keep repeating the same story over and over, you finally begin to doubt it yourself, because the words stop making sense. That was an important fact, but he couldn't say it because they would all make capital out of it. Even Ellie. Walter got up from the table and walked away, then turned around suddenly.

"Bill, I don't know if Corby told you also that Clara tried to kill herself last September."

"No," Bill said solemnly.

"She took sleeping pills. That's why she had that stay in the hospital. She had suicide on her mind. I wasn't going to say anything about it, but in view of this—these other facts—I think you ought to know about it."

"Well, we heard something of that," Bill said.

"We heard the *rumor*," Betty Ireton corrected carefully. "I think it was Ernestine who told us. She thought so. Not from anything definite, but she's very intuitive about things like that. She knew Clara was in a bad state." Betty spoke with the sweetness and decorum befitting the dead.

Betty and Bill still looked at him, expectantly. It took Walter aback. He had thought the sleeping pill episode would fairly prove that she killed herself. They were looking at him with the same question in their faces as before.

"I wonder what I'm supposed to do?" Walter burst out. "Who'll ever prove anything in a case like this?"

"Walter, I don't think they're investigating *you*," Betty repeated. "You shouldn't feel so nervous—*personally*. My goodness!"

"That's very easy to say. I wouldn't like to be up against Corby myself," Bill said. "I mean—I see what he's trying to do."

"I'm sure he explained it," Walter said. "He explains it to everybody."

"I do want to tell you, Walter—not that I have to say it, I hope—that I told Corby I was absolutely sure you'd never do a thing like this. I know what they say about people who *do*. I mean, that you never can tell about them. I feel differently about this." Bill gestured with his open hands. It didn't make his words any stronger. "Even though you didn't get along, you never would have killed her."

To Walter it sounded like total nonsense, and insincere nonsense at that. He wasn't even positive that Bill *had* said it to Corby. Walter swallowed down what he wanted to say about Corby, and came out with only a croaking "Thanks."

There was another silence. Bill looked at Betty. They exchanged a long, trout-solemn look, and then Bill stood up.

"Guess we better be taking off. Let's go, hon." Bill often proposed leaving before his wife did.

Betty hopped up obediently.

Walter felt like holding them physically while he said one

thing more, one thing that would make them believe him. These were supposed to be his best friends in the neighborhood! He went with them to the door, stiffly, his hands in his jacket pockets. They were ready to turn against him, already were turned against him. The old favorite sport of the human race, hunting down their fellows.

"Good night!" Walter called to them. He managed to make it sound actually cheerful. He shut the door and turned to Ellie. "What do you make of that?"

"They're behaving like any other average people. Believe me, Walter. Probably better than most."

"Well, have you seen any worse—toward me?"

"No, I haven't." She began to clear the table. "If I had I'd tell you."

From her tone, Walter felt she wanted him to change the subject. But if I can't talk to you, he thought, who the hell can I talk to? Suddenly he imagined Jon being told about the Kimmel clipping, and Walter felt a sickening sink in his stomach. He imagined that pushing Jon over a brink of doubt into certainty. He began to help Ellie with the things on the table. Ellie already had it nearly done. She knew where everything went. She was faster than Claudia. The coffee was already started in the Chemex. She was going to wash up the dishes, but he told her to leave them for Claudia tomorrow morning. By the time they had straightened the kitchen, the coffee was ready, and they took it into the living room. Walter poured it.

Ellie sat down and put her head back tiredly against the sofa pillow. The light from the end of the sofa lay on her curving, Slavic cheekbone. She was thinner than she had been in summer, and she had lost nearly all her tan, but Walter thought her more attractive now than before. As he bent over her, she opened her eyes. He kissed her on the lips. She smiled, but he saw a wary, wondering look in her eyes, as if she did not know what to make of him. She put her arm around his shoulder and held him, but she did not say anything to him. Nor he to her. He kissed her forehead, her lips, drawing peace and a kind of animal comfort from her body in his arms. But it was wrong that they didn't speak to each other, he thought. It was wrong that they kissed like this—he because she was there and available, and she because she wanted him, physically. He could sense it in her tense restraint, her held breath, and in the way she turned herself to him. It did not appeal to Walter, but still he held her and kissed her.

When Ellie got up to get a cigarette, Walter could feel her desire like a pull, a drain on him across the space that separated them. He stood up to light her cigarette. She put her arms around his neck.

"Walter," she said, "I want to stay here tonight."

"I can't. Not here."

Her arms tightened around his neck. "Let's go to my place then—please."

The pleading in her voice embarrassed him. And then he was ashamed of his own asinine embarrassment. "I can't, Ellie. I can't—yet. Do you understand?" He took his hands from her.

Slowly she picked up the lighter and lighted her own cigarette. "I'm not sure I do. But I guess I'll have to try."

Walter stood there tongue-tied. It wasn't the house, or even his own indifference tonight that he should have explained, he thought, or should be explaining. What rendered him speechless was that he couldn't even tell her that it would be different one day, that he had any plans at all where she was concerned.

"It'd be nice some time if we'd coincide—about the way we feel," she said, giving him a sidelong look. But she smiled and there was humor in the smile. "So—Boadicea and I'll be going home."

"I wish you wouldn't."

"I'd rather." She was gathering up her pocketbook and her gloves.

He was being unfair, he told himself, deliberately using her and hurting her. He followed her and went out to the car with her. She said a pleasant good night to him through the window, but she did not wait for his kiss.

Walter went back into the empty house. Did he hang onto the house, he wondered, only because it kept a barrier between him and Ellie? The house didn't depress him—it depressed Ellie, actually—but he knew he would never be at ease with Ellie here because Clara had been here, was still here. Upstairs, Claudia had rearranged the bedroom without his asking her to: the bed was in the rear corner, and Clara's dressing table, its top empty of perfume bottles, powder boxes and the photograph of her and himself, stood between the two front windows. But the closet was full of her packed suitcases, her coats that still hung. He must do something with her clothes soon, he thought, give them away, give them to Claudia to give to people she knew. He had been putting it off.

The telephone rang. Walter was standing in the living room. He had a feeling, as strong as if the telephone bell had been a human voice, that it was Corby calling him. On the fourth or fifth ring, Walter made a start to go and answer it, but he didn't. He stood in the living room, rigid, listening, while the hair crept on the back of his neck, until after about a dozen rings, it stopped.

29

ABOUT FIVE hours later, Kimmel was awakened in his house by Lieutenant Lawrence Corby, made to dress and come to the 7th Precinct Headquarters in Newark.

In his haste to dress, Kimmel had not put on any underwear. The wool of his suit scratched the delicate skin of his buttocks, and he felt half naked. The police station was an ugly, square building with two outside flights of steps going up to the main entrance, steps that made the word *perron* spring to Kimmel's mind and Vienna's Belvedere Palace which had such steps—though the nineteenth-century hideousness of the building's architecture made such an association ludicrous—and as he climbed the steps Kimmel was repeating the word in his mind, "*Perron, perron, perron,*" in a terrified way, like a kind of personal and protective incantation against what might befall him in the building. The basement room where Corby took him was lined with small hexagonal white tiles, like a huge bathroom. Kimmel stood under a light. The glare of the light on the tiles made his eyes sting. There was nothing in the room but a table.

"Do you think Stackhouse is guilty?" Corby asked.

Kimmel shrugged.

"What do you *think*? Everybody's got an opinion about Stackhouse."

"My dear Lieutenant Corby," Kimmel said grandly, "you're so convinced that everybody's fascinated by murder and can't rest until the murderer is brought to justice—by *you*! Who cares whether Stackhouse is guilty or not?"

Corby sat down on the edge of the wooden table and swung his leg back and forth. "What else did Stackhouse say?"

"That's all."

"What else did he say?" In the empty room, Corby's voice grated like a metal file.

"That's all," Kimmel repeated with dignity. His plump hands twisted and twitched, touching fingertips lightly together below the bulge of his belly.

"It took Stackhouse nearly twenty minutes to apologize then?"

"We were interrupted several times. He just stood in the back of my shop by my desk and chatted with me."

"Chatted. He said, 'I'm so sorry, Mr. Kimmel, to have caused you all this trouble.' And what did you say? 'Oh, that's quite all right, Mr. Stackhouse. No hard feelings.' Did you offer him a cigar?"

"I told him," Kimmel said, "that I did not think either of us had anything to worry about, but that he had better not come to see me again, because you would attach a meaning to it."

Corby laughed.

Kimmel held his head higher. He stared at the wall, unmoving except for his twisting, lightly playing hands. He was standing on one leg, the other was gracefully relaxed, and his body was somewhat turned from Corby. Kimmel realized it was the same statuesque position in which he sometimes surveyed himself, naked, in the long mirror on his bathroom door. He had assumed it without thinking, and though in a secret part of his brain it made him feel shame, he felt it gave him a certain indestructible poise. Kimmel held the pose as if he were paralyzed.

"Guilty or not, I suppose you know that Stackhouse pointed the finger at you, don't you, Kimmel?"

"That is so obvious, I don't think it needs mentioning," Kimmel answered.

Corby kept swinging his leg over the edge of the table. The brown wooden table suggested a primitive, filthy operating table. Kimmel wondered if Corby was going to fling him onto it finally with a jiujitsu hold on him.

"Did Stackhouse explain why he had the newspaper clipping?" Corby asked.

"No."

"Didn't make a complete confession then, did he?"

"He had nothing to confess. He said he was sorry he had brought the police down on my head."

"Stackhouse has a lot to confess," Corby retorted. "For an innocent man, his actions are very peculiar. Didn't he tell you why he followed his wife's bus that night?"

"No," Kimmel replied in the same indifferent tone.

"Maybe you can tell me why."

Kimmel pressed his lips together. His lips were trembling.

He was simply bored with Corby's questioning. Stackhouse was being hammered at, too, Kimmel supposed. For a moment, a defiant sympathy for Stackhouse rose in him, tangled with his loathing of Corby. He believed what Stackhouse had told him. He did not think Stackhouse was guilty. "If you so doubt my report of what Stackhouse said to me, you should have sent a spy into the shop to listen!"

"Oh, we know you're an expert at spotting police detectives. You'd have warned Stackhouse and he would have stopped talking. We'll get it out of both of you finally." Corby smiled and came toward Kimmel. He looked fresh and fit. He was working on a nightshift now, he had told Kimmel. "You're protecting Stackhouse, aren't you, Kimmel? You like murderers, don't you?"

"I didn't think you thought he was a murderer."

"Since finding the clipping, I do. I told you that as soon as I'd found it!"

"I think you think there is still ample room for doubt about Stackhouse, but that you will not *let* yourself be fair with Stackhouse because you have decided to break a spectacular case!" Kimmel shouted, louder than Corby. "Even if you invent the crimes yourself!"

"Oh-h, Kimmel," Corby drawled. "I didn't invent the corpse of your wife, did I?"

"You invent my participation in it!"

"Did you ever see Stackhouse before I brought him to your shop?" Corby asked. "Didn't you?"

"No."

"I thought he might even have come to see you," Corby said speculatively. "He's that type."

Kimmel wondered if Stackhouse had been stupid enough to tell Corby that he had come. "No," Kimmel said, a little less positively. Kimmel took off his glasses, blew on them, reached for his handkerchief and not finding it, scoured the lenses on his cuff.

"I can imagine Stackhouse coming to see you, looking you over—maybe even expressing his sympathy for you. He might have looked you over to see if you really looked like a killer—which you do, of course."

Kimmel put his glasses back on and recomposed his face.

But fear had begun to grow in him like a tiny fire. It made him shift on his feet, made him want to run. Kimmel had felt until Corby that he had enjoyed a supernatural immunity, and now Corby himself seemed possessed of supernatural powers, like a Nemesis. Corby was not fair. His methods were not those commonly associated with justice, and yet he enjoyed the immunity that official, uniformed justice gave him.

"Had your glasses repaired?" Corby asked. Corby walked toward him like a little strutting rooster, his fists on his hips holding back his open overcoat. He stopped close in front of Kimmel. "Kimmel, I'm going to break you. Tony already thinks you killed Helen. Do you know that?"

Kimmel did not move. He felt physically afraid of Corby and it angered him, because physically Corby was a wraith. Kimmel was afraid in the closed room with him, with no help within call, afraid of being hurled to the hard tile floor that looked like the floor of an abattoir. He could imagine the vilest tortures in this room. He imagined that the police hosed the blood down from the walls after they worked a man over here. Kimmel suddenly had to go to the toilet.

"Tony's working on our side now," Corby said close in his face. "He's remembering things, like your saying to him just a few days before you killed Helen that there were ways of getting rid of the wrong wife."

Kimmel did remember that—sitting with Tony in a booth at the Oyster House, drinking beer. Tony had been there with some of his adolescent friends and had sat himself down in the booth uninvited. Kimmel had actually talked so boldly because he had been annoyed at Tony's sprawling himself down before he had been asked to sit down. "What else does Tony remember?" Kimmel asked.

"He remembers that he tried to come by your house after the movie that evening and you weren't home. You didn't get home until long after midnight that night, Kimmel. What if you had to say where you were?"

Kimmel gave a laugh. "It's absurd! I *know* that Tony did not try to come to see me. It's absurd to try to reconstruct the dullest, quietest evening in the world more than three months later when everybody's forgotten it!"

"The dullest, quietest evening in the world." Corby lighted

a cigarette. Then his hand flashed out suddenly, and Kimmel felt a sharp sting on his left cheek.

Kimmel wanted to take off his glasses before it was too late, but he did not move. The sting in his cheek continued, burning, humiliating.

"Getting hit is the only thing you understand, isn't it, Kimmel? Words and facts never bother you, because you're insane. You refuse to attach a meaning to them. You live in your own private world and the only way to break into it is by hitting you!" Corby's hands came up again.

Kimmel dodged, but Corby had not struck him, was only removing the glasses that Kimmel felt suddenly yanked from his ears. The room jumped and became blurred, and Kimmel tried to focus the black smudge of Corby's figure moving toward the horizontal blur of the table. Quickly, Kimmel put his spread hand before his face, saw it, and whipped it behind him, clasped with the other.

Corby came back.

"Why don't you admit that you know Stackhouse is guilty? Why don't you admit that he told you enough to make you sure of it? You can't make me believe that you love Stackhouse so much that you're going to protect him, Kimmel."

"We are both innocent men in very much the same position," Kimmel said in a monotonous voice, "as Stackhouse pointed out. That is why he came to see me."

Corby hit him in the stomach. It doubled Kimmel over, like the blow in his house. Kimmel waited for the hurling into the air, the crash to the floor. It didn't come. Kimmel stayed bent over, recovering his breath little by little. He saw black spots on the floor, more came as he watched, and then he realized that his nose was dripping blood. He had to open his mouth to breathe, and then he tasted it, a terrifying salty orange taste. Corby was walking around him and Kimmel turned with him, keeping his black figure always in front of him. Kimmel suddenly grabbed his nose and blew it violently, flinging his wet hand out to one side of him. "You should have blood on this floor!" Kimmel shouted. "You should make the walls run with it! Men you have tortured!"

Corby seized Kimmel by the shoulders and pushed his knee into his belly.

Kimmel was down on hands and knees, gasping for breath again, with a deeper pain than before.

"Admit that you know Stackhouse is guilty!"

Kimmel simply ignored it. His mind was entirely occupied with feeling sorry for himself. Even the recovery of his breath was an involuntary process, a series of painful, soblike gasps. Then Corby kicked him or pushed him in the hip, and Kimmel fell soddenly to the floor. He lay on one hip, his head raised.

"Get up, you old bitch," Corby said.

Kimmel didn't want to get up, but Corby kicked him in the buttocks. Kimmel got onto his knees and slowly hauled himself erect, his head up, though he had never felt weaker or more passive. The closer Corby strutted around him, the flabbier he felt himself, as if Corby hypnotized him. He ached, he stung in a dozen places. Kimmel was aware that he felt intensely feminine, more intensely than when he spied upon his own sensuous curves in the bathroom mirror, or when he read books sometimes and for his own diversion, imagined, and he was aware that it gave him pleasure of a kind he had not felt in years. He waited for the next blow, which he anticipated would strike his ear.

As if Corby understood him, he struck the side of Kimmel's head.

Kimmel screamed suddenly, releasing in one shrill blast a frantic shame that had been warring with his pleasure. He heard Corby's laugh.

"Kimmel, you're blushing!" Corby said. "Shall we change the subject? Shall we talk about Helen? About the time she threw out your Encyclopaedia Britannica? Out of sheer malice? I heard you paid fifty-five dollars for that set secondhand, and at a time when you really couldn't afford it."

Kimmel heard Corby bouncing on his heels, triumphantly, though Kimmel was still too ashamed to look at him. He made a tremendous effort to think who could have told Corby about the Encyclopædia Britannica, because it had happened way back in Philadelphia.

"I've also heard about the time Helen was manicuring her friends' fingernails for pin money. You must have loved that—women coming in and out of the house all day, sitting around gabbing. That's when you decided you could never educate Helen up to your level."

But the manicuring had lasted only a month, Kimmel thought. He had stopped it. Kimmel looked off to one side, though he was still wary of a darting attack from Corby. Kimmel felt goose-pimples under his trousers, as if he were naked and a cool wind were blowing on him.

"But even before that," Corby went on, "you'd reached the point where you couldn't touch her. She was loathsome to you, and gradually the loathing transferred itself to other women, too. You told yourself you hated women because they were stupid, and the stupidest of all was Helen. That was strange for you, Kimmel, who'd been so passionate in your youth! Did you begin to get it all out of pornographic books?"

"You disgust me!" Kimmel said.

"What could disgust you?" Corby came closer. "You married Helen when you were twenty, too young really to know anything about women, but you were very religious in those days, and you thought you ought to be married before you enjoyed their— You must have a name for it, Kimmel."

"It fits you!" Kimmel spluttered. He wiped his mouth with the back of his hand.

"Do you want your glasses?"

Kimmel took them and put them on. The room and Corby's thin face came into focus again. Corby's lips were sneering under the little mustache.

"Anyway, it was a sad day for Helen when she married you. Little could she know—a simple girl out of the Philadelphia slums. She made you impotent, you thought. That wasn't so bad, because you could blame it on Helen and enjoy hating her."

"I didn't hate her," Kimmel protested. "She was actually feeble-minded. I had nothing to do with her."

"She wasn't feeble-minded," Corby said. "Well, to continue this, a woman you had a big fiasco with came and told Helen about it and Helen began to taunt you."

"She did not! There was no woman!"

"Yes, there was. Her name was Laura. I've talked to Laura. She told me all about it. She doesn't like you. She says you gave her the creeps."

Kimmel stiffened with shame, seeing it again as Corby told it, the furtive afternoon in Laura's apartment when her husband was at work—he'd always told himself it was the furtiveness that had caused everything that day, but whatever had caused it, he had never had the courage to try again after that—seeing Laura climbing the stairs of his own house the next day to tell Helen. Kimmel had not seen her climbing the stairs, but he always imagined it very clearly, because Laura limped in one foot and had to pull herself up by banisters. Kimmel could see the two women laughing at him, then covering their mouths like idiot children, ashamed of what they had said. Helen had told him about Laura's visit that very night, and Helen had still been giggling about it, jeering at him. Helen had murdered herself that very night with her insane jeering!

"You thought after that that everybody knew about you," Corby said, "so you moved to Newark. The last straw was here in Newark—that insurance salesman Ed Kinnaird."

Kimmel twitched. "Who told you that?"

"That's a secret," Corby said. "It's too bad you didn't kill him instead of Helen, Kimmel, you might have gotten off. That lout! And Helen picked him up on the sidewalk like a prostitute—at the age of thirty-nine, a sagging old woman having a last fling. To you it was repellent! And she was proud of him, boasting all over the neighborhood about what he could do. You couldn't stand that, not when you were carrying on scholarly correspondences with college professors all over the country. By that time you'd built up quite a reputation in Newark as a bookdealer who knew his business."

"Who told you about Kinnaird?" Kimmel asked. "Nathan?"

"I don't reveal my sources," Corby said smiling.

Nathan had been at the house the night before, Kimmel thought, the night Helen and Kinnaird had come in, yet he didn't believe Nathan would tell, not about that night, anyway. Lena could have told him about Kinnaird, or Greta Kane—any of the lowest people in the neighborhood Helen had used to blabble to! But what bothered Kimmel most was that with all Corby's investigations in the neighborhood, no one had come and informed him.

"It wasn't Nathan," Corby said, shaking his head, "but Nathan did tell me about the night you and he were playing pinochle and Helen came in with Ed Kinnaird to change her clothes before she went out somewhere dancing. Kinnaird walked in as unconcerned as you please. Nathan knew what was going on. And you might as well have been a fat eunuch sitting there!"

Kimmel staggered forward, grappling for Corby with both arms. Kimmel's stomach heaved, his feet left the floor, and something smashed against his shoulder blades. For an instant, his face was pressed against his belly. His legs were propped against the wall. *Every bone in my body is broken!* Kimmel thought. He did not even try to move, though the pain in his spine was excruciating.

"You told her to get out of the house—right in front of Nathan. It wasn't the first time, but you meant it this time. Ed got out and she stayed, wailing it all to Lena over the phone."

Kimmel felt a kick in his legs. His feet hit the floor and began to sting. Nathan who never talked, Kimmel thought. That was why Nathan had not come to see him in so long. Kimmel knew from the Newark police that Nathan had never even said: "He *might* have done it" when he was questioned. But maybe the Newark police had never gone into that story of the night before. Nathan had betrayed him—the high-school history teacher whom Kimmel had considered a gentleman and a scholar! A bitter disappointment in Nathan, like a private inner hell, filled Kimmel's mind, balancing the outer hell of the room. He had lost his glasses again.

"Lena told Helen to go to her sister's in Albany for a while. A very unlucky move. Really, Kimmel, with all the people who knew about your fracas that night, you've gotten off amazingly well till now, haven't you?"

Kimmel was beyond speaking. He lay in a heap. The black spot not far from his eyes was his shoe, he thought. He reached for it and his hand pressed against something cool, but whether it was floor or wall, he didn't know.

"You didn't kill Helen because she was going with Kinnaird so much as because she was stupid. Kinnaird was only the match that touched it all off. So you followed your wife in the bus that night and killed her. Admit it, Kimmel!"

Kimmel's tongue was limp in his mouth. In a sense, he had even closed his ears to Corby's voice. He cringed on the floor like a dog, painfully aware that he was like a dog, yet enduring it because he knew there was no alternative. No alternative to Corby's rasping, screaming voice, Corby's hands yanking him up by the shoulders with their terrifying strength and propping him against the wall, cracking his head against the wall. Kimmel couldn't see anything. It was dimmer than before.

"Look at yourself! Pig!" Corby shouted. "Admit that you know Stackhouse is guilty! Admit that you know you are here because of Stackhouse and that he's as guilty as you are!"

Kimmel felt his first passionate thrust of resentment against Stackhouse, but he would not have betrayed it to Corby for anything because Corby wanted him to. "My glasses," Kimmel said in a squeaky voice that didn't sound like his own. He felt them pushed into his hand, felt the nosepiece crack even as he took them. Half of one lens was gone. He put them on. They fell to one side, below his eye level, and he had to hold them up to see anything.

"That's all for today," Corby said.

Kimmel did not move, and Corby repeated it. Kimmel did not know which way the door was, and he was afraid to look, afraid even to turn his head. Then he felt Corby yank him by one arm and shove him in the back. Kimmel nearly tripped over his big dragging feet. Something bounced in front of him on the floor. It was his shoe that Corby had thrown after him. Kimmel started to put it on, had to sit down on the floor to get it on. The floor felt icy beneath him. Kimmel got himself up the stairs to the ground level of the building. Corby had disappeared. He was alone. There was a policeman reading a newspaper at a desk in the hall, who did not even look at him as he passed. Kimmel had a ghostly feeling, as if he might be dead and invisible.

Kimmel went down the steps clinging to the banister and thinking of Laura doing it. He held to the end of the banister, trying to think where he was. He started off, then turned again and went in the other direction, still holding up his glasses so he could see. It was morning now, though the sun had not risen. When he felt the cold wind on him, he realized that he had wet his trousers. Then his teeth began to chatter, and he did not know if it was from cold or fear.

As soon as he reached home, Kimmel dialed Tony's home number. It was Tony's father who answered, and Kimmel had to pass the time of day with him before he put the telephone down to call Tony. Tony senior sounded just as usual, Kimmel thought.

"Hello, Mr. Kimmel," Tony's voice said.

"Hello, Tony. Can you come over to my house please? Now?"

There was a startled silence. "Sure, Mr. Kimmel. Your *house?*"

"Yes."

"Sure, Mr. Kimmel. Uh—I didn't have breakfast yet."

"Have your breakfast." Kimmel put the telephone down, and went with as much dignity as he could in his damp trousers upstairs to his bedroom, removed the trousers and hung them to dry before taking them to the cleaners.

He washed his shoes carefully in the bathroom, put his socks to soak in the basin, and drew himself a hot bath. He bathed slowly and exactly in the manner in which he always bathed. Yet he felt he was being watched, and he did no more than glance at himself in the long mirror when he stepped out of the tub, and it was a furtive, disapproving glance. In his bedroom, he took a clean white shirt from the stack in his drawer, put it on and put his robe on over it. His fingers caressed the starched white collar absently and appreciatively. He loved white shirts more than almost any tangible object in the world.

What proof could Tony give them? he asked himself suddenly. What if Tony did turn against him? That would prove nothing.

The doorbell rang as he went downstairs to put on coffee. Kimmel let him in. Tony came softly, a little reluctantly. Kimmel could see the apprehension in his black eyes. Like a small dog afraid of a whipping, Kimmel thought.

"I stepped on them," Kimmel said in anticipation of Tony's question about his glasses. "Will you come into the kitchen?"

They went into the kitchen. Kimmel motioned Tony to a straight chair and set about making coffee, which was difficult because he had to hold his glasses.

"I hear you have talked to Corby again," Kimmel said. "Now what did you tell him?"

"The same old thing."

"What else?" Kimmel asked, looking at him.

Tony cracked his knuckles. "He asked me if I'd seen you after the show. I said no—at first. I really didn't see you. You know, Mr. Kimmel."

"What if you didn't? You weren't looking for me, were you, Tony?"

Tony hesitated.

Kimmel waited. A stupid witness! Why had he chosen a stupid witness? If he had only kept looking that night, looked around in the theatre, he might even have found Nathan! "Don't you remember? You never said you were looking for me. We spoke to each other the next day." Kimmel felt repelled by the shiny black hairs that grew over Tony's thick nose, connecting his eyebrows. He was hardly a cut above a juvenile delinquent in appearance, Kimmel thought.

"Yes, I remember," Tony said. "But I might have forgotten."

"And who told you *that*? Corby?"

"No. Well, yes, he did." Tony put on his earnest, frowning expression that was no more intelligent than his normal one.

"Told you you might have forgotten. Said I could have been miles away killing Helen by nine-thirty or ten, didn't he? Who is *he* to tell you what to think?" Kimmel roared with indignation.

Tony looked startled. "He only said it was possible, Mr. Kimmel."

"Possible be damned! Anything is possible! Isn't it?"

"Yes," Tony agreed.

Kimmel could see that Tony was staring at the pink blotch on his right jaw, where Corby had hit him. "Who is this man to come here and make trouble for you and me and the whole community?"

Tony hitched himself to the edge of his chair. He looked as if he were really trying to think just who Corby was. "He talked to the doctor, too. He said—"

"What doctor?"

"Mrs. Kimmel's doctor."

Kimmel gasped. He knew: Dr. Phelan. He might have known Helen would have gone to have a talk with Dr. Phelan. He had cured her of arthritic pains in her back. Helen thought he was a miracle man. Kimmel even thought he could remember the time when Helen must have been going to him, about a month before she died, when she was wrestling with herself as to whether to give up Ed Kinnaird or defy her husband and indulge herself in that last fling. Dr. Phelan would have told her to indulge herself, of course. But Helen would have told Dr. Phelan about his own efforts to stop her. "What did the doctor say?" Kimmel asked.

"Corby didn't tell me that," Tony said.

Kimmel frowned at Tony. All he saw in Tony's face was fear and doubt now. And when a primitive mind like Tony's began to doubt—Tony *couldn't* doubt, Kimmel thought. Doubt demanded a mind capable of entertaining two possibilities at once.

"Corby did say—the doctor told him about Ed Kinnaird. Something like that. A fellow—"

Everybody knew, Kimmel thought. Corby had circulated like a newspaper.

Tony stood up, sidling from his chair. He looked afraid of Kimmel. "Mr. Kimmel, I don't think—I don't think I should be seeing you so much any more. You can understand, Mr. Kimmel," he went on faster, "I don't want to get myself in no more trouble over this. You understand, don't you? No hard feelin's, Mr. Kimmel." Tony wavered, as if he were about to extend a hand, but he was far too frightened to extend a hand. He sidled a few steps toward the door. "It's okay with me, Mr. Kimmel, whatever you say. Do, I mean."

Kimmel roused himself from his trance of astonishment. "Tony—" He stepped toward him, but he saw Tony retreat and he stopped. "Tony, you are in this—to the extent that you are a witness. You saw me *in* the theatre. That's all I've ever asked you to say, isn't it?"

"Yes," Tony said.

"That's the truth, too, isn't it?"

"Yes. But don't be angry, Mr. Kimmel, if I don't—don't have so many beers with you any more. I'm scared." He nodded. He looked scared. "I'm scared, Mr. Kimmel." Then he turned and trotted down the hall and out the front door.

Kimmel stood still for a minute, feeling weak, physically weak and lightheaded. He began to walk up and down his kitchen. A concatenation of curses rattled steadily through his mind, curses mild and foul in Polish and in German but mostly in English, curses directed at no one and nothing, then at Corby, then at Stackhouse, then at Dr. Phelan and Tony, but he checked the curses at Tony. He lumbered round and round his kitchen, chin sunk in the fat collar of flesh that flowed into his rounded chest.

"Stackhouse!" Kimmel shouted. It echoed in the room like pieces of glass falling around him.

"I WANT fifty thousand," Kimmel said. "No more and no less."
Walter reached for the cigarettes on his desk.

"You can pay it in installments, if you like, but I'd like it all within a year."

"Do you think I would even begin? Do you think I am guilty in the first place? I am innocent."

"You could be made to look very guilty. I could make you guilty," Kimmel replied quietly. "Proof is not the thing. Doubt is the thing."

Walter knew it. He knew what Kimmel could make out of the first visit to his shop, the visit that he could prove by the book order. And he knew why Kimmel was here, and why his glasses were broken and tied with string, and he understood that he had at last been driven to desperation and revenge; yet Walter's uppermost emotion was shock and surprise at seeing Kimmel here and being threatened by him. "Still," Walter said, "rather than pay a blackmailer, I'll risk it."

"You are most unwise."

"You're trying to sell me something I don't want to buy."

"The right to live?"

"I doubt if you can do me that much damage. What proof have you got? You have no witnesses."

"I've told you I'm not interested in proof. I still have the dated order you left in my shop. The date can be confirmed by the people I wrote to for the book. I can weave a fatal story for the newspapers around that day, the day you first came to me." Kimmel's eyes were stretched expectantly behind the glasses that reduced them.

Walter studied those eyes, looking for courage, determination, confidence. He saw all three. "I don't buy," he said, walking around his desk. "You can tell Corby what you wish."

"You make a terrible mistake," Kimmel said without moving. "Shall I give you forty-eight hours to think it over?"

"No."

"Because in forty-eight hours I can begin to show you what *I* can do."

"I know what you can do. I know what you're going to do."

"That's your last word?"

"Yes."

Kimmel stood up. Walter felt that Kimmel towered over him, though actually Kimmel was only a couple of inches taller.

"I protected you this morning," Kimmel said in a different tone. "I was beaten—tortured about whether I had seen you before your wife's death. I did not betray you." Kimmel's voice shook. He was convinced that he had come through hellfire, and for Stackhouse's benefit. He was convinced that Stackhouse owed him something. It had shamed him to ask for money, and he had done it only because he thought he deserved it. He had degraded himself once more in coming here this morning, and now to be refused by this stupid, ungrateful blunderer!

"That protection wasn't entirely altruistic, was it?" Walter asked. "I'm sorry you were beaten. You don't have to protect me. I'm not afraid of the truth."

"Oh, you are not afraid of the truth! I could have told them this morning. I could have told them more than the truth!"

Walter noticed the horrible smell of the bookshop clinging to Kimmel, or his clothes, emanating from them. It gave him a feeling of being closed in and trapped, which was made worse by the soundproofed ceiling that muffled Kimmel's muted, passionate voice. "I realize that. But what's going to happen is that I'll tell Corby the truth myself, you see. You can embellish it, if you like. I'll take the chance—but I'll never pay you a dime for anything!"

"I'd like to say you're a man with courage, Stackhouse, but you're only a fool and a coward from start to finish."

Walter started to swing the door open for Kimmel to go out, but he paused with his hand on the knob. He did not want Joan to hear anything. "Have you finished, Mr. Schaeffer?"

Kimmel scowled. His huge, smooth face looked like a scowling baby's. "Had you rather I'd given my real name?"

Walter yanked the door open. "Get out!"

Kimmel walked through lightly, his head up. He turned. "I shall call you, however, in forty-eight hours."

"That'll be too late."

Walter closed his door, went to the window, and stared at the empty sky beyond the edge of a building. The idea of talking to

Corby before Kimmel did was dissolving under him. The more he talked, the more of the truth he revealed—at this late date—the worse it would look for him. Walter could see Corby gloating when he confessed the first visit. Corby wouldn't possibly believe he had come by accident, or for the purpose he *had* come, just to look at Kimmel. Corby would think, well, what purpose did looking at Kimmel have? Of course it had a purpose, somewhere. No action could be totally without purpose, or without explanation.

Walter imagined himself stealing into Kimmel's shop, rifling the desk until he found the order slip. He squirmed and turned around. Kimmel wouldn't have it there anyway. It was probably hidden. Or Kimmel carried it on him now. He looked at the telephone and wondered where he could reach Corby at this hour of the morning? Or was it better to wait forty-eight hours and let Kimmel call again? Something could happen by then. But what? What ever happened? He only sank deeper, that was what happened. Walter gripped his thumbs inside his fingers. He reached for the telephone on a frightened impulse, then realized that he wouldn't have the nerve to tell Jon this. He had spent an evening with Jon two days ago. Jon had acted perfectly natural, and apparently had accepted the Kimmel clipping as pure coincidence. Corby had told him about the clipping. Jon knew he tore items out of the newspapers. So far as Walter could see, Jon hadn't given the Kimmel clipping a bit of weight, but if Jon were to know he had been in Kimmel's shop. . . . That would be the final thing, and the rest would suddenly crystallize.

Walter went quietly out of his office and took the elevator down. He went into a hotel across the street and called the Philadelphia Police, Homicide Department, and asked for Lieutenant Lawrence Corby. He was switched to another line, and he had to wait. For a few moments, he debated hanging up, because it had just struck him that Corby might not believe Kimmel at all about the visit or the order slip. The order was written in pencil, Walter remembered, and Kimmel could have written his name on an order that had been somebody else's. Kimmel wouldn't have written his name in the letters he sent to other bookstores, asking for the book. It was the kind of thing Kimmel would try to do, to hit back at him, and Corby would know that. But Walter knew Corby would prefer to seize on it, whether he believed it or not, and defy him to disprove it. Personal belief didn't influence Corby in the least. Walter squeezed the telephone.

"Lieutenant Corby is in Newark today. I don't expect him back for forty-eight hours. This is Corby's chief, Captain Dan Royer."

"Thanks," Walter said.

"May I ask who's calling?"

"It doesn't matter," Walter said.

He started for Newark at 5:30.

31

THE FIRST two precinct headquarters Walter telephoned had never heard of Corby. Walter wondered if he were working absolutely on the loose in Newark. He tried a third and got a response: Corby had been there early in the morning. They couldn't say when he would be back.

Walter got back in his car, discouraged. He decided to drive by the last place he had called and leave a sealed note for Corby with a message in it to call him. On the way to the precinct headquarters, Walter recognized the street where he had parked his car the day he went to see Kimmel to tell him that he was innocent. Walter turned his car into Kimmel's street. Just as he saw the projecting windows of the bookshop, their lights went out. Walter slowed down. Kimmel's big figure backed out of the door, stood for a moment locking the door, then turned, within ten feet of Walter's car. Walter watched him take a half dozen steps down the sidewalk—bent forward, head down as if he had to hurl his huge body forward to make progress—and then Walter's car passed him. Walter stepped on the gas pedal as if Kimmel were pursuing him. *My God*, Walter thought, *my God*! He kept saying it over and over in his mind.

It was the craziness of it. Kimmel—beaten in the morning, closing shop at night, carrying around a little hell in his head, a plan for vengeance against him. And what had he to do with a stranger in a dark street of Newark?

A police officer in the precinct headquarters said that he expected Corby to come in between nine and midnight. "He's working on a case around here," the man said casually. "He's in and out."

Walter waited in his car. Then he drove around for a while to ease his tenseness, came back and inquired again, and waited. He wondered if he could possibly prevail on Corby not to put the story of his first visit to Kimmel in the newspapers, and to stop Kimmel from doing it. He wondered, even if Corby were to think or pretend to think that he was guilty after hearing Kimmel's version of the visit, if Corby could be persuaded to wait until all the proof was collected. But Corby might say this was all the proof he needed. *But I haven't done anything*, Walter thought. Before, he had felt it buoying him up, that fact that he hadn't done anything. Now the buoyancy felt hollow and unreal.

As he stared in front of him, Walter saw Corby's long loose figure emerging out of the darkness on the sidewalk, and he got out of his car.

Corby's narrow face lighted under the dapper brim of his hat. "Good evening, Mr. Stackhouse!"

"I came to talk to you," Walter said.

"Would you like to come in?" Corby gestured to the dismal building, as graciously as if it were his home.

"It's very private. I'd rather sit in the car."

"You're not supposed to park here. However, it's such a small offense." He smiled his boyish smile, and got into the car.

Walter began as soon as they had closed the doors. "Kimmel came to me today with a proposition of blackmail. I'm telling you what it's all about before he does. I saw Kimmel in October a couple of weeks before my wife's death."

"You *saw* him?"

"I went to his shop. I ordered a book from him. I knew he was Kimmel—the one whose wife had been killed. I mentioned it to him—that I knew about it. But that's all that was said. I left my name and address when I ordered the book."

"Your name and address!" Corby sat upright, smiling. "Did you!"

"I had no reason not to," Walter said. "I still haven't. I did *not* kill my wife!"

Corby shook his head as if this were all just too incredible to be believed. "Do you concede, Mr. Stackhouse, that you at least thought about killing her?"

"Yes."

"And you didn't do it?"

"No."

"And you also guessed how Kimmel did it."

"How Kimmel *might* have done it."

Corby laughed and opened his hands. "What is this? Both of you defending each other now?"

Walter frowned. "If you've got so much against Kimmel, why don't you arrest him?"

"We're getting there. I'm only collecting some more facts from the neighbors," Corby said, pulling the limp brown tablet out of his pocket. "Motivations."

"Can you convict a man on motivations? Or on circumstantial evidence? It doesn't take a lawyer to know that you haven't got enough to indict us, Corby. If you had what you needed, we'd be in jail!"

Corby was writing in the tablet. He looked around and turned on the car light so he could see better. "Kimmel will crack finally. He's got a peculiar psychic structure—" Corby mouthed the words like a pedantic schoolboy—"full of little cracks. I just have to find the weakest."

"You won't find any in me."

Corby ignored it. "Do you mind telling me the date of your visit to Kimmel? Was there more than one?"

"No. As near as I can remember it was around the seventh of October." Walter remembered the date exactly, because it was the day he had first gone to Ellie's Lennert apartment.

"How long did you stay there?"

"About ten minutes."

"Can you tell me everything you said? Everything you both said."

Walter related it, and Corby took notes. It was very brief, because they had exchanged very few words.

"Kimmel's probably going to tell you that I talked with him about murdering my wife," Walter said. "Or he's going to say that I asked so many questions that what I wanted to find out was obvious."

"What did you want to find out?"

"I meant, what Kimmel's going to *say* I wanted to find out. Actually—the truth is that I wanted to see Kimmel, just see him. I did think that Kimmel might have killed his wife. It fascinated me. I wanted to see Kimmel to see if he looked like he could have done it."

"It fascinated you." Corby looked at him with interest, the bright schoolboy look again, as if he were comparing Walter to some textbook criminal type that he knew thoroughly.

Walter regretted using the word. "It interested me. I'm admitting it!"

"Why didn't you admit it sooner?"

"Because—because of the position I was in," Walter said desperately. "I'm admitting to you now that Kimmel has an order slip with my name and the date on it to prove my visit. I'm warning you in advance that Kimmel's going to tell you God knows what about that visit!"

Corby's half-smiling expression did not change. "Mr. Stackhouse, I don't believe *your* story at all."

"All right, get it from Kimmel!"

"I will. Stackhouse, I think you did not discuss murder with Kimmel, but I think you killed your wife. I think you're as guilty as Kimmel is."

"Then you're not being logical! You're so determined to prove me guilty, you're no longer capable of looking at the facts or judging anything!"

"But I am looking at the facts. They're pretty damning, from anybody's point of view. The more you furnish, Stackhouse—" Corby left it unfinished and smiled. "Maybe next week we'll have the last installment. Is this all for tonight?"

Walter set his teeth together. He felt he had exhausted every defense he had, every fact, and that there was not another word he could say. He felt he was sliding down a sewer.

"Not a stupid man, Kimmel. You are, Stackhouse." Corby got out of the car and slammed the door.

Walter heard his quick steps running up one of the flights of stairs that led to the door of the police building. How absurd he had been to think that he would be believed! How absurd to think that he could ask Corby not to print what he had just told him. Walter felt that Corby needed something explosive to shake the Kimmel-Stackhouse case into a new stage. This was really a much more spectacular story than merely finding the clipping.

A curious feeling came over Walter as he sat there. It took him a moment to understand what it was. Then he did: he was giving up. He didn't care any more. He'd tell Ellie. He'd tell Jon, everybody. He'd lose them all. He'd go down the drain alone.

Walter started the car. Ellie would be the first, he thought. It was after nine o'clock now. He wondered if he should call her from Newark to make sure she was in, and then suddenly he remembered this was the night of *Hansel and Gretel*.

Thanksgiving Eve. Ellie was playing in the Harridge School auditorium now, and he was supposed to be there. He had his ticket in his pocket. Walter stopped the car, cursing, feeling completely rattled. The story would break on Friday evening, if Kimmel succeeded in putting it in the papers. He wouldn't be able to do a thing about it at the office until Monday. By Monday, Dick Jensen would be ready to say, "It's no go, Walter. Count me out." They were planning to move into the new office December first. Cross would tell him he was through at the office, and he'd better get out and stay out. Walter wondered if by Monday he'd even have the courage to go to the office?

His hands were sweaty on the steering wheel. He drove for the tunnel. He wondered what excuse he would make to Ellie for not coming to the show? Well, this one, of course. The truth for once!

32

ELLIE WAS not home by eleven, though Walter knew the show got out at ten. Walter drove to Lennert and sat in his car across the street from her house, waiting. He became terribly sleepy and had to fight against falling asleep in the car.

Ellie's car turned into the street at about a quarter to twelve, and Walter got out and walked toward the parking lot where she always put Boadicea.

"What happened to you?" Ellie asked.

"I'll explain it upstairs. Can we go up?"

"Corby again?"

He nodded.

She gave him a look, a look of exasperation, nothing else, then she unlocked her door and they went upstairs. Walter was carrying the box from Mark Cross, the alligator bag he had had initialed for her and had picked up that morning before he went to the office. He handed it to her when they were in her apartment.

"This is for Thanksgiving," he said. "I'm sorry I wasn't there tonight, Ellie. How'd it go?"

"All right. I've just been with Virginia and Mrs. Pierson. They liked it better than last year's." She looked at him, smiled a little, then began to open the box.

It was in a big square box, and under tissue. Ellie gasped when she saw it: shining brown alligator with a gilt clasp and a strap.

"Big enough?" he asked.

Ellie laughed. "Like a suitcase."

"I ordered the largest. Otherwise you'd have had it a couple of weeks ago."

"Tell me about Corby," she said.

"I had to go to Newark," Walter said and stopped. He began to feel he couldn't tell her. "Really nothing happened," he said. "I—I met Kimmel."

"Kimmel! What is he like?"

There was only curiosity in Ellie's face, Walter thought,

simple curiosity. "He's a big fat fellow, about forty, intelligent, cold-looking—"

"Do you think he's guilty?"

"I don't know."

"Well, what happened? Were you in a police station?"

"Yes. Kimmel's not under arrest. He may not be guilty. Corby's hipped, you know. Corby's a zealot out for a promotion at anybody's expense."

"But what *happened*?"

Walter looked at her. "He wanted to know if there was any connection between Kimmel and me—other than the clipping I had. Of course, there wasn't." Walter spoke in a tone of desperate conviction that actually fooled himself. This may be the last time you'll ever talk to her, he thought, the last time you'll stand in this room, after she finds out you've lied. If it weren't in the papers Friday, Corby would get around to telling everybody he knew. Walter went on, "He didn't third-degree us or anything, just asked questions."

"You look exhausted."

He sat down on the sofa. "I am."

"And what else?" she asked, folding the tissue that had come in the box.

Walter knew she was going to save the tissue for something. Clara would have saved it, too, he thought. "That's all," he said. "I had to go. I was just sorry to have missed the show tonight."

She looked at him a moment, and Walter wondered if she believed that was all, though there was really not the least doubt in her face now. "Have you had anything to eat?" she asked.

Walter couldn't remember. He didn't answer, only looked at her. A lump was growing in his throat, like panic, like terror. He didn't know what it was. He suddenly wished he was married to Ellie, had married her right after Clara's death, and in the next moment was ashamed of wishing it.

"I'll fix you some scrambled eggs. There's nothing here but eggs." She went into the kitchen. "Why don't you take a nap? We'll have coffee and eggs in fifteen minutes."

Walter continued to sit upright on the sofa. It was unreal to him, the way she took it. Even his not being at the show tonight. An idea that she might be pretending, before she cut him off from her with one fell swoop, made the atmosphere even more unreal.

"Do you know you're getting too thin?" Ellie asked as she worked in the kitchen. "Can't you remember to eat occasionally?"

He said nothing. He put his head back and closed his eyes, but sleep was far from him now. After a few minutes, he got up to help her put dishes on the coffee table by the sofa. They ate scrambled eggs with toast and marmalade.

"We'll have a nice day tomorrow," Ellie said. "Let's not let anything spoil that."

"No." They were going to have Thanksgiving dinner at a restaurant near Montauk and then drive around, probably walk along a beach somewhere, which Ellie loved to do.

After he had eaten, Walter felt too tired even to smoke a cigarette. His arms and legs were heavy, as if he had been drugged. He could hardly feel Ellie's fingers pressing his hand as they sat on the sofa.

"Can I stay here with you tonight?"

"Yes," she said quietly, as if he had asked her many times before.

But they sat there for a long while before they moved to put dishes away and to open the sofa which made a double bed.

Coward, Walter said to himself. Walter Stackhouse, a coward and a bastard.

Walter only lay in her arms and she held him as if she did not expect him to make love to her. But toward dawn, after he had slept for a while, he did. And it seemed more than the first time, better than the first time, and more desperate also, because Walter was afraid it was the last time, and Ellie's intensity made him imagine that she knew it, too. Walter had a vision of a little window. It was a beautiful little square window, just out of his reach, filled with light blue sky with a suggestion of green earth below.

33

Dick and Pete jumped up to help him, but there was nothing they could do except stand there while he bent over the basin, retching. There was not even anything in his stomach except the coffee he had drunk for breakfast, but the retching lasted ten minutes or so, and it was too constricting for him even to tell Dick and Pete to go back to Cross and forget him. And as he bent there, staring at the pale green porcelain of the little basin, listening to the symphonic ringing in his ears, Walter told himself he was sick of the job Cross had for him and Dick to do, bored and sick of it, and that it was one of the last jobs they'd ever do at the office and what was the use in reacting like this? But Walter knew he was sick because he expected the call from Kimmel at 11:30, when the forty-eight hours would be up.

"Where'd you have that turkey yesterday?" Dick asked him, trying to sound cheerful, patting him on the back.

Walter did not try to answer. He'd been going to tell Kimmel to go to hell, to do his worst. Now he hadn't the guts to stand up. His clothes stuck to him with sweat. Dick had to help him to the leather sofa in the corner, and if not for the cold towel over his face, he thought he might have fainted.

"Think you've got a touch of ptomaine?" Dick asked.

Walter shook his head. He was aware of Cross's swarthy, pouchy face looking over his shoulder from his desk, looking annoyed. You go to hell, too, Walter thought. Walter finally stood up and said he would try to pull himself together in his own office.

"I'm very sorry," Walter said to Cross.

"*I'm* sorry," Cross said crisply. "Go home if you're not feeling well."

Walter got the bottle of scotch from a lower drawer of his desk and took a pull on it. It made him feel slightly better.

He left the office around 10:30.

It was five to twelve when he got home. The house was empty. Claudia would have left at eleven. Walter wondered if Kimmel had called before eleven and spoken to Claudia?

Walter went directly to his study and got out his portable typewriter. He tried to move briskly, though he was still weak and shaking. He addressed a letter to the Administration Department of Columbia Law School, and wrote that he was opening a law office for small claims clients in Manhattan, and that he would like two or three senior students to work as his assistants on various day shifts. He asked that a notice be posted on the bulletin board of the school, so that any students interested could get in touch with him. His thoughts did not come out smoothly, and he had to retype the letter.

In the middle of his typing, the telephone rang.

Walter answered it in the hall.

"Hello, Mr. Stackhouse," Kimmel's voice said.

"The answer is still no."

"You are making a great mistake."

"I've talked to Corby," Walter said. "If you add anything to what I told him, Corby's not going to believe you."

"I'm not interested in what you told Corby. I'm interested in what I tell the newspapers. You should be, too."

Through Kimmel's dead calm, Walter heard his resentment because his game had been spoiled. "They won't believe you. They won't print it."

Kimmel gave a hooting laugh. "They'll print everything I tell them, as long as I hold myself responsible for it—which I shall do with pleasure. Don't you want to change your mind for a mere fifty thousand dollars?"

"No."

Kimmel was silent, but Walter kept holding the phone, waiting. It was Kimmel who finally hung up.

Walter went back to his letter. Even his hands were weak and damp with sweat, and he had to type very slowly. He added another paragraph, feeling a little insane, like the crackpots who put ads in newspapers to sell an estate they haven't got, or offering to buy a yacht they can't afford:

> I am especially interested in securing a few serious students, young men who would otherwise not be able to acquire practical experience so early in their careers and who would prefer this kind of work to the more

tedious and impersonal tasks they would be given if they took jobs as junior lawyers in bigger law firms.

I should appreciate an acknowledgment of this letter at your convenience.

Yours sincerely,
WALTER P. STACKHOUSE

He gave the address and telephone of Cross, Martinson and Buchman as well as the address of the new office in Forty-fourth Street, where he and Dick were supposed to be by Tuesday. Walter had discussed with Dick the advisability of hiring a couple of law students to help out in the office, and Dick had thought it a good idea. Now it seemed to Walter that he had written the letter today in order to have anybody at all in the office with him, as if he knew that the next time he saw Dick, Dick was going to tell him he wasn't going into partnership with him.

Walter drank a straight scotch, and felt better so quickly, he knew that the therapeutic effect of the liquor was purely mental. Well, mentally, hadn't he decided he didn't care any more, Wednesday night sitting in his car outside the Newark police station? That he felt so weak physically was an accident today, he thought. What the hell if Kimmel got his crazy story printed? It was one more lie, that was all. He'd already weathered so many lies: *why* he was at the bus stop, *why* he had the Kimmel clipping, *why* he had gone back to talk to Kimmel in his shop. Well, now he was going to hear *why* he had come to Kimmel's shop the first time, and he'd weather this one, too. When the crazy custodians of justice came to seize him—finally—they would find him hard at work in a law office on Forty-fourth Street. Maybe alone. He took a second large drink.

Then he went into the kitchen and found a can of tomato soup in the cupboard, opened it, and put it on to heat. The kitchen was silent except for the purring of the gas flame. Walter stood there, waiting, and finally began to walk up and down the floor to break the silence. Then he heard Clara's steps upstairs and he stopped abruptly. It was getting his brain, too. He'd actually *heard* her steps, as clearly as if they had been a little rill of music—six or seven steps.

Walter realized he was standing halfway up the staircase, staring at the empty hall. Did he expect to see Clara? He didn't even remember starting up the steps. When he went back to the kitchen the tomato soup was boiling over. He poured some into a bowl and began to eat it at the kitchen table.

He heard Clara's voice, uttering little shadowy whispers. He cocked his head, listening, and the more he concentrated, the more definite it seemed that he *did* hear them, though they were not distinct enough for him to be able to hear what she was saying. They were sibilant phrases, laughing phrases, as if he were overhearing her as she played with Jeff. Or as she really had talked to him a few times in the first months they had lived in this house. Jeff was curled up in the living room in a chair, Walter knew. If there *were* anything to the sounds, Jeff would—

Walter stood up. Maybe he *was* going insane. Maybe it was the house. He ran his fingers through his hair, then quickly went to a window and threw it open.

He stood there, trying to make himself think, decide, remember, remember Clara here, and the times they had been happy here, before it was too late to remember, and after a few crazy, agonized seconds, realized that he wasn't thinking at all, wasn't even feeling anything except confusion.

He went to the telephone and dialed the Knightsbridge Brokerage number. Its familiarity to him was pleasant and terrifying. It was as if Clara were alive again. The phone rang and rang, and Walter knew it meant the Philpotts had not opened their office today, but he let it ring about fifteen times before he gave up.

He called Mrs. Philpott's home number. Mrs. Philpott was in, and he told her he wanted to sell the house right away. He said he could easily be out by Monday, and he would see about selling some of the furniture tomorrow. The transaction would be very simple, she said: the Knightsbridge Brokerage would buy the house for $25,000.

"It just happens," she said, "that I've a man coming tomorrow to do some appraising—a furniture appraiser in particular. Suppose I come over with him tomorrow morning? Will you be home around noon?"

"I can be here at noon," Walter said.

"I know about such things as furniture appraising. I don't want you to get cheated," she said with a laugh.

That afternoon, Walter began to sort out the things he would give to Claudia. His father and Cliff might be willing to take some of the living room furniture, Walter thought. He should answer his brother's letter. It had come ten days ago—the third or fourth letter from Cliff since Clara's death—full of such brotherly affection and Cliff's shy, roundabout sympathy that Walter had been touched almost to tears over it. But he hadn't answered.

He went upstairs and began to put all the linens out on the bed, but he got discouraged after a few minutes and decided to wait until Claudia came that evening so she could help him.

He started to call Ellie to tell her he was selling the house, actually went to the telephone, then changed his mind. He decided to drive to Benedict to mail his letter to Columbia. He got into his car and drove to Benedict.

Then it was 3:12. He debated parking the car somewhere and taking a long walk in the woods. Or going home and getting drunk all by himself. Ellie was gone by now. She would have started off for Corning around two to visit her mother, and she would be gone overnight. But they had newspapers in Corning, too, of course. Ellie might see it tonight, certainly by tomorrow morning. He wondered if he would ever see Ellie again? He whipped the car around and headed for New York. He was going to do what he wanted to do, wait around in Manhattan for the evening papers to come out. He would put the car somewhere and walk, anywhere. He had always loved to walk in Manhattan. Nobody looked at him, nobody paid any attention. He could stop and stare into shopwindows at rows of glistening scissors and knives, and feel like nothing but a pair of eyes without an identity behind them.

He went, and walked, and waited. He drank brandies and cups of coffee, and walked some more. But the story was not in the papers by 10 P.M. For hours he had been debating calling Corby and asking him to stop Kimmel, swallowing his pride and begging Corby to stop him. In between his debates with himself, his pride would suddenly soar, and he would take an arrogant, desperate attitude of not caring. Corby as a savior was an absurdity, anyway. He'd be on Kimmel's side about this.

Or rather, he'd back either of them, whichever one was trying to accuse the other.

There was another edition around midnight. Walter waited for it, and still there was nothing in it about him. Walter began to wonder if Kimmel was not going to tell the newspapers after all. Or was Kimmel sitting in some room in Newark, waiting for a telephone call from him, saying that he had changed his mind?

Or was Corby beating up Kimmel again tonight? Kimmel perhaps hadn't had time to tell the newspapers. But Walter couldn't imagine Corby detaining him if he had such an important mission.

Walter stood on the corner of Fifty-third Street and Third Avenue, looking up at the old elevated structure over his head, wincing as a taxi's brakes shrieked. The glare of light in the Riker's shop beside him hurt his eyes. As he looked up the dark tunnel under the elevated, a bus slid silently toward him with headlights like the eyes of a monster. Walter shivered.

He was in hell.

34

HE LAY awake, listening for the feathery impact of the paper striking the front door. The paper generally came at a quarter to seven. By then, he hadn't heard it, and he went downstairs, turned the front door light on to see the steps. The paper had not come. He went back upstairs and got dressed.

The paper had arrived when he started out the front door. Walter looked at it by the hall light.

NEWARK MAN TELLS OF PLANNED MURDER
OF BENEDICT WOMAN

Nov. 27—An amazing story—with nothing but a pencil written order for a book and a tortured man's grim and earnest statements to back it up—was unfolded late last night in the offices of the Newark *Sun.* Melchior J. Kimmel, owner of a bookshop in Newark, stated that Walter Stackhouse, husband of the late Clara Stackhouse of Benedict, Long Island, came to his shop two weeks before Mrs. Stackhouse's death in October, and asked him pertinent questions about the murder of his own wife, Helen Kimmel. . . .

Walter stuck the paper under his arm and ran out to his car. He wanted to get the other papers, all of them at once. But he put the light on in his car and glanced at the solid double-column box again.

"I was horrified," Kimmel stated. "I started to turn the man in as a criminal psychopath, but on second thought decided to wash my hands of the whole thing. In view of later developments, I bitterly regret my cowardice."

Walter started his car. It was still almost dark, and his headlights fell on Claudia walking toward him on Marlborough Drive. Walter saw her step quickly to the edge of the road, and he felt she shied away from him more than from his rushing car. He wondered if she had seen it yet, or had talked to the woman she sometimes rode with on the bus?

He drove to Oyster Bay and stopped at the first newsstand. He saw it on the front pages of two New York papers. He bought all the morning papers and took them back to his car. He began to read them all at once, skipping over them, looking for the worst.

The body of Helen Kimmel was found in the woods near a bus stop in Tarrytown, New York, on August 14. The body of Clara Stackhouse was found at the bottom of a cliff near Allentown, Pa., on October 24. Police, who listed the death of Mrs. Stackhouse as a suicide, have not commented on the Kimmel story as yet.

NEWARK BOOKDEALER ASSERTS STACKHOUSE
"PLANNED" MURDER OF WIFE AT BUS STOP

The New York *Times* account was not very long but it amounted to plain accusation of murder, with Kimmel's statements cushioned by "alleged . . . according to Kimmel . . . Kimmel attested . . ."

A New York tabloid had a very long account with a photograph of Kimmel talking vociferously with raised finger, and a picture of the order slip with his own name very legible on it. And the date.

Melchior Kimmel, forty, impressively huge with alert brown eyes behind the thick-lensed glasses of a scholar, told his story in rolling phrases and with a thundering conviction that made his statements hard to disbelieve, said Editor Grimler of the Newark *Sun*. . . .

The conversation about the murder occurred, said Kimmel, after Stackhouse (a lawyer) had placed an order for a book called "Men Who Stretch the Law." Kimmel produced the dated order for the book to substantiate his statement. Kimmel stated that Stackhouse appeared to assume he (Kimmel) had killed his wife Helen, and said that he intended to kill his own wife by the "same method," that is, attacking her during a rest stop on a bus trip.

The Kimmel account goes on to state that Stackhouse proposed to follow the bus in his own car, speak to his wife during the rest stop, and persuade her to a secluded spot where he could attack and kill her without being seen, a method Kimmel says Stackhouse appeared to assume he, Kimmel, had used.

"This," Kimmel charged yesterday, "is what Stackhouse did."

Kimmel further asserted that Stackhouse came to see him again on November 15, in order to make him a "maudlin apology" and to confess his guilt in the murder of his wife. Stackhouse, who denies any part in his wife's death, Kimmel said, "suffers under a psychotic fixation on me." Kimmel hinted at frequent visits from Stackhouse, which he said he "did not want to go into." The November 15 visit of Stackhouse was confirmed by Lieutenant Lawrence Corby, Philadelphia Police Homicide Squad detective, who has been investigating the Kimmel and Stackhouse cases for the past several weeks.

Kimmel stated that Stackhouse's alleged actions "disrupted his life," causing the police to begin investigating his (Kimmel's) movements on the night of his wife's murder. It is this, he said, which prompted him to reveal the story of Stackhouse's October visit at this late date.

"I am not a vindictive man," Kimmel said, "but this man is obviously guilty and moreover has ruthlessly disrupted my personal and professional life in an effort to besmirch me with guilt. I say, let justice be done where justice is due!"

Kimmel's allegations follow earlier disclosures by the police that Stackhouse was seen and identified at the scene of his wife's death at 7:30 P.M. October 23, though in his first statements to the police, Stackhouse declared he had been in Long Island the evening of his wife's death.

A newspaper story of Helen Kimmel's murder was found in Stackhouse's possession on October 29. An admission by Stackhouse that he had torn the story out of a newspaper and kept it in a scrapbook was corroborated by Lieutenant Corby when Editor Grimler of the Newark *Sun* telephoned him to check on it.

Lieutenant Corby reminded Grimler that Kimmel himself was not entirely clear of suspicion in his wife's murder, and that he would not accept responsibility for anything Kimmel said against Stackhouse, unless he personally corroborated it. . . .

But Corby did corroborate Kimmel in practically everything he said, Walter thought. Corby might have been briefing Kimmel all afternoon yesterday, to make sure he told every fact, to make sure he spoke forcibly enough when he made up his fiction!

Walter stamped on his starter and turned automatically toward home.

He found Claudia standing in the kitchen with her coat and hat still on and a newspaper in her hands. She looked stunned. "Myra give me this on the bus this morning," she said, indicating the newspaper. "Mr. Stackhouse, I come here this morning to tell you that I'd like to quit—if you don't mind, Mr. Stackhouse."

Walter couldn't say anything for a moment, only stare at her face that looked rigid and shy and terrified at the same time. He walked toward the center of the kitchen and saw her step back from him, and he stopped, knowing that she was afraid because she thought he was a murderer. "I understand, Claudia. It's all right. I'll get your—"

"If you don't mind, I'll just collect my shoes out of the closet and a couple of other things."

"Go ahead, Claudia."

But she turned back. "I didn't believe it when I heard it from Myra this morning, but when I read it myself—" She stopped.

Walter said nothing.

"Then I don't like these police to question me all the time, neither," she said a little more boldly.

"I'm sorry," he said.

"He told me not to tell you about it—Mr. Corby. But now

I guess it don't matter. I couldn't stop him from coming, but I don't want to have anything to do with it."

Slimy bastard, Walter thought. He could see him pumping Claudia of every detail. Walter had wanted to ask Claudia weeks ago if Corby had come to see her. He had never dared to.

"I never told Mr. Corby anything against you, Mr. Stackhouse," Claudia said a little frightenedly.

Walter nodded. "Go ahead and get your shoes, Claudia." He went to the hall stairs. He had to get his billfold to pay her. He'd forgotten it this morning and gone off with only change in his pocket.

Walter stopped in the act of taking the bills from the billfold: he imagined he heard an outcry from Clara—shocked and reproachful—because Claudia was leaving them, and through his own fault. For a moment, Walter suffered that familiar sensation of shame, sudden anger and resentment, because he had committed a blunder that Clara was reproaching him for. Then he moved again and ran downstairs with the money and his checkbook. He made out a check to her for two weeks' pay and handed it to her with three ten-dollar bills.

"The tens are just for your good service, Claudia," he said.

Claudia looked down at them, then handed the check back. "I didn't work but four days this week, Mr. Stackhouse. I'll just take what's due me and no more. I'll just take the thirty dollars."

"But that's not quite enough," Walter protested.

"This'll be fine," Claudia said, moving away. "I'll be going now. I think I've got everything."

He couldn't even give her a reference, Walter thought. She wouldn't want one, from him. She was carrying a bulging paper bag in her arms, and Walter opened the door for her. She edged away with a real physical fear of him as she passed him. No use offering to drive her to the end of Marlborough to the bus stop, no use saying anything else. He watched her as she descended the slope in the lawn to the road, watched her turn and walk under the row of willow trees. It was hard to realize that he'd probably never see Claudia again. And it was astonishing how much her leaving hurt him.

Walter closed the kitchen door. He felt suddenly alone and desolate. And this was only the maid. What about the others?

What about Ellie? And Jon? And Cliff and his father? And Dick? Walter set about mechanically making his coffee. He wondered if Mrs. Philpott would come this morning, if she would call and make an excuse, or not even call?

The telephone rang just before nine. It was a toll call, and Walter waited while the quarters dropped in. He knew it would be Ellie calling from Corning. Then Jon's voice said:

"Walter?"

"Yes, Jon."

"Well, I've seen it."

Walter waited.

"Just how true is it?" Jon asked.

"The visits are true—most of them. What he says I said—that isn't true." Even his voice sounded spent and hopeless, not to be believed. And Jon was silent a long time, as if he didn't believe him.

"What are they going to do to you?"

"Nothing!" Walter said explosively. "They're not going to put me in jail or anything logical like that. They haven't got the facts, anyway. They make no attempt to prove anything. Any man can get up and say anything, that's their technique!"

"Listen, Walter, when you cool down a bit, you'd better make a statement and tell them the whole thing," Jon said in his deep, calm voice. "Tell them whatever you've left out and get it—"

"I haven't left out anything."

"These visits—"

"There were only three visits, the second with Corby himself who *knows* every visit I made!"

"Walter, it seems to me that something new is turning up every week. I'm suggesting that you get it all down in writing and swear to it and prove it."

Now Walter heard the coldness in Jon's drawling words, heard the impatience and the withdrawing.

"If you're innocent," Jon added casually.

"I suppose you doubt it," Walter said.

"Listen, Walter, I'm only suggesting that you tell the whole story instead of parts—"

Walter hung up.

He was thinking of what some paper had said: that it was

very strange, if Kimmel's story was *not* correct, that Stackhouse had chosen to go to an obscure bookshop in Newark for a book he could have got more easily at several New York bookstores.

Walter got the brandy bottle and poured himself a drink.

Where did they go with him from here? He could issue a statement to the press, all right. It would be the truth, but who would believe him? The truth was so dull, and Kimmel's story so spectacular.

He took Jeff out for a walk around the woods at the end of Marlborough Road. Jeff had stopped watching for Clara, but he was a sadder little dog. Even when Walter played his favorite game of swinging him out on an old rag until Jeff had shredded it completely with his teeth, Jeff's face never had the cocky, silly look it had used to have when Clara was alive. Ellie noticed it, and had offered to take Jeff if Walter no longer wanted to keep him. But Walter did want to keep him: he tried to take as good care of him as Clara had, give him a good run once a day, and Walter generally fixed his food himself, mornings and even when Claudia was there. But if something should happen to him, Walter thought, he ought to make sure Jeff went to Ellie, or to the Philpotts.

He made Jeff's breakfast of warm milk poured over a piece of buttered toast, and stood watching him eat it. His heel jittered on the linoleum floor, from tiredness. Jeff looked up from his breakfast at the sound, and Walter pressed his heels against the floor.

Walter heard the telephone.

It was Mrs. Philpott calling to ask if he would be able to see Mr. Kammerman, the furniture appraiser, right away. Walter said he would. Mrs. Philpott's still tranquil, polite voice baffled him. Then she said: "I hope you'll excuse me if I don't come after all, Walter. Something's just come up that I've got to attend to this morning."

35

WALTER CALLED the Newark police station from New York. They said that Corby was in Newark, but his exact whereabouts were unknown. Walter went on to Newark.

It was 1:15. It had begun to rain lightly.

Corby was not at the police station when he got there. An officer asked Walter his name, but Walter refused to give it. He got back in his car and drove to Kimmel's bookshop. The shop was closed. There was a long crack in one of the front windows, a crystalline scar in its middle where something hard had struck it, and seeing it, Walter felt a leap of blood lust in himself, glanced on the sidewalk for the brick, but it was gone.

Walter drove to a filling station, had his gas tank filled, and looked in a telephone book for Melchior Kimmel's address. He remembered it was not listed, but now he saw a Helen Kimmel entry on Bowdoin Street. The filling station attendant did not know where Bowdoin Street was. Walter asked a traffic policeman, who had a general idea, but when Walter followed it, he could not find Bowdoin. It made him so furious, he had a hard time controlling his voice when he asked a woman on the sidewalk where it was. She knew, exactly. He was four streets off.

It was a street of frame houses. The number was 245—a small, red-brown two-story house set back from the sidewalk by an extremely narrow strip of neglected lawn with a meaningless fence of low iron pickets around it. All the shades were drawn. Walter looked up and down the sidewalk. Then he got out of his car and walked up the wooden steps to the strip of porch. The doorbell made a shrill yelp. But there was no sound from inside the house. Walter imagined Kimmel watching him from behind one of the drawn shades. A physical fear crept over him, and his body tensed to fight, but there was no one. He rang the bell again, louder. He tried the door. The corners of the metal knob hurt his hand. It was locked.

Walter went back to his car, stood by it a moment, feeling his fear turn to a frustrated anger. Maybe they were all at the Newark *Sun* again. Maybe that was where he should go, and make a statement in his own defense. They probably wouldn't even print it, Walter thought. He wasn't to be trusted any more. He would need Corby to back him up, a fine, upstanding, young police detective to corroborate what he said. He swung the car around and headed back for the police station.

Walter was told that Corby was in the building, but that he was busy.

"Tell him Walter Stackhouse wants to see him."

The police sergeant gave him another look, then opened a door in the hall and went down some stairs. Walter followed him. They went down another hall and stopped at a door where the sergeant knocked loudly.

"Yes?" Corby's voice called muffledly.

"Walter Stackhouse!" the sergeant shouted against the door.

The bolt slid. Corby opened the door wide, smiling. "Hello! I was expecting you today!"

Walter came in, his hands in his overcoat pockets, and he saw Corby glance at them as if he suspected he had a gun. Walter stopped suddenly: Kimmel sat in a straight chair, his huge body twisted strangely as if he were in pain. Kimmel stared at him as if he did not recognize him at all. There was only a numbed, naked expression of terror on Kimmel's face.

"We are confessing today," Corby said genially. "Tony has already confessed, Kimmel comes next, and then you."

Walter said nothing. He glanced at the scared-looking dark-haired boy in the other straight chair. The room was tile-lined, cold and white and glaring with light. Kimmel's huge face was wet, either with tears or sweat. His collar was ripped open and his still-knotted tie hung down.

"Want to sit down, Stackhouse? There's nothing left but a table."

Walter saw that the door was closed with a big sliding bolt on the inside, like the bolts on the inside of refrigerated rooms where butchers work. "I came here to ask you what happens next. I want a showdown. I'm perfectly willing to be tried, but I'm not going to take a bunch of lies from you or anybody—"

"You'd shorten everything if you'd only admit what you did, Stackhouse!" Corby interrupted him.

Walter looked at his conceited stance, his scowling, under-sized face—little demagogue, safe behind his badge. Suddenly

Walter grabbed Corby's arm and pulled him around, threw his other fist at Corby's jaw, but Corby grabbed his fist before it landed and yanked Walter forward. Walter slipped on the tile floor and would have fallen, except that Corby kept hold of his wrist and swung him up again.

"Kimmel's found out I can't be touched, Mr. Stackhouse. You'd better find it out, too." Corby's bony cheeks had flushed. He moved his shoulders, readjusting his clothes. Then he took off his overcoat and tossed it on the wooden table.

"I asked you what comes next," Walter said. "Or is that supposed to be a surprise? Who do you think you are, releasing lies to the newspapers?"

"There's not a lie in any paper. Only one possible untruth, which is stated everywhere as uncorroborated and therefore a possible untruth."

A hell of a word, Walter thought, untruth. He watched Corby's lean, arrogant figure circle Kimmel's chair as if Kimmel were an elephant he had trapped, an elephant not yet dead. Kimmel's face and head were entirely wet with sweat, though the room was icy. Walter saw Kimmel flinch as Corby passed close by him, and he realized suddenly why Kimmel looked so ugly and naked: he hadn't his glasses. Corby must have grilled him hard, Walter thought, probably all night. And after all Kimmel's good work at the newspaper offices! Walter's fists clenched harder in his pockets. Corby was glancing at him at every lap he made around the chair. Then Corby said suddenly: "I've tried a quiet method with you, Stackhouse. It doesn't work."

"What do you mean, quiet?"

"Not printing in the papers all that I might have. I wanted you to see the stupidity of concealing what you know to be true yourself. It didn't work. I'll have to use pressure. Today's papers are only the beginning. There's no limit to the pressure I can put on you!" Corby stood with his feet apart, scowling at Walter. A twitch in one lid of his straining eyes heightened his look of drunken intensity.

"Even you have superiors," Walter said. "Maybe I should go and have a talk with Captain Royer."

Corby frowned harder. "Captain Royer backs me completely. He's completely satisfied with my work, and so are *his* superiors. I've done in five weeks what the Newark police couldn't do in two months when the trail was fresh!"

Outside of Hitler, Walter thought, outside of an insane asylum, he had never seen anything like it.

"Tony here," Corby said gesturing, "has agreed that Kimmel could have left the movie theatre immediately after he saw him, at eight-five. Tony even remembers trying to find Kimmel at his house that evening after the movie and Kimmel not being there."

"He didn't—he didn't say he tried to," Kimmel protested nervously in a strange adenoidal voice. "He didn't say he *went—*"

"Kimmel, you're so guilty, you stink!" Corby shouted, his voice rasping in the hollow room. "You're as guilty as Stackhouse!"

"I didn't, I didn't!" Kimmel said in the pattering, nasal voice, thick with a foreign accent that Walter had never heard in it before. And there was something pathetic in Kimmel's desperate denials, like the last twitchings of a body in which every bone might have been broken.

"Tony knows your wife was having an affair with Ed Kinnaird. Tony told me this morning. He's heard it from all the neighbors by now!" Corby yelled at Kimmel. "He knows you'd have killed Helen for that and for a lot less, wouldn't you? Didn't you?"

Walter watched aghast. He tried to imagine Tony on a witness stand—a terrified, unintelligent hoodlum who looked as if he would say anything he had been paid to say or terrorized into saying. Corby's methods were so crude, and yet they got results. Kimmel looked as if he were wilting, melting, like a huge gob of grease. Then he said again, in a high voice:

"I didn't, I didn't!"

Corby suddenly kicked at Kimmel's chair, and when he failed to kick it from under him, reached down and wrenched the two back legs sideways, so that Kimmel rolled with a thud onto the floor. Tony half stood up, as if he were going to give Kimmel assistance, but he didn't. Corby shoved Kimmel with the flat of his shoe, and Kimmel slowly got up, with the exhausted dignity of a wounded elephant. Corby's voice went on and on, exhorting Kimmel to confess, hammering into him that he hadn't a leg to stand on. Walter knew exactly what Corby was going to say when his turn came: he would go over the visits to Kimmel, he would pretend he believed Kimmel implicitly about the discussion of murder, his confession to Kimmel later, pretend to believe that everybody else believed it, too, and that his position was as hopeless as anyone's could be. Walter watched Corby gesticulating, coming toward him, rasping out as if to a huge audience: "—*this* man! *This* man brought it all down on you, Kimmel! Walter Stackhouse—the blunderer!"

"*Shut up!*" Walter said. "You know that I'm not guilty! You said so once, twice, God knows how many times! But if you can invent a spectacular story and win a pat on the head from some stupid bastard above you, then you'll lie and perjure a thousand times to prove your cockeyed idea is right!"

"*Your* cockeyed idea!" Corby said, not at all ruffled.

Walter swung at him. His fist cracked against Corby's jaw and he saw Corby's legs flying in the air against the white of the wall for an instant, and then Corby on the floor, tugging at his jacket. Corby leveled a gun at him and slowly stood up.

"Another move like that and I'll fire this," Corby said.

"Then you'd never get your confession," Walter said. "Why don't you arrest me? I've struck an officer!"

"I wouldn't arrest you, Stackhouse," Corby snarled. "That would give you too much protection. You don't deserve it."

Corby was standing still, but he kept the gun leveled at Walter. Walter studied his tight little face again, the icy pale-blue eyes, and wondered if Corby could possibly really believe he was guilty? And Walter decided that he did, for the negative reason that there was no possible chink left in Corby for any doubt of his guilt, whatever fact might turn up on the side of his innocence. Walter looked at Kimmel: Kimmel was staring at him with an absolutely blank and exhausted expression. Corby had driven him insane, Walter thought suddenly. They were both insane, Corby and Kimmel, each in his own way. And that half-wit boy sitting in the chair!

Walter said, "I'm either arrested, or I'm getting out of here." He turned and walked to the door.

Corby jumped between him and the door with the gun. "Get back," he said close in Walter's face. There was sweat on his bony, freckled forehead and a pink spot on his jaw where Walter had hit him. "Where do you think you're going to, anyway? What do you think there is for you outside, freedom? Who's going to talk to you? Who's your friend now?"

Walter did not step back. He looked at Corby's face, intense and rigid as a madman's, and was reminded of Clara. "What are you going to do? Threaten me with a gun to make me confess? I'm not going to confess even if you shoot me." That unnatural calm that always came over him when Clara raged at him had come over him now and he was no more afraid of the gun than if it had been a toy. "Go ahead and shoot," Walter said. "You'll get a medal for that. Certainly a promotion."

Corby wiped his mouth with the back of his hand. "Get over there by Kimmel."

Walter turned slightly, but he did not walk. Corby walked closer to Kimmel, still keeping the gun on Walter. Walter thought: there is no real way out of here, because Corby is a madman with a gun.

Corby rubbed his jaw with his free hand. "Tell me how you felt this morning when you saw the papers, Stackhouse."

Walter didn't answer.

"Tony here—" Corby gestured with the gun. "It made him see the light. Tony decided it wasn't too impossible that Kimmel could have murdered his wife. In the same way you did."

"When he saw the papers?" Walter gave a laugh.

"Yes," Corby said. "Kimmel meant to expose you, but it backfired on him. He showed Tony what might have happened. Tony's been a very bright and co-operative boy," Corby said smugly, strolling toward Tony, who looked like a scared wretch.

Walter laughed louder. He bent back and roared out a laugh, and it roared back at him from the walls. He looked at Tony, whose doltishly anxious expression had not changed, and then at Kimmel, who was now beginning to look offended, personally offended at his laughter. He felt as insane now as any of them, and he began to laugh at the insane sounds of his own laughter. He rocked on his feet, though a part of his brain that remained perfectly steady was thinking that he laughed only from nerves and tiredness, and that he was making an idiot of himself as well as a blunderer. He was thinking, Corby no more represented the law than Kimmel or Tony did, and he was a lawyer and he could do nothing about it. That impartial judge that Walter had imagined—a calm, wise man with gray hair and a black robe, who would listen to him and hear his story out to the end, and then pronounce him innocent—that figure existed only in his imagination. No one would ever hear him out before an army of Corbys interrupted, and no one would believe what had really happened—or what had *not* happened.

"Why do you laugh, you idiot?" Kimmel asked, standing up slowly from his chair.

Walter watched Kimmel's flabby face hardening with wrath, and Walter's smile diminished. He saw the righteousness, the adamant resentment that he had seen the day he came to Kimmel to tell him he was innocent. He felt suddenly afraid of Kimmel.

"Look what you have done, and yet you laugh!" Kimmel said, still in the adenoidal tone. His hands trembled and their fingertips played together in curiously childlike and dainty movements. Yet his pink-rimmed eyes bored their shocked hatred into Walter.

Walter looked at Corby. Corby was watching Kimmel with a look of satisfaction, as if his elephant were performing properly, Walter thought. And he realized that Corby's objective was to goad Kimmel into more and more hatred against him, to make Kimmel attack him physically if he could. Walter saw in Kimmel's face the maniacal conviction of his own innocence, of the injustice of the fate that had befallen him, and Walter felt suddenly ashamed, as if he actually had drawn an innocent man into a trap from which he could not hope to escape. Walter wanted to leave, to say a few words of apology that didn't exist, and back out of the room and flee.

Kimmel took a step toward him. His huge body seemed to topple and catch itself, though he still held to the back of his chair. "Idiot!" he shouted at Walter. "Murderer!"

Walter glanced at Corby and saw that Corby was smiling.

"You may go now," Corby said to Walter. "You'd better."

Walter hesitated a moment, then turned and with a crushing sense of shame and of fleeing walked to the door. The bolt did not slide at once, and he worked with another lever under-neath it, worked frantically as the sweat broke out and he imagined Corby leveling the gun behind him, or Kimmel ad-vancing behind him. Then the bolt slid, and Walter yanked the door open by the knob.

"*Murderer!*" Kimmel's voice roared behind him.

Walter ran up the steps to the main hall. His knees wobbled. He went down the outside stairs, then stood for a moment, holding to the cold iron knob at the end of the banister. He had a feeling of suffocating, or being paralyzed. It was like a dream, the paralyzed end of a dream. There was insanity be-hind him in the basement room. And he had laughed at it. He remembered Kimmel's passionate face when he had laughed, and then he pushed off from the banister, frightened, and be-gan to walk.

36

"YOU DON'T seem to understand me yet," Ellie said. "If you had killed her—I could even imagine that and maybe I could even forgive it. That's not impossible for me to imagine. It's the lies I can't forgive."

They were sitting side by side in the front seat of her car. Walter looked at her steady eyes. They were calm and clear, almost as he had seen them many times before, almost as they had always looked when they looked at him. But not quite. "You said you didn't believe Kimmel's story," Walter said.

"I certainly don't believe you went and discussed murder with him. But you've admitted the visits."

"Two," Walter said. "If you could only realize, Ellie, that this is a series of circumstances—accidents. That it all could have happened and I'd still be innocent—" He expected her to protest that she did believe him innocent of murder, but she didn't.

She kept her eyes turned on him, alertly, not moving.

"You can't believe I'm guilty of murder, Ellie!" he burst out.

"I'd rather not say anything."

"You have to answer me that!"

"Let me have that privilege at least," she retorted. "I'd rather not say anything."

Walter had wondered at her calmness on the telephone that morning when he called her, at her willingness to make an appointment with him. Now he knew she had decided yesterday when she saw the papers how she felt and how she was going to act.

"What I'm trying to say is that I could probably have taken all of it, if you'd only been honest. I don't like this, and I don't like you any more." She was sliding her thumb back and forth on the leather keycase in her hands, as if she were eager to be off. "It can't be too upsetting to you. You've never made any plans about us anyway, certainly not about marriage."

Walter thought suddenly, she holds that last night against me, too, that last night at her house. The very night he had intended to tell her that Kimmel's exposé in the newspapers was coming. Walter wondered now if he hadn't concealed what he knew that night, and hadn't made love to her, only so that she *would* react like this now, and he would lose her. He knew he had never even made up his own mind about marrying her. And yet he remembered poignantly now his elation after that first night with her, when in spite of the barriers all around him, he had been convinced that they would finally be together because they loved each other. He remembered his own conviction that he loved her—that night he had called her from the Three Brothers, when he had been unable to see her. He remembered his pride because she was so near to the ideal he had always imagined—loyal, intelligent, kind, and simply, in contrast to Clara, healthy. Now it seemed to him that he had played every card wrong, and moreover, deliberately. Or as if Clara's negative, inimical volition had made itself felt and had dominated, even now that she was dead.

"I suppose this is the last time we'll see each other," Ellie said in a quiet tone, as deadly and quiet as a surgeon's scalpel cutting through a heart. "I'm moving next week—somewhere in Long Island but not in Lennert. I want to get out of that apartment."

Walter's restless fingers touched the dashboard of her car. "You said you didn't believe Kimmel. Is that true?"

"Does that matter?"

"That's the only thing that happened yesterday. That's the only thing that's changed anything!"

"No, it isn't. That's my point. You admit that you saw him in early October, so you lied to me."

"But it's not my point at the moment. I asked if you chose to believe Kimmel—about Clara—after all I've told you about Kimmel."

"Yes," she said softly, still looking at him. "I can also say that to some extent—I suspected you all along."

Walter stared back at her, thunderstruck. He saw a different expression growing in her face now: fear. She looked as if she were afraid of a physical retaliation from him. "All right," he said through his teeth. "I don't care any more. Do you understand that?"

She only looked at him. Her tense, full lips looked as if they were even smiling at the corners.

"I'd like to make that clear to you and to everybody," Walter said. "I'm sick of it! I don't care any more what anybody thinks. Do you understand that?"

She nodded and said, "Yes."

"If nobody understands the truth, then I'm tired of explaining. Do you understand that?" He opened the car door and started out, then looked back. "I think this—this last meeting of ours is absolutely perfect. It fits in with everything else!" He closed the door after him, and strode across the street toward his own car. He was staggering from weakness as if he were drunk.

37

The office was simple, wonderfully simple. Walter just walked into George Martinson's office—it was one of the days Willie Cross was not in, though Walter wished he had been—and announced that he was leaving, and Martinson gave his assent with a minimum of words. Martinson looked at him as if he were amazed that he was still, at least to the eye, a free man.

Everybody looked at him that way, even Peter Slotnikoff. Nobody said anything but a mumbled hello to him. Everybody looked as if he were waiting for somebody else to take the initiative and spring on him and hold him, or put him in jail. Even Joan looked afraid of him, afraid to say one friendly word. Walter didn't care. Something—his indifference that had become total and genuine or his physical exhaustion that felt like a kind of drunkenness—gave him a sense of wearing an armor that protected him against everyone and everything.

Dick Jensen came into his office while he was clearing out his desk and collecting his books. Walter straightened up and watched him approach, his chin sunk reflectively down on his collar, the morning sun glinting handsomely on the gold-coin watchfob that hung out of his vest pocket.

"You don't have to say anything," Walter began. "It's perfectly all right."

"Where are you going?" Dick asked.

"To Forty-fourth Street."

"You're starting the office alone?"

"Yes." Walter went on with his drawer-emptying.

"Walt, I hope you understand why I can't come in with you. I've got a wife to support."

"I understand," Walter said evenly. He stood up and took out his billfold. "Before I forget, I want to give you back your share of the rent. Here's a check for two hundred twenty-five." He laid it on the edge of the desk.

"I'll take it on condition that you take the *Corpus Juris*," Dick said.

"But that's yours."

"We were going to use it together."

The *Corpus Juris* was at Dick's apartment, part of his private library. "You'll be needing it one day yourself," Walter said.

"Not for a long time yet. Anyway—I'd like you to have it. And the State Digests, too. They'll be way out of date before I open an office."

"Thanks, Dick," Walter said.

"I saw the notice about the office in the paper this morning."

Walter hadn't seen it yet. It was the little notice he had put in defiantly on Saturday morning, just before he went to Newark. "I was careful not to mention our names," Walter said. "Your name. I'll have my own name on the second ad this week."

Dick's big, soft brown eyes blinked. He looked surprised. "I wanted to say, Walt, that I admire your courage."

Walter waited, hungry for something else. But apparently Dick was not going to say anything else. Walter watched him pick up the check and fold it. "I'll be glad to come and get the books sometime myself in the car. Some evening when it's convenient for you. I'm going to be living in Manhattan now, starting today. I'll still consider the books just a loan until you need them."

"Oh, I'll bring them over some time during office hours," Dick said. "I'll bring them to your office." He moved toward the door.

Walter followed him, involuntarily. In spite of Dick's word-less backing out on him, Dick's reluctance to say what he was thinking, Walter couldn't end four years of friendship like this. "Dick," he said.

Dick turned. "What?"

"I want to ask you— Do you think I'm guilty? Is that it?"

Dick frowned and wet his lips. "Well, I—I guess I just don't *know*, Walter. If you want me to be perfectly honest—" Dick looked at him, still embarrassed, but he looked straight at Walter, as if he had just said all that Walter could expect any-body to say.

And Walter knew it was so, and that he could not blame Dick for what Dick couldn't help. But as he stared at Dick, he felt that the last remnant of their confidence in each other, their loyalty, their promises to each other, had been suddenly swept away, and that there was an ugly, bitter emptiness in its place.

"You're going to fight back, aren't you?" Dick asked. "What *is* going to happen?"

"I am innocent!" Walter said.

"Well—aren't you going to make a statement at least?"

"Do I have to *prove* myself innocent?" Walter burst out. "Is that the new system?"

"All right," Dick said. "Your principle is absolutely correct, but—"

"Do you think if I were guilty I'd be standing here? They haven't even enough to indict me."

"But a lot of people like me—"

"Be damned to the people like you! I'm good and sick of them, and sick of talk with no facts behind it! I don't give a damn any more what *anybody* says!"

"I hope you survive," Dick said, but in an extremely cold tone. He turned and went out the door.

Walter went back to his desk and continued stacking his papers.

Joan came in just as he was about to leave. She closed the door behind her. "You're leaving today?" she asked. "Starting the new office?"

"Yes." He saw she was embarrassed, and to help her he said, "I understand, Joan. Don't feel you have any obligation to me. I mean, as far as working for me goes."

She hesitated. For a moment, he thought she was going to say in her quiet, even voice that she still believed in him and that she still wanted to come and work for him, because she believed he would come through all this. For a moment, he dared to hope it. Then she said: "I thought I ought to tell you that I've changed my mind about leaving the office—this office. I think I prefer to stay here."

He nodded. "All right." He kept staring at her, waiting for her to say something stronger, something more precise. She had given him two years of her loyalty. He felt suddenly as embarrassed as she. "It's perfectly all right, Joan. Don't worry about it." He walked past her to the door. "You've been a very fine secretary," he added.

Joan said nothing.

Walter turned quickly and went out.

This was the way it would go, he thought, one after another. Like his friends when Clara was alive. This was like the quintessence of Clara. Isolation! Pretty soon he would know what isolation was. Soon it would be total. He didn't *really* believe any young man would apply for a job in his office, not after he found out his name. He was only going doggedly about a task he had set himself, just as he had doggedly gone about the task of dismantling the house, and just as he would this afternoon set about finding himself an apartment hotel to live in, and pay a month or two's rent in advance, with no anticipation at all of being there more than a week or so. Some kind of end would surely come: a hand would fall on his shoulder, a gun would point and a bullet fly out of the darkness at him. Or Kimmel's hands would close around his throat. But before that, everyone would have drawn back from him. There would be no one who would speak to him. The earth would become like the moon, and he as lonely as if he were the only man on it.

38

For the fourth time, Kimmel went to Bausch & Skaggs Opticians' shop on Phillston Avenue and ordered a new pair of glasses. This time, the young attendant not only smiled but laughed outright. "Dropped them again, Mr. Kimmel? You'd better tie a string on them, hadn't you?"

From the uncontrollable mirth in his voice, Kimmel knew he knew why the glasses were broken. He had no doubt that the clerk told everyone he knew about Kimmel's broken glasses. Kimmel would have ordered them from some other shop, except that Bausch & Skaggs were the quickest, and he could depend on their getting the measurements right.

"May I ask you for a deposit, Mr. Kimmel?"

Kimmel took out his wallet and removed a bill from the right side of the bills, which he knew would be a ten.

"They'll be ready tomorrow morning. Shall I send them over?" the clerk asked with mock deference.

"If you will. I'll write you a check for the rest at the house."

Then for the fourth time, Kimmel went out and crossed the sidewalk to the waiting car, though now it was not his own car with Tony in it; it was a taxi. Kimmel began to feel hungry as he drove toward home, really hungry despite his large breakfast an hour ago. He debated, examining his sensations of emptiness as if they were a palpable problem that he investigated with his fingertips. It evoked a vision of a liverwurst sandwich with sliced onion on rye bread and beer.

"Driver, will you stop at—at Twenty-fourth Street and Exeter, please. The Shamrock Delicatessen."

In front of the delicatessen, Kimmel hauled himself from the taxi again, crossed the sidewalk as cautiously as if it were a thoroughfare full of cars, and entered the shop. He ordered a liverwurst sandwich and several cans of beer. The sandwiches here could not compare with Ricco's, but Kimmel did not go to Ricco's any more. Tony fled when he saw him. His father no longer spoke to him when they passed on the street. Kimmel carried the sandwich and the beer back to the taxi, and told the driver to go to his house. He opened the waxed paper to take a bite of the sandwich, but by the time he got home, the sandwich was three-quarters eaten and he wished he had ordered two. The taxi meter said $2.10, according to the driver. Kimmel could not see it, and he did not believe the driver, but he paid it.

Kimmel drank two cans of beer at home, ate the rest of the sandwich and a piece of bread with cream cheese, then sat down in the living room to wait. He wished he could read, at least, but he couldn't. There was nothing he could do but wait, wait for the glasses and wait for Corby to come and break them again. He thought of the broken window in his shop. Someone had thrown a brick at it last Friday, when he had been there. The brick hadn't made a hole in the window, but there was a long crack going the whole way diagonally. Kimmel was afraid to stay there now during the daytime. Somehow he dreaded a fight in his shop more than in his house. Or maybe it was that everyone knew Kimmel's bookshop belonged to Melchior Kimmel, but not everyone knew where he lived.

Kimmel stood up and went back to the kitchen. He got a piece of the dressed pinewood which he bought from a lumber-yard for his carvings, took it back to the living room and began to whittle off a length of about seven inches. The wood was cut square. Kimmel made it round, like a cigar. He could not see enough to make decorations on it, but he could prepare it. He worked quickly with his sharp knife whose blade, though still strong, had been whetted so often that it was narrow and came to a long, rounded point that was as sharp as a razor.

He thought of Stackhouse's laughter again, and it was like a jolt to his brain, like a kick from Corby. His mind began to spin in a storm of anger. He could only think of crushing Stackhouse, stabbing him, when he thought of his laughter. Kimmel stood up and threw the knife and the wood on the sofa and began to walk around the room, his hands in the pockets of his voluminous trousers. He was torn in his mind between forgetting Stackhouse completely as he had forgotten Tony, simply striking him out of his memory, or crushing him physically to ease his terrible hunger for revenge. Stackhouse was like a cowardly wretch who murdered, lied, laughed at his victims and went miraculously scot-free—even when his crimes were exposed! Corby had never laid a hand on him. And he had money as well! Kimmel pictured Stackhouse living on

something approaching the category of an estate in Long
Island, living in luxury with a couple of servants (even if they
had quit him, Stackhouse could hire more) and perhaps a
swimming pool in his back lawn. And the selfish, stupid ass
had been too stingy to part with fifty thousand of it to save his
own name from being made a little blacker! Kimmel was not
only repelled by what he considered a stupid decision on
Stackhouse's part, but he felt that Stackhouse owed him fifty
thousand dollars, at the very least, for the damage he had done
his life.

Kimmel opened the refrigerator and took out the plate with
the half cervelatwurst, started to go to the breadbox for bread,
but the spicy, smoky smell of the cervelat was too tempting,
and he picked it up and bit off a piece, working his teeth to get
the inside without the skin. He took another can of beer out.
Then he went back to his seat in the living room, and picked
up the knife and the wood again.

He could go to another town, he thought. Nobody was
stopping him from doing that. Corby would undoubtedly follow him, but at least for a while there could be no staring
neighbors, or the friends and acquaintances who didn't speak
to him when he saw them. If the new town—Paterson or
Trenton—finally ostracized him, it would not be so painful as
Newark, where his friends were of longer standing.

He began to make crisscrossing cuts in the wood. He hoped
Stackhouse was losing all his friends. Kimmel hollowed out
circular pits with the rounded point of the knife. Then he
made X's in the pits, trueing them up by feeling for the right
angle with his thumbnail. He could not do any of the fancy
braided designs without his glasses, but it amused him now to
work only by the sense of touch. He was happy with his work,
though as he worked more quickly and surely, he began to feel
angry and tense again. He was thinking that the only proper
punishment for Stackhouse was castration. He was wondering
how dark it was around Stackhouse's house in Long Island.
Kimmel snorted as he sank his knife into the wood. He realized
that he had begun to assume Stackhouse was guilty, and that at
first he had believed him innocent, but to Kimmel this shift
seemed not important at all. Rather, whether Stackhouse had
really killed his wife was of no importance at all. The curious

thing about Corby, Kimmel thought, was that he apparently felt the same way. Kimmel distinctly remembered that Corby had thought Stackhouse innocent, even when he found the newspaper story about Helen's death. Corby had only begun to *say* he thought Stackhouse guilty, and to treat him as if he were. The results were the same, Kimmel thought, whether Stackhouse was guilty or not: his wife was dead, it looked as if he had killed her, and Stackhouse had brought hell down on a man who had been living perfectly peaceably before. Kimmel was conscious that he *preferred* to think Stackhouse guilty, because Stackhouse's guilt plus the immunity he enjoyed made him all the more loathsome. Kimmel imagined Stackhouse with a couple of his loyal friends—loyal with that supercilious, upper-crust loyalty that would pretend to believe a man like Stackhouse incapable of as bestial a crime as murder—drinking good scotch with him and trying to assure him that he had been the victim of a horrible plot, a most unfortunate set of circumstances. Maybe they even laughed about it! Kimmel suddenly realized that he had been cutting a deep gash around the middle of the piece, as if he were going to cut it in half. He stopped and began to smooth out the gash. But he didn't like the thing now. He had really ruined it. Kimmel jumped as the doorbell rang.

Kimmel had heard no step on the porch. The hall was dark to him, and he looked carefully around the edge of the door curtain, saw the blurred silhouette of a hat and shoulders and recognized them as Corby's.

"Open it, Kimmel, I know you're there," Corby said as if he could see him, and Kimmel was not sure he couldn't.

Kimmel opened the door.

Corby came in. "I looked for you in your shop. You're not working there any more? Oh, the glasses again!" Corby said, smiling. "Of course." He walked past Kimmel into the living room.

Kimmel tripped on the rug. He went straight to the sofa, recovered first his knife and then his piece of wood, which he put in his pocket. He held the knife down at his side, its handle between his thumb and fingertips.

"What've you been doing with yourself?" Corby asked, sitting down.

Kimmel did not answer. Corby had seen him last night until 3 A.M. Corby knew everything he had done, everyone he had seen—which was no one—since the session they had had at the police station.

"Stackhouse has opened a new office on Forty-fourth Street, all by himself. I went up to see him this morning. He seems to be getting along very well, considering."

Kimmel continued to stand, waiting. He was used to these visits from Corby, to these bits of information dropped like bird dung.

"Your denunciation of Stackhouse didn't do you much good, did it, Kimmel? No money from him, you have to close your shop because of some new enemies, and Stackhouse is able to open a new office under his own name! Kimmel, the luck's just not with you, is it?"

Kimmel wanted to hurl the knife into Corby's teeth. "It's of no interest to me what Stackhouse does," Kimmel said coldly.

"Can I see your knife?" Corby asked, reaching his hand out.

It irritated him to see Corby slouched on his sofa, to know that if he did lunge at him, Corby could probably parry it. Kimmel handed him the knife.

"It's a beauty," Corby said with admiration. "Where'd you get it?"

Kimmel smiled a little, grimly, yet with pleasure. "In Philadelphia. It's an ordinary knife."

"Good enough to do plenty of damage. It's the knife you used on Helen, isn't it?"

Oh, yes, Kimmel wanted to say casually. He said nothing. His heavy lips pressed together. He stood waiting, outwardly calm, though the anger within him churned like a poison and actually made him feel a little dizzy, a little sick at his stomach. He was anticipating the next minutes, Corby standing up to strike him in the face, to strike him in the stomach, and if he retaliated in any way, Corby would strike him harder. Kimmel liked to imagine getting his hands on Corby's throat, even one hand. If he ever did, he would never turn loose, no matter how or where Corby might hit him. He would never turn loose, and perhaps that might happen today, Kimmel thought, taking a little solace from the hope. Or it would be so simple to stab Corby in the back of the neck as he was leaving. Or would he be lying as usual in a throbbing heap on the living room floor by then?

"Don't you think that's interesting about Stackhouse? Doesn't seem to have hurt his popularity at all." Corby was opening and closing the knife.

In Corby's hands, the familiar sound of the knife was hateful to Kimmel. "I've told you, I don't care!"

"When do you get your glasses?" Corby asked indifferently.

Kimmel did not answer. This would make $260 that Corby's destruction of his glasses had cost him.

Corby got up. "I'll be seeing you again, Kimmel. Maybe tomorrow." Corby walked out of the living room.

"My knife!" Kimmel said, following him.

Corby turned around at the door and handed it to him. "What would you do without this?"

39

O N THE following night, Kimmel took his car and drove out to Benedict, Long Island. He drove to Hoboken first, caught a ferry at the last minute, and then in Manhattan took an extremely circuitous route up the west side and down Park Avenue before he cut over east to the Midtown Tunnel, in an effort to shake off the Corby man who he knew would be following him from his house. Being followed irritated him, almost as much as Corby's face-to-face insults irritated him. Whenever he spotted the man—and he often did, though Corby changed his man all the time—on his way to the shop or on his way to the grocery store, Kimmel flushed with anger, he squirmed, though at the same time a surge of dignity went through him to confuse him and prevent him from doing anything about the man, or even feeling anything about him except a quiet and murderous desire to twink out the man's life with his fingers, if he ever got within range, as he would the life of a mosquito. He did not see his trailer the night he went to Benedict, but he imagined him, even after he was logically sure he should have shaken him, and that was irritating enough. Kimmel was in a morose and restless mood.

He had obtained a map at a filling station, but it was not detailed enough to include Marlborough Road in Benedict. Kimmel made an inquiry at a delicatessen in a shopping center outside the town. The man knew where Marlborough Road was, and he did not seem at all interested in his question, Kimmel thought. The potato salads and rollmops and sausages behind the glass counter looked particularly fresh and attractive, but Kimmel found himself without hunger and he did not buy anything.

Kimmel parked his car on the main street near the turnoff into Marlborough Road, locked it and began to walk. It was a dark dirt road with only two or three houses on it so far as he could see in the darkness. He could see no numbers on them at all, but with his pen flashlight he saw the names on the mailboxes at the edge of the road. Neither of the names was Stackhouse, and Kimmel went on toward the white house behind the trees. Kimmel looked behind him. There was no car light and no sound. He got to the mailbox and flashed the thin light on it. W. P. Stackhouse. Not a window was lighted in the house. Kimmel looked at his watch. It was only 9:33. Stackhouse was probably out for the evening, with one of his loyal friends. Still he approached the house cautiously across the lawn. He went on tiptoe, his great weight throwing his body from one side to the other, and yet there was an oily grace in his progress, much more grace than when he walked. He bent smoothly to avoid a low-hanging vine in the garden and went on, circling the house. There was no light.

Kimmel stood again before the front door. He debated ringing the bell. It would be pleasant to irritate Stackhouse, to start him seriously worrying about his physical welfare. Stackhouse wasn't nearly worried enough. He could even kill Stackhouse tonight, now that he had shaken off his shadower, and to hell with an alibi. He would leave no traces. He would lie again. Kimmel trembled as he thought of crushing Stackhouse's throat between his hands, and then suddenly he realized where he was standing, where Stackhouse might conceivably see him against the slightly light strip of road, realized that he had come tonight only to satisfy his curiosity as to where Stackhouse lived. Stackhouse was most probably not at home. He should consider himself lucky that Stackhouse was not at home, because he could get a much better look at the house now.

Slowly he went close to the front door, stuck his flashlight against the glass in its upper part and looked in. The light shone on part of an empty hall, a shining dark floor. The hall looked absolutely empty, though the beam did not go farther than four feet. He found a window at ground level on one side of the house. He pointed his light. The beam picked out a white wall, an empty floor. And there were no curtains. It dawned on Kimmel that Stackhouse could have moved out, and a sudden vexation swung him around and made him walk briskly back to the front door.

He pressed the doorbell. It made a soft chime sound. He waited, then pressed it again. He felt annoyed and angry. He was angry because he felt now that he had made the long tedious drive for nothing, and that Stackhouse had given him the slip, and he was as resentful of it as he would have been if

Stackhouse had vanished with all his possessions only five minutes ago as he approached the house. Kimmel leaned on the doorbell, pressing it with a rhythmic pumping, filling the black, empty house with the repeated, banal tune of the chimes. He stopped only when his thumb began to hurt, and turned around, cursing out loud.

If he wanted to see Stackhouse, he thought, he could, and no one could stop him, not even Corby's men. Stackhouse's old office would be glad to give out his new office address. He could imagine Stackhouse's face when he saw *Kimmel* waiting for him downstairs, waiting to follow him where he lived. Stackhouse *could* be scared. Kimmel had seen that ever since the first day he had come into his shop. Kimmel wanted to scare him thoroughly, and then perhaps kill him, on some night like this, somewhere. It was a real pity Stackhouse was not here tonight, Kimmel thought. All of it might have happened tonight.

Kimmel suddenly strode away from the door, across the lawn, his head indifferently up and his heavy arms swinging. Just the kind of place he had expected Stackhouse to live in, ample and solidly expensive as a book bound in white vellum yet without being ostentatious—Stackhouse was so much the man of taste, so smugly within his rights behind the barrier of his money, his social class, his Anglo-Saxon good looks. Kimmel stopped at one of the willow trees beside the road and urinated on it.

40

WALTER PICKED up the telephone. "Hello?"

"Hello. Is this Mr. Stackhouse?"

"Yes." Walter glanced at the man who was lingering inside the door.

"This is Melchior Kimmel. I should like to see you. Can you make an appointment with me this week?"

Walter wished the man would go. They had finished talking, yet he lingered, watching him. "I have no time this week."

"It's important," Kimmel said with sudden crispness. "I'd like to see you one evening this week. If you don't, I'll—"

Walter put the telephone down slowly, cutting off the voice, and stood up slowly and approached the man at the door. "I'll be able to get the case in court the first part of next week. I'll let you know as soon as there's a decision."

The man looked at him as if he could not quite believe it. "The people tell me, never fight with a landlord. They say, don't try it."

"That's what I'm here for. We'll try it, and we'll win it," Walter said, opening the door.

The man nodded. The suspicion that Walter had imagined he saw in his face had been only apprehension, Walter thought, apprehension that he might not recover the $225 he had over-paid a gouging landlord in the last eight months. Walter watched him go down the hall to the elevator. Then he turned back into his office.

Walter stared down at the two form sheets on his desk: one, the landlord case, the other, a case of unwarrantable detention for drunkenness. And that was all. The office was silent now. The telephone was silent. But this was only the eighth day, he thought. One couldn't expect a landslide of clients in eight days, and maybe he had missed some calls, anyway, when he had been out two mornings at the library. Maybe there had even been a call from a student, asking to work for him. Maybe he should advertise again, put in a bigger ad than before.

He looked at the folded newspaper on the corner of his desk

and thought of the paragraph in the gossip column. Headed "Haunted House? . . . The mystery of a certain young lawyer's part in the death of his wife remains unsolved, but there is no mystery as to his whereabouts. Apparently undaunted, he has set up business on his own in Manhattan. We wonder if clients are staying away in as big droves as they are from his Long Island mansion, now up for sale? Local folks say the place is haunted. . . ."

He really couldn't do a much better job of advertising than that. Walter smiled one-sidedly, listening to the steps in the hall, steps that went by. He had hoped it was the mailman. He wondered what this morning's mail would bring?

Did Kimmel want to gouge him for money again? Or did Kimmel want to kill him? What was Corby doing? Corby had been silent for a week. What were Corby and Kimmel planning together? Walter lifted his head, trying to reason. He couldn't. He felt there was a wall in front of his brain. He stood up, as if he could push it aside by movement, and began to walk in the small space around his desk.

A flash of white dropped by the door. Walter jumped for it. There were four letters. He chose the plain envelope that was type addressed.

It was a letter from a student named Stanley Utter. He was twenty-two and in his third year of law school, and he hoped his present training would be sufficient, because he was specializing in penal code. He asked for an appointment and said that he would telephone. It was a very serious, respectful letter, and it touched Walter as much as any personal letter he had ever received. Maybe Stanley Utter would be just the kind of young man he wanted. Maybe Stanley Utter would be worth ten other applicants.

Walter laid to one side an envelope that looked like an advertisement, and opened the one with the Cross, Martinson and Buchman return address.

DEAR WALT,

I think I ought to warn you that Cross is going to do all he can to get you disbarred. They can't disbar you unless you're proven guilty, of course, but meanwhile, Cross can raise enough smoke to ruin your new office. I don't know what advice to give you, but I thought it only fair to tell you.

Dick

Walter folded the letter, then automatically tore it up. He had been expecting this, too. It would be like all the rest. They wouldn't officially stop him from practicing, ever. Only unofficially. Only enough talk about disbarment to put him out of business.

41

SHOULD HE give them all one more chance?

Walter laughed, a nervous laugh that made him hunch his shoulders in fear and shame as he walked in the room. He looked down at the floor, at the patterned red and green carpet.

The room was waiting. The two high-backed chairs standing against the wall were waiting, the plain, empty bed, the ormolu clock that didn't run was waiting for him. Everything was waiting except Jeff. Jeff slept in the seat of the armchair, just as he had always slept at home.

But Ellie. Jon. Dick. Cliff. The Iretons and the McClintocks. They must be waiting, too, for something to happen, for him to admit he was whipped.

"How're you feeling, Walt?" Bill Ireton had asked three days ago. "Well, we'll be seeing you some time." Walter winced at the hollow, horrible words that had nothing but curiosity behind them, a lying hypocrisy safe at the far end of a telephone wire. He wondered if Bill would get curious enough to try it again.

Walter stood looking at Jeff, trying to remember if he had fed him tonight. He couldn't remember. He went into the little kitchen, opened the refrigerator and looked at the half-empty can of dog food, which didn't recall anything to him. He put some out in a pan, heated it, and took it in to Jeff. He watched Jeff eat all of it, slowly.

He should go out and mail the letter to Stanley Utter, he thought. It lay ready on the foyer table.

He wanted to call Jon. Not with any hope of anything, but just to say the last word that Walter felt never got said. Last week he had called Jon and apologized for hanging up when Jon had called him in Long Island. Jon hadn't been angry, he had sounded exactly the same as the day he had called long distance: "When you calm down, maybe you can talk straight to me, Walter." "I *am* calmed down. That's why I'm calling." And he had been about to ask Jon when he could see him, when Jon said: "If you'd stop being a coward about the facts, whatever they are . . ." and then Walter had realized they were at the same place as before, that he *was* a coward about the facts, because he was afraid that Jon wouldn't believe him even if he fought the whole long way back in words, because nobody else had believed him. "Let's let it go," Walter had said finally to Jon, and they had let it go, and hung up, and Jon had not called back.

"Tell me what really happened, Walt," Cliff had written last week. "Until you tell what really happened, there's no end to this . . ."

"Oh, yes," Corby had said, "this'll go on forever, unless you confess."

And Ellie: "It's the lies I can't forgive . . . I can also say that I suspected you all along."

He wanted to call Jon. He would say: "I've been suspended. Let it all come down. Look at me! You can gloat! You can all congratulate yourselves! You've succeeded, I'm licked!"

What became of someone like him?

You became a living cipher, Walter thought. The way he had felt with Clara sometimes, standing on somebody's lawn in Benedict with a drink in his hand, asking himself why he was there, and where was he going? And why? And never finding an answer.

He looked at Jeff in the chair. *I love you, Clara*, he thought. Did he? Did a cipher have the capacity to love? It didn't make sense that a cipher could love. What made sense? He wished Clara were here. That was the only definite wish he had, and it made the least sense.

Walter took his overcoat from the closet and put it on quickly, realized that he had not put on a jacket, and let it go. He swung a woolen muffler around his neck, remembering mechanically and with complete indifference that it was very cold tonight. He picked up the letter to Stanley Utter.

He walked westward, toward Central Park. He could see the dark mass of its trees, and it seemed to offer shelter, like a jungle. He kept his eye out for a mailbox, but he did not see any. He pushed the letter in his overcoat pocket and put his hands in his pockets because he had no gloves. If the park were a jungle, he thought, he would keep on walking deeper and deeper into it, so far that no one could find him. He would keep walking until he dropped dead. No one would ever find his body. He would simply vanish. How did one kill oneself so that there was no trace? Acid. Or an explosion. He remembered the explosion of the bridge in the dream he had had. It seemed as real as anything else that had happened.

He entered the park. A path curved ahead of him, lighted by a lamppost, a finite length of curving gray cement. And around the curve lay another. It was so cold, there was no one in the park, he thought. And then he came on a couple sitting on a bench in a line of empty benches, embracing each other and kissing. Walter turned off the path and began to climb a hill.

In the darkness, he stumbled over a rock. The wiry underbrush caught at his trouser cuffs. He kept walking in steady, climbing strides. He was thinking of nothing. The sensation was pleasant and he concentrated on it. *I am thinking of the fact that I am thinking of nothing.* Or was that possible? Wasn't he really thinking of all the people and all the events that he was at this moment excluding? And if you thought of excluding something, weren't you really thinking of it?

He imagined he heard Ellie's voice saying very distinctly, "I love you, Walter." Walter stopped suddenly, listening. How many times had she said that? And what did it mean? It did not seem to mean half so much as Clara's saying it, and Clara had said it, and in her way she had meant it. He began walking again, but almost immediately he stopped and looked behind him.

He had heard the sound of a shoe stubbing on a rock.

He stared into the blackness below him. He heard nothing now. He glanced around for a path. He did not know where he was. He kept on in the direction he had been going. Perhaps he had imagined the sound. But for an instant, he had been absurdly frightened, imagining Kimmel behind him, puffing up the hill, angry, looking for him. Walter made himself walk in long slow paces. The ground began to slope downward.

A twig snapped behind him.

Walter took the rest of the slope in leaping strides, and jumped finally down a rock face onto a path. He stepped quickly into the shadows of an overhanging tree. The path was only dimly lighted by a lamp several yards away, but Walter could see distinctly the high rock he had jumped down, and the gentler slope of ground on the other side of it, down to the path.

Now he could hear steps.

He saw Kimmel come to the edge of light above the rock, look all around him, then descend by the gentler slope. Walter saw Kimmel look in both directions on the path, then walk toward him. Walter pressed himself against the sloping rock face of the hill. Kimmel's huge face turned to right and left as he walked. He held his right hand in a strange way, as if he carried an open knife whose blade he kept hidden in his sleeve. Walter stared at the hand, trying to see, after Kimmel passed him.

Kimmel must have followed him from the apartment, Walter thought, must have been watching the building.

Walter waited until Kimmel was too far away to hear his footsteps when he moved, and then he stepped out on the path and walked in the other direction. He took several steps before he looked behind him, but just as he looked, Kimmel turned around: Walter could see him very clearly in the light from the lamppost, and in the second that Walter stood still he thought that Kimmel saw him, because Kimmel started quickly toward him.

Walter ran. He ran as if he were panicked, but his mind seemed to work calmly and logically, asking: *What are you running for? You wanted a chance to fight it out with Kimmel. This is it.* He even thought: Kimmel probably hasn't even seen me, because he's nearsighted. But Kimmel was running now. Walter could hear the heavy ringing steps in the cement paved tunnel he had just come through.

Walter had no idea where he was. He glanced for a building that would orient him. He saw none. He climbed a hill off the path, clutching at bushes to pull himself up. He wanted to hide himself and he also wanted to see, if he could, where to get out of the park. The hill was not high enough to reveal any buildings above the dark wall of trees. Walter stopped, listening.

Kimmel went by at a trot on the path below. Walter saw him, a huge dark shadow, through the leafless branches of a tree. Walter waited until he thought three or four minutes had passed, then he began to descend the slope. He felt suddenly spent, and more out of breath now than when he had been running.

He heard Kimmel coming back. Walter was almost down the slope. He clung to the branch of a tree for a moment, his shoes sliding, listening to the steps that were coming straight toward him, only a few paces away, and he knew there was no hiding now, that Kimmel would surely see his feet, or hear him if he started climbing again. Walter cursed: why hadn't he kept on going across the hill? He tensed himself, ready to spring on Kimmel, and when he saw the dark figure just below and in front of him, Walter jumped.

They both crumpled with the impact and fell. Walter hit with all his strength. Half kneeling on him, Walter hit his face as fast and hard as he could, then lunged for the throat and held it. He was winning. He felt intensely strong, felt that his arms were strong as iron and that his thumbs were driving into the throat as deep and hard as bullets. Walter lifted the heavy head and banged it again and again on the cement path. He lifted and threw down the head until his arms began to ache and his movements grew slower and slower and there was a pain in his chest so sharp he could hardly breathe. He flung the head down for the last time and sat back on his heels, taking slow gulps of air.

He heard a step and staggered to his feet, prepared to run. But he stood without moving as the tall figure approached him.

It was Kimmel.

A wave of sickness and terror broke over him. He took a step back, but he could not make himself run as Kimmel came toward him, lifting his huge right arm to strike him.

Kimmel struck him across the side of the head, and Walter fell. The hard shins of the dead man were under him, and Walter scrambled to roll away, but Kimmel crashed down on him and held him down like a black mountain.

"Idiot!" Kimmel said. "Murderer!"

Kimmel's fist smashed against his cheek. Walter could smell, like another complicated word in the cold air, the musty, sweetish smell of Kimmel's shop, Kimmel's clothes, Kimmel. Walter's arms twitched unavailingly, and he felt Kimmel's hand grappling for a grip on his throat, taking it. Walter tried to scream. He saw Kimmel's right hand rise, and then in his open mouth felt the sting of a knifeblade through his tongue, felt the sting again in his cheek, and heard the blade's grate against his teeth. The hot pain in his throat spread down into his chest. This was dying. A thin coolness flashed across his forehead: the knife. He heard a roaring in his ears like a steady thunder: that was death and Kimmel's voice. Calling him murderer, idiot, blunderer, until the meaning of the words became a solid fact like a mountain sitting on top of him, and he no longer had the will to fight against it. Then he seemed to glide away like a bird, and he saw the little blue window he had seen with Ellie, bright and sun-filled, and just too small and too far away to escape through. He saw Clara turn her head and smile at him, a quick, soft smile of affection, as she had smiled in the first days he knew her. *I love you, Clara*, he heard himself say. Then the pain began to stop, swiftly, as if all the pain in the world were running out through a sieve, leaving him empty and pleasantly light.

Kimmel stood up, looking all around him, mashing his slippery knife clumsily shut, and trying to listen for sounds above the roar of his gasping. Then he faced the darker direction and began to walk. He did not know where he was going. He wanted only to go where it was dark. He felt extremely tired and contented, just as he had felt after Helen, he remembered. He recovered his breath carefully, still listening, though by now he had assured himself that no one was around him.

Two corpses! Kimmel almost laughed, because it was almost funny! Let them figure that one out!

There was Stackhouse, anyway! Enemy number one! Corby was next. Kimmel felt a surge of animosity go through him, and he thought, if Corby only were here, he would finish him off tonight, too.

Kimmel saw the lights of some windows in a building ahead of him.

"Kimmel?"

Kimmel turned around and saw about ten feet away the figure of a man, saw the dull shine on the barrel of a gun pointed at him. The man came closer. Kimmel did not move. He had never seen the man before, but he knew it was one of Corby's men: the paralysis had come over him already. In those seconds that the man advanced, he knew he would not move, and it was not because he was afraid of the gun or of death; it was something much deeper that he remembered from his childhood. It was a terror of an abstract power, of the power of a co-ordinated group, a terror of authority. Kimmel realized it intensely now, and he had realized it a thousand times before, and reasoned with himself that despite terror, he ought to act, but now he could not any more than at any other time. His hands had raised automatically, and this Kimmel hated more than anything, but when the man came very close and motioned with the gun for him to turn and walk, Kimmel turned with an absolute calm and with no personal fear at all, and began to walk. Kimmel thought, this time I am finished and I shall die, but he was not at all afraid of that, either, just as if it did not register. He was only ashamed of being physically so close to the smaller man beside him, and ashamed that they had any relationship.

BEAST IN VIEW

Margaret Millar

For

BETTY AND JOHN MERSEREAU

best friends and

unseverest critics

Chapter 1

T HE VOICE was quiet, smiling. "Is that Miss Clarvoe?"
"Yes."

"You know who this is?"

"No."

"A friend."

"I have a great many friends," Miss Clarvoe lied.

In the mirror above the telephone stand she saw her mouth repeating the lie, enjoying it, and she saw her head nod in quick affirmation—*this lie is true, yes, this is a very true lie*. Only her eyes refused to be convinced. Embarrassed, they blinked and glanced away.

"We haven't seen each other for a long time," the girl's voice said. "But I've kept track of you, this way and that. I have a crystal ball."

"I—beg your pardon?"

"A crystal ball that you look into the future with. I've got one. All my old friends pop up in it once in a while. Tonight it was you."

"Me." Helen Clarvoe turned back to the mirror. It was round, like a crystal ball, and her face popped up in it, an old friend, familiar but unloved; the mouth thin and tight as if there was nothing but a ridge of bone under the skin, the dark brown hair clipped short like a man's, revealing ears that always had a tinge of mauve as if they were forever cold, the lashes and brows so pale that the eyes themselves looked naked and afraid. An old friend in a crystal ball.

She said carefully, "Who is this, please?"

"Evelyn. Remember? Evelyn Merrick."

"Oh, yes."

"You remember now?"

"Yes." It was another lie, easier than the first. The name meant nothing to her. It was only a sound, and she could not separate or identify it any more than she could separate the noise of one car from another in the roar of traffic from the Boulevard three floors down. They all sounded alike, Fords and Austins and Cadillacs and Evelyn Merrick.

"You still there, Miss Clarvoe?"

"Yes."

"I heard your old man died."

"Yes."

"I heard he left you a lot of money."

"That's my business."

"Money is a great responsibility. I might be able to help you."

"Thank you, I don't require any help."

"You may soon."

"Then I shall deal with the problem myself, without help from any stranger."

"Stranger?" There was a rasp of annoyance in the repetition. "You said you remembered me."

"I was merely trying to be polite."

"Polite. Always the lady, eh, Clarvoe? Or pretending to be. Well, one of these days you'll remember me with a bang. One of these days I'll be famous, my body will be in every art museum in the country. Everyone will get a chance to admire me. Does that make you jealous, Clarvoe?"

"I think you're—mad."

"Mad? Oh no. *I'm* not the one who's mad. It's you, Clarvoe. *You're* the one who can't remember. And I know why you can't remember. Because you're jealous, you've always been jealous of me, you're so jealous you've blacked me out."

"That's not true," Miss Clarvoe said shrilly. "I don't know you. I've never heard of you. You're making a mistake."

"I don't make mistakes. What you need, Clarvoe, is a crystal ball so you can remember your old friends. Maybe I should lend you mine. Then you could see yourself in it, too. Would you like that? Or would you be afraid? You've always been such a coward, my crystal ball might scare you out of your poor little wits. I have it right here with me. Shall I tell you what I see?"

"No—stop this . . ."

"I see you, Clarvoe."

"No . . ."

"Your face is right in front of me, real bright and clear. But there's something wrong with it. Ah, I see now. You've been in an accident. You are mutilated. Your forehead is slashed open, your mouth is bleeding, blood, blood all over, blood all over . . ."

Miss Clarvoe's arm reached out and swept the telephone off the stand. It lay on its side on the floor, unbroken, purring.

Miss Clarvoe sat, stiff with terror. In the crystal ball of the mirror her face was unchanged, unmutilated. The forehead was smooth, the mouth prim and self-contained, the skin paper-white, as if there was no blood left to bleed. Miss Clarvoe's bleeding had been done, over the years, in silence, internally.

When the rigidity of shock began to recede, she leaned down and picked up the telephone and placed it back on the stand.

She could hear the switchboard operator saying, "Number please. This is the operator. Number please. Did you wish to call a number, *pulllease*?"

She wanted to say, *Give me the police*, the way people did in plays, very casually, as if they were in the habit of calling the police two or three times a week. Miss Clarvoe had never called the police in her life, had never, in all her thirty years, even talked to a policeman. She was not afraid of them; it was simply a fact that she had nothing in common with them. She did not commit crimes, or have anything to do with people who did, or have any crimes committed against her.

"Your number, please."

"Is that—is that you, June?"

"Why, yes, Miss Clarvoe. Gee, when you didn't answer, I thought maybe you'd fainted or something."

"I never faint." Another lie. It was becoming a habit, a hobby, like stringing beads. A necklace of lies. "What time is it, June?"

"About nine-thirty."

"Are you very busy?"

"Well, I'm practically alone at the switchboard. Dora's got flu. I'm warding off an attack of it myself."

Miss Clarvoe suspected from the note of self-pity in her voice and the slight slurring of her words that June had been warding off the flu in a manner not approved by the management or by Miss Clarvoe herself. She said, "Will you be going off duty soon?"

"In about half an hour."

"Would you—that is, I'd appreciate it very much if you'd come up to my suite before you go home."

"Why, is there anything wrong, Miss Clarvoe?"

"Yes."

"Well, gee whiz, *I* didn't do any . . ."

"I shall expect you here shortly after ten, June."

"Well, all right, but I still don't see what I . . ."

Miss Clarvoe hung up. She knew how to deal with June and others like her. One hung up. One severed connections. What Miss Clarvoe did not realize was that she had severed too many connections in her life, she had hung up too often, too easily, on too many people. Now, at thirty, she was alone. The telephone no longer rang, and when someone knocked on her door, it was the waiter bringing up her dinner, or the woman from the beauty parlor to cut her hair, or the bellboy, with the morning paper. There was no longer anyone to hang up on except a switchboard operator who used to work in her father's office, and a lunatic stranger with a crystal ball.

She had hung up on the stranger, yes, but not quickly enough. It was as if her loneliness had compelled her to listen; even words of evil were better than no words at all.

She crossed the sitting room and opened the French door that led on to the little balcony. There was room on the balcony for just one chair, and here Miss Clarvoe sat and watched the Boulevard three flights down. It was jammed with cars and alive with lights. The sidewalks swarmed with people, the night was full of the noises of living. They struck Miss Clarvoe's ears strangely, like sounds from another planet.

A star appeared in the sky, a first star, to wish on. But Miss Clarvoe made no wish. The three flights of steps that separated her from the people on the boulevard were as infinite as the distance to the star.

June arrived late after a detour through the bar and up the back staircase which led to the door of Miss Clarvoe's kitchenette. Sometimes Miss Clarvoe herself used this back staircase. June had often seen her slipping in or out like a thin, frightened ghost trying to avoid real people.

The door of the kitchenette was locked. Miss Clarvoe locked

everything. It was rumored around the hotel that she kept a great deal of money hidden in her suite because she didn't trust banks. But this was a common rumor, usually started by the bellboys who enjoyed planning various larcenies when they were too broke to play the horses.

June didn't believe the rumor. Miss Clarvoe locked things up because she was the kind of person who always locked things up whether they were valuable or not.

June knocked on the door and waited, swaying a little, partly because the martini had been double, and partly because a radio down the hall was playing a waltz and waltzes always made her sway. Back and forth her scrawny little body moved under the cheap plaid coat.

Miss Clarvoe's voice cut across the music like a knife through butter. "Who's there?"

June put her hand on the door jambs to steady herself. "It's me. June."

The door was unchained and unbolted. "You're late."

"I had an errand to do first."

"Yes, I see." Miss Clarvoe knew what the errand was; the kitchenette already reeked of it. "Come into the other room."

"I can't stay only a minute. My aunt will . . ."

"Why did you use the back stairs?"

"Well, I didn't know exactly what you wanted me for, and I thought if it was something I'd done wrong I didn't want the others to see me coming up here and getting nosy."

"You haven't done anything wrong, June. I only wanted to ask you a few questions." Miss Clarvoe smiled, in a kindly way. She knew how to deal with June and people like her. One smiled. Even in an agony of fear and uncertainty, one smiled. "Have you ever seen my suite before, June?"

"No."

"Never?"

"How could I? You never asked me up before, and I didn't get my job here until after you moved in."

"Perhaps you'd like to look around a bit?"

"No. No thanks, Miss Clarvoe. I'm in kind of a hurry."

"A drink, then. Perhaps you'd like a drink?" One smiled. One coaxed. One offered drinks. One did anything to avoid being alone, waiting for the telephone to ring again. "I have some nice sherry. I've been keeping it for—well, in case of callers."

"I guess a nip of sherry wouldn't hurt me," June said virtuously. "Especially as I'm coming down with flu."

Miss Clarvoe led the way down the hall into the sitting room and June followed, looking around curiously now that Miss Clarvoe's back was turned. But there was very little to see. All the doors in the hall were closed; it was impossible to tell what was behind any of them, a closet or a bedroom or a bathroom.

Behind the last door was the sitting room. Here Miss Clarvoe spent her days and nights, reading in the easy chair by the window, lying on the davenport, writing letters at the walnut desk: *Dear Mother: I am well . . . glorious weather . . . Christmas is coming. . . . My best to Douglas. . . . Dear Mr. Blackshear: Regarding those hundred shares of Atlas . . .*

Her mother lived six miles west, in Beverly Hills, and Mr. Blackshear's office was no more than a dozen blocks down the Boulevard, but Miss Clarvoe hadn't seen either of them for a long time.

She poured the sherry from the decanter on the coffee table. "Here you are, June."

"Gee, thanks, Miss Clarvoe."

"Sit down, won't you?"

"All right. Sure."

June sat down in the easy chair by the window and Miss Clarvoe watched her, thinking how much she resembled a bird, with her quick, hopping movements and her bright, greedy eyes and her bony little hands. A sparrow, in spite of the blonde hair and the gaudy plaid coat, a drunken sparrow feeding on sherry instead of crumbs.

And, watching June, Miss Clarvoe wondered for the first time what Evelyn Merrick looked like.

She said carefully, "I had a telephone call an hour ago, June, about nine-thirty. I'd be very—grateful for any information you can give me about the call."

"You mean, where it came from?"

"Yes."

"I wouldn't know that, Miss Clarvoe, unless it was long distance. I took three, four long distance calls tonight but none of them was for you."

"You recall ringing my room, though, don't you?"

"I don't know."

"Think hard."

"Well, sure, Miss Clarvoe. I *am* thinking hard, real hard." The girl screwed up her face to maintain the illusion. "Only it's like this, see. If someone calls and asks for Miss Clarvoe, then I'd remember it for sure, but if someone just asks for room 425, well, that's different, see."

"Whoever called me, then, knew the number of this suite."

"I guess."

"Why do you guess, June?"

The girl fidgeted on the edge of the chair, and her eyes kept shifting toward the door and then to Miss Clarvoe and back to the door. "I don't know."

"You said you *guessed*, June."

"I only meant I—I can't remember ringing 425 tonight."

"Are you calling me a liar, June?"

"Oh no, Miss Clarvoe, I should say not, Miss Clarvoe. Only . . ."

"Well?"

"I don't remember, is all."

They were the final words of the interview. There were no thank-you's or farewells or see-you-soon's. Miss Clarvoe rose and unlocked the door. June darted out into the corridor. And Miss Clarvoe was alone again.

Laughter from the next room vibrated against the wall and voices floated in through the open French door of the balcony.

"Honestly, George, you're a kick, a real kick."

"Listen to the girl, how cute she talks."

"Hey, for Pete's sake, who took the opener?"

"What do you think the good Lord gave you teeth for?"

"What the Lord gaveth, the Lord tooketh away."

"Dolly, where in hell did you put the opener?"

"I don't remember."

I don't remember, is all.

Miss Clarvoe sat down at the walnut desk and picked up the

gold fountain pen her father had given her for her birthday years ago.

She wrote, Dear Mother: It has been a long time since I've heard from you. I hope that all is hell with you and Douglas.

She stared at what she had written, subconsciously aware that a mistake had been made but not seeing it at first. It looked so right, somehow: *I hope that all is hell with you and Douglas.*

I meant to say well, Miss Clarvoe thought. It was a slip of the pen. I hold no resentment against her. It's all this noise—I can't concentrate—those awful people next door . . .

"Sometimes you behave like an ape, Harry."

"Send down for some bananas, somebody. Harry's hungry."

"So what's so funny?"

"Take a joke, can't you. Can't you take a joke?"

Miss Clarvoe closed and locked the French doors.

Perhaps that's what the telephone call was, she thought. Just a joke. Just someone, probably someone who worked in the hotel, trying to frighten her a little because she was wealthy and because she was considered somewhat odd. Miss Clarvoe realized that these qualities made her a natural victim for jokers; she had become adjusted to that fact years ago, and behind-the-hand snickers no longer disturbed her the way they had in school.

It was settled, then. The girl with the crystal ball was a joke. Evelyn Merrick didn't exist. And yet the very name was beginning to sound so familiar that Miss Clarvoe was no longer absolutely certain she hadn't heard it before.

She pulled the drapes close across the windows and returned to her letter.

I hope that all is hell with you and Douglas.

She crossed out hell and inserted well.

I hope that all is well with you and Douglas. I don't, though. I don't hope anything. I don't care.

She tore the sheet of paper across the middle and placed it carefully in the wastebasket beside her desk. She had nothing really to say to her mother, never had, never would have. The idea of asking her for advice or comfort or help was absurd. Mrs. Clarvoe had none of these things to give, even if Helen had dared to ask.

The party in the next room had reached the stage of song. Down by the Old Mill Stream. Harvest Moon. Daisy, Daisy. Sometimes in close harmony, sometimes far.

A hot gust of anger and resentment swept through Miss Clarvoe's body. They had no right to make so much noise at this time of night. She would have to rap on the wall to warn them, and if that didn't work she would call the manager.

She started to rise but her heel caught in the rung of the chair and she fell forward, her face grazing the sharp edge of the desk. She lay still, tasting the metallic saltiness of blood, listening to the throbbing of the pulse in her temples and the panic beat of her heart.

After a time she pulled herself to her feet and moved slowly and stiffly across the room toward the mirror above the telephone stand. There was a slight scratch on her forehead and one corner of her mouth was bleeding where the underlip had been cut by a tooth.

. . . *"I have a crystal ball. I see you now. Real bright and clear. You've been in an accident. Your forehead is gashed, your mouth is bleeding. . . ."*

A cry for help rose inside Miss Clarvoe's throat. Help me, someone! Help me, mother—Douglas—Mr. Blackshear . . .

But the cry was never uttered. It stuck in her throat, and presently Miss Clarvoe swallowed it as she had swallowed a great many cries.

I am not really hurt. I must be sensible. Father always boasted to people how sensible I am. Therefore I must not become hysterical. I must think of something very sensible to do.

She went back to her desk and picked up her pen and took out a fresh sheet of note paper.

Dear Mr. Blackshear:
    You may recall that at my father's funeral you offered to give me advice and help if the occasion should ever arise. I do not know whether you said this because it is the kind of thing one says at funerals, or whether you sincerely meant it. I hope it was the latter, because the occasion, you may have already inferred, has arisen. I believe that I have become the victim of a lunatic. . . .

Chapter 2

. . . IT IS distressing to me to have to confide these sordid details to anyone. I do not lightly cast my burdens on other people, but since you gave my late father such expert counsel, I would very much appreciate your advice in the situation I have described to you.

If you would be so kind as to telephone me when you receive this letter and let me have your opinion in the matter, I would be extremely grateful. I intend, of course, to express my gratitude in more practical terms than words.

Yours very truly,
Helen Clarvoe

The letter was delivered to Mr. Blackshear's office and then sent on to his apartment on Los Feliz because he had gone home early. He no longer appeared regularly at his office. At fifty, he was retiring gracefully, by degrees, partly because he could afford to, but mostly because boredom had set in, like a too early winter. Things had begun to repeat themselves: new situations reminded him of past situations, and people he met for the first time were exactly like other people he'd known for years. Nothing was new any more.

Summer had passed. The winter of boredom had set in and frost had formed in the crevices of Blackshear's mind. His wife was dead, his two sons had married and made lives of their own, and his friends were mostly business acquaintances whom he met for lunch at Scandia or the Brown Derby or the Roosevelt. Dinners and evening parties were rare because Blackshear had to rise long before dawn in order to be at his office by 6 o'clock when the New York stock exchange opened.

By the middle of the afternoon he was tired and irritable, and when Miss Clarvoe's letter was delivered he almost didn't open it. Through her father, who had been one of Blackshear's clients, he had known Helen Clarvoe for years, and her constrained prose and her hobbled mind depressed him. He had never been able to think of her as a woman. She was simply

Miss Clarvoe, and he had a dozen or more clients just like her, lonely rich ladies desiring to be richer in order to take the curse off their loneliness.

"Damn the woman," he said aloud. "Damn all dull women."

But he opened the letter because on the envelope, in Miss Clarvoe's neat, private-school backhand, were the words Confidential, Very Important.

> . . . Lest you think I am exaggerating the matter, I hasten to assure you that I have given an exact account both of the telephone call and my subsequent conversation with the switchboard operator, June Sullivan. You will understand, I am sure, how deeply shocked and perplexed I am. I have harmed no one in my life, not intentionally at any rate, and I am truly amazed that someone apparently bears me a grudge. . . .

When he had finished reading the letter he called Miss Clarvoe at her hotel, more from curiosity than any desire to help. Miss Clarvoe was not the kind of woman who would accept help. She existed by, for, and unto herself, shut off from the world by a wall of money and the iron bars of her egotism.

"Miss Clarvoe?"

"Yes."

"This is Paul Blackshear."

"Oh." It was hardly a word, but a deep sigh of relief.

"I received your letter a few minutes ago."

"Yes. I—thank you for calling."

It was more like the end of a conversation than the beginning. Somewhat annoyed by her reticence, Blackshear said, "You asked me for advice, Miss Clarvoe."

"Yes. I know."

"I have had very little experience in such matters, but I strongly urge you to . . ."

"Please," Miss Clarvoe said. "Please don't say anything."

"But you asked me . . ."

"Someone might be listening."

"I have a private line."

"I'm afraid I haven't."

She must mean the girl, June Sullivan, Blackshear thought.

Of course the girl would be listening, if she wasn't busy elsewhere; Miss Clarvoe had probably antagonized her, or, at the very least, aroused her curiosity.

"There have been new developments." Miss Clarvoe's voice was guarded. "I can talk about them only in the strictest privacy."

"I see."

"I know how busy you are and I hate to impose on you, but—well, I must, Mr. Blackshear. I *must.*"

"Please go on." Behind her wall of money, behind her iron bars, Miss Clarvoe was the maiden in distress, crying out, reluctantly and awkwardly, for help. Blackshear made a wry grimace as he pictured himself in the role of the equally reluctant rescuer, a tired, detached, balding knight in Harris tweeds. "Tell me what you want me to do, Miss Clarvoe."

"If you could come here to my hotel, where we can talk—privately . . ."

"We'd probably have more privacy if you came over here to my apartment."

"I can't. I'm—afraid to go out."

"Very well, then. What time would you like me to come?"

"As soon as you can."

"I'll see you shortly, then, Miss Clarvoe."

"Thank you. Thank you very much. I can't *tell* you how . . ."

"Then please don't. Good-bye."

He hung up quickly. He didn't like the sound of Miss Clarvoe's gratitude spilling out of the telephone, harsh and discordant, like dimes spilling out of a slot machine. The jackpot of Miss Clarvoe's emotions—*thank you very much.*

What a graceless woman she was, Blackshear thought, hoarding herself like a miser, spending only what she had to, to keep alive.

Although they communicated quite frequently by letter, he hadn't seen her since her father's funeral the previous year. Tall, pale, tearless, she had stood apart from the others at the grave; her only display of feeling had been an occasional sour glance at the weeping widow, Verna Clarvoe, leaning on the arm of her son Douglas. The more tears her mother shed, the more rigid Helen Clarvoe's back had become, and the tighter her lips.

When the services were over, Blackshear had approached Miss Clarvoe, aware of her mute suffering.

"I'm sorry, Helen."

She had turned her face away. "Yes. So am I."

"I know how fond you and your father were of each other."

"That's not entirely accurate."

"No?"

"No. I was fond of him, Mr. Blackshear, not he of me."

The last time he saw her she was climbing stiffly into the back seat of the long black Cadillac that was used to transport the chief mourners, Mrs. Clarvoe, Helen and Douglas. They made a strange trio.

A week later Blackshear received a letter from Miss Clarvoe stating that she had moved, permanently, to the Monica Hotel and wished him to handle her investments.

The Monica was the last place in the world he would have expected Miss Clarvoe to choose. It was a small hotel on a busy boulevard in the heart of Hollywood, and it catered not to the quiet solitary women like Miss Clarvoe, but to transients who stayed a night or two and moved on, minor executives and their wives conducting business with pleasure, salesmen with their sample cases, advertising men seeking new accounts, discreet ladies whose names were on file with the bellhops, and tourists in town to do the studios and see the television shows. All the kinds of people Miss Clarvoe would ordinarily dislike and avoid. Yet she chose to live in their midst, like a visitor from another planet.

Blackshear left his car in a parking lot and crossed the street to the Monica Hotel.

The desk clerk, whose name plate identified him as G. O. Horner, was a thin elderly man with protuberant eyes that gave him an expression of intense interest and curiosity. The expression was false. After thirty years in the business, people meant no more to him than individual bees do to a beekeeper. Their differences were lost in a welter of statistics, eradicated by sheer weight of numbers. They came and went; ate, drank, were happy, sad, thin, fat; stole towels and left behind toothbrushes, books, girdles, jewelry; burned holes in the furniture, slipped in bathtubs, jumped out windows. They were all alike, swarming around the hive, and Mr. Horner wore a protective net of indifference over his head and shoulders.

The only thing that mattered was the prompt payment of bills. Blackshear looked solvent. He was smiled at.

"Is there anything I can do for you, sir?"

"I believe Miss Clarvoe is expecting me."

"Your name, please."

"Paul Blackshear."

"Just a moment, sir, and I'll check."

Horner approached the switchboard, walking softly and carefully, as if one of his old enemies had scattered tacks on the floor. He talked briefly to the girl on duty, hardly moving his mouth. The girl looked over her shoulder at Blackshear with sullen curiosity and Blackshear wondered if this was the June Sullivan Miss Clarvoe had mentioned in her letter.

Blackshear returned her stare. She was an emaciated blonde with trembling hands and a strained white face, as if the black leech of the earphone had already drawn too much blood.

Horner bent over her but the girl leaned as far away from him as she could and started to yawn. Three or four times she yawned and her eyes began to water and redden along the upper lids. It was impossible to guess her age. She could have been a malnourished twenty or an underdeveloped forty.

Horner returned, his fingers plucking irritably at the lapels of his black suit. "Miss Clarvoe didn't leave any message down here, sir, and her room doesn't answer."

"I know she's expecting me."

"Oh, certainly, sir, no offense intended, I assure you. Miss Clarvoe frequently doesn't answer her telephone. She wears ear plugs. On account of the traffic noises, a great many of our guests wear . . ."

"What is the number of her suite?"

"Four-twenty-five."

"I'll go up."

"Certainly, sir. The elevators are to your right."

While he was waiting for an elevator, Blackshear glanced back at the desk and saw that Horner was watching him; he had lifted his protective veil of indifference for a moment and was peering out like an old woman from behind a lace curtain.

Blackshear disappeared into the elevator and Mr. Horner lowered his net again, and let the lace curtain fall over his thoughts: *That suit must have cost a hundred and fifty dollars. . . . These con men always put up a good appear-*

ance. . . . I wonder how he's going to take her and for how much. . . .

Miss Clarvoe must have been waiting behind the door. It opened almost simultaneously with Blackshear's knock, and Miss Clarvoe said in a hurried whisper, "Please come in."

She locked the door behind him, and for a few moments they stood looking at each other in silence across a gully of time. Then Miss Clarvoe stretched out her hand and Blackshear took it.

Her skin was cool and dry and stiff like parchment, and there was no pressure of friendliness, or even of interest, in her clasp. She shook hands because she'd been brought up to shake hands as a gesture of politeness. Blackshear felt that she disliked the personal contact. Skin on skin offended her; she was a private person. The private I, Blackshear thought, always looking through a single keyhole.

The day was warm for November, and Blackshear's own hands were moist with sweat. It gave him a kind of petty satisfaction to realize that he must have left some of his moisture on her.

He waited for her to wipe her hand, surreptitiously, even unconsciously, but she didn't. She merely took a step backward and two spots of color appeared on her high cheekbones.

"It was kind of you to go to all this trouble, Mr. Blackshear."

"No trouble at all."

"Please sit down. The wing chair is very comfortable."

He sat down. The wing chair was comfortable enough but he couldn't help noticing that it, like all the other furniture in the room, was cheap and poorly made. He thought of the Clarvoe house in Beverly Hills, the hand-carved chairs and the immense drawing room where the rug had been especially woven to match a pattern in the Gauguin above the mantel, and he wondered for the dozenth time why Miss Clarvoe had left it so abruptly and isolated herself in a small suite in a second-rate hotel.

"You haven't changed much," Blackshear lied politely.

She gave him a long, direct stare. "Do you mean that as a compliment, Mr. Blackshear?"

"Yes, I did."

"It is no compliment to me to be told that I haven't changed. Because I wish I had."

Damn the woman, Blackshear thought. You couldn't afford to be nice to her. She was unable to accept a compliment, a gift of any kind; they seemed to burn her like flaming arrows and she had to pluck them out and fling them back with vicious accuracy, still aflame.

He said coldly, "How is your mother?"

"Quite well, as far as I know."

"And Douglas?"

"Douglas is like me, Mr. Blackshear. He hasn't changed either. Unfortunately."

She approached the walnut desk. It bore no evidence of the hours Miss Clarvoe had spent at it. There were no letters or papers visible, no ink marks on the blotter. Miss Clarvoe did not leave things lying about. She kept them in drawers, in closets, in neat steel files. All the records of her life were under lock and key: the notes from Douglas asking for money, her bank statements and canceled checks, gardenia-scented letters from her mother, some newspaper clippings about her father, an engraved wedding invitation half torn down the middle, a bottle of sleeping pills, a leash and harness with a silver tag bearing the name Dapper, a photograph of a thin awkward girl in a ballet dress, and a sheaf of bills held together by a gold money clip.

Miss Clarvoe picked up the sheaf of bills and handed it to Blackshear.

"Count it, Mr. Blackshear."

"Why?"

"I may have made a mistake. I get—flustered sometimes and can't concentrate properly."

Blackshear counted the money. "A hundred and ninety-six dollars."

"I was right, after all."

"I don't understand."

"Someone has been stealing from me, Mr. Blackshear. Perhaps systematically, for weeks, perhaps just once—I don't know. I do know that there should be nearly a thousand dollars in that clip."

"When did you discover some of it was missing?"

"This morning. I woke up early while it was still dark. There was some argument going on down the hall, a man and a woman. The woman's voice reminded me of the girl on the telephone, Evelyn Merrick, and I—well, it upset me. I couldn't go back to sleep. I began to wonder about Miss Merrick and when—whether I would hear from her again and what she hoped to get out of me. The only thing I have is money."

She paused, as if giving him a chance to contradict her or agree with her. Blackshear remained quiet. He knew she was wrong but he didn't feel that anything could be gained, at this point, by stating it: Miss Clarvoe had another thing besides money which might interest a woman like Evelyn Merrick, and that was the capacity to be hurt.

Miss Clarvoe continued quietly. "I got up and took a pill and went back to sleep. I dreamed of her—Evelyn Merrick. I dreamed she had a key to my suite and she let herself in, bold as brass. She was blonde, coarse-looking, made up like a woman of the streets—it's so vivid, even now. She went over to my desk and took my money. All of it." Miss Clarvoe stopped and gave Blackshear a long direct stare. "I know such dreams mean nothing, except that I was disturbed and frightened, but as soon as I woke up again I unlocked my desk and counted my money."

"I see."

"I told you about the dream because I wanted to make it clear that I had a *reason* for counting the money. I don't usually do such a thing. I'm not a miser poring over a hoard of gold."

But she spoke defensively, as if someone in the past had accused her of being miserly.

"Why do you keep such a large amount of cash in your room?" Blackshear said.

"I need it."

"Why?"

"For—well, tips, shopping for clothes, things like that."

Blackshear didn't bother pointing out that a thousand dollars would cover a lot of tips, and the black jersey dress Miss Clarvoe was wearing indicated that her shopping trips were few and meager.

The silence stretched out like tape from a roller until there seemed no logical place to cut it.

"I like to have money around," she said, finally. "It gives me a feeling of security."

"It should give you the opposite."

"Why?"

"It makes you a target."

"You think that's what Evelyn Merrick wants from me? Only money?"

He realized from her stressing of the word "only" that she, too, suspected other factors were involved.

"Perhaps," he said. "It sounds to me like an extortion racket. It may be that the woman means to frighten you, to harass you, until you are willing to pay her to be left alone. It may be, too, that you'll never hear from her again."

Miss Clarvoe turned away with a little sighing sound that whispered of despair. "I'm afraid. I'm afraid sometimes even to answer the phone."

Blackshear looked grave. "Do you know more than you're telling me, Helen?"

"No. I wrote everything in my letter to you, every word that was spoken. She's—she's crazy, isn't she, Mr. Blackshear?"

"A little off-balance, certainly. I'm no specialist in these matters. My business is stocks and bonds, not psychoses."

"You have no advice for me, then?"

"I think it would be a good idea if you took a vacation. Leave town for a while. Travel. Go some place where this woman can't find you."

"I have no place to go."

"You have the whole world," Blackshear said impatiently.

"No—no." The world was for couples, for lovers, for husbands and wives, mothers and daughters, fathers and sons. Everywhere in the world, all the way to the horizon, Miss Clarvoe saw couples, like her mother and father, and, now, Douglas and her mother, and the sight of them spread ice around her heart.

"England," Blackshear was saying. "Or Switzerland. I'm told St. Moritz is very lively in the wintertime."

"What would I do in such a place?"

"What do other people do?"

"I don't really know," she said seriously. "I've lost touch."

"You must find it again."

"How does one go about finding things that are lost? Have you ever lost anything, Mr. Blackshear?"

"Yes." He thought of his wife, and his endless silent prayers when she was dying, his bargains with God: take my eyes, my arms, my legs, take anything but leave me Dorothy.

"I'm sorry," Miss Clarvoe said. "I didn't realize—I'd forgotten . . ."

He lit a cigarette. His hands were shaking with anger and remembered grief and sudden loathing for this awkward woman who did everything wrong, who cared for no one and gave nothing of herself even to a dog.

"You asked me for advice," he said with no trace of emotion. "Very well. About the missing money, you'll have to report that to the police. Whether you like it or not, it's your duty as a citizen."

"Duty." She repeated the word after him, slowly, as if it had a taste that must be analyzed, a flavor pungent with the past: castor oil and algebra and unshed tears and hangnails and ink from leaky pens. Miss Clarvoe was a connoisseur. She could pick out and identify each flavor, no matter how moldy with age.

"As for the woman, Evelyn Merrick, I've already given you my advice. Take a vacation. There are certain disordered persons who get a kick out of making anonymous phone calls to strangers or people they know slightly."

"She gave me her name. It wasn't an anonymous call."

"It was as far as you're concerned. You don't know her. You've never heard of her before. Is that right?"

"I think so. I'm not sure."

"Do you ordinarily remember people well—names, faces, conversations?"

"Oh yes." Miss Clarvoe gave a nod of bitter satisfaction. "I remember them."

Blackshear got up and looked out of the window at the traffic below. After-five traffic, with everyone hurrying to get home, in all directions; to Westwood and Tarzana, to Redondo Beach and Glendale, to Escondido and Huntington Park, to Sherman Oaks and Lynwood. It was as if the order had gone out to evacuate Hollywood and the evacuation was taking place with no one in command but a single traffic cop with a tin whistle.

Blackshear said, over his shoulder, "You're not good at taking advice."

"What you suggest is impossible. I can't leave Los Angeles right now, for personal reasons." She added vaguely, "My family."

"I see. Well, I'd like to help you but I'm afraid there isn't anything I can do."

"There is."

"What?"

"Find her."

He turned, frowning. "Why?"

"I want to—I must see her, talk to her. I must rid myself of this—uncertainty."

"Perhaps the uncertainty is in yourself, Helen. Finding a stranger may not help you."

She raised her hand in an autocratic little gesture as if she meant to silence him. But almost immediately her hand dropped to her side again and she said, "Perhaps not. But you could try."

"All I have to go on is a name."

"No. There's more than that. Remember what she said, that one of these days she'd be famous, her—her body would be in every art museum in the country. That must mean that she poses for artists, she's a model."

"Models are a dime a dozen in this town."

"But it at least gives you a place to start. Aren't there such things as model booking agencies?"

"Yes."

"You could try there. I'll pay you, of course. I'll pay . . ."

"You're forgetting something."

"What?"

"I'm not for hire."

She was quiet for a moment. "Have I offended you by mentioning money? I'm sorry. When I offer to pay people, I don't mean it as an insult. It's simply all I have to offer."

"You have a low opinion of yourself, Helen."

"I wasn't born with it."

"Where did you get it?"

"The story," she said, "is too long to tell, and too dull to listen to."

"I see." But he didn't see. He remembered Clarvoe as a tall, thin, quiet-mannered man, obviously fond of and amused by his frilly little wife, Verna. What errant chromosomes or domestic dissensions had produced two such incongruous children as Helen and Douglas, Blackshear could not even guess. He had never been intimate with the family although he'd known them all since Helen was in college and Douglas was attending a military prep school. Once in a while Blackshear was invited out to the house for dinner, and on these occasions the conversation was conducted by Verna Clarvoe who would chatter endlessly on the I—me—my level. Neither of the children had much to say, or, if they had, they had been instructed not to say it. They were like model prisoners at the warden's table, Douglas, fair-skinned and fragile for his age, and Helen, a caricature of her father, with her cropped brown hair and bony arms and legs.

Shortly after Clarvoe's death, Blackshear had been surprised to read in the society page of the morning paper that Douglas had married. He had been less surprised when a notice of annulment followed, on the legal page, a few weeks later.

"I know what you are thinking," Miss Clarvoe said. "That I should hire an experienced investigator."

Nothing had been further from his thoughts but he didn't argue. "It seems like a good idea."

"Do you know of anyone?"

"Not offhand. Look in the yellow pages."

"I couldn't trust a stranger. I don't even tr—" Her mouth closed but her eyes finished the sentence: I don't even trust you. Or mother, or Douglas. Or myself.

"Mr. Blackshear," she said. "I . . ."

Suddenly, her whole body began to move, convulsively, like that of a woman in labor, and her face was tortured as if she already knew that the offspring she was going to bear would be deformed, a monster.

"Mr. Blackshear—I— Oh, God . . ."

And she turned and pressed her forehead against the wall and hid her face with her hands. Blackshear felt a great pity for her not because of her tears but because of all the struggle it had taken to produce them. *The mountain labored and brought forth a mouse.*

"There, there, don't cry. Everything's going to be all right. Just take it easy." He said all the things that he'd learned to say to his wife, Dorothy, whenever she cried, words which didn't mean anything in themselves, but which fulfilled Dorothy's need for attention and sympathy. Miss Clarvoe's needs were deeper and more obscure. She was beyond the reach of words.

Blackshear lit another cigarette and turned to the window and pretended to be interested in the view, a darkening sky, a dribble of clouds. *It might rain tonight—if it does, I won't go to the office in the morning—maybe the doctor was right, I should retire altogether—but what will I do with the days and what will they do to me?*

He was struck by the sudden realization that he was in his way as badly off as Miss Clarvoe. They had both reached a plateau of living, surrounded by mountains on the one side and deep gorges on the other. Blackshear had at one time scaled the mountains and explored the gorges, Miss Clarvoe had not done either; but here they were, on the same plateau.

"Helen . . ." He turned and saw that she had left the room.

When she returned a few minutes later, her face was washed and her hair combed.

"Please excuse me, Mr. Blackshear. I don't often make a fool of myself in public." She smiled wryly. "Not such a *damned* fool, anyway."

"I'm sorry I upset you."

"You didn't. It was—the other things. I guess I'm an awful coward."

"What are you afraid of, the thief or the woman?"

"I think they're the same person."

"Perhaps you're interpreting your dream too literally."

"No." Unconsciously, she began to rub her forehead, and Blackshear noticed that it bore a slight scratch that was already healed over. "Do you believe that one person can influence another person to—to have an accident?"

"It's possible, I suppose, if the suggestion is strong enough on the part of the first person, and if it coincides with a desire for self-punishment on the part of the second person."

"There are some things you can't explain by simple psychology."

"I suppose there are."

"Do you believe in extrasensory perception?"

"No."

"It exists, all the same."

"Perhaps."

"I feel—I feel very strongly—that this woman means to destroy me. I *know* it. If you like, call it intuition."

"Call it fear," Blackshear said.

She looked at him with a touch of sadness. "You're like my father. Nothing exists for you unless you can touch or see or smell it. Father was tone-deaf; he never knew, in all his life, that there was such a thing as music. He always thought that when people listened to music they were pretending to hear something that wasn't really there."

"It's not a very good analogy."

"Better than you think, perhaps. Well, I won't keep you any longer, Mr. Blackshear. I appreciate your taking time out to come and see me. I know how busy you are."

"I'm not busy at all. In fact, I've practically retired."

"Oh. I hadn't heard. Well, I hope you enjoy your leisure."

"I'll try." What will you do with the days? he asked himself. Collect stamps, grow roses, sit through double features, doze in the sun on the back porch, and when you get too lonely, go to the park and talk to old men on benches. "I've never had much leisure to enjoy. It will take practice."

"Yes," Miss Clarvoe said gently. "I'm afraid it will."

She crossed the room and unlocked the door. After a moment's hesitation, Blackshear followed her.

They shook hands again and Blackshear said, "You won't forget to report the missing money to the police?"

"I won't forget to do it, Mr. Blackshear. I will simply *not* do it."

"But why?"

"The money itself isn't important. I sit here in my room and get richer without even raising my hand. Every time the clock ticks I'm richer. What does eight hundred dollars matter?"

"All right, then, but Evelyn Merrick matters. The police might be able to find her for you."

"They might, if they bothered to look."

Blackshear knew she was right. The police would be inter-

ested in the theft but there wasn't the slightest evidence that
Evelyn Merrick was the thief. And as far as the phone call was
concerned, the department received dozens of similar complaints every day. Miss Clarvoe's story would be filed and forgotten, because Evelyn Merrick had done no physical harm,
had not even voiced any definite threats. No search would be
made for the woman unless he, Blackshear, made it himself.

I could do it, he thought. It isn't as if I'd be investigating a
major crime where experience is necessary. All I have to do is
find a woman. That shouldn't require anything more than ordinary intelligence and perseverance and a bit of luck. Finding
a woman is better than collecting stamps or talking to old men
on benches in the park.

He felt excitement mounting in him, followed by the sudden and irrational idea that perhaps Miss Clarvoe had contrived the whole thing, that she had somehow tricked or willed
him into this reversal of his plans. *Do you believe in extrasensory perception, Mr. Blackshear?" "No."*

No? He looked at her. She was smiling.

"You've changed your mind," she said, and there was no
rising inflection of doubt in her voice.

Chapter 3

THE FOLLOWING afternoon, after spending the morning at the telephone, Blackshear arrived at the establishment advertised in the yellow pages of the Central Los Angeles phone book as the Lydia Hudson School of Charm and Modeling. It was one of two dozen similar schools listed, differing only in name, location and degree of disregard for the laws of probability: We will make you a new person. . . . Hundreds of glamorous jobs awaiting our graduates. . . . We guarantee to improve your personality, poise, posture, make-up, figure, and mental outlook. . . . Walk and talk in beauty, our staff will teach you. . . .

Miss Hudson performed her miracles on the second floor of a professional building on Vine Street. The outer office was a stylized mixture of glass brick and wrought iron and self-conscious young women in various stages of charm. Two of them were apparently graduates; they carried their professional equipment in hatboxes, and they wore identical expressions, half-disillusioned, half-alert, like commuters who had been waiting too long for their train and were eyeing the tracks for a handcar.

They spotted Blackshear, and immediately began an animated conversation.

"You remember Judy Hall. Well, she's *finally* engaged."

"No! How did that happen?"

"I wouldn't *dare* to guess. I mean, her methods are pretty stark, aren't they?"

"They have to be. She's let herself go terribly in the past year. Did you notice her complexion? And her posture?"

"It isn't her posture that's so bad. It's her figure."

"I bet Miss Hudson could do wonders . . ."

Walk and talk in beauty, our staff will teach you.

Blackshear approached the reception desk and the commuters stopped talking. Another train had passed without stopping.

"I have an appointment to see Miss Hudson. The name is Blackshear."

The receptionist's eyelids drooped as if from the weight of her mascara. "Miss Hudson is in Conversation Class at the moment, Mr. Blackshear. Will you wait?"

"Yes."

"Just have a seat over there."

She undulated across the room, walking in beauty, and disappeared behind a frosted glass door marked Private. A minute later a short woman with hair the color of persimmons and a mouth to match came out of the same door. She didn't undulate. She walked briskly with her shoulders back and her head thrust forward at a slightly aggressive angle, as if she expected to be challenged by a high wind or a disgruntled client.

"I'm Lydia Hudson." Her voice was incongruously soft and pleasant, with a faint trace of a New England accent. "Sorry to keep you waiting, Mr. Blackshear."

"You didn't."

"I was rather surprised by your phone call. You sounded so mysterious."

"Let's say mystified, not mysterious."

"Very well." She smiled a professional smile, without disturbing her eyes. "You're not a policeman, are you, Mr. Blackshear?"

"No."

"Maybe you're a lawyer, and the Merrick girl is a long-lost heiress. That would be fun."

"It would."

"But that's not it, eh?"

"No."

"It never is." Miss Hudson glanced at the two models who were making a noble pretense of not listening. "Your call hasn't come through yet, girls. Sorry."

One of the models put down her hatbox and started across the room. "But, Miss Hudson, *you* said be here at two and here we . . ."

"Patience, Stella. Patience and poise. One moment of distemper can be as damaging to your skin as two éclairs."

"But . . ."

"Remember, you're a *graduate* now, Stella. You can't afford to behave like a freshman." To Blackshear, she added softly, "Come into my office. We can't talk here in front of these morons."

Miss Hudson's office was artfully devised for the acquisition of new students. On each side of the desk where she sat was a lamp with a pink shade that flattered her complexion and made her hair look almost real. The other side of the room, reserved for prospective clients, was illuminated from the ceiling with fluorescent rods that gave a dead white light, and two of the walls were decorated with full length mirrors.

"This is our consultation room," Miss Hudson said. "I never give the girls any personal criticism. I simply let them study themselves in the mirrors and *they* tell *me* what's wrong. That way, it makes for a more pleasant relationship and better business. Please sit down, Mr. Blackshear."

"Thanks. Why better business?"

"I often find that the girls are much harder on themselves than I would be. They expect more, you see?"

"Not quite."

"Well, sometimes a very pretty girl comes in and I can't find anything the matter with her at all. But *she* can, because she's probably comparing herself to Ava Gardner. So, she takes my course." Miss Hudson smiled dryly. "Results guaranteed, naturally. Cigarette?"

"No thanks."

"Well, now you know as much about my business as I do. Or," she added, with a shrewd glance, "as much as you care to, eh?"

"It's very interesting."

"Sometimes the whole thing makes me sick, but it's a living, and I've got three kids to support. The youngest is fourteen. When I get her through college or married off to some nice steady guy, I'm going to retire. I'm going to loll around the house all day in a bathrobe and bedroom slippers and I'm never going to open another jar of face cream as long as I live, and every morning when I get up I'm going to look in the mirror and chortle myself silly over a new wrinkle and another gray hair." She paused for breath. "Don't mind me. I'm only kidding. I think. Anyway, you didn't come here to listen to my blatting. What do you want to know about this Evelyn Merrick?"

"Everything you can tell me."

"It won't be much. I only saw her once and that was a week

ago. She read my ad in the *News* offering a free consultation for a limited time only, and in she came, sat in the same chair you're sitting in now. A scrawny brunette very poorly dressed and made up like a tart. Pretty impossible, from a professional point of view. She had one of those Italian boy haircuts gone to seed. They're supposed to look casual, you know, but actually they require a lot of expert care. And her clothes . . ." Miss Hudson stopped sharply. "I hope she's not a friend of yours?"

"I've never seen her."

"Why do you want to find her, then?"

"Let's stick with the long-lost heiress story," Blackshear said. "I'm beginning to like it."

"I always have."

"You gave her the free consultation?"

"I did the usual thing, tried to put her at ease, called her by her first name and so on. Then asked her to stand up and walk around and watch herself in the mirror and tell me what she thought needed correction. Ordinarily the girls are embarrassed at this point, and sort of giggly. She wasn't. She acted—well, odd."

"In what way?"

"She just stood there looking into the mirror, without making a sound. She seemed fascinated by herself. I was the one who was embarrassed. . . ."

"Walk around a bit, Evelyn."

The girl didn't move.

"Are you satisfied with your posture? Your skin? How about your make-up?"

She didn't speak.

"It is our policy to let our prospective students analyze themselves. We cannot correct faults that the student doesn't admit having. Now, then, would you say that you are perfectly happy about your figure? Take a good honest look, fore and aft."

Evelyn blinked and turned away. "The mirror is distorted and the lights are bad."

"They are not bad," Miss Hudson said, stung. "They are—realistic. We must face facts before altering them."

"If you say so, Miss Hudson."

"I say so, I— How old are you, Evelyn?"

"Twenty-one."

She must consider me a fool, Miss Hudson thought. "And you want to be a model?"

"Yes."

"What kind?"

"I want to pose for artists. Painters."

"There's not much demand for that kind of . . ."

"I have good breasts and I don't get cold easily."

"My dear young woman," Miss Hudson said with heavy irony. "And what else can you do besides not get cold easily?"

"You're making fun of me. You simply don't understand."

"Understand what?"

"I want to become immortal."

Miss Hudson lapsed into a stunned silence.

"I couldn't think of any other way to do it," the girl said. "And then I saw your ad, and the idea came to me suddenly, suppose someone paints me, a really great artist, then I will be immortal. So you see, it makes sense, if you think about it."

Miss Hudson didn't care to think about it. She had no time to worry about immortality; tomorrow was bad enough. "Why should a young woman like you be concerned about death?"

"I have an enemy."

"Who hasn't?"

"No, I mean a real enemy," Evelyn said politely. "I've seen her. In my crystal ball."

Miss Hudson looked at the cheap rayon dress stained at the armpits. "Is that how you make your living, telling fortunes?"

"No."

"What do you work at?"

"Just at the moment I'm unemployed. But I can get money if I need it. Enough to take your course."

"You understand we have a waiting list," *Miss Hudson lied.*

"No. No, I thought . . ."

"I shall be most happy to put your name on file." *And leave it there. I want no part of your immortality. Or your crystal ball.* "How do you spell your last name?"

"M-E-R-R-I-C-K."

"Evelyn Merrick. Age, 21. Address and phone number?"

"Well, I'm not sure. I'm moving out of my present place tomorrow, and I haven't decided just where I'll go."

No address, Miss Hudson wrote on her memo pad. Good. It will give me the perfect excuse for not calling her.

"I'll phone you when I get settled," Evelyn said. "Then you can tell me if you have an opening."

"It might be quite some time."

"I'll keep trying anyway."

"Yes," Miss Hudson said dryly, "I believe you will."

"I'll call you, say, a week from today?"

"Listen to me a minute, Evelyn. If I were you, I'd reconsider this modeling business, I'd . . ."

"You are not me. I will call you in a week. . . ."

"The week was up yesterday," Miss Hudson told Blackshear. "She didn't call. I don't know whether I'm glad or sorry."

"I think," Blackshear said, "that you ought to be glad."

"I guess I am. She's a real mimsy, that one. God knows my girls aren't mental giants, not one of them has an *I.Q.* that would make a decent basketball score. But they're not really *screwy*, like her. You know what I wonder, Mr. Blackshear?"

"No."

"I wonder what she saw in that mirror when she stood there half-hypnotized. What did she see?"

"Herself."

"No." Miss Hudson shook her head. "*I* saw herself. She saw somebody else. Gives you the creeps, doesn't it?"

"Not particularly."

"It does me. I felt sorry for her. I thought, suppose it was one of my kids—suppose something happens to me before they're safe and grown-up, and they're cast out into . . . Well, we won't go into that. Very depressing. Besides, I'm healthy and I drive carefully. Also, I have a sister who's perfectly capable of taking over the kids if anything happened to me. . . ." In sudden fury, Miss Hudson reached out and slapped the fragile mauve and white desk with the palm of her hand. "*Damn* that girl! You go along for years, doing your best, not worrying about dying, and then something like this happens. Some screwball comes along with a bunch of crazy ideas and you can't get them out of your head. It's not fair. Damn her hide. I'm sorry I tried to help her."

Blackshear raised his brows. "How exactly did you help her, Miss Hudson?"

"Maybe I didn't. But I tried. I could tell she was broke, so I gave her the name of a man. I thought he might give her an odd job to tide her over until she came to her senses if any."

"What kind of job?"

"Posing. He's an artist, a good one, too, which means he has to teach to make ends meet. He uses live models in his classes, not just pretty girls, but all kinds and shapes and sizes. I figured it wouldn't do any harm to send Evelyn over there. He might take a fancy to her earlobes or her big toe or something. Moore's a stickler for details."

"Moore?"

"Harley Moore. His studio is on Palm Avenue, just off Sunset near Santa Monica Boulevard."

"Has she actually done any posing, do you know?"

"She said she had. She said she'd done some work for Jack Terola. He's a photographer, ten or twelve blocks south of here. I don't know much about him except that he pays pretty well. He does photo illustrations for one of those confession magazines—you know, where the wife is standing horrified watching her husband kiss his secretary, or the young Sunday school teacher is being assaulted in the choir loft—that sort of thing. My youngest kid reads them all the time. It drives me crazy trying to stop her. Stuff like that gives kids the wrong idea about the world—they get to thinking all secretaries get bussed by the boss and all Sunday school teachers are assaulted in choir lofts. Which isn't true."

"I hope not."

"Well, there you are."

Blackshear wasn't exactly sure where he was. But he knew where he was going.

The means to charm were apparently more profitable than its ends: Miss Hudson could afford glass bricks and mahogany paneling; Terola's place was a long narrow stucco building between a one-way alley euphemistically named Jacaranda Lane and a rickety three-story frame house converted into apartments. Black stenciling on the frosted glass window read:

PHOTOGRAPHIC WORKSHOP

JACK TEROLA, PROPRIETOR

PIN-UP MODELS • LIFE GROUPS FOR AMATEURS
AND PROFESSIONALS • RENTAL STUDIOS FOR ART GROUPS

Come in Any Time

Blackshear went in. In spite of the rows of filing cabinets and the samples of Terola's work which lined the walls, the office still looked like what it had been originally, somebody's front parlor. Near one end of the room was a dirty red-brick fireplace which had a desolate and futile appearance, as if it had become, from long disuse, a mere hole in the wall which a careless workman had forgotten to plaster over. To the right of the fireplace was a curtained alcove. The curtains were not drawn and Blackshear could see part of the interior: a brown leather chair, the seat wrinkled with age, a day bed partly covered with an old-fashioned afghan, and above it, the stenciled front window. The alcove reminded Blackshear of his childhood in the Middle West—all the best people had had a "sun porch," which was indescribably hot in the summer and equally cold in the winter and no good for anything at all except social prestige.

Terola's sun porch seemed to be not a mark of prestige but a sign of necessity. The day bed was obviously used for sleeping; a dirty sheet dribbled out from under the afghan and the pillow was stained with hair oil.

There was no one in sight, but from behind the closed door at the other end of the room came sounds of activity, the scraping of equipment being moved across a wooden floor, the rise and fall of voices. Blackshear couldn't distinguish the words but the tones were plain enough. Somebody was giving orders and somebody else wasn't taking them.

He was on the point of knocking on the closed door when he noticed the printed sign propped against the typewriter of Terola's desk: FOR ATTENTION, PLEASE RING.

He rang, and waited, and then rang again, and finally the door opened and a young girl came out, wearing a printed-silk bathrobe. She wore no make-up and her face glistened with grease and moisture. Water dripped from the ends of her short black hair and slid down her neck, and the damp silk of the bathrobe clung to her skin.

She seemed unconcerned. "You want something?"

"I'd like to speak to Mr. Terola."

"He's busy right now. Sit down."

"Thank you."

"I'm supposed to be drowning but Jack can't get the water right. It's supposed to be Lake Michigan, see."

Blackshear nodded politely to indicate that he saw.

"Jack's a sucker for drowning scenes," the girl added. "Me, I like to stay dry. The way I look at it is, I could just as easy been stabbed. All this fuss trying to make like Lake Michigan. Don't you want to sit down?"

"I'm perfectly comfortable."

"Well, all right. You here on business?"

"In a way. My name is Paul Blackshear."

"Pleased to meet you. I'm Nola Rath. Well, I better get back now. You want a magazine to read?"

"No, thanks."

"You may have quite a wait. If Jack gets this shot right he'll be out here in a jiffy, but if he don't, he won't."

"I'll wait."

"I could just as easy been stabbed," the girl said. "Well, I'll tell Jack you're here."

She left behind a trail of water drops and the smell of wet hair.

Nola Rath. Blackshear repeated the name to himself, wondering how old the girl was. Perhaps twenty-five, only a few years younger than Helen Clarvoe, yet a whole generation seemed to separate the two. Miss Clarvoe's age had very little to do with chronology. She was a middle-aged woman because she had had nothing to keep her young. She was the chosen victim, not only of Evelyn Merrick, but of life itself.

The thought depressed Blackshear. He wished he could forget her but she nagged at his mind like a broken promise.

He looked at his watch. Three-ten. A wind had come up. The curtains of Terola's alcove were blowing in and out and the cobwebs in the fireplace were stirring, and somewhere in the chimney there was a fidgeting of mice.

"You wanted to see me?"

Blackshear turned, surprised that he had not heard the opening of the door or the sound of footsteps.

"Mr. Terola?"

"That's right."

"My name's Blackshear."

They shook hands. Terola was in his early forties, a very thin, tall man with an habitual stoop as if he were trying to scale himself down to size. He had black bushy brows that quivered with impatience when he talked, as if they were silently denying the words that came out of the soft feminine mouth. Two thin parallel strands of iron-gray hair crossed the top of his bald pate like railroad ties.

"Just a minute." Terola walked over to the alcove and drew the curtains irritably. "Things are in a mess around here. My secretary's home with the mumps. Mumps, yet, at her age. I thought they were for kids. Well, what can I do for you, Blackshear?"

"I understand you employ, or have employed, a young woman called Evelyn Merrick."

"How come you understand that?"

"Someone told me."

"Such as who?"

"Miss Merrick used your name as a reference when she went to apply for training as a model. She claimed she had done some work for you."

"What kind of work?"

"Whatever kind you had to offer," Blackshear said, attempting to conceal his impatience. "You do quite a bit of—shall we call it art work?"

"We shall and it is."

"Have it your way. Do you remember Miss Merrick?"

"Maybe I do, maybe I don't. I'm not answering a lot of questions unless there's a good reason. You got a good reason, Mr. Blacksheep?"

"Blackshear."

"It's not that I don't want to co-operate, only I kind of like to find out first who I'm co-operating with, in what and for why. What's your business, mister?"

"I'm an investment counselor."

"So?"

"Let's say that there's an estate to settle and Evelyn Merrick may get a piece of it."

Terola spoke tightly, barely moving his mouth, as if he was afraid there might be lip-readers around peering in through the curtains of the alcove or the chinks in the chimney: "The kind of piece that babe gets won't come out of any estate, mister."

"She came here, then?"

"She came. Gave me a hard-luck story about a dying mother, so I let her have a couple of hours' work. I'm a sucker for dying mothers, just so's they don't change their minds and stay alive, like mine did."

"Did the Merrick girl give you any trouble?"

"I don't take trouble from chicks like that. I bounce them out on their ear."

"Did you bounce her?"

"She got nosey. I had to."

"When was this?"

"Couple of weeks ago, maybe less. When they get nosey, they get bounced. Not," he added with a wink, "that I have anything to hide. I just don't like snoopers. They get in my hair, what's left of it."

"What else did she do besides snoop?"

"Oh, she had some screwy idea about me making her immortal. At first I figured she was kidding and trying for a laugh. I have a pretty good sense of humor so I laughed, see? She got sore as hell. If you want the truth, I don't think she's playing with all her marbles."

"Exactly what kind of work did you give Evelyn Merrick?"

"She posed."

"For you personally? Or for one of your 'art' groups?"

"What difference does it make?"

"It might make a lot of difference to me."

"How so?"

"If she posed for you, for a magazine story layout, you might give me a print of the picture. If she worked with your art group, I don't think you will."

Terola ground out the stub of his cigarette in an ashtray. "I never give away prints."

"What do you do, peddle them?"

"Peddle is a very nasty word. You'd better leave before I push it back down your throat."

"I didn't realize what a sensitive fellow you were, Terola."

"I don't want any trouble with your kind. Blow."

"Thank you for the information."

Terola opened the door. "Go to hell."

Blackshear walked down the alley and got into his car. It was the first time in thirty years that he'd been close to having a fight and the experience aroused old memories and old fears and a certain primeval excitement. His hand on the ignition key was unsteady and anger pressed on his eyeballs like iron thumbs. He wanted to go back and challenge Terola, fight him to the finish, kill him, if he had to.

But as he drove in the direction of Harley Moore's studio, the brisk sea wind cooled his passions and neutralized the acid in his mind: I'm not as civilized as I like to think. There was no need to antagonize him. I handled everything wrong. Maybe I can do better with Moore.

Chapter 4

BERTHA MOORE had waited more than fifteen years for a child, and when the child, a girl, was born, Bertha could not quite believe in her good fortune. She had constantly to reassure herself. At all hours of the day and night she tiptoed into the nursery to see if the baby was still there, still alive. She could not settle down to read or sew even for a minute; she seemed to be half-suspended in air like a gas-filled balloon held captive only by a length of string. At the other end of this string, fixed and stationary, was her husband, Harley.

She did not make the mistake of ignoring Harley after the birth of the baby. She was, in fact, extremely kind to him, but it was a planned and unemotional kindness; at the back of her mind there was always the thought that she must take deliberate pains to keep Harley contented because the baby would be healthier and better adjusted if it had a happy home and a good father.

What spare time Bertha had was spent in conversations with friends and relatives about the perfections of her child, or in frantic calls to the pediatrician when it regurgitated its food or to Harley when it cried without apparent reason. During nearly twenty years of marriage Bertha had learned not to disturb Harley at his studio. She unlearned this in a single day, easily, and without the slightest compunction. These calls were "for the baby's sake," and as such were beyond reproach and above criticism. The baby flourished, unaware of its demands on its parents. Bertha called her Angie, which was short for Angel and had no connection with her registered name, Stephanie Caroline Moore.

At 4 o'clock Angie was in no mood for her bottle. Bertha was waltzing her back and forth across the living room when the telephone rang. She shifted the baby gently from her left arm to her right and picked up the receiver.

"Hello?"

"Hello. Is that Mrs. Moore?"

"Yes."

"You don't know me, but I'm a friend of your husband's."

"Really?" Bertha said, in a lively manner, though she was hardly paying any attention. The baby's hair felt so soft against her neck and its warm skin smelled of flowers and sunshine.

"I'm Evelyn Merrick. Perhaps your husband has mentioned me?"

"He may have." With considerable effort the baby turned her head to listen to the conversation, and she made such a droll face that Bertha laughed out loud.

"Are you alone, Mrs. Moore?"

"I'm *never* alone. We have a new baby, you know."

There was a pause. "Of course I knew."

"She was just four months old yesterday."

"They're so sweet at that age."

"Aren't they, though. But Angie's more like six months than four, even the doctor says so." This was practically true. The doctor had, after considerable prompting from Bertha, agreed that Angie was "quite advanced," and was "developing nicely."

"That's such a cute name, Angie."

"It's only a nickname, really." What a nice voice the woman had, Bertha thought, and how interested she was in the baby. "Speaking of names, I'm afraid I didn't catch yours."

"Evelyn Merrick. Miss Merrick."

"It does sound familiar. I'm almost sure Harley's mentioned you. Most of the time I'm so busy with the baby I don't hear what people are saying. . . . Stop that, Angie. No, no, mustn't touch. . . . She's trying to pull out the telephone cord."

"She sounds just adorable."

"Oh, she is." Bertha had admired other women's babies for so many years—telling the truth, if the baby was cute, fibbing if it wasn't—that she felt it only just that other women now had to admire hers. The nice thing was that none of them had to fib about Angie. She was perfect. There was no compliment about her so bulky, no piece of flattery so huge, that Bertha couldn't swallow with the greatest of ease and digest without the faintest rumble.

"Does the baby look like you or like Harley?"

"Oh, like me, I'm afraid," Bertha said with a proud little laugh. "Everyone thinks so."

"I'd love to see her. I'm quite—mad about babies."

"Why don't you come over?"

"When?"

"Well, this afternoon, if you like. Angie's restless, she won't go to sleep for hours." It would be fun to show the baby off to one of Harley's friends, for a change. Harley was very modest about Angie and hardly ever brought anyone to see her. "Harley won't be home until six. We can have some tea and a chat, and I'll show you Angie's baby book. Are you an artist, by any chance, Miss Merrick?"

"In a way."

"I just wondered. Harley says the baby's too young to be painted, but I—well, never mind. You will see for yourself. You know our address?"

"Yes. It will be a pleasure meeting you, Mrs. Moore."

They said good-bye and Bertha hung up, feeling a pleasant glow of anticipation and maternal pride.

She was not, by nature or experience, a suspicious woman— Harley had dozens of friends of both sexes—and it didn't strike her as odd that Evelyn Merrick hadn't explained the purpose of her call.

"A nice lady," she told Angie, "is coming to admire you and I want you to be utterly captivating."

Angie chewed her fingers.

When the baby's diaper and dress had been changed and her half-inch of hair carefully brushed, Bertha went back to the phone to call Harley.

Harley himself answered, sounding sharp and distrustful the way he always did over the telephone, as if he expected to be bored or bamboozled.

"Har? It's just me."

"Oh. Anything wrong with the baby?"

"Not a thing. She's bright as a dollar."

"Look, Bertha, I'm awfully tied up right now. There's a man here who . . ."

"Well, I won't keep you, dear. I just wanted to tell you not to hurry home, I'm having company for tea. A Miss Merrick is coming over to see the baby."

"Who?"

"A friend of yours. Evelyn Merrick."

"She's coming there?"

"Why, yes. What's the matter, Har? You sound so . . ."

"When is she coming?"

"Well, I don't know. It was kind of indefinite."

"Listen to me carefully, Bertha. Lock the doors and stay in the house until I get home."

"I don't under—"

"Do as I say. We'll be there in fifteen minutes."

"What do you mean, we?"

"There's a man in my studio right now looking for that woman. He says she's crazy."

"But she sounded so sweet—and she was so interested in Angie and wanted to see . . ."

But Harley had hung up.

She stood, wide-eyed and pale, hugging the baby to her breasts. Angie, sensing the sudden tension, and resenting the too tight and desperate embrace, began to cry.

"Be a good girl now, Angie," Bertha said, sounding very calm. "There is nothing the matter, nothing to be afraid of."

But the calm voice did not reassure the baby; she heard the quickened heartbeat, she felt her mother's trembling muscles, and she smelled fear.

"We will simply lock the doors and wait for daddy. There's nothing to cry about. My goodness, what will the neighbors think, such a little girl making so much noise. . . ."

Carrying the howling child, Bertha locked the three outside doors and pulled the heavy drapes across the bay window in the living room. Then she sat down in the rocking chair that Harley had bought her because she'd said no one could raise a baby without one. The darkened room and the gentle rocking motion quieted the child.

"That's a sweet girl. You settle down now and go to sleep. My goodness, we mustn't get excited about a little thing like a crazy . . ."

The door chimes pealed.

Without even glancing toward the door, Bertha carried the sleeping child to the nursery and laid her in the crib and covered her with a blanket. Then she walked slowly back to the front hall as the chimes pealed again.

She stood, waiting and listening, her face like stone. There were no sounds of cars passing or children playing or women hurrying home from the super market. It was as if everyone, forewarned of danger, had moved to another part of town.

"Mrs. Moore?" The voice came, soft but persistent, through the crack of the oak door. "Let me in."

Bertha pressed the back of her hand tight against her mouth as if afraid words might come out without her volition.

"I hurried right over. I'm dying to see the baby. Let me in. . . . I know you're there, Mrs. Moore. What's the matter? Are you afraid of me? I wouldn't harm anyone. I only want to see Harley's baby. . . . Harley and I may have a baby, too."

The words seeped through the crack of the door like drops of poison that could kill on contact.

"Does that shock you, Mrs. Moore? You don't know much of what goes on in that studio of his, do you? What do you think happens after I pose naked?"

Make her stop, Bertha prayed silently. She's lying. She's crazy. Harley would never—he's not like that—he told me they were all like pieces of wood to him. . . .

"Oh, don't think I'm the only one. I'm just the latest. After the posing it comes so natural, so inevitable. Have you been fooled all these years? Haven't you wondered, in the back of your mind? Aren't you wondering now? I should lend you my crystal ball. Oh, the things you'd see!"

And she began to describe them, slowly and carefully, as if she were instructing a child, and Bertha listened like a child, not understanding some of the ugly words she used but hypnotized by their implications of evil. She couldn't move, couldn't get out of range of the poison. Drop by drop it burned into her heart and etched nightmares on her mind.

Then, quite suddenly, from the corner, came the quick, tinkling song of a Good Humor man. "My Bonnie lies over the ocean. . . . Oh, bring back my Bonnie to me." The song ended and began again, but in the interval Bertha heard the tap of heels on concrete. Moving lifelessly, like a dummy on hinges, she walked into the living room and parted the heavy drapes on the bay window.

A woman was running down the street, her dark hair lashing furiously in the wind, her coat flapping around her skinny legs. She turned the corner, still running, heading south.

Bertha went back to the nursery. Angie was sleeping on her side with her thumb in her mouth.

Bertha stood by the crib and looked down at the baby, numbly, wondering what kind of man its father was.

"Bertha. Are you all right, dear?"

"Of course."

"We got here as soon as we could. This is Mr. Blackshear. My wife, Bertha."

"How do you do." She shook hands with Blackshear. "Would you like a drink?"

"Thanks. I would," Blackshear said.

"I will, too. I was going to have tea, but . . ." I was going to have company for tea. A nice lady was coming to admire the baby. I dressed Angie up and brushed her hair. I was feeling happy, I remember. That was a long time ago.

"Bertha, you're sure you're feeling all right?"

"Yes," she said politely. How odd Harley looked, with his crew cut and his sunburn and his horn-rimmed glasses. Not like a painter at all. Perhaps that was because he didn't do much painting any more—other things went on in his studio that were more important. . . .

Harley mixed her a bourbon highball. It tasted weak and sour, and after the first sip she just held the glass to her lips and looked over the rim of it at Blackshear. Quiet, dignified, respectable. But you couldn't tell. If you couldn't tell about Harley, you couldn't tell about anyone in the whole world.

Her hand shook, and some of the highball spilled down the front of her dress. She knew both the men had seen the little accident. They were staring at her in a puzzled way, as if they realized that something was wrong and were too diffident or polite to ask what.

"She was here," Bertha said. "She asked me to let her in, and when I wouldn't, she talked at me through the crack of the door. I didn't answer, or make any noise, but somehow she knew I was there, listening." She glanced quickly at Harley and away again. "I can't tell you what she said, in front of a stranger."

"Why not?"

"It was about you, your relations with her."

"I had no relations with her except one day last week when she came to the studio for a job and I turned her down."

"She said she was one of your—models."

"Go on," Harley said grimly. "What else?"

"She said you and she—she used terrible words—I couldn't repeat them to anyone. . . ."

The blood had drained from Harley's sunburned face, leaving it gray-tan and lifeless, like sandstone. "She implied that I had sexual relations with her?"

"*Implied.*" Bertha began to laugh. "*Implied.* That's funny, it really is. If you could have heard her . . ."

"You listened to her, Bertha?"

"Yes."

"Why?"

"I don't know. I didn't want to, I hated it, but I listened."

"Did you believe what she said?"

"No."

He accepted the faint and unconvincing denial without pressing her further. He even tried to give her a reassuring smile, but he looked sick and exhausted as he turned to Blackshear. "Is this the kind of mischief the Merrick woman goes in for?"

"It's a little more than mischief, I'm afraid."

"Well, she may be insane, but she seems to know a lot about human frailties."

"She does." Blackshear thought of the things Evelyn Merrick had said to Miss Clarvoe. She had used Miss Clarvoe's own special set of fears as she had used Mrs. Moore's, and to a lesser extent, Lydia Hudson's, not creating new fears but working on ones that were already there. In each case she had taken a different approach, but the results were the same, uncertainty, anxiety, dread. Miss Hudson had a strong enough personality to settle her own problems; Helen Clarvoe's, perhaps, would never be settled; but Mrs. Moore had a need for, and the ability to accept, help.

Blackshear said, "Evelyn Merrick gets her satisfactions out of other people's pain, Mrs. Moore. Today it was yours. But there have been others."

"I didn't—know that."

"It's true. There is absolutely no limit to what she would say to cause trouble, and perhaps in your case she had an extra motive. Mr. Moore tells me that he was busy at the time she came to the studio and he gave her a quick brush-off."

Bertha smiled, very faintly. "Harley's quite good at that."

"The Merrick woman may have wanted to pay him back. Little episodes like that, which the ordinary person would pass off easily and forget about, often become terribly exaggerated in the mind of an unbalanced woman."

"Of course, I didn't believe her for a minute," Bertha said, in a very firm, reasonable voice. "After all, Harley and I have been happily married for nearly twenty years. . . . I suppose Harley's told you about our little girl?"

"He did."

"Would you like to see her?"

"I'd like it very much."

"Let me get her," Harley said, but Bertha had already risen.

"I'll get her," she said, smiling. "I have something to tell her."

Angie was still asleep. She woke up, at Bertha's touch, and made a squeak of protest that turned into a yawn.

Bertha spoke softly into her tiny ear. "Your father is a good man. We mustn't either of us forget that. He is a *good man*."

She carried the child into the living room, walking fast, as if she could get away from the whispers that echoed against the walls of her memory: *You don't know much of what goes on in that studio. . . . Have you been fooled all these years? . . . Oh, the things you'd see in my crystal ball. . . .*

Bertha listened.

Chapter 5

"HELEN? Is that you, Helen dear?"

"Yes."

"This is mother."

"Yes."

"I must say you don't seem very happy to hear from me."

"I'm trying." Helen thought, she sounds the same as ever, like a whining child.

"Please speak *up*, dear. If there's one thing I can't bear it's telephone mumblers. Helen? Are you there?"

"I'm here."

"That's better. Well, the reason I wanted to speak to you, I just had a very mysterious phone call from Mr. Blackshear. You remember, that broker friend of your father's whose wife died of cancer?"

"I remember."

"Well, suddenly out of a blue sky he called and asked if he could come and see me tonight. You don't suppose it has anything to do with *money*?"

"In what way?"

"Perhaps he's discovered some misplaced stocks or bonds that belonged to your father."

"I hardly think so."

"But it's possible, isn't it?"

"Yes, I suppose."

"Wouldn't it be a lovely surprise, say just a few shares of AT&T stuck away in a drawer and forgotten. Wouldn't that be *fun*?"

"Yes." She didn't bother pointing out that her father had never bought any shares of AT&T, and if he had, they wouldn't be stuck in a drawer and forgotten. Let Verna find it out for herself; she had a whole closetful of punctured dreams, but there was always room for one more.

The expectation of money, however remote, put a bright and girlish lilt into Verna's voice. "I haven't seen you for ages, Helen."

"I realize that."

"How have you been?"

"Fine, thank you."

"Are you eating properly?"

It was an impossible question to answer, since Verna's ideas of proper eating varied week by week, depending on which new diet attracted her attention. She dieted, variously, to grow slim, to gain weight, to correct low blood sugar, to improve her complexion, to prevent allergies, and to increase the flow of liver bile. The purpose of the diet didn't matter. The practice was what counted. It gave her something to talk about, it made her more interesting and unusual. While her liver bile continued at the same old rate, Verna flitted from one diet to another, making other women who could and did eat anything look like clods.

"*Do* speak *up*, Helen."

"I didn't say anything."

"Oh. Well. The fact is, Dougie and I are having lunch to-morrow at the Vine Street Derby. It's so close to where you are that I thought you might like to join us. Would you?"

"I'm afraid not. Thanks just the same."

"But it's quite a special occasion. In the first place, it's Dougie's birthday, he'll be twenty-six. *Tempus fugit*, doesn't it? And in the second place, someone else will be there whom I'd like you to meet, Dougie's art teacher, a Mr. Terola. I'm told he's a terribly fascinating man."

"I didn't know that Douglas was interested in painting."

"Oh, not painting. Photography. Dougie says there's a big future in photography, and Mr. Terola knows practically every-thing there is to know about it."

"Indeed."

"I do wish you'd make an effort to come, dear. We'll be at the Derby at 1 o'clock sharp."

"I'll try to make it." She knew why her mother was anxious for her to be there. She expected her to bring a check for Douglas as a birthday present.

"Are you still there, Helen?"

"Yes."

"These long silences make me nervous, they really do. I never know what you're *thinking*."

Helen smiled grimly into the telephone. "You might ask me some time."

"I'm afraid you'd answer," Verna said with a sharp little laugh. "It's all set, then? We'll see you tomorrow at one?"

"I won't promise."

"My treat, of course. And listen, Helen dear. *Do* wear a little lipstick, won't you? And don't forget it's Dougie's birthday. I'm sure he'd appreciate some little remembrance."

"I'm sure he would."

"Until tomorrow, then."

"Good-bye."

Helen set down the phone. It was the first time in months that she had talked to her mother, but nothing had changed. Animosity still hung between them like a two-edged sword; neither of them could use it without first getting hurt herself.

"A hundred dollars," Verna said aloud. "Or two, if we're lucky. She wouldn't miss it. And if Mr. Blackshear has found those shares of AT&T, we'll be able to keep going for a little while anyway."

Verna was down to a single car, a second mortgage and a part-time servant. She had had the telephone company take out the extra phones in her bedroom and in the patio, and she'd covered the bare spot in the dining-room carpet with a cotton mat, and hung a calendar over the cracking plaster of the kitchen wall. In brief, she had done everything possible to cut expenses and keep the household running. But the household didn't run, it shuffled along like a white elephant, and each week it got farther and farther behind.

There were occasions, usually at the beginning of the month when the bills poured in, when Verna thought it would be a good thing if Douglas went out and got a job. But most of the time she was content to have him around the house. He was good company, in his quiet way, and he did a great deal of the gardening and the heavier work, when he wasn't studying. In Verna's opinion, Douglas was a born student. He hadn't finished college because of some highly exaggerated incident in the locker room of the gym, but he had continued studying on his own and had already covered ceramics, modern poetry, the

French impressionists, the growing of avocados, and the clarinet. The clarinet hurt his lip, the avocado seedlings in the back yard had withered and no one seemed interested in exhibiting his ceramics or listening to him read Dylan Thomas aloud.

Through all this Douglas remained good-natured. He didn't openly blame the public for its stupidity or the nurseryman for selling him defective avocados, he simply let it be understood that he had done his best and no one could expect more.

No one did, except Verna, and the day he'd sold his clarinet, even though she hated the shriek of it, she went up to her bedroom and wept. The sale of the clarinet wasn't like the gradual loss of interest in ceramics and poetry and all the other things. There was an absolute finality about it that hit her like a fist in the stomach. Her pain was so actual and intense that Douglas sent for the doctor. When the doctor came he seemed just as interested in Douglas as he was in Verna herself. "That boy of yours looks as if he needs a good tonic," the doctor had said.

The "boy" would be twenty-six tomorrow.

"Two hundred dollars at least," Verna said. "After all, it's his birthday and she's his sister."

She covered the canary cage for the night, checked the kitchen to see if the maid had tidied it properly before she left, and went into the den where Douglas was lying on the couch, reading. He was wearing beaded white moccasins and a terry-cloth bathrobe with the sleeves partly rolled up revealing wrists that were so slim and supple they seemed boneless. His coloring was like Helen's, dark hair and the kind of chameleon gray eyes that changed color with their surroundings. His ears were like a woman's, very close-set. In the right ear lobe he wore a circle of fine gold wire. This tiny earring was one of the things he and Verna frequently quarreled about, but Douglas would not remove it.

When he heard his mother enter the room, Douglas put down his book and got up from the couch. Verna thought, with satisfaction, *at least I've brought him up to show some respect for women*.

She said, "Go and put some clothes on, dear."

"Why?"

"I'm having company."

"Well, *I'm* not."

"Please don't argue with me, dear. I have one of my headaches coming on." Verna had a whole battalion of headaches at her disposal. They came on like a swarm of native troops; when one of them was done to death, another was always ready to rush forward and take its place. "Mr. Blackshear is coming to see us. It may be about money."

She explained about the shares of AT&T that might have got stuck in a drawer, while Douglas listened with amiable skepticism, tugging gently at his golden earring.

The gesture annoyed her. "And for heaven's sake take that thing off."

"Why?"

"I've told you before, it makes you look foolish."

"I don't agree. Different, perhaps, but not foolish."

"Why should you *want* to look different from other men?"

"Because I am, sweetheart, I am."

He reached out and touched her cheek lightly.

She drew away. "Well, it seems to me . ."

"To you, everything seems. To me, everything is."

"I don't understand you when you talk like that. And I won't have another argument about that earring. Now take it off!"

"All right. You don't have to scream." There was a thin line of white around Douglas' mouth and the veins in his temples bulged with suppressed anger. He unfastened the earring and flung it across the room. It ricocheted off the wall onto the blonde plastic top of the spinet piano, then it rolled forward and disappeared between two of the bass keys.

Verna let out a cry of dismay. "Now look what you've done!"

"I'm sick of being ordered around."

"You've wrecked my piano. Another repair bill to pay . ."

"It isn't wrecked."

"It is so." She ran over to the piano, almost in tears, and played a scale with her left hand. The C and D keys were not stuck but they made a little plinking sound. "You've ruined my piano."

"Nonsense. I can fix it easily."

"I don't want you to touch it. It's a job for an expert." She rose from the piano bench, her lips tight as if they'd been set in cement.

Watching her, Douglas thought, there are some women who expand with the years, and some who shrink.

Verna had shrunk. Each week she seemed to grow smaller, and when Douglas called her old girl, it wasn't a term of endearment, it was what he really thought of her. Verna was an old girl.

"I'm sorry, old girl."

"Are you?"

"You know I am."

"Will you go up and change your clothes, then?"

"All right." He shrugged as if he'd known from the very beginning that she would get her own way and it no longer mattered because he had his own methods of making her regret her authority.

"And don't forget to put on a tie."

"Why?"

"Other men wear ties."

"Not all of them."

"I don't see why you're in such a difficult mood tonight."

"I think it's the other way around, old girl. Take a pill or something."

As he passed the piano on his way out of the room, he ran his forefinger lightly along the keys, smiling to himself.

"Douglas."

He paused in the doorway, holding his bathrobe tight around his waist. "Well?"

"I met Evie and her mother downtown this afternoon."

"So?"

"Evie asked after you. She was really very pleasant considering what happened, the annulment and everything."

"I will be equally pleasant to her, if and when."

"She's such a lovely girl. Everyone said you made a very attractive couple."

"Let's not dredge that up."

"I don't suppose there's any chance you might want to see her again? She didn't ask me that, of course, but I could sense she was still interested."

"You need a new crystal ball, old girl."

When he had gone, she began to circle the room, turning on the lamps and straightening the odd-shaped ceramic pieces on the mantel which had been Douglas' passing contribution to the art. Verna didn't understand what these pieces represented any more than she understood Douglas' poetry or his music. It was as if he moved through life in a speeding automobile, now and then tossing out of the windows blobs of clay and notes in music and half-lines of poetry that he had whipped up while stopping for the red lights. Nothing was ever finished before the lights changed, and what was tossed out of the windows was always distorted by the speed of the car and the rush of the wind.

Verna Clarvoe greeted Blackshear with an effusiveness he didn't expect, desire or understand. She had always in the past made it obvious that she considered him a dull man, yet here she was, coming out to the car to meet him, offering him both her hands and telling him how simply marvelous it was to see him again and how well he looked, not a day, not a minute, older.

"You haven't changed a bit. Confess now, you can't say the same about me!"

"I assure you I can."

She blushed with pleasure, misinterpreting his words as a compliment. "What a charming fibber you are, Mr. Blackshear. But then, you always were. Come, let's talk in the den. Since Harrison died we practically never use the drawing room. It's so big Dougie and I just rattle around in it. Helen no longer lives at home."

"Yes, I know that. In fact, that's one of the reasons I'm here."

"You've come about *Helen*?"

"Yes."

"Well," she said with a sharp little laugh. "Well. This is a surprise. I thought perhaps you were coming to see me about money."

"I'm sorry if I gave you that impression."

"It wasn't an impression, Mr. Blackshear. It was a *hope*. Very silly of me." She turned her face away. "Well, come along, we'll have a drink."

He followed her down the dimly lit hall to the den. A fire was spluttering in the raised fieldstone firepit and the room was like a kiln. In spite of the heat Verna Clarvoe looked pale and cold, a starved sparrow preserved in ice.

"Please sit down, Mr. Blackshear."

"Thank you."

She mixed two highballs, talking nervously as she worked. "Harrison always did this when he was alive. It's funny what odd times you miss people, isn't it? But you know all about that. . . . That's some of Dougie's work on the mantel. It's considered very unusual. Do you know anything about art?"

"Nothing at all," Blackshear said cheerfully.

"That's too bad. I was going to ask your opinion. Oh well, it doesn't matter now, Dougie's taken up something new. Photography. He goes into Hollywood to classes every day. Photography isn't just taking pictures, you know."

This was news to Blackshear but he said, "Tell me more."

"Well, you have to study composition and lighting and filters and a lot of things like that. Dougie's crazy about it. He's a born student."

She crossed the room, carrying the drinks, and sat down beside Blackshear on the cocoa rattan couch.

"What shall we drink to, Mr. Blackshear?"

"It doesn't matter."

"All right. We'll drink to all the millions of things in this world that don't matter. To them!"

Blackshear sipped his drink uneasily, realizing that he had never actually known Verna Clarvoe. In the past he had seen her in character, playing the role she thought was expected of her, the pretty and frivolous wife of a man who could afford her. She was still onstage, but she'd forgotten her lines, and the props and backdrop had been removed and the audience had long since departed.

She said abruptly, "Don't stare at me."

"Was I? Sorry."

"I know I've changed. It's been a terrible year. If Harrison only knew . . . Do you believe that people who have passed on can look down from heaven and see what's happening on earth?"

"That wouldn't be my idea of heaven," Blackshear said dryly.

"Nor mine. But in a way I'd like Harrison to *know.* I mean, he's out of it, he's fine, he has no problems. *I'm* the one that's left. I'm—what's that legal term? Relict? That's what I am. A relict." She gulped the rest of her drink, making little sucking noises like a thirsty child. "This must be very boring for you."

"Not at all."

"Oh, you're always so *polite*. Don't you ever get sick of being polite?"

"I do, indeed."

"Why don't you get *im*polite then? Go on. I dare you. Get *im*polite, why don't you?"

"Very well," Blackshear said calmly. "You can't hold your liquor, Mrs. Clarvoe. Lay off, will you please?"

"Please. *Please*, yet. You just can't help yourself, you're a gentleman. A born gentleman. Dougie's a born student. He's learning photography. Did I tell you that?"

"Tell me again, if you like."

"Mr. Terola is his teacher. He's a very interesting man. Not a born gentleman, like you, but very interesting. You can't be both. Tragic, isn't it. Why don't you be impolite again? Go on. I can't hold my liquor. What else?"

"I came here to talk about Helen, Mrs. Clarvoe, not about you."

Blotches of color appeared on her cheekbones. "That's impolite enough. All right. Go ahead. Talk about Helen."

"As you may know, for the past year I've been handling her investments."

"I didn't know. Helen doesn't confide in me, least of all about money."

"Yesterday she asked me to serve in another capacity, as an investigator. A woman in town has been making threatening and obscene telephone calls; Helen is one of her victims. From what I've learned about this woman today, I believe she's dangerous."

"What do you expect me to do about it? Helen's old enough to take care of herself. Besides, what are the police for?"

"I've been to the police. The sergeant I talked to told me they get a dozen similar complaints every day in his precinct alone."

The effects of the drink were beginning to wear off. Verna's hands moved nervously in her lap and a little tic tugged at her left eyelid. "Well, I don't see how *I* can help."

"It might be a good idea if you invited her to come and stay here with you for a while."

"Here? In my house?"

"I'm aware that you're not on very friendly terms but . . ."

"There are no buts, Mr. Blackshear. None. When Helen left this house I asked her never to come back. She said unforgivable things, about Dougie, about me. Unforgivable. She must be out of her mind to think she can come back here."

"She doesn't know anything about the idea; it was entirely my own."

"I ought to have guessed that. Helen wouldn't ask a favor of me if she were dying."

"It isn't easy for some people to ask favors. Helen is shy and insecure and frightened."

"Frightened? With all that money?" She laughed. "If I had all that money I wouldn't be scared of the devil himself."

"Don't bet on that."

With a defiant toss of her head, she crossed the room and began mixing herself another drink. As was the case with the first drink, she began reacting before she'd even uncorked the bottle.

"Mrs. Clarvoe, do you think it's wise to . . ."

"No, it's not wise. I'm a very stupid and ignorant woman. So I'm told."

"Who told you?"

"Oh, a lot of people, Harrison, Dougie, Helen, lots of people. It's a funny thing being told you're stupid and never being told how to get unstupid." She raised her glass. "Here's to all us birdbrains."

"Mrs. Clarvoe, do you do this every night?"

"Do what?"

"Drink like this."

"I haven't had a drink for months. As you said, I can't take the stuff. And I don't usually try. But tonight's different. Tonight's an end of something."

She held the glass in both hands, rotating it as she talked so that the clink of ice cubes punctuated her words.

"You think of an end as being definite, being caused by something important or calamitous. It's not like that at all. For me tonight is final, but nothing special happened, just a lot of little things. Some bills came in, the maid was rude about waiting for her salary, I met Evie on the street, the girl Dougie married, Dougie put on his earring and I made him take it off and he threw it and . . . You see? Just little things." She stared into the glass, watching the bubbles rise to the surface and burst. "Evie looked so sweet and pretty. I thought what lovely children they might have had. My grandchildren. I don't mind getting old but I'd like to have something to show for it, like grandchildren. Mr. Blackshear . . ."

"Yes?"

"Do you think there's something the matter with Douglas?"

A trickle of sweat oozed down the side of Blackshear's face, leaving a bright moist trail like a slug. "I'm afraid I can't answer that."

"No. No, of course not," she said quietly. "I shouldn't have asked. You don't know him, really. He's a—very sweet boy. He has many fine qualities."

"I'm sure he has."

"And he's extremely talented, everyone says that. Harrison was so strict with him, I tried to make it up to Dougie on the side, I encouraged him to express himself." She put the half-empty glass on the mantel and leaned closer to the fire, her bony little hands stretched out until they were almost touching the flames. "Harrison was a very cruel man sometimes. Does that surprise you?"

"Not much. Most of us are cruel on occasion."

"Not the way Harrison was. He used to . . . But it doesn't matter now. I can tell I'm depressing you." She turned from the fire, making an obvious effort to control her emotions. "You've listened to my troubles, now you may tell me yours, if you like."

"They aren't very interesting."

"All troubles are interesting. Perhaps that's why we have them, to keep ourselves from being bored to death. Go on, tell me yours."

"Sorry, there isn't time, Mrs. Clarvoe."

"Don't leave yet. You haven't seen Dougie. He's upstairs getting dressed. Tomorrow's his birthday. We're having a little party at the Brown Derby."

While the maid waits for her salary, Blackshear thought grimly. "Wish Douglas a happy birthday for me."

"I will."

"There's just one more thing, Mrs. Clarvoe. Do you know a young woman named Evelyn Merrick?"

She looked surprised. "Well, of course."

"Of course?"

"She's Dougie's wife. She was, I mean. The marriage was annulled and she took back her maiden name."

"She lives here in town?"

"In Westwood. With her mother."

"I see." It was as simple as that. There'd been no need to ask Miss Hudson or Terola or Harley Moore. Evelyn Merrick wasn't a waif or a stranger. She had been Douglas Clarvoe's wife, Helen Clarvoe's sister-in-law. "Did Helen know the girl?"

"Know her? Why, that's how Douglas first met her. Evie and Helen went to a private school together years ago in Hope Ranch and Helen used to bring Evie home for week-ends. After graduation they went to different colleges and lost touch, but Evie used to come over here once in a while, mostly to see Douglas. Douglas had always adored her, she was such a lively, affectionate girl. She used to tease the life out of him but he loved it. There was never any malice in her teasing."

There is now, Blackshear thought. "Tell me about the wedding."

"Well, it was a very quiet one, being so soon after Harrison's death. Just the family and a few friends."

"Was Helen there?"

"Helen," she said stiffly, "had already moved out. She was invited, of course, and she sent a lovely gift."

"But she didn't come?"

"No. She was ill."

"How ill?"

"Really, Mr. Blackshear, I don't know how ill. Nor did I care. I didn't want her to come anyway. She might have ruined the wedding with that gloomy face of hers."

Blackshear smiled at the irony. Helen might have ruined the wedding, but Verna had ruined the marriage.

"Besides," Verna said, "she and Evie weren't best friends any more, they hardly ever saw each other. They had nothing much in common, even when they were at school together.

Evie was quite a bit younger, and the very opposite in temperament, full of fun and laughter."

"You saw her this afternoon."

"Yes."

"Is she still full of fun and laughter?"

"Not so much any more. The breakup of the marriage was hard on her. Hard on all of us. I wanted grandchildren."

The second drink had brought color to her face and made her eyes look like blue glass beads in a doll's head.

"I wanted grandchildren. I have nothing to show for my life. Nothing."

"You have Helen. I think perhaps the two of you have reached the stage where you need each other."

"We won't discuss that again."

"Very well."

"I don't want any advice. I hate advice. I don't need it."

"What do you need, then?"

"Money. Just money."

"Money hasn't helped you much in the past. And it's not helping Helen much now. She's in the position of being able to indulge her neurosis instead of trying to do something about it."

"Why tell me?"

"I think you're the logical person to tell, since you're her mother."

"I don't feel like her mother. I never did, even when she was a baby. The ugliest baby you ever saw, I couldn't believe it belonged to me. I felt cheated."

"You'll always be cheated, Mrs. Clarvoe, if you put your value on the wrong things."

She raised her clenched right fist and took a step forward as if she meant to attack him.

Blackshear rose to meet her. "You asked me to be impolite."

"I'm asking you now to get out and leave me alone."

"All right, I'll go. Sorry if I've disturbed you."

Her hands dropped suddenly and she turned away with a sigh. "I'm the one who should apologize. I've had—it's been a bad day."

"Good night, Mrs. Clarvoe."

"Good night. And when you see Helen, tell her—tell her hello for me."

"I'll do that."

"Good night."

As soon as he had gone, she went upstairs to Douglas' room, leaning heavily on the bannister for support. I must be firm, she thought. We must reach some decision.

The door of his bedroom was open.

"Dougie, there are some things we should . . . Dougie?"

He had changed his clothes as she had ordered him to—the terry-cloth robe and the beaded moccasins he'd been wearing were on the floor beside the bed—but once again he'd made her regret the order. Instead of coming down to the den to meet Blackshear, he had left the house.

She said, "Dougie," again, but without hope. She knew he was gone, she could even visualize the scene. Douglas coming downstairs, pausing at the den door, listening, hearing his name: *Do you think there's something the matter with Douglas, Mr. Blackshear?*

She turned and moved stiffly toward the staircase. As she walked through the empty house she had a feeling that it would always be empty from now on, that the day had held a finality for Douglas as well as for herself, and he had fled the knowledge of it.

Pressing her fists against her mouth, she thought, I mustn't get silly and hysterical. Of course Dougie will be back. He's gone out to get a pack of cigarettes. Or for a walk. It's a lovely evening. He likes to walk at night and name the stars.

The telephone in the hall began to ring. She was so sure that it was Douglas calling that she spoke his name as soon as she picked up the receiver.

"Douglas. Where are . . . ?"

"Is that the Clarvoe residence?"

The voice was so muffled and low that Verna thought it was Douglas playing one of his tricks, talking through a handkerchief to disguise his identity. "Where on earth did you disappear to? Mr. Blackshear was . . ."

"This isn't Douglas, Mrs. Clarvoe. It's me. Evie."

"Evie. What a coincidence, I was just talking about you."

"To whom?"

"A friend of mine, Mr. Blackshear."

"Did you say nice things?"

"Of course I did." She hesitated. "I said hello to Douglas for you. He was very pleased."

"Was he?"

"I—I know he'd love to see you."

"Would he?"

"He said, why don't you come over some time, we'll talk about old times."

"I don't want to talk about old times."

"You sound so funny, Evie. Is anything wrong?"

"Nothing. I only called to tell you something."

"What about?"

"Douglas. I know you're worried about him. You don't know what's the matter with him. I'd like to help you, Mrs. Clarvoe. You were always kind to me, now I will repay you."

She began to explain in detail what was the matter with Douglas and some of the things that went on in the rear of Mr. Terola's studio.

Long before she had finished, Verna Clarvoe slumped forward on the floor.

Chapter 6

IT WAS nine-thirty.

The woman had been in the telephone booth for half an hour and Harry Wallaby was still waiting to call his wife in Encino and tell her the old Buick had broken down and he was going to spend the night with his brother-in-law.

"You'd think the dame's tongue'd drop off," Wallaby said over his third beer.

The bartender, a middle-aged Italian sporting a bow tie in Princeton colors, shook his head knowingly. "Not hers. The more exercise it gets, the stronger it gets. Phoneitis, that's what she has, phoneitis."

"Never heard of it before."

"It's like a disease, see. You gotta phone people. With her it's bad."

"Who is she?"

"Just a dame who comes in once in a while. Everytime it's the same routine. A couple of drinks and it hits her, wham. She gets a buck's worth of dimes and parks herself in the phone booth, and there she sits, yackity, yackity, yackity. I've often wondered what in hell she talks about."

"Why don't you find out?"

"You mean go over and listen?"

"Sure."

"It wouldn't look right, me being the owner and proprietor," the bartender said virtuously.

"The same don't go for me. Is there a law says a guy can't stand beside a telephone booth, innocent-like?"

"It's a free country."

"Damn right it's a free country."

With an elaborate pretence of casualness, Wallaby slid off the bar stool, walked toward the front entrance as if he intended to leave, and then crept up on the telephone booth from the left side. He listened a moment, his hand cupping his ear, and returned to the bar, grinning a little sheepishly.

The bartender raised his eyebrows in silent inquiry.

"She's talking about some guy called Douglas," Wallaby said.

"What about him?"

"I don't know."

"Didn't you hear anything?"

Wallaby flushed. "I must of heard wrong. I mean, I must of. Jeez, I never heard nobody talk like that before."

"Well, for Pete's sake, tell me."

"I need another drink first."

At a quarter to ten Evelyn Merrick stepped out of the telephone booth, stretched her left arm to relieve the cramp and smoothed her skirt down over her hips. Usually, after making a series of telephone calls, she felt a certain relief and relaxation, but tonight she was still excited. The blood drummed double-time in her ears and behind her eyes, and she lurched a little as she made her way back to the bar. Her old-fashioned was untouched on the counter. She didn't pick it up, she just sat down, staring at it suspiciously, as if she thought the bartender had added something to it in her absence.

"O.K., Wallaby," the bartender said loudly and pointedly, "you can phone your wife now."

Evelyn caught his meaning at once and looked up, a flush spreading across her cheekbones. "Did I use the telephone too long?"

"Just nearly an hour, that's all."

"It's a public phone."

"Sure, it's a public phone, meaning it's for the public, for everybody. Someone like you ties it up and the rest don't get a chance. If this was the first time, I wouldn't beef."

"Do you talk to all your customers like this?"

"I own the joint. I talk how I please. People that don't like it don't gotta come back. This includes anybody."

"I see." She stood up. "Is that your liquor license beside the cash register?"

"Sure, it's my license. Paid for and up to date."

"Your name's Florian Vicente?"

"That's right."

"Well, good night, Mr. Vicente."

Vicente's jaw dropped in astonishment at her pleasant smile

and friendly tone, and he felt a little ashamed of himself for being so brusque with her. After all, she was harmless.

Outside, the first rain of the season had begun, but Evelyn Merrick didn't notice. She had more important things to think about. Mr. Vicente had been rude and must be taught a lesson in manners.

She began walking along Highland toward Hollywood Boulevard, repeated the bartender's name to imprint it on her memory. Florian Vicente. Italian. Catholic. Very likely a married man with several children. They were the easiest victims of all, the married ones with children. She thought of Bertha and Harley Moore and threw back her head and laughed out loud. The rain sprayed into her open mouth. It tasted fresh and good. It tasted better than Mr. Vicente's old-fashioneds. Mr. Vicente should serve drinks like that. *Give me a double rain, Mr. Vicente. In the morning I will phone Mrs. Vicente and tell her her husband is a pimp.*

She tripped down the slippery street, her body light and buoyant, bobbing like a cork on the convulsed seas of her emotions.

People huddling in doorways and under awnings looked at her curiously. She knew they were thinking how unusual it was to see such a gay pretty girl running alone in the rain. They didn't realize that the rain couldn't touch her, she was waterproof; and only a few of the smart ones guessed the real reason why she never got tired or out of breath. Her body ran on a new fuel, rays from the night air. Occasionally one of the smart ones tried to follow her to get her secret, to watch her refueling, but these spies were quite easy to detect and she was always able to evade them. Only in the strictest privacy did she store up her rays, breathing deeply first through one nostril and then the other, to filter out the irritants.

She turned east on the Boulevard, toward Vine Street. She had no destination in mind. Somewhere along the way there would be a small bar with a telephone.

She hurried forward across the street, not seeing the red light until a woman yelled at her from a passing car and a man behind her grabbed her by the coat and pulled her back up on the curb.

"Watch your step, sister."

She turned. The man's face was half-hidden by the collar of his trenchcoat and the pulled-down brim of a green fedora. The hat splashed water like a fountain.

"Thank you," she said. "Thank you very much."

He tipped his hat. "Welcome."

"You probably saved my life. I don't know how to . . ."

"Forget it."

The light turned green. He brushed past her and crossed the street.

The whole episode had not taken more than half a minute, but already it was expanding in her mind, its cells multiplying cancerously until there was no room for reason. The half-minute became an hour, the red light was fate, the touch of his hand on her coat was an embrace. She remembered looks that hadn't been exchanged, words that hadn't been spoken. Lover. Dear one. Beloved. Beautiful girl.

Oh, my dear one, wait for me. I'm coming. Wait. Lover. Lover dear.

Soaked to the skin, exhausted, shivering, lost, she began to run again.

People stared at her. Some of them thought she was sick, some thought she was drunk, but no one did anything. No one offered her any help.

She refueled in an alley between a hotel and a movie house. Hiding behind a row of garbage cans, she breathed deeply first through one nostril and then the other. The only witness was a scrawny gray tomcat with incurious amber eyes.

Inhale. Hold. Count four.

Exhale. Hold. Count three.

It must be done slowly and with proper care. The counting was of great importance. Four and three make seven. Everything had to make seven.

Inhale. Hold. Count four.

By the time she had finished refueling, she had completely forgotten about lover. The last thing she remembered was Florian Vicente who had called her wicked names because she had discovered his secret, that he was a pimp. What a shock it would be to his wife when she found out. But the poor woman must be enlightened, the truth must be told at all costs, the word must be spread.

Shaking her head in sympathy for poor Mrs. Vicente, Evelyn walked on down the alley and into the back door of the hotel bar. She had been here before.

She ordered a martini, which had seven letters.

A young man sitting on the next stool swung round and looked at her. "It's still raining, eh?"

"Yes," she said politely. "It doesn't matter, though."

"It matters to me. I've got to . . ."

"Not to me. I'm waterproof."

The young man began to laugh. Something about the sound of his laughter and the sight of his very white, undersized teeth reminded her of Douglas.

"I'm not joking," she said. "I *am* waterproof."

"Good for you." He winked at the bartender. "I wish I was waterproof, then I could get home. Tell us how you did it, lady."

"You don't do anything. It happens."

"Is that a fact?"

"It just happens."

"Is that a fact?"

He was still laughing. She turned away. She couldn't be bothered with such an ignorant fool who had teeth like Douglas. If he persisted, of course, if he became really rude like Mr. Vicente, she would have to get his name and teach him a lesson. Meanwhile, there was work to be done.

She paid for the martini, and without even tasting it she approached the phone booth at the rear of the room and opened the folding door.

She didn't have to look up any numbers. She forgot other things sometimes, she had spells when the city seemed foreign as the moon to her and people she knew were strangers and strangers were lovers, but she always remembered the telephone numbers. They formed the only continuous path through the tormented jungle of her mind.

She began to dial, shaking with excitement like a wild evangelist. The word must be spread. Lessons must be taught. Truth must be told.

"The Monica Hotel."

"I'd like to speak to Miss Helen Clarvoe, please."

"I'm sorry, Miss Clarvoe has had a private telephone installed in her suite."

"Could you tell me the number?"

"The number's unlisted. I don't know it myself."

"You filthy liar," Evelyn said and hung up. She couldn't stand liars. They were a bad lot.

She called Bertha Moore, but as soon as Bertha recognized her voice, she slammed down the receiver.

She called Verna Clarvoe again. The line was busy.

She called Jack Terola's studio, letting the phone ring for a full minute in case he was busy in the back room, but there was no answer.

She called the police and told them a man had been stabbed with a scissors in the lobby of the Monica Hotel and was bleeding to death.

It was better than nothing. But it wasn't good enough. The power and excitement were rotting away inside her like burned flesh, and her mouth was lined with gray fur like the tomcat's in the alley.

The cat. It was the cat that had ruined everything, it had contaminated her because it saw her refueling. She liked animals and was very kind to them, but she had to pay the cat back and teach it a lesson, not with a phone but a scissors. Like the man in the lobby.

The man was no longer part of her imagination but part of her experience. She saw him clearly, lying in the lobby, white face, red blood. He looked a little like Douglas, a little like Terola. He was Douglas-Terola and he was dead.

She returned to the bar. One of the bartenders and the young man who had laughed at her were talking, their heads close together. When she approached they pulled apart and the bartender walked away to the other end of the bar. The young man gave her a hurried uneasy glance and then he got up and he, too, walked away toward the back exit.

Everyone was deserting her. People did not answer their phones, people walked away from her. Everyone walked away. She hated them all, but her special hate was reserved for the three Clarvoes, and, of the three, Helen in particular. Helen had turned her back on an old friend, she had walked away, first and farthest, and for this she must suffer. She couldn't hide forever behind an unlisted telephone number. There were other ways and means.

"I'll get her yet," Evelyn whispered to the walls. "I'll get her yet."

The fur in her mouth grew long and thick with hate.

Chapter 7

DAWN CAME, a misty, meager lightening of the sky. The storm had intensified during the night. A banshee wind fled screaming up and down the streets, pursued by the rush of rain.

But it was not the wind or the rain that awakened Miss Clarvoe. It was the sudden stab of memory.

"Evie," she said, the name which had meant nothing to her for a long time was as familiar as her own.

Her heart began to pound and tears welled up in her eyes, not because she remembered the girl again, but because she had ever forgotten. There was no reason to forget, no reason at all. Right from the beginning they had been the closest of friends. They exchanged clothes and secrets and food from home, giggled together after the lights were out, met between classes, invented language of their own to baffle the interceptors of notes, and shared the same crush on the science master who was married and had four children and large romantic brown eyes. Other crushes, too, they shared, but they were all Evie's to begin with. Helen just followed along, content to have Evie take the lead and make the decisions.

We were friends, always. Nothing ever happened that I should forget her. There's no reason, no reason.

They had attended their first dance together one Hallowe'en, dressed alike, at Evie's suggestion, in gypsy costumes. Evie carried a goldfish bowl as a substitute for a crystal ball.

The dance, to which all the upper school girls had been invited, was held in the gymnasium of a private boys' school in the valley. Mr. Clarvoe drove Helen and Evelyn to the school and left them at the gym door. They were nervous and excited and full of the wildest hopes and the most abysmal fears.

"I can't go in, Evie."

"Don't be silly. They're only *boys*."

"I'm scared. I want to go home."

"We can't walk ten miles dressed like this. Come on in, be a sport."

"Promise you won't leave me?"

449

"I promise."

"Cross your heart."

"Listen to the music, Helen. They've got a real orchestra!"

They went inside and almost immediately they were separated.

The rest of the evening was a nightmare for Helen. She stood in a corner of the room, rigid, tongue-tied, watching Evie surrounded by boys, laughing, humming snatches of music, floating gracefully from one partner to another. She would have given her soul to be Evie, but no one offered her the chance.

She went into the lavatory and cried, her forehead pressed against the wall.

When the dance was over, her father was waiting in the car outside the gym.

He said, "Where's Evie?"

"A boy asked to take her home. She's going with him."

"She's altogether too young for that sort of thing. If she were my daughter I wouldn't allow it." He pulled away from the curb. "Did you have a good time?"

"Yes."

"Tell me about it."

"There's not much to tell. It was fun, that's all."

"That's not a very good description. Your mother and I went to considerable trouble to get you to this dance. We'd like some report on it at least."

She knew from his tone that he was angry but she didn't know what caused the anger and why it should be directed against her. "I'm sorry if I kept you waiting, daddy."

"You didn't." He'd been waiting for three-quarters of an hour but it was not her fault. He had come early deliberately, because it was her first dance and he was as uneasy about it as she was. He had sat in the car, listening to the chaos of laughter and music coming from the gym, imagining the scene inside, and Helen in the very center of it, bright and gay in her gypsy costume. When at last she came out, alone, with that stiff sullen look on her face, disappointment rose up and choked him so that he could hardly breathe.

"Did you dance with anyone?"

"Yes."

"Who?"

She didn't want to lie but she knew she had to, and she did it well. Without hesitation she described some of the boys she'd seen dancing with Evie and gave them names and invented conversations and incidents.

She talked all the way home, while her father smiled and nodded and made little comments. "That Jim sounds like a real cut-up." "Too bad the Powers boy was shorter than you." "Now, aren't you glad we made you go to dancing school?"

Later, when she kissed him good night, he gave her an affectionate little pat on the bottom.

"I'll have to watch out for you now, young lady. One of these days I'll be driven out of house and home by those little idiots hanging around."

"Good night, daddy."

"I forgot to ask about Evie. Did she have as good a time as you did?"

"I guess so. I was too busy to pay her any attention."

She went to bed, half-believing in her own lies because her father's belief was so complete.

The following day the dean of Helen's school, who had been one of the chaperones, telephoned Mr. Clarvoe. She wanted, she said, to check up on Helen and see if she was all right, she'd been so unhappy at the dance.

Nothing was said at dinner in front of Verna and Douglas, but later Mr. Clarvoe called Helen into the den and shut the door.

"Why did you lie, Helen?"

"About what?"

"The dance."

She stood, mute, scarlet with humiliation.

"Why did you lie?"

"I don't know."

"If it had been just one lie—but it was a whole string of them. I can't understand it. Why?"

She shook her head.

"Nothing of what you told me was true?"

"No, nothing," she said with a kind of bitter satisfaction, knowing he was hurt almost as much as she was. "Not a word."

"All the boys—they weren't even real?"

"I made them up."

"Helen, look at me. I want the truth. I demand it. What really happened at the dance?"

"I hid in the lavatory."

He stepped back, as if the words had struck him across the chest. "You hid—in the lavatory."

"Yes."

"Why? For God's sake, *why*?"

"I couldn't think of anything else to do."

"My God, why didn't you phone me? I'd have come and taken you home. Why didn't you let me *know*?"

"I was too—proud."

"You call that pride? Skulking in a lavatory? It's almost obscene."

"I couldn't think of anything else to do," she repeated.

"What about Evie? Was she with you?"

"No. She was dancing."

"The entire evening she was dancing and you were hiding in the lavatory?"

"Yes."

"For heaven's sake, why?"

"She was popular and I wasn't."

"Going off and hiding like that, you didn't give yourself a chance to be popular."

"I wouldn't have been anyway. I mean, I'm not pretty."

"You'll be pretty enough in time. Why your mother is one of the prettiest women in the state."

"Everyone says I take after you."

"Nonsense. You look more like your mother every day. What on earth put the idea in your head that there's anything the matter with your appearance?"

"The boys don't like me."

"That's probably because you're too standoffish. Why can't you try to be more friendly, like Evie?"

She didn't tell him what he should have known for himself— that she would have given anything in the world to be like Evie, not just at the dance, but any time, any place.

His anger, which in the beginning had boiled out like lava, was now cooling, leaving a hard crust of contempt. "You realize, of course, that I'll have to punish you for lying?"

"Yes."

"Are you sorry you lied?"

"Yes."

"There's only one true test of penitence. If you had a chance to repeat the lies, knowing you wouldn't be found out, would you do it?"

"Yes."

"Why?"

"It would have made both of us happier."

It was true and he knew it as well as she did, but he shook his head and said, "I'm disappointed in you, Helen, extremely disappointed. You may go to your room."

"All right." She lingered wanly at the door. "What about my punishment?"

"Your punishment, Helen, is being you, and having to live with yourself."

Later in the evening she heard her parents talking in their bedroom and she crept down the dark hall to listen.

"Well, heaven knows I've done everything *I* can," Verna said. "You can't make a silk purse out of a sow's ear."

"What about my idea of giving her a big party, inviting a bunch of boys . . ."

"What boys?"

"We must know some people who have boys about her age."

"I can think of exactly two, the Dillards and the Pattersons. I loathe Agnes Patterson, and besides, the whole idea of a party wouldn't work."

"We've got to think of something. If she goes on like this she may not even marry."

"I just don't understand you, Harrison. For years you've been treating Helen as if she were about four, and now suddenly you're thinking about her marriage."

"Are you blaming the situation on me?"

"Someone's to blame."

"But never you."

"I," Verna said righteously, "am bringing up Dougie. The girl is the father's responsibility. Besides, she takes after you. Half the time I don't even understand her. She won't speak out, let anyone know what she's thinking or how she feels about things."

"She's shy, that's all. We must find a way to get her over her shyness."

"How?"

"Well, for one thing, I think we should encourage her relationship with Evie. The girl's a good influence on Helen."

"I agree." There was a silence, and then a sigh, "What a pity we didn't have a girl like Evie."

Barefooted, shivering with cold and fear, she trudged back to her room and got into bed. But the walls and ceiling seemed to contract, to press down on her until they fitted her like a coffin. She knew then that her father had been right. This was her punishment, to be herself, and to have to live with herself forever, a living girl inside a locked coffin.

She lay awake until morning, and the emotion that was strongest in her heart was not resentment against her parents but a new and bitter hatred for Evie.

She did nothing about this hatred. It was buried with her inside the coffin and no one else knew it was there. Things went on as before, with her and Evie, or almost as before. They still shared a crush on the science master with the romantic eyes, they wrote notes in their secret language, and exchanged clothes, and food from home, and confidences. The difference was that Helen's confidences were not real. She made them up just as she'd made up the boys, and the incidents at the dance, for her father.

At the end of the spring semester, when Evie acquired a boy friend, Helen acquired two. When Evie was promised a horse as a reward for good grades, Helen was promised a car. It became as difficult for Evie to accept these lies as it was for Helen to keep on inventing them, and the two girls began to avoid each other.

There was trouble about it at home, but Helen had anticipated it and she was ready.

"Why didn't you bring Evie with you for the week-end?" her father asked.

"I invited her to come. She didn't want to."

"Why not?"

She hesitated just the right amount of time to rouse his curiosity. "I promised not to tell."

"I'm your father, you can tell me."

"No, I can't."

"Well, is it anything *we've* done?"

"Oh no. It's just—she's busy, she wanted to stay at school and study for the Latin test."

"That doesn't sound like Evie to me, staying at school when she could be here having a good time."

"Oh, she'll be having a good—I mean, she likes to study."

"You mean she's not going to be studying, isn't that it?"

"I promised not to tell."

"This sounds like the kind of thing I'd better get to the bottom of, right here and now. Where is Evie?"

"At school."

"Why?"

"I can't tell you. I made a solemn vow."

"I want an immediate and truthful answer to my question, do you hear me, Helen?"

"Yes. But . . ."

"And no but's, if's and when's, please."

"She—she has a boy friend."

"Yes? Go on."

"She doesn't want her parents to find out about him because he's a Mexican."

"A *Mexican*."

"He works on a lemon ranch near the school. She climbs out of the window after the lights are out and meets him in the woods." She began to cry. "I didn't want to tell. You made me. You made me a liar!"

Miss Clarvoe lay in bed with her right arm across her face as if to shield herself from the onslaught of memories. The ceiling pressed down on her, the walls contracted, until they fitted her like a coffin, tight, airless, sealed forever. And locked in with her were the mementos of her life: *"Your punishment is being you and having to live with yourself." "What a pity we didn't have a girl like Evie!"*

Chapter 8

THE HOUSE was set in the middle of a tiny walled garden on Kasmir Street in Westwood. An engraved card in a slot above the doorbell read: Mrs. Annabel Merrick, Miss Evelyn Merrick.

The house needed paint, the woman who answered Blackshear's ring did not. She looked like a farmer's wife, plump and tanned and apple-cheeked, but her clothes were city clothes, a smart black-and-white-striped suit that hinted at severely disciplinary garments underneath.

"Mr. Blackshear?"

"Yes."

"I'm Annabel Merrick." They shook hands. "Come in, won't you? I'm just making breakfast. If you haven't had yours, I can pop another egg in the pan."

"I've eaten, thank you."

"Some coffee then." She closed the front door after him and led the way through the living room into the kitchen. "I must say I was surprised by your early phone call."

"Sorry if I got you out of bed."

"Oh, you didn't. I work, you know. In the flower shop of the Roosevelt Hotel. Sure you wouldn't like an egg?"

"No, thanks."

"I've been divorced for several years, and of course alimony payments don't rise with the cost of living, so I'm glad to have a job. Somehow it's not so much like work when you're surrounded by flowers. Delphiniums are my favorite. Those blues—heavenly, just heavenly."

She brought her plate of eggs and toast to the table and sat down opposite Blackshear. She appeared completely relaxed, as if it was the most normal thing in the world to entertain strange men before 8 o'clock in the morning.

"Blackshear, that's an odd name. Do people ever get mixed up and call you Blacksheep?"

"Frequently."

"Here's your coffee. Help yourself to cream and sugar. You didn't tell me what business you were in."

"Stocks and bonds."

"Stocks and bonds? And you want to see Evelyn? Heavens, you're barking up the wrong tree. Neither of us is in a position to invest a nickel. As a matter of fact, Evelyn's out of a job right now."

"It won't hurt to talk to her."

"I guess not. As I told you on the phone, she's not here at the moment. She's spending two or three days with a friend whose husband is out of town. The friend hates to stay alone at night and Evelyn's always anxious to oblige. She's that kind of girl, she'd do anything for a friend."

Her tone was proud and maternal and Blackshear deduced from it that Mrs. Merrick was as blind about her daughter as Verna Clarvoe was about her son. He said, "May I have this other woman's name and address?"

"Certainly. It's Claire Laurence, Mrs. John Laurence, 1375 Nessler Avenue, that's near U.C.L.A. Evelyn won't be there during the day, she's looking for a job, but she'll arrive around dinnertime, I expect."

"What kind of job is she looking for? I might be able to help."

"I'm afraid stocks and bonds aren't in Evelyn's line."

"What is her line, Mrs. Merrick? Is she stage-struck? Does she want to be a model, or something like that?"

"Good heavens, no! Evelyn's a sensible and mature girl. What on earth gave you the idea she might want to be a model?"

"A lot of pretty girls do."

"Evelyn's pretty enough, but she's not vain, and she has far too many brains to enter a profession that's so temporary. Evelyn wants a future. More coffee?"

"No, thank you." But she didn't seem to hear him. She poured more coffee into his cup, and he noticed that her hand was trembling.

He said, "I hope I haven't upset you in any way, Mrs. Merrick."

"Perhaps you have. Then again, perhaps I was upset to begin with."

"Are you worried about Evelyn?"

"What else does a mother worry about, especially when

there's only one child? I want Evelyn to be happy, that's all I
ask for her, that she be happy and secure."

"And isn't she?"

"I thought she was, for a while. And then she changed. Ever
since her marriage she's been different." She looked across the
table with a bleak little smile. "I don't know why I should tell
you that, you said on the phone you don't even know Evelyn."

"I don't. I've heard of her, though, through the Clarvoes."

"The Clarvoes are friends of yours?"

"Yes."

"You know about the marriage, then?"

"Yes."

"Is that why you're here? Did Verna send you to make
amends?"

"No."

"I thought perhaps—well, it doesn't matter now. It's over.
Spilled milk and all that." She took her empty plate to the sink
and began rinsing it under the tap. "My own marriage failed. I
had high hopes for Evelyn's. What a fool I was not to *see*."

"See what, Mrs. Merrick?"

"You know what." She turned so suddenly that the plate fell
out of her hands and crashed in the sink. She didn't even notice. "My daughter married a homosexual. And I let her. I let
her because I didn't know it, because I was blind. I was taken
in, the way Evelyn was, by his gentleness and his pretty manners and his so-called ideals. I thought what a kind and consid-
erate husband he would make. Do you begin to see the picture
Evelyn had of him?"

"Yes, clearly."

"I guess it's happened to other girls, but it wouldn't have
happened to Evelyn if I hadn't been divorced, if her father had
been here. He'd have known right away that there was something wrong with Douglas. As it was, we had no hint, no warning at all.

"They went to Las Vegas for their honeymoon. I had a
post card from Evelyn saying she was fine and the weather
was beautiful. That was all, until the doorbell rang one night
a week later, and when I opened the door there was Evelyn
standing on the porch with her suitcases. She didn't cry or
make a fuss, she just stood there and said in a matter-of-fact

way, 'I've left him. It wasn't a marriage. It was only a wedding.'

"It was a terrible shock, terrible. I kept asking her if she was sure, I told her some men were like that at first, timid and embarrassed. But she said she was sure, all right, because he had admitted it. He had apologized. Can you beat it? He apologized for marrying her! I know now how much suffering that apology cost him. I'm not blaming Douglas any more. How can I? But at the time all I cared about was Evie.

"She left her suitcases out on the porch, wouldn't even let me bring them into the house, and the next day she took them down to the Salvation Army, her whole trousseau, wedding dress and all. When she came back around lunchtime she looked so pale and exhausted my heart turned over with pity—yes, and guilt, too. I should have known. I've been around. I was responsible."

Mrs. Merrick turned back to the sink, gathered up the bits of broken plate and tossed them into the trash can. "A plate breaks and you throw it away. A person breaks and all you can do is pick up the pieces and try to put them together the best way you can. Oh, Evelyn didn't break, exactly. She just—well, sort of lost interest in things. She'd always been an outgoing and lively girl, very quick to express her opinions or her feelings. On the night she came home she should have made a fuss, I ought to have encouraged her to talk and cry out a little of the hurt. But she was withdrawn, detached. . . ."

"Evelyn, dear, did you have dinner?"

"I think so."

"Let me heat up a little soup for you. I made some corn chowder."

"No, thank you."

"Evelyn—baby . . ."

"Please don't get emotional, Mother. We have to make plans."

"Plans?"

"I'll get an annulment, I suppose. Isn't that what I'm entitled to when the marriage wasn't consummated, as they say?"

"I think so."

"I'll see a lawyer tomorrow morning."

"There's no need for such haste. Give yourself a chance to rest up."

"*Rest up from what?*" Evelyn said with a wry smile. "*No. The sooner the better. I've got to shed that name Clarvoe. I hate it.*"

"*Evelyn. Evelyn dear. Listen to me.*"

"*I'm listening.*"

"*He didn't—mistreat you?*"

"*You have,*" Evelyn said distinctly, "*quite the wrong picture. I'll give you the right one, if you like.*"

"*Not unless you feel like it, dear.*"

"*I don't feel one way or the other. I just don't want you to get the idea in your head that I was physically abused.*" As she talked she rubbed the third finger of her left hand, as if massaging away the marks of her wedding ring. "*It began on the plane when he became sick. I thought at the time it was airsickness, but I realize now he was sick with fear, fear of being alone with me.*

"*When we arrived at the hotel, he went into the bar while I unpacked. He stayed in the bar all night. I waited for him, all dressed up in my flossy nightgown and negligee. Around 6 o'clock in the morning two of the bellboys brought him up and poured him out on the bed. He was snoring. He looked so funny, yet so pathetic, too, like a little boy. As soon as he began to show signs of waking up, I went over and spoke to him and stroked his forehead. He opened his eyes and saw me bending over him. And then he let out a scream, the queerest sound I ever heard, an animal sound. I still didn't know what the trouble was, I thought he merely had a hangover.*" Her mouth twisted with distaste and contempt. "*Well, he had a hangover, all right, but the party had been years and years ago.*"

"*Oh, Evelyn. Baby . . .*"

"*Please don't fuss.*"

"*But why, why in heaven's name did he marry you?*"

"*Because,*" Evelyn said dryly, "*he wanted to prove he was a man.*"

Blackshear listened, pitying the woman, pitying them all; Evelyn waiting in her flossy nightgown for the bridegroom, Douglas sick with fear, Verna trying desperately to hide the truth from herself.

"Yesterday," Mrs. Merrick continued, "Evelyn met me downtown at noon to do some shopping. For the first time since the wedding we saw Verna Clarvoe. I was quite upset, I could think of nothing but bitter things to say. But Evelyn was perfectly controlled. She even asked about Douglas, how he was and what he was doing and so on, in the most natural way in the world."

"Verna went into that spiel of hers—Dougie was fine, he was taking lessons in photography, and doing this and doing that. It seemed to me that she was trying to start the whole business over again, trying to whip up Evelyn's interest. And then it struck me for the first time, she doesn't *know*, Verna still doesn't know, she still has hopes, doesn't she?"

"I think she has."

"Poor Verna," she said quietly. "I feel especially sorry for her today."

"Why especially?"

"It's his birthday. Today is Douglas' birthday."

Chapter 9

DOUGLAS' DOOR was locked; it was the only way she had of knowing that he had come back some time during the night, perhaps because he wanted to, perhaps because he had no place else to go.

She knocked and said, "Douglas," in a harsh heavy voice that was like a stranger's to her. "Are you awake, Douglas?"

From inside the room there came a mumbled reply and the soft thud of feet striking carpet.

"I want to talk to you, Douglas. Get dressed and come downstairs. Right away."

In the kitchen, the part-time maid, a spare elderly woman named Mabel, was sitting cross-legged at the breakfast bar, drinking a cup of coffee and reading the morning *Times*. She didn't rise when she saw Verna, who owed her back wages in civility as well as cash.

"There's muffins in the oven. Yesterday's. Heated up. You want your orange juice now?"

"I'll get it myself."

"I made a grocery list. We're out of eggs and coffee again. I need a drop of coffee now and then to steady myself and there's barely a cup left in the pot."

"All right, go and buy some. You might as well do the rest of the shopping while you're at it. We need some 100-watt bulbs and paper towels, and you'd better check the potato bin."

"You want I should do it now, before I have a bite to eat?"

"Our understanding was that you were to eat before you come here."

"We had *other* understandings too."

"You'll be paid this week. I expect a check in the mail today."

When the maid had gone, Verna took the muffins out of the oven and tested one. It was rubbery, and the blueberries inside were like squashed purple flies.

She added water to the coffee and reheated it, and then she poured some orange juice out of a pitcher in the refrigerator. It smelled stale. The whole refrigerator smelled stale, as if Mabel had tucked odds and ends of food into forgotten corners.

Hearing the wheeze and rattle of Mabel's ancient Dodge as it moved down the driveway, Verna thought, I'll have to let her go, as soon as I can pay her. How awkward it is to have to keep her on because I can't afford to fire her.

Douglas came in as she was pouring herself a cup of coffee. He hadn't dressed, as she'd asked him to. He was wearing the terry-cloth robe and beaded moccasins he'd had on the previous night before Blackshear's visit. He looked haggard. The circles under his eyes were like bruises, and from his left temple to the corner of his mouth there ran three parallel scratches. He tried to hide the scratches with his hand, but the attempt only drew attention to them.

"What happened to your cheek?"

"I was petting a cat."

He sat down beside her, on her left, so that she would only see the uninjured side of his face. Their arms touched and the physical contact jabbed Verna like a needle. She got up, feeling a little faint, and walked over to the stove.

"I'll get you some muffins."

"I'm not hungry." He lit a cigarette.

"You shouldn't smoke before breakfast. Where did you go last night?"

"Out."

"You went out and petted a cat. A real big evening, eh?"

He shook his head wearily.

"What kind of cat was it that you petted?"

"Just an ordinary alley cat."

"Four-legged?"

"Most cats are four-legged."

"Not the one that scratched you."

"I don't know what you're getting at, I really don't." He turned his eyes on her, dove-colored, full of innocence. "What are you so angry about, Mother? I went for a walk last night, I saw this cat, I picked it up and tried to pet it and it scratched me. God help me, that's the truth."

"God help you, yes," she said. "No one else will."

"What brought on this somber mood?"

"Can't you guess?"

"Certainly I can guess."

"Go ahead, then."

"You tried to borrow money from Helen and she turned you down."

"Wrong."

"Mabel asked for her back wages."

"Wrong again."

"It has something to do with money, that's for sure."

"Not this time."

He got up and started toward the door. "I'm tired of this guessing game. I think I'll go up . . ."

"Sit down."

He stopped at the doorway. "Don't you think I'm too old to be ordered around like . . ."

"Sit down, Douglas."

"All right, all right."

"Where did you go last night?"

"Are we going to start that all over again?"

"We are."

"I went out for a walk. It was a nice night."

"It was raining."

"Not when I left. The rain started about 10 o'clock."

"And you just kept on walking?"

"Sure."

"Until you got to Mr. Terola's place?"

He stared at her across the room, unblinking, mute.

"That was your destination, wasn't it, one of the back rooms of Terola's studio?"

He still didn't speak.

"Or perhaps it wasn't Terola's, perhaps it was just anybody's back room. I hear your kind isn't particular." She heard herself saying the words but still she didn't believe them. She waited, her fists clenched against her sides, for the reactions she wanted from him: shock, anger, denial.

He said nothing.

"What goes on in that studio, Douglas? I have a right to know, I'm paying for those so-called 'photography' lessons of yours. Are you really learning anything about photography?"

He walked unsteadily back to the breakfast bar and sat down. "Yes."

"Are you behind the camera or in front of it?"

"I don't know—what you mean."

"You must know, other people do. I heard it myself last night."

"Heard what?"

"About the kind of pictures Terola takes. Not the sort of thing one would want in a family album, are they?"

"I wouldn't know."

"Who would know better than you, Douglas? You pose for them, don't you?"

He shook his head. It was the denial she'd been waiting for, praying for, but it was so fragile she couldn't touch it for fear it would break.

"Who's been talking to you?" he said.

"Someone called me last night after you went out."

"Who was it?"

"I can't tell you."

"If rumors are going around about me, I have a right to know who's passing them along."

She clutched at the straw. "Rumors? That's all they are then, Douglas? None of it's true? Not a word?"

"No."

"Oh, thank God, thank God!"

She rushed at him across the room, her arms outspread.

His face whitened and his body tensed as he braced himself for her caress. She stroked his hair, she kissed his forehead, she touched the scratches on his cheek with loving tenderness, she murmured his name, "Dougie. Dougie dear. I'm so sorry, darling."

Her arms entwined around him like snakes. He felt sick with revulsion and weak with fear. A scream for help rose in his throat and suffocated there: *God. God help me. God save me.*

"Dougie dear, I'm so sorry. You'll forgive me, won't you?"

"Yes."

"Oh, what a horrible mother I am, believing those lies. That's all they were, lies, lies."

"Please," he whispered. "You're choking me."

But the words were so muffled she didn't hear them. She pressed her cheek against his. "I shouldn't have said those terrible things, Dougie. You're my son. I love you."

"Stop it! Stop!"

He tore himself out of her grasp and ran to the door, and a

moment later she heard the wild pounding of his feet on the stairs.

She sat for a long time, stone-faced, marble-eyed, like a deaf person in a room of chatterers. Then she followed him upstairs.

He was lying spread-eagled across the bed, face down. She didn't go near him. She stood just inside the door.

"Douglas."

"Go away. Please. I'm sick."

"I know you are," she said painfully. "We must—cure you, take you to a doctor."

He rolled his head back and forth on the satin spread.

Questions rose on her tongue and died there: When did you first know? Why didn't you come and tell me? Who corrupted you?

"We'll go to a doctor," she said more firmly. "It's curable, it must be curable. They cure everything nowadays with all those wonder drugs they've got, cortisone and ACTH, things like that."

"You don't understand. You just don't *understand*."

"Try me. What is it? What don't I understand?"

"Please. Leave me alone."

"Is that what you want?"

"Yes."

"Very well," she said coldly. "I'll leave you alone. I have an errand to do anyway."

Something in her voice alerted him, and he rolled over on the bed and sat up. "What kind of errand? You're not going to see a doctor?"

"No, that's your duty."

"And what's yours?"

"Mine," she said, "is to see Terola."

"No. Don't go there."

"I must. It's my duty, as your mother."

"Don't go."

"I must confront this evil man, face to face."

"He's not an evil man," Douglas said wearily. "He's like me."

"Have you no shame, no sense of decency, defending a man like that to me, to your own mother?"

"I'm not defen—"

"Where's your self-respect, Douglas, your pride?"

He had so many things to say to her that the words became congested in his throat and he said nothing.

"I'm going to see this Terola and give him a piece of my mind. A man like that being allowed to run around loose, it's a disgrace. He's probably corrupted other young men besides you."

"He didn't corrupt me."

"What are you saying, Douglas? Of course he did. He was responsible. If it weren't for him you'd be perfectly normal. I'll see to it that he pays the . . ."

"Mother. Stop it."

There was a long silence. Their eyes met across the room and went on again, like strangers passing on a street.

"Terola," she said finally. "He wasn't the first, then."

"No."

"Who was?"

"I've forgotten."

"When did it happen?"

"It was so long ago that I can't remember."

"And all these years—all these *years* . . ."

"All these years," he repeated slowly, using the words like weapons against both her and himself.

He didn't hear her leave, but when he looked up again, she was gone and the door was closed.

He lay back on the bed, listening to the beat of rain on the roof, and the cheep-cheep of a disgruntled house wren complaining about the weather from under the eaves. Every sound was clear and sharp and final: the cracking of the eucalyptus trees as the wind increased, the barking of the collie next door, Mabel's old Dodge wheezing up the driveway, the slam of a car door, the murmur of the electric clock beside his bed.

It seemed that he had never really listened before, and now that he had learned how, each sound was personal and prophetic. He was the wren and the rain, he was the wind and the trees bending under the wind. He was split in two, the mover and the moved, the male and the female.

All these years, the clock murmured, *all these years.*

Verna tapped on the door again and came in. She was dressed to meet the weather, in a red plaid raincoat and a matching peaked cap.

She said, "Mabel's back. Keep your voice down. She has ears like a fox."

"I have nothing to say, anyway."

"Perhaps you'll think of something by the time I get back."

"You're not going to see Terola?"

"I told you I was."

"Please don't."

"I have some questions to ask him."

"Ask me instead. I'll answer. I'll tell you anything you want to know."

"Stop wheedling like that, Douglas. It annoys me." She hesitated. "Don't you see, I'm only doing my duty? I'm only doing what your father would have done if he were still alive. This man Terola, he's obviously corrupt, and yet you're trying to protect him. Why? You said you'd tell me anything. Why?"

He lay motionless on the bed, his eyes closed, his face gray. For a moment she thought he was dead, and she was neither glad nor sorry, only relieved that the problem had been solved by the simple stopping of a heart. Then his lips moved. "You want to know why?"

"Yes."

"Because I'm his wife."

"His . . . *What did you say?*"

"I'm his wife."

Her mouth opened in shock and slowly closed again. "You filthy little beast," she said quietly. "You filthy little beast."

He turned his head. She was standing by the bed watching him, her face distorted with loathing and contempt.

"Mother. Don't go. Mom!"

"Don't call me that. You're no part of me." She walked decisively to the door and opened it. "By the way, I forgot. Happy birthday."

Alone, he began to listen again to the clock and the wren and the rain and the trees; and then the sound of the Buick's engine racing in response to Verna's anger. She's leaving, he thought. She's going to see Jack. I couldn't stop her.

He got up and went into the bathroom.

For almost a year, ever since his marriage to Evelyn, he'd been saving sleeping pills. He had nearly fifty of them now, hidden in an epsom-salts box in the medicine chest, capsules in various gay colors that belied their purpose. He swallowed five of them without any difficulty, but the sixth stuck in his throat for a few moments, and the seventh wouldn't go down at all. The gelatin coating melted in his mouth and released a dry bitter powder that choked him. He did not try an eighth.

He removed the blade from his safety razor, and standing over the washbasin he pressed the blade into the flesh that covered the veins of his left wrist. The razor was dull, the wound was hardly more than a scratch, but the sight of his blood oozing out made him dizzy with terror. He felt as if his knees were turning into water and his head was filling with air like a balloon.

He tried to scream, "Help! Mother!" but the words came out like a whimper.

As he fell forward in a faint his temple struck the projecting corner of the washbasin. The last sound Douglas heard was sharp and clear and final, the crack of bone.

Chapter 10

AT 10 O'CLOCK, Miss Clarvoe, who had slept late, was just finishing her breakfast. When she heard the knocking on the door, she thought it was one of the busboys from the dining room coming to collect her tray and his tip.

She spoke through the crack of the door. "I haven't quite finished. Come back later, please."

"Helen, it's me. Paul Blackshear. Let me in."

She unlocked the door, puzzled by the urgency in his voice. "Is there anything the matter?"

"Your mother's been trying to reach you. The telephone company wouldn't give her your unlisted number so she called me and asked me to come over."

"To tell me she's canceled the birthday luncheon, I suppose."

"She's canceled it, yes."

"Well, she needn't worry about Douglas receiving a present from me. I sent a check out last night, he should get it today."

"He won't get it today."

"Why not?"

"Sit down, Helen."

She went over to the wing chair by the front window, but she didn't sit down. She stood behind it, moving her long thin hands nervously along its upholstered back, as if to warm them by friction.

"It's bad news, of course," she said, sounding detached. "You're not an errand boy, even mother wouldn't use you as an errand boy to tell me about a canceled luncheon."

"Douglas is dead."

Her hands paused for a moment. "How did it happen?"

"He tried to commit suicide."

"Tried? I thought you said he was dead."

"The doctor believes Douglas swallowed some sleeping capsules and cut one of his wrists, but the cause of death was a blow on the head. He struck his temple against the washbasin as he fell, probably in a faint."

She turned and looked out of the window, not to hide her

470

grief, but to hide the grim little smile that tugged at the corners of her mouth. Poor Douglas, he could never finish anything properly, not even himself.

"I'm sorry, Helen."

"Why should you be? If he wanted to die, that was his affair."

"I meant I was sorry for you."

"Why?"

"Because you don't feel anything, do you?" He crossed the
room and stood facing her. "Do you?"

"Not much."

"Do you ever feel anything? For anybody?"

"Yes."

"For whom?"

"I—I wish you would not get personal, Mr. Blackshear."

"My name is Paul."

"I really can't call you that."

"Why not?"

"I just can't, that's all."

"Very well."

"I . . ." She stepped back and stood against the wall with
her hands behind her back, like an embarrassed schoolgirl.
"How is mother taking it?"

"I'm not really sure. When she called me on the telephone
she seemed more angry than anything else."

"Angry at whom?"

"Evelyn Merrick."

"I don't understand. What had Evelyn to do with Douglas'
death?"

"Your mother holds her responsible for it."

"Why?"

"Evelyn called your mother last night and gave her some
information about Douglas and Jack Terola, the man who's
supposedly been giving Douglas lessons in photography. I
won't repeat the information. It wasn't pretty, though, I can
tell you that. This morning your mother taxed Douglas with it
and he admitted that some of it, at least, was true. Your mother
wanted a showdown with Terola and actually started out to see
him. Whether she saw him or not, I don't know for sure. She
says she didn't, that she turned around and came back to the
house. Meanwhile, the maid had found Douglas' body when

she went to clean his room, and she called the doctor. The doctor was there when your mother arrived. She tried to get in touch with you immediately, and failing that, she called me and asked me to come over here."

"Why?"

"The telephone company . . ."

"I meant, why was she so anxious to have me informed right away? So she could be sure I'd send a nice fat wreath, as I sent a nice fat check?"

"That's uncharitable, Helen."

"Yes, I guess it is. I'm sorry. Life has taught me to be suspicious. I've learned the lesson too well."

"Perhaps you can unlearn it some day."

"Perhaps. It's harder to unlearn, though."

"I can help you, Helen."

"How?"

"By giving you something that's been too scarce in your life."

"What?"

"You can call it love."

"*Love.*" Violent pink spread up from her neck to her cheekbones. "No. No. You—you're just trying to be nice to me."

"I'm not trying," he said with a smile. "I *am* being nice to you."

"No. I don't want your love, anyone's. I can't accept it. It—embarrasses me."

"All right. Don't get excited. There's no hurry. I can wait."

"Wait? What will you wait for?"

"For you to unlearn some of those lessons you've been taught."

"What if I can't. What if I never . . ."

"You can, Helen. Just tell me you'll try. Will you?"

"Yes, I'll try," she whispered. "But I don't know where to start."

"You've already started."

She looked surprised and pleased. "I have? What did I do?"

"You remembered Evelyn Merrick."

"How do you know that?"

"You referred to her quite casually a few minutes ago as Evelyn. Do you remember her clearly now?"

"Yes."

"In her phone call to you the other night, when she said you'd always envied and been jealous of her, was she right, Helen?"

"She was right."

"That's no longer true, is it?"

"No. I don't envy her any more. She's to be pitied."

"Pitied, yes," he said, "but watched, too. She's all the more dangerous because she can appear quite rational on the surface."

"You've seen her, then."

"Not yet, I'll see her tonight. But I discussed her with your mother last night before the phone call, and early this morning I talked to Evelyn's own mother. Neither of them had the faintest suspicion that the girl is insane. She appears to have a completely split personality. On the one hand, she's the affectionate, dutiful daughter, as well as your mother's idea of a perfect daughter-in-law—and the latter would take quite a bit of doing, since your mother's not easy to please."

"I'm aware of that."

"On the other hand, the girl is so full of hatred and vengeance that she wants only to destroy people by turning them against one another. She's crafty, she hasn't had to do any of the destroying herself. She just throws in the bone and lets the dogs fight each other over it. And there's usually some meat of truth on the bone."

She thought of her mother and Douglas, and how they had fought throughout the years, not like dogs, or like boxers in a ring face to face, but like guerrillas stalking each other in a dark forest. Into this forest Evelyn had thrown a giant flare which lit up the trees and the underbrush and scorched the enemies out of their cover.

Poor Douglas. He was always a boy, he could never have grown up in a dark forest.

"I sent him a check for his birthday," she said dully. "Perhaps if I'd sent it sooner . . ."

"A check wouldn't have made any difference, Helen. The doctor found nearly fifty sleeping capsules in the medicine chest. Douglas had been planning this for a long time."

"Why does mother blame Evelyn for it, then?"

"She has to blame someone. And it can't be herself."

"No," she said, thinking, mother was trapped in the forest just as much as Douglas was. Years ago someone should have led them out, but there was no one except father and me, and father was too harsh and I was lost myself.

She covered her face with her hands and tears slid out between her fingers.

"Don't cry, Helen."

"Someone should have helped. Years ago someone should have *helped*."

"I know."

"Now it's too late, for Douglas, for mother." She raised her head and looked at him, her eyes softened by tears. "Maybe it's too late for me, too."

"Don't think that."

"Yes. I feel inside me that I've lived my life, I'm only waiting, like Douglas with his hoard of sleeping capsules. Perhaps I'll get another phone call, perhaps it will light up the underbrush and I won't be able to bear what I see."

"Stop it." He put his arms around her, but her body grew stiff as wood at his touch and her hands clenched into tight fists. He knew the time had not yet come, and perhaps never would.

He walked away to the other side of the room and sat down at the desk, watching the change come over her at his retreat, the relaxation of her muscles, the easier breathing, the leveling off of color in her face. He wondered if this was how they must remain for all time, a room's width away from each other.

"You're very—kind," she said. "Thank you, Paul."

"Forget it."

"I suppose now I must go home and stay with mother. That's what is expected of me, isn't it?"

"By her, yes."

"Then I'll get ready, if you'll excuse me."

"I'll drive you over, Helen."

"No, please don't bother. I'll call a cab. I don't want to interfere with your investigation."

"My investigation, as such, is almost finished. You asked me to find Evelyn Merrick. Well, I've found her."

"You think it's all over, then? Everything's settled?" Her voice was insistent. "You have no further work to do on the case?"

"There's work to be done but . . ."

"More than ever, in fact."

"Why more?"

"Because there's been a death," she said calmly. "Evelyn's not going to stop now. I think Douglas' death will actually spur her on, give her a sense of power."

It was what Blackshear himself feared but he hadn't wanted to alarm her by saying so. "It could be."

"Where did she get her information about Douglas?"

"From Terola himself, I guess."

"You mean they could be together in some extortion racket?"

"Perhaps Terola intended it that way, but Evelyn needs deeper satisfactions than money can give."

"But you think they were partners?"

"Yes. When I went to see Terola about her, he was pretty cagey. I got the impression he knew the girl a lot better than he admitted."

"So if there's any evidence against her, this man Terola would have it?"

"Evidence of what?"

"Anything that can be used to put her away some place. So far she's done nothing actionable. In Douglas' case she didn't even tell a lie. She can't be sued or sent to jail just for phoning mother and telling her the truth. And yet, to a certain extent, she's morally guilty of Douglas' death. You've got to stop her, Paul, before she goes on." She turned so that he couldn't see her face. "I may be next."

"Don't be silly, Helen. She can't call you, she doesn't know your number. And if she comes to the door, don't let her in."

"She'll think of some other way. I feel she's—she's waiting for me."

"Where?"

"I don't know."

"Look, if you're nervous about going over to your mother's house, let me drive you."

She shook her head. "I'd rather you went to see Terola. Tell him about Douglas, force him to talk, to give you information that can be used in court."

"That's a tall order, Helen. Even if he knows Evelyn like a

book, he's not going to read it aloud to me. He'd incriminate himself."

"You can try, can't you?"

"That's about it. I can try."

He waited while she went into the bedroom to dress for the street. When she came out she was wearing a dark gray woolen coat and an old-fashioned black felt hat with a broad brim turned down over her forehead. The outfit made her look as if she'd stepped out of the previous decade.

"Helen."

"Yes?"

"Mind if I say something personal?"

"You usually do, whether I mind or not."

"You need some new clothes."

"Do I?" she said indifferently. "I never pay much attention to what I wear."

"It's time you started."

"Why?"

"Because you and I will be going places together. All kinds of places."

She smiled slightly, like a mother at the exaggerated plans of a small boy.

They took the elevator downstairs and walked through the lobby together. Mr. Horner, the desk clerk, and June Sullivan, the emaciated blonde at the switchboard, watched them with undisguised curiosity and exchanged small ugly smiles as they paused at the swinging door that led to the street.

"My car's a couple of blocks away. Sure you don't want me to drive you over to your mother's?"

"It isn't necessary."

"I'll come there later to see you, if you like."

"I'm afraid it won't be a very cheerful household. Perhaps you'd better not."

"Shall I call you a cab?"

"The doorman will."

"All right. Good-bye, then."

"Good-bye."

Outside, on the busy street, Evelyn Merrick was waiting for her.

Chapter 11

T HE WIND had blown the storm out to sea and the streets, which had been fairly quiet half an hour before, now came alive, as if the end of the rain was an all-clear signal for activities to resume immediately and simultaneously. People marched briskly up and down the sidewalks like ants patroling after a storm, but on the road traffic came almost to a standstill. Cars moved slowly, if at all, defeated by their own numbers.

It took Blackshear ten minutes to get his car out of the parking lot and another thirty to reach the long narrow stucco building on Vine Street which served as Terola's studio.

For the second time Blackshear read the black stenciling on the frosted-glass window, but now the words had more sinister implications:

PHOTOGRAPHIC WORKSHOP

JACK TEROLA, PROPRIETOR

PIN-UP MODELS • LIFE GROUPS FOR AMATEURS
AND PROFESSIONALS • RENTAL STUDIOS FOR ART GROUPS

Come in Any Time

The office was exactly as it had been the previous afternoon except that someone had recently used the old brick fireplace. The remains of a fire were still smoking, and whatever had been burned had generated enough heat to make the room uncomfortably hot.

The heat drew out other odors, the smell of boiled-over coffee and of a sharp, musky perfume. The coffee smell came from Terola's alcove, concealed from view by a pair of dirty flowered-chintz curtains. The odor of perfume came from the girl seated behind, and almost hidden by, the old-fashioned rolltop desk. She was leaning back in the swivel chair at an awkward angle, and her eyes were closed. She appeared to be asleep.

Blackshear recognized her as Nola Rath, the young girl who'd been posing for one of Terola's magazine layouts the preceding day. At that time her long black hair had been wet and she'd worn no make-up. Now her hair was compressed into a roll on top of her head and she had on a layer of cosmetics so thick it was like a mask. She looked years older.

He approached the desk, diffident and a little embarrassed, feeling that he was intruding on her privacy by watching her in her sleep.

"Miss Rath?"

Slowly, as if the movement hurt her, she opened her eyes. There was no recognition in them, of Blackshear, or of anything else. She seemed dazed.

"I'm sorry if I woke you up."

"I wasn't—asleep." Her voice matched her eyes; it was flat and dull and expressionless. She held her hand to her throat as if the act of speaking, like the act of moving her eyelids, was painful to her.

"Are you feeling all right, Miss Rath?"

"All right."

"Let me get you a glass of water."

"No. No water." She shifted her weight and the chair creaked under it. "You better get out of here."

"I just came."

"That don't matter, you better go."

"I'd like to see Mr. Terola, if I may. Is he in?"

"He's not seeing anybody."

"If he's too busy right now, I'll come back later."

"He's not busy."

"Well, is he ill or something?"

"He's not ill. He's something. He's very something." She began to move her head back and forth. "I been sitting here. I don't know what to do. I been sitting. I ought to get out of here. I can't move."

"Tell me what's happened."

She didn't answer but her eyes shifted toward the alcove. Blackshear crossed the room, drew back the curtains of the alcove and stepped inside.

Terola was lying on his back on the day bed with a pair of barber's shears stuck in the base of his throat. A soiled sheet and a blood-spattered pink blanket covered the lower half of his body; the upper half was clothed in an undershirt. On a

table near the foot of the day bed the hot plate was still turned
on and the coffee pot had boiled dry. It looked as though
Terola had got up, turned on the coffee, and then gone back
to bed for a few more minutes. During those few minutes he'd
had a visitor.

Whoever the visitor was, Terola had not been alarmed.
There were, except for the blood, no signs of violence in the
room, no evidence of a struggle. Terola's hair was not even
mussed; the same thin parallel strands of gray crossed the top
of his pate like railroad ties. Either Terola had known the visitor well and been taken completely by surprise, or else he'd
been killed in his sleep.

The thrust of the scissors had been deep and vicious and
accurate. It was a woman's weapon, a scissors, but the hand
that used it had a man's strength.

In life Terola had been unprepossessing enough, in death he
was monstrous. The eyes bulged like balls of glass, the fleshy
mouth hung slack, the tongue, grayish pink and thick, lolled
against the tobacco-stained teeth. Blackshear thought of Douglas and his youth and good looks, and he wondered what dark
paths had led him to Terola.

Without touching anything, he returned to the girl in the
office.

"Have you called the police?"

She blinked. "Police? No."

"Did you kill Terola?"

"No. For God's sake, no! He was my friend, he gave me a
job when I was down and out, he treated me good, never
slapped me around like some."

"You found him the way he is now?"

"Yes, when I came to work."

"When was that?"

"Fifteen, twenty minutes ago, I guess. Be here at noon, he
said, only I always come a little early so's I can get ready."

"Was the door locked when you arrived?"

"No. Jack doesn't—didn't keep it locked unless he's—unless
he was out."

"Did Terola always sleep at the office?"

"No. He and his mother and his brother have a little ranch
out in the valley where they raise avocados, only Jack wasn't

stuck on the place, or the company either, I guess, so he often just stayed here in town." She pressed a handkerchief to her eyes. "Oh God, I can't believe he's dead. He was going to do big things for me, he said. He said I had a great future, all I needed was some publicity. He promised he'd get me all the publicity I wanted."

Blackshear was firm. "Well, he kept his promise."

"Kept it? No, he didn't. What do you mean?"

"You'll get all the publicity you want, Miss Rath. Maybe more."

Her reaction was not what he expected. "My God, that's right. Say, there'll be newspaper photographers and everything. The works. How do I look?"

"Great."

"Gee, maybe I could even write an article for the Sunday papers about what a stinker Jack was, except to me. How's that for an angle? Here is this bum Terola, who everybody hates his guts, only he puts himself out to be kind to a down-and-out orphan girl. How does that sound?"

"Are you an orphan, Miss Rath?"

"I could be," she said with a cold little smile. "Depending on the stakes, I could be anything."

"Including a liar."

"Oh, that. Sure."

"You didn't phone the police, did you?"

She shrugged. "No. I will, though. As soon as you get out."

"Why should I get out?"

"Because you'll wreck everything for me. My future depends on this. It's gotta be done right, see?"

"I don't see."

"Well, put it this way. Suppose I didn't have so many clothes on, and suppose I run screaming into the street that I found a murdered man—get the picture?"

"Vividly."

"Then you see how you'd gum things up by being here." She stood up and leaned across the desk toward him. "I didn't kill Jack and I won't touch anything, I promise. Go away, will you, mister? I need a chance. A real chance."

"And you think this is a real chance for you?"

"It's *got* to be. I'll never get another. Now will you go? Will you *please* go, mister?"

"After you call the police."

She picked up the phone and dialed. While she waited for an answer, she began unbuttoning her dress.

Blackshear went out to his car. He would have liked to stay behind the wheel for a few minutes to witness Nola Rath's performance, but he had a more important matter to attend to. Sometime, during the morning Verna Clarvoe had set out to see Terola. Had she, in spite of her story to the contrary, seen him, talked to him? Or had she despaired of words as a weapon and used a scissors instead? Perhaps other people had motives for killing Terola, but Verna's was fundamental, for in her, love and hate had merged and exploded like two critical masses of uranium. In the explosion, Douglas had died. Perhaps Terola was the second victim of the chain reaction.

Chapter 12

A RED-EYED maid answered the door.

Blackshear said, "May I see Mrs. Clarvoe, please?"

"She's not seeing anybody. There's been an accident."

"Yes, I know. I have something urgent to tell Mrs. Clarvoe."

"What's more urgent than being allowed to be alone with your grief, I'd like to know?"

"What's your name?"

"Mabel."

"Mabel, I want you to tell Mrs. Clarvoe that Paul Blackshear is here on important business."

"All right, but I warn you, she's been carrying on something awful. When the hearse came to take him away, she screamed, such screaming I never did hear in all my born days. I thought she'd bust a blood vessel. She called someone on the telephone and kept shouting things about a girl named Evelyn. It was fierce."

"Didn't the doctor give her a sedative?"

"Some pills he gave her. *Pills.* Pills is a pretty poor substitute for a son." She opened the door wider and Blackshear stepped into the hall. "I'll go up and tell her. I don't guarantee she'll come down, though. What can you expect, at a time like this?"

"Has Miss Clarvoe arrived yet?"

"*Miss* Clarvoe?"

"Douglas' sister."

"I didn't even know he had a sister. Fancy that, no one mentioning a sister."

"She should be arriving any minute now," Blackshear said. "By the way, when she comes, you needn't let on that she isn't mentioned around here."

"As if I'd do a thing like that. Will she be staying, I mean, sleeping and eating and so forth?"

"I'm not sure."

"Well, it's a queer household, make no mistake about that."

"I won't."

"You can wait in the drawing room, if you like."

482

"I prefer the den."

"I'll show you . . ."

"I know the way, thanks."

The den smelled of last night's fire, and the morning rain. Someone had started to clean the room and been interrupted; a vacuum cleaner was propped against the davenport, and a dust cloth and a pile of unwashed ashtrays were sitting on the piano bench. The glass door that led out to the flagstone patio had been slid back and the November wind rustled across the floor and spiraled among the ashes in the fireplace.

Verna Clarvoe came in, her step slow and unsteady as if she was wading upstream in water too deep, against a current too strong. Her eyes were swollen almost shut, and there were scratches around her mouth as if she'd clawed herself in a fury of grief.

She spoke first. "Don't say you're sorry. Everyone says they're sorry and it doesn't matter, it doesn't *matter* whether they're sorry or not." She slumped into a chair. "Don't look at me. My eyes, they always get like this when I cry. I've forgotten where I put my drops. It's so cold in here, so *cold*."

Blackshear got up and closed the door. "I talked to Helen. She offered to come home."

"Offered?"

"Yes, offered." It was true enough. He hadn't suggested it. "She should have been here half an hour ago."

"She may have changed her mind."

"I don't think so."

"Why didn't she come with you?"

"I had some business to attend to first. It concerns you, Mrs. Clarvoe. If you're feeling well enough, I think I'd better tell you about it now."

"I feel all right."

"Terola is dead."

"Good."

"Did you hear what I said, Mrs. Clarvoe?"

"You said Terola is dead. I'm glad. Very glad. Why should you be surprised that I'm glad? I hope he suffered, I hope he suffered agonies."

"He didn't. It happened pretty quickly."

"How?"

"Someone stabbed him with a scissors."

"Someone murdered him?"

"Yes."

She sat, quiet, composed, smiling. "Ah, that's even better, isn't it?"

"Mrs. Clarvoe . . ."

"He must have been scared before he died, he must have been terrified. You said he didn't suffer. He must have. Being scared is suffering. A scissors. I wish I'd seen it happen. I wish I'd been there."

"And I wish," Blackshear said, "that you could prove you weren't."

"What a silly remark."

"Perhaps, but it had to be made."

"I told you on the phone, I started out to see Terola but I changed my mind and came back."

"How far did you get? As far as the studio?"

"Yes."

"But you didn't go in."

"No. The place looked so squalid. I lost my nerve."

"Did you get as far as the door?"

"No. I never left the car. There's a yellow curb in front of the place, I just stopped there for a while."

"For how long?"

"A few minutes."

"Did anyone see you?"

"I was there, people must have seen me."

"What kind of car do you drive?"

"A black Buick sedan, last year's. There are hundreds like it, if that's what you're getting at."

"It is."

"Well, I didn't race up in a flame-red Ferrari. There's no reason why anyone should have paid any particular attention to me."

"Let's hope no one did."

"What if they did?"

"If they did," Blackshear said patiently, "you'll probably be questioned by the police. You had a pretty good reason for hating Terola."

"If I killed everyone I hated, people would be dying like flies all over town."

"I don't believe that, Mrs. Clarvoe."

"Oh, stop. Stop that boy-psychiatrist approach. You don't know me. You don't understand. I'm filled with hatred. How can I help it? I've been cheated, duped, tricked—what do you expect? Everyone's let me down, everyone. Harrison, Douglas, they're out of this mess of a life. I'm the one that's left, always the one that's left."

From the driveway came the squeal of a car's moist brakes. They both heard it simultaneously, Verna with dread, Blackshear with relief. He hadn't admitted even to himself that he'd been worried about Helen's delayed arrival.

"That must be Helen now," Verna said. "I don't know what I'll say to her, how I'll act. We've been apart for so long, we're strangers."

"Then act like strangers—they're usually polite to each other, at least."

Blackshear went to the glass door and looked out across the patio toward the driveway. A woman was paying off the cab driver, a plump gray-haired woman in a black-and-white suit. When the cab backed out toward the street, she stood for a moment staring at the house as if she wasn't sure it was the right one. She saw Blackshear and appeared to recognize him. Instead of going to the front door she started across the patio toward the den with quick, aggressive strides.

Sensing trouble, Blackshear went out to meet her, closing the glass door behind him.

"Hello, Mrs. Merrick."

Her face was stiff and hostile. "Is she in there?"

"Yes."

She tried to brush past him but he reached out and clasped her arm and held it.

"Wait a minute, Mrs. Merrick."

"The sooner this is done, the better. Let go of my arm."

"I will, after you tell me what you have in mind."

"You mean, am I going to strangle the little bitch? No. Much as I'd like to."

He released her arm but she didn't move away from him. "Much as I'd like to," she repeated. "The things she said about

Evelyn—incredible, terrible things. I can't, I won't, let her get away with it. No mother would."

"When did she make these remarks?"

"Less than an hour ago. She called me at the office—at the office, mind you; God knows who heard her, she was shouting so loud. She made the most terrible accusations against Evelyn. I can't even repeat them, they were so vile. She kept shouting something about giving Evelyn a dose of her own medicine. I don't know what she meant. Evelyn's always been so nice to her. Then she said that Evelyn was a murderer, that she murdered Douglas. I hung up, but she called back right away. I had to take the call, there were other people around. When she finally finished, I asked the boss for the rest of the morning off and here I am. I've got to get to the bottom of this."

"Isn't it rather a bad time?"

"It's a bad time, but it's not going to get any better. I have to find out why she said those things about Evelyn. If she's crazy with grief over Douglas, well, all right, I can undersand that, I've had a few griefs of my own. But why should she take it out on Evelyn of all people? My daughter has never hurt anyone in her life, it's so *unfair* that she should be attacked like this. She isn't here to defend herself, but I am. I'm here. And don't try and stop me this time, Mr. Blackshear. *I'm going to see Verna Clarvoe.*"

He watched her go into the house.

The two women faced each other in silence for a long time.

"If you've come for an apology," Verna said finally, "you won't get one. A person isn't obliged to apologize for telling the truth."

"I want an explanation, not an apology."

"You have the explanation."

"You've said nothing yet. Nothing."

"I gave Evelyn back some of what she gave me. The truth." Verna turned away, pressing her fingertips against her swollen eyelids. They felt hot, as if they'd been scalded by her tears. "She called me last night. She was quite friendly at first, she said I'd always been kind to her and she wanted to do me a favor in return. Then she told me about Douglas, the kind of life he was leading, the friends he had—sordid terrible things, in words so vile I don't see how a girl like Evelyn would know them, let alone speak them. That's your explanation, Mrs. Merrick."

"You can't be talking about Evelyn. Not *my* Evelyn."

"Why not?" Verna said, through clenched teeth. "She was talking about *my son*."

"I don't believe it. Evelyn would never do such a thing. She felt vindictive, perhaps, for a time after the marriage, but she's all over that. She has no hard feelings now. You saw that for yourself when you met us yesterday. She was pleasant and friendly, wasn't she? Wasn't she nice to you? You said yourself she bears no grudge."

"I am not arguing. I am too tired to argue. I told you what happened."

"You must be mistaken." Mrs. Merrick's plump face was like rising dough. "At least admit the possibility that you're mistaken."

"There's no such possibility."

"What time did she—what time was the call?"

"About ten."

"There. You see? You're wrong. Evie stayed with some friends last night. They had tickets for a play at the Biltmore Bowl."

"It was Evelyn who called me. I recognized her voice. And no one else, no woman, anyway, would know such things about Douglas."

"These things—how can you be sure they were true?"

"Because he admitted them, my son admitted them. And then he killed himself." She began to sway back and forth, her arms hugging her scrawny breasts. "Dougie. Dougie is dead. It's his birthday. We'd planned a little party . . . Oh God, go away, leave me alone."

"Mrs. Clarvoe, listen to me."

"No, no, no."

"I'd like to help you."

"Go away. My son is dead."

She left the way she had come, across the patio. Blackshear was waiting for her on the driveway, his suit collar turned up against the wind, his lips blue with cold.

He said, "I'll drive you back to work, Mrs. Merrick."

"No, thanks. You'd better go in to her." She began putting on her suede gloves. "At least Evelyn is alive. No matter what she's done, at least she's *alive*. That's enough to thank God for."

She turned and walked briskly into the wind, her head high.

Chapter 13

THE WET patches on her dress, where she'd washed off the blood in the lavatory of the public library, were dry now, and it was safe to venture out into the street again. Even if the wind should blow her coat open, people wouldn't notice the faint stains left on her blouse, or if they did, they couldn't identify them.

She closed the book she'd been pretending to read for the past hour and returned it to the reference shelf. She knew no one in the library, and no one knew her. Still, it was dangerous to sit too long in any one place, especially a quiet place, because sometimes her mind clicked noisily like a metronome and spies could tell from its frequency what she was thinking.

One of these spies was an old man sitting at a table near the information desk, half-hidden behind a copy of *U.S. News and World Report*. How innocently engrossed he seemed, like a child gazing at a picture book, but something about the angle of his head gave him away. She began to hum, quite loudly, so he couldn't hear her thoughts. He lowered the magazine and gave her a sour look, realizing that he'd been outwitted.

As she passed the table, she bent toward the old man and whispered, "It won't do you any good to follow me." Then she headed for the door, pulling her coat tight around her.

The victory was hers, of course. Still, the clicking of her mind was becoming annoying. It came and went at odd moments, varying with the intensity of her thoughts, and if she was excited by an idea the noise was almost deafening, enough to drive her crazy.

Crazy. Not a word to use lightly. Terola had tried.

She walked quickly down the library steps and turned north, thinking of Terola. She'd been perfectly nice to him, perfectly polite. He had had no reason to act as he did.

When he had answered the door he was wearing striped pajama bottoms and an undershirt.

"Hello, Mr. Terola."

"What do *you* want?"

"I just thought I'd pop in and . . ."

"Look, kid, pop out again, will you? I'm hung over."

He started to close the door but she was too quick for him. "I could make you some coffee, Mr. Terola."

"I've been making my own coffee for years."

"Then it's high time you tried mine. Where's the stove?"

Yawning, he led the way to the alcove and sat down on the edge of the day bed while she plugged in the hot plate and filled the coffee pot with water.

"How come the ministering angel act, kid?"

"I like to do a favor for a friend, now and then."

"And then the friend is supposed to do a favor right back at you?"

"That would be nice."

"What's the angle?"

"Those pictures you took of me," she said. "Burn them up."

"Why?"

"They didn't do me justice."

His eyebrows humped like black bushy caterpillars. "So?"

"So burn them up and take new ones. Good ones, the kind they hang in museums."

"Look, Elaine, Eileen, whatever your name is . . ."

"Evelyn."

"Look, Evelyn, you go home now like a good girl and I'll consider your proposition."

"You don't mean it."

"Sure, sure I do." He lay down on the bed and pulled the covers up to his waist.

"Do you promise, Mr. Terola?"

"Promise what?"

"To make me immortal."

"You crazy or something?" he said, punching the pillow irritably. "People hear you talking like that, they'll haul you off to the loony bin."

"Mr. Terola . . ."

"Blow, will you? I'm tired. I had a big night."

"Mr. Terola, do you think I'm pretty?"

"Gorgeous," he said, closing his eyes. "Just gorgeous, sweetheart."

"You're making fun of me."

"No, I'm not. Why should I make fun of you? Now blow, like a good girl, Eileen."

"Evelyn," she said. "*Evelyn*."

"All right. Sure."

"Say it. *Say Evelyn*."

He opened his eyes and saw her standing over him. "What's the matter with you, kid? Are you crazy?"

Crazy. Not a word to use lightly.

As she turned the next corner she looked back toward the library. The spy, disguised as an old man, was standing on the steps watching her, with the *U.S. News and Report* tucked under his arm. She began to run.

The old man went back into the library and stopped at the information desk where a red-haired girl sat surrounded by telephone directories from all over the country.

The girl smiled and said, "Here I thought you were running off with one of our magazines again, Mr. Hoffman."

"Not this time. Did you happen to notice the young woman who just left? The one with the dark coat?"

"Not particularly. Why?"

"I've been observing her for the past half-hour. Very peculiar, she seemed to me."

"We get a great many peculiar people in here," the girl said cheerfully. "Public institution, you know."

"I thought perhaps—well, the fact is, I couldn't help noticing she had stains on the front of her dress."

"She probably had spaghetti for lunch. You know how it dribbles."

"All the time I was watching her she kept a book open in front of her but she wasn't reading. A book on birds, I believe, though my eyes aren't what they used to be. Then, as she was leaving, she leaned down and whispered something to me. I didn't quite catch it. Odd, wouldn't you say?"

"Rather."

"I was wondering if I should, perhaps, report it to the police?"

"Now there you go again, Mr. Hoffman, imagining things!"

Because of the clicking of her mind and the danger of spies, she tried never to go into the same bar twice, but it was difficult to tell one from another, they were so similar. It was as if the decorations, the neon signs, the furniture, the customers, the bartenders, had all come from the same warehouse in a package deal.

The important difference was the location of the pay phone. At the Mecca it was in the rear, near the entrance to the men's room and cut off from the view of the people at the bar by a massive tub of philodendron.

With the folding door of the phone booth shut tight, she felt safe and warm and secluded, beyond the reach of society, like a child in a playhouse or a poet in an ivory tower.

She dialed, smiling to herself, breathing the stale air deeply into her lungs as if it were pure oxygen. Crestview 15115. As she waited for an answer, she totaled the numbers. Thirteen. Add one and divide by two, that made seven. Everything had to make seven. Most people didn't know this, and even when they were told, exhibited skepticism or frank disbelief.

On the fifth ring (plus two) a woman's voice said, "Hello."

"Is this the Clarvoe residence?"

"Yes."

"Mrs. Clarvoe?"

"She's not in."

"But I recognize you, Mrs. Clarvoe."

A sharp sound came over the wire, like a metallic object striking the floor. "Who . . . Is that you, Evelyn?"

"Didn't you expect to hear from me again?"

"Yes. Yes, I expected to."

A pause at the other end of the line, then a flurry as if people were moving about, and a man's voice, low and hurried, but distinct: "Ask her about Helen. Ask her where Helen is."

"Who's that with you?" Evelyn said. As if she didn't know. Poor old bungling Blackshear, looking for her all over town, like a blind man feeling his way through a forest. One of these days I will pop out at him from behind a tree.

"No one's with me, Evelyn. There was, but I—I sent him away. I felt you—you and I could talk better alone. Evelyn? Are you still there?"

Still there. Safe, warm, secluded, the poet in the playhouse, the child in the ivory tower.

A man, barrel-chested, bald, passed the phone booth, and she peered out at him through the dirty, narrow glass door. But he didn't even notice her. His mind was on other things.

"Evelyn? Answer me. *Answer me.*"

"Well, you needn't shout," Evelyn said coldly. "I'm not deaf, you know. I have what you might call 20-20 hearing."

"I'm sorry I—shouted."

"That's better."

"Listen to me, please. Have you seen Helen? Have you talked to her?"

"Why?" She smiled to herself because she sounded so sober and earnest when all the time she was bursting with laughter. Had she seen Helen? What a marvelous joke. Prolong it. Draw it out. Make it last a bit. "Why do you want to know about Helen, Mrs. Clarvoe?"

"She was due here hours ago. She said she was coming home."

"Oh, that."

"What do you mean? Have you . . . ?"

"She changed her mind. She didn't really want to come home anyway. She didn't want you to see her in her present condition."

"What is her—condition?"

"I promised not to tell. After all, we were friends once, and I ought to keep a promise to a friend."

"Please. For God's sake . . ."

"You keep shouting. I wish you wouldn't."

"All right," Verna whispered. "I won't shout. Just tell me, where's Helen and what's the matter with her?"

"Well, it's a long story." It wasn't really. It was short and sweet, but Mrs. Clarvoe must be taught a lesson. It was rude to shout.

"Evelyn, please, I beg of you . . ."

"No one has to beg me for the truth. I give it freely, don't I?"

"Yes."

"Whatever else people say about me, I'm not a liar."

"No. Of course not. You're not a liar. About Helen, she's all right, isn't she?"

"I don't know."

"But you said . . ."

"I didn't say she was all right or all wrong. All I said was that she changed her mind, she's not coming home."

"Where is she?"

The barrel-chested man passed again, on his way back to the door. He had glass eyes and wooden lips.

"She's working," Evelyn said, "in a call house."

She had begun to tremble in excitement and anticipation, waiting for Verna's reaction, shock, disbelief, protest. None came.

"Did you hear me, Mrs. Clarvoe? Helen's working in a call house. It's down on South Flower Street. No place for a lady, I can tell you. But then, Helen never wanted to be a lady. A little excitement, that's what she needs. She'll get it, too. Oh my, yes. She'll get it."

Still no answer, not even the click of the receiver. The excitement began to spill out of her, like blood from a severed artery. She stuffed words into the wound to stem the flow.

"I got her the job. I met her outside her hotel this morning. She said she was sick of the idle life she was leading, she wanted to have something interesting to occupy her time. So I said I knew of something. Come with me, I said. And she came."

"Now I know you're lying," Verna said flatly. "Helen would never have gone anywhere with you. She's been warned."

"Warned? About me?"

"What have you done with her?"

"I told you, I got her a job."

"That's preposterous."

"Is it?" She hung up softly.

It was preposterous, nothing could be more preposterous than poor old Helen in a call house. Yet it was true.

She began to laugh, not ordinary laughter, but sounds with claws that tore at her chest and at the tissues of her throat. Burning with pain, she stumbled out into the street.

Chapter 14

DURING CLASSES she was known as Dr. Laurence, but after five she was Claire and she lived near the U.C.L.A. campus in Westwood with her husband, John, and an overweight spaniel called Louise. She was a tall, well-built young woman with long beautiful legs and black hair which she wore in a coronet of braids. The style was old-fashioned and not particularly becoming, but it made her look unique, and she was well aware that this was about as much as she could expect with her limited equipment.

Frank, intelligent and unpretentious, she got on well with her students and had a great many friends, most of them university people. Her closest friend, however, had nothing to do with the faculty.

She had met Evelyn Merrick about eight months previously on a double date with one of John's fraternity brothers. On the way home she asked John, "Well, how do you like her?"

"Who?"

"Evelyn Merrick."

"She's O.K.," John said.

"You certainly are enthusiastic."

"Thank God *one* of us doesn't form snap judgments of people."

"Snap judgments are the only valid ones."

"How so?"

"Otherwise you get to like people just because they satisfy a need in you and not because of their intrinsic worth."

"Don't look now but your Ph. D. is showing."

"Let it show," Claire said. "I'll bet she's suffered. And don't say *who* again. You know perfectly well who."

"Most of us suffer here and there."

"I don't think it was here and there with Evelyn. It seems to me that she's had a tremendous shock of some kind, and not too long ago, either."

"Maybe she had shock treatments."

"You meant that to be funny, I suppose."

"Very, very slightly funny."

"As a matter of fact, I've seen people after they've had shock treatments, and they often show the same kind of wary attitude. Even if they hear a question the first time, they like to have it repeated. Things like that."

"So you think your new friend is a parolee from Camarillo."

"I think nothing of the sort," Claire said briskly. "My opinion is that she's suffered a shocking experience. I wonder what it could have been."

"Well, if I know you, angel, you'll have the whole story out of her the second time you meet."

He was wrong. During the next few months the two women met quite frequently, sometimes accidentally, since they lived only eight blocks apart, and sometimes by arrangement, for lunch or dinner or an early movie; but whatever Evelyn's shock had been, she didn't mention it, and any hints that Claire put out or direct questions she asked, were met with silence or a gentle remonstrance. At first, Evelyn's ability to keep a secret tantalized and annoyed Claire, but in time she came to respect it.

When John, who taught in the biology department, had to go away on field trips, Evelyn frequently came over to spend the night because Claire was nervous about being alone.

John liked to tease his wife about these occasions. "Afraid of the dark, at your age and weight."

"I can't help it."

"What did you do before you were married?"

"Before I was married, I lived in an apartment house with people below me, above me, and on both sides of me. The walls were so thin you could hear a pin drop, so there wasn't much chance of being murdered in your bed. It's quite different living in a house, like this. You're cut off from people."

"By a driveway and two flower beds."

"No, you know what I mean."

He knew exactly what she meant. She'd been brought up in a large family and lived in dormitories at school. There had always been people around, brothers and sisters, and friends and cousins and cousins of cousins. Being left in a house by herself made Claire feel insecure, and John was grateful to Evelyn for keeping her company in his absence. He had long since lost his original distrust of Evelyn and he believed now that, in her quiet way, she was just about the nicest girl in the world.

On Wednesday morning John took some of his freshmen students on a field trip to Los Padres National Forest and in the late afternoon Evelyn came over to the house to have dinner with Claire and spend the night. The two women had planned on going to see a play at the Biltmore Bowl but the arrangements were canceled when Claire arrived home with a severe cold. She went to bed at eight, drugged with antihistamines and codeine, and slept around the clock.

She woke up the next morning to the sound of dishes rattling and the smell of burning bacon. Slipping on her husband's old paisley bathrobe, she went out into the kitchen and found Evelyn making breakfast.

Claire said, yawning, "I could eat a horse."

"You may have to. I just ruined the last of the bacon."

"I like it well-done."

"It isn't well-done, it's charred."

"Well, Johnny says everybody should eat a certain amount of carbon. It acts as a purifying agent."

"You're making that up."

"It sounds rather plausible, though, doesn't it?"

"I can tell you're feeling better this morning."

"Oh, I am. How about you?"

Evelyn turned, her face white and aloof. "Me? There was never anything wrong with me."

"You're looking rocky. If I didn't know you better, I'd say you'd been out on a binge."

"Binges aren't much in my line."

"I was just kidding. I didn't mean to offend you."

"I'm afraid I offend easily these days."

"I know you do. John and I—well, we've noticed, and we couldn't help wondering."

"Wondering what?"

"If you shouldn't get married."

Evelyn was silent.

"I mean," Claire said with awkward earnestness, "marriage is a wonderful thing for a woman."

"Oh?"

"It really is. I don't know why you're looking so amused. What's funny?"

"I'm afraid," Evelyn said, smiling, "you wouldn't understand."

On Thursday afternoon Claire arrived home from her classes a little earlier than usual, around four-thirty. It was already getting dark and she didn't notice the car parked at the curb until she let the cocker spaniel out. The dog streaked across the lawn toward the car and began pawing at the door.

A man wearing a gray felt hat leaned out of the window and said, "That's not doing the finish of my car much good."

"So I see." She picked up the squirming spaniel.

"You're Mrs. Laurence?"

"That's right."

"I'm Paul Blackshear. I called you at the University this afternoon."

"Oh, yes."

"Is Miss Merrick here?"

"Not yet. She will be, though. If you'd like to come inside and wait . . ."

"Thanks, I would."

She led the way across the lawn, feeling apprehensive about letting the stranger into the house and yet unable to think of an adequate reason or a polite way to get rid of him.

In the living room she turned on all four of the lamps and left the drapes open, and when Blackshear had settled himself on the davenport she sat down in a straight-backed chair at the opposite end of the room.

"My husband," she lied firmly, "will be home at any minute."

Blackshear gave her a quizzical look. "Good. I'll need all the help I can get."

"Help with what?"

"I am trying to find a woman. I have reason to believe that Evelyn Merrick knows where this woman is."

"You mean you think Evelyn helped her to disappear?"

"I mean that, yes, but not in exactly the same sense that you do."

"I don't understand."

"The woman's disappearance was involuntary."

Claire stared at him, her face pale and astonished, her clenched fists pressed against her thighs. "What are you—implying?"

"It's obvious, isn't it, Mrs. Laurence?"

"No, it's not obvious. Nothing is obvious. I'm confused. I don't understand."

"I don't understand either, but I'm trying to. That's why I'm here. The woman who disappeared is Helen Clarvoe, a friend of mine. She was also, at one time, a friend of Evelyn Merrick's."

"At one time. Does that mean they quarreled?"

"Let's say they lost touch. Until last Monday night. At that time Miss Merrick telephoned Helen Clarvoe at her hotel. I won't go into detail but I assure you it wasn't an ordinary call from one old friend to another. As a result of it, Miss Clarvoe asked me to try and find Evelyn Merrick."

"Why?"

"She was disturbed and frightened by Miss Merrick's remarks. During the course of the week I've discovered that unusual telephone calls are Evelyn Merrick's specialty. Some people, when they have a grievance, blow their top, some brood, some write crank letters. Evelyn Merrick telephones."

"Nonsense," Claire said sharply. "I don't believe it. Ev hates to talk on the phone. I should know, I'm her best friend."

"Look, Mrs. Laurence, there may be some things about this woman that even her best friend doesn't know because Miss Merrick herself may not know them."

"That's not possible. Unless she's—are you trying to tell me she's insane?"

"It's a form of insanity."

"What is?"

"Multiple personality."

Claire rose abruptly and began to pace the room. "Ev is my best friend. You're a stranger. You come here and tell me some monstrous things about her and expect me to believe them. Well, I can't. I won't. What right have you got to go around diagnosing people as multiple personalities?"

"The theory isn't mine. It was advanced as a possibility by Miss Merrick's own doctor. I talked to him this afternoon. Miss Merrick has already suffered two emotional disturbances, one after her parents were divorced and her father went east to live, and the other after the breakup of her own marriage last year."

"Marriage," Claire repeated. "Ev's never been married."

"It's a matter of record."

"She's never said a word to me about it. I—why, just this morning we were talking and I said something about marriage being good for a woman and she—well, it doesn't matter now."

"Go on, Mrs. Laurence. She what?"

"Nothing. She just smiled, as if I'd said something unintentionally funny."

"You did."

"It wasn't a happy marriage, then?"

"No."

"Who is the man?"

"Helen Clarvoe's brother, Douglas." Blackshear hesitated, feeling a sudden and acute distaste for the job he had to do. "The young man died this morning."

"Why do you say it in that particular tone?"

"I wasn't aware of my tone."

"I was. You sounded as if you thought Evelyn had something to do with the man's death."

"There's no question in my mind. And two men have died."

She was shaken but obstinate. "There must be some terrible mistake. Ev is the gentlest creature in the world."

"Perhaps the one you know is. The other . . ."

"There is no other!" But the strength had gone out of her. She slumped into a chair, the back of her right hand pressed against her trembling mouth. "How—how did her husband die?"

"He killed himself."

"And the other man?"

"He was stabbed in the throat with a barber's shears some time this morning."

"My God," she said. "My God." And her hand slid down to her throat as if to try to staunch an invisible flow of blood. "She'll be here any time. What am I going to do?"

"Nothing. Act as if nothing's happened."

"How can I?"

"You must. Helen Clarvoe's life may be at stake."

"There's no chance you've—made a mistake?"

"There's always that chance, Mrs. Laurence, but it's pretty small. When she called Mrs. Clarvoe about Helen this afternoon she made no secret of her identity, she was even proud of herself."

He told her the content of the telephone call. She listened in stunned silence, rubbing the same place on her neck over and over again.

Outside, the spaniel began to bark. Blackshear turned and looked out of the window. A young woman was coming up the walk, laughing, while the spaniel jumped around her in frenzied delight. As she reached the steps of the porch, she leaned down and put out her arms and the spaniel leaped up into them. Both the girl and the dog looked very pleased with themselves at this remarkable feat.

It was Blackshear's first sight of Evelyn Merrick, and he thought how ironic it was that he should see her like this, laughing, greeting a dog—*the gentlest creature in the world*, Claire Laurence had said.

He turned and looked back at Claire. There were tears in her eyes. She brushed them away with the back of her hand as she went to unlock the door.

"Did you see that, Claire? She finally did it, jumped right up into my arms! John said he's been trying to teach her that for years. How's your cold?"

"Much better, thanks," Claire said. "We have company."

"Company? Good."

"Come in and meet Mr. Blackshear."

"Just a sec, I'll shed my coat."

When she came into the room she was smiling slightly, but it was a guarded smile, as if she already suspected that the company wasn't the kind she would enjoy. She had short dark hair and gray eyes that borrowed a little blue from the shirtwaist dress she was wearing. When Blackshear had first seen her greeting the spaniel, she had seemed strikingly pretty. Now her animation was gone and she looked quite commonplace. When she shook hands, her clasp was limp and uninterested.

Blackshear said, "I heard Mrs. Laurence call me company. The term isn't quite accurate."

She raised her dark straight brows. "No?"

"I would like to ask you some questions, if I may, Miss Merrick."

"You may. I may even answer them."

"Mr. Blackshear is trying to find a woman who disappeared," Claire said. "I told him you probably don't know a thing about it." She caught Blackshear's warning glance and added, "I'll go and make some coffee."

When she had gone, Evelyn said lightly, "This sounds very intriguing. Tell me more. Is it anyone I know?"

"Helen Clarvoe."

"*Helen.* Good heavens, I think that's the last name in the world I expected to hear. You say she's disappeared?"

"Yes."

"That is odd. Helen just doesn't do that sort of thing. She's, shall we say, on the conservative side."

"Yes."

"Still, she's old enough to do what she likes and if she wants to disappear why should anyone try and find her?"

"I'm not sure she wanted to."

"Oh really?" She seemed amused. "Helen isn't quite as dull as she acts, you know. There may be a man involved."

"I doubt that."

"In any case, I don't see how *I* can help you, Mr. Blackshear. I'll try, though."

"Thank you."

"Fire ahead."

"Are you acquainted with South Flower Street, Miss Merrick?"

"South Flower? That's downtown, isn't it?"

"Yes."

"I suppose I've driven along it. It's not the kind of section I'm familiar with, however."

"How long is it since you've seen Helen Clarvoe?"

"Over a year."

"Have you talked to her on the telephone?"

"Of course not. Why should I? We have nothing to discuss."

"There's no bad feeling between you?"

"There's no feeling at all between us. Not on my side, anyway."

"You were good friends at one time."

"In school, yes. That," she added with a shrug, "was a long time ago."

"You married Helen's brother, Douglas."

"I wouldn't say married. We went through a ceremony. Do you mind if I ask *you* a question now?"

"Not at all."

"Where did you get all your information about me?"

"From your mother."

She looked genuinely amused. "I might have guessed. Mother's a great talker. She bares her soul to the milkman or the boy who delivers the groceries. Unfortunately, she bares mine too."

"Have you seen Douglas recently, Miss Merrick?"

"No, I haven't seen him. I've talked to him, though."

"When?"

"He telephoned me last night."

"Here?"

"Yes. After Claire had gone to bed."

"How did he know you were here?"

"I presume he called the house first and mother gave him this number."

"Do you think that's likely, in view of the resentment she feels toward him?"

"He probably didn't give his name." She added with a touch of scorn, "I assure you *I* haven't been keeping in touch with him. As far as the Clarvoes are concerned, I've had it. They're a good family to stay away from."

"What was Douglas' reason for calling, Miss Merrick?"

"I don't know. It's the first time I've heard from him since the annulment. He sounded lonely and confused. I was a little of both, myself, so we talked. Mostly about old times, years ago when Helen and I were at school together and I used to go home with her for holidays and week-ends. Dougie, we called him then, and he was always tagging around after us, no matter how much we teased him. Even Helen was happy in those days. Funny how everything's turned out."

But she spoke with complete detachment, as if the Evelyn of those times had no connection with herself. Blackshear wondered when the split in her personality had begun. Perhaps it had been there from infancy and no one suspected. Or perhaps it had started during her teens, during the very times she'd been reminiscing about to Douglas, the "happy" days. It was possible that those were the "happy" days because she had already started on her flight from reality.

Of one thing he was almost certain, the split in her personality was complete. The woman he was talking to was unaware of the existence of her deformed twin. She remembered talking to Douglas on the telephone the previous night, and yet he knew that if he told her she had also talked to Mrs. Clarvoe, and in quite a different fashion, she would be incredulous and probably very angry. Nothing would be gained by antagonizing her. His job was to wait until the change occurred and the twin took over. Only the twin knew what had happened to Helen Clarvoe and where she was now. South Flower Street was miles long and had more brothels than restaurants.

Even if it had been safe to do so, there was no way of precipitating the change in Evelyn Merrick because no one knew what caused it. It could be something external, a word, a smell, a sound, a chance phrase of music, or it could be something inside, a sudden chemical change in the body itself.

"It was funny," she said, "hearing from Douglas again. I expected to feel all sorts of resentment against him, but I didn't. Odd, isn't it, how people plan what they'll do and say in a certain situation and then when the situation actually occurs, they don't do any of the things they've planned."

"What did you plan?"

"To make him feel like a worm. But I knew as soon as I heard his voice that I didn't have to say anything. He feels worse than any worm."

"Miss Merrick, how did you spend the day?"

"Looking for a job."

"Any particular kind of job, such as modeling, for instance?"

"*Modeling*. What on earth would give you that idea?"

"You're a very pretty girl."

"Nonsense. Thanks just the same, but it really is nonsense. I want a job with a future."

"You haven't been home, then, all day today?"

"No."

"Have you seen your mother?"

"No. I tried to get her at the flower shop this afternoon but they told me she was taking the rest of the afternoon off."

"She went to see Mrs. Clarvoe."

"Verna? Why on earth would she do that?"

"Douglas died this morning."

Evelyn sat quietly, her eyes lowered, her hands folded on her lap. When she spoke finally her voice was clear and distinct: "The coffee must be ready by now. I'll get you a cup."

"Miss Merrick . . ."

"What do you expect me to say, that I'm sorry? I'm not. I'm not sorry he's dead. He's better off. I'm only sorry he wasn't happier while he was alive."

It was the kindest thing he'd heard anyone say about Douglas since his death.

She asked, "How did it happen?"

Blackshear explained the circumstances of Douglas' death, while she sat with her head half-averted, looking contemplative, almost serene, like a child listening to a story she'd heard a dozen times before.

When he had finished, she said with a sigh, "Poor Douglas. In some ways he was the best of the bunch, of the Clarvoes, I mean. He at least had some warmth in him. Directed toward the wrong people, perhaps, but at least it was there."

"Helen has it, too."

"Helen is cold to the very marrow of her bones."

A premonition of disaster struck Blackshear like a spasm of pain. He had a feeling that her remark was intended to be quite literal, that the woman was trying to tell him Helen was already dead.

"Miss Merrick, I will ask you again."

"Yes?"

"Have you seen Helen Clarvoe today?"

"No."

"Do you know where she is?"

"No."

"Do you know if she's alive?"

"No."

"Do you remember telephoning her at her hotel last Monday night around 10 o'clock?"

"I can't remember something that never happened," she said

gently. "I wish I could help you, Mr. Blackshear, but I'm afraid I don't know any of the answers."

It's useless he thought, and turned toward the door. "Thank you for trying, anyway."

"You're welcome. When you find Helen, let me know."

"Why?"

"Auld lang syne or curiosity, you name it. I'll make a little bet with you, Mr. Blackshear."

"Such as?"

"When you do find her, I'll bet she has a man with her."

Anger rose in him like an overflow of bile, leaving a green and bitter taste on his tongue and a rawness in his throat. He couldn't trust himself to speak.

He opened the door and stepped outside. In spite of the lighted houses and the street lamps, the darkness seemed as impenetrable as a jungle.

Chapter 15

SHE OPENED her eyes and closed them again quickly because the light was so blinding, but in that instant she saw that she was in a small white room like a cubicle in a hospital and the enormous woman bending over her was dressed all in white like a nurse.

The woman said in a harsh tired voice, "She's coming to. Give her some more of that whiskey."

"If she's drunk already, what you want to give her more of the same for, Bella?"

"Shut up and do as I say. Nothing brings a drunk around faster than the smell of another drink. Hand me the bottle, Mollie."

"O.K."

"Now hold her head up while I pour. Ha ha ha, sounds like a society tea, eh? Madame Bella poured."

Miss Clarvoe tried to protest. She did not want the whiskey; it burned like acid. She jerked her head to one side and began to scream, but a hand closed over her mouth.

"You don't want to do that, dear," the woman called Bella said quite softly. "Maybe you're seeing things, eh? Maybe little animals running around, eh? Just take a nip or two of this and they'll go away."

"No, no! I don't want . . ."

"What's the matter, dear? You tell Bella. Everybody tells Bella their troubles. Maybe you got a monkey on your back, eh, dear?"

Miss Clarvoe shook her head. She didn't know what the woman was talking about. There was no monkey on her back, no little animals running around.

"Tell Bella, dear."

"I can't tell, I don't know," Miss Clarvoe said, her voice muffled against the fleshy palm of the woman's hand. "Let me go."

"Certainly, dear, just so long as you don't scream. I can't have you disturbing my other customers. A man comes in after a hard day at the office, he wants a nice quiet massage, he don't want to hear a lady screaming, it upsets him."

Customers. Massage. It wasn't a hospital, then, and the woman in white wasn't a nurse.

"No more carryings-on, eh, dear? Promise Bella."

"Yes. I promise."

Miss Clarvoe opened her eyes. She was lying on a couch, and at the foot of the couch a very pretty blonde girl with acne was standing with a bottle of whiskey in her hand. The other woman, Bella, was enormously fat; her flesh quivered at the slightest movement and her chins hung in folds against her swarthy neck. Only her eyes looked human. They were dark despairing eyes that had experienced too much and interpreted too little.

The mere exertion of talking made her pant, and when she removed her hand from Miss Clarvoe's mouth she pressed it against her own heart as if to reassure herself that it was still beating.

"That's good material in her coat," the blonde girl said. "Imported from Scotland, it says, see right there on the label?"

"You can get back on the job now, Mollie."

"I don't have any more appointments for tonight."

"Then go home."

"What if she starts kicking up a fuss again?"

"I can handle her," the fat woman said. "Bella can handle her. Bella knows what the trouble is. Bella understands."

"Yeah, sure," the blonde girl said with a contemptuous little smile. "I'll bet you do. Well, you can have it. *I* like the normal ones."

"Shut up, dear."

"I wonder what's so special about material imported from Scotland."

"Blow, dear, and close the door after you."

The blonde girl left and closed the door behind her.

Miss Clarvoe pressed her fingertips against her eyes. She couldn't understand what the two women had been talking about, none of it made sense to her. She felt nauseated and dizzy and her head ached just behind her left ear as if someone had struck her there.

"My head," she said. "My head hurts."

"Her head hurts yet, listen to that. Naturally your head hurts, dear. You've been hitting the bottle."

"No. I never drink, never."

"You were reeking of the stuff when I found you out cold on my doorstep. I was saying good-bye to one of our regular customers who came in for his treatment, and when I opened the door there you were, lying against it. Stiff, dear. But stiff."

"That's impossible. I don't drink."

"Just rinse your mouth out now and then, eh?" The fat woman was laughing, every inch of her was laughing, mouth, chins, belly, breasts. When she had finished she wiped the moisture from her face and neck with a handkerchief. "That's my trouble, I'm too jolly. I laugh too much. It makes me sweat. Oh, how I sweat, dear, it's just not human the way poor Bella sweats. How about another nip of whiskey, dear?"

"No. No!" Miss Clarvoe tried to get up, lost her balance and rolled over on to the floor. "I must—I must get home—they're waiting for me."

The fat woman put her hands under Miss Clarvoe's armpits and helped her to her feet. "Who's waiting for you, dear?"

"I—don't know."

"Well, if you don't know, there's no hurry, is there? Lie down for a bit. Bella will make you feel better."

"No, no." The fat woman's breath was hot against the back of her neck and smelled overpoweringly of aniseed. "I must . . . They're waiting." Someone was waiting for her, she knew that, but she couldn't remember who it was. The faces in her memory were blurred and indistinct, people were shadows, places were all alike. She leaned against the wall and said faintly, "May I—have some water?"

"Certainly, dear."

The woman brought her some water in a paper cup and watched her while she drank.

"Feeling better now, dear?"

"Yes."

"Your coat's dirty. Give it to me and I'll brush it off for you."

"No. No." She clutched the coat tightly around her body.

"Ah, you're one of the shy ones. Bella knows. Bella's been in this business for a long, long time. You don't have to be shy with Bella. By the way, who recommended me, dear?"

"I don't understand."

"How did you get my name?"

"I didn't. I don't know your name."

The fat woman stood very still. Her eyes, tucked away under folds of flesh, were dead and purple like grapes. "How come you picked my place?"

"I didn't. I didn't pick any . . ."

"We mustn't tell fibs, dear. Bella hates fibs, they stir her to anger. Who gave you my name?"

"No one."

"You just came here by a lucky accident, eh? Is that right, dear?"

"I don't remember," Miss Clarvoe whispered. "I can't remember—Evelyn . . ."

"Is that who you are, dear? Evelyn?"

"No. No! I was—I was with Evelyn. She brought me here. She said . . ." Miss Clarvoe paused, holding her hands against her trembling mouth.

"What did she say, dear?"

"She said I belonged here."

The fat woman nodded and smiled and rubbed her chins. "She's a discerning girl, that Evelyn, oh my, yes."

"I don't understand what she meant."

"Don't you, dear. Well, lie down and rest a bit and Bella will tell you later. Let me take your coat, dear. What sweet ankles you have. I used to have a well-turned ankle myself in the old days. Now I eat. I eat and eat because nobody loves me. Nobody loves Bella, she is fat as an elephant, yes, but she's smart. Give me your pretty little coat, dear."

Miss Clarvoe stood stiff with terror.

"I revolt you, eh, dear? Is that it? Bella revolts you?"

"Stay away from me."

"Or is it that you're just shy, dear?"

"You monstrous old slut," Miss Clarvoe said and lunged toward the door.

But the fat woman was there ahead of her. She stood with her back pressed against the door, her arms crossed on her enormous breasts.

"Bella hates to be called names, dear. It stirs her to anger."

"If you don't let me out of here, I'll scream. I'll scream until the police come."

Bella was quiet a moment, then she said bitterly, "I believe you would, you're a nasty piece if I ever saw one. Well, that's gratitude for you. . . . I take you in, I look after you, you lap up my good whiskey, I say pretty things to you, none of them true, of course. Your ankles are lousy, they're like pipe-stems. . . ."

"Open that door."

Bella did not open the door but she moved away from it, still talking, half to herself: "All the things I do for people, and what do I get in return? Dirty names and looks. Bella is human. Maybe she is as fat as an elephant, but she is human, she likes a little gratitude now and then. It's a wicked world, there's no gratitude in it. Get out of here, you nasty girl, get out. Bella is stirred to anger. Get out, get out."

But the nasty girl had already left, and she was talking to an empty room. She sat down heavily on the couch, one hand pressed against her heart. It was still beating, fluttering like a captive bird under smothering folds of flesh.

"People are no damned good," Bella said.

Helen Clarvoe couldn't run. Her legs felt weak, as if the muscles had atrophied from long disuse, and the pain in her head had become worse. When she tried to think, her thoughts melted and fused and only one stood out clearly and distinctly from the others: I must get away. I must escape. I must run.

It was not important where she ran to. She had no plan. She didn't even know where she was until she reached the corner and saw the street signs: South Flower Street and Ashworth Avenue. She repeated the names to herself, hoping they would form a pattern in her mind, but neither of the names meant anything to her, and the neighborhood was strange. She knew she had never seen it before just as she knew that she didn't drink. Yet she'd come here, had walked or ridden or been car-ried, and when she arrived she was drunk. *Stiff*, Bella had said, *but stiff. Naturally your head hurts, dear, you've been hitting the bottle.*

"I never drink," Miss Clarvoe said. "I never touch liquor. Someone must have poured it down my throat. Someone. Evelyn."

An old man waiting at the corner for the traffic light to

change looked at her over the top of his bifocals with interest and pleasure. He often talked to himself. It was nice to know other people did it, too.

Miss Clarvoe saw him looking and she turned away and color flooded her cheeks, as if he had caught a glimpse of her, naked.

"Heh, heh, heh," the old man said and shuffled across the street, his shoulders shaking with mirth. Even the young ones talked to themselves these days. It was the age of the atom. Madmen have taken over. "Heh, heh, heh."

Miss Clarvoe touched her face. It was burning with humiliation. The old man had seen her talking to herself, perhaps he'd seen more than that. Perhaps he'd been walking by when she came out of Bella's place and he knew all about what kind of place it was. She must get away from the old man.

Miss Clarvoe turned and began running in the opposite direction, her coat billowing behind her, her thin legs moving stiffly.

At the next corner she stopped, gasping for breath, and held on to a lamppost for support. The sign on the post read Figueroa Street. I am not lost, she thought. I know Figueroa Street, I will wait here on the corner until an empty taxicab comes along. But something in her mind, some sixth sense, warned her not to stand still, and she started out again. Not running. The running had attracted too much attention. She must be casual, ordinary. No one must find out that somewhere, along these streets, or other streets, she had lost the day. It was night. The day had gone, passed her by, passed without touching her.

She walked on, her head bent, as if she were searching the sidewalk and the gutters for her lost day. People passed, cars roared by, the night was filled with noise and light and movement, but Miss Clarvoe did not raise her head. *I must pretend*, she thought. *I must pretend not to know I'm being followed.*

If she was clever enough, if she could control her panic, she might be able to find out who it was. Bella? The old man who'd caught her talking to herself? One of Bella's friends? None of them had anything to gain by following her, not even money. She had lost her purse, along with the day.

A bus was unloading at the next intersection and she quickened her pace and mingled with the crowd that was getting off the bus. Secure for a moment, she looked back, peering through the moving jungle of faces. Only one face stood out among the others, pale, composed, half-smiling. Evelyn Merrick. She was standing in the shadowed doorway of a small TV repair shop, leaning idly against the plate-glass window as if she had just paused for a rest during an evening stroll. But Miss Clarvoe knew it was not an evening stroll, it was a chase, and she was the beast in view. She moved in sudden terror. The woman at the window also moved. For an instant, before fear blacked out all thought, Helen realized that the woman was her own image.

She turned and began to run across the street, blind and deaf and numb with panic. She did not even feel the impact of the car that struck her.

When she returned to consciousness she was lying against the curb and people were standing over her, all talking at once.

"Saw her with my own eyes, out she dashed . . ."

"Red light . . ."

"Drunk, for sure. You can smell it a mile away."

"Honest to God, I didn't *see* her!"

"Let's get out of here. I don't want to be called as a witness."

"Come on, Joe, come on. I just can't stand the sight of blood."

Blood, Miss Clarvoe thought. I'm bleeding, then. It's all come true, what she said to me the first night. She saw it in her crystal ball, I was to be in an accident, bleeding, mutilated.

"What's a little blood, you watch prize fights all the time, don't you?"

"Must of been drunk . . ."

"With my own eyes . . ."

"Somebody call an ambulance."

"The lady in the green hat went to phone her husband, he's a doctor."

A young man wearing a cabdriver's uniform took off his coat and tried to put it under Miss Clarvoe's head. She thrust it away and sat up painfully. "I'm all right. Leave me alone."

The words were muffled and indistinct but the young man heard them. "You're supposed to lie there until the doctor comes."

"I don't need a doctor."

"I took a course in first aid and it says that in the book. Keep the patient warm and . . ."

"I'm not hurt." She dragged herself to her feet and began wiping the moisture off her face with a handkerchief, not knowing which was blood and which was sweat from all the running she'd done.

The crowd began to disperse—the show was over, no one was killed, too bad, better luck next time.

Only the young man in the cabbie's uniform lingered on, looking fretful. "It wasn't *my* fault. Everyone could see it wasn't my fault. You dashed right out in front of my cab, didn't give me a chance to stop, craziest thing I ever saw in my life."

Miss Clarvoe looked back at the doorway of the shop where she'd seen Evelyn Merrick just before the accident. The girl had left. Or else she had stepped farther back into the shadows to wait. That was the game she played best, waiting in shadows, walking in the night, watching for the unwary.

The cabbie was still talking, aggrieved and belligerent. "Everyone could see I did the best I could. I stopped, didn't I? I tried to minister first aid, didn't I?"

"Oh stop it, stop it! There's no time for argument. No *time*, I tell you."

He stepped back looking surprised. "I don't get . . ."

"Listen to me. What's your name?"

"Harry. Harry Reis."

"Listen, Harry, I must get away from here. I'm being followed. She was—I saw her in that doorway over there a few minutes ago. She intends to kill me."

"You don't say." A faint derisive smile stretched his mouth. He didn't even glance back at the doorway she was pointing at. "Maybe you escaped from somewheres, huh?"

"Escaped?"

"Sure. Escaped. Climbed over the wires."

She shook her head in mystification. He seemed to be talking in riddles like the fat woman, Bella. Monkeys on the back, little animals running around, wires to climb over. They were all English words but Miss Clarvoe couldn't understand them. She thought, perhaps I am the foreigner, perhaps I have been out of touch too long; the language has changed, and the people. The world has been taken over by the Bellas, and the Evelyn Merricks and little men like Harry with sly insinuating smiles. I must get back to my own room and lock the door against the ugliness.

"I must . . ."

"Sure," Harry said. "Sure. Anything for a lady."

He led the way to his cab. Miss Clarvoe dropped the bloody handkerchief on the curb and followed him. She wasn't aware yet of any pain, only of a terrible stiffness that seemed to cover her entire body like a plaster cast.

She got into the back seat of the cab and pulled her coat close around her. She remembered the blonde girl in Bella's place asking what was so special about fabric imported from Scotland. Miss Clarvoe didn't know, and it seemed important for her to figure it out. There were sheep, plenty of sheep, all over the world, but perhaps the Scottish sheep had finer wool. Wool. Sheep. Blackshear. She had forgotten about Mr. Blackshear. He was miles and years away, she couldn't even recall his face except that it looked a little like her father's.

The inside of the cab was dark and warm and the radio was turned on to a panel discussion on politics. All of the people on the panel had very definite ideas, firmly spoken. All of them knew exactly where the day had gone and what to expect from the night.

Harry got in and turned the radio off. "Where to?"

"The Monica Hotel."

"You live there?"

"Yes."

"You been living there long?"

"Yes."

"All the time steady?"

"Yes."

She could tell he didn't believe her. What did he believe? What were the wires she was supposed to have climbed over? She had never seen Harry before, never, she was sure of that. Yet he acted as though he knew secrets about her, ugly secrets.

"I will pay you," she said. "I have money in my hotel suite."

"Yes, ma'am."

"I'll send the boy down with it."

"Yes, ma'am."

She knew from his tone that he didn't expect any money, that he was humoring her as he would any drunk or liar or madman who happened to be his passenger. The customer is always right.

The headlights of the car following shone into the rear-view mirror and Miss Clarvoe saw Harry's face for a minute quite clearly. It was young and pleasant and very, very honest. A nice open face. No one would suspect what kind of mind lay behind it. The fat woman wore her malice and her miseries for all the world to see; Harry's were hidden underneath the youthful blandness of his face, like worms at the core of an apple that looks sound from the outside.

Yet even Harry, even apple-cheeked, wormy-brained Harry knew where his day had gone. She had lost hers, dropped it somewhere like a handkerchief and picked it up again, soiled, from the dirty floor of a slut.

"Harry."

"Yes, ma'am." His tone was still sardonically polite.

"What day is this?"

"Thursday."

Thursday. Douglas died this morning. Mr. Blackshear came to the hotel to tell me about it. I promised to go home and keep mother company. Mr. Blackshear offered to drive me, but I refused. I didn't want him to touch me again. I was afraid. I went and waited in front of the hotel for a cab. People kept passing, strangers, hundreds of strangers. I felt very nervous and upset. The people terrified me and I didn't want to go home and face mother and hear her carry on about poor dead Douglas the way she did about father. I knew what a dreadful show she would put on. She always does, but none of it's real.

Cabs kept passing, some of them empty, but I couldn't force myself to hail one. Then someone spoke my name and I turned and saw Evelyn Merrick. She was standing right beside me, smiling, very sure of herself. The strangers, the traffic, didn't bother her. She'd always liked crowds and people, the more the merrier. I held my head up high, pretending I was just as poised and confident as she was. But it didn't work. I could never fool Evelyn. She said, "Scared, aren't you?" and she took my arm. I didn't mind. I usually hate people to touch me, but somehow this was different. The contact made me feel more secure. "Come on, let's have a drink some place," she said.

Come on, let's have a drink, let's lose a day, let's drop a handkerchief.

"You say something, ma'am?"

"No."

"Like I told you, if you want to change your mind and go back . . ."

"Go back where?"

"Back where you came from."

"I don't know what you're insinuating," she said as calmly as possible. "I *am* going back where I came from. I live at the Monica Hotel. I have a permanent suite there and have had for almost a year. Is that clear to you?"

"Yes, ma'am." His tone added, clear as mud. Harry had been around, he knew a thing or two, sometimes even three, and he was pretty certain that the woman had been playing around with narcotics, probably yellow jackets. She was obviously a lady and ladies didn't go in so much for heroin. Nembutal was more genteel both to use and to procure. You didn't have to hang around a street corner or the back booth of a café waiting for your contact. You could get yellow jackets just sitting in a nice upholstered chair in some fancy doctor's office, telling how you were nervous and worn-out and couldn't sleep.

Sleep wasn't always what they got, though. Sometimes the stuff went into reverse, and they did crazy things like taking off all their clothes in the middle of Pershing Park or racing up Sunset Boulevard at eighty miles an hour and fighting with the police when they were arrested. Ladies could sometimes behave worse than women.

He glanced back at Miss Clarvoe. She was crouched in the right-hand corner of the cab, her arms pressed tautly across her chest, her lips moving slightly as if in prayer: She took my arm, I remember that, she took my arm like an old friend and said, "*Godiona gavotch.*" It was our secret password in school when we were in trouble and needed help. "Godiona gavotch," I repeated, and suddenly it was as if the years had never passed, and we were friends back in school, giggling after the lights were out and plotting against the French mistress and sharing the treats from home. "Come and have a drink," she said. It was always like that. Evelyn was the one who initiated things, who formed the ideas and made the suggestions. I was the one who tagged along. I worshipped her, I wanted to be exactly like her, I would have followed her anywhere, like a sheep, the goat, the victim. I was marked, even then, and the marks have not faded with the years but have grown more distinct. Even Harry knows. He looks at me with contempt and his voice drips with it.

Apple-cheeked Harry, I see your worms.

"You want to go in the front or the back, ma'am?" Harry said.

"I am not in the habit of using a service entrance."

"I just thought, being you were messed up a little . . ."

"It doesn't matter." It did matter, she wanted nothing more than to go in the back entrance and sneak up to her room unnoticed, but it was impossible. Her keys had been in the purse she'd lost. "About the fare, I'll send a bellboy down with the money. How much is it?"

"Three dollars even." He stopped the cab at the marquee of the hotel but he made no move to get out and open the door for her. He didn't expect a tip, he didn't even expect the fare, and for once it didn't matter much to him. She was a creepy dame, he wanted to see the end of her.

Miss Clarvoe opened the door for herself and stepped out onto the sidewalk and pulled her collar up high to hide the wound under her ear. The torn stockings, the rip in her coat, she couldn't hide; she could only move as rapidly as possible through the lobby, trying to outrun the stares of the curious.

Mr. Horner, the elderly desk clerk, was busy registering some new guests, but when he saw Miss Clarvoe he dropped everything and came over to her, his eyes bulging and his mouth working with excitement.

"Why, Miss Clarvoe. Why, Miss *Clarvoe*, for goodness sake . . ."

"I lost my keys. May I have a duplicate set, please?"

"Everybody's been looking for you, Miss Clarvoe. Just everybody. Why, they . . ."

"They need look no further."

"But what happened to you?"

She answered without hesitation. "It was such a nice day I decided to take a little trip into the country." Had it been a nice day? She didn't know. She couldn't remember the weather of the day any more than she could its contents. "The country," she added, "is very beautiful this time of year. The lupine is in bloom, you know. Very lovely." The lies rolled glibly off her tongue. She couldn't stop them. Any words were better than none; any memory, however false, was better than a blank. "Unfortunately, I tripped over a boulder and tore my coat and my stockings." As she talked the scene came into sharper focus. Details appeared, the shape and color of the boulder she'd fallen over, the hills blue with lupine and dotted with the wild orange of poppies, and beyond the hills the gray-green dwarfs of mountains with their parched and stunted trees.

"You should," Mr. Horner said with reproach, "have let someone know. Everyone's been in a tizzy. The police were here, with a Mr. Blackshear."

"Police?"

"I had to let them into your suite. They insisted. There was nothing I could do." He leaned across the desk and added in a confidential whisper, "They thought you might have been kidnapped by a maniac."

Color splashed across Miss Clarvoe's face and disappeared, leaving her skin ashen. Kidnapped by a maniac? No, it wasn't like that at all. I went with an old friend to have a drink. I was frightened and confused by all the strangers and the traffic, and she rescued me. She put her hand on my arm and I felt secure. By myself I was a nothing, but with Evelyn there beside me I could see people looking at us with interest and curiosity, yes even admiration. "Come and have a drink," she said.

I could have stood there forever, being looked at, being admired—it is a wonderful feeling. But Evelyn likes excitement, she wanted to be on the move. She kept saying, come on, come on, come on, as if she had some very intriguing plan in mind and wanted me to share it. I said, "I promised to go home and stay with mother because Douglas is dead." She called each of them an ugly name, mother and Douglas, and when I looked shocked she laughed at me for being a prude. I've never wanted to be a prude; I've simply never known how to be anything else. "I've got a friend," Evelyn said. "He's a lot of fun, a real joker. Let's go over and have some laughs."

Douglas was dead, my own brother; I shouldn't have felt like laughing, and yet I did. I asked her who the friend was who was such a joker and I remember what she answered. It's odd how the name has stuck in my mind when I've forgotten so many other things. Jack Terola. "He is an artist with the camera," Evelyn said. "He's going to take pictures of me that will be shown all over the country. He's going to make me immortal." I felt the knife of envy twisting in my heart. I wanted to be immortal, too.

"I had to co-operate with the police," Mr. Horner said. "I didn't have any choice. It was a question of handing over the keys to your suite or having them taken from me."

"I dislike the idea of anyone prying into my personal affairs."

"Everyone acted in your best interests, Miss Clarvoe."

"Indeed."

"After all, anything might have happened."

"What happened," she said coldly, "is that I went into the country with a friend of mine."

"Ah, yes. To see the lupine in bloom."

"That's correct."

Mr. Horner turned away, his lip curling slightly. It was November. The lupine wouldn't be in bloom for another three or four months.

He returned with the duplicate set of keys and laid them on the desk. "There are some messages for you, Miss Clarvoe. You are to call Mr. Blackshear immediately; he is at your mother's house."

"Thank you."

"Oh yes, and someone asked me to put this note in your box. A young lady."

The note was written in an ostentatious backhand on hotel stationery which had been folded twice:

I am waiting in the lobby. I must see you at once. Evelyn Merrick.

She wanted to run but her legs ached with weariness; they would not carry her farther. She'd already run too far, too fast, down too many strange and terrifying streets.

Chapter 16

SHE TURNED and saw Evelyn Merrick coming toward her across the lobby, picking her way fastidiously through the crowd. The day, which had changed Miss Clarvoe, had changed Evelyn too. She wasn't smiling and self-assured as she'd been when they met on the street. She was a grim-faced, cold-eyed stranger, dressed all in black as if in mourning.

"I see you got my note."

"Yes," Miss Clarvoe said, "I have it."

"We must have a talk."

"Yes." Yes, we must. I must find out how I lost the day, how the minutes passed overhead without touching me, like birds in a hurry. Wild-geese minutes. I remember father took us hunting once, Evelyn and me. Father was angry with me that day because the sun gave me a headache. He said I was a spoilsport and a crybaby. He said, *"Why can't you be more like Evelyn?"*

"Everyone's been worried about you," Evelyn said. "Where have you been?"

"You know, you know very well. I was with you."

"What are you talking about?"

"We went into the country together—to see the lupine—we . . ."

The stranger's voice was harsh and ugly. "You've always told fantastic lies, Helen, but this is going too far. I haven't seen you for nearly a year."

"You mustn't try to deny it. . . ."

"I'm not *trying* to deny it. I am denying it!"

"Please keep your voice down. People are staring. I can't have people staring. I have a reputation, a name, to protect."

"No one is paying the least attention to us."

"Yes, they are. You see, my stockings are torn, and my coat. From the country. You have forgotten how we went into the country, you and I, to see the lupine. I tripped over a boulder and fell." But her voice trailed upward into a question mark, and her eyes were uncertain and afraid. "You—you remember now?"

"There's nothing to remember."

521

"Nothing?"

"I haven't seen you for nearly a year, Helen."

"But this morning—this morning you met me outside the hotel. You asked me to have a drink with you, you said you were on your way over to see a man who would make you immortal and you wanted me to come along."

"It doesn't even make sense."

"Yes, yes, it does! I even remember the man's name. Terola. Jack Terola."

Evelyn's voice was quiet, insistent. "You went to see this man Terola?"

"I don't know. I think we—we both went, you and I. After all, I wouldn't go to such a place alone and besides Terola was your friend, not mine."

"I never heard the name before in my life. Until I read the evening papers."

"Papers?"

"Terola was murdered shortly before noon today," Evelyn said. "It's important for you to remember, Helen. Did you go there this morning?"

Miss Clarvoe said nothing, and her face was blank.

"Did you see Terola this morning, Helen?"

"I must—I must go upstairs."

"We have to talk."

"No. No, I must go upstairs and lock my door against all the ugliness." She turned, slowly, and began walking toward the elevator, her shoulders hunched, her hands jammed into the pockets of her coat as if she wanted to avoid all physical contact with other people.

She waited until one of the elevators was empty. Then she stepped inside and ordered the operator to close the door immediately. The operator, an old man, was no bigger than a child, as if the years he'd spent inside the tiny elevator had stunted his growth. He was accustomed to Miss Clarvoe's idiosyncrasies, such as riding alone in elevators, and he'd been well enough tipped, in the past, to indulge them.

He shut the door and as the elevator began to ascend he kept his eyes on the floor indicator. "A wintry day, Miss Clarvoe."

"I don't know. I lost mine."

"Beg pardon, ma'am?"

"I lost my day," she said slowly. "I've looked everywhere for it but I can't find it."

"Are you—are you feeling all right, Miss Clarvoe?"

"Don't call me that."

"Ma'am?"

"Call me Evelyn."

"Yes, ma'am."

"Well, say it. Go ahead. *Say Evelyn*."

"Evelyn," the old man said and began to tremble.

Back in her suite she locked the door and without even taking off her coat she went immediately to the telephone. As she dialed, she felt the excitement rising inside her like molten lava in a crater.

"Mrs. Clarvoe?"

"Is that—that's you, Evelyn?"

"Certainly it's me. I've done you another favor."

"Please. Have mercy."

"Don't snivel, I hate that, I hate snivelers."

"Evelyn . . ."

"I just wanted to tell you that I've found Helen for you. I have her all locked up in her hotel room, safe and sound."

"Is she all right?"

"Don't worry, I'm looking after her. I'm the only one who knows how to treat her. She's been a bad girl, she needs a little discipline. She tells lies, you know, awful lies, so she must be taught a lesson or two like the others."

"Let me talk to Helen."

"Oh no. She can't talk right now. It isn't her turn. We have to take turns, you know. It's very inconvenient because Helen won't voluntarily give me my turn so I just have to go ahead and take it. She was feeling weak from the accident, and her head hurt, so I simply took over. I feel fine. I'm never sick. I leave that to her. All the sordid things like being sick or getting old, I leave to her. I'm only twenty-one; that old crock is over thirty. . . ."

Evelyn Merrick was waiting for Blackshear in the lobby when he arrived twenty minutes later.

"I got here as soon as I could," Blackshear said. "Where is Helen?"

"Locked in her room. I followed her up and tried to talk to her, but she paid no attention to my knocking. So I listened at the door. I could hear her inside."

"What was she doing?"

"You know what she was doing, Mr. Blackshear. I told you when I called you. She was telephoning, using my name, my voice, pretending to be me."

Blackshear was grim. "I wish that's all it was, a child's game, like pretending."

"What else is it?"

"She has a rare form of insanity, Miss Merrick, the disease I thought you had. A doctor would call it multiple personality. A priest might call it possession by a devil. Helen Clarvoe is possessed by a devil and she gives your name to it."

"Why should she do that to me?"

"Are you willing to help me find out?"

"I don't know. What must I do?"

"We'll go up to her room and talk to her."

"She won't let us in."

"We can try," Blackshear said. "All I seem able to do for Helen is try. Try, and fail, and try again."

They took the elevator up to the third floor and walked down the long carpeted hall to Miss Clarvoe's suite. The door was closed and locked. No light showed around its edges, but Blackshear could hear a woman talking inside the room. It was not Helen's voice, tired, uninterested; it was loud and brash and shrill, like a schoolgirl's.

He rapped sharply on the door with his knuckles and called out, "Helen? Let me in."

"Go away, you old fool, and leave us alone."

"Are you in there, Helen?"

"Look at the mess you've got me in now. He's found me. That's what you wanted, isn't it? You've always been jealous of me; you've always tried to cut me out of your life. Now you've done it, calling in that man Blackshear and the police to hunt me down like a common criminal. I'm not a common criminal. All I did to Terola was touch him with the scissors to teach him a little lesson. How was I to know his flesh was soft as butter? An ordinary man wouldn't even have bled, my touch was so delicate. It wasn't my fault the poor fool died. But the police won't believe that. I'll have to hide here with you. Just you and me, how about that? God knows if I can stand it, you should be able to. You're dull company, old girl, you can't deny that. I may have to slip out now and then for a bit of fun."

Blackshear tried to call out again but the words died of despair in his throat: *Fight, Helen. Fight back. Stand up to her.* He began pounding on the door with his fists.

"Listen to that, will you? He's trying to break the door down to get to his sweetheart, isn't that touching? Little does he know how many doors he'll have to break down; this one's only the first. There are a hundred more and that pitiful idiot out there thinks he can do it with his fists. Funny boy. Tell him to go away, Helen. Tell him not to bother us. Tell him if he doesn't go away he'll never see you alive again. Go on. Speak. *Speak*, you ugly crone!"

A pause, then Helen's voice, a tattered whisper, "Mr. Blackshear. Paul. Go away."

"Helen, hang on. I'm going to help you."

"Go away, go away."

"Hear that, lover boy? Go away, she says. Lover boy. God, that's funny. What a romance you had, eh, Helen? Did you *really* think anyone could fall in love with you, you old hag? Take a look in the crystal ball, you crow."

She began to laugh. The sound rose and fell, a siren screaming disaster, and then there was a sudden silence, as if the loud night were holding its breath.

Blackshear pressed his mouth against the crack of the door and said, "Helen, listen to me."

"Go away."

"Unlock your door. Evelyn Merrick is here with me."

"Liar."

"Unlock your door and you can see for yourself. You are not Evelyn. Evelyn is out here with me."

"Liar, liar, liar!"

"Please, Helen, let us in so we can help you. . . . Say something to her, Miss Merrick."

"We are not trying to fool you," Evelyn said. "This is really Evelyn, Helen."

"Liars!" But the lock clicked and the chain slid back and

slowly the door opened and Miss Clarvoe's tormented face peered out. She spoke to Blackshear, her pale mouth working painfully to form the words: "Helen is not here. She went away. She is old and sick and full of misery and wants to be let alone."

"Listen to me, Helen," Blackshear said. "You are not old and sick. . . ."

"*I'm* not, no. *She* is. You're mixed up. I'm Evelyn. I'm fine. I'm twenty-one. I'm pretty, I'm popular, I have lots of fun. I never get sick or tired. I'm going to be immortal." She stopped suddenly, her eyes fixed on Evelyn Merrick, fascinated, repelled. "That girl—who is she?"

"You know who she is, Helen. She's Evelyn Merrick."

"She's an impostor. Get rid of her. Tell her to go away."

"All right," Blackshear said wearily. "All right." He turned to Evelyn. "You'd better go down to the lobby and call a doctor."

Miss Clarvoe watched Evelyn go down the hall and get into the elevator. "Why should she call a doctor? Is she sick?"

"No."

"Why should she call a doctor, then, if she isn't sick?" She added peevishly, "I don't much like you. You're sly. You're a sly old man. You're too old for me. Not much use your hanging around. I'm only twenty-one. I have a hundred boy friends. . . ."

"Helen, please."

"Don't call me that, don't say that name. I'm not Helen."

"Yes, you are. You're Helen, and I don't want you to be anybody else. I like you exactly as you are. Other people will, too, if you'll let them. They'll like you just as you are, just for yourself alone, Helen."

"No! I'm not Helen, I don't want to be Helen! I hate her!"

"Helen is a fine young woman," Blackshear said quietly. "She is intelligent and sensitive—yes, and pretty too."

"Pretty? That crock? That hag? That ugly crone?"

She started to close the door but Blackshear pressed his weight against it. She released the door and stepped backward into the room, one hand behind her back, like a child concealing a forbidden object. But Blackshear did not have to guess what she was concealing. He could see her image in the round mirror above the telephone stand.

"Put down the paper knife, Helen. Put it back on the desk where it belongs. You're very strong, you might hurt someone accidentally. . . . How did you meet Terola in the first place, Helen?"

"In a bar. He was having a drink and he looked over at me and fell in love with me at first sight. Men do. They can't help it. I have this magnetism. Do you feel it?"

"Yes. Yes, I feel it. Put down the knife, Helen."

"I'm not Helen! I am Evelyn. Say it. Say I'm Evelyn."

He stared at her, saying nothing, and suddenly she wheeled around and ran across the room to the mirror. But the face she saw in it was not her own. It was not a face at all, it was a dozen faces, going round and round—Evelyn and Douglas and Blackshear, Verna and Terola and her father, Miss Hudson and Harley Moore and the desk clerk and the little old man in the elevator—all the faces were revolving like a ferris wheel, and as they revolved, they moved their mouths and screamed out words *"What's the matter with you, kid, are you crazy?" "You've always told the most fantastic lies." "What a pity we didn't have a girl like Evelyn." "You can't make a silk purse out of a sow's ear." "Why can't you be more like Evelyn?"*

The voices faded into silence, the ferris wheel of faces stopped, and there was only one image left in the mirror. It was her own face, and the mouth that moved was her own mouth, and the words that came out were uttered by her own voice: "God help me."

Memory stabbed at her with agonizing thrusts. She remembered the bars, the phone booths, the running, the strange streets. She remembered Terola and the odd, incredulous way he looked just before he died and the acrid smell of the coffee boiling over on the stove. She remembered taking the bills from her own money clip and then thinking later that they'd been stolen. She remembered the cat in the alley, the rays from the night air, the taste of rain, the young man who'd laughed because she was waterproof. . . .

"Give me the knife, Helen."

In the mirror she could see Blackshear approaching, slowly and cautiously, a hunter with a beast in view.

"It's all right, Helen. Don't get excited. Everything's going to be all right."

A pause, and then he began to talk again in a low, persuasive voice, about doctors and hospitals and rest and care and the future. Always the future, as if it was definite and tangible, rosy and round like an apple.

She stared into the crystal ball of the mirror and she saw her future, the nights poisoned by memories, the days corroded by desire.

"It's only a matter of time, Helen. You'll be well again."

"Be quiet," she said. "You lie."

She looked down at the knife in her hand and it seemed to her that it alone could speak the truth, that it was her last, her final friend.

She pressed the knife into the soft hollow of her throat. She felt no pain, only a little surprise at how pretty the blood looked, like bright and endless ribbons that would never again be tied.

FOOLS' GOLD

Dolores Hitchens

Chapter One

THE FIRST time they drove by the house Eddie was so scared he ducked his head down. Skip laughed at him. Above the rattling of the motor, Skip jeered, "What's the matter with you? Afraid the old woman's got X-ray eyes or something? She's a mind reader, maybe? She's looking out now and spotting us? You nuts?" What he really meant, as Eddie knew, was that Eddie was chicken.

Now that they were past the house, headed downhill past empty lots, Eddie cast a glance back. "Hell, it's such a doggone big place, that's all. Important-looking." And in this hour of near twilight, in his opinion, kind of spooky and ominous.

"The bigger they come the harder they fall," Skip pronounced. He was peering ahead to the corner where the side street entered the main boulevard from Pasadena. Suddenly he chucked Eddie in the ribs. "Hey, there's the chick now!" His tone had taken on a certain confidential excitement.

A girl of around seventeen sat on the bench at the bus stop. She had a couple of books in her lap, one open between her hands, and her head was bent over it, the book slanted so that its pages caught the last thin light from the sky. Her hair was short and curly, a soft lustrous brown. "Look at that. A dish," Skip was saying. As they went by Eddie gave her a single nervous glance and Skip an all-out stare, but she didn't look up. She wore a plain blue coat that looked old for her, white sandals, and a small white handbag hung from her wrist. Her lashes and little winglike brows were dark against the creamy color of her skin.

"She's on her way to night school now," Skip explained. "Taking a secretarial course. The old lady tried to goose her into nursing school, but she wouldn't bite. You want to meet her tonight? I could introduce you when typing class is out. Be in the hall."

"Maybe one of us ought to kind of lay low," Eddie said. "I mean——" He paused to watch what Skip was doing with the car. Skip had waited for a lull in the traffic on the boulevard, then cut sharply into a U-turn. "Hey, for the lova Pete!"

531

"Just going back for another look. We've got to have that layout down pat."

"Oh, Lord." Eddie hunkered down into the seat, trying to squirm out of sight of the bench. "You want her to know we've been out *here*?"

"Why not? It's a free country." Skip often pretended to be dense like this.

"Look, afterwards, when the thing happens, won't they begin to ask about strangers hanging around, other people in the neighborhood——"

"Oh, relax, for Chrissakes." Skip swung the car jauntily close to the bench on which the girl sat, then whistled his wolf call. She lifted her face at that, staring at the car; but Eddie sensed that she hadn't recognized Skip. She wore a confused, foggy expression, as if her mind were on the book or as if her eyes, tired from reading, had trouble adjusting to the distance.

The old car puffed and rumbled as it started back up the grade. Skip nursed it with gas from the choke. Eddie said, "She didn't seem to know you."

"Getting dark," Skip said. "Anyhow, we'll meet her tonight at school."

He had already dismissed Karen Miller from his mind, Eddie saw, and was again fascinated by the house. The roof made a tall, turreted line against the darkening sky. It was an aloof and aristocratic old house, settled in amid dusty cedars and deodars, surrounded by almost a square block of lawns and shrubs. A mansion, Eddie thought, and the idea of fooling around it and the old woman who owned it made prickles of icy bumps crawl on his arms.

Suddenly a couple of lights went on inside, one upstairs and one down. "Doggone!" Skip muttered. "You see that? Both at once? Somebody's there with her. I'll find out from Karen tonight who it is."

"Maybe a maid." Eddie needed to do something with his hands, so he took cigarettes and a pack of matches from his jacket pocket and lit a smoke.

Skip shook his head. "She doesn't keep a servant. Too cheap. She makes the chick help her and together they do it all, a hell of a job from what Karen tells me. A regular moperoo."

"A place that big . . . must be a hundred rooms——"

"Nah. All she has is a gardener. He comes by the day, three times a week. Old guy, deaf as a post. Lives miles from here."

"Well, then, this relative of hers——"

Skip's teeth gleamed as he smiled. He was small and wiry, a reddish blond with pale, stony eyes, and when he smiled he looked like a fox. "Yeah, it must be him, the guy from Las Vegas." They were past the house now. Looking back at it through the masking branches of trees, Eddie caught a cold, faint twinkle of light like a star's, and this somehow seemed a warning, making the place more dangerous, more impregnable than ever. He choked over words he couldn't get out.

The car picked up speed as the street leveled out. Beyond the Havermann place the street skirted vacant hilly acres rising to foothills, then descended again to another through boulevard, this one cross-town from Los Angeles, the route they'd taken to get here. Neon signs and street lamps were beginning to flare against the dusk. "Well, what do you say?" Skip asked. "Want a hamburger and coffee before we go on?"

"Sure," Eddie said, trying to sound easy. His hands were cold and his fingers kept wanting to twitch; he felt a repeated need to swallow. He hoped that Skip didn't notice his nervousness, and at the same time he envied Skip's cool manner. This was something to keep you bug-eyed.

They parked near a diner and went in. It was fairly full, but they found a couple of stools near the end. When the waitress had come, taken the order and gone again, Skip began to toy with a pencil on a paper napkin. He muttered to Eddie, "I'll bet it's at least fifty grand." He wrote it out on the napkin: $50,000.00, and Eddie broke into a sweat. They were right in the open, under lights, next to other people. He grabbed the napkin and shoved it in his pocket and Skip laughed.

"What's the matter, Eddie?"

"Well, that just wasn't smart."

"Who says?"

"I do." But Eddie didn't back it up with a glance at Skip; he fiddled with the coin receiver for the juke box, reading the array of record titles, finally dropping in a dime for a tune.

"You got a complaint? You want to run this show?"

"It's still your show," Eddie said stiffly.

Skip stared for another moment and then his mood underwent one of its quick causeless changes. He stuffed the pencil into his coat pocket and slumped on the stool, bracing his head with his hand. "Oh, what the hell." He began to watch an old man working behind the counter, cleaning off the dirty dishes into a big tin tray. The man was about sixty, going to fat, had watery eyes and almost no hair, wore a white tee shirt and a white duck apron. His big arms were pocked with scars and a network of broken veins. "See him? You know what? In a few years that's you and me, Eddie old boy. Restaurant swampers. Or dishwashers. If we're lucky. If we aren't lucky we'll be hobos, freezing in rags in a culvert."

Eddie felt cornered. "Ah, don't start singing the blues for Chrissakes."

But Skip slumped lower, his eyes dull. "Figure it out. I'm twenty-two. You're almost as old. Who're we trying to fool, going to night school, me taking typing and bookkeeping and you studying metalwork. Who's going to hire us when we finish?"

Eddie looked at him. "We could get a break."

"Who from? Some personnel manager? Some cluck too dumb to want to know what we've been doing up to now?"

Eddie shifted his position, began to fish for another dime to drop into the record player. But Skip grabbed his wrist and held it, his finger digging into his flesh. "They give you a form to fill in, see? Every year for the past five years——" With his free hand Skip sketched five imaginary lines on the counter. His lips were pulled off his teeth in a fierce, foxy grin. "Where were you last year, friend? And the year before that? Weren't you in some kind of little trouble? Would you care to give us your former address? Wasn't it out in the country and weren't you sort of working for the state?"

Skip released Eddie's hand suddenly and Eddie sat huddled, wondering who had been watching.

After a minute in a low tone Eddie said, "Look, Skip, I've told you I didn't——"

"You mean they took those two years for nothing?"

"Yes."

"That's kind of expensive nothing. Don't you think you might have some change coming?" The waitress came and put down the food and the coffee, and there was silence while they dug out the money to pay her. "Now look. Afterwards, when we're swamping dirty crockery, we can't say we never had a chance. We had a big one. We had four cherries and a bell going bong-bong-bong and everybody screaming jackpot. We just pushed it away, that's all."

"Who's pushing it away? I'm not," Eddie said humbly.

"You're not?"

They began to eat. Eddie wondered why Skip had the recurring urge to test and torment him. He ate and thought. Under the uneasiness he knew that Skip was right; there were freakish circumstances here which wouldn't be apt to happen again. How often did you run into a girl like Karen, an odd ball, trusting Skip and telling him all that stuff about the old woman and the guy from Las Vegas and the money? In some ways Karen must be a dope, because what did she know about Skip? If she had known the truth, she wouldn't have told Skip a word about anything bigger than a nickel.

Skip chewed slowly and then he said, "What we ought to do now is to go back to the house and scout around. It'll be dark. With lights on inside we might see something."

Eddie looked at him. Skip was all right again, friendly, sure of himself. "What about classes?"

"So we're fifteen minutes late." Skip shrugged.

Eddie didn't argue because he wouldn't admit even to himself the squeamish dismay in his own vitals. He had to measure up and quit being a drag on Skip. He and Skip had been friends for years, ever since grammar school, with Skip the leader and organizer and Eddie the follower. Even the separations, while one or the other served time in reformatories and jails, hadn't broken the pattern. "What do you think you'll see? The money?" he asked finally.

They went out to the car again. Skip said, "I've got to make sure it's on the up-and-up and Karen isn't just handing me a line. I want to see the old woman and the inside of the house, and check what Karen told me. If I see the relative counting his dough, all the better."

Eddie sensed that Skip, in spite of what he said about Karen, was pretty sure of her. Skip had never had any trouble with women lying to him. Something in his face and manner discouraged it.

They drove back the way they had come. The last of the twilight had faded and the street lamps had a yellow brightness against the night. In the block next to the Havermann property a thin grove of young eucalyptus trees straggled down from the hilly rising almost to the curb. Here and there were a few wild and neglected lantana thickets almost as high as a man's head. Eddie parked, got out, looked around. He nodded toward the hills. "Up there. Get it?"

Eddie could make out only the line of hills against the sky, the thicket dark among the trees. "What do you mean?"

"High ground. We go on up there and circle around, we can look *down*. Down into the house." Skip shuffled his shoes. "Anything looks interesting, we'll creep in close."

He started off with Eddie following in his tracks. Dead leaves crackled underfoot and occasionally out of the dark the lantana brushed them with a thorny prickle. When they came to a clear spot Eddie paused and looked back and was surprised at how far they'd climbed above the road. The lights of Pasadena across the Arroyo Seco made a great glow to the east and south. To the right, far away, downtown L.A. lit up the horizon.

"Come on," Skip muttered. He circled east toward the upper end of the Havermann place. There was lawn here, glimmers of light through the thick old trees. "Well, let's try a little closer."

There was a sudden loud crashing and bounding through the shrubs and Eddie turned hot with fright. He knew at once what it must be and that Karen hadn't said a word about a dog. Skip was cursing, and then the dog jumped on him out of the dark and Skip thrashed to the ground. There was a lot of racket and Eddie stood frozen, expecting someone to follow, a light to shine on them, a gun pointed, anything. Instead the dog leaped off Skip and bounded around playfully, letting out little yelps. He wanted Skip to chase him.

Skip got up, still cursing, and brushed at his clothes. There was enough light for him and Eddie to see the dog, still leaping around and wagging his tail. "Hell," Skip said, "the damn dog didn't even bark."

"Let's go back," Eddie said suddenly.

"No, look, this is important. Karen never said a word about

a dog, and I kind of hinted, too. She's holding out on me. Who does she think she is?" Under his breath he cursed the girl fiercely. "The thing is, the important thing, he's no good for a watchdog." Skip squatted and whistled softly, and the big collie came over and tried to lick his face. The dog made whining sounds and Skip patted his head.

"You don't know what he'll do next," Eddie argued. "I'll bet he's used to people hiking along up here, kids playing hooky or hunting jackrabbits. If we try to go near the house, he'll raise hell."

"Well, let's test him." Skip jumped to his feet and strode off downhill through the trees toward the lights of the house. Eddie stood rooted in the dark. The dog whined a couple of times, circling Eddie as if asking a question about what to do next, then suddenly sat down on his haunches. Eddie moved into a still darker spot, then clucked to the dog; and the collie ran to him, frisking.

"Hey, boy. Nice boy." Eddie rubbed the dog's warm silky head, feeling the hard bones of the collie's skull under the fine fur. He liked dogs generally, most especially big golden dogs with a friendly way.

Skip whistled a summons, an eerie killdeer kind of noise, but Eddie hung back, telling himself he and Skip would be better off if he stayed to keep the dog from the house. He didn't move until Skip returned, which must have been more than ten minutes later. Skip was walking lightly, confidently, hissing the killdeer cry between his teeth. He came up to Eddie, and Eddie sensed the grin.

Skip patted the dog. "The mutt likes us."

"He's a good dog."

Skip said, "I was right down there, real close, looking in the windows. Chrissakes it's big, but it's old—old furniture and high ceilings and regular granny shelves full of knickknacks. I didn't see the old lady. There's a man inside, though. He's in a room, must be a library, looking at something on a desk. I thought maybe account books, but I couldn't be sure." Skip cuffed the dog playfully, and the dog growled and pretended to chew his hand. "The guy from Vegas. He's brought more dough."

"That's a crazy place to keep money!" Eddie blurted.

"You trying to knock this thing?" Skip cried in sudden anger.

"No, of course not."

"I got a good look at the guy," Skip boasted, "real good. I'd know him anywhere. You know what I'm going to do? Before we pull this, that is? I'm going to hitchhike to Vegas and look him up."

Eddie felt his heart lurch against his ribs. "That'd be crazy!"

"Oh, I'm not going to charge in and let on I'm itching for his green stuff. What this'll be—making *sure*. Karen *thinks* he's big in Nevada, has a chunk of one of the clubs on the Strip, but she could be wrong. He could be tinhorn, full of wind, maybe even making a play for the chick. One thing more, is he really old lady Havermann's ex-son-in-law? I'll need to check on it."

"He'll have you thrown out," Eddie said.

"You think I'm dumb enough to speak to him, let him get a look at me?" Skip was outraged, on the verge of violence. "The thing is, if he's who Karen thinks he is, and he's coming here every few weeks, staying overnight, why not, if not to stash some winnings?"

"And why should Karen tell you about it?" Eddie cried from his own uncertainty.

"Because." Skip leaned toward him in the dark beneath the trees. "She's mine any time I want her. Just any time, any-where, anyhow. Want me to prove it?"

"What do you mean?"

"We'll come back here when classes are out, I'll show you. Right here on the ground under these trees."

"Ah, can it."

"No, I'm serious."

They started to walk west, then downhill out of the trees. They had forgotten the dog, and he rushed by them suddenly, scattering leaves and dirt, and Eddie stumbled with fright. Skip whirled to look back, as if someone might have sent the dog after them: but there was only the bank of towering ever-greens and the glimmer from the house.

The dog jumped around, wanting to play, but Skip ignored him.

Finally they started off again. Skip didn't say anything until they got to the car. The dog frisked off home, and Skip faced the street light and said, "If anything goes wrong on this thing, someone's going to get hurt. Bad hurt." His tone was sharp and mean.

Eddie thought, Skip's thinking about Karen. But he couldn't be sure. Skip might be thinking about him, too. It was right at that moment, stepping into the car, that Eddie realized how utterly intent Skip was on getting the money.

Chapter Two

KAREN MILLER laid her coat across the back of the chair and looked with a touch of shyness around the room. A few students were already at their typewriters, one or two pecking desultorily at the keys, but most were still in the hall, smoking a last cigarette or lingering to finish a conversation. Karen sat down, adjusted her skirt across her knees. Her motions were deft and graceful. She put out her hands, settling her fingers on the keys of the typewriter. She ticked off a few imaginary phrases.

A buzzer sounded in the hall. There was a bustle of entry, chairs scraping, a last whisper of talk. The teacher, a tall thin man with a storklike gait, came in from the hall and smiled at the assembled class. He laid a couple of books on the desk. "Good evening, students."

The chorus answered as usual, "Good evening, Mr. Pryde."

Karen opened the exercise book on the desk beside the machine, and the memory of a whole series of nights like this, Mr. Pryde and his greeting, the waiting, hopeful, or indifferent ones around her, ticked off in her mind. The faces, the figures were familiar, and Karen thought of them as friends, though in some way she was not able to comprehend she seemed unable to make the opening overtures which might lead to actual acquaintance. It was part shyness but mostly a lack of practice in social give-and-take. She felt awkward in the presence of strangers. It seemed to Karen a sort of miracle that Skip had sought her out and forced her to talk to him.

She knew that Skip must be in his place behind her now. A feeling of warm awareness stole through her; she could almost feel his gaze on her. She wanted to glance back at him, afraid at the same time that this glance would betray all that she felt.

Mr. Pryde left his desk and stalked over to the old phonograph in the corner. He wound the old machine. "Time for an exercise in rhythm. You ain't got a thing, you know——" He paused for effect. "—if you ain't got that swing."

Titters answered the sally, not because of any humor in it, but because poor old Mr. Pryde had worn the remark to death.

Karen felt a surge of sympathy for him. Mr. Pryde glanced at his watch. "Page twenty-two. Keep in time to the music. Now. *Dum dum de dum*." A Sousa march, hoarse and brassy, roared from the machine. Karen began to type rapidly.

When the exercise was finished she took a quick glance behind her and was surprised to find Skip's place vacant. He didn't come in until the first period was almost over. He crowded close to Karen as the class poured out into the hall for the break. "Hiya."

She looked at him shyly, pink color coming into her face. "How are you?"

"Really want to know?" He made it sound as if he kept a dangerous secret, teasing her.

"Oh, tell me." They were in the hall now, strolling away from the others. She noted a certain real excitement in Skip's manner. "You must have had a good reason to miss the rhythm exercise."

He caught her elbow and took her through the door, out upon the terrace which overlooked the grounds. Lights bloomed across the campus lawns; a sprinkler sent a shower of silver over the dark shrubbery. "I feel like cutting class—period. Never coming back." With his fist he chucked up her chin, put his mouth on hers, pressed hard. Finally she drew away, gasping. "What do you mean?"

"Ah, I'm disgusted, I'm not getting anywhere." He took out a cigarette and snapped flame to it from a match, all with an elaborate air of anger.

"Oh no, Skip! You mustn't get discouraged!"

He leaned on the railing, smoking moodily. Karen stood close, as if her nearness might soothe him. "Is anything the matter? More than usual?"

"Does it have to be more than usual? Isn't the regular grind enough?"

"You're bored, Skip? Is that it?"

"Aren't you, babe?"

"No. Mrs. Havermann wants me to learn something to make a living at. She thought nursing, but I couldn't stand that. I was sick a couple of years ago, I had to have my appendix out, and I saw how those nurses worked and what they had to do. I know I'd never be a success at it. I'm not patient

enough, kind enough. Why, a woman in our ward used to——"
She broke off suddenly.

Skip was interested. "Used to what?"

"Oh, it wasn't a nice thing, the thing she did."

"Well, what was it?" When Karen remained abashedly silent
he said, "For Chrissakes, what do you think I am? A baby? The
woman wet the bed, I bet."

Karen looked embarrassedly back at the door. "Well, it was
something like that, only worse. She'd use the bedpan, and
then when the nurse came to take it she'd make it spill. Over
and over. They must have known she did it on purpose. You
could see she got a kick out of it. But those nurses just cleaned
and cleaned—and I'd have blown my stack."

"So now you're taking typing," Skip put in.

"It's not exciting, but it's something I can do," Karen said.

Skip turned to her and grinned. "You know what I'd have
done? I'd have taken the nursing course like Mrs. Havermann
wanted. And then I'd have looked around for some rich old
geezer to nurse, some old bachelor or widower loaded with
dough, not too bright, and I'd have married him."

Karen was disgusted. "Some sick old man? Oh, heavens!"

"And then, being a nurse, I'd have helped him get sicker and
sicker until finally he croaked and I had the dough for myself."

The thought shocked her. "That's an awful thing to say."

He moved closer and put a hand behind her head and
pushed her mouth against his own. All of Skip's kisses had an
experimental quality about them, as though the act of embracing contained some novelty he couldn't get used to. "Now
I've made you mad."

"Well, I'm getting over it." She kissed him in return, solemnly, and as if humbly offering a gift. The buzzer sounded;
he yanked her back.

"I don't think I'm going in there."

"Why not? You're doing as well as anybody. Don't quit just
because tonight you're bored and disgusted," Karen begged.
"They'll give your place in class to someone else, and then
you'll have to start all over again next semester, just like a be-
ginner."

"I don't know——" He seemed to hesitate. "What about
afterwards?"

"You asked before; I told you how Mrs. Havermann gets nervous if I'm not there on time. She doesn't like being alone."

"Yeah, yeah. She's crazy about you."

"No, she's not. I'm not her child. It's because of her own feelings."

"Suppose there was a meeting after class, you had to stay for it?"

"There never is."

"She knows there never is?"

"Oh, Skip, I don't want to worry her!"

He nodded indifferently. "Sure. I see exactly how it is. Go on inside then. I'll see you around sometime."

She hesitated in the doorway, her expression harried and anxious. "You make it seem as if I'm letting you down."

He shrugged, turned to lean on the railing, lit a fresh cigarette, and expelled smoke into the dark. The stony eyes looked past her as he glanced into the hall. "They're all inside. You'd better hurry."

She rushed back to him headlong. "What would we do? I couldn't take time to eat, or go dancing, or anything like that."

He laughed shortly in surprise. "Who the hell said anything like that?"

"Well, then . . ." She was confused.

"I'll drive out somewhere close to the house, a lonesome spot, we'll sit in the car for a while."

She couldn't help coloring a little. "I'm not supposed to do anything like that."

"Like that? Or like this?" He threw away the cigarette, put both hands against her waist, backed her against the wall. He kissed her. "We'll leave a little early, give us plenty of leeway." He put up a hand and touched her throat with his fingers, lazily.

The idea he suggested, parking near the house in the car, the thought of the warm and dark interior and she and Skip enclosed in its privacy, filled Karen with a rush of almost dizzying sensations. A melting weakness poured through her. She nearly tottered, there against the wall with Skip's fingers touching her throat.

Then Skip muttered, "I've got to pick up a friend in metal class."

She was looking at him as if dazzled. "You mean someone's

coming with us?" It didn't fit into the mental picture she had created; her thoughts whirled in confusion. But suddenly Skip moved off, taking her with him into the building. "Tell old man Pryde you've got a headache. I'll just walk out as if getting a drink of water or something. Meet you outside that door in thirty minutes."

She stumbled to her place, began mechanically working on the machine, meanwhile trying to sort sense from what Skip had told her. Under the emotional uproar she was aware of something else, a kind of dread at what she might be willing to do for Skip.

During the years of growing up which she had spent in the Havermann house, certain taboos had been instilled, not by anything as direct as spoken advice, since Mrs. Havermann never mentioned such things, nor lovingly by example, because temptation had no truck with that household, but rather by punctilious omission. Mrs. Havermann no longer lived in a world where people worried about anything more compelling than running out of sugar. Passion was a pale flare on the horizon of memory, growing dimmer year by year. The things she recalled from her marriage were the turmoil of its social obligations and the tantrums of her husband over his mislaundered shirts. And in some way of which both women were unconscious Mrs. Havermann had imposed her withdrawal upon the young girl.

Now Karen sat before a typewriter, the bulwarks trembling, and tried to force herself to be clear-headed, tried to keep from drowning in the emotional tide.

Skip meant to pick up a friend, she reminded herself. This must be Eddie, the one he had mentioned to her previously. Perhaps he just meant to give Eddie a lift first, before driving her home.

She wondered if Skip's friend would be able to see how she felt, to sense the turmoil inside her. The thought was disturbing and at the same time steadying. She found herself drawing a deep, relaxing breath. What she felt for Skip was too strange, too raw and new, to be betrayed to anyone. It was a secret which she must keep to herself.

Skip parked the car by the curb and Eddie and Karen stepped out. All the way from school Karen had been puzzled and embarrassed, and Eddie knew it. He knew that she kept glancing at him as if wondering when he would leave them. On his part, Eddie wished in disgust that he had refused to return with Skip. Skip had a new air about him, and the way he drove and the way he whistled through his teeth told Eddie that he was feeling mean.

Skip came around the car, carrying the old blanket he used to cover the car's torn upholstery. "Let's go somewhere and talk," he said. Remembering what Skip had promised on the previous trip here, Eddie felt his face go tight and hot. He tried to mutter something about getting home, but Skip ignored it. Above them the trees climbed the rising ground, and all was as dark as a tomb.

Karen said in a shivery voice, "I thought we were going to sit in the car."

Skip gave an elaborate start of surprise. "Damned if we weren't. But it would be kind of crowded with Eddie in there, wouldn't it?" He walked uphill to the dark trees, the girl and Eddie following, and when he found an open spot he spread the blanket on the ground and flopped on it. There was nothing but a little starshine. Skip sighed and stretched out. "Come on, you two. Sit down."

Karen tucked in her skirt and sat down gingerly at the edge of the blanket. Eddie didn't sit down at all. He was beginning to get an idea that Skip was having a big joke here, that this amused him. He was tickled by their embarrassment and by their uncertainty over what he meant to do next. He felt that he held them in his power. He could do some outrageous thing, or nothing at all; it was just up to him.

"Sit down, Eddie. You're blocking the view."

Eddie said, "Ah, I'm not tired right now. I want to stretch my legs."

"Sit down anyway." The tone was a trifle ugly. Skip lay on his back and lit a cigarette and blew smoke at the sky. Eddie sat down. He could see the girl's face turned his way, a pale patch against the dark; he couldn't make out her eyes. He wondered what she was thinking, what she expected Skip to do. Around them the young trees whispered under a touch of wind, and there was a wild dusty smell. It was quiet, a long way from the city.

"Who's home at your place?" Skip asked all at once.

The girl didn't catch on at once; then she said, "You mean at Mrs. Havermann's?"

"Sure I mean at Mrs. Havermann's."

"Well, Mr. Stolz is there. He came this morning. There's her, and me, and that's all."

"How long is Stolz going to be there?"

"I don't know."

"Does he ever make a play for you, get fresh or funny, anything like that?"

"Why, of course he doesn't. He's real nice. You'd hardly know he was in the house. He reads, or types in the library, or takes walks. He's friendly and . . . just sort of keeps to himself."

"Does he ever count his money where you can see him?"

Karen threw a glance toward Eddie; Eddie saw the quick turn of her head and sensed her eyes on him. She was beginning to realize that Skip was in an unpredictable mood; perhaps she was wondering, too, how much he had told Eddie. "No," she said uncertainly, "I've never seen the money."

"But you know it's there."

"Mrs. Havermann thinks it's there."

"*Thinks?*" Skip jerked himself indignantly up on one elbow. "Now wait a minute. What is this? You expect us to go ahead on just what the old woman thinks?"

"What do you mean, go ahead?" Her tone was scared, a scared whisper.

"Why, what we were talking about, how to get hold of some of that dough for ourselves," Skip said, maddeningly offhand. Eddie recognized the trick since Skip had played it a thousand times on him: delivering a jolt as if you were supposed to know all about it.

Karen seemed to huddle in the coat, shrinking down inside it. "You must be crazy, Skip. Just as crazy as can be."

Skip was bolt upright now, his manner angry and astounded. "You mean you've been feeding me a bunch of lies? It's all something you've made up in your head?"

He had confused her now. She said pleadingly, "You mistook what I said for something else. The money belongs to Mr. Stolz. He keeps it at Mrs. Havermann's place on account of some tax business."

"He's cheating the government," Skip pointed out nastily, "and he deserves to be cheated a little himself." It was infantile reasoning, but Skip put heat and conviction into it. "He's a crook. I ought to turn him in to the income-tax cops."

"Oh, don't do that!"

"I'm not going to. I just said I ought to. I'm going to help myself to some of the money; I'll let him pay me for keeping my mouth shut."

She sat so still, like a crouched animal, not saying anything, that Eddie knew she was afraid to have the conversation go on. She was afraid of what Skip would say next. At the same time she must have been doing some agonizing recapitulation, trying to recall all she had told him.

"We've got to make plans." Skip circled his knees with his arms, leaned his head on them as if thinking. "You'll have to find out exactly where the money is. Does he keep his room locked?"

"No, but I'm not supposed to ever go in there!" she cried.

"Where is his room?" He waited, and she said nothing, and Skip went on: "Upstairs? Near where you sleep?"

"No. Downstairs, next to the library. Oh, Skip, don't do this crazy thing!"

"Crazy, crazy, is that all you've got in your head?" He reached for her, pulled her nearer; she almost sprawled on her face. "It's up to you, this first part of it, finding the money and seeing how much it is, or a rough guess, and making sure we hit the place just after he's gone and when he won't be coming back for a while very soon. You get it?"

"I couldn't do it!"

"Chick, you've already done the main job, fingering the guy."

"What's that?"

"Letting somebody know who can use the information."

"I was just . . . talking. Passing time."

"Not with me you weren't." Her head was bent close and Skip was stroking her hair; Eddie could see the movement of his hand against her head. He heard crying, too. Karen was crying in desperate entreaty. "I like you a lot and you like me, and we can pull this off with Eddie here to help——"

"I'd have to leave home!" she wept.

"For Chrissakes, don't you want to? You want to live with that old dame, taking her charity, all your life?"

She hung there in silence, as if on the point of some terrible decision. "She's been awfully——"

"Good to you?" Skip mocked. "Treated you like a daughter?"

Skip's tone told Eddie this much: Skip knew Karen hadn't been treated as a daughter. For all that Skip had some sort of blind spot, unable to see himself, he could always pounce unerringly on the flaws in anyone else. Now he grabbed for Karen suddenly, pulled her over so that she lay across his knees, her shoulders against his chest. He looked at Eddie and said, "I'll meet you at the car."

Eddie got up and went quickly down through the trees. He felt an immense relief. There had been a moment when he had thought the girl wasn't going to co-operate, and he'd been afraid of what Skip might do to her. She was a kind of nice girl. Young and inexperienced. More than that, worse than that— ignorant. The girl was just ignorant enough to think Skip was interested in her instead of the money.

Eddie got into the car and put his head back and shut his eyes. He was half asleep when Skip came back alone. The girl had gone home by herself through the trees.

Skip got into the car, started the motor. He was grinning in the light from the dash, and his air was satisfied. The dog, he told Eddie, was a new arrival. Mrs. Havermann had taken it off the hands of a friend. It was just a pet, Karen said. "I think there's more to it," Skip concluded, "even if Karen doesn't know it. The old woman's nervous over all that money in the house. Bound to be."

They turned from the hillside roads into lower and shabbier streets, heading for home.

"It must be like sitting on a bomb," Skip said all at once, amused. "Yeah. Mrs. Havermann must feel that way." He drove as if musing over it. Eddie knew then that Skip was thinking of the old woman and her fear and of what sort of reaction she'd have on learning that someone else knew about the money and had come to get it.

Chapter Three

EDDIE LET himself in quietly at the back door. The smells of the house swept over him, garlic and chili spices and stale coffee and an undefinable aroma of ingrained dirt. He stood still in the kitchen and listened. By now his dad should be asleep, fogged out on wine, but his mother might be up, reading or telling her beads. He had noted a light in the front room as he had come into the yard.

When he heard no sound, he went into the tiny hall and then on into the living room. His mother sat asleep in a chair, a magazine on her lap. She was a short, heavy woman, her neck thickened by a goiter, her gray hair thin and straggling. Her mouth had fallen open, and Eddie could see the gold tooth shining, the tooth put in in Mexico when she had been a girl.

As if his presence had signaled her sleeping mind, her eyes came open. They were large brown eyes, as gentle as a doe's; and Eddie never saw his mother's eyes without a recognition of the goodness, the loving charity within. She said sleepily, "Well, you're home now. Class was late a little?"

"A little." Eddie moved around the room to the door of his own room and stood awkwardly, wanting to go on in.

"Sit down, son."

There was a chair beside the door. It was springless, the arms mended with twined wire, a cushion covering the hole in its seat. "Yes, Mama, what is it?"

"I want to know about the class, how you're doing in it, what the teacher thinks of you." Her glance was pleased and eager.

"Oh, I'm doing all right. The teacher says I'm coming along."

"Today your father was talking to Mr. Arnold in the metal shop. Maybe you could go to work there, Eddie. Maybe the other thing, the trouble you've had, wouldn't stand in your way if you didn't mention it."

"Does Mr. Arnold know about my record?"

"No, I don't think so."

"He'd find out," Eddie said without bitterness.

"Well, it's a while yet before you finish the classes, isn't it? Maybe Mr. Arnold would let you help around the shop, not paying anything, until the class is done, and then he'd know what a good boy you are and he'd think the trouble didn't matter."

His mother was always planning these schemes for Eddie; he rejected this one without heat. Without hope, either. "Mama, the railroad doesn't let people come and work without paying them. And they don't take men with a police record, either. Dad's wasting his time talking to Arnold. Tell him to leave Arnold alone."

Her glance dropped from Eddie's face, settling on the magazine in her lap. "It seemed like such a fine idea."

"I know, Mama." Eddie avoided looking at his mother now. He knew that her life, hard as it was, and exposed to the violence of his father's drunkenness as it was, still protected her from many of the common cruelties and frustrations. She could not conceive of a few mistakes—as she thought of them, tolerantly—barring her son from a multitude of jobs. "We'll talk about it some other time. Maybe I'll come up with something of my own."

She spread her work-knotted hands on the cover of the magazine. "Yes. We'll think of something, you and I." She smiled gently. "You are too fine a boy not to have a fine job, Eddie." The glance she gave him was full of love. "Go to bed now. Don't worry, don't lie awake thinking about your troubles."

Eddie lay awake but briefly in the small overcrowded room. In those moments of wakefulness he thought of Skip and Skip's plan to rob the Havermann house of its store of money. Skip had talked of nothing else for more than a week. Karen seemed to be under his control now. Eddie allowed himself a brief wishful glimpse of riches, of buying a car for himself and something nice for his mother. A necklace, a nice dress, a big plastic purse like those in the fancy shopwindows. Maybe something for the house, too. To Eddie the house was familiar, its shabbiness acceptable; but he knew from remarks dropped now and then by his mother that she wanted the place fixed up. A new rug and a couple of chairs would bring a glow of joy to her brown eyes.

He woke in the early dawning, hearing his father pounding

out to the kitchen, the rattle of glassware and the rush of water from the faucet. His father always downed about a pint of water before taking a pickup. Then he was ready for coffee, a couple of doughnuts, a second pickup, and so off to the job at the roundhouse.

Eddie's mother glanced in at him. She was huge inside the shapeless flannel gown, the gray hair tied up in skimpy braids, her enormous, bulbous throat hanging over the neck of the gown. "Cover up, Eddie. It's cool this morning."

He grunted, burrowing into the pillow. He went back to sleep. There was nothing to get up for. He'd given up hunting a job, even a temporary job to fill in until he was through the metalwork class, a long time ago.

Skip awoke in the room above the garage, raised himself on an elbow, and looked out at the morning. It was foggy, overcast, and a dull gray light lay over the neighborhood. Next to the garage was a big bank of shrubbery, then a plot of flowers, then the paved tennis court and the high brick wall surrounding the house next door. It was a district of once-exclusive homes now mostly broken up into housekeeping apartments and rooms-for-rent. Only a few of the original owners still lived here, among them Mr. Chilworth, who owned the big house at the front of the lot.

Skip sat up and rubbed the hair out of his eyes, yawned, put his bare feet on the floor. His uncle was already gone. He had made his bed on the other side of the room; it was neat and square under the white cotton counterpane. His uncle was probably already in the house now, cooking Mr. Chilworth's breakfast. After cooking, and washing up the dishes, he'd start cleaning the house. In the afternoons his uncle worked in the garden. Mr. Chilworth was a bachelor, eighty-six years old, still hating women so badly he refused to keep a cleaning woman on the place. Skip's uncle performed as cook, maid, gardener, and chauffeur; and because Mr. Chilworth was practically impoverished now, the wages were poor, but Mr. Chilworth was broad-minded about a man with a prison record, and Skip's uncle had one. A long one.

Mr. Chilworth's charitable attitude was based in part upon the fact that there was nothing around worth stealing.

Skip went to the tiny bathroom and showered, brushed his teeth, shaved. He then looked over his uncle's shirts in the bureau drawer and chose one that he disliked less than the rest. His uncle was about his size, a slim wiry little man; he had Skip's foxy expression, though it was much subdued. He had learned to keep his eyes down. He walked with a shuffle. Mr. Chilworth's one complaint about his man of all work was that he came upon you silently, without warning. At first, seven months ago, Mr. Chilworth had found it annoying.

When Skip was through dressing, he went down the outer staircase to the yard, through the yard to the rear door of the big house. Here was a large screened porch, on it some of the overflow from the kitchen, boxes of pots and pans no longer needed, cases of health food and vegetable juices, an old refrigerator minus its door where Mr. Chilworth kept oranges and grapefruit. Skip went through to the enormous kitchen. His uncle Willy was sitting at a breadboard pulled out from the cabinet, drinking coffee and reading a racing sheet. Uncle Willy nodded without speaking. His gaze lingered for a moment on his shirt.

"How's for breakfast?" said Skip, the usual greeting.

Skip's uncle rose and went to the stove and lit a fire under a skillet. It had already been used for Mr. Chilworth's meal and had some scraps of egg in the bottom. Uncle Willy broke two eggs in a bowl, beat them with a fork, grated some cheese over them, added a dollop of cream, dumped the whole into the pan. "Watch it," he said, going back to his stool by the breadboard.

Skip whistled between his teeth, stirring the eggs with the fork with which Uncle Willy had beaten them. When the mass congealed, he pushed it out upon a plate, salted it, took it to the sinkboard near his uncle. His uncle meanwhile had shoved a piece of bread in the toaster and poured a second cup full of coffee. Skip ate standing. "What looks good today?"

His uncle grunted, sucked his teeth with an air of disgust, folded the racing sheet, and tossed it over.

"When's he going to let you go out there?"

Uncle Willy shrugged, implying that Mr. Chilworth hadn't said when he might take an afternoon off for the races.

"Well, when did you go last?" Skip asked.

"Three weeks."

Skip considered. "You know, this isn't much of a job you've got here, Unc. The wages are nothing. You scrub and wash, mow the lawn and dig crab grass, and he doesn't even give you a day off for the races."

Uncle Willy waited for a moment before answering. "I'm eating. So are you," he pointed out with a dry air.

"So? It's not hard to eat now. Times are pretty good. Even the panhandlers are fat. For what you do here, working your tail off from morning to night, you ought to do better."

"You know where I can do better?" Uncle Willy asked mildly.

"An experienced man like you," Skip added with a sidelong glance.

An oddly quiet and attentive look came over his uncle. He put down the cup of coffee and regarded Skip for a moment in silence. The buzzing of a fly on the pane over the sink was the only sound in the room.

Skip said, "How old are you now? Fifty? By now you must have caught on to a lot of angles."

"I might have." Under the attentive expression was a sort of question.

"What were you in for?"

"I don't want to talk about that, Skip. One thing I've learned here, learned from Mr. Chilworth, is that the past is as dead as you let it be. And I want mine to be really forgotten."

Skip nodded indifferently. "Sure. You're right." He seemed ready to abandon the line of conversation.

"I made my mistakes, just as you did, Skip; but we both paid for them with time out of our lives. You're lucky, you're young, you haven't lost all the middle years." The tone had the air of sermon in it, but Uncle Willy's eyes had taken on a certain sharpness. He studied Skip warily, prying at him with little glances.

"Just blowing off my big mouth," Skip said apologetically.

"Nothing specific in mind?"

"No, not a thing."

When he had finished eating Skip went back to the room above the garage, threw the bedding together, and flopped on the bed. He had some planning to do; he had to get to Las

Vegas by the day after tomorrow, when Karen said that Stolz would probably return. His jalopp would never hold up for such a grind. He considered going by bus; but though the fare would only be a little over fifteen dollars roundtrip, Skip had little hope of getting the amount out of his uncle. Karen either. Old lady Havermann kept her on nickels and dimes. The answer, obviously, was to hitchhike. Take a local bus for two bits, get as far out on the highway as possible, use his thumb. The prospect bored him, but getting to Las Vegas and checking on Stolz was a necessary precaution. Skip was innately suspicious.

When Skip was fifteen he'd been arrested for the first time for driving a stolen car. The car had been loaned him by a school friend who had been positive it belonged to his old maid aunt, who didn't mind who drove it. In this way Skip got his name in the police records, and he learned distrust. Before he did anything about the money in the Havermann house he intended to check its source.

It was one thing to rob an old woman who would start screaming for the cops, and another to steal from a gambler hiding his dough from Uncle Whiskers and the tax collectors.

He had also to think up an excuse to give to the typing teacher and the bookkeeping teacher for a two- or three-day absence. In spite of what he had told Karen, he had no intention of giving up the classes until the other thing had been accomplished and the money was in his possession. Uncle Willy only allowed him to stay here sharing Mr. Chilworth's spare bounty because he was learning a trade.

He decided to palm off a story on the teachers about his brother in Fresno, sick, wanted to see him. Skip had a brother who lived near Fresno, ran a vineyard, a winery and a fig orchard, and, sick or well, wouldn't want anything further to do with him. He had a Presbyterian wife and three kids. The whole family was, in Skip's opinion, fantastically law-abiding.

Skip was digging in the closet for a zipper bag he recalled having seen there when he heard his uncle come softly up the stairs and into the room. "Skip? You in here?"

Skip backed from the closet, the dusty bag in his hand. "Yeah. Look, do you mind if I use this for a couple of days?"

His uncle studied the bag. "Why do you want it?"

"I'm going to make a short trip, need it for shaving stuff and so on." Skip knew from experience that a hitchhiker with any sort of luggage had a better chance of getting a ride than one without. The one without had a look of foot-loose mischief from which most drivers shied away. A bag, even a small one, implied possessions and a destination.

"Where are you going?"

"Oh, not too far," Skip said vaguely, unzipping the bag and glancing into it.

"You're giving up your classes?" Skip's uncle went to his bed across the room and sat down lightly on its edge. For the first time Skip noted the steadily attentive manner; it made him uneasy. "I don't think that would be the wise thing to do. Learning is money, Skip. It enables you to rise above the common herd. Look at me, grammar grade education, prison record; all I can get is the kind of slavery I do here. Work that nobody else would take." His prying eyes were full of questions.

"Education isn't the only thing," Skip muttered.

"Well, what else is there?"

"A break."

"You're getting a break somehow? This trip is a break?"

Skip felt that his uncle's persistence was drawing from him things he would have preferred not to divulge. He saw where that moment of incaution in the kitchen, that desire to hint and boast, had led. He looked at his uncle. "I can't talk about it."

"I think you'd better."

"Huh?"

"I think you'd better explain. I'm real curious about this trip and whatever else you're planning. And then, too, I might be able to give you some advice."

Skip thought about it while he took a soiled shirt off a hook and dusted out the interior of the bag. His uncle had not been a successful thief, though he had once had the reputation of moving with a big-time mob. Long prison sentences had sapped his body, curdled his manner into silent submission, slowed his walk to a shuffle. "Ah, there's nothing you could tell me."

"Maybe not. Maybe so. Who's in this with you?"

"Who's in what?"

"This break you're talking about."

They were circling verbally. Skip wished he had made up a story for Uncle Willy, something like being invited to stay with Eddie for a couple of days. "Oh, a guy I know."

"Eddie Barrett?"

"Yeah." Skip threw the dirty shirt into a hamper in the bathroom, came out, began to look around for something to stick into the bag. There was no need to pack yet, but he didn't want to have to sit down and face Uncle Willy and parry his questions.

Uncle Willy sat in silence as if thinking. Finally he said, "Is it a big thing? Something worth taking a risk for?" When Skip didn't answer he went on, "Because Eddie might not be up to it. There might be a catch somewhere and Eddie could let you down."

"Eddie's okay." Skip shrugged it off. "Anyway, he's not carrying the ball. I am. It's my baby."

"In any job," said Uncle Willy, "the least man, the man with almost nothing to do, can bitch you up. That's what happened to me, that's why I'm a two-time loser. That's why, even if you told me all about it, I couldn't go in with you or have the least thing to do with it."

Skip said, "That's right, you couldn't. Three times and you're out."

"So you can tell me whatever you want." Uncle Willy moistened his lips. "I can say what I think and that's all. Right now I'm telling you, watch Eddie Barrett. He's a punk kid in a lot of ways."

"Yeah, maybe you've got something there." Skip went into the bathroom and inspected his meager array of shaving stuff, as if making a note of what he needed to take.

"Now, where's this trip you're taking?"

"Las Vegas." In an expansive mood, Skip began to tell Uncle Willy about Stolz and the money in old lady Havermann's house.

Chapter Four

"WHO IS this girl, this Karen Miller?" Uncle Willy wanted to know.

"Old Mrs. Havermann never adopted her legally. Karen's dad was a friend of Mr. Havermann in the old days before he made his money, and when Miller died Karen was left all alone, an orphan kid about ten years old, and the Havermanns took her in. Havermann died about a year later. Karen stayed on with the old woman, helped with the housework for her keep."

"How does the old lady treat her?"

"Okay, I guess. Hell, she's not her mother. She wants Karen to earn what she hands out to her."

"No animosity there, you think?"

"No, Karen likes the old woman."

"How does Stolz fit into the picture?"

"He was married to Mrs. Havermann's daughter. They were divorced. The daughter—she's around thirty, I guess—she lives back East somewhere. The old woman stayed friends with Stolz. Maybe he pays her something, I don't know. Karen doesn't think so. She thinks the old woman is kind of sweet on Stolz even if he is about fifteen years younger than her."

Uncle Willy sucked his teeth and twiddled his thumbs thoughtfully. "You were right about going to check up in Las Vegas. That's the thing to do. Make sure. You got a good look at Stolz through the window?"

"Ah, I'd know him anywhere," Skip said.

"When are you leaving?"

"Day after tomorrow. That's when Stolz is supposed to go. Karen will let me know for sure, of course, when it happens."

"You might not run into him over there, you might have to inquire around, and you'd better handle that pretty carefully. Some of those boys in Nevada own those clubs sort of under the counter, so to speak. Silent partners. There's a reason. Nobody with a record is supposed to have any piece of the gambling over there."

"For Chrissakes, you think I'm a nut or something?"

557

"It takes thinking about, more than you might realize."

"I'll do okay."

Skip came out of the bus depot, into the bright hot Nevada sunlight, and looked around for a cab to take him out to the Strip. Karen was sure that Stolz would be there by now, in one of the big hotels. She was sure that he had nothing to do with any of the downtown clubs, catering to the less-well-heeled and the more transient suckers. Old Mrs. Havermann and Stolz had never mentioned the name of the hotel where he was supposed to live and in which he had a share, but Skip and Uncle Willy had done a little figuring. Stolz had been coming to Mrs. Havermann's house off and on for a little more than three years, according to Karen's memory, and it would seem logical that he had acquired his gambling interests at about that time. Several of the biggest and most lavish hotels had opened since then, and these could be ignored, provided Stolz hadn't switched his investment.

Uncle Willy thought it most likely that Stolz had bought into one of the older establishments. He had telephoned a friend who had Nevada contacts, and from the friend had obtained a list of probabilities. Skip carried the list in his pocket, along with the return bus ticket financed by Uncle Willy in a burst of generosity.

When a cab drew in to the curb, Skip read off the name of the first hotel on the list; the cabbie nodded. They rapidly left the downtown area for through boulevards heading west. Skip had been through Las Vegas several times. He was always interested, when passing through the Strip, to see the new hotels which were constantly being added to the long line on either side of the highway stretching toward Los Angeles. Great piles of million-dollar masonry, glass and brick, they rose like fantastic palaces set amid tropic gardens. He read the names: the Sands, the Sahara, the Flamingo, Desert Inn, the Dunes, Thunderbird; and the vision of their opulence filled him with excitement. Only the knowledge of his own flattened wallet kept him from vainglorious dreams.

By seven that evening he was in the third hotel of the list Uncle Willy had prepared, and getting nowhere. He had found himself the recipient of cool evaluation by pit bosses, room clerks, and bar waitresses. Skip had no money to spend; he could only look. He knew that the category *flat broke* was pinned on him by the dealers within ten minutes of his entering the casinos. A stubborn anger had begun to burn.

He was at a crap table. The dice were in the hands of a thickset man with an alcohol flush, expensive clothes, diamond stickpin and solitaire. Two blond chippies clung to him, slipping ten-dollar chips into their gilt bags when opportunity presented. The man was loud, much the worse for liquor, and held up the game for long periods while he argued with one or both of the girls. What Skip took in was the attitude of the dealers at the table, the hovering pit boss: they wore fixed smiles and they ignored or pacified complaints from other players. Plainly here was big money working.

He waited and watched the stack of chips dwindle. All at once he found the man staring at him across the crap table.

"Hey, you?"

Skip was stupefied. "Who?"

"You. Young fella. You come around here." He beckoned with a weaving arm. Skip looked around, too dumfounded to know what to do. He caught the eye of the pit boss, the faint nod that commanded him to obey. Skip went around the table and the old man pushed one of the chippies away roughly and pulled Skip in close. "Uh-huh. You remind me of my boy. Did remind me. I mean, he used to look like you." The thickset man hiccuped loudly. "Foxy boy. In England now. Long way off." He was fumbling chips and pushing them into Skip's hands.

Skip wanted to stare at them; he knew they were worth ten dollars apiece and the old man had given him more than a dozen.

"Play 'em," the thickset man commanded.

Skip put one down tentatively; the old man shot the dice; the dealer raked in the bets. The old man had brought in a two-spot, craps. Skip put down another chip.

"Naw," the old man said. "Lookee here. Fix 'em up. You get nowhere piddling along." He raked Skip's hands clean and dribbled the orange chips across the green felt, betting the line, the big six and eight, come bets, everything. Skip's brief riches were all spread out waiting for the throw. Skip felt breath die out in his lungs, his heart's thumping. Maybe . . .

Craps again. The old man had neglected that particular item. Skip stepped back into the shadows, expecting to be dismissed, but the old man turned bloodshot eyes to search him out. "Hey, you!"

The chippie was staring into Skip's face as if the least thing would set her to clawing his eyes. "I'm . . . I'm broke," Skip muttered.

"Sure. Sure. I've been broke a million times," the old man boomed. "Had to clean spittoons in Fairbanks, Alaska. Drove a mule team between Barstow and Daggett—one hundred and ten in the shade and there wasn't any shade. Never knew what it was in the sun. Afeared to look." He was throwing bills across the green felt to the dealer, who poked them into a slot in the table and replaced them with more orange chips. "What you want to remember, boy—luck's gonna change. Nobody ever has bad luck all the time."

Skip wanted to say, "You sure about it?" but he held his tongue. The old man had pulled him back to the table, given him a double fistful of the chips and was telling him how to play. Skip glanced at his shoulder, feeling pressure there. A girl's palm was outspread. Skip shrugged and turned away. The girl said, "You little son of a bitch!"

"Get lost."

"You'd better stay away from Mr. Salvatorre! These people at the hotel keep an eye on him!" she hissed at him.

"They'd better watch you," Skip told her.

She didn't leave. He was aware of her warm flesh, the perfume, the silver glitter of her hair. She had on a red sheath dress, cut so tight Skip didn't understand how she could breathe. She wore a clutter of platinum bangles on her wrists. Her bare legs above gold sandals were chocolate-colored from the sun. "Nasty little man. You belong on skid row. Why don't you go away and quit trying to crash the party?"

Skip didn't answer. He was interested in what was happening to his money. The old man had given him over two hundred dollars, and now by a rapid calculation he found that he was down to eighty.

"Play up, boy, play up!" The old man leaned his belly on the rim of the table and chanted to the dice. Afterward he bought more chips.

An ugly feeling of disappointment surged through Skip. He wasn't going to come out of this with anything. It was a con game, a racket. The old fool must be a shill, playing on house money. Or else he was a nut. Skip was himself too unpredictable and too insecure to endure eccentricity in others.

He was trying desperately to think of a way to back off with even a few of the chips left when Salvatorre suddenly decided he'd had enough of dice. Now it was time to try the slot machines. He dragged Skip along to another part of the big casino, ordered drinks for everybody in sight, passing out quarters and half dollars as fast as he could buy them from the change girl. The two blondes made Skip think of hovering vultures. They did everything but crawl into Salvatorre's pockets. Skip noted that very little of what the old man gave them went into the machines. They rapidly switched the change back into bills and tucked the bills away into the bulging gilt bags.

The tempo around Salvatorre increased. The old man was almost in a frenzy. He had a half dozen slots going, was stuffing change into the girls' hands and tossing Skip an occasional batch of quarters. Skip noticed that the pit boss in the distance was keeping an eye on things. It could be true that the old man was a valued and familiar patron.

All at once Mr. Salvatorre was staring into his empty hands in a way that was almost tearful. "Broke. I'm broke, boy," he cried to Skip.

It was crazy. Skip knew that Salvatorre still had money in his wallet. One of the change girls glided up, smiling, to say, "Why, we'd be pleased to cash a check for you, Mr. Salvatorre."

All around them the slots were clanging; Salvatorre shook his head as if unable to hear. She repeated what she had just said, but Salvatorre blinked his eyes sadly. "Broke. Going to call it a night." He glanced around, noticed the bright-eyed chippie in the red sheath, saw Skip in the shadows. "We'll have a nightcap, the three of us. Come on, we'll go up to my room now; you'll order whatever you want."

Skip was wary, more than half disgusted. He saw the girl throw a victorious cat-smile at the other chippie, who appeared to take it philosophically and began to inspect the loot in her handbag. The girl in red then snatched Salvatorre's arm. "Not him," she mouthed, nodding toward Skip. "Let's leave him out of it."

It would have suited Skip; he had four or five dollars in quarters and half dollars and two ten-dollar chips. He had no desire to get better acquainted with the eccentric old man.

But Salvatorre roared a protest, threatening to dislodge the chippie on his arm. "Leave him here? Course not! Going to buy the boy a drink. Makes me think of my boy Al, over in England. Foxy boy, good boy, needs a drink."

"Tell him you're under age, darling," the blonde purred to Skip.

"Twenty-two," Skip said, unwilling to oblige her.

She showed her teeth at him.

The three of them went from the casino into the huge lobby. Outside, beyond great glass doors, was the pool, lit with pink light at its edges, surrounded by late swimmers and a few diners at the little tables in the dusky distance. Inside here was an air of carpeted quiet and the watchful eyes of two clerks at a desk in a niche across the way. Skip knew their gaze was for him, and he tensed with a sense of danger. The girl, that was expected, but they had cold stares for Skip. He might be up to something with their valuable Mr. Salvatorre, who had just provided a good chunk of the overhead for the day.

Skip stared back in defiance, but his heart wasn't in it. There was power here, concealed, it was true, under a show of hospitality, but nevertheless capable of swift and ruthless action. He had no illusions as to what would happen to him if he should try to slip off, say, with an added chunk of Mr. Salvatorre's money.

In Mr. Salvatorre's room the air-conditioning ducts hummed softly. There were flowers, bottles of good wine, a tray of snacks. Salvatorre ignored all this and rang for room service. The waiter came so quickly that Skip wondered if he had been stationed in the hall. "Drinks!" Mr. Salvatorre commanded, motioning toward the girl on the couch and Skip standing over by the windows.

The waiter looked patient and obedient; his attitude was one of simple politeness and not that of the cold hostility of the desk men.

"A stinger," the blonde said languidly, stroking the fat side of the gilt handbag.

"A double Scotch with water back," said Skip.

"Good boy!" the old man approved. "That's what my Al would say. And waiter, I want Irish whiskey with Coca-Cola in it."

Now that's a drink for you, Skip thought in distaste. He listened to the sounds from outside, where swimmers were splashing in the pool and a girl was laughing in a high-pitched squeal. He thought of the old dun-colored house, Uncle Willy's garage apartment, Mr. Chilworth and the amount of work he got from Uncle Willy for practically nothing; and he looked with disbelieving eyes on Salvatorre. How did a crazy old man like this acquire so much money?

He said tentatively, "You made it in mining, I'll bet."

"Some in mining," said Salvatorre, nodding his head, sitting down by the blonde and playfully squeezing her knee through the red sheath dress. "Some in oil. All by accident, boy. A man owed me some debts and all he owned, all he had left, was some desert land out in the middle of nowhere. Worth nothing. So he gave it to me and I forgot it and I went on working until five years ago. Then came the oil. I was a butcher for more than thirty years." He looked the girl over, as if she were some toy he meant to see perform before the evening was over. The blonde had taken a tiny vial of perfume from the overstuffed bag and was dabbing her ears and her palms with scent.

Skip thought, now why in hell couldn't something like that have happened to Uncle Willy? Uncle Willy had spent his years desperately planning how to scrounge a little money here and there, and being sent to prison for his efforts, and here was this stupid old coot who'd had it handed to him, who'd done nothing. The unfairness of it was stupefying.

The waiter brought the drinks. Salvatorre paid him and ordered refills at once, before they had even started on the first ones. Skip sat and drank, trying not to look very often at the couch. It was embarrassing, the old man almost paralyzed with booze and the skillful and willing chippie, whose skill and willingness weren't enough. Presently Skip took his drink into the bathroom and stayed there a long time. He heard the second arrival and departure of the waiter. Finally he went back into the other room. The sight he saw was curious.

Salvatorre lay stretched out on his back on the couch, obviously dead to the world. The blonde was at the dresser, fluffing her hair with a little silver comb. "Hi," she said to Skip. There was no animosity in her now. She winked at him in the mirror. "I'm going back to the casino. He'll be passed out for hours." She slipped the comb back into the purse and Skip saw the enormous roll of bills.

"Give me some," he said.

She crinkled her nose at him. "Oh, now, let's be realistic."

"You didn't give him anything for his money," Skip persisted, "because he was too drunk to take it. You've charged him for nothing. I want a cut of it."

She adjusted the neck of the sheath, tucking it a little lower over her sharply pointed breasts. "Don't get funny here, lover boy. You'd better take your small change and blow. The management will be along pretty soon to look Mr. Salvatorre over and maybe put him to beddy-bye. And they'll kick you out then if you haven't already gone."

Skip stepped close and put a hand at the back of her neck, where the skull joined the fragile spine, and he closed his fingers slowly. She tried to lunge forward, out of his grip, but the dresser held her. Then she tried to twist sidewise and away and Skip put an arm tight around her waist. He went on pinching the base of her skull and she turned white and started to scream and he lifted his free hand and slapped her hard. "Give," he said. He let up on the pressure at her neck and her head sagged forward drunkenly.

"My head! My head!" she moaned.

"It'll ache a little," he agreed. He pushed her aside and inched his fingers into her purse and extracted a chunk of money.

"Don't . . . take it all!"

"I'm not. I'm leaving you plenty."

He had a bad moment when he opened the hall door. A big man stood there, beefy inside a neat blue suit, hands like slabs of granite, a cold green eye. Skip repressed a start of fright. He said quietly, "I'm just leaving."

"Fine," said the man with the green eyes. He looked inside the room at the girl in front of the dresser. "You leaving too, Tina?"

"Yes, I'm leaving," Tina got out.

The big man waited, intending to see that Mr. Salvatorre was comfortable and alone. Skip started down the hall, and then from nowhere at all came a curious hunch, a thing to say. He obeyed it instinctively. He paused and looked back at the beefy man in Salvatorre's doorway. "I don't suppose it means anything."

"What's that?"

"What Mr. Salvatorre was telling me. He said if I wanted a job here in Las Vegas, he'd speak to somebody he called Mr. Stolz."

No change in the green eyes or the patient manner; the beefy man looked at Skip as from a vast distance, somebody looking at nobody, or a man on a curb watching a bit of trash blow by in the gutter.

"This . . . this Stolz. Is he anybody?"

The granite lips parted. "Mr. Stolz has retired for the evening. If I were you I wouldn't try to come back to see him. Mr. Salvatorre might not recall what he promised to do."

"Mr. Stolz owns the hotel?"

"A partner." The beefy man turned away to look at Tina inside the room.

Skip went away, through the lobby and into the desert night outside. He looked for a cab. In a freakish way he could never have foreseen he had found out about Stolz and made a little money into the bargain.

Chapter Five

U NCLE WILLY got off the bus in Beverly Hills and walked two blocks north of Sunset, up the hill where the big homes and apartment houses towered perchlike against the sky. He entered a small open courtyard. The low one-storied building surrounded it on three sides. There was a great deal of tropical shrubbery and a tiny fountain in a copper bowl. On the left was the door of a dentist's office, to the right were a couple of doctors. In the rear, beyond a screen of bougainvillea, was a door on which, in gilt letters, was printed R. Mocksly Snope, Attorney At Law. Uncle Willy crossed the courtyard and entered.

An artfully cosmeticked redhead in a tan sleeveless dress was seated in the outer office. The thing she was seated behind might have been a desk or it might have been a slab of metallic substance which had fallen through the roof off an airplane; Uncle Willy couldn't make up his mind which.

"Yes, sir?" The smile was careful, the eyes amused.

"I'd like to see Mr. Snope."

"Do you have an appointment, sir?" She clipped legal-sized pages together and stacked them at the edge of the metallic structure before her.

"No. Just tell him it's Willy Dolman. He knows me."

"Mr. Snope is very busy today."

"I'll wait." Uncle Willy looked around for a chair and found some contorted steel tubing and black plastic foam. He sat down. The thing fitted you strangely close, he thought, once you got into it.

She lifted a section of the metallic desk and peered into it, as if she might have a cake baking inside; then she spoke, softly inaudible words and afterward she listened. Then she looked in surprise at Willy.

"Mr. Snope will see you now," she said, as if she could scarcely believe it. She rose and walked to a door and opened it. Uncle Willy, with his hat in his hands, went on in. Snope was grinning at him from the other side of the room. Snope's carpet was a deep garnet red and his desk had no resemblance to a wing fallen off a plane; it was solid mahogany, six feet across, and shone like a mirror.

"Well, long time no see. Have a chair," Snope said, and opened a leather box and offered Willy a cigar.

Snope was about sixty, a stout man with a ruddy skin. He wore a gray hard-weave suit which must have cost around three hundred dollars in Willy's opinion. There was a peculiarity about Snope; in spite of his obvious age he had a certain juvenile softness and cheerfulness, an odd innocence, considering his class of clients and the seamy side of the legal profession he practiced.

"I was glad to hear you were out, Willy. How are things with you?"

"Not too bad." Willy explained about Mr. Chilworth and his job.

"Well, that's fine." Snope lit their cigars with a silver lighter. "I'm glad to know that you've settled down and aren't planning any more mischief."

"I'm settled down, all right," Willy said.

"You were a good man, a clever man, in your day. But we all get old. We all get to a certain point, and then it's time to take stock and think a bit and figure what the odds are. Sometimes the odds are such that we have to quit taking chances." Under Snope's mild tone was a warning, and Willy sensed it.

"I know I'm too old to plan any more jobs. I haven't any ideas along that line at all."

"Fine, fine. You're looking well, too. Taking on a little tan."

"That's the yard work," Willy explained. "What I came about is something else entirely. Not a job of mine. It's one I got wind of by accident."

Snope's face closed coldly and he inspected the cigar as if he thought it might harbor some species of insect life. "Now . . . Willy, I've advised you to the best of my knowledge——"

"It's not *my* job," Willy insisted. "I wouldn't touch it, in fact. But the thing is, the people who are planning it are punks. They don't know how to organize. It's going to skyrocket unless somebody with know-how takes over." He waited, a careful moment. "If someone with experience, the right person, got into it there might be a big payoff."

There was a tick-tock of such silence that Willy could hear Miss Redhead typing rattledy-clack in the outer office.

"Well, then——" Snope put his cigar into a crystal ash tray and stuck his hands palm down on the desk. His mouth had tightened. "Whom do you want to see?"

"I thought, well . . . Big Tom, if he isn't too busy."

"Big Tom." Snope thought about Big Tom, revolved Big Tom in his brain and inspected him from various angles. "It's his kind of job?"

"No."

Snope allowed a touch of suspicion to come up under the juvenile cheer, and Willy saw as usual and with the usual surprise that the youthful optimism was as false, really, as Mr. Snope's beautiful white teeth.

"I owe Big Tom a favor," Willy explained. "I've waited a long time to pay off. You know, when that last job went sour, when we were keeping our heads down and the heat was so bad we could hardly breathe, it was Big Tom did me a good turn. He loaned me a car and some money and it was just chance he didn't get pinched over it."

"I see." Snope twiddled his fingers on the mahogany. Then he said abruptly, "How big?"

"I don't know that yet."

"Will you know it before you pull the job?"

"Hope to."

Snope nodded. He had said nothing yet about his cut; and Willy understood that this was taken for granted. Snope got up from his chair and went to a steel file cabinet and extracted a folder. He studied the folder for a while; it contained some items about car accident statistics and the legal settlement of the same, but Mr. Snope seemed to be reading between the lines. After a while he said, "All right. Here's the address."

Willy copied down what Snope told him.

Snope laid the folder on his desk. "How many more?"

"I'll let Big Tom handle it."

Snope nodded. "Fine." He was smiling youthfully, his manner full of boyish good will. "Leave a phone number with Miss Weems. Don't call me, I'll call you." On the way to the door he clapped Willy cheerfully on the shoulders.

There was wind in the canyon, the smell of sage and sycamores, the old dry taste of summer dust, heat, a muffled quiet. Uncle Willy paused on the rutted road to wipe the sweat off his face with his handkerchief. He hated not having a car. Being afoot in southern California meant depending on a public transportation system which would have been insufficient for 1890.

Above him a pink-trimmed cabin peeped from a grove of trees. Uncle Willy looked up at it, narrowing his eyes against the glare. Steps led up from the unpaved road. There were patches of ivy and geraniums on the slope, and, seeing these, a look of recognition flickered in Willy's eyes. Big Tom had always been great for gardening. Gardens and cats. Sure enough, there was a big yellow cat on the porch above, looking down at Willy with the air of watching a mouse.

Willy climbed the steps, went up on the porch, rapped at the door. It wasn't a big place, but there was a great deal of privacy. From the porch there were no other houses visible, just the road leading off into the lonely sunlight. Willy heard a stir in the room, steps, then the door opened before him. "Hi, you old son of a gun," Willy said, and the man inside let forth a great cackle of laughter.

"Well, for God's sake, look who's here!"

Big Tom wore a pair of jeans and a knitted white tee shirt. His big toes were hooked into rubber sandals. He had a great mane of gray hair, stiff as wire, pale skin matted with freckles, a broad face, a heavy mouth. He was fat now; Willy commented at once upon how much fatter Big Tom was than when he had last seen him.

"Hell, you were salted away a long time, Willy!" They were seated by now. Big Tom gazed suddenly at Willy with his hazel-colored eyes. "Who gave you the address here?"

"Snope."

"What the hell were you doing with him?" Then an air, quiet and watchful, settled over Big Tom. "Wait a minute. You've come on business?" Big Tom shook his head decisively. "Afraid you're barking up the wrong tree. Don't plan on me, Willy. I'm all through."

Willy nodded mildly. "I know, it's not even your kind of job.

I wanted to offer it, though, because of the favors you did me in the past."

"Forget it." Big Tom turned the talk to other subjects: the house, the yard and the flowers, his family of cats. They were outdoors presently and Big Tom led Willy toward the lath house. "Begonias in here. I'm slipping some gardenias and camellias—not hard to do, but it takes them forever to start growing. See this fern? Jap gave it to me. The Japs irradiate or poison the damned fern some way; it comes all crinkly like that, like green lace."

Willy nodded over the ferns. He thought the place smelled mossy and fungus-like. He said, "There's this guy from Vegas, owns a chunk of a hotel over there. He's got some dough hid out in an old barn of a place in Pasadena. Nobody around but an old woman and a young girl. The girl won't make any trouble."

Big Tom rearranged some potted plants and ran a hose over some fuchsias. "I'm sorry to hear that you're meddling around with such things, Willy. You know and I know that you can't afford it."

"I'm not going to have any part of it," Willy said. "I'm just offering you the information because you tried to help me a long time ago when nobody else would have spit on me if I was afire."

Big Tom thrust a finger into a basket. "Getting dry. That's the trouble with the canyon, the wind through here drying everything out. I water these fuchsias three, four times a day. Can't keep 'em damp otherwise. Not even here, under the lath." He worked his way around the bench.

"You always went for this stuff," said Willy, trying not to walk on the fine green creeping growth on the floor.

"I'd of sure been better off if I'd done what the old gardener wanted me to. You know, that first time I was inside—they let me help Mr. Wilcox and he taught me to garden and grow things. Vegetables, too, that was the work end of it; we had to supply the tables at Preston. Then the flowers—he showed me how—that was the fun end of it, the beauty end, and I almost got a job gardening when I got out. Only, there was my brother. You remember Buddy."

"Yeah. I remember."

Two yellow cats came in and rubbed themselves against Big Tom's legs. Big Tom shoved them off with his toe. "If I had gone to gardening after that first hitch, it would have changed my whole life." He mused over some begonias with reddish hairy leaves and a long spate of crimson bloom. He said, "What's Snope want out of it?"

"He'll want the usual ten per cent."

"What do you want?"

"I'll settle for the same. Ten."

"That's not much."

"If what I think is there is there, it could be plenty. A half million wouldn't surprise me none. Look, this has been going on for more than three years. You know the kind of lettuce they cut over there in Nevada."

"Could be."

Willy's eyes had begun to gleam. He had a sudden vivid picture of himself at the track. The horses were parading to the post. He was all dressed up, and there was a wad of money in his hand. He'd just cashed a slew of tickets on a fifteen-to-one shot. Willy grew so excited under the compelling reality of the dream that he could scarcely stand still.

Big Tom was studying quietly over something. "What's been done so far?"

"My punk nephew got acquainted with the girl. She just lives there, works for her keep. She told him about this guy named Stolz and the money. Skip's got some wild idea he can pull it off with the help of another punk named Eddie Barrett. Believe me, this Eddie is from nothing. It's going to fall on their heads."

"Maybe not."

"Chrissakes, they don't know anything!" Willy cried. "They think they'll walk in there and tie up the old woman and heist the dough and take the girl with them when they walk out. Just like that!"

"They might get away with it," Big Tom said.

"Look. If Stolz is big in Nevada, he'll have connections here. Hot ones. You think he'll sit still for it? Nuts." Willy almost backed into the ferns. "He'll peg out their hides in his lobby, that's what he'll do."

Big Tom said, "Well, let's go inside and have a beer. We'll

talk it over. Before I'd go ahead with it I'd have to know more about the money."

"The girl's going to find out about that."

"You've met her?"

"Never. Don't intend to. That's what I mean about these punks not knowing anything. They're careless; they even drive around and look the place over by daylight; they run around with the girl."

Big Tom led the way back, shaking his head sadly.

Eddie went into the kitchen and looked into the coffeepot. There was a dark greasy cupful swimming in the bottom. He turned the gas on under it. From his mother's room he heard the creak of bedsprings.

"Eddie? You're up? You want something to eat?"

"I'll get it, Ma."

"Tortillas in the oven, beans on the stove."

"I want some eggs."

"In the icebox." She was in there resting, Eddie knew. Her heart bothered her a lot; she was short of breath, needed an operation for the goiter. The first thing I do, Eddie thought, thinking of the money—the first thing is the operation. Then some clothes for her, a good coat, maybe a fur one.

He saw his father's wine bottle on the sink and said to himself, For him, a kick in the guts.

He was frying the eggs when he heard her in the doorway and looked around. She had on a blue cotton house dress, bedroom slippers, an old green wool sweater thrown across her shoulders. "Eddie, I've been thinking. You know, about the job you might get with Mr. Arnold."

"Arnold doesn't do the hiring, Mama. He just works for the railroad like anybody else. Sure he's a straw boss, over the metal-shop, but it doesn't mean he could recommend me or anything. I'd have to fill out an application at the office and put down everything I've ever done. Including time I've served, and that would let me out right there."

He saw her desperate anxiety and pleading but closed his mind to it. "Sometimes I get scared. I think maybe you'll do something you shouldn't, maybe get into trouble again." She tried to pry into his closed face.

"I'm okay. I'm studying, I'll find something. They need metalmen. Even with records, they need them."

"Sure." The smile lighted her face; she half turned away. "You need money for carfare tonight? I could give you a dollar."

"Yes, I'll need it."

Skip wouldn't be there tonight, he was in Las Vegas. Eddie was to meet Karen and see what news she had, whether she'd gotten a chance to inspect Stolz's room and count up any of the money.

At eight o'clock Eddie was in the hall outside the typing room, waiting for the break. When Karen came out he gave her a shy smile, not quite sure how to act toward her in Skip's absence. She was Skip's girl. He wanted to be friendly, not in any way fresh. She seemed young and to Eddie terribly inexperienced. "Hello."

She looked at him blankly and started off. They went down to the end of the hall where the big double doors stood open to the terrace and the outside stairs. Lights bloomed here and there, illuminating shrubbery and paths. She turned on the terrace to face him. For the first time Eddie noticed her manner, how tight with strain she seemed, how excited.

She put a hand on his arm. "I saw it."

For a moment he failed to understand. Then he remembered. "You found the money?"

"There's too much of it! I couldn't begin to count it. I'm scared. I'm afraid Skip won't leave it alone." She trembled; her hand quivered on Eddie's arm. "It's tied up in paper bands, stacks and stacks, and somehow it's not like real money at all."

Some of her keyed-up mood communicated itself to Eddie. "It's really there." He moistened his lips with his tongue, staring off into the dark.

"You'll have to explain to Skip—it's too big. There's too much of it, and taking even a little would be dangerous."

"How could I tell him?" Eddie said reasonably. "He'd say I was crazy. Don't you know anything about him? Don't you see the way he is?"

She gazed at him as if trying to understand what he wanted to tell her. "It's not like real money at all," she said, wanting to make that point. "There's too much, it's just like paper. Like green, printed paper."

He shook his head, feeling sorry for her. "It'll seem real enough to Skip."

She wanted to draw back and didn't know how. She wanted to get Skip's mind off the money and still keep him interested in her. She was scared because she had told Skip about what was hidden in the Havermann house, and now nothing on earth could stop this thing from happening that was going to happen.

The wind touched her dark hair, blowing it in feathery streaks across her face. Her eyes were young and frightened. Eddie tried to find words to comfort her, but it was too late. It had been too late the first time she had opened her mouth to Skip about that money.

Chapter Six

A T SEVEN o'clock Skip stepped off the bus at the depot in downtown L.A. He felt stiff, tired, and gritty. He went into the coffee shop adjoining and had a cup of coffee, sitting hunched over it, his mind a blank. His only desire was to get home and have about eight hours' sleep. Then he'd gas up the jalopp and run over to see Eddie.

He passed Mr. Chilworth's big house and walked through the overgrown yard to the rooms above the garage. He looked around, in case his uncle was about, but saw nobody. He went up the stairs, the zipper bag swinging from his fingers, and opened the door. Uncle Willy was there and so was someone else, a big old man with a pale freckled face and a great shock of gray hair. Skip said, "Uh. Hello." He tossed the zipper bag to his bed.

"Sit down, Skip. We want to talk." His uncle nodded toward the other man. "This is Tom Ranigan. Big Tom to his friends."

"Hiya," said Skip. He sat down and pulled off his shoes and scratched the back of his neck.

"How did you do in Las Vegas?"

Skip's head jerked up. He fixed his gaze on Big Tom. "Hey," he said.

"That's right. Big Tom knows all about it."

"Well, I'll be damned. Cook me for crowbait," said Skip incredulously.

"It's this way, Skip. You and Eddie are a couple of inexperienced young punks. You've got hold of something here, maybe. Maybe not. If it's real and there are possibilities in it you're going to find yourselves with a wildcat's tail in your mitt."

"Now let's get this all straight," Skip said between his teeth. "You've brought in this old gazoo to run things?"

"Now don't speak disrespectfully of Big Tom," Willy advised. "He's a man with a great reputation. Earned it hisself, I might add."

Skip was staring evilly at Willy. "I oughta bust you in the

snoot. Tipping my plans to some broken-down has-been. What is it, really? You figuring on a cut for yourself?"

"Don't get excited."

Skip was full of a cold rage. He went on to describe in detail just what he should do to Willy, and what Willy could do with Big Tom. The two older men listened for a short while in silence; Willy in a warning stillness and Big Tom biting his lips. Then Big Tom said, "This isn't getting us anywhere."

"You'd better listen to us," Willy warned. Skip went on with the bitter tirade, and Big Tom stood up on his chair and all at once there was a gun in his hand. It was a shining and well-kept-looking Luger, not new but quite businesslike. Big Tom walked over to Skip, and Skip's words died in his throat.

"It's like this, kid." Big Tom whipped the gun against Skip's face, not edgewise but cupped flat in his hand. The skin burst in a few places and Skip spun sidewise, catching himself at the rim of the bed. He felt as if the bones of his jaw and of his face in front of his ear had snapped to splinters. He sucked a breath in agony. He saw Big Tom through a whipping red haze. "Now that wasn't anything," Big Tom said, "but just a tap. I can do better if I have to, lots better. I like bouncing punks around. If you weren't Willy's kin I'd show you how I like to do it."

Skip pushed erect and touched his face with a shaking hand, not sure there was anything but pulp there. His head still rang from the blow, the blow that hadn't looked like anything when he'd seen it coming. It occurred to him that this man called Big Tom had a freakish strength and power in his hands.

There was something else here, too, something that frightened Skip more than the blow. The old man exuded a terrific authority. He was boss, kingfish, top banana, and he knew it. Skip tried to feel his way past that bulwark of power, and couldn't. There was no softness, no pity. The old man stood over Skip with the Luger balanced in his palm and he had Skip under control as he would have controlled a puppy.

Skip crouched, rubbing his aching head, and stared across the room at Uncle Willy. Willy looked back with a sort of mild sympathy, as if he was sorry that Big Tom had had to do what he had done. Skip tried to figure out where his uncle had located this character so quickly, and came to the conclusion that Willy must still have some connections with his old organization. He had dug Big Tom out of his past, and now the job was being taken away from Skip and given over to this old con. Skip thought he would have pegged Tom for an old con even in passing him on the street.

Willy said mildly, "Now straighten up, Skip, and listen to reason."

Skip said nothing. Words boiled in his mind, but he knew what he would get in return if he spoke them.

"He'll be all right now," said Big Tom, putting the gun back into his belt at his belly. "He just needed a little lesson."

The ringing was leaving Skip's ears. The pain remained at the side of his skull. He looked from Willy to Big Tom and thought, *There's going to be a way to pay this back.*

Big Tom sat down again. "I want to talk to you about this Eddie Barrett." He waited, as if he might expect some remark from Skip. "I want to know what he expects out of this thing."

"Money," said Skip gratingly.

"Don't get sassy with me," Big Tom warned. "I mean, what're his plans? What's he want to do afterwards?"

Skip blinked, then lowered his eyes. He knew that some importance attached to his answer. He wished he knew in what way so that he could reply in a way to screw things up. Everything he could do now, short of outright rebellion, he meant to throw in their way.

Finally he thought, It's too soon. I don't know enough yet. He said, "Eddie's mother is sick. He wants to help her, pay for a doctor or something. The old man drinks and raises hell. Eddie wants to get away from him. At least, that's what he talks about."

"What does he want for himself? Clothes? A car?"

"Yeah, a car."

"Does he have a girl?"

"Not that I know of."

Big Tom sat in silence, as if digesting this information. Willy said, "Tell us about Las Vegas, now. What did you find out?"

"Stolz is over there. He's a partner at the Solano Sea."

Willy nodded. "One of the big ones. Well established. You saw plenty of play in the casino, I bet."

Skip said, "Yeah, it looked okay."

Willy moistened his lips. "The next step, the girl. You've got

to make sure this Karen knows where the money is, how much
it is, how long before Stolz might get back. When will you see
her? Not before tonight?"

"I'll see her in class."

Big Tom said, "We want to ease this Eddie Barrett out of it.
Can you handle it?"

"I don't know. Suppose I can't?"

"It would be better for him if you do it," Big Tom said.

"He's going to be surprised," Skip said. "I don't know how
he'll take it."

"This is the way he'd better take it. He'll forget he knows
Karen or ever heard of the money. He'll think you changed
your mind."

Eddie might believe he'd changed his mind, Skip thought.
He might even want to believe it. Eddie wasn't nearly as keen
on the job as Skip was. But Skip made a mental note: he
wouldn't follow any directions in regard to Eddie. Eddie might
turn out to be what Skip needed. He could be the one to foul
them up, if Skip could plan it. "Oh, he'll go along," Skip said
to Big Tom. "I'll convince him it wasn't a good idea, there
wasn't any money there after all, or something like that."

Big Tom said, "You let us know exactly what he says, how
he takes it."

"Sure. Sure."

"There are going to be two other men in this. You won't
meet them," Big Tom continued. "I'm just telling you about
them so you'll understand about the split. We're letting you in
for ten per cent."

Skip said nothing. His rage was already throttled down; if
anything, this lessened it. He saw with a cold certainty how
Willy had rooked him, conned and betrayed him. Willy had
taken the great golden opportunity, the once-in-a-lifetime
chance, and turned it over to his friends. For what?

As if Willy knew what he was thinking, he said, "That's what
I get too, Skip. Between us—twenty per cent. Twenty per cent
of possibly a million. Nothing to do, just sit tight." He leaned
forward as if trying to rouse some hint of enthusiasm from
Skip. Or perhaps an uneasy warning stirred in him, the knowledge of what Skip was like when he was frustrated or crossed.

Skip didn't look at his uncle. He said to Big Tom, "Are you

cutting Karen out, too? She gives you the information and you leave her there with nothing, leave her for the old woman and the cops? Karen's kind of young. She's liable to squawk. She'll squawk about me. For ten per cent, I'm the pigeon?"

"You don't have to be," said Big Tom easily. "You can handle her the way you do Eddie Barrett. Tell her it's all off, you've changed your mind. Or if you want, take her away somewhere when the job comes off." He made an emphasizing gesture, lifting a hand, the thick fingers curled above the fleshy palm. Skip noted the broad and powerful wrist. "There's this, though. When she leaves they'll look for her. They find her, they've got you then. They'll work on your alibi. It had better be a good one."

"In the can on drunk and disorderly is best," said Willy.

"I'm not crazy about it," Big Tom argued. "Still, they can't blink away a jail booking."

Skip got the complete picture now. He was going to be paid off to keep out of it, to build an unassailable alibi in case he was picked up. Willy would be paid for information given. The girl and Eddie were to be brushed aside as expendable. They would have no knowledge of Big Tom, represented no danger, had nothing with which to trade. The hog's share of the loot would go to Big Tom and his two faceless helpers; plus, Skip suspected, something put aside for the organization.

"Why won't you use me on the job so I could rate a bigger cut?" Skip begged, testing them.

Big Tom nodded in judicious approval. "In anything smaller I'd do just that. For Willy's sake. But, kid, I've got experienced men I've worked with before. I know just how good they are and, even more, that in an emergency they won't lose their heads and goof off. They'll never break where the bulls are concerned, either. They've been tested." His eyes mocked Skip with a wolfish humor.

"Skip," said Uncle Willy, as if making a last plea for understanding, "it's not just the job. It's the beef, the squawk afterwards. Things can go haywire in a hell of a hurry. Somebody's singing your name to the wrong folks before you even know it. Now just picture it, because I know you never did, but try: you and Karen and Eddie with all that dough. What were you going to do afterwards?"

Skip didn't answer. He had nothing at all to say to Willy. He looked at Big Tom politely and said, "If you don't mind, I'd like to get some sleep now. I've been up all night and I'm beat."

"Sure. Get your sleep." Big Tom stood up and nodded to Uncle Willy and they went out and down the steps to the yard. Skip gave them a couple of minutes. Then he rose and, walking silently in his socks, he went into the bathroom and inspected his face in the mirror. An area of bruised flesh was swelling and darkening in front of his ear. He turned sidewise, inspecting it, and curses growled in his throat. He ran cold water into a towel, squeezed it lightly, patted the swollen place. It was going to look like hell tonight; and in class, under the bright lights, he'd feel like a fool. He decided then not to attend class but to wait for Karen outside on the break.

He went back to the bed and lay down on top of the covers and stared at the ceiling. The picture was clear, but his own part in it was not.

Uncle Willy and Big Tom went out to the alley, where Tom's Ford sedan was parked. An old lime tree was blooming against the fence and the air was sweet with the smell of its blossoms. Willy said, "He'll be okay. He got a little excited there at first, but that was natural. He's settled down now."

Big Tom said slowly, "When you get a chance, talk to him. He has a chance here he'll never get again."

Willy nodded excitedly. "Sure. Nothing to do. A wad of dough just for sitting still. What more could he ask?"

"Keep an eye on him," Big Tom said. "I'll be back tonight around eleven."

"We'll be waiting for you." Uncle Willy turned and hurried through the yard to the rear door of the big house at the front of the lot. In the kitchen was Mr. Chilworth in pajamas and robe; he'd already had breakfast and Uncle Willy was surprised to find him here. Mr. Chilworth was staring nearsightedly into one of the kitchen drawers.

"What is it, Mr. Chilworth?"

"Oh, there you are!" Mr. Chilworth opened a second drawer. "I need a screw driver. One of the pulls on my dresser drawer is loose."

"I'll fix it, Mr. Chilworth."

"Would you? That's fine." He was near the back windows now; through the screened porch the stairs of the room above the garage were plainly visible. For a moment Uncle Willy worried whether Mr. Chilworth might have seen him with Big Tom, an item Big Tom wouldn't have liked; but then he reminded himself of Mr. Chilworth's extremely bad sight. There was nothing to be worried about.

Mrs. Havermann walked along the upstairs hall to the stair railing. From above she could see the lower hall, wide and shadowy, and through an open archway a part of the parlor. She leaned on the railing and stood still for a moment as if listening, then called, "Karen! Karen, are you down there?"

In Stolz's room Karen was on her knees before the open door of the old-fashioned wardrobe. She had a hand stretched to touch the heap of money inside. Her expression was one of fascinated fright. When she heard Mrs. Havermann's voice she jerked her hand back as if from something hot. Quickly she got to her feet, shut the walnut panel, and walked across the room. She brushed at her face, then glanced at the sweat on her fingers in surprise. She opened the door just a crack.

"Karen!"

She was safe. From upstairs Mrs. Havermann couldn't see the door of Stolz's room. Karen came out, stumbled a dozen feet, looked up.

"Oh. There you are. Come up here, Karen, I've something to show you." Mrs. Havermann indicated some linens over her arm. As Karen mounted the stairs she moved away from the railing to meet her. "I've been looking into the hall closets. Here are some sheets nearly worn through. We'll cut them up for pillowcases and dish towels. The nice thing about a sheet . . . when it wears, there's so much left to do things with."

Karen came up the last of the stairs. Her heart still thumped and she couldn't keep her breathing steady. As she took the linens from Mrs. Havermann she expected some comment, some notice—surely Mrs. Havermann would see her excitement. But as Karen ventured to lift her eyes, she found Mrs. Havermann's gaze focused just beyond her. The look in Mrs. Havermann's eyes was as always vaguely pleasant and cheerful.

In that instant it occurred to Karen that through the years Mrs. Havermann had always regarded her like this. As if she were a shadow through which Mrs. Havermann must peer. As if she were not quite a living being. As if there lay between them a vast distance, an ocean of indifference.

Karen saw this now because in her fright she expected the attention of the other woman.

Mrs. Havermann transferred the sheets to Karen's arm and then said unexpectedly, "Were you in the kitchen just now?"

Karen, caught off guard, could only stammer, "No, I wasn't."

Through the rimless glasses Mrs. Havermann's gaze seemed mildly puzzled. "I have the strangest impression lately that you drop out of sight now and then. Just disappear. You aren't hiding kittens in the cellar again, are you?" The tone was not exactly chiding, nor was there much curiosity in Mrs. Havermann's attitude.

Struck with guilt, her tongue thick, Karen got out, "No, I'm not."

There was no argument, no real interest on Mrs. Havermann's part. She was picking at the sheets. "Measure the towels by those in the kitchen. Be sure to get them square. Don't forget to change the bobbin on the machine. Black's on it now." She smiled vaguely and turned away. She was short and stout and heavily corseted. The artificial tightness of the corset lengthened her torso, flattened the softness around her middle. She walked as though encased in a barrel whose contents must be kept in delicate balance. Her gray hair she piled high on her head in an effort to gain height.

Mrs. Havermann had stood near, had looked at her and had turned away, and to Karen it was at once a miracle and a revelation. She had never quite realized before how indefinite and withdrawn Mrs. Havermann's manner was toward her. Along with gratitude over her escape from discovery Karen felt almost a sense of shock that Mrs. Havermann had paid so little real attention.

Karen went back downstairs. Past Stolz's room—she gave it a quick guilty glance—and then on to where the hall made a right-angle turn in the direction of the pantry, the huge kitchen, and the rear entry. In the sewing room, once a maid's room, stood a long cutting table made of boards laid on a pair of sawhorses. Karen put the sheets here, got scissors from the sewing machine, and set to work. She had no objection to the task at hand. She was not lazy, and the solitude of working alone gave her time to think.

The thing on which her thoughts fastened most desperately was the great store of money in Stolz's room. It at once fascinated and repelled her. Most of all, from it she absorbed a stunning sense of danger.

She had worked for a short time when she heard Mrs. Havermann's quick step in the hall. The door opened and the older woman stared in at her. There was no vagueness now; behind the rimless glasses Mrs. Havermann's eyes were sharp. "Karen, have you been in Mr. Stolz's room today?"

On the heels of fright, the denial was automatic. "I never go in there."

Mrs. Havermann hesitated in the doorway, her excitement subsiding. "Well, it's rather odd. There's something out of place in there. I can't remember seeing it earlier." She tapped the door lintel with a nail, obviously puzzled.

Karen's heart filled with fear. She knew exactly what must be out of place in that room; Stolz's overcoat was lying on the bed. Stolz kept it folded on top of the money so that in first opening the wardrobe you didn't see the heap of bills. When she had gone in to stare in fascination at the treasure she'd put the coat on the bed, and when Mrs. Havermann had called her she'd forgotten to replace it.

"Perhaps Mr. Stolz changed things around," she managed to get out.

"It's not the furniture." Mrs. Havermann turned back into the hall. "I wonder . . . could he have laid it out for the cleaners and I not noticed?"

Karen waited. Concerning Stolz, Mrs. Havermann was close-mouthed, inclined to sentimental secrecy; Karen decided that she would not be told all about the coat. "Didn't he send suits out when he was here?"

"No, that was time before last." Mrs. Havermann nodded, as if deciding for herself what to do with the coat. "That's it—he wants it sent off to be cleaned."

Karen was at a loss, though she saw the pitfall she had

constructed for herself. When Stolz returned there would be conversation about the coat, where it had been found and what had been done with it; and whether she was able to argue Skip out of what he wanted to do, or not, she was in trouble up to her neck.

She looked mutely after Mrs. Havermann. She needed help, needed to confide; but Mrs. Havermann was already too far away.

Chapter Seven

K AREN WALKED out to the terrace when class was dismissed for the mid-evening break, and she was startled to find Skip there waiting, smoking a cigarette, grinning at her. He pulled her close and kissed her, and something in Karen, constricted and repressed, born of her life at Mrs. Havermann's, seemed to burst and flood her with warmth. She returned the kiss hungrily, clutching the shoulders of his jacket. Then she lay against him, grateful; here was someone to whom she could confide the disaster with the coat. She told Skip about it all in a rush.

Skip listened, at first with indifference. He'd heard already from Eddie of Karen's reaction to the money, her frightened excitement about it. It took a moment to realize that this wasn't more of the same, the reaction of an inexperienced girl, but that a bad break had really occurred. Then it struck him with irony that this would be exactly what was needed if he meant to string along with Big Tom and Uncle Willy. Now was the time to pretend everything was off, that he was afraid Stolz would be warned and have the money guarded. But even as he opened his mouth to speak Skip changed his mind. He noticed that Karen was looking at him closely in the dim light.

"What happened to your face?"

His hand jumped automatically to touch the sore spot. "I . . . auh . . . I fell, getting off the bus in Vegas."

"It looks terrible! You should have a bandage on it."

"No, it's okay."

She lifted a hand gently but he brushed it aside.

"How much money does Stolz keep there?"

"I don't know."

"You haven't counted it? What's the matter? Scared or something?"

"It scares me," Karen admitted, wide-eyed. "There's so much of it. Too much to count." She touched his arm timidly. "Leave it alone, Skip."

He flipped the cigarette into the dark. "Big bills?"

"All I saw were hundreds."

Skip rubbed his hair, stretched lazily. "Sounds as if Eddie and I ought to do it tonight."

Her eyes were stark. "Why . . . how could you?"

"The way we planned. You let us in around midnight, keep an eye out for the old woman, keep the dog quiet. How long will it take? Not over a couple of minutes. It'll be a breeze."

"It won't turn out the way you think. I know it." She stood in the direct light from the door, trying to make Skip look at her; but now his gaze had a vagueness that reminded her of Mrs. Havermann's. He peered beyond her at the hall, and she blurted: "What will happen when Stolz gets back?"

"To you? Nothing. You could lie your way out of it. Or come to me." He reached for her, pulled her close again; he could feel her heart thumping like a rabbit's, and the knowledge of her fright and torment filled him with amusement. "What about the old lady? You ever tell her my name, mention seeing me in school?"

"I guess she knows I talk to you. I've told her things you've said."

"Chrissakes, that was a dumb thing to do. Now she'll have a line on me."

"No. Rather than have anyone suspect you, I'll stay and make up a story; someone's been prowling around when I got home at night, and I saw them. I'll describe somebody. A stranger."

Skip stood musing, wondering if Karen were capable of carrying it off. Then he wanted to laugh at himself. Of course Karen wouldn't be able to stand up to the characters Stolz would bring in. They'd have her babbling the whole thing in a couple of minutes. He let his mind dwell on some possible methods they might use, grinned, shook his head, while she watched. "You wouldn't back down? Even to Stolz?"

He was just having fun though she didn't know it. "I'd never give you away. Never." She put her arms around him, tucked her head against his shoulder. The warning bell rang in the hall, signaling the end of the break.

"You know old lady Havermann could come to class, check up on whoever you've been seen with."

Karen gave a troubled sigh.

Again, Skip thought, the opportunity presented itself. Say

now to her that you're calling it off, go out and build a rock-solid alibi, take the ten per cent from Big Tom and keep your lip buttoned. But again perversity, or perhaps the memory of the gun in Big Tom's fist, kept him from speaking. He was even beginning to enjoy himself, the opportunities offered and shrugged off because, as Uncle Willy would say, he was just a punk and didn't know better.

"I'm just a damned punk," he said aloud, amused with it.

"No, you're not. I love you."

Abruptly he shook her arms free. "Now what the hell kind of talk is that?"

"Well, it slipped out. But I do."

"Listen, Karen. You cut it out. There's not going to be any crap like that here, not between us."

"Sure, Skip."

"Come out this way when class is over. I'll be waiting for you."

She turned away. The wind brushed at her short dark hair, tumbling it; she held it off her face, glancing back at Skip. At the door she blew him a small, light kiss from her fingers.

What a sap she was, Skip thought.

At eleven o'clock Big Tom went into the bath of Uncle Willy's room above the garage, drew a glass of water, stepped to the open door to drink it. "He's always here by eleven?"

"Has been, up to now. Even earlier sometimes." Uncle Willy sat on his small bed with a garden-seed catalogue in his hands. Mr. Chilworth had expressed a fantastic but determined whim for snapdragons and phlox. He wanted them along the side of the house and along the front walks. It was crazy, an abominable amount of work for Uncle Willy. "Class runs to ten, seven o'clock to ten. He ought to of been here by now."

"Why in hell doesn't he go to school daytimes?"

"Well . . . Skip's an adult. Adult classes are almost all at night. You know, most people work."

Big Tom frowned. "He's staying out later for some reason. I smell something funny."

Uncle Willy said soothingly, "Oh, Skip wouldn't try anything."

"He'd better not. I don't want any preliminary fooling

around, a job I handle. There's been too much already." Big Tom put the glass back into its holder above the small basin, came back, sat down on Skip's bed.

As if to get Big Tom's attention off Skip, Uncle Willy asked, "You got somebody in Las Vegas already?"

"Benny Busick. He flew over, going to look around and see if Stolz has had a tax beef in the last few years."

"If Stolz has—it'll be tax dough?"

"Probably not. It's the ones the tax bulls haven't looked at who still feel like hanging onto their little nest eggs."

"I'll bet Stolz is robbing the tax bulls blind," Uncle Willy decided with a grudging touch of admiration.

Big Tom leaned his arms on his knees, rubbed his chin, frowned at the open light in the middle of the ceiling. "I don't know. There's something screwy about the setup, a chunk like that left unlocked and unguarded in a house with an old woman and a girl. It's careless-like, and a boy such as Stolz isn't careless, ever. It's almost like he's got some kind of guarantee. Something to keep everybody away."

"There's a dog," Uncle Willy offered.

"Oh, hell, I'm not talking about a dog."

"Maybe he's keeping it for a friend."

Big Tom smiled slightly, as if Uncle Willy had cracked a joke.

They wasted forty-five minutes in the hamburger joint and afterward let Karen out at the corner where the bus stopped. "Now we'll go on to the vacant place and circle around through those trees," Skip told her. She was standing under the glow of a street light and staring across the wide lawn at the house. The house was dark except for a small bulb burning in the enormous cavern of the porch.

"Did you hear me, for Chrissakes?"

"Sure. Sure I heard you."

"The back door. We'll be at the back door."

"What about afterwards?"

"Stay and size it up for a day or two. If she gets wise the money's gone and starts to get hold of Stolz, or makes a squawk for the cops, run. Don't bother to pack a bag or any of that kind of crap. Just walk off."

"Where? Where should I walk, Skip?"

"I'll figure a place. Get going."

Eddie was alone in the car with Skip now. As the car labored up the grade to the rising ground and the trees, Eddie said, "I felt sorry for her there."

"For what? We'll be doing her a favor, getting her out of the dump. The old woman works her tail off, and look at the clothes the chick wears. Not a goddamn thing you wouldn't put on your old maid aunt. She wears cotton underpants, for Chrissakes!"

"She told you?"

Then Eddie knew that Skip was laughing at him, and he shut up. The car labored up the rise and drew to a stop beside the dark curb. Eddie got out. He heard Skip shut the door on the opposite side, not slamming it, ticking the lock quietly. "I wonder why we've never seen a patrol car through here," Eddie said. "Big homes and all. You'd think they'd keep an eye on things."

"They've got an eye on you right now, friend," Skip jeered. "They're reading your mind with a goofus machine. Wait'll we get to the back door. They'll jump out of the bushes."

"Ah, shut up," Eddie said mildly.

It seemed easier this time; they were familiar with the ground and the extent of the grove of trees. They came to a point where they could see the dark bulk of the house, a dim light in one of its upper windows, a little window like a bathroom's; and all at once Eddie was struck by the panic, the aversion and fright he had felt before. His feet grew leaden, his palms sweated. A cloying tightness shut off his breath.

"What's the matter with you?" Skip had paused; by starshine Eddie could see him looking back.

"I . . . Just a minute." He sucked in a deep breath and tried to force himself to relax, tried to force the freezing scare out of his mind. He tried to blank out all thought, since the panic seemed rooted in thinking. But through his mind poured memories of other times, things that he and Skip had done. Most of the jobs had come off all right. They'd sneaked tires and junk off wrecking lots, lanterns and fusees and tools out of freight yards, even cigarettes, a whole huge carton of them, from a half-plundered freight car on a siding. They'd stuck up old man Fedderson's candy shop . . . twice. Stockings over their heads, cap pistols. It had been fun. For God's sake, why did he have to feel like this now?

Was it because of the times things hadn't turned out okay? Like when he rolled the bum in the alley, a dead-end passage behind a garage and a bar and a warehouse, and the patrol car had turned in on him with its lights blazing?

Or the time Skip had whistled from the back yard, the kill-deer call, and he'd gone and Skip had been white and sweating. Skip had borrowed a couple of bucks and had walked to the corner and had been picked up right there, still within sight of the house. Later that day Eddie found out that Skip had been caught robbing a market storeroom of a case of whiskey.

Was it the failures that drained him now of strength?

Skip was standing still, a little way off. "What are you doing there? Are you . . . For Chrissakes, are you getting ready to chicken out on me?"

Eddie's stumbling answer died in his throat.

Skip took a lithe step toward him. "If you are, goddammit, get on with it. Faint. Or drop dead. Or start running. Don't just stand there with your legs locked together. Why in hell should I care what you do? I can't think why I needed you in the first place."

"You said . . . if something went wrong——"

"It is. It is," Skip said wryly. "You're punking out just like Unc said you would."

Eddie failed to catch the revelation at the moment; he was too busy with his own miseries. But the harshness of Skip's tone had the usual effect; it dried up his terror. There was more to be feared from Skip's contempt than from the mysteries of the old house in the dark below them. "Oh, God," Eddie said, "there for a minute . . . I don't know. It just hit me."

"What are you going to do now?"

"I'll be okay. Let's go."

"Sure." Skip stepped closer still and his fist shot out. The blow to Eddie's midsection was small and sharp, and it hurt. Eddie grabbed his stomach; his tongue curled out over his teeth; breath whistled in his nostrils. "Now," Skip said. "Now we'll go."

Eddie stumbled after him. Karen was down there, outside the back door; Eddie could make out that she'd taken off her coat and shoes. She padded toward them. "Be quiet! She's in bed but I heard her turning over; I don't think she's asleep."

Skip was looking up at the house. "Where?"

"The corner there upstairs."

"Open windows?"

"No. She's scared of the night air. Leaves the bathroom window open, the light on in there. I don't know why, maybe because she's nervous."

"What the hell are we beating our gums for out here? Let's go in," Skip said.

"I don't dare turn on a light," Karen whispered. "You'll have to follow me. Don't fall over anything."

"Just lead me to the dough," Skip said. "I won't make any racket."

They crept into the house. This was a windowed porch. Eddie could see the shining white enamel ledges of laundry trays, a black door open in a white wall; he smelled disinfectant and soap.

"This is the washroom," Karen whispered. "We'll go through the kitchen and on to the hall. There's a big table in the middle of the kitchen, pots stacked on a shelf underneath. For God's sake don't touch that table."

"Where's Stolz's room?"

"I'll have to show you."

Feeling his way in the dark, Eddie saw with incredulous wonder how stupid they had been. He and Skip should have known all about the house, every obstacle; should have managed to look it over during the old woman's absence, or drawn a map from Karen's description. Now they had to be led along as if blind; and above him he felt the old woman on her bed, wide awake and waiting to hear them stumble. He fought panic again, glad that Skip couldn't see.

They got through the kitchen. Eddie's eyes were adjusted to the dark; he could see the white rectangle of the table's surface, so there was no problem in avoiding it. He kept expecting to bump into something invisible, though. Or to kick some pan or dish left for the dog to eat or drink from.

Where was the dog?

He wanted to ask Karen, but she was ahead of Skip and his voice might carry, might rouse the old woman upstairs.

The hall was darker, closed in and stuffy. The house was old; you could smell age in it, old varnish and dead wax and underpinnings touched with mold, all clean and swept on the surface. There was none of the familiar effluvium of home, where the choking goiter and a palpitating heart kept his mother all but bedridden, and flies and dirt grew thicker day by day. Eddie's shoes brushed the carpet, roused no smell of dust, just that of old wool and mothproofing. He all but ran into Skip. Skip and Karen had paused before a door.

"Where's the dog?" Eddie got out.

"Upstairs. I shut him in my room."

Skip said, "What the hell's the matter with the door?"

"It doesn't open!"

"Here, let me try it." Skip moved; Eddie heard his soft dry step on the wood beyond the carpet; he heard a sort of grunt and a faint click of metal. "For Chrissakes, it's locked!"

"No, it couldn't be!" Karen whispered in a positive way.

"Well, it goddamn well is. Here, Eddie, have a go at it and see if it isn't locked."

Eddie tried the knob, warm from Karen and Skip's hands. "Sure it's locked." He said in Karen's direction, "Maybe she's always locked it at night and you didn't know it."

"It's never been locked before," Karen said positively. Her voice was beginning to quiver.

"What about the windows?" Skip asked.

"You'd need a ladder."

"Well, for Chrissakes get me a ladder!" Skip was angry and he was losing control, forgetting to keep his voice low. Eddie expected at any moment to be bathed in light, to find the old woman standing and looking at them from the other end of the hall.

"The ladder's in the garage. I'll have to get the garage key from the hook in the kitchen."

After agonizing minutes of creeping back through the dark house, of delay while Karen put on her shoes and got the garage key and opened the garage and found the ladder, of the risk of noise and exposure, of Skip's climbing the high old wall of the house above the basement windows, it came out——

The windows of Stolz's room were locked as tight as its door.

Chapter Eight

Eddie carried the ladder back to the garage and Karen, moving beside him in the dark, showed him where to stow it away. They came outside again and found Skip. He stood without moving, utterly silent, and Eddie had a sudden sense of warning. The next moment Skip had turned on Karen. He grabbed her and slammed her into the wall and then jerked his hand back and hit her with the edge of his fist. Her head snapped and Eddie heard the bump it gave against the garage wall. "You goddamn bitch!"

Eddie said, "Skip, cut it out. We can't have a racket here."

Skip paid no attention. "I'll show you!" He snatched at her hair, got his fingers into it, jerked her forward almost off balance. She tried to catch his knees to keep from falling; he slapped her hands away. She'd begun to whimper. She stumbled around Skip, off balance, and then he yanked her head up again and she gave a small shrill cry.

Eddie moved then. His action was involuntary, without plan. He put out a foot and then with a quick tentative step he was closer and pushing Skip in the face with his open hand. Skip tried to hang onto the girl and handle Eddie, but he couldn't do it. Eddie got a good leverage under his chin and jabbed hard and Skip fell over backward. He was on his feet again in an instant, like a dropped cat. He moved in with a flurry of blows.

Eddie wasn't Skip's kind of fighter. Skip danced and flicked his fists and tormented an opponent, while Eddie just stood and took punishment and waited; but pretty soon Eddie found what he was looking for and he let loose a solid heavy blow that snapped Skip's head back and flung him off his feet. He sat there under the starshine, not hopping up as before, but stunned, groggy. "You leave her alone," Eddie said. "From now on."

There seemed an eternity of quiet out there in the dim dark beside the old garage. Eddie stood over Skip. He was tensed, a hot fiddle-string tautness filling him, his fists hard as hammers. He was ready for Skip to move. Skip sat bent, his head hanging.

His light-colored hair shone a little in the gloom, but his face was in shadow, and Eddie couldn't even guess what sort of expression was on it. One thing he knew, Skip didn't accept defeat. His reaction was always simply to be meaner and tougher and cleverer than ever.

Oddly enough, Skip didn't say much. He got to his feet, grunted, brushed at his clothes, and then looked around as if for Karen.

Karen was across the open space, near the house. The light from the little window high in the wall shone down on her, and Eddie could see the look of shock she had, the tear shine on her face and the frightened attitude of her body. When Skip walked toward her she backed to the wall.

Skip stood, balancing on the balls of his feet, his hands in his pockets. He said almost indifferently, "You're okay, aren't you?"

Eddie wondered why she didn't run into the house. She was scared; Skip's violence had astounded her. But he heard her whisper, "Yes, I'm okay."

"Sore at me?"

"You didn't have to hurt me," Karen said. "Finding the door locked was just as big a surprise to me as it was to you." She was looking at Skip now as if something about him was new and unfamiliar.

Skip stood quietly, almost meekly. It was an act, of course. Eddie had seen Skip do it a thousand times, and though it was false, a fantastic pretense, he could almost believe—as Karen must—that Skip was sorry for what he had done. "Well, sure, I blew my stack over nothing. Why do you think she locked the door if she's never done it before?"

"On account of the coat," Karen said wearily. "Mr. Stolz kept it lying on the money, covering the money so you didn't see it if you accidentally opened the door of the wardrobe. Maybe she knew where the coat belonged or maybe she didn't recognize it because Mr. Stolz never wears it. I don't know. She got excited when she found it lying on the bed."

After a while Skip said musingly, "What a rotten break."

Karen didn't say anything. She knew that Skip blamed her.

Skip said, "Well, you'll have to find that key tomorrow."

"Oh no, Skip! Please! It's too dangerous. It's time to stop now."

"You'll find it," Skip insisted. He didn't take any step nearer, but something in his eyes that Karen could see, that Eddie couldn't see from where he stood, seemed to frighten her. "You'll be sure that door's not locked tomorrow night, and we'll be here right on schedule. Then afterwards we'll have fun."

Eddie wished there was some way he might have comforted her. She looked as if her world were coming apart at the seams.

Eddie let himself into the rear of the house. There was no one in the living room tonight. From the bedroom he heard his father's snoring. He knew that his mother must be lying in there awake and miserable, trying to rest because that was what the doctor had told her to do, but kept from sleeping by the grunts and snorts of her husband.

The bastard abused her even in sleep, Eddie thought, tiptoeing across to his own door. Inside, he pulled off his jacket and shirt and flung them over a chair and sat down on the bed to unlace his shoes. They were tennis sneakers and quite shabby; the laces had knots in them and Eddie had to pluck with his nails until they loosened enough for him to shuck off the shoes.

The money in Stolz's room would buy a hell of a lot of shoes. A million other things besides, too. Eddie threw the tennis sneakers under the chair and sat thinking of what he would buy with his share of the loot when they pulled off the job. There would be a tremendous amount of cash. Enough for dozens of suits, shirts, sharp new shoes, a car. An operation for his mother, removing the ugly balloon at the base of her throat. Clothes for her, all kinds of silk dresses, a fur coat, new furniture for the house if she wanted it. And all this, dazzling as it was, would only scratch the surface.

An odd uneasiness stirred in his mind.

It was hard to conceive of all the possibilities wrapped up in the bundle of money in Stolz's wardrobe. When you were used to a dollar or two, even a hundred seemed more than you could count. A thousand was fabulous. With five thousand you'd feel like doing something silly, maybe, just to be spending, something crazy like buying a gold-plated switch blade . . . or taking dancing lessons so you could do fancy steps better than anybody . . . or buying all silk shirts with monograms . . . His imagination sought for other images, roamed in a dazzle of overwhelming splendor.

Under the dazzle the uneasiness increased. Eddie put his finger on it. The natural, crazy things you did with a lot of money were the things he and Skip had to be careful not to do.

They needed a plan. He hunted around through the cloud of dissatisfaction and apprehension in his mind and decided that what worried him was Skip's apparently deliberate lack of planning. Skip was either unable or unwilling to choose a course of action and stick to it. He wanted to improvise, to make his decisions when the time came for them; and even Eddie could see the danger in it.

Eddie roused himself, shed his pants, snapped off the light, and crawled under the thin covers. He stretched his body on the bed. To hell with worrying. This job was Skip's baby. Let Skip do the worrying.

He found himself thinking of Karen then. The idea came abruptly; she was too young for Skip. The clothes the old woman put on her made her look old for her years; but inside, Karen was terribly unadult. It was as if she'd been stunted at about the age of twelve, never allowed to grow further, so that in addition to the youngness there was an inner hunger and craving, a need. The need had sent her to Skip, as if he might show her how to grow up and be a woman.

You got smart around Skip, Eddie thought, but you didn't grow up because Skip has never grown up and has no idea how to show anyone else to do it.

Eddie sat up in the dark, rubbing his head. The memory of the moment came back, how he'd stood over Skip with his fists knotted, wanting Skip to get up and dance around him some more so that he could land another scorcher.

Now why did I want to do that? Eddie wondered. Why in Chrissakes should I get so worked up over Karen, when she's Skip's girl and he ought to be able to treat her the way he wants to?

Skip was twenty-two. My God, he ought to know by now how women should be treated.

Skip stood in the dark at the foot of the steps to Willy's room. He smoked a cigarette, listened to the voices from upstairs. That big bastard was there again with his uncle and Skip had an ominous feeling that his coming in late was a mistake.

Finally he went on upstairs and opened the door. Uncle Willy sat on his cot in his pajamas and cotton robe. His skinny feet, the toes knobbed with corns, were tucked Buddha-fashion at his knees. He smiled nervously at Skip. "Well. Hello. You're pretty late tonight. Something keep you?"

Skip knew all at once that his clothes and his face showed the effects of his bout with Eddie. "I had a fight over a bitch."

"Now that's interesting. Who's the lady?"

"Karen Miller." Skip hadn't moved away from the door. He was waiting for some action from Big Tom, who was standing across the room. The big brush of gray hair caught the light; the freckles were brilliant against the pale skin. A typical con, Skip thought in disgust. He thought he'd never seen a guy who showed prison like Tom did.

Big Tom began to walk toward him on the balls of his feet. He exuded authority and power. He could run over Skip or anybody like a hippo over a mouse. Skip hated him so fiercely it was dizzying.

Big Tom stopped about two feet from Skip. "Who'd you fight?"

"Eddie Barrett."

"That half-Mex punk?" Uncle Willy cried. "You still messing around with him?"

"Tell us about it," Big Tom suggested.

The tone warned Skip. He had to take this easy. He said, "Well, this girl, this Karen Miller, she's trying to make a play for me. She wouldn't talk about the money unless I took her home in the car. Eddie came along."

"You went out to the house?" Big Tom asked sharply.

"Not all the way. I got her to the neighborhood, near enough to walk, and I asked about the dough, Stolz's money, and she got cute. I was . . . uh . . . urging her a little when Eddie blew up. Oh, hell, in the end it wasn't anything. But it took time." Skip thought, Time's what I've got to explain. That's all they give a damn about.

"Eddie got sore over what you were doing to the girl?" Big Tom asked. "That doesn't sound so good."

"Ah, he's soft in the head. I'm glad now I'm not going through with it with him."

Big Tom was watching him sharply. "You explained about that?"

"Oh, sure, once Karen had spilled, I let on I'd turned cold on the idea."

"How did Barrett take it?"

"Just . . . nothing." Skip shrugged. "He didn't have any complaints. Hell, he wouldn't know what to do with a sawbuck if he got that much together."

"He heard everything Karen had to say?"

"Yeah, I couldn't get rid of him." Skip was feeling his way cautiously, wary for any sign of violence from Big Tom, any indication Big Tom needed to prove who was boss again. "He's just a sap, he doesn't know what it's all about. He's busy thinking all the time about his mother being sick and his old man steamed up on vino."

Big Tom seemed to believe Skip. He walked over and sat down on one of the battered straight chairs, a discard from Mr. Chilworth's place up front, reversing the chair and folding his big arms across the back. "I want to know about the place. The house, inside. The money. Where it is and how much."

"Well . . . as for the house . . ." Skip sat down on his bed. "The way Karen describes it, there's a hall from the kitchen. Several doors in it. Stolz's room is to the right. He keeps the money in a wardrobe, a kind of thing Karen says is half drawers and half a kind of cupboard for clothes."

"I know about wardrobes."

"Well, the money is in the big half under a coat, just piled there. She hasn't counted it. Looks like a lot."

"The room's never locked?"

"Nah, it's never locked." Skip forced himself to meet Big Tom's gaze with an air of frankness. *It'll be locked when you get there, you bastard. There won't be anything inside, though.*

"That's what I don't like. The carelessness." Big Tom was frowning. Uncle Willy picked up a flower-seed catalogue off the cot and riffled its pages nervously. "If it was anyone but

Stolz . . . If it was the old woman, for instance. I could believe she'd stuff the money in there and be stupid enough to
think no one would find it. Hell, they do it all the time, little
old ladies keeping a wad in a teapot or a tomato can."

Skip shook his head. "The money belongs to Stolz. Karen's
sure of it."

He had a flash of hope that Big Tom would worry himself
right out of the job, but the hope faded. Big Tom got up and
picked up his coat, shrugged into it. "Well, there's a reason,
God knows what. I don't expect to move, though, until I hear
from Benny in Las Vegas. That should be tomorrow. I'll get in
touch with you, Willy. You and Skip can be figuring out where
you'll be. I happened to think—— Skip being in class, that
would be good enough. You need to be where people will see
you, Willy; I don't believe I'd do the jail routine."

"You can't argue with a jail record," Uncle Willy repeated.

"It makes you look bad," Big Tom said firmly. "Do something else."

"All right."

"I'll see that Snope is notified; he'll be standing by in case
we need him." Big Tom went to the door, paused there to give
Skip a studying glance. "I don't think we'll have any trouble.
Getting it shouldn't amount to much. Keeping out of Stolz's
way afterwards might take a little work. Or it could be he can't
afford a squawk and there's nothing to be afraid of."

And I handed it over to you by blabbing to Uncle Willy,
Skip thought, his expressionless eyes on Big Tom's face.

Big Tom went out quietly, closing the door. His steps went
down softly on the stairs to the yard. A minute later they heard
his Ford start up in the alley. Uncle Willy said, "It's going to
work out fine, Skip. You'll see, we'll have a fat cut, no work or
effort, nothing pinned on us by the bulls."

"Just as you say." Skip stood up and began to undress. In his
shorts he went into the bathroom, washed his teeth, scrubbed
his face and hands and arms with soap. He looked at his face in
the mirror above the basin. There was no doubt but that he
and Uncle Willy bore a strong resemblance to each other. To
Skip, however, Willy was hideous with the wasting of time, of
frustration, poverty, and denial. It was the way Skip would

look after years of small jobs and petty thefts and jail. Damned if I will, Skip told himself. There's this one big chance and it's got to be for me.

Tomorrow night Big Tom and his friends would move in on old lady Havermann. He and Eddie had to be there first. There was this one break; he didn't have to account for himself to Tom; he was supposed to be in class. Tom had been a sap to trust him, but everybody makes mistakes. Tom must have made plenty or he wouldn't have that old burned-out look of a con.

He went back into the other room. Uncle Willy was in bed, the covers pulled up around his skinny shoulders, facing the wall.

"Turn out the light. Good night, Skip."

"Night."

Skip clipped off the light and lay down. Just before dropping off to sleep he thought briefly of Karen as he had seen her last, standing in the faint glow from the little window high in the old woman's house. She'd looked scared to death. Eager, too, eager to be sure that Skip wasn't really mad at her, that lashing out at her had been the impulse of a moment. Skip thought drowsily, I can do anything I want to with her. I can beat her half to death and she'll come crawling back, wearing that same sappy look, wanting to be sure I'm not really mad at her. Why are dames like that? Why don't they, for Chrissakes, have any guts?

Skip smiled to himself in superior humor and then drifted off to sleep.

Big Tom was awakened by the clamor of the phone in the other room. It was still dark. The dry canyon wind blew in at the open window. A couple of cats on the bed near his feet lifted their heads as he stirred and reached for the rubber sandals.

He snapped on the little lamp and looked at the clock. A quarter of four. "What the hell . . ." The phone was ringing like a fire alarm in the quiet of the lonely house. Big Tom padded into the front room and lifted the receiver. "Yeah?"

"Benny Busick here."

"Huh. You calling from Vegas?"

"That's right. Look . . . uh, this transaction we were discussing. There's something here I can't put my finger on. Working at it. You didn't need that information for a day or so, now, did you?"

"Today, you crumb. I need it right now. What in hell are you doing over there?"

"Don't blow your goddamned stack at me. I'm just telling you. It's an angle. I'm working on it and I need time."

"By noon today or don't bother."

"Okay, I'm still trying. Take my advice. Lay off until you hear from me." Benny's gravelly voice was wheedling.

"It's noon or nothing." Big Tom put the telephone back in its cradle and sat there yawning and rubbing the mane of gray hair off his forehead. Three of the cats who had been sleeping on chairs awoke and looked around as if it might be time for breakfast.

Big Tom scratched and yawned himself fully awake and then took stock of the conversation just concluded. Hell, there had been no reason for him to snap Benny off like that. Just because he'd been irritable from interrupted sleep and Benny hadn't seemed to have anything definite except a request that Big Tom wait.

That was it, he decided. Benny's desire for a delay, a need for time to search and listen—that had roused the sudden anger.

For a moment Big Tom felt a sense of shock, and then he wanted to laugh at himself. Here he'd been so convinced that there'd never be another job in his life, just this little dump of a house and the plants and the cats—and all the time the hungry impatience had been building in him, the determination to have one more big one.

He was shaking his head over it as he went back to bed, snapped off the light and lay down. The moment of insight passed quickly from his mind, leaving only the crystallized decision to have Stolz's money at the first opportunity.

Chapter Nine

MRS. HAVERMANN never got out of bed much before nine. She usually came downstairs around nine-thirty, always completely dressed and with her hair combed and pinned high and with a touch of powder on her cheeks. She always paused in the lower hall to look over yesterday's bouquet on the table there and to make up her mind what she wanted in the vase today. Then, if the mail had come, she inspected that. There was ordinarily very little—ads addressed to Householder, or perhaps a few bills.

After her husband had died Mrs. Havermann had dropped almost all of her social contacts and had gradually taken on the habits of a recluse. This came about from choice, though not consciously so. It was a matter of a weathered ship finding haven in a peaceful pond. She had been married for many years to a demanding and autocratic man. He had loved social functions and had had many friends. When he wasn't hard at work in his contracting business he played with equal gusto at being a host, gourmet, horse bettor, traveler, or yachtsman. The pace had been stormy.

Though she had never admitted it to herself, her sensations on hearing of her husband's death in a plane accident had been mostly of relief.

The withdrawal from social participation had been accompanied by an emotional withering. She no longer wanted to be involved with other people; she wanted peace. She protected herself, unconsciously, by the pleasant air of vagueness, by concentration upon household trivia, and by a mild daydreaming about Stolz. The fact that he was much too young and too sophisticated to return that interest was also, indirectly, another part of her defense. There was no real danger that the daydreams might become reality and burst the emotional vacuum in which she lived.

Mrs. Havermann had no comprehension of how her futile and barren situation affected Karen. She considered herself as acting properly in the capacity of mother to the girl. There were food, shelter, and clothing, a training at a trade as well.

Behind her wish for Karen to become a nurse had been the unrealized idea that if in the future she should become ill or bedridden Karen could care for her properly. The thought of Karen serving her in her helplessness involved nothing more emotionally moving than that Karen would thus be repaying her for the years of keep.

Karen had refused to go into nursing school. In reproof, Mrs. Havermann had declined to finance a course at business school, had instead made the girl study commercial subjects in adult classes.

On the morning following Skip's and Eddie's abortive attempt to enter Stolz's room, Mrs. Havermann came downstairs at twenty-five minutes past nine. She picked over the flowers on the hall table and then examined the three letters which Karen had brought in. The first was a dental bill, the second a notice of a sale on some hosiery at a department store where she kept an account. The third letter, also an ad, caught her instant attention. It was the notice of the opening of a new local office by a locksmith.

The incident of the coat being out of place had focused her thoughts on Stolz's room, and now the coincidental arrival of this ad had for her an odd, superstitious impact. She turned and stared at the door of Stolz's room, just visible in the corner where the hall turned. She tucked the locksmith's ad back into the envelope, and then, wearing a thoughtful look, she went out to the kitchen.

Karen was at the kitchen table with classwork spread out before her. Mrs. Havermann glanced at her briefly, then looked quickly around the room. Karen's eyes seemed red and swollen. Mrs. Havermann wondered momentarily if Karen could be coming down with a cold. "Well, it's a nice bright day," Mrs. Havermann said, going to the kitchen range. There was coffee hot in the percolator and Mrs. Havermann poured herself a cup of it. "What would you like for breakfast today, Karen?"

"Whatever you'd like, Aunt Maude." Karen was gathering up her books and papers. Her manner was dull and depressed. She put the books into a locker and took dishes and silver from another cupboard.

The exchange was so routine that Mrs. Havermann would

have been astonished had Karen actually offered a preference in food. She carried her cup of coffee to a window and stood there to drink it while looking out at the sky. The sun bathed the yard in bright morning light. Frowning, Mrs. Havermann noticed that the lawn between the house and garage had a trampled appearance, and this annoyed and puzzled her. She sipped at the coffee and thought about it. She didn't speak of her impression to Karen but decided to go out after breakfast and look more closely at the area. Suddenly she thought again of the locksmith's notice and an odd alarm ran through her.

When the coffee was gone she set the cup on the table, went to the refrigerator, took out a bowl of leftover cereal, two small eggs, and a package of bacon. At the stove she reheated the oatmeal, boiled the eggs, fried two slices of bacon.

Karen was abnormally listless and untalkative, and her obvious depression penetrated even Mrs. Havermann's aloofness. But Mrs. Havermann at once dismissed it from her mind; she wanted to think about the trampled grass and other household matters. Biting into her breakfast toast, she said, "I'm going into town today."

Karen showed a trace of curiosity. "Downtown?"

"Not into downtown L.A. It's just too far. I have an errand a few blocks from here. The shopping center."

Karen nodded indifferently. Her unhappy melancholy was so obvious that for once Mrs. Havermann almost reversed her attitude of cheerful inattention, almost asked Karen what was wrong. But habit was ingrained. Instead she urged on the girl a second cup of coffee.

She would not have dreamed of explaining to Karen that she was thinking of putting a new lock on Stolz's door. As it was now, the door was fastened by the primitive apparatus installed when the house was built—fifty years, she thought, if it was a day. She'd had a terrible time locating a key for it. For her own peace of mind, best to reinforce it with something new.

Her secrecy in regard to Stolz had had its origins in the breakup of his marriage to her daughter Margaret. Margaret, just out of school, had met and been attracted to the older, worldly man, and when the mother had met him she too had been charmed. The marriage had been brief, though ironically friendly. Margaret had met another man and Stolz had amiably stepped aside. Mrs. Havermann's attitude had been incredulous. Compared to her own difficult, tempestuous marriage, Margaret's had been ideal. She disliked the new son-in-law. She felt a deep disappointment over what she considered Margaret's foolishness.

All this had happened a little over nine years ago, when her husband had brought Karen into their home. It had been the natural thing not to explain the involved situation to a child. Afterward, especially since Havermann's death, the habit of secrecy had become a part of her withdrawal from normal communication. Stolz remained on friendly terms, visiting frequently, and now he was almost the only person besides Karen and the gardener whom Mrs. Havermann saw much of. Her mildly sentimental daydreams about him she kept entirely to herself.

The hints she had dropped to Karen, that Stolz might have money here, had been the result of a moment's desire to brag, to let someone else see how much Stolz trusted her. Perhaps, too, to convince herself he might be as interested in her as she was in him.

When they had finished breakfast Karen cleared away the table and washed the dishes and the stove. Mrs. Havermann went into the front of the house and looked around. She had not forgotten her idea of giving the back yard a close inspection. She wanted to figure out a way to have Karen away from the rear of the house.

She could not quite pin down why she didn't want Karen watching when she went outdoors. Certainly she felt no distrust of the girl.

Mrs. Havermann thought, Karen might think me a fool if she saw me out there staring at the ground. This summed it up for her, though there was something more she didn't try to analyze.

She returned to the kitchen shortly. Karen was sweeping a few crumbs from the floor around the table. Mrs. Havermann said, "That reminds me, dear, I think the front hall could use the dust mop this morning. The wax is there; it just needs a good buffing. Use a little pressure."

"Yes, Aunt Maude. What about flowers?"

"Well, the ones Mr. Dooley picked yesterday still look pretty fresh. Daisies and lupines wear well." Mrs. Havermann went out into the service porch. "I'll be sorting laundry while you do the hall."

Karen went out of the kitchen, and Mrs. Havermann heard her at the mop and broom closet in the pantry. When the sound of Karen's steps had quite died out Mrs. Havermann went quickly into the back yard. She walked around inspecting the grass, which somehow upon close view didn't show the disorder she had noted from a distance. It was hard to see any definite markings; the old tough growth of Bermuda lawn grew every which way, with patches here and there devastated by moths or by inadequate watering. She made up her mind to speak to Mr. Dooley. He had charged her last week for insecticide and manure, and heaven knew the water bill was big enough. There should be a luxurious green carpet here.

She went over and glanced in at the small side door of the garage. It was dim inside and smelled musty. Her old-fashioned Packard limousine sat on its blocks. She never used it any more. The car hadn't even had a license renewal for the past two years. Probably the tires were rotted, she thought, looking at the dust on them.

She went back into the yard, and some feeling which another person would have identified as a hunch took her over toward the windows in Stolz's room. Old Mr. Dooley had turned the earth here, wet it deeply, and scattered zinnia seeds. The bed was in an excellent state to retain impressions, and Mrs. Havermann could see quite clearly the twin marks made by the feet of the ladder and a man's shoeprint. The shoeprint was that of a ribbed rubber sole such as a tennis shoe.

She felt frozen, locked in panic, hanging there over the marks in the earth while the blood pounded in her throat and temples. Her hands turned cold. Her knees shook. This was nightmare.

After a moment she hurried back to the garage, went inside, and snapped on the light. The ladder sat in its usual spot. No, not quite. Mr. Dooley had used the hose yesterday, and now one of the feet of the ladder was placed on a stray end of the hose, squeezing it flat. The ladder must have been moved since Mr. Dooley had put the hose in the garage. Had Dooley himself used the ladder? She was certain he had not. Nor would he have left it like this, possibly to damage the plastic hose by its pressure.

Mrs. Havermann knelt down and rubbed shaking fingers around the bottom of the ladder and some crumbs of earth came off. She rubbed the crumbs to powder between her fingertips, and the earth still held a trace of moisture, as it would if it had come from the wetted bed of zinnia seed.

Someone had used the ladder to gain entry to Stolz's room. Had they succeeded? She rushed a second time to the zinnia bed and looked upward. What she could see reassured her. There was no indication that the sills had been prized, and she could see the locks in place on the crosspieces.

She felt a little calmer. Someone had tried to get in, but they hadn't risked a forced entry. Sneak thief, she thought. She looked at the footprint in the earth and a sly, menacing figure seemed to build itself in the air above it. Mrs. Havermann shuddered, averting her eyes as from a living criminal, and then she went quickly back to the laundry room.

I can't just go to pieces, she thought. I must go at this sensibly. She stood by the white enamel tubs and forced herself to consider, to think the situation through. The best and most obvious course was to go to the police and report an attempted burglary.

Would Stolz want her to do this? Somehow she thought not. She remembered vividly the scene in the library more than two years past—she and Stolz sharing a brandy, the room warmly lit, Stolz's darkly handsome face looking at her over the brandy snifter, and his voice: "I'm going to ask a favor. Don't be afraid to turn me down, Maude. I'd like to keep a bit of money here."

She'd said promptly, a little coquettishly, "Well, why shouldn't you?"

"Would it make you nervous?"

"I keep money in the house, Dan."

"This might be much more than what you're accustomed to having around. If I leave it here, shall it be our secret, yours and mine? I don't have to warn you about careless talk."

"I wasn't born yesterday." She had smiled at him, inwardly delighted. Not only at his trusting her so far but, as well, that the storing of money in her home made a kind of tie between them and a guarantee of his continuing visits.

"If anyone ever tries to question you——" A touch of sharpness in his glance; she noted it.

"I'd tell them nothing, never fear."

His emphasis on caution and secrecy had impressed her. True, she had hinted about the money to Karen, but she quickly dismissed the memory. She was positive that Karen had too much honor and good sense to go babbling about it to outsiders.

She again thought of Stolz's words: ". . . shall it be our secret, just yours and mine?"

He wouldn't want her to call the police and explain about the money, she decided. At least, not yet.

The first thing to do, if she was to pursue a sensible course, was to check and make sure the money was still there. Though she had dropped hints to Karen, on her own part Mrs. Havermann had maintained a curious sense of honor; she had felt that Stolz wouldn't want her spying on his hoard and so she had given in to her curiosity only once, some six months after he had requested permission to leave the money here; and at that time she had found over fourteen thousand dollars in one of his wardrobe drawers.

Now, composing herself in case she met Karen in the hallway, she went upstairs to her room. The key was in her bureau under a box of handkerchiefs. As she took it out, she heard Karen in the bathroom adjoining. "Karen?"

"I'm washing the tile. I didn't get finished yesterday."

"That's good." The bathroom faced the rear yard, overlooking the area between the house and the garage. Had Karen looked out of the window a few minutes before, she would have seen Mrs. Havermann below, but Mrs. Havermann had shut the frosted pane tight upon arising, as usual; there was no reason for Karen to have opened it. The girl hadn't seen anything.

These ideas trailed through Mrs. Havermann's mind as she stood there with the key in her fingers, and something more followed. She always kept the bathroom light burning at night. She'd read somewhere long ago that such a light was one most apt to keep off burglars, seeming to indicate that one was up out of bed either using the toilet or taking medicines—in either case relieving a condition which had made one wakeful. Now it occurred to her that the bathroom light being on during the night had been what had kept the burglar from making a forced and perhaps not entirely silent entry. He had thought that someone was awake upstairs.

She nodded to herself, pleased in spite of her worries that her small precaution had paid off. She went downstairs, unlocked the door to Stolz's room, went in, relocked the door, and looked around. She had been here only yesterday, checking to see if she should dust; her eyes flew at once to the coat on Stolz's bed.

She had almost convinced herself, since first finding it, that the coat had actually been on the bed all of the time since Stolz's departure and that she had somehow overlooked it. But now a new conviction startled her. Someone had already been in the room, searching for the money.

Puzzled over this, as well as sure that her conclusion was the right one, Mrs. Havermann opened the drawer where she had once seen and counted the fourteen thousand dollars. To her surprise there was no money here now, only some of Stolz's shirts and underwear. She opened other drawers in the wardrobe, and then looked into a set of drawers built into the closet. Such drawers as did not hold clothing were empty.

He's taken the money away, she thought vaguely, aware that her sensations were a mixture of relief and disappointment. The next instant she became illogically convinced that the thief had been successful, the money stolen! In fright she finished her search by throwing open the door of the wardrobe compartment designed to hang clothes. At sight of the enormous heap of green packets she stood transfixed, and as she comprehended the size of the heap and the amount of money which must be here, she gave a shrill cry and almost fell to her knees.

She was as stunned as if she had come upon some monstrous growth which in stealth and darkness had increased beyond all bounds. While she stood tottering a couple of packets slid off to the floor, and she jerked her foot away as from a poisonous and malignant fungus.

She managed finally to slam the wardrobe door, then went to the bed and sat down groggily. Fear seemed to have congealed in her marrow. Under the poleaxed numbness some thoughts fluttered: one, that there must be something illegal in Stolz's hiding such a vast amount; and also, a brief feeling of outrage that he had chosen to put it here. In that instant she nearly grasped how illusory was the sentimental dream she'd built up around him.

She rose from the bed and, without another glance at the wardrobe, went into the hall and locked the door.

She passed Karen on the stairs. Karen carried cleaning materials in her hands, had her eyes fixed where she must step. For a moment Mrs. Havermann paused. Her emotions had been stirred as they had not been in years. She was on the verge of panic and the need to talk to someone was almost overpowering. She blurted, "Karen!" and the girl looked at her.

Like an electric spark there seemed to flow between them a blaze of sympathy and compassion. There was in both a terrible need to communicate. Mrs. Havermann's stark eyes and chalky skin brought out in Karen the yearning to console, to listen and reassure. And for the first time in Mrs. Havermann's life she felt the girl there as a living human being on whom she could depend, whose love she had earned and deserved.

Mrs. Havermann put out a hand, opened her lips to speak. In the next moment she would have spilled her panic and confusion, and Karen would have confessed all of Skip's plans.

But the words wouldn't come. In the years of repression, of rejection, the loving and confiding words had withered and died. Now there was only awkward silence, the ticking away of the moments as she and Karen faced each other on the stairs.

Mrs. Havermann licked her lips. The warm turmoil was dying in her, and Karen seemed to be receding to a more proper perspective. She tried to think of something to say. "I'll be going soon," she got out.

Karen waited as if still not giving up hope, her face full of the ache to be accepted. But Mrs. Havermann brushed by her and went on up the stairs.

Chapter Ten

"WHEN MRS. Havermann came out of the front door, wearing her hat and coat and carrying a purse, she found the big collie lying on the porch. His fur was golden in the sun. He lifted his head and wagged his tail, blinking his eyes against the light. She stopped abruptly to stare at him. Where had he been during the night? She hadn't heard a bark out of him, though his little house was just beyond the garage.

He greeted everyone, she knew, with a happy frisking, often too exuberant to be welcome. But surely, if a stranger had gone so far as to put a ladder on the wall, he'd have at least barked a little. The dog's silence became a part of the menacing and incomprehensible whole, like the misplacement of the coat on Stolz's bed and the thief's directness in going straight to Stolz's window and no other.

She hurried down the front walk, then down the paved street to the main boulevard where the bus passed. A cab happened to come by before the bus did, and she took that. She got out at the shopping center.

The locksmith had a small office in a corner of one of the supermarkets. There was a counter, beyond it a desk and a table full of tools, shelves of stock, and some key-cutting equipment. The man who came forward when she stopped was about thirty, very clean-looking in a smart gray apron. "Yes, ma'am."

She had taken his mailed notice from her bag. "I received this today."

"One of our ads. What can I do for you?" He was sizing her up and perhaps he saw the fear she tried to repress, for his glance sharpened with interest.

"I wish to have a lock installed. Locks, rather. A door and two windows."

"Yes, ma'am. Any particular make or type in mind?" He was pulling a scratch pad and a pencil toward him on the counter.

"The best. The very strongest. You choose them."

"We have some remarkable new locks for windows now," he said pleasantly. "Absolutely burglar-proof. What's the address, please?"

She gave the address of the tall old house, and he wrote it down. She stammered then, "There is another thing I want to mention. I don't care to have anyone come to the house in a . . . any kind of truck with a sign on it. That is, if anyone happened to be . . . to be around outside . . ." She stumbled to a halt, her face alternately blanched and crimson. He was looking at her directly now, a stare of open curiosity.

"It's not an outer door?"

"No. A bedroom."

"You prefer that we come in a private automobile?"

"Yes, please."

"What about our satchel of tools? The boxes of locks?"

She saw gratefully that he had quickly grasped her need of secrecy. "Could you disguise them somehow? If I were to buy some groceries——"

He thought it over for a moment, tapping his teeth with the pencil. He had the air, she thought, of entering into a game. Could it be, she wondered briefly, that he considered that he was humoring a crocked old lady? "I have even a better idea. Now, you just don't want to advertise that you're bringing in a locksmith, is that it?"

She nodded mutely.

"Well, what about a plumber?"

She looked blankly into his friendly gaze, not understanding.

"I know of a plumber's truck I could borrow. Has the plumber's sign on it."

"Why, that would be fine!"

"How about tomorrow morning?"

For an instant she didn't grasp it, and then she felt the blood drain from her skin. "Oh, but this must be done today!" She had a moment's horrifying image of herself lying awake tonight listening for the thief.

"I'm not sure that I can borrow the truck today, the other truck. Besides, you see, I have a partner in this business. He's out now on a commercial job and won't be back till late. I could hardly leave the office for such a length of time."

She was desperate. "Ten dollars extra if you'll come today!"

He nodded. "For ten dollars I'll come right this minute."

"No. There's someone that I . . . Could you make it at

one o'clock?" A plan had come spinning into her head from
nowhere. Karen loved the big downtown stores. She'd pretend
she hadn't found what she wanted here and send Karen downtown for the afternoon to look for it. Something inexpensive
and hard to find, some certain brand of wax or polish. But no.
In Karen's unusual mood she might become discouraged too
quickly. Here Mrs. Havermann, recalling that moment on the
stairs, had a twinge of guilt. Best to give the girl something to
look for that she'd find interesting, some folderol thing.
Cosmetics. Or clothes. Or perfume. That was it, some kind of
cologne they didn't make any more. Keep her running to perfume counters, a pleasant chore.

This all ran through her head with the speed of light; the man
behind the counter must have seen how she had cheered up.

"One o'clock on the nose," he said in a friendly manner.

She felt better now, enough to wonder what he thought of
her behavior. "I guess you don't get many requests like mine,"
she said with a small effort to be cheerful.

"More than you'd think, ma'am." He smiled in a reassuring
manner.

She went back outdoors. The sunlight seemed garish, almost
scalding. She saw a cab pull into the parking lot, raised her
hand in a signal. An old friend and neighbor got out, old Mrs.
Potts, and she had to stop and commiserate over the woes of
arthritis and colitis. Once in the cab and headed for home, a
confused panic almost overwhelmed her. She was aware of her
aimless, bumbling behavior. Perhaps she was, after all, doing
the wrong thing. Surely the logical action would be to call
Stolz in Las Vegas.

She could pretend she hadn't investigated his room, hadn't
seen the money, was merely worried over indications of attempted entry.

She could ignore the emphatic request, repeated since the
time he had begun staying overnight, that she never try to
contact him in Nevada. A silly rule. Obviously he didn't want
anyone over there knowing of his private retreat in her house—
but suppose a fire or other catastrophe had wiped out his
money? Wouldn't he want to know? She rapped on the glass
panel between herself and the driver.

"Yes, ma'am?"

"Stop at the first public telephone."

He nodded, braked, swung toward a drugstore on a corner.

Inside it was cool and dim. The druggist, in a white jacket, was squatted before an array of rubber beach toys, building a pyramid. He rose and looked at her. "The phone," she said.

Then she saw it, the black box inside its cubbyhole at the rear. It seemed to promise relief from intolerable anxiety and tension. She went into the phone booth and drew the door shut after her.

Stolz, however, was not at the Solano Sea. She had to leave a message for him, to be delivered if and when he came in.

Big Tom was sitting in a chair by the telephone, his expression glowering when the call came at eleven forty-five from Benny Busick.

"Benny here."

"Yeah. Yeah."

"Take it easy, now, for God sakes. Keep the lid on."

Big Tom hitched himself closer to the phone. "Look, crumb, why aren't you on the way back here? I need you outside to-night. I've got things to tell you."

"Not me, you don't. No, sir, I don't want any part of it."

"What do you mean?" Big Tom felt like biting the phone. "You don't want what we lined up—you crazy?"

"I don't think you know *what* you've got lined up." Benny's tone had grown high and squeaky with defiance.

"Spill, crumb."

"Look. This . . . this information you got. It's known here in Las Vegas, and the ones who know aren't doing a damned thing about it. Lay off, Tom. Don't touch it."

"You must have a screw loose," Big Tom growled into the phone.

"Maybe I have. I got a nose, too. This deal smells funny."

"Now you lay it on the line or, by God, when we meet again I'll stomp you flat." The words were bitten off crisply, and Big Tom knew the effect they'd have on Benny in Las Vegas. Benny's narrow face would be wet with sweat and his chest would be heaving. He'd be staring into the phone like a wild-eyed tomcat.

"I'll . . . I'll call you when I've got something," Benny said in an almost inaudible voice. "Stick around." To Big Tom's disgust, the wire went dead. Benny Busick had hung up.

Big Tom slammed the receiver into its cradle. For a moment he remained in the chair, staring at the opposite wall. Then, with a hard angry look on his face, he went out to the kitchen. He stood by the drainboard and drummed his nails on the tile, looking out of doors through the window over the sink.

When his anger had subsided somewhat he went to the kitchen range, heated a cup of coffee left in the pot, drank it standing in the middle of the floor. A couple of cats had roused themselves from a midday nap and now came looking for lunch. Big Tom grumbled at them, meanwhile spooning processed fish into their bowl.

He went back to the living room, sat down, dialed a number on the phone. It rang twice before someone lifted the instrument at the opposite end of the wire. "Yeah? Hello?"

"Ranigan here."

"Oh. Hey, wait a minute, will you?" The voice turned from the phone and spoke to someone else. "Doll . . . run down t' the corner and get me some smokes, huh? Couple a cartons."

A girl's voice whined a complaint, dim in the distance.

"Be a good kid, huh? Filter tips, king size. The kind like it says on the TV, not a burp in a bellyful."

The girl's voice rose sharply in sarcasm. "Oh, Harry, you're killing me!"

"Don't forget t' bring matches, two, three them little packs."

She grouched: "Oh, okay, I'm going."

Dimly Big Tom heard a door close behind her. Harry said, "She's a good little twist; I just don't want t' explain everything t' her."

"Same one you had last year?" Big Tom said evenly.

"You mean Eva? Ah, she ran off with a bum, played the cornet in a dive, him and her are over t' Phoenix now."

"Well, I wouldn't confide in this one either. She might not last any longer than the others."

"Who's confiding? I never confided the time of day t' none a them." Harry sniffled into the phone. "Business is business and dolls is dolls. That's my motto!"

Big Tom dropped it. "Busick just called."

"Yeah, what's he say now?"

"More of the same. Lay off, it don't smell right. He's got butterflies in his underpants."

"Well, what you going t' do?" Harry asked uncertainly.

"I'm going to pull it. To hell with him." He waited, and Harry said nothing. "I don't see what could be wrong."

"Well, like you said yourself, it's funny that it's laying there where it is and nothing guarding it."

"I've made up my mind to get it and take a look at it," Big Tom said. "Then if there's something queero we can have a bonfire. I wanted Busick outside just in case, but he won't come back now."

"Ah, we can do it ourselves, you and me," Harry said with renewed confidence. "It'll be a snap."

"You know what to bring," Big Tom told him. "Be here by ten."

"Sure, I'll be there."

Big Tom put the phone into its cradle. The look of anger and disgust had smoothed from his face. He went out into the small kitchen again and found three newcomers mewing into the fish bowl. He fed them, then went out the rear door to the yard. Shaded by a big pepper tree, this area was cool and breezy. He walked the narrow bricked path back to the lath house. Before stepping inside he looked around carefully.

He watered the potted fuchsias and the ferns. He had another look outside. Then he went into a corner of the lath house and lifted a flat stone set into the creeping green moss. Below the stone was a small compartment lined with brick. From among other things Big Tom selected a plastic-wrapped object which had, in spite of the wrappings, the unmistakable shape of the Luger.

Carrying the wrapped gun, he went back into the house. He stood for a minute in his small front room, listening to the silence of the canyon. Then he sat down, unwrapped the Luger and inspected it thoroughly, meanwhile whistling through his teeth.

Skip went into the bathroom and examined his face. What Eddie had done looked like a mere scratch; the damage wrought by Big Tom darkened the whole side of his face. Skip washed and dried himself, brushed his teeth. He'd slept later than usual. Well, that was all right. He'd be up later tonight, too. He looked at himself again in the mirror, and the thought of Big Tom brought flickering lights into his eyes.

He went back to the outer room, dressed, went downstairs, and crossed the yard to the big house. Uncle Willy was in the outer porch on his hands and knees, wielding a scrub brush. A pail of soapy water stood by him. "Watch it," he yelped at Skip. "It's all wet in here. Go around to the side door. Watch that kitchen. Where it's still damp, I don't want it all tracked up."

"Give me fifty cents, I'll get something down at the corner."

"Fifty cents, hell. I'll be through here in a minute. Ten minutes, it'll be dry as a bone here. Those eats in the kitchen are free, Skip. Don't forget that. Don't try to fifty-cent me when there are free eats for the cooking."

Skip moved a little closer. "You ought to try to start getting used to having dough, Unc. Now handing out fifty cents would be a good beginning. Practicing, you could say." Uncle Willy was shooting poisonous looks at him and jerking his head toward the inner recesses of the house where Mr. Chilworth might be listening.

"You weren't worried about him hearing you talk about his free eats," Skip pointed out reasonably. "What's wrong now? Chrissakes, he's got it bugged out here or something?"

Uncle Willy propped himself on his heels. A thin lock of gray hair had fallen over his eyes. "Skip, you try me. You really do. If you weren't my own sister's boy, I swear I'd kick your butt in."

"Want to try?" But Skip went around to the side door and let himself into the pantry, walked on to the kitchen, and looked around for something to eat. Willy scrubbed his way to the rear door. He propped the mop there, dumped the water on the shrubbery, and came to the side door and was soon in the kitchen with Skip. By now Skip was frying three eggs in about an equal quantity of butter.

Willy heated the coffee, poured two cups full.

"Oh, God, that damned business of working on your hands and knees always did get my back to aching. I bet I washed ten thousand miles of corridor when I was inside. It just wore my spine out. I can't hardly stand to get down like that any more."

Skip flipped the eggs around to get them thoroughly covered by the butter. "You won't have to work like this much longer. You'll be flying high."

Uncle Willy frowned at him across the cup. "Are you nuts? I'm not going to make a move for a year. What I learned, I learned the hard way, but I got a few things that stuck with me and one is—one important one is—you flash it, they nab you. You want a collar, just start living high and throwing it around." His voice was low, little more than a whisper. "And that's my word to you, Skip. Look poor and talk poor and ride poor. A Cadillac will get you the jug as sure as the sun rises."

"Yeah, yeah." Skip took a plate out of the cupboard, dumped the eggs on it, took bread from the toaster and buttered it. He ate standing up at the sink as usual. "Suppose the law never hears about it? Suppose Stolz can't afford to let on what's happened?"

"That'll be even worse," Uncle Willy whispered. "That chance, that Stolz is hiding tax dough, is what made me take the job away from you and give it to Big Tom. Big Tom can protect himself. If the heat's too bad he'll make a deal. He'll sell it back to Stolz himself, for a cut, of course. Now how would you and Eddie ever have handled that?"

"You talk like Stolz is the bugger-man," Skip jeered, but a memory jumped into his mind: the big man with granite fists who had stood outside Mr. Salvatorre's door in the Solano Sea.

The man with the granite fists was one of Stolz's little helpers. He could crush you like a marshmallow with one wallop. Under the repose, the cumbersome politeness, lay a well of savagery. You saw it in his cold and measuring stare.

Skip looked at Uncle Willy; a nervous smile flitted across his face. Willy didn't see. He was staring into his coffee.

"What are you going to use for an alibi?" Skip wondered.

Chapter Eleven

A T SIX-THIRTY Uncle Willy was dressed in a blue suit, a pale
blue shirt, red bow tie; and his black shoes shone like Mr.
Chilworth's front windows. Skip, too, had on the outfit he
usually wore to go out, slacks and the leather jacket. He had
scrubbed, his hair was combed neatly, and a faint dusting of
talcum subdued the bruise along his jaw. Uncle Willy came out
of the bathroom drying his hands. He was smiling foxily. "I've
really got a good one this time."

"You really have," Skip agreed. "Who's this bird who's going
to pick you up?"

"Name of Mitchell, he said over the phone. The meeting's
out on West Larchmont. My God," Uncle Willy said wonderingly, "just think! I'll be sitting in a meeting of Alcoholics
Anonymous telling the folks my drinking problems when Big
Tom is pulling that job."

"It's a real good alibi," Skip agreed again. Privately he was
surprised that Uncle Willy had thought up so original an idea.

"You know," Uncle Willy went on, his tone warming, "at
first when Big Tom nixed the idea of being in the can, I
thought of going to a bar, talking to somebody there, making
an acquaintance. But then I thought, hell, the bastard would
be drinking and, with my luck, he wouldn't be able to pick me
out of a line of midgets when the time came. So then I thought,
What's the opposite of a goddamn bar? And the answer came,
Why—Alcoholics Anonymous." He beamed at Skip in pride.
"I figured it out all by myself."

True, Skip thought. Everybody at the A.A. meeting would
be interested, observant, and sober. You couldn't ask for a
better batch of witnesses. "It's okay," he said.

Uncle Willy brushed some lint off his pants with a flick of
the damp towel. "I'll be hard put to keep from laughing,
though. I'll be thinking to myself of all that dough I'm making. Just sitting there and spinning yarns, and I'll be making
more money than anybody else ever did for one night at A.A."

Skip glanced at him coldly. "You're right." He thought it
over for a moment while he checked the stuff in his pockets,

change and keys and cigarettes. "You never were a drunk. You're going to have to make it convincing."

"Oh, hell," Uncle Willy said cheerfully, "I had a cellmate in Quentin had been on every skid row from here to Brooklyn. The stories he told, I could keep gabbing for a week. You know, the damnedest thing, he said one time when he was in Seattle—at that time they didn't sell any liquor on Sunday, and this was Sunday—and he and some pals got some canned heat and strained it through a rag. Damned near blinded 'em."

A faint honk sounded from the street beyond Mr. Chilworth's house.

"That must be him," said Uncle Willy. He straightened his coat, picked his hat off the table, and ran out.

Skip listened to his dying footsteps with a sour look. He lit a cigarette, went into the bathroom for a last look at himself, ran the powder puff over his darkened jaw, snapped off the light. Outside in the alley the fragrance of the lime tree lay heavy on the air. There was no light at this point; the last traces of twilight, dying in the west, gave his hands on the lock a ghostly grayness. Skip opened the garage. Inside to the left was Mr. Chilworth's ancient Buick. Skip ran the jalopp out into the alley, closed the doors again, and drove away.

There was no way he could pay Uncle Willy back for bringing Big Tom into the job, or at least none at present. The loss of the money would have to suffice.

Karen was in the classroom, though the bell hadn't yet rung. She was sitting motionless before the typewriter. Skip slid into the empty chair in front of her, swinging a leg over so that he faced her, putting his hands on the chair back. "Hiya. Got the key?"

The little wing-like brows looked very dark against her pale skin, and her eyes, when she raised them, seemed buried in black lashes. "It wouldn't have done any good." Her voice was hoarse, and Skip caught the listless note and his attention sharpened. "She sent me downtown for the afternoon," Karen went on, "and when I got back there were all new locks on Stolz's room—the door, the windows too. I could see the new brass fixtures from the yard."

"How does she act to you?"

"I thought for a moment——" Karen bit her lip. "I thought she was going to talk to me about it."

Skip leaned closer, his stare narrowing. "How does she look at you? As if she thinks you're up to something? You'd catch that, wouldn't you?"

"She looks at me the way she always does."

"That's good." Skip thought about it, teetering on the legs of the chair. A few early arrivals were coming in; he lowered his tone to a whisper. "Look, I don't really care what kind of damned lock is on the door. Not tonight. This is the night we roll. If she's scared, scared enough to give us the key, good. If not——"

Karen seemed panic-stricken. "You'd let her see you?"

Skip nodded. "Why not? I'll fix it so she'll never recognize me."

Her hands fluttered on the keys of the machine. All color had left her face and her eyes burned with fright. "I won't let you in to hurt her or scare her."

Skip shrugged. "You getting ready to tip the old woman off?"

"I wouldn't do that."

"Look, you don't seem to understand the choice you've got here. You either line up with Eddie and me and help us in the house, or you tip off the old woman and she calls the bulls. There isn't going to be any way for you to chicken out, do nothing, keep your goddamn skirts clear." He reached, grabbed one of her hands, twisted the fingers painfully. "If you help us, you help all the way. See? A nice quick job, and we'll be cleared out and miles away by nine-thirty, if we leave class right at nine."

He got out of the chair and went quickly from the room. He had no doubts about Karen. Besides, he had an errand to do. He crossed the street from the school and entered a drugstore and asked to see some rubber gloves. If there had to be work done on that door they'd need these. He was particular, inspecting several pair. Finally he chose two pair, light in weight, in natural rubber, paid for them, stuffed the package into his jacket pocket. Too keyed up to return to class, he killed time then by strolling around and smoking cigarettes.

He didn't waste even a moment worrying about Mrs.

Havermann and her new locks. You busted locks when you had to, and she was nothing. There was danger if she had called Stolz already, but this was a chance he had to take.

At a quarter of nine Eddie came out of class, having told the instructor a lie about a stomach-ache. He and Skip went for Karen. When she came out into the hall Eddie saw at once how bleak and depressed she looked, and he wanted to say something but held his tongue in front of Skip. At twelve minutes past nine they swung up the driveway of the Havermann house, motor cut and lights out. Skip guided the car into the dense shadow of some shrubbery. Skip and Eddie got out of the car, Karen dragging after them, and then Skip said to her, "Take off your stockings."

She didn't catch on at once, and Skip cursed her under his breath. Then when she had taken off her shoes and removed the nylon hose he and Eddie pulled a stocking apiece over their heads. Their features flattened weirdly, the skin whitening over the bones, eyes pinched up between folds of flesh. When Eddie looked at Skip he wanted to shudder.

Skip took the package from his pocket, removed the gloves, gave a pair to Eddie.

There were several lights on inside the house: the kitchen, upstairs, a room on the lower floor near the front of the house. "Now this is what you do," Skip said to Karen, his voice distorted and muffled by the flattening of his lips. "First, the dog. Shut him up where he won't get out, won't bark or bother us. Then come to the back door and fix it so we can get in. Then go and tell the old woman there's something she ought to look at in the kitchen. You smell gas leaking there, or something."

"She's going to be terribly scared," Karen protested. "Can't you do it some other way?"

"How? Now how could we do it another way?" Skip's manner was mild now, almost patient, but Eddie sensed the violence just under the surface, and Karen must have felt it too.

"Promise me," Karen got out, "that when she gives you the key you'll leave her alone. You won't hurt her."

"Now why would I do that?" Skip wondered.

"Promise," Karen insisted.

"Okay, okay. Now snap it up." Skip stretched inside the leather jacket as if he were almost bored. The light silk encasing his head gave him a strange brightness, almost a halo, in the dimness. It was crazy, Eddie thought, to think of Skip with a halo. Any time.

Karen walked away, the sound of her steps diminishing; the dark swallowed her, and then a few moments later Eddie could hear the front door rattle. The interval following seemed unending to Eddie; he kept expecting some disastrous eruption of sound from the house, the old woman screaming, perhaps, as Karen betrayed their presence and their intention. He breathed thickly through the silk fabric pressing his face and felt as if he would choke.

Suddenly in the light reflected through the kitchen door they saw Karen in the porch. She fumbled with the lock, then moved quickly out of sight again. Skip turned toward Eddie and jerked his head in a summoning motion. They walked to the door. Eddie tried to lick his lips; his tongue snagged in the knitted silk and he was almost sick.

They went into the laundry room, not making any noise, and then Skip padded on into the kitchen and stood close to the wall on one side of the door to the hall and motioned Eddie to stand opposite. They hadn't been there more than a few seconds when Mrs. Havermann walked in. At the sight of the old woman, the realization that they were actually embarked on this thing, Eddie's heart gave a great lurch.

Mrs. Havermann went several feet past the door and then looked back over her shoulder. She glanced at Eddie, then switched her head all the way around to look at Skip. She turned a little, as if she meant to face them, and then her knees must have given out, for she reached a hand to prop herself against the table in the middle of the room.

"Who are you?" The words were plain enough in her high-pitched old woman's squeal, but they were mechanical and called for no reply. She knew who Eddie and Skip were: they were the double image of her nightmare, and her face shook and twitched at the shock of recognition. Then, "Go away!" she muttered in her throat. "Karen! Karen, send them away!"

Karen appeared in the hall. She was crying, making no attempt to wipe away the tears. She looked terribly young in her distress. She said, "I don't know what to do, Aunt Maude!" It had the ring of terrified truth.

Skip had put his hand in his jacket pocket, Eddie noticed, and had a finger poked forward to make it seem he held a gun. Eddie thought Mrs. Havermann was too stunned with fright to notice. She seemed ready to drop. As he watched, she actually tottered, then recovered. "Please don't . . . don't do anything violent," she stammered.

"That depends on you," Skip said in a perfectly indifferent manner. He was smiling a little, and the effect of the flesh moving and whitening under the knitted silk was uncanny. "We want the key to Stolz's room and then we want you to keep out of our way."

There was a moment of waiting while she made up her mind about it, or gained control of her shaking limbs, and then she slowly led the way out of the kitchen. They passed Karen, who shrank aside, then upstairs. At the top of the stairs Mrs. Havermann turned to face them. She seemed to have better control of herself. "You're wasting your time," she said to Skip. "There is nothing of value in Mr. Stolz's room."

"How about letting us see for ourselves?" Skip was easy and unworried. "Let's have the key, huh?"

Karen was about halfway up the stairs. She came on up as Mrs. Havermann turned into her bedroom and opened a closet door. Skip tensed, perhaps thinking she had a gun hidden, but when she had fumbled for a moment in the pocket of a hanging coat she came out with the key. It had a new look; the ridges were sharp-cut. Skip grabbed it and nodded.

He glanced from Eddie to Karen. "Okay. Now tie her up."

Karen cried, "You promised!" and Skip said coolly, "Tie her up or I'll knock her out."

Mrs. Havermann licked her lips. "You tie me, Karen."

Skip was grinning twistedly inside the mask, and Eddie wondered if Karen knew how she had betrayed herself, crying out like that. Mrs. Havermann had a very thoughtful look as she sat down on the edge of the bed, where Skip motioned her. She looked as if she were thinking of things which had happened long ago, or over a long period of years. She looked as if there might be a bitter taste in her mouth.

"Turn over on the bed," Skip said to Mrs. Havermann. "Karen, tie her arms behind her. Tight. Wrists, then higher. And put juice in it."

"What shall I use?"

"For Chrissakes, tear up a towel or something."

Mrs. Havermann turned her head. "Karen, do you know these men?"

"I never saw them before," Karen answered, a confused childish lie. Everything she did showed that she knew Skip, was aware of his every move and glance. "What shall I use to tie you?"

"Don't destroy something good," Mrs. Havermann said, much more calmly now. "Go to the linen closet and get one of the worn things."

Karen hurried out, came back in a moment with some pillowcases over her arm. She tore strips and tied Mrs. Havermann's arms and then, at Skip's orders, her ankles.

"Any cotton in the bathroom?" Skip demanded. "That fuzzy stuff."

"I guess so," Karen stammered, her eyes full of dread.

"Go see."

Karen backed around the edge of the bed, and Mrs. Havermann said in a low tone, "Please don't put a gag in my mouth. I promise I won't call out."

"Who's running this thing?" Skip inquired of the room. He went into the bathroom and came out with a blue box of absorbent cotton. He threw it on the bed. "Stuff her mouth with it. A rag over it to hold it." He looked at Karen, who hadn't moved.

"Please!" Mrs. Havermann gasped from where she lay. She had turned her eyes so that she could glimpse Skip. "I promise not to make a bit of trouble."

"You've got a choice," Skip said, unconcerned. "A gag. Or I'll clip you behind the ear and you won't see or hear anything for a while. Would you like that better?" He stepped forward, as if thinking she might really want him to knock her out, and she cringed on the counterpane, trying to inch her head away.

"No. No, I wouldn't want that."

"Okay. Karen, you'd better get busy." Skip regarded the shaking girl with a wry amusement. "Time's wasting."

Karen moved tremblingly nearer the older woman and said uncertainly, "Will you open your mouth, Aunt Maude?"

"I'm not your aunt," Mrs. Havermann said, looking directly

into Karen's eyes. "I wonder why I asked you to call me that. I wonder why I sheltered and fed you—now you've brought these two into my home."

Karen looked at Mrs. Havermann as if in an agony of regret.

"I don't know how you became acquainted with these two, the kind of creatures they seem to be. You've never been sly and secretive, slipping out at night, or acting in any way delinquent. You've seemed a straightforward girl. And now you've done this."

"Gag her, for Chrissakes," Skip said, his temper rising.

"The other one never says anything, does he?" Mrs. Havermann remarked harshly, looking at Eddie. Eddie knew that he was sweating through the silk mesh. It did not occur to him that his features were as distorted, as unreadable as Skip's.

Now Mrs. Havermann spoke directly to Eddie. "If you are sensible, young man, you'll leave now before a serious crime is committed."

An indignant growl escaped from Skip. He grabbed up a wad of cotton, and as Mrs. Havermann finished speaking he jabbed it between her teeth. Mrs. Havermann worked her jaws, trying to spit the cotton out, and then Karen rushed to pull it away and Skip straight-armed the girl back into the wall. He looked at Eddie.

"Take it easy, for Chrissakes," Eddie muttered.

Skip took a length of cotton cloth and wrapped it over the lower part of Mrs. Havermann's face and tied it tight. Mumbling noises came through the gag. Mrs. Havermann's skin grew red, then darkened.

Skip said to Eddie, "Take Karen out in the hall."

Eddie went over to Karen. "She's passed out, she doesn't feel anything." He didn't want to look at Mrs. Havermann's flabby, suddenly sprawled body.

Karen was crouched against the wall, staring at Skip. "I'll have to stay with her. Don't touch me."

Skip held the key; he was tossing it, and the bright brass color sparkled in the light. "You're coming with us," he said to Karen. "I don't trust you much up here with the old woman. What the hell's the matter with you? I didn't do anything to her." He went to Karen and gripped her upper arm between his fingers, lifting her, and Eddie heard the gasp of pain she gave. "Now come along."

Karen went as if she were sleepwalking. Eddie was nervous, and Skip walked jauntily, snapping the key into the air and laughing under his breath. Skip unlocked the new lock on Stolz's door and they went in. Karen remained by the door. She seemed utterly indifferent now to the fascination of the money. Skip snapped on the light and hurried to the old-fashioned mahogany wardrobe against the inner wall. He stretched a hand to its door. The look of his curled fingers was hungry. He threw open the door and stood there blanked out with shock. Finally he looked at Eddie, then at the girl.

The wardrobe was empty.

Skip and Eddie searched hastily for the next few minutes, every cranny and hidey-hole in the room, expecting at any moment to run across the money. When it was obvious that the money wasn't in the room Skip would have turned on Karen. Eddie knew it, knew that his being here was the only thing which saved her from Skip's violence.

Trying to control his voice, Skip said to her, "We'll go back and see the old woman. Maybe you can get her to understand—we want the money Stolz kept here. We're going to get it."

Upstairs, they found Mrs. Havermann conscious again. Above the gag her eyes bugged at them.

Eddie felt hot and sick. He wished he had never seen the house or the old woman, never heard of the money.

It didn't occur to him to wish that he had never known Skip.

Chapter Twelve

THE CITY spread below the foothills made a great blaze in the sky and frosted the tips of the hills with reflected light; but here in the canyon it was dark, quiet except for the rustle of trees under the wind, and nothing moved except the small car creeping up the grade. The car rolled to a stop below Big Tom's house, the motor died, the lights went out, and a short stocky man in a black suit got out and looked all around. The only light in all that darkness was beside Tom's door.

Harry sniffed the breeze, noting the absence of exhaust fumes and city smoke. He looked back down the hill, toward the turnoff from the canyon highway. There was no traffic whatever. The canyon might have been a thousand miles from L.A. Big Tom had certainly picked him a spot.

Harry climbed to Big Tom's porch and rattled the screen door. The door within opened promptly. Big Tom was all dressed, ready to leave. A couple of cats were sitting attentively in the middle of the room, looking at their master as if wondering what possible business he had out at this hour.

"Just a minute. I want to check the back door." Big Tom started away, and the phone began ringing. Big Tom ignored it, went into the kitchen for a minute, then came back. Harry had his head inside, holding the screen ajar with his shoulder.

"Aren't you going t' answer the damned phone?"

"I know who it is. Benny." Big Tom walked by the table where the phone sat, didn't give it a glance. "To hell with him."

"Maybe he knows something," Harry said. "Maybe you ought t' hear what he says, anyhow."

"I know what he says. He's been saying it all day."

"Well, then, maybe I ought t' hear what he says," Harry declared. A touch of truculence had come into his manner. He stepped into the room.

Big Tom gave him a cool stare. "Are you going with me, or aren't you?"

"I might be going, after I hear from Benny. He saved me one hell of a blowup in Frisco. I just want t' hear what he says."

"Oh, hell, go ahead and listen." Big Tom sat down on a

628

chair and folded his hands between his knees and looked un-lovingly at the cats sitting together in the middle of the rug.

Harry went to the phone and lifted it out of its cradle and put it to his ear. "Yeah. No, this is Harry. We're ready t' roll." He listened and pretty soon his tongue came out and licked at his lips. "You think it's on the level?"

The silence made a cup, a kind of vacuum, around the house, and Big Tom sat moveless as if he might be listening for some scratch of sound, the tiniest indication of a break in that envelopment. He didn't look at Harry. Harry's nervous fright rolled from him in waves, like a smell.

Harry put the phone into its cradle, went to a chair facing Big Tom, sat down. "My God," he said. He took out a white linen handkerchief and mopped at his neck under the collar. "What a hell of a break." Big Tom made no reply, showed no curiosity, just waited; and Harry went on: "All day Benny's been following this character, buying him drinks and trying t' chum him up . . . when he wasn't ducking out t' phone you . . . and he finally got the character drunk enough and he talked. He talked about Stolz."

Big Tom grabbed one of his cats and inspected behind its ears for fleas. He didn't look in Harry's direction.

"This boy Benny's been with is a real hard-nose. Tough. Benny thinks he's a gun from El Paso, somebody he met once. Worked for Stolz for a year or so. Not working for him now. Uses a different moniker. Won't be needing any moniker at all if he blabs much what he's been blabbing t' Benny."

"Well, I'm glad you're working around to the big news," Big Tom said.

"The news is bad, real bad," Harry answered, his eyes shining like wet soap. "The word is that Stolz bought a chunk of the Hartfield ransom. Got it for about ten cents on the dollar. No bargain at that. You remember about the Hartfields?"

Big Tom put the cat down carefully on all four feet. "Yeah, I remember."

"The job was a ripperoo all the way around," Harry went on breathlessly. "The punks who snatched Hartfield and his wife didn't have sense enough t' specify the kind of money. So they got hundreds, all consecutive, every goddamn number taped—— Oh, my god! And we nearly walked int' that!"

Big Tom lifted his eyes slowly. "You're not going?"

"Good God! Good God!" Harry cried loudly. "You're not going either!"

"Yes, I am."

Harry lowered his face and peered at Big Tom as through a haze. "Now, now wait up——"

"I'm going," Big Tom affirmed. "I didn't know it myself until just now. I kept thinking all day, if Benny dug up something smelly I'd have to drop it, but then I quit answering the phone so I wouldn't hear what he said. All the time I knew I was going and didn't realize I'd made up my mind. Till now."

"What in the blazing hell," Harry wondered, his mouth puckering, "can you do with dough as hot as that?"

"Stolz must have had a plan for it," Big Tom said. "Maybe I can figure out what it was, use it myself." He stood up, checked his keys, adjusted the gun inside his belt against his belly. He said as if to himself, excluding Harry, "I'll have to go it alone."

"You sure will," Harry agreed.

Big Tom walked over to the door. "Will you phone Snope for me?"

"He'll blow his stack. They don't want hot moola!"

"It's his cut anyway," Big Tom said. "Hot or cold." He had a look of ironic amusement as he went out, not even bothering to shut the door. Harry sat for a minute or more as if undecided. He plucked at his lip. He heard Tom's Ford, first inside the garage down by the road, warming up, then out in the open. Finally Harry stood up, went to the front door to listen. The sounds of Tom's car died in the distance, and Harry shook his head in relief.

He said to the listening cats, "He's crazy as a bedbug. He ought t' be in the loony bin."

Harry went out, snapping the lock but leaving all the lights on. The cats wandered around the room for a brief while, annoyed at being alone, then settled in the shabby chairs to sleep.

And then after all, along with the terrific fright there was desperate defiance. Mrs. Havermann had had time to gather her forces somewhat. When Skip had taken out enough of the cotton wadding so that she could speak she croaked, "Mr. Stolz is on his way here. I'm doing you a favor by telling you.

When he comes he won't stand for any nonsense, and he certainly won't let you take his money!"

For the first time Skip's assurance slipped. He grabbed Mrs. Havermann by the shoulders and dragged her up and shook her. "When? When's he coming?" Karen, trying to interfere, got in his way then, and he jabbed viciously with an elbow, still hanging onto Mrs. Havermann. Karen gave a cry and put a hand to her cheek. "When? When is Stolz coming?"

"Any minute now." She was tied, helpless, and the nerves twitched in her face, but she kept her eyes angrily on Skip. "You'd better leave at once."

Perhaps she thought she really had frightened him. Skip grew quiet, bent over the bed, his foxy eyes suddenly still and watchful. So she pressed it a little further. "I believe I hear Mr. Stolz at the front door downstairs now."

The three of them waited, frozen, listening for some sound from below. Skip went softly out into the hall, listened, came back. "She's giving us a line of crap. I'm going to work her over."

Karen flung herself between him and Mrs. Havermann. "Don't hurt her! You promised. I wouldn't have let you in if you hadn't promised!"

Mrs. Havermann writhed up on one elbow and the head of the bedstead. "Karen, look at me." When Karen had turned, Mrs. Havermann went on: "I don't want you pleading for me. I don't want a word from you in my behalf. You no longer mean anything to me. The love and loyalty I might have expected from you are ashes. I want nothing from you. You owe me nothing." Tears filled Karen's eyes, ready to spill; and then Mrs. Havermann forced her head forward a little, and from between the cotton-flecked lips she spat into Karen's face.

Skip laughed. Eddie moved to the rim of the room, anxious, hating the delay, hating his own feelings of fear and inadequacy.

"Why do we take time to argue?" Eddie said. "She's hidden the money to save it for Stolz. So we find it. We don't have to hurt anybody."

"In this place we find it?" Skip hollered.

"Karen can help. She'll know the places it could be hidden."

Karen had gone away from Mrs. Havermann and the bed.

She had wiped the spit off her face with her sleeve. At the moment Mrs. Havermann had leaned forward and spat, a look of unbelieving shock had flooded Karen. But now she seemed to have regained a dull composure.

"How about it?" Skip demanded of Karen.

She looked around at them, at Eddie and Skip. She didn't look at Mrs. Havermann. "Yes, I guess so."

They split up. Karen said she'd take the attic and the upper bedrooms, let Eddie and Skip search the easier area downstairs. There was a basement too, she told them; nothing in it but the oil furnace, though they'd have to check.

In the kitchen, in a lower cupboard behind a stack of canned dog food, Skip found two packets of hundred-dollar bills. For an instant he was about to let out a shout, thinking he'd located the hoard; but then in sizing it up he noted that the two packets were out of the way in a dark spot, as if Mrs. Havermann might have started to put the money in there and then changed her mind, retrieving what she had stored. These two packets had escaped her searching fingers.

Skip, wary for steps outside the kitchen door, flipped through the money. It looked new. He studied it closely; it wasn't counterfeit; the bills were perfect. He noted a number on a bill, then two, then three. This new money was numbered consecutively, as if it might have just come from the mint. Skip shook his head and grinned. Stolz had converted something—surplus profits, a payoff, a sale of shares—into this easily stored and beautifully legitimate currency. The newness of the bills, the consecutive numbering were to Skip an indication that there was nothing wrong here. Stolz had his cash where he could get it and spend it easily if he wanted to. He'd just forgotten to keep an eye on it!

Skip rose, having made sure there were no other packets scattered in the depths of the cupboard. He put the two packets inside his shirt against his skin, buttoned his shirt over them. He kept on smiling to himself, the smile distorted by the silken mask. The old woman hadn't been so smart after all. She was just a stupid, panicky old bag, putting new locks on doors and then getting scared the locks weren't enough and trying a trick or two. She was the kind of old bag would keep dimes and quarters in a sugar bowl. He wished he could go up and be allowed to punch her face in.

He happened to be looking toward the door when Eddie appeared there. "I've been thinking about what Mrs. Havermann said about Stolz," Eddie told Skip. "If he's really on his way here, apt to arrive any time, it might be better to have Mrs. Havermann out of sight."

Skip regarded him thoughtfully.

"If he comes in," Eddie continued, "you and I could hear him in time to slip out the other door. Then if he caught Karen upstairs she could pretend nothing was wrong, the old lady was out seeing some friends or something. If she wasn't out where he could see her, tied up like that, he'd have no way of knowing right off that anything was going on."

"Sure, you're right." They went down the hall, passing the open door of the parlor where Eddie had been searching. Karen met them at the top of the stairs. Skip stopped and said, "We're going to put Mrs. Havermann out of sight. So if Stolz comes he won't see her right away. And you can tell him she's out visiting, until you have a chance to slip out."

Karen started to say something. Probably she intended to remind Skip again of his promise that there would be no violence. But the words died before she spoke them. She looked tired and drawn. Her cheek was swelling where Skip had struck her with his elbow. There was a deeper wound somewhere inside; her eyes were sick with the pain of it.

Skip said to Karen, "Stay out here and keep an eye on that front door while we're in there."

Skip actually wasn't much scared that Stolz would arrive; he thought that Mrs. Havermann had made up a yarn to frighten them. But he had begun to worry a little about Big Tom and his friends. They had to be out of here before Big Tom arrived.

On the bed Mrs. Havermann lay with her eyes shut. Her mouth was pinched and she seemed pale, almost bluish. "We'll put the gag back," Skip said, gathering up the scattered cotton.

Mrs. Havermann opened her eyes. "You are a wicked person," she said. "God knows what you are doing here; He sees your every act. And He will punish you for it."

For some reason it triggered Skip's rage. He bent over her and slapped her hard and repeatedly. He had his fists doubled then, ready to pump blows into her face, when Eddie dragged him away. Eddie was yelling, "*Sancta Maria!*" and in a flood of Spanish he commanded Skip to leave her alone, not even realizing which tongue he used. He and Skip stood with their eyes not more than a couple of feet apart, and he heard Skip calling him a half-Mex bastard, and then he knew what he had said.

"Chrissakes, don't beat up an old woman!" he told Skip.

"What was all that yap in Mex?"

"Just that. Don't hurt her."

Skip showed his teeth through the silk mask. "She knows where that money is."

"Well—just ask her, then."

"Ah, she'd never tell us." By main force Skip got the wadding of cotton back into Mrs. Havermann's unwilling mouth. He pushed it in hard, then wrapped her face in the piece of cloth.

"Not too tight," Eddie warned.

"She'll keep her yap shut now," Skip said savagely, giving the wrapping another knot.

Eddie was uneasy, but he didn't want another fight with Skip. He went to the closet door, opened it, and looked in. It was a big closet, neatly arranged, well filled with clothing. Skip inched Mrs. Havermann off the bed, carrying her by the shoulders, and he and Eddie got her into the closet under the hanging garments. She struggled and bumped around, made frantic muffled noises under the gag. Skip stood and watched interestedly from the closet doorway.

Eddie said nervously, "Please, Mrs. Havermann, just lie still. We won't bother you again. Mr. Stolz will come and find you, and you'll be all right."

Mrs. Havermann thrashed and convulsed. Her thick legs whipped back and forth with surprising force, scattering some shoes set in a row along the closet wall.

"She acts like she's having a doggone fit," Skip said musingly.

A shrill noise now came from under the gag, as if Mrs. Havermann had swallowed a toy whistle. The whipping motion of her lower limbs was slowing down. She tried to push herself erect by means of her bound hands, but soon fell back.

Eddie had gone out of the room. "You just take a nice little nap," Skip said to Mrs. Havermann, and kicked her foot back into the closet and shut the door.

They went back to the search. Skip looked through Mrs.

Havermann's room before leaving it, inspecting a sewing box, a big basket of mending, a small black trunk. Everything the old woman owned, he thought, stank of moth balls. When he lifted the trunk lid the odor was almost stifling. He noted that in the top tray there lay a large framed photograph, the picture of a stout man with an autocratic and arrogant expression.

Havermann, he thought.

He rifled the trunk, threw stuff back into it, shut the lid. Hell, there was no money in this room. Nor in this part of the house, either. He thought about the cupboard where he'd found the two packets hidden behind the dog food. There ought to be a clue there. Something had made her change her mind. She'd thought of a better spot. Skip tried to figure out what there was about the cupboard or the stored dog food to remind her of some better place, tried to think as Mrs. Havermann would have thought, and failed. Neither the cupboard nor the dog food reminded him of a thing.

There was an especially loud thump from the closet, as if Mrs. Havermann had made one last try for the door with a heel. Then there was silence.

Skip left the room, went downstairs, and then, taking care to move silently, he went out into the rear yard. He needed to reassure himself that Big Tom wasn't out there. He scouted around the car, looked down the driveway to the street. It would be a hell of a note if Big Tom showed up and caught them here in the middle of the search. Skip pulled off the stocking from his face, smoked a cigarette, sheltering the lighted tip inside his palm, watching the street and trying to think his way past the stalemate. The old woman had outfoxed them, beaten them. Skip hissed the killdeer cry between his teeth and thought of what he would like to do to her.

All at once he saw Eddie in the porch used as a laundry room. Eddie moved over to the door and peered out and said, "Skip, we've got to get out of here!"

Skip walked toward him, pulling on the mask. "You can say that again," he growled.

"I've been thinking. Mrs. Havermann's going to have to tell us. Not by hurting her. But we could threaten to do something. Like burn the house down."

"Okay. What happens if she doesn't bite?"

"Maybe she'll bite," Eddie said hopefully.

They went back through the hall to the stairs. Karen was there, standing as if all life, all emotion, had drained out of her. Her eyes seemed set deep in her head, burned dark with strain. She said in a little above a whisper, "Let her go, Skip."

"Sure," Skip agreed. "We're going to let her go. Right now." He ran up the stairs with Eddie following, and crossed Mrs. Havermann's room and threw open the closet door. Mrs. Havermann's contorted form fell out into the room, dragging some fallen clothes with her. Somehow, after he'd shut the door on her, she'd writhed around to lie against it. Skip bent over her, got a good look at her, and he knew.

Mrs. Havermann was dead.

Chapter Thirteen

SKIP AND Eddie looked at the dead, contorted face and then slowly at each other; and the silence was like the ear-bursting backslap of an explosion or like the vast sucking up after a great wind had passed or like the final stillness after the toppling of a tidal wave.

Eddie said unbelievingly, "I stood right here and let you do it!"

"What do you mean, let *me* do it?" Skip's mouth thinned to an ugly line and his hands balled to fists. "Hell, you were in it; you helped me get her into the closet where she suffocated."

"You murdered her," Eddie said slowly.

Skip's fists knotted tightly, and he knocked Eddie down with one blow. Eddie had been dazed, not looking, too shocked to react, to protect himself. He hit the wall and slid down, and then in an automatic response to terror he started to scramble for the door. Skip had run out swiftly. He collided with Karen at the top of the stairs, and they half fell part of the way down before they could stop and disentangle themselves. Karen cried, "What's wrong up there? What's happened?" Her face was wild with fear.

"Go to hell." Skip stiff-armed her, and she toppled away and staggered on down to the lower hall.

Eddie came out of the room, got to his feet, stood there hanging horrified on the railing. He looked down at Karen. "She's dead. The gag was too tight, and it choked her to death."

Karen gave a choked scream and tried to run back up the stairs, and again Skip stiff-armed her and she backed away, crying breathlessly, holding her stomach.

"We're leaving, you sap. Aren't you coming?" Skip said to her.

He ran past her, on down the hall. Eddie came downstairs quickly. Karen looked at him with stunned, uncomprehending eyes and said, "It isn't true, is it? She's all right."

"She's dead." He saw the shock of these words go through her like a blow, draining her skin of color, her eyes of life.

637

There wasn't time for gentleness, but Eddie had to be gentle with her. He put an arm around her. "Don't go back and look at her. Not if you liked her, and I guess you did."

She said: "Liked her? I loved her. I just never could . . . She never let me show her." She covered her face then and would have wept against him, but Eddie pushed her gently away.

"We've got to leave. Quick. Come on."

He took her hand, and she let him lead her out through the rear door. At the car Skip had stripped off mask and gloves and was inside fitting the key into the switch. Eddie and Karen ran around to the other side and got in, Karen in the middle.

Skip started the motor, and then it coughed gently and died. He tried again, nursing it, giving it gas, and Eddie could hear the tired sparkless rattle as it turned over without catching, and the noise of loose fittings and the gradual wearing down of the battery. And over all this, Karen's exhausted crying.

Eddie had stripped off the stocking from his face, the gloves. He was sweating now; his heart was pounding. The old motor ground and ground, and each time it turned over the sound was weaker and more dragging.

Skip looked at them jeeringly. "Anybody got any suggestions?"

"For Chrissakes get it started," Eddie said.

The motor caught for a second time, hesitated for an instant that seemed an eternity, and then settled into its rackety rhythm. Eddie let out a long aching breath, unaware that he'd even been holding it.

The car slipped down the drive in the dark, and once in the street Skip switched on the lights and let it pick up speed.

Eddie said hotly, "I wish I'd never heard of that goddamn money."

"We just had bad luck, that's all," Skip answered evenly. He was beginning to calm down somewhat, to reconsider what had really happened. He didn't believe their situation to be completely hopeless. It was too bad of course that they couldn't leave Karen here to palm off some yarn to the homicide dicks about strange, unknown men breaking in and killing Mrs. Havermann and mistreating herself. In his present mood he was more than ready to mark Karen up to leave the right im-

pression with the cops. But he had no illusions about Karen
standing up under questioning. She was too young and soft,
too easily hurt. Skip jerked his head over his shoulder in the
direction of the house. "Well, good-by Stolz's dough, wherever you are." He laughed a little under his breath.

Karen tried to draw away from him. "How can you make a
joke . . . how can you act as if nothing had happened?"

"You and Eddie go ahead and tear your hair and squall,"
Skip said. "Me, I've got to drive the jalopp. It's never learned
to drive itself. And I can't see to drive if I'm crying."

He had turned into the busy boulevard. A big transit bus
rolled by, a scattering of people in it, tired faces turned to the
windows. In a rear seat a small wrinkled hatless man looked
especially discouraged and weary. His eyes were almost covered with drooping, parchment-like lids. As the car gathered
speed, Skip found himself staring up at the bus window, keeping pace; and the wheel wobbled between his hands.

"Hey!" Eddie said. "Watch it, we don't want a ticket now."

The bus sped on, and they kept abreast of the rear window.
Skip could see the tired, wrinkled face just above; the washed-
out old eyes seemed dead beneath the parchment lids. "Look
at that," Skip said between his teeth. "Look at this old geezer
by the window. You know what?"

"What?" said Eddie uneasily. He couldn't see the old man
from where he sat, but he heard the anger in Skip's tone.

"We had a chance," Skip said. "The old woman ruined it for
us, the only decent chance we'll ever have."

"It's over," Eddie said, his tone hardening. "We were lucky
to get out."

"All we needed was the dough," Skip went on. "She didn't
have to act like a son of a bitch over it. She could have cooper-
ated a little."

He glanced up again at the bus window. The old man sat
with his forehead sagging toward the window, his tired eyes
fixed on nothing. He had glanced once at Skip, almost sharply,
but now seemed withdrawn again into his private limbo. He
had only the night, the passing cars, the gloomy and uninter-
esting way home. He was the kind of old man who existed in
an endless rut. Lives in some rattrap rooming house, Skip
thought. His feet hurt. He must have a job where he stood up

all day. Maybe he was a dishwasher. Skip pictured the old man over a steamy sink, scraping garbage, stewing his hands for hour after hour in hot soapy water. Once in a while ducking out to a littered alley for a cigarette. What a life, what a dirty rotten break. Such rage rose in Skip that he had difficulty in keeping it under control.

The through boulevard swung to the east in a slight curve. In the distance, across vacant rising ground, the Havermann house among its trees glittered with light. Eddie said, "Oh, for God's sake, look at it. Like a Christmas tree! Why didn't we turn off the lights?"

"Yeah, why didn't you?" Skip said.

"What do the lights matter?" Karen cried as if bewildered.

They were passing the hamburger diner when Skip braked the car sharply and turned in at the parking lot.

"You're not . . . stopping?" Karen gasped.

"I'm hungry as hell," Skip said. "I didn't get any dinner. My unc was too worked up to cook anything for me."

"What was he worked up about?" Eddie said quickly, suspiciously.

It had been a slip, but Skip didn't worry about it. He parked the car and cut the motor, took the keys from the lock. "Ah, he was going to an A.A. meeting for the first time."

"I didn't know he drank," Eddie said, still curious.

"Well . . ." Skip spoke with mock reluctance. "God knows Unc should have learned better by now, but I think he's planning some sort of con on those A.A. people. He thinks he'll get their sympathy, sing them a hard-luck story, maybe cop a little dough."

"They'll know right away he's a phony," Eddie said positively.

"I don't see how you can worry about Skip's uncle and whether he drinks or not and what he's doing with the A.A. people," Karen said with frantic urgency. "If we don't want to be caught . . . just please, please don't stop here!"

Skip glanced at her. "Well, it's good to see that you've started to collect your marbles. You're worrying about getting away instead of about the old woman. But you're right in a way—someone might know you, this close to home. So you stay in the car, and Eddie can stay with you while I go in and have a bite." He got out, brushed back his hair where the stocking mask had disarranged it, and walked away across the graveled lot.

He sat over a hamburger and coffee, frowning in thought. He couldn't get the image of the old man in the bus out of his mind. There seemed some sort of carry-over, some connection with himself. A threat.

The old man who swamped dishes in the diner came out and began to clean the counter. Skip watched him, thinking that this old character with the gray face and the white tee shirt resembled in some way the old man on the bus and seeing that the pattern could have been laid out to enfold himself.

In the car Karen was weeping on Eddie's shoulder, and Eddie held her, at first loosely and then more closely, feeling the shudders that racked her young bones beneath her flesh.

Big Tom parked two blocks from the house, down the boulevard where there were a liquor store and a drugstore, both open, and a closed barbershop and shoeshine stand. He parked his car out of the direct light, went into the drugstore, and looked around, walked out quickly, went briskly away down the dark sidewalk to the cross street. He strolled uphill, eyes and ears alert. When he finally got within sight of the Havermann house and saw all the lights in it, he was filled with a ravaging disappointment. It had all the signs of a four-bell alarm.

Still he continued, drawn by bitter frustration, and walked on past. He had expected to see cars in the driveway, indications that the police were there, but it all seemed quiet enough. Not a soul moved in the grounds.

A full-fledged conviction had come into his mind that Skip and his friend had moved in early, forestalling him, had botched it and been discovered by the old woman. Now he wasn't so sure.

On an impulse he ducked into the heavy shrubbery bordering the drive, crouched there, waited. He could hear a dog barking in the distance, perhaps inside the house. There was no other sound at all. He pushed further into the shrubs and came out into a sort of lane, overhung by dusty evergreens and ditched for irrigation purposes, which led up directly to the house. Big Tom stole forward, careful to make no noise, and in a couple of minutes he had sized up the house, both front and rear, and was more puzzled than ever.

He retreated into the shadowy darkness to figure things out. It seemed now that no public alarm had been given; the place was much too silent for that. The old woman might be inside, scared, with all the lights on, having been alarmed by some preliminary boobery by Skip. Or—his mind seized on a new idea—Skip and his friend might be in there searching, the old woman having outwitted them somehow.

Stolz could be there, of course, a grimmer possibility to Big Tom than the presence of the police. Big Tom chewed a lip, squinted at the lights, considered thoughtfully.

Common sense and every instinct for danger he possessed warned him to get out of here, forget the job, forget he'd ever heard of the old house and the money in it. But Big Tom hesitated. He was curious. His hands itched for the money, the great beautiful green heap—hot or not.

All at once he caught a movement at an upper window, stiffened, his eyes narrowed with fright. Something yellow bobbed against the pane, an indistinct furry mass; and then the dog had his paws on the window sill and seemed to be peering out at the dark and barking as if to summon help.

"Now that's a funny thing," Big Tom said under his breath. He waited, and the dog bounced there, pawing at the pane, and the echo of his barking drifted out upon the night. "He's shut in. He's raising hell about it."

Big Tom went on thinking. If the old woman was in there scared, with the lights on to drive away potential prowlers, she wouldn't have the dog shut up that way. The dog would be downstairs, or outside, watching the place.

If Skip and Eddie were in there, though, messing around, shutting the dog up out of the way would be the first thing they'd do.

A faint smile touched Big Tom's lips. He pushed the dark cap back off his head a little; a few locks of the stiff gray hair escaped. He scratched around at his hairline. "By God, that must be it. They're in there doing something. Or they've just left." The thought that they might have just escaped with the money sent Big Tom hurrying from the bushes to the back door. He stopped there, took an old pair of gloves from his pants pocket, and slipped them on his hands. He patted the gun against his belly. Then he tried the screen door. It opened under his touch.

Like a man made of smoke, he drifted silently through the outer porch, glancing at the washing machine and the tubs in passing, and entered the kitchen and paused to listen. The dog's barking echoed sharply from upstairs. He couldn't hear another sound. No voices, footsteps, no clatter of struggle or search. He wondered briefly if the house, except for the disturbed dog, could be entirely empty.

With the greatest caution he crept into the hall. He saw the open door of the pantry, the light burning within, the sewing room across the hall, beyond these more doors, and then, at a point where the hall turned in a right angle, the edge of a hall runner and a bright glow from above. He recalled the location of Stolz's room as described by Skip, and noted that ahead and to the right a closed door had a bright, brass-colored, apparently new lock set into the wood.

Walking softly, walking on the edges of his shoes, he went to the door and tried the knob; the door opened at once. Inside the light burned in the overhead fixture. His gaze swept the room and took in the wardrobe, the open door of its clothes compartment gaping on nothing, the spilled drawers and other signs of search. Alarm caught him, froze him in the doorway. Everything seemed to hammer to a stop inside him: his heart, his breath, thought itself. He stood arrested by fright, gawking, until he remembered the hall and his unprotected back and moved on into the room.

He went over to the wardrobe and looked at it for a moment and then touched it with his gloved hand, shutting the little door. He looked around then, and certain facts occurred to him. If the money had been where Skip had expected it to be, there wouldn't have been a search.

The search had been successful, though, or they'd still be here.

It occurred to Big Tom to wonder where Mrs. Havermann was.

He stood in the middle of the room, undecided, listening for any scratch of sound. The sense of warning drilled through him again, but he resisted it. The curiosity was like a nagging itch inside his brain. He wanted to see what was in the rest of the house, make sure what had happened here, allay the hope that the money might remain.

He waited for another minute, listening to the creaking stillness punctuated now and then by the dog's yapping, and then went back into the hall.

Skip walked out to the car and approached it opposite the driver's seat. He heard Eddie say something, and Karen lifted her head and smoothed her hair; and a slight smile touched Skip's mouth, increasing the foxy look, narrowing his thin lips. He stood close to Eddie's door, and Eddie rolled down the glass.

"I'm going back," Skip said.

The two in the car looked out as if not understanding what he'd said. Karen's wet eyes gleamed in the dimness. All at once Eddie caught on and said, "Chrissakes, for why? You must be nuts."

"Ah, I just . . ." Skip's manner was completely relaxed. "I just want one more chance. The dough's there. Got to be."

"But she's dead in there," Karen said, leaning past Eddie, her voice shaking. "You can't go back!"

"Yell a little louder," Skip encouraged. "I don't think they quite heard that in the diner."

"Please! Please—let's not go back," she begged.

"Like I say," he went on, "the money's in there, maybe lying some perfectly ordinary place we just forgot to look at, some place I'd notice right away if I went back."

"You're crazy," Eddie said. "How do you know the cops aren't there right now?"

"Why should they be?" Skip demanded.

"Didn't you hear what she said about Stolz coming?" Eddie's nervous tension made his words jump.

"Ah, she just made it up to get rid of us." There was a moment of silence and then Skip said, "You remember what Karen told us, she was kind of sweet on Stolz? Hell, she must have been. She died trying to save his dough for him."

Karen cried brokenly then, and Eddie was distracted, trying to comfort her. He looked around, found that Skip had opened the door beside him. "We're going to change places. You'll do the driving now. You're going to drive by and drop me off at those trees. I'll work my way back to the house."

Eddie got out, went around the car. It was absolute insanity to stay in the neighborhood, much less go anywhere near that house. He wondered in an instant of self-revelation why he let Skip dictate this crazy course to him.

Skip got in on the other side of the car, shut the door. "Give me thirty minutes. I'll come out the same way, through the trees. If I'm not there give me another half hour before you come back again. But go by the house, size it up, before you stop anywhere either time."

"What'll we do?"

Skip looked slyly from Eddie to Karen. "Just drive around. And keep out of trouble."

Chapter Fourteen

UNCLE WILLY was surprised, a little disappointed, to see what a large gathering it was. The place was a grammar school auditorium. He and his sponsor slipped into their seats just as the proceedings opened. A big husky-looking guy on the stage at the front of the room rapped a gavel on a table and said, "Will the meeting please come to order?"

Willy looked all around. He had to make enough of an impression here so that he would be remembered, his time accounted for. A smaller group would have been better, easier to handle.

The chairman waited until the rustling and whispering subsided. Then, looking directly and rather fixedly at the people nearest the platform, he said, "Good evening, folks. My name is Jerry. I'm an alcoholic."

The audience answered in unison, "Hello, Jerry."

"He's an alcoholic?" Willy whispered to Mitchell. Willy thought he'd never seen a healthier specimen in his life than the man in front of the room. Mitchell nodded, smiling encouragement.

"He got his five-year pin a couple of weeks ago," Mitchell replied.

Jerry, the chairman, now said, "You all know Betty. Betty, will you please open our meeting by reading the twelve steps?"

Betty stood up in the front row, turned around holding the A.A. manual. She was a woman of around thirty, smartly dressed, rather good-looking. She read the twelve steps of the A.A. program in a firm clear voice.

"That's another one?" Willy wondered, squinting at her.

"Look," Mitchell said, "this is a closed meeting. Everybody here has been through the mill. Some of these people would be dead if it weren't for A.A. All these people, sober and presentable, interested in helping each other, were once just as confused and lost as you are."

On the way here Willy had given Mitchell a line composed equally of imagination and the recollections of his old cellmate.

Now he wondered if he might have overdone it a little. No matter. Mitchell's expression was friendly, and he was safely in the midst of a group with all their wits about them. Willy nodded to Mitchell and gave his attention to the program.

The speaker of the evening had come all the way from Riverside to be with them. He came forward smiling after Jerry's introduction, a stocky man nearly bald, and looked out over the audience and said, "Yes, folks, this is me—Bob. I'm an alcoholic. Hello, everybody."

The murmur responded from the listeners, "Hello, Bob."

As a preamble, Bob began: "Whenever I address a meeting like this I always wonder how many first-timers there are to hear what I have to say. I'd like to see hands of any first-timers here tonight."

Mitchell glanced at Willy, smiling. Willy raised his hand. A woman down the row, who had a hatbrim pulled over her eyes as if afraid she might be recognized, also put up her hand.

Bob counted the scattering of hands. "Six. Well, that's fine. I'm especially interested in you beginners. If I could, to encourage you, I'd turn the clock back and show you, for a couple of minutes, how I looked, acted, and felt just three years ago." Bob shook his head over the memory. Then his voice hoarsened, took on an edge of authority. "I was a bum," he stated bluntly. "I was down in the gutter. I *mean* gutter—I laid in it or near it night after night right here in L.A. skid row. I was a thief, too. Anything I could find that wasn't nailed down I sold to a junk dealer for money to buy wine. I panhandled. I rolled other drunks. I'd have stolen the dimes off my dead grandmother's eyes if I could have gotten to them. Lucky for her, my grandmother is perfectly healthy and lives in Iowa. She never knew what a close call she had."

The audience responded with a ripple of mirth. The stocky balding man had won his listeners. What he lacked in skill as a speaker he more than made up in sincerity and force. In spite of a determined inward cynicism and a wish to disassociate himself and daydream over the money, Willy found himself engrossed and impressed. My God, what the man had done with himself was almost unbelievable!

Bob went on to tell other details of his life as an alcoholic. His attitude was without bitterness, had instead a rather clinical air of reflection. Somehow, Willy sensed, Bob had made peace with whatever demons had driven him.

Bob related incidents which in other company would have been the cause of raised eyebrows, the bum's rush, or even calling the cops. He confessed to crimes committed under the influence of drink, horrible involvements with other skid-row denizens, blackouts, jail sentences, narrow escapes from death. His audience listened tolerantly, respectfully, laughing once in a while, and occasionally someone would nod as if an anecdote had hit home.

Bob told of the loss of home, family, and friends. His wife had deserted him early in his downward progress. His mother and father had forbidden him ever to set foot in their home. His brothers and sisters refused to recognize him on the street.

"In skid row and in jail I seemed to have come home at last," Bob said. "The environment made a kind of shelter, taking the place of all I had lost through alcoholism. I knew I couldn't adjust to normal people, normal surroundings. I kept myself stupefied on drink and stayed where I felt at home—in the gutter."

Willy was almost overwhelmed with a sense of compassionate brotherhood. True, he'd never been a drunk. Thievery had been his compulsion, separating him from decent companions and decent surroundings as effectively as liquor had done for Bob. In Willy's mind he translated what Bob had said into circumstances which applied to himself and was astounded at the parallel.

Bob's voice dropped to a confidential, hopeful note. "Well, one night when it seemed all that was left to me was a wretched death and a drunkard's grave," he went on, "by accident I found myself in the back room of a mission where an A.A. meeting was going on. I don't remember how I got into the place. I think I might have gone in there with the idea of stealing a snooze under a bench—out of sight of the mission people, who might have wanted me to bathe and eat and get my clothes laundered. I needed a bath. Yes, I remember that much. I noticed that a bum, almost as bad-looking a bum as I was, moved away when I sat too close to him."

Bob smiled cheerfully over the memory, and the audience smiled with him. Willy felt something run down his cheek from the corner of his eye. He put up an inquiring finger, found a damp streak. Oh, God, he was crying! Making an ass of himself! At the same moment he felt Mitchell's hand patting his arm. Willy wanted to run.

Bob continued: "And so, stinking and sick, hardly able to sit erect on the bench, I waited out the meeting. Somehow—this was a miracle—some of the meaning of the A.A. program got through to me. I got to talking to the bum who had moved away on the bench. He said he'd been a member for three weeks now and had tapered down to one quart of wine a day."

The audience laughed.

Bob waited until the amusement subsided. "When the meeting was over I went up to the front of the room and collared the speaker and said something to him—I don't remember what. This man, someone I'd never seen before and have never seen again—took time to sit down and discuss my problems with me. He urged me to stay at the mission, get some rest, clean up. He even—now get this—he even offered to take me home with him to help me straighten up."

There was a silence now, a few sighs. Willy thought, My God, that guy was a sucker, offering to take a drunk home, maybe get his place torn up by a maniac with the D.T.s. At the same time, the generosity of the offer touched him immensely, and he sensed that it had made a great change in Bob.

Bob continued soberly, "In the days that followed, while I wandered in a drunken haze, the thought of this man's trust and confidence kept coming back. Finally I returned to the A.A. meeting on another night at the mission. I won't try to fool you and say that I changed overnight or never had any trouble with liquor afterwards, or any such lies. It was tough. There were days when I didn't think I could make it."

Willy was shaking his head now, trembling. Again he noticed Mitchell's hand on his arm.

Mitchell whispered, "You just wait and see, friend. Things are going to be different for you, too. From here on out."

Willy wanted to be caught up in the peace and security that seemed to surround these people. God knows, he thought, being a thief and not able to stop is a lot like being a hopeless drunk. If I could find some way to get over the craving . . . What's being poor, what's working my ass off for old man

Chilworth, if I had a little self-respect and could know in my heart that I'd never be in trouble again? Why, that feeling would be the most wonderful thing in the world! To be safe. To be absolutely clean. Forever.

Willy leaned forward and put his face in his hands. He was almost swept away by an intense welling of emotion, as though Bob's speech had touched old, forgotten springs. The shell of silence and suspicion built up by the years in prison was crumbling. He felt newborn, and scared to death, and utterly naked mentally—all at once.

Bob's voice went on, and Willy shivered and shook under its sound and Mitchell kept patting his arm to comfort him.

Finally Mitchell leaned closer and spoke. "Don't worry, don't be afraid. Let yourself go. You'll be around the corner and on your way before you know it. Nothing can stop you now."

Befuddled, Willy glanced up at him. "Really?"

"Absolutely."

"How do you know?"

"Experience." Mitchell winked at him. "Just between us— I've never reminded Bob of it, and he's never remembered me. He was pretty soused that night. But I'm the guy who wanted to take him home from the mission."

Eddie had no watch, no way of keeping track of the time so he would know when to go back for Skip. He began to drive close to the curb, looking for a clock in some shop window. Finally, in a closed barbershop, he saw a clock on the back wall, made out the time by means of the light reflected from the street. It was a little past ten-fifteen.

Karen sat huddled opposite. She hadn't said a word while he was dropping Skip, while Skip was giving instructions as to when he must return. She wasn't asleep, though. Her eyes were fixed straight ahead, as if she were watching something that kept pace with them just outside the windshield. He kept glancing her way. His impression was that she was beginning to get over the first shock of Mrs. Havermann's death, beginning to accept and believe it, and that new torments were rising in her.

Finally she said, "What will they do to us?"

"Who?"

"When they catch us." She licked her lips. "When the police catch us."

"There's something you've got to remember," Eddie said, "if you get caught and they want you to talk, and promise you things, promise they'll make it easy for you, or argue with you. It's this. Keep your mouth shut. It's the only way to stay out of trouble. If you answer just one time, correct them on one little detail they've got wrong on purpose, they'll have you tripping over your own feet before you know it."

Her eyes moved around to study him. "You mean, just say nothing at all?"

"Don't even nod your head or blink your eyes. Shut yourself up inside yourself and think about something else. Don't listen to them. Count things, remember things. Try to remember all the shoes you've ever owned, all the shoes you've worn all the way back as far as your memory goes. Or count the shows you've seen. The movies. Try to think of the titles. But don't let their words get through to you."

Her eyes were big now. "You've done that?"

He nodded. "I had to. Somebody told me about it a long time ago, and it's the only way to beat them. Just don't listen."

She went back to staring through the windshield. Eddie was driving aimlessly. He was scared all the way through, sick over the old woman's death, and if he'd had his way would have headed out of town as fast as the jalopp would take them. But of course they had to go back for Skip. Skip was still trying to find the money.

They were in the hills above Altadena now, on a rough rutted road. Eddie looked around, seeing the sudden dropping away of lights. They had come to a section where new homes were being built. A cluster of red lanterns loomed up ahead, topping the piled earth of a new excavation. Eddie braked to a halt.

Karen roused and looked out. Some of the houses were just framework buttressed with chimneys, not roofed over. Others were almost completed. Karen said tonelessly, "Look, it's a new neighborhood."

"I've got to turn around, go back. We can't get past that ditch."

Karen was looking out now with a touch of interest. "No,

let's stop here for a while. We've got to wait somewhere. Do you think there's a watchman out here?"

"I don't know. Probably not," Eddie answered, thinking of the times he and Skip had stolen things out of unfinished houses. Karen was opening the car door on her side. "Where are you going?"

She said, "I just want to get out of the car. I just want some fresh air." She stood with her head back, looking at the stars, and then moved off across the dark, rubble-dotted ground. Eddie doused the lights, got out, shut the car door. It was quite dark here now; there were crickets in the distance that only seemed to emphasize the silence around them. The red lanterns at the excavations in the distance looked like glowing coals. He could make out Karen, a dim shape under the star-shine, going toward a half-finished place with a big front porch. She sat down there facing the street, put her elbows on her knees, leaned her face on her palms. She looked small and unutterably lonely.

"Why do things happen . . . the way they happen?" she asked when Eddie sat down close beside her.

"Gosh, I don't know. If I knew that, I'd be a magician." Eddie thought it over some more. "I'd be God."

The porch was brick, hadn't been swept yet, and crumbs of mortar lay on it. The interior of the house behind them gave forth a strong fragrance of sawn wood, the smells of paint and putty. He saw that Karen had cupped her eyes with her hands and was crying again.

Eddie moved closer and put an arm around her. She moved her face against his jacket. "I didn't even get to say good-by to her," she wept. "I didn't get to tell her . . . not even once . . . how I felt about living there all those years. And at the end she hated me. She hated me because I brought Skip and you to her house." She choked over her words, and Eddie stroked her hair softly. "When I first met Skip and talked to him about the money, I just thought it was a kind of joke."

Eddie was amazed at her idea. "Skip never thought money was a joke."

She cried for a while against his coat, wiping tears away with the back of her hand. Then she said, "You're different from Skip, Eddie. I'll bet you don't even know it, but you're entirely different. There's a kind of . . . gentleness about you, and Skip doesn't have it. Not a bit of it."

"Ah, Skip's okay, I guess," Eddie said uncomfortably.

"No, there's something lacking. I used to think he was tough, awfully brave, and that what was inside him was strength. But tonight I saw that wasn't it at all. Inside, Skip is—is kind of hollow. Not in a physical way. I don't quite know how to put it."

Eddie recalled something from the past. "When we were in high school I heard the principal raising hell with Skip once and he told Skip that he was immature. Something in him wasn't growing up along with the rest of him. That's all that's wrong with Skip; he just isn't all grown up yet," Eddie said.

"He's never going to grow up." She waited then as if thinking, then said suddenly, "Let's not go back for him!"

The treasonous thought was to Eddie like ice water thrown over his body. He began to protest.

"Well, we won't argue about it," she said quickly. She pulled herself closer, as if sheltering from a wind. "I don't want to argue with you. I like you. If anything separated us I'd just die."

She was awfully young and afraid—Eddie had sense enough to know this, to suspect that her clinging was based on the circumstances of the moment. But he could not help but respond to her softness, her nearness. All at once she lifted her face to his, and their lips met and clung.

She was warm and yielding. He found himself trembling. She whispered something against his face, her voice husky, almost drowsy. He spoke then, staccato, the words ripped off short with tension and urgency. "We won't go back. You're right. We'll leave Skip where he is. And to hell with him."

Chapter Fifteen

SKIP STOOD in the shadows beside the back door for several minutes, listening. When he had first emerged from the shrubbery and stolen toward the porch it had seemed as if a sound reached him, not the sort of sound somehow that he connected with the bouncing and yapping of the dog upstairs. But now that he had waited and listened there was nothing; the house was empty and still and something in its stillness had the feeling of death about it.

Skip went into the screened porch, passing the tubs and the washing machine, on into the kitchen, then the hall. The door of Stolz's room stood open, and for a moment this startled him; but then, thinking back, he couldn't remember whether it had been closed or shut when they had fled from the house. He went into Stolz's room and pushed the door shut, not quite catching the lock. Stolz's room was his objective. Mulling things over in the diner, it had occurred to him that finding the money behind the canned dog food might have a different meaning than the one he had put on it.

Old Mrs. Havermann might have hidden the money in the kitchen *before* she'd thought of putting the new locks on Stolz's room. After the new locks were installed, she could have reclaimed the treasure from the cupboard and returned it to Stolz's room—somewhere they hadn't thought to look. Skip remembered looking under the bed, but not *in* it.

Could the money have been carefully hidden between the covers, or under the mattress, spread out thin so it made no bulge or wrinkle?

He meant to find out.

Skip went to the bed and stripped back the covers, pulled them off into a heap on the floor. Nothing. He lifted the mattress at the head of the bed. Beneath the mattress were the springs, not enclosed like box springs but the older coil type, so that Skip could see through them to the floor. There was a little dust on the floor, some rolls of cottony fuzz, and that was all. Skip dropped the mattress into place. His conviction that the money must be in Stolz's room was beginning to weaken.

He was careful about touching anything which would retain a print. He'd forgotten the rubber gloves, left them on the shelf back of the car seat along with Eddie's.

He started to take out cigarettes and matches, and then with a muttered "Oh, what the hell," went to the foot of the bed and flipped up the other end of the mattress and for a moment felt a great leaping shock of joy. There was a white-wrapped bundle there, not big; it could be a part of the money. Skip dropped the cigarette in his fingers. His hands were shaking. But then the moment he touched the wrapped object he knew it wasn't bills.

He undid the white cloth, which turned out to be a pillow slip. Inside was a gun. It was quite small and flat with an extremely short barrel. It looked like a toy. Skip had trouble breaking the cartridge clip loose. But when he had it out, it proved to be full of neat little bullets.

For a moment he was so taken with the tiny, deadly-looking gun that he almost forgot the money. He lined up the sights, squinting at himself in Stolz's mirror across the room.

"Neat," he said, examining the weapon. "Real neat."

He put it into his pocket and then couldn't leave it there. He took it out again and kept it in his hand while he looked over the rest of the room. He found nothing, and everywhere he searched, he and Karen and Eddie had searched before.

He stood in the middle of the floor, thinking. He couldn't understand why Big Tom and his friends hadn't shown up, and then he remembered the way the house had looked, all lit up, when they had seen it across the vacant lots. To Big Tom and his friends the effect would have been the same as if the place had been on fire. Skip grinned to himself. Well, leaving the lights on had been smart . . . for a time. But now it was better to turn them out. Somebody besides Big Tom might take notice. Skip clicked off Stolz's light as he went out, circled back to the kitchen, doused the lights there, then clicked off all but one in the lower hall. He darkened the rooms where Eddie had searched and then went softly up the stairs.

He felt funny about going up here, so near the dead woman, but he wanted one more glance around. He had the gun in his hand; he liked the feel of it, the compact deadly weight of it, like a pair of brass knucks that spit fire. He passed close to Mrs.

Havermann's door, and then from within the room he heard a slight noise.

The dog? Skip froze to listen. No, the dog was still down the hall, yapping and bumping around, nowhere near Mrs. Havermann's bedroom.

Mrs. Havermann . . . Hell, she wasn't dead then! She'd revived somehow. What was she doing in there?

The conviction that Mrs. Havermann had made the faint sound, like a slow-moving person shifting some article in the room, was so strong that no thought of Big Tom intruded to warn him.

I'll scare her with the gun, Skip thought. Nobody else is here now to interfere. I can beat her up a little. She ought to be plenty ready to talk by this time. He threw open the door and started inside.

Big Tom was across the room beside the open closet. He had entered the room only a minute before, had seen the woman sprawled under some fallen clothes. In that instant his mind had gulped in a vast lump of knowledge: the punks had been here; they'd bungled it; they'd run out in a panic just as he would have expected, and his own situation here in the house with a corpse was the kind of thing he dreamed about on the bad nights when he suffered from nightmares.

He ripped off his right-hand glove and bent forward to touch her, not through any instinct of mercy or a desire to revive her, but rather to convince himself that this ultimate boobery on the punks' part had actually happened, and at the same moment he heard someone come into the room behind him. His hand clawed for the gun in his belt, the big heavy gun, and then he had pulled it free and was ready to fire even as he swung around to face the room. The Luger spoke, but at this instant fiery gnats were stinging his flesh. There was no sense of impact or penetration; it all seemed to lie in his skin, a spray of needles. The bullet from the Luger entered the floor at Skip's feet. Big Tom folded forward slowly and struck the rug with his head.

Skip stood near the doorway. His expression was one of surprise, as if things had happened too quickly to be believed. The gun in his hand had seemed to act of itself. It was a very clever, quick, and willing little gun. He gazed at it and then at the big man convulsing on the floor, as if wondering at the connection between the weapon and the condition of the man.

Skip waited. Big Tom quit writhing and jerking so badly and tried to get his fingers on the fallen Luger, so Skip walked over and kicked it into the closet with the dead woman. Big Tom tried to prop himself up by means of an outspread right hand, and when the hand moved it had left a print in blood, quite distinct on the polished light-colored wood, and Skip regarded it with interest.

"You give me ideas, old man," he said. He put his own weapon in his pocket, grabbed Big Tom by the arm, pulled him nearer the closet, and then, holding Big Tom's palsied fingers outspread, he made a big beautifully distinct print on the white-painted door.

Big Tom's breathing sounded as if he were doing it through a ten-foot length of hose. "Goddamn . . . goddamn punk . . . I told Willy——"

"Shut up." Skip went to the closet and got Mrs. Havermann, brought her out and laid her beside Big Tom, and then, using Big Tom's hand as he would a paintbrush, he daubed and smeared her with his blood. "That ought to do it." He went to the door, clicked off the lights, ran down the stairs and out through the rear of the house. He was positive he hadn't left a print on any surface which might retain it. Nobody was going to raise any prints on old lady Havermann except the bloody ones of Big Tom's fingers. Skip felt like whistling.

He waited in the trees above the vacant road. The night faded toward midnight, and a sense of danger stole over him. All at once some sixth sense told him what had happened to Eddie and Karen. Skip's reaction was not one of anger. He had the only amount of loot the night had produced, some three or four thousand dollars at a guess, and he had no wish to share it with them.

He left the trees at the far end of the block and walked rapidly down to the cross-town boulevard, where he caught a bus for Uncle Willy's. He was busily packing his belongings—all of them, this time—when Willy came in.

Big Tom awoke and looked at the dark, and the phantoms fled from his brain. He knew where he was, he even knew what the thing was lying next to him, the thing whose inert pressure he felt whenever he moved. He recalled Skip at the doorway. He had not seen any gun in Skip's hand and so the source of the bullets confused him, though he had no doubt of their reality. They nested in his flesh now like fiery eggs. He was light headed, almost drained dry of blood, and he had to get out of here.

He inched and wriggled his way across the room to the door, out into the hall. Then he slithered down the stairs. The lower hall had one light burning in a bracket beside the front entry. He looked up at it and it swam, exploded into a red and purple nimbus, and blacked out. Big Tom lay on his face, thought and consciousness gone, and Mrs. Havermann's big clock, the one she had brought from France when she was twenty-seven, ticked lonesomely in the silence.

When he roused again he forced himself to his knees and reached for the front doorknob. He fell down again before he could get hold of it. He tried to figure out another way to open the door without reaching the knob, and failed. Then he remembered seeing a telephone inside the door of the parlor. He turned and crawled toward the open door across the hall.

There was enough light; he could see the phone on its little spindling table, a doily under it, lace hanging down around the rim of the table. The doily pulled off with the phone, fell on his face. It smelled of ironed starch and dust. It seemed an eternity while he fought to lift his hand, to get it away from his mouth and nose so that he could breathe again.

When he had dialed, when the phone at the other end of the wire had rung six or seven times, Harry answered. Harry sounded cross and sleepy. "Yeah? Yeah?"

"Say . . . Harry."

"Who is it?" Harry yawned. "Speak up. Say something."

"Tom. This is Tom."

"Oh." Harry seemed to withdraw slightly from the receiver. "Well, where are you? What's cooking?"

"Need . . . help."

Harry took even longer to think about this. "You calling from a public phone, huh? A bar or someplace?"

"Hav . . ." Big Tom had to stop, to catch himself against

the little table. He was only half propped up; now he lay flat on the floor, the phone on the floor beside him. "Havermann house. My car's on the boulevard, near a dru . . . a drugstore." Each word involved the effort of thinking about it, forming it with his lips, summoning the breath to speak. He lost all sense of what he had said; the present word was the aim, the hope, the hurdle.

"You sound sick," Harry said. "Something happen t' you?"

"Shot."

"Man, oh man. You better get out of that house."

"Going to try." Big Tom's senses faded; fear that he would black out again, lose the phone connection, lose Harry, washed through him like an icy pulse. "Can you meet me? Drive . . . car?"

Harry wasn't willing; the silence, the waiting told Big Tom that. But finally Harry said grudgingly, "Now where did you say the car is?"

Big Tom tried to think of the name of the big boulevard. He grappled with his memory. It supplied names, other streets, other towns. Now this one—— Suddenly he had it, he said it into the phone, and Harry, still unwilling, promised to meet him at the car.

No use asking Harry to come here to help him. Harry wouldn't do it. And the refusal would harden him and then he'd refuse to wait at the car. I'll make it alone, that far, Big Tom promised himself. He dragged his drained, burning body back to the front door and tried again for the knob. He passed out there, still trying.

When he became conscious again, he stared around him in amazement. This was a miracle! He was far down the sloping lawn of the Havermann grounds, almost to the curb. He had no memory of opening the front door, getting down off the porch, or inching across the turf.

Could someone—Harry? Benny?—have found him, helped him? He looked all around, but he was alone. Back across the shadowed lawns, the Havermann house looked tall and lonely. The front door stood open, the beams of the light in the bracket shone out upon the porch. The rest of the place was dark.

He felt a renewal of confidence and strength. He pulled himself to his knees, and then on hands and knees he traversed the two blocks, long vacant blocks, to the boulevard. And then it was time to rise up and to walk.

He squeezed himself over against a building, out of the light, and forced his body slowly upward. There were strangenesses: odd tremors and loosened joints and a tearing sensation all through the middle of his lungs, as if his lungs were made of tissue paper and the breath trapped in them was forcing a hole slowly wider and wider. Sweat came out all over him; he tottered off balance; a great roaring filled his ears.

"Walk, feet." Had he said it aloud? No matter. There was no one about now; the drugstore had closed. Passing, he could see inside it, the night light above the prescription counter glowing ruby red in an enormous jar of colored liquid. And then by another miracle he was at the car. He slid inside and fell across the seat.

A long while later he heard a whispering voice. It insinuated itself into his brain, rousing him from the compulsion to sleep.

"Hey! Hey! Can you sit up? Look, are there any cops around here?"

Tom listened dreamily to the voice.

"Who shot you?"

Tom said, in his mind, "The little bastard threw a handful of bullets at me—just threw them, mind you—and the damned things went all the way in, exactly as if he had used a gun. It was remarkable, very remarkable." In his dream, then, he was telling this to a screw he had known in prison, and in reply the screw, who had always been short-tempered, raised an enormous leg and kicked him between the shoulder blades and a long quivering slice of pain ran through his body from back to front. That'll teach me to pass the time of day with a goddamn screw, Tom said to himself in his mind. But then, anyway, he went on explaining: "And I didn't even see him raise his arm. What I saw, it seemed he just had his finger pointed at me and . . . zzzzzz! Like bees!"

"For God's sake, are you laughing?" cried the whispering voice.

Big Tom opened his eyes. Harry had the door open on the other side of the car, was leaning in, his face not more than six inches from Big Tom's. "I'll get you t' Doc. You remember Doc. He won't like it," Harry whispered, "but he'll do it." He grunted, pushed Tom erect, got him propped into the other corner of the seat. "Where's the key? Tom, Tom!" He was slapping Tom's face.

"Shirt . . . pocket."

Harry squeezed into the seat, poked into the pocket, got a closer look at the mess on Tom's clothes. "Jeez! My God, it's like a sieve. I've *really* got t' get you t' Doc!"

"You . . . really . . . do," Tom whispered in answer.

The motor hummed into life. Harry let in the clutch. "You had a gun? How come you didn't use it?"

"Surprise . . ."

"What about the dough?"

"I don't know. Maybe they . . . got it. Old woman's dead."

"What?" Harry's voice was a yelp.

"Dead . . . inna . . ." Too hard to say; he'd forgotten the other word. "Dead," he repeated simply.

"You plugged her?"

"Already dead."

"Who did it then? Who plugged you, for God's sake?"

"The punk." Big Tom fell over against Harry, and Harry had to fight to hold onto the wheel, to keep from crashing into a row of parked cars. "Hey, look, you're getting blood all over me! You got t' bleed like that? You got t' bleed on *my* clothes?"

Big Tom's answer was a hoarse, dragging breath which died in a sudden strangle. Harry drew the car into a side street, slowed down, studied Big Tom's bobbing face anxiously.

"You okay?"

Big Tom's mouth opened; he lifted a hand aimlessly as if to locate his lips, to see why they no longer obeyed his commands, no longer formed words, just hung loosely and fluttered with his breath. As the hand lifted, his head bowed as if to meet it. His whole body staggered forward to crash against the front of the car.

Blood began to drip heavily to the floor.

"Hey!" Harry waited a moment, looking out anxiously—this was a quiet residential street, old houses set close together in a lot of shrubs and flowers. Harry licked his lips, swallowed several times. His face was greenish in the light from the dash. "Tom?" he said softly.

The dripping was slowly decreasing and there was no answer from Big Tom, not even the sound of a breath.

Harry took out his handkerchief, carefully wiped the steering wheel, the door rim, and then used the handkerchief, wrapped around his hand, as a sort of glove while he set the brakes and doused the lights and switched off the motor. He opened the car door and slipped out and laid the handkerchief on the door handle before closing the door. Then he backed from the car a few steps and paused. He could see Big Tom in there, lying forward on the dashboard; he thought Big Tom looked exactly like a passed-out drunk and wouldn't be noticed seriously for hours, not before morning, perhaps, when it would be light enough to see the blood all over him.

"I'm sorry t' have t' do this," Harry muttered. "I just can't afford t' get messed up in it." He started away, then glanced back and whispered, "If I could help, I would. But nothing's going t' help now."

He went back to the main cross-town street and looked around. He'd taken a cab all the way out here, answering Big Tom's urgent summons, but that was before he had known what had happened. Now he wanted no one connecting him with the district, with Big Tom, or even with the city of Pasadena. He couldn't risk a cab.

He waited for a bus, and when one came he sized it up; it was quite crowded, a bunch of noisy young people in the back and the others looking tired and indifferent, not paying any attention to each other. He got on. He crouched quickly into a seat near the door before anyone could notice the blood on the side of his suit.

When he reached his flat the blond girl was in bed asleep, naked as usual, reeking with sexy cologne.

Harry sponged the suit in the bathroom, put on his pajamas, took several aspirin and a couple of sleeping pills. When he sat on the side of the bed to yawn the girl roused and grunted at him, and he said, "Shaddap!" Finally he snapped off the bedside lamp and put his head on his pillow and lay there looking at the dark.

"Just like that!" Harry whispered to himself. "What a hell of a way t' go!"

Chapter Sixteen

THE LONG black car snaked into the drive, paused, then continued almost silently toward the house. The man behind the wheel, a huge black-haired man with a look of granite hardness about him, said, "Mr. Stolz, the front door's open."

"Yes, I see that it is," Stolz said quietly. His dark, narrow, handsome face held only a touch of dismay. He was smoking a cigarette in a gold and ivory holder; now he removed it, crushed it out in the dashboard tray, put the holder into his breast pocket. He looked closely at the house as they rolled nearer. "All dark, darker than she would have it. Someone's been here. We're late."

Marvitch nodded, guiding the car back into the shadowy area near the garage. When Marvitch had set the brakes, cut the motor and lights, Stolz got out and walked toward the back door. Marvitch caught up with him there. "This door isn't locked," Stolz said. "I know she was careful about keeping it latched after sundown."

They went in. Stolz knew the house, didn't put on a light until they had reached the hall. He went at once into his own room. He and Marvitch surveyed the mess. "She had moved it," Stolz said. "I kept it in there." He indicated the wardrobe, walked over, opened the little door that Big Tom had closed. "They made a search." Stolz looked at the upturned end of the mattress. He shook his head. "I hate to lose the little automatic. It was quite a toy. Besides that, it might turn up somewhere later to embarrass me."

Marvitch said, "We'd better look around for the old lady and the girl. Maybe they're tied up somewhere."

"That's likely." Stolz led the way back into the hall. "Mrs. Havermann's room is upstairs. Let's look there first."

Stolz ran lightly up the carpeted steps. He kept himself lean and fit. He watched his diet, ate a lot of fruit and yogurt and bran crackers, and swam in the hotel pool. The desert sun kept him well tanned. Marvitch was slower, weighter. Marvitch lived on rare steaks and bourbon whiskey and eighteen-year-old brunettes. He, too, in his own way was in excellent shape.

When Stolz saw what was in Mrs. Havermann's bedroom he paled yellow, and when Marvitch saw it he made a sharp indignant sound like a squeezed duck.

"Oh, my God, what a horrible thing to have happened to her," Stolz said. He sounded as if he meant it. He looked at Mrs. Havermann and then glanced away, as if the dreadful sight sickened him. "They've killed her."

"They sure have." Marvitch stared around at the room. "I wonder where the girl is?" He had never seen Karen, but Stolz's description of her had interested him.

Stolz looked quickly through the other rooms. "She doesn't seem to be here." He shook his head, as if dismissing the problem of Karen from his mind. "We have to plan very carefully now."

"I don't see how we can clean this up enough to keep it away from the bulls," Marvitch said.

"Oh, we'll have to call the police. This is murder, Marvitch." He looked Marvitch in the eyes and Marvitch understood: this was a *special* kind of killing, not the sort you did and dumped in an alley or left for the buzzards out the other side of Hoover Dam, in the desert. This old lady had to be all legally accounted for, examined, and investigated. "Yes, sir," Marvitch answered. "But when, Mr. Stolz?"

Stolz's eyes were bitter. "We've got to find that damned money first."

"I should think so," Marvitch agreed.

Stolz appeared to think it over. He said, "I know the house better than you do. You don't know your way around at all."

"Money's money, Mr. Stolz. I'd recognize it anywhere."

Stolz smiled slightly.

"Not only that," Marvitch went on, "I've had things hidden from me before, and I never had much trouble finding them."

"There's no one to question, unfortunately."

"I don't mean like that. I mean cold turkey, looking for it. I had me a girl in Chicago once; I gave her a diamond brooch, and then afterwards she decided she liked another dealer better than me and she gave me the gate. I wanted the pin back. I couldn't touch her; her new friend had connections. So I hunted in her place and I——"

Stolz held up his hand. "We haven't much time."

Marvitch demanded, "You know where she had that diamond pin hidden?"

Stolz sighed. "No. Where?"

"In a box of very personal apparel, if you get what I mean."

Stolz nodded. "That was unfair, wasn't it?"

"Didn't fool me a minute."

"Go downstairs," Stolz said briskly, "and start looking. Not in my room. Everywhere else. Including the garage, the old car she kept jacked up out there."

Marvitch was glad that Mr. Stolz had allowed him to conclude his little yarn about the diamond pin. He rushed downstairs and began to turn over again the things Eddie and Skip had once tonight overturned.

Nearly an hour's work got them nothing. They concluded that the money had been taken by the thieves. Much disturbed now, uneasy and angry, Stolz called for the help of the police.

They awaited the arrival of the cops in Mrs. Havermann's parlor. The dog had been released from his prison upstairs and now lay at Stolz's feet. After obvious cogitation Marvitch said, "You know, there are some funny things about the old lady's death. She has all the marks of a strangling job. But then there's all that blood—bloody prints on the closet door, blood all the way down the hall and the stairs. There's even some over there." He pointed to the large stain in the rug by the table holding the phone. He had found the phone off the hook and on the floor when he had come searching here for the money. Off the hook, and covered with bloody prints. "I think one of *them* got shot. We ought to go out and see if there's a trail outdoors and where it leads."

"It's obvious that one of them was shot," Stolz said impatiently. "But we won't hunt for him. That's for the police. We don't dare meddle with evidence. This isn't Nevada." He was looking hard at Marvitch. "We'll be walking a tightrope here. Watch what you say, watch how you act. We just got here, and we're stunned."

They practiced looking stunned, and the dog slept until the cops came with red lights, sirens, and bright gold badges.

————

Skip slammed the lid of the suitcase, locked it. It was bigger than the zipper case and quite old and battered. "Well, that's that."

Uncle Willy, pale and shaken and twitchy with nervousness, sat across the room on the other bed. "Can't you tell me everything that happened? I don't want to be left in the dark. After all, I got my friends into this. Important people." Uncle Willy was thinking of Snope and of Snope's methods when he became displeased.

"You're better off not knowing," Skip said. "Just believe me, the job went sour. Big Tom goofed. Real bad. I knew when you dragged him in on it, it was a mistake."

Uncle Willy chewed a nail. "I can't understand anything going wrong for Big Tom. He's a real careful operator. Maybe you shouldn't have gone anywhere near the house tonight. Maybe if you hadn't been there, prying around——"

"Just be glad I was," Skip said. "Just be glad I was smart enough to do a little checking. If I hadn't heard those shots and seen what I had, you might be a sitting duck right now."

"No, no, I'm in the clear. Perfectly in the clear. Skip, I don't mind telling you this job washes me up. I'm all through. I'm never going to have anything more to do with anything crooked."

"Now you're getting smart," Skip commended.

"I'm not going to ask you any more questions, either," Uncle Willy went on with an air of withdrawing from something wicked. "I've got a whole new slant on life. It doesn't have to be a rat race." His coat hung over a chair, the pockets heavy with A.A. leaflets; Uncle Willy looked over that way, his face brightening. "Yessir, I've crossed a kind of bridge and I never intend to go back the way I came."

Skip nodded, looking around to see if he had missed anything. He paid little attention to Uncle Willy's meanderings.

Uncle Willy said, "I had my eyes opened tonight. I'm not going to kick any more about working for Mr. Chilworth. I'm not going to grouch to myself and think all the time about the chances I missed and the jobs I might have pulled off, and things like that. I'm going to concentrate on myself, my own shortcomings and failures. You know, the harm I've done others, and so on. I'm going to straighten myself out. It's just a miracle, you might say, that I called A.A. and they sent me this Mr. Mitchell."

"You liked him, huh?" Skip picked up the zipper bag and went into the bathroom for his shaving stuff.

"He's the best man I ever met in my life," Uncle Willy said fervently.

"That's fine; you stick with him," Skip advised.

Uncle Willy's gaze followed Skip as he moved around the room. "There's no money coming at all?" he ventured timidly.

Skip glanced over at him. "You'd better forget you ever heard of any money."

"And you didn't . . . uh . . . get a chance to——"

"From outside?" Skip demanded scornfully. "With them plugging away at each other in there like a shooting gallery?"

"I just can't understand it." Uncle Willy rubbed a hand around over his thin head of hair. "To think Big Tom and those men he knew would have a blowup like that."

"They did, and that's why I have to clear out. If the girl talks I'm cooked. If they find her, that is."

"She's not waiting somewhere for you?" Uncle Willy demanded, having forgotten his decision not to ask any more questions. "I thought she had your jalopp, maybe, was outside in the street, or maybe running an errand."

"Eddie has the jalopp," Skip said. "If he brings it back here, push it in the garage, will you? If he doesn't, it's okay." Privately Skip thought: He took the bitch off my hands, he's welcome to the heap. He had the two bags stuffed with his clothes and belongings now, the zipper bag and the old battered case. Skip went over to the door. "Well, so long, Unc. I'll be seeing you. Remember, if the bulls give any sign of thinking you were in on this thing tonight, you know from nothing."

"I was at the A.A. meeting," Uncle Willy said, the new light beginning to shine again in his weary eyes.

In Union Station, Skip went into the men's room, entered a cubicle and shut the door, and then, standing spraddle-legged above the bags, he unbuttoned his shirt and took out the two packs of bills and counted them. One pack had twenty hundred-dollar bills and the other had twenty-five. He was the possessor of forty-five hundred dollars in crisp legitimate currency. He extracted two of the bills, put the rest back inside his shirt, unlatched the door, picked up the bags, and returned to the main lobby.

His real desire was to get to Las Vegas and try to run the money into an important sum with luck; but Las Vegas was Stolz's territory and it was just possible the money might be recognized over there in some manner. Not probable, Skip thought, but possible to the degree that he felt nervous over it. The next best, though much farther away, was Reno.

He bought a ticket to Portland, Oregon. This would take him through Sacramento, where he would get off the train and buy another ticket east.

In case anyone wished to trace him there would be a little difficulty. He wasn't thinking now of the police, but of Stolz. He had no desire ever to meet again the big man with the granite face and the granite fists. People like that were, in Skip's opinion, just plain undesirable citizens.

Eddie parked the car in the alley, some two or three doors from home. Karen whispered, "Will you be long, Eddie? Will it take much time?"

"I've got to pack a few things, not much."

Her face floated in the dark, pale as a flower, and Eddie could make out the endearing curve of lip and cheek, the fringe of lashes, the soft gleam of her eyes. Already Karen's face had taken on the familiar aspect of the well-beloved. It seemed to Eddie that he had known her forever. He leaned into the car to kiss her once again. She put up her hands to frame his face, to pull his mouth to hers. When the kiss ended she whispered, "You're just wonderful, Eddie. You really are!"

Eddie felt wonderful. He had the sensation of having found a small, exclusive, and rather unbelievable treasure much more to be prized than the mundane one of money. Karen belonged to him. He belonged to her. It had happened on the front porch of a house being built in an unknown part of Altadena. No matter who eventually bought and owned that house, a little bit of it would always be his and Karen's.

He went quickly down the dark unlit alley to the slatternly back fence, found the gate, went in past the heaps of unboxed refuse and wine bottles, to the back door of the house. He let himself in. The smell left by his mother's cooking, the chili, the masa and grease, the coffee, was rank in the kitchen. He stole through to the main room, crossed it softly in the dark, and tapped on the bedroom door.

He heard the bedsprings creak, some sort of muffled drunken jabber from his father, his mother saying, "Go back to sleep. I'll see to it." The door opened and there she stood, dimly visible in the vast white cotton gown. "Eddie?"

"Come out and close the door."

She obeyed. She came into the room, shut the door without rattling the catch, then went to a table and switched on a lamp there. She looked over the lamp at Eddie, and he saw the worry, the anxious dread in her eyes. "Something's happened?" she whispered.

"I have to go away tonight. Right away."

She pulled the edge of the gown up over the lump at the base of her throat. She stood by the lamp for another moment, then sat down slowly. Her face crumpled; she hid it in her hands. She was crying.

"Don't worry about me," Eddie said. "All I need is a few dollars. You do have something hidden away, don't you, Mama?"

She nodded without lifting her head from her hands. The enormous goiter bulged from between her wrists like the head of a baby under the skin there, a baby which had worked its way up there trying to be born. She trembled, her flesh quivered, but the big lump under her skin was firm and quiet as though it were not a part of her. "Can you tell me?" she whispered.

"I'd better not. Then you won't know; they can't threaten you."

"I wouldn't tell anyone anything," she said through her shaking hands.

"No, Mama."

"Is it . . . really bad?"

"Yes, it's bad. It's as bad as it can get."

She lifted her eyes, her mouth still covered, perhaps to conceal its trembling. Her eyes were already reddening. "Somebody killed?"

Eddie looked away, not answering. His mother picked up the sleeve of the gown between her fingers and rubbed her eyes on the cotton. "I had a feeling. A long time I've had a feeling. I kept saying to myself, No, it's just the class Eddie's interested in. He's going to get a job, make honest money. All those troubles are behind him, the bad company he kept and all that talk about how to live easy without working."

Eddie walked around the room a little. He knew his mother had the right to say what she was saying. She had stood by him in every scrape he'd been in, from the earliest time when he'd still been in grammar school and had been caught stealing money from the teacher's purse. He and Skip. He hadn't told anyone that Skip had been in it with him. He'd kept his mouth shut; the principal had whipped him with a wooden paddle, had warned his mother that a second offense would mean the juvenile court. And she had taken the principal's harsh words with dignity, with composure, and, going home, she had stopped on a street corner and shyly, softly, she had asked Eddie if he would like a chocolate soda at the drugstore fountain. Eddie couldn't remember a time when this Mexican mother of his had not had love and patience and gentleness in her, and so now he listened to her grieving and kept his mouth shut and waited.

"I will say a prayer first, and then I will get you the money," she said. "Kneel down, my son."

He knelt down, feeling a little awkward, and she began saying the Our Father in Spanish. After that she prayed to the Blessed Virgin, asking the help of the Mother of Christ for her son, asking that this most pure and merciful Mother who had known terror and despair in her time on earth should now listen to the anguish of another for her child.

When the prayer was finished she rose, crossing herself, and went into the kitchen. She brought a broken-backed chair from beside the door and placed it in front of a cupboard. She said to Eddie, "On the top shelf. The red can, the tomatoes. Take what is in there."

Eddie got the can down, opened it.

"There is fifty-six dollars," his mother told him. "Not much. It will take you a little way. Write to me when you get where you are going. Not here, send it to Mrs. Valdez. She'll give it to me at church."

Eddie stuffed the money into his pants pocket. They exchanged a last embrace. His mother's body was big and flabby inside the gown; her hair smelled of oil; she had a faint odor of wine, too, from being around his father, from being shut up in the bedclothes with a stinking drunk.

"I'll write to Mrs. Valdez," Eddie promised.

"Go with God," said his mother in farewell.

Chapter Seventeen

THEY DROVE up the coast. The night had turned chill and patches of fog swept in from the sea, obscuring the highway. Eddie began to yawn, to have difficulty keeping his eyes open. Above Santa Monica they came to an oceanside park and campground. It was full of trailers and tents, but Eddie pulled in anyway, crowding the jalopy in among some squatty evergreens. Karen got out. She was shivering. She had no wrap of any sort. Eddie stripped the blanket off the seat, the old Army blanket Skip had used to cover the holes in the original upholstery. He spread it on the needles, leaves, and trash under the trees and then he and Karen lay down and rolled themselves up in it. Down here next to the earth, sheltered from the seawind, they were fairly warm. During the night Eddie was awakened by Karen's crying. When he touched her hair softly it was damp with tears.

At about eight o'clock the clatter of the other campers awakened them. Eddie unwrapped himself from the blanket, helped Karen to her feet. Karen staggered, gained her balance, looked around. It was a dark, overcast morning, quite foggy and cold. She rubbed her bare arms with her hands, licked her lips. There was a grainy exhaustion and heat behind her eyes. Her mouth tasted sour and soiled. She thought suddenly of the big Havermann house, its quiet and its security, clean hot water and towels, food waiting to be cooked, and a sense of loss and desolation shook her. For the first time she seemed to see, in a material way, what Mrs. Havermann had given her.

She walked over to the car, not wanting Eddie to see her tears, and waited while he replaced the blanket on the torn upholstery. She noticed that Eddie had an air of confidence, of knowing what he was about, even of meeting a challenge, and this comforted her a little.

They kept headed north. When they got close to Oxnard Eddie said, "We've got to eat. We need every dime we've got with us, though. I'm going to try something."

I need a comb and a towel, Karen said to herself. I never knew you could feel so dirty, just sleeping out one night by the roadside. I feel as if I could soak for a week. She closed her eyes; the thought of food didn't interest her.

Eddie passed up several rather nice-looking cafés after studying them briefly. Finally he swung in beside a somewhat shabbier café, small, sitting by itself a little distance from the highway. There was a graveled lot growing up with weeds. The signs all needed repainting. On the roof of the café a metal vent had fallen over and lay at the rim of the rain gutter. Eddie cut the motor, set the brake, got out of the car. "Wait here," he said. He bunched his jacket over his chest against the chill air, went to the door of the café and entered.

The only person inside was a woman of about sixty. She wore a clean cotton housedress and a blue calico apron, a blue cap over her thin gray hair. She had coffee going in an old-fashioned pot, grease on a griddle, bowls set out with little boxes of cereal in them. Eddie spraddled a stool. "Cup of coffee," he said.

She looked out the window at the car, then back at Eddie. "Cold this morning, ain't it?"

"It sure is."

"Along the coast here, some days you'd never know what time of year it is. Just always foggy and cloudy and cold. Yessir." She poured coffee into a thick mug and put it down for Eddie.

Eddie said, "I'd like breakfast, a real breakfast, but I'm too broke to buy it."

"Well, that's too bad." Her tone didn't betray any interest or sympathy. She started to turn away, then looked back. "Who's that out in the car?"

"My wife," Eddie said.

"If she's cold and wants a cup of coffee, I'll give her one," the old lady said. "Free."

"Well . . . I do appreciate it." Eddie stood up. "What we need is pancakes and bacon and eggs. I sure wouldn't mind working for it if you'd let me. I could do dishes."

"Dishes are done," she snapped back. Then, as if relenting a little, "Say, you are kind of husky. How are you with a pick and shovel?"

Inwardly Eddie instantly shied off; he hadn't had any intention of involving himself in anything more laborious than an hour or so of pearl diving. But under the old lady's alert, somewhat cynical glance he found himself saying, "Well, maybe I'm no expert, but I'm willing."

She put both knuckly hands on the counter. "I'll tell you what happened. My husband—he and I run this place—he's been digging a ditch for the new septic tank out back. County said we had to have one, gave us sixty days to do it. Well, he's been digging every day for a week and yesterday he ain't feeling so good and today he can't hardly move a muscle. He's almost seventy. Shouldn't a done it at all, of course."

She was watching Eddie closely. Her mouth was pursed up now, her expression one of penny-pinching miserliness. "If you're hungry, you and your wife—well, there's a job for you."

Eddie put a dime on the counter and shook his head. "That would be a kind of big job in trade for a meal. Thanks anyway."

"Now, wait a minute." She swallowed a couple of times as if the next words were coming hard. "I ain't said just trade for a meal. We need the ditch dug. We got to get it dug, somehow. Them damned plumbers want four dollars a hour." By an instantly regretful expression, Eddie knew she wished she hadn't parted with this bit of information. She stumbled around then and finally said, "How's this—I'll pay a dollar an hour. Two days if it takes that long."

Eddie reached for the cup, downed the last of the coffee. "I'm sorry. It's not enough."

"Meals throwed in. You and your wife."

They stared at each other measuringly. She was the kind of little old woman, Eddie thought, that if she'd been left on a farm all her life wouldn't have known the time of day, but being exposed to the sharpers and chiselers among the touring public, was as sharp as a pin. "A dollar and a half an hour, I might think it over."

She came back instantly, "Dollar'n' a quarter. That's my top limit."

"Meals too? All we want?"

She peered out the window, probably trying to size up the girl in the car, wondering how much she'd eat. Eddie was big and, exposed to the labor of ditch-digging, could be expected to be ravenous. The little old lady gulped down some thrifty objections, nodded her head, and said, "It's a bargain."

Eddie hurried back to the car, opened the door on Karen's

side. "I've made a deal. We eat here. Order whatever you want."

She brushed back her hair and looked at him in a dazed, indifferent manner. Eddie, knowing how she must feel, urged her out of the car. "You'll feel a lot better when you eat. You'll be surprised at what some hot coffee will do."

A lot of anxiety went out of the old lady's expression when she saw how small and slender Karen was. She drew a cup of coffee quickly, put it on the counter, took Eddie's cup and refilled it. "Now," she said, "Ham and? Toast?"

"Pancakes," Eddie said. "Plenty of butter and syrup." He took off the jacket and laid it on a stool and saw the little old lady sizing up his muscular arms. He thought, We need a name. He remembered the name of a classmate in metal class, Arnold Dykes. He said, "I'm Arnold Dykes and this is my wife Kay." Kay for Karen. Karen glanced at him as if she hadn't quite caught what he had said.

The little old lady shifted the pancake turner to her left hand, offered her right to the girl. "I'm Mrs. Mosby. You can call me Ellie if you've a mind. Kay's a pretty name. You're a right pretty girl, too."

She seemed taken by Karen. Perhaps something in the girl's hunted, exhausted look touched her. When the food was put before her, Karen ate it indifferently, almost mechanically; but Eddie noted that her color was better almost at once, that some of the dazed look went out of her eyes.

They were finishing a third cup of coffee when a couple of trucks pulled in next to the place and four truck drivers entered. They were big men, hungry as horses; Mrs. Mosby scurried around, chattering with them, and Eddie saw they were regulars, the kind she depended on to keep the café in business. He was surprised, then, when Karen got up and took all their dishes out to the kitchen, found a rag behind the counter, wiped up.

He caught her wrist across the counter. "Hey," he said in a low tone, "you don't have to do that."

"I'd rather, than just sit." She went back to the kitchen and came back with a blue apron tied around her middle. The truckers were showing signs of interest, and Mrs. Mosby was openly pleased.

"It wasn't in the deal," Eddie said stubbornly, standing up from the stool. Karen looked at him tiredly.

"I'll make my own deal, then." Suddenly tears stood in her eyes; her expression seemed weak and sick. "Oh, Eddie, let's don't quarrel. Things are too bad to add that along with the other. Let's just be friendly."

He shrugged. Mrs. Mosby was pleased, and Karen perhaps would have something to take her mind off their predicament. When Mrs. Mosby had served the truckers she led Eddie out behind the café. The restrooms were here at the back, and the sewer lines from them and from the kitchen drains lay exposed in the hard brown earth. She indicated where Eddie was to dig, and how deep.

"Over there." She was pointing now to a small house, half hidden in a clump of young pepper trees. "That's our place. My husband's in there now, him and his lame back. He'll be watching you, but don't let it bother you. He won't get out to try to run things." By a certain vindictive tone in her words Eddie judged that she was somewhat put out with her ailing husband.

The morning passed slowly. Eddie took a coffee break about eleven. In the café a couple of Japanese truckers, their load of lettuce outside, were finishing coffee and doughnuts. Karen was washing up in the kitchen. Old Mrs. Mosby was as chipper and cheerful as a sparrow.

Why not? Eddie thought uncomfortably. Hell, the two of us working—she's got us over a barrel. Or thinks she has. A sudden strong dislike for the old lady came over him.

Close to noon, she took off across lots for the house in the pepper trees, and as soon as she was out of sight Eddie put down the shovel and went into the café. Karen was alone there, polishing the griddle. Eddie went to the cash register, pushed the no-sale button, and inspected the amount of money in the till. About ten dollars, he thought, mostly in quarters, half dollars, and dimes. He slammed the drawer.

"Now, what did you do that for?" Karen demanded, staring at him.

"For nothing."

"She's a nice old lady," Karen said.

"I didn't say she wasn't."

"You don't like it because I'm helping her, do you?"

"I don't care." Eddie was conscious mainly of boredom. The job in the back yard meant nothing to him. He stared out of the window at Skip's jalopp, the shabby little car, and wished he'd never stopped. At the same time he knew that what he was doing now his mother would call honest work, and she would never understand his dissatisfaction and lack of interest. In order to have understood her son his mother would have had to follow him through his whole life, first as a half-Mexican in a mixed school, belonging to neither faction, and then as a friend of Skip and being molded by Skip's opinions and desires.

Skip got off the bus in Reno, checked his suitcases in the station, and went out at once to look the town over. He had never been in Reno, though he knew it was different in some ways from Las Vegas. There was no Strip, for one thing, no long arm of luxury hotels and casinos stretching toward sucker-land in California. Reno lay close to the High Sierras, the Donner Pass country, and it seemed at once more of a frontier town and at the same time more compact and sophisticated, like a city. Once inside the gambling clubs, however, the resemblance to Las Vegas was startling. Here were the same vast ranks of slots, the identical green tables, craps, roulette, twenty-one, the same clang of coins and, for Skip, even the same faces, the expressionless know-nothing masks of players and club employees alike.

Skip turned in one of the hundred-dollar bills at the cashier's cage, getting tens in exchange. He went to a crap table, watched the action for a couple of minutes, then tossed three of the tens across to the dealer, who stacked thirty silver dollars in front of him. Skip put five dollars on the line. There were about a dozen men at the table. The shooter was an old fellow with the withered, weather-worn look of a desert rat. On his first shot he threw a seven and Skip's money was increased by five. Skip let it ride, added ten. Again the old fellow threw a five and a two. Skip withdrew his winnings on some psychic impulse, fortunately, for the old fellow crapped out on his next throw.

Skip went to the next table. When he finished there he was more than five hundred dollars to the good. Feeling hungry and thirsty, he headed for the café at the rear of the club.

In the cashier's cage the assistant manager was counting and examining the money taken in and took a second and longer look at Skip's hundred-dollar bill. He nodded to the girl cashier. "Wait a minute. Something I want to check." He took the bill with him, went to a door set flush on the wall, touched a button, and waited. In a moment he was admitted to an inner office, a steel-lined room built like a vault.

He took an FBI flyer from a desk drawer and began to study numerals on it and compare them with the numbers on the bill.

In the café Skip had just been served a New York-cut steak, Caesar salad, whipped Idaho potatoes, fresh green peas, and coffee royal. He ate dreamily, looking at the Gold Rush murals painted around the walls.

Eddie said, "Look, it's nearly five. I'm going to knock off."

Mrs. Mosby was drawing him a cup of coffee. "Sure, that's all right. You've done fine. Got a lot more digging done than I thought you would." She glanced at him anxiously as she put the coffee down in front of him on the counter, perhaps sensing his mood of disgust and boredom. "Tell you what, I'll close up about seven, you and your wife can have the place to yourselves. There's a cot stowed in the rafters, up above those shelves in the storeroom. It ain't much, just a double cot and a pad. I'll get you some bedding. What I thought, it'll save you the price of a room."

Karen was stacking dishes under the counter. "That's nice of you, Ellie." She hadn't looked up. She'd been acting funny, in Eddie's opinion, ever since the middle of the afternoon. Scared, more than ever. Dry-mouthed with fright, eyes big, hands quivering.

He noted a paper down the counter, pulled it toward him. It was an L.A. paper, and as soon as he saw the headlines he knew what was eating Karen.

RICH WIDOW SLAIN IN PASADENA
TEEN-AGER, WOMAN'S WARD, MISSING

Eddie glanced at Mrs. Mosby, saw she had turned away and wasn't paying any attention, and began reading the news article avidly. The information was scant but bewildering. The last Eddie had seen of old Mrs. Havermann she'd been in the door of the closet, stiffening, cooling, showing signs of strangulation but otherwise not marked up. Here in the paper it stated she had been found in a blood-smeared room, evidence of a savage gunfight all around her, and the cause of death was undecided.

Eddie felt as if his head whirled. *What was this?*

He licked his lips and read on. Stolz had told the police he had arrived at the Havermann house at around eleven-thirty, answering a phone call from Mrs. Havermann to Las Vegas. Mrs. Havermann's message, delivered to him at the hotel, had said that she was nervous over the possible presence of burglars. According to the paper, the police were quite curious as to why the elderly woman had appealed for protection to an ex-son-in-law as far away as Las Vegas, but Stolz stuck to his tale that Mrs. Havermann had lived almost alone and had grown eccentric. He had also informed the police of the disappearance of the young girl whom Mrs. Havermann had raised from the age of nine or ten. There then followed a good description of Karen.

There were photographs on an inner page: the Havermann house from outside, Stolz—coming out the front door with his hat up as if accidentally shielding his face—and a picture of Karen with braids at about the age of twelve. It still looked a lot like her, Eddie noted uneasily.

In a framed box was a detailed description of the girl, with an appeal from the police for anyone seeing her to get in touch with them.

The general belief seemed to be that Karen had been kidnaped by the robbers who had invaded the house, had had a gunfight, and had decamped.

Stolz said that nothing seemed to be missing.

Not a word about the money, Eddie thought. He put the paper down, tried to figure out what had happened. Stolz had his money safe, that was sure. He was keeping quiet about it, too. Then another hunch struck Eddie with dreadful impact.

Skip had been shot in that room. Stolz had killed him and

hidden his body, dumped it somewhere. Or else Skip was wounded and was hiding somewhere and perhaps dying slowly.

A terrific sense of treasonous guilt shot through Eddie. His course was plain to him. He would have to go back to L.A. and find Skip.

Chapter Eighteen

Mrs. mosby locked the front door of the café and clicked off all the lights in the dining area. She showed Eddie where the cot was, stuck up high in the rafters, the pad tied in a roll beside it; and while he was getting the cot down, setting it up and unrolling the pad, she went to her house and brought back two pillows in fresh cases, a couple of sheets and a blanket.

When she had gone again, when the bed was made, Eddie flopped on it and stretched himself with a sigh. "I'm beat. Chrissakes, I'm beat to the socks," he said. Then he looked around for Karen. She had disappeared into the kitchen. "Hey, what are you doing?"

"I've got to scrub and wash my hair," Karen called back.

Eddie lay and listened to the wet splashy noises from the sink, and then he drowsed. He hadn't worked so hard since the last time he'd been in honor camp, repairing the roads in a county park. He woke when Karen sat down beside him. She'd found an old broken comb, was using it to straighten her hair. She smelled fresh and clean. He lifted himself and pulled her close, loving the clean smell and the softness. Then he had to talk about what he'd read in the paper.

"I've been trying to figure it out. Stolz must have caught Skip and shot him, but Skip somehow got away. He'll need help; my God, he might be bleeding to death somewhere this minute."

A bleak frightened look settled in her eyes. "Don't talk about him. Don't think about him. Forget him."

"I can't do it." Eddie spoke in resignation, bitterly.

"We have each other," she said desperately. "We don't need him."

"I shouldn't have run away, ditched him like that. It wasn't any kind of a thing to do."

"No, it was the right thing to do." She lay down close to Eddie and tucked her head against his chin, and he saw the fluff of her hair against the dying twilight.

He pulled up her face, kissed her, forgot the tiredness and

began to stroke the soft line of her back beneath the slip she'd kept on as a nightdress. Then the discomfort of his own guilt intruded. "I've got to go back and see what's happened to him."

She pulled away, rose on an elbow. "What? What did you say?"

"I've got to go back." Eddie's brown eyes, so brown they seemed black, were thoughtful in his dark, square face. "It's this way. Skip and I—well, we were always a team. Always together! We never let each other down."

"I'll bet he's let you down plenty of times," Karen said in sudden anger. "I'll bet he's tricked you and left you out on a limb over and over again."

Eddie sat up; he felt irritated and insulted. Still, he couldn't blame Karen for being upset; she was young and inexperienced. He controlled the rush of angry words. "This is what I planned, why I planned it. Now look. We were going to sleep here tonight, weren't we?" Karen nodded; he went on: "So if I slip out and drive back to L.A. during the night, get back here by daylight, who's going to know about it, and what difference will it make?"

Karen had moved away to sit crouched at the foot of the bed. Inside the rayon slip she looked slim as a child, frail, defeated. Her skin glowed with a white shine under the dim light from the window high in the storeroom wall. "Please don't go. Oh, please, Eddie! Stay here with me. Or if you want, tomorrow we can go on somewhere else."

The tone was so desperate, so pleading, that Eddie almost relented.

As if sensing that he was on the verge of giving in, Karen rushed on: "If you go anywhere near that house, the police will grab you. I'll bet they'd grab you if you drove by a block away and even looked over at it."

"I wouldn't go out to *your* place," Eddie said. "What I'd better do, the first thing to do, is check with Eddie's uncle."

"You can do that over the telephone!"

"I don't know the number."

"Well, you know Skip's name!" Her voice grew higher, shriller, with every word she spoke.

"It's not in Skip's name, or his uncle's name. His uncle works for a man—I've heard Skip mention the man's name but

I can't remember it. I wouldn't want to put in a long-distance call anyway, asking about Skip. You know, if the cops are wise, the phone could be bugged, or the uncle even taken in on suspicion—oh, hell, anything could have happened!"

She flung herself at him, clutched him, squeezed so tight that Eddie was astonished at her frantic strength. "Don't go! Don't go!"

Eddie loosened her grip patiently. "Now of course Skip's uncle doesn't know anything about the Havermann job," he went on, thinking aloud. "So he won't know, unless Skip got to him, that Skip needs help. That's what I've got to do, get to him and explain that Skip's in trouble, must be shot up and ought to be found and taken to a doctor."

She threw back her head, brushed at her hair, looked directly into his eyes. "I know it isn't Skip who's hurt. He's too smart, too clever and quick. If anyone is shot, it's somebody else."

"It has to be Skip," Eddie explained. "Stolz is okay. The paper said so."

At the last Karen offered Eddie the one gift she thought would keep him, and he accepted it instantly and delightedly, loving her passionately for the offering of it; but when it was done he got up from the bed and put on his clothes and went out, instructing her to lock the door after him.

Thinking to cut some distance from the trip, he took the Ventura Boulevard route for San Fernando Valley, planning to enter L.A. through North Hollywood and Cahuenga Pass; and in an isolated part of the west valley, surrounded by walnut groves and areas of rocky hills, everything but what the headlights showed blanketed in moonless dark, the old car burned out a bearing, the engine exploded with a grinding breakage, and he was stranded. He was nowhere near L.A., had no idea what the next town might be or where it was. Karen and Mrs. Mosby's café might as well have been a thousand miles from him. All he could do was to wait in the car until daylight.

When Mrs. Mosby came over from her own place at about seven, Karen was already up and dressed, had the cot folded and stacked in a corner, the pad rolled and tied, the borrowed bedding placed neatly on top. She was in the dining room, stacking dishes. Coffee water was boiling.

Mrs. Mosby exclaimed with pleasure and surprise. There wasn't a lazy bone in the girl's body. She was young and pretty, the truckers would be attracted. Mrs. Mosby made plans to keep them here—and then noticed the absence of Eddie. "Now where'd he take himself off to?" She peered out through the front windows. "Car gone, too, huh?"

"He went over to see a friend," Karen said stumblingly. "Last night. He . . . didn't come back."

Mrs. Mosby studied Karen, saw that tears were just under the surface and that the girl was terribly frightened and upset. Had a fight, she concluded from her own experience, remembering the long ago years when she had been a bride, easily hurt and dismayed. "Well, we'll just go ahead and have breakfast, and he'll show up. You scold him good when he comes. Make him eat crow. Ain't every young fellow has as pretty a wife as you."

They ate. The food was hearty and filling. Mrs. Mosby emptied her change bag into the cash register, unlocked the front door, and the place was open for business.

Karen worked as if afraid to stop. She scrubbed up all the out-of-the-way spots, stacked canned goods in the storeroom, tidied the soaps and brushes beneath the sink. She seemed determined to keep her hands occupied, to keep thought, introspection, and self-concern at bay.

At about eleven-thirty Mrs. Mosby went back home to attend to her husband's wants. During this time Karen was alone in the café. A trucker came in with an L.A. morning paper. He left it when he finished eating. Karen read it in panic. Her description was boxed on the front page now, in large black type. Mrs. Havermann's death had been attributed to heart failure brought on by asphyxiation. Murder. A man identified as the intruder in her home had been found dead of gunshot wounds in a car some distance from the Havermann house. Reading this, Karen had an almost unbearable surge of relief, thinking Skip was dead and Eddie would know it and come back—but the paper's account continued, to say that the dead man had been identified as a middle-aged ex-convict named Thomas Ranigan, commonly known among his criminal associates as Big Tom.

His fingerprints matched the bloody ones found in the dead

woman's room and on her person. The police were now trying to trace Ranigan's movements on the night of the murder and to account for the accomplices who must have quarreled with him and shot him.

Karen felt almost dizzied by this crazy story which seemed to have no connection with the facts as she knew them. Eddie had made a frightening mistake in going back. Probably he was in the hands of the police right now. As the paper dropped from her fingers, the black-boxed description of herself seemed to boom almost audibly from the page: *seventeen years old, five feet three to four, slender build, dark brown hair, blue eyes, attractive appearance.* It never occurred to Karen that the items listed in the box could apply to thousands of other young girls. She felt picked out, spotlighted. She felt as if a million eyes, a million pointing fingers, searched out her shrinking body. She was convinced that the next customer to walk into Mrs. Mosby's café would recognize her instantly.

The place was empty temporarily. It was chance, perhaps her only one. She ran to the cash register, punched a key, removed a handful of bills, half dollars, quarters. She rushed around the counter and out the front door. Beyond the parking lot the highway hummed with traffic.

She walked, turning whenever she heard a car coming, trying not to look guilty and scared, trying to look like an ordinary girl out for a walk, needing a ride. She was in the outskirts of Oxnard now, among orange-packing plants, lots selling farming equipment, truck lots.

The big tanker began slowing some distance behind her. By the time Karen looked around, she could see that it was going to stop. The big tires spun gravel off into the roadside ditch, the brakes whooshed with a sound like a giant sigh. Then from the cab the driver was leaning across to look down at her. He had a heavy face, black eyebrows, signs of a beard beneath his skin. "Hey, kiddo. You going someplace? Want a ride?"

She nodded swiftly. "Yes, I want a ride. Please."

"Where you headed?" He smiled now, the lips drew back from his teeth, his heavy chin widened.

"Where are you going?"

"Don't care, huh?" He put an elbow on the rim of the cab window. "I'm headed for Salinas; from Salinas I'm taking a

load north. Eureka. Know where that is?" He smiled, waited;
but Karen was struck dumb, and he added, watching her curiously, "Three hundred miles north of San Francisco."

She said from a dry mouth, "That's fine."

She took a step toward the cab door and he put his hand
down inside as if about to touch the door latch there. Then he
sized her up a little more closely. Perhaps something young
and inexperienced about her warned him off. His look clouded
and he said, "Well, now, wait a minute." After a pause he
added, "That's a hell of a long trip. Sure you want to go so
far?"

He was stalling, she saw. She looked up at him. The heavy,
sweating face was like a mask hung in the sky above her, denying her, shutting her away from escape.

She tried to think of some way to convince him he should
take her, to force some hint of invitation and knowingness into
her eyes so that he might be attracted to her, but she was too
inexpert and too unsophisticated to bring it off. She could not
summon any coaxing remarks. She looked up at him mutely.

"You really got to go?" he asked softly.

She nodded.

His hand dropped to the door latch, and the wide door
swung out and for a moment she saw the wide padded leather
seat and his thick legs and his booted foot on the brake pedal.
"Get in," he said.

She took a single step on the gravelly shoulder of the road,
and then wordlessly she turned and, running, almost falling,
she went headlong back the way she had come.

Skip awoke and looked around the hotel room. He felt good,
in spite of the long hours at the crap tables the night before,
plus the drinking he had done after midnight in order to stay
awake. He rolled over, took the phone off the cradle, asked
the desk for the time. It was a quarter past ten. Skip asked to
be transferred to room service, requested a shot of Scotch,
coffee, and tomato juice sent up at once.

He crawled out of bed, inspected the roll in his pants pocket.
He had over seven hundred in tens, twenties, and fifties. The
remainder of the money he'd found in the Havermann house
was still intact. After some thought he took an envelope and

paper from the writing desk across the room, wrapped the Havermann money into the writing sheet and sealed it in the envelope, wrote his name across the envelope; and when the boy came with the whiskey, coffee, and juice, Skip tipped him two dollars and asked that he turn the envelope over to the desk with instructions to lock it in the safe.

Skip then lay in bed and enjoyed his breakfast.

He made plans for the day. Blackjack first. He used to be pretty good at it. An old con in the road camp had showed him a trick or two. But while Skip was dressing he became displeased with his clothes. Hell, they were rags. He postponed the gambling until he had bought a new suit, shirt, shoes, and tie. Then he hit the blackjack tables, three clubs one after the other, and by ten minutes to two he was broke. He went back to the hotel and requested his envelope from the safe.

He thought that the clerk handed it over with a glance of cynical amusement, knowing what was inside, thinking of the sucker being peeled of his money, and inwardly Skip cursed and raged.

He went back to Virginia Street and by chance, recognizing the façade, re-entered the club at which he had begun gambling the evening before. He gave the girl a hundred-dollar bill and she seemed to delay changing it, fussing with money in the cash drawer below the counter; and then, distinctly, perhaps because some sixth sense was tuned for an alarm, Skip heard a buzzer sound somewhere in the rear of the club, near the entrance to the café.

He put his face close to the grill. "Something wrong with my dough, sister?"

She met his gaze calmly. "No, sir. I've had to call for some small bills. The manager will be here in a minute."

Skip looked around. A tall man dressed in a tux, white shirt, black tie was coming toward him through the ranks of slots. He had his eyes fixed on Skip in a way which Skip recognized. He was memorizing Skip's face. Skip reached at once inside the cage, snatched his bill back, and turned for the door. "Just a minute," called the manager in a voice of authority.

Skip walked rapidly, bumping into people, shoving others flat against the machines as he passed. One old woman screeched at him, "You better watch it, buddy!"

There was a cop on the sidewalk, twirling his club; Skip went right past, not looking up, the bill clutched tightly out of sight in his palm. He heard voices behind him, looked back briefly. The manager was talking to the cop, his arm raised to point Skip out.

Skip opened his hand and took one incredulous look at the bright new bill. What in hell was wrong with it? There were no visible defects. If it had been counterfeit the girl cashier, long trained to detect phonies, would have spotted it last night. He glanced behind him, found the cop making purposeful progress in his direction. Skip darted into an alley.

It was not an ordinary alley. It was paved and walled with tile, bursting with neon light even by day, the entrances of several gambling clubs open, patrons idling there in the doorways. Skip started to run.

The cop shouted behind him. Skip darted into a club, worked his way across it, found himself at a dead end. There was no other exit on this side.

A sliding door clicked open and he saw the inside of an elevator. He rushed into it. The operator looked at him politely and said, "Sorry, sir, we're going down. Basement offices." His look invited Skip to leave before he was suspected of being a holdup artist.

Skip ran for the front of the club, out upon the sidewalk, across Virginia Street, down the block, around the corner beside a bank. Here was a cross street, not as crowded, no gambling clubs but cafés and small stores. He went into a souvenir store and pretended interest in some painted ties; and then in another two minutes the cop was out there, staring in at him.

There wasn't anything else to do. Skip grabbed for the little gun in his pants pocket, the tiny toy he had inherited from Stolz. The little gun spoke quickly and willingly, and a spray of little holes danced across the plate glass at the front of the store. The cop ducked. Something big and black sprang into his hand. The sound it made was nothing like the small *pocketypock* of Skip's tiny automatic. It went *booomp*.

Skip went down, clutching the rack of ties.

He had three bullets in his liver, one in his groin, and by the time he reached the hospital in the city ambulance he had only moments to live. A nurse bent over him, asking his name, his home address, and Skip spoke to her in return.

The doctor came toward the stretcher with a hypo in his hand. "What did he tell you?" he asked of the nurse.

"I can't repeat it," she said. "It was too nasty."

The doctor reached for Skip's arm, then suddenly for his pulse. But Skip was dead.

Chapter Nineteen

Eddie woke at about daybreak. He was chilled, his muscles stiffened by the long hours in the seat of the car. He had spent a lot of time in thought; and the conclusion, though he hated to face it, was that he did not have money enough to repair the jalopp, even if the old car had been worth it.

He hitched a ride eastward with a chicken farmer who had a pickup with crates of white leghorn fryers in the back. The old man chewed snuff and talked about raising pullets and the price of chicken feed and how much he got for chicken manure and feathers. Eddie learned for the first time, though he didn't think about it long, that chicken feathers were used for fertilizer.

At a roadside garage Eddie got out, while the chicken farmer waited for him, and rang the night bell. The mechanic stuck his head out of a window at the back. "Yeah?" Eddie went back there to talk to him. He described what had happened to the car, its age and condition, and the mechanic shook his head. "Tell you what, after I've finished breakfast I'll run out there and take a look at it. Won't cost you nothing," he added, perhaps because Eddie showed so few signs of having a bankroll. "Where you headed now?"

"L.A."

"Stop here on your way back to the car and I'll tell you what I think, what it'll cost to fix it, and if I think you might as well junk the heap, or what."

"Thanks a lot."

The chicken farmer let him out in Reseda, and on the far outskirts of the town Eddie caught a second lift, this time from an expensively dressed heavy man driving a Cadillac. The man had whiskey on his breath and proceeded to unload his troubles on Eddie. He had spent the night with his girl friend, and his wife was going to raise hell. She was getting ready to take the kids and leave, and he was scared to death she wouldn't even be home when he got there. His father-in-law was threatening to run him down with a shotgun. At the same time he couldn't leave this other woman alone. She was his former secretary, married to an airline pilot who was gone a lot. She had red hair and weighed one hundred and fifteen pounds and had been a New York model.

Eddie was glad to escape in Studio City.

He caught a bus, using some of the money his mother had given him. It was getting later by now, the sun was high, and he began to worry about Karen. She'd think he wasn't coming back. He should have telephoned from Reseda.

In downtown L.A. he tried to call the Mosby café in Oxnard, but the operator could find no number listed for it. Eddie recalled distinctly the big black phone on the wall at one end of the counter and told the operator about it, and she suggested that it may have been a pay phone and told him that such phones were not listed under the name of the establishment; there was a separate list for them and it would take a little time to check this. Eddie told her he couldn't wait and hung up.

By means of several bus transfers he finally reached Uncle Willy's home. He went up the stairs softly, rapped at the door. Uncle Willy didn't answer; but presently, from up there, Eddie saw him come out of the rear door of the big house at the front of the lot and throw some bread crumbs on the lawn for the birds.

Eddie went down there. Uncle Willy noticed him and stood by the back door, waiting.

"Is Skip around?"

"Skip?" Uncle Willy looked innocent and wily, his old face with its startling foxy resemblance to Skip turned up to the sky as if expecting something to fly by within his field of vision. "Skip who?"

"Your nephew." Eddie had never met the uncle before, but the family pattern was too marked to be mistaken. "I'm Eddie. You know."

"You're Eddie?" A touch of vindictive dislike appeared for a moment on Uncle Willy's features, to be smoothed away at once as if by magic. "Oh yes. Eddie. Been a friend of Skip's for a long time, haven't you? You boys have been in trouble together, lots of trouble." Uncle Willy came down the steps and faced Eddie closely. "Let me tell you just one thing. It's time to change. It's time for you to change and for Skip to change, to remake your lives, to give up the things that are going to ruin all the years ahead."

This was not the sort of talk Eddie would have expected, since he knew from Skip of his uncle's record.

"Now, Skip has gone," Uncle Willy went on. "He was here packing his bag when I got home from the A.A. meeting and I talked to him, as much as he'd let me, and then he left. I'm not sure how much of an impression I made. Maybe I didn't put it right. Maybe I should have waited until he was ready to listen. But now you're here, and my conscience wouldn't let me rest unless I'd told you a few facts for your own good." He looked earnestly and determinedly into Eddie's reluctant eyes. "The life you and Skip have led is nothing but a blind alley. It'll get you nowhere."

Eddie said, "Where is Skip, please? I wanted to make sure he was all right, not hurt, not shot up or anything."

"He's fine, perfectly fine," Uncle Willy said. "It was Big Tom was shot up. Skip sneaked over there, wasn't supposed to, of course, and heard it going on. Big Tom must of made a terrible booboo somehow. You just be thankful, Eddie my boy, that Skip eased you out of that job when he did. It could have been *you* on the receiving end of those bullets." With a final, emphatic nod Uncle Willy went into the rear porch and shut the door.

Eddie rapped on the door, full of anxious questions, but Uncle Willy called from the kitchen, advising him to go away and behave himself. Finally Eddie left the place, went down the block to an intersection, bought a paper off a newsstand, and read the account of the finding of Big Tom, dead in his car, and the identification of Big Tom as the intruder at the Havermann house. There was no mention whatever of Skip, nor of himself or Karen.

Eddie couldn't figure out this puzzle, but some things were obvious. Skip hadn't been injured. He had been packing to leave when his uncle had reached home. He had apparently heard some sort of shooting inside the house where the dead woman lay. Could it have been possible that some other outfit had planned to get Stolz's dough on the same night that they had?

Much confused, as well as relieved about Skip, Eddie set about the long chore of returning to Oxnard.

Anxious over the long delay in returning to Karen, he decided not to stop and see about the mechanic's report on the jalopp. He had a hunch what the mechanic had to say, anyhow. Something about throwing good money after bad—if he was honest, and he'd looked honest. Eddie bought a ticket on a Greyhound bus and rode straight through. At Mrs. Mosby's café he found the elderly woman working at a counter full of customers, Karen nowhere in sight. Mrs. Mosby jumped on him for leaving Karen so long, and between scurryings told him Karen was feeling poorly. She was in bed, on the cot in the storeroom.

When Eddie entered the storeroom, closing the door behind him, he could see Karen lying there on her back, face to the ceiling, eyes big and quiet, almost dreamy. She looked thinner, fine-downed. Mrs. Mosby had tacked some cotton material over the window, dimming the light, but Karen glanced over and saw Eddie at once. She said weakly, "I can't really believe it's you. I was sure the police had caught you."

He sat down, put his arms under her, lifted her close. "Not a chance. It's all over now."

"It's just beginning," she whispered against his face.

"*We're* just beginning," he agreed.

"No, I don't mean that. What I mean is, we're going back. I thought of calling the police here, but it might make trouble for Mrs. Mosby. And she's been kind. We'll have to go back to L.A. and get hold of a policeman there."

Eddie put her down slowly. His expression was one of stunned amazement. "You don't mean it."

"Yes, I do. As soon as I get over this chill, or whatever it is, I'm going to dress and leave." She was looking up into his eyes with a steady, earnest gaze. "Don't you see, what we were talking about in connection with Skip, that he wasn't grown up, that there was something in him that would never develop; well, that would apply to us, too, if we didn't go back and clear our consciences."

Eddie pounded his shirt. "I don't have a conscience! Chrissakes, a conscience to make you put your head in a noose, I wouldn't want a thing like that!"

"Yes, you do. And I do. We're grown up now, Eddie. We can take what's coming to us. Perhaps it won't be too bad.

Perhaps, a long time from now, we can see each other again."
She moved closer, twined her hand in his. She gazed at him in
a wholly new way, Eddie saw, calm and unafraid and utterly
loving. A convulsion seized Eddie; he thought he was going to
be sick. The thought of the cops, the questionings, the ordeal
of being charged and condemned and put away ran through
his mind like a leaping fire.

"You must have a fever," he said to her. "You're out of your
head. Crazy."

"No, I'm not. I've just got over being sort of crazy, I guess. I
thought I could run away, leave everything. Leave everything
I'd done, what I'd been. When you didn't come back I panicked;
I tried to hitch a ride on the highway. And then I saw"—her
voice sharpened—"I saw what my whole life would be from
then on. Just running. And not really getting away at all."

He argued with her. But nothing moved her or changed her.
And finally, in some way Eddie couldn't comprehend, some of
her assurance and the peaceful acceptance transferred themselves to him. He didn't try to fool himself about the actual
situation. It was going to be tough; God, was it going to be
tough! But since they'd be turning themselves in, confessing,
perhaps there would be something to look forward to a long
time from now. With everything wiped clean, paid up, no need
to run and hide.

He lay down close to her, and she stroked his hair and murmured to him. It seemed then to Eddie that the years he had
known with Skip, along with Skip's values and Skip's outlook
on life, dropped completely away so that for the first time he
was really himself.

Eddie's mother had spent a wretched, sleepless, and tearful
night. In the early dawn she arose, taking care not to wake
her snoring husband, and went out to the kitchen. In the
back of a cupboard, hidden from sight, was a box in which
she had stored some mementos of Eddie's growing up—
school cards and various items of correspondence garnered
through the years. Some she'd kept to reassure herself, good
grades, encouraging notes from teachers. Other bits she'd
retained to worry and puzzle over.

During the night she had decided, in view of the circumstances, to burn all of this material. In some way, in the future, something in it might be damaging to her son.

She took the box to the sink, brought matches from the stove, and then began to burn the cards and notes, one by one.

A handwritten letter which had worried her particularly, coming as it had from an official in the California Youth Authority, someone who had taken an interest in Eddie, caught her eye just as she set a match to it. The words were distinct on the white page.

> *. . . your son, I feel, is in danger of becoming a type of person called, in modern parlance, a socio-path. In other words, someone without moral sense in whom all ethical feelings are stunted. A man without compassion or con-science . . .*

The flame crept upward. She felt the heat in her fingers. She dropped the sheet into the sink, and it became crackling ash.

"Not my Eddie," she said, looking down at the blackened, curling remains. "I know better."

The page gave a final pop. She turned to the next item in the box.

On the morning of the third day the patrolman on guard at the rear of the Havermann house took notice at last of the anxious dog. He went to the rear door of the house and rapped, and Stolz interrupted his breakfast in the kitchen to answer. "This dog's hungry or something," said the cop. He was a young husky cop with alert eyes and a square, business-like chin. "You got anything to feed him?"

"I've been feeding him well," Stolz answered, regarding the dog with indifference. "He's just restless, I suppose, since his mistress is dead." Stolz wore crimson pajamas and a light silk dressing gown, oriental straw mules. He hadn't been up long. He was eating scrambled eggs with yogurt and stone-ground whole-wheat toast. He had made Marvitch hunt up a health-food store. In the store Marvitch had tried to become ac-quainted with the eighteen-year-old brunette clerk. "Perhaps you'd better tie him out beside his doghouse," Stolz offered. "Then he won't be in anyone's way."

The cop took the patient, anxious collie out to his doghouse beyond the garage, squatted inside the heavy blue uniform, reached for the chain attached to the side of the opening. Then he got lower on his haunches, actually put one neat blue knee on the dirt, and peered hard inside. "Well, I'll be switched," the patrolman said to the dog. "No wonder you were worried. There isn't enough room in there for your fleas." He wooled the dog's head with his hand, and the big collie jumped around, overjoyed at this show of friendliness. "What is all this stuff?"

The cop reached inside and pulled out a plastic pillowcase, zippered shut, which through its pink color seemed marked faintly green and white. The cop unzipped the opening and stared in upon what he had found.

He tried to say something, but his tongue froze.

It was money, an unbelievable amount of cold green cash, and finding it like this, outside a bank or similar reservoir, had the funny effect of making it look like a lot of printed paper. He jiggled it, and other packets came to view, all fresh hundred-dollar bills packed into pads of similar size.

He shoved off the bouncing dog, got to his feet, and with the plastic case swinging from his fingers he went through the kitchen to the phone in the front of the house, passing Stolz at the table on his way.

Stolz got quickly to his feet, went into his room, and dressed in nothing flat. Marvitch had returned to Las Vegas; there was no way he could reach him at the moment. Marvitch would simply have to look after himself.

Stolz was on his way out the front door when the dog met him, bouncing and barking, tremendously happy that these human beings had arranged at last a place for him to sleep. Stolz aimed a kick at the collie; at the next instant some instinct warned him to look behind him.

The cop was there, the money in one hand and an authoritative gun in the other. "You'll please wait, sir. Inside."

Stolz went back inside. He braced himself. He was sharp and fit and clear-headed, healthy as an ox, and it was surprising that a shock like this could make him feel so disorientated and dizzy.

He said to the officer, "I had nothing to do with the kidnaping, nothing at all; even the FBI will understand that. I just bought a piece of the loot." He shrugged and the motion almost sent him off balance, as if he were drunk.

"It's a hell of a lot of dough," the cop said.

Stolz looked at it shimmering with newness inside the plastic case. "Ruin and death," he said, blurting it out with melodramatic suddenness. "Ruin and death."

He put his hands over his face and began to weep.

BIOGRAPHICAL NOTES

NOTE ON THE TEXTS

NOTES

Biographical Notes

CHARLOTTE ARMSTRONG Born Charlotte Armstrong on May 2, 1905, in Vulcan, Michigan, to Frank Armstrong, a mining engineer and inventor, and Clara Pascoe Armstrong. Graduated from Vulcan High School in 1921. Attended Ferry Hall junior college in Lake Forrest, Illinois, for one year, serving as editor-in-chief of student publication *Ferry Tales*. Attended University of Wisconsin–Madison for two years before transferring to Barnard College, where she received a bachelor's degree. Took a job writing classified advertisements for *The New York Times*; later worked as a fashion reporter for the buyer's guide *Breath of the Avenue* and as a clerk in a certified public accountant's office. Published three poems in *The New Yorker*, 1928–29. Married Jack Lewi, an advertising executive, in 1928, and had a daughter and two sons. Wrote the plays *The Happiest Days* (1939) and *Ring Around Elizabeth* (1941), both produced on Broadway. Published mystery novels *Lay On, Mac Duff!* (1942), *The Case of the Weird Sisters* (1943), and *The Innocent Flower* (1945). Turned to suspense with *The Unsuspected* (1945), whose sale to Hollywood enabled Armstrong and her family to move to California; the film version, directed by Michael Curtiz, came out in 1947. Published novels *The Chocolate Cobweb* (1948), *Mischief* (1951, filmed as *Don't Bother to Knock* with Marilyn Monroe), *The Black-Eyed Stranger* (1952), *Catch-as-Catch-Can* (1953), *The Trouble in Thor* (1953, as Jo Valentine), *The Better to Eat You* (1954), *The Dream Walker* (1955), and *A Dram of Poison* (1956), which won the Edgar Award for Best Novel. Published short story collection *The Albatross* (1957) and novels *Incident at a Corner* (1957), *The Seventeen Widows of Sans Souci* (1959), *The Girl With a Secret* (1959), and *Something Blue* (1959). Wrote three teleplays for *Alfred Hitchcock Presents* ("Sybilla," directed by Ida Lupino; "The Five Forty-Eight," adapted from a John Cheever short story; and "Across the Threshold") and an adaptation of *Incident at a Corner* for the television series *Startime* in 1959, with Hitchcock directing. Later novels were *Then Came Two Women* (1962), *The One-Faced Girl* (1963), *The Mark of the Hand* (1963), *Who's Been Sitting in My Chair?* (1963), *The Witch's House* (1963), *A Little Less Than Kind* (1964), *The Turret Room* (1965), *Dream of Fair Woman* (1966), *The Gift Shop* (1966), *The Balloon Man* (1968), *Lemon in the Basket* (1968), *Seven Seats to the Moon* (1969), as well as the short story collection *I See You* (1966). Died July 7, 1969, of cancer in Glendale, California. Her final novel *The Protégé*

(1970) was published posthumously by Coward-McCann, publisher for all of her novels.

PATRICIA HIGHSMITH Born Mary Patricia Plangman on January 19, 1921, in Fort Worth, Texas, the only child of artist Jay Plangman and the former Mary Coates; parents divorced shortly after her birth, and she moved to New York City with mother and stepfather, Stanley Highsmith; grew up mostly under care of maternal grandmother. Graduated from Barnard College in 1942. Published short story "The Heroine" in *Harper's Bazaar* in 1945. Worked as a freelance comic book scriptwriter, 1942–48, including romance comics for Marvel precursors Timely Comics and Atlas Comics. In 1948 stayed at Yaddo, artists' colony in Saratoga, New York, along with Chester Himes, Truman Capote, and Katherine Anne Porter. Published first novel *Strangers on a Train* in 1950; rights purchased for small amount by Alfred Hitchcock, whose film version starring Farley Granger and Robert Walker was released the following year. Published *The Price of Salt*, a novel with a lesbian theme, as Claire Morgan in 1952; did not publicly acknowledge pseudonym until shortly before her death. Published *The Blunderer* (1954), followed by *The Talented Mr. Ripley* (1955), in which she introduced the continuing character Tom Ripley. Published *Deep Water* (1957), *A Game for the Living* (1958), and, with Doris Sanders, the children's picture book *Miranda the Panda is On the Veranda* (1958). Moved to Sneden's Landing, New York, where she lived briefly with the novelist Marijane Meaker. Published *This Sweet Sickness* (1960). Moved to Europe, living in Italy, England, and France. Published novels *The Cry of the Owl* (1962), *The Two Faces of January* (1964), *The Glass Cell* (1964), *The Story-teller* (1965), *Those Who Walk Away* (1967), and *The Tremor of Forgery* (1969), as well as a guide for writers, *Plotting and Writing Suspense Fiction* (1966). Returned to Tom Ripley with *Ripley Under Ground* (1970), *Ripley's Game* (1974), *The Boy Who Followed Ripley* (1980), and *Ripley Under Water* (1991). Published short story collections *Eleven* (1970), *Little Tales of Misogyny* (1974), *The Animal Lover's Book of Beastly Murder* (1975), *Slowly, Slowly in the Wind* (1979), and *The Black House* (1981), as well as novels *A Dog's Ransom* (1972), *Edith's Diary* (1977), and *People Who Knock on the Door* (1983). Moved to a small village near Locarno, Switzerland, in 1981, where she remained for the rest of her life. Published novel *Found in the Street* (1986) and the short story collections *Mermaids on the Golf Course* (1985) and *Tales of Natural and Unnatural Catastrophes* (1987). Received Chevalier dans l'Ordre des Arts et des Lettres from the French Ministry of Culture in 1990. In 1991 Highsmith's mother died at the age of ninety-five. Died February 4, 1995, of aplastic anemia in Locarno, Switzerland, at the age of seventy-four. A final novel, *Small g: A Summer Idyll*, was published posthumously in 1995, as was the short story collection *Nothing That Meets the Eye: The Uncollected Stories* (2002).

DOLORES HITCHENS Born Julia Clara Catherine Dolores Birk on December 25, 1907, in San Antonio, Texas. Published poems while completing graduate studies at the University of California; enrolled in a nursing school. She worked as a nurse at Hollywood Hospital, and later became a teacher before pursuing a professional writing career. Married T. K. Olsen, whom she later divorced. Married Hubert Allen "Bert" Hitchens, a railroad investigating officer, who had a son, Gordon (later founder of *Film Comment* and contributor to *Variety*). Together they had a son, Michael. As D. B. Olsen, published two novels featuring Lt. Stephen Mayhew, *The Clue in the Clay* (1938) and *Death Cuts a Silhouette* (1939); twelve novels featuring elderly amateur sleuth Rachel Murdock: *The Cat Saw Murder* (1939), *The Alarm of the Black Cat* (1942), *Catspaw for Murder* (1943), *The Cat Wears a Noose* (1944), *Cats Don't Smile* (1945), *Cats Don't Need Coffins* (1946), *Cats Have Tall Shadows* (1948), *The Cat Wears a Mask* (1949), *Death Wears Cat's Eyes* (1950), *Cat and Capricorn* (1951), *The Cat Walk* (1953), and *Death Walks on Cat Feet* (1956); and six novels featuring Professor A. Pennyfeather: *Shroud for the Bride* (1945), *Gallows for the Groom* (1947), *Devious Design* (1948), *Something About Midnight* (1950), *Love Me in Death* (1951), and *Enrollment Cancelled* (1952). Published play *A Cookie for Henry* (1941) as Dolores Birk Hitchens; novel *Shivering Bough* (1942) as Noel Burke; and novels *Blue Geranium* (1944) and *The Unloved* (1965) as Dolan Birkley. Cowrote five railroad detective novels with Bert Hitchens: *F.O.B. Murder* (1955), *One-Way Ticket* (1956), *End of Line* (1957), *The Man Who Followed Women* (1959), and *The Grudge* (1963). As Dolores Hitchens, published two private detective novels featuring California private eye Jim Sader: *Sleep With Strangers* (1955) and *Sleep With Slander* (1960); as well as stand-alone suspense novels *Stairway to an Empty Room* (1951), *Nets to Catch the Wind* (1952), *Terror Lurks in Darkness* (1953), *Beat Back the Tide* (1954), *Fools' Gold* (1958), *The Watcher* (1959, adapted for the television series *Thriller* in 1960), *Footsteps in the Night* (1961), *The Abductor* (1962), *The Bank with the Bamboo Door* (1965), *The Man Who Cried All the Way Home* (1966), *Postscript to Nightmare* (1967), *A Collection of Strangers* (1969), *The Baxter Letters* (1971), and *In a House Unknown* (1973). Jean-Luc Godard adapted *Fools' Gold* into the 1964 film *Band of Outsiders*. Died in August 1973 in San Antonio, Texas.

MARGARET MILLAR Born Margaret Ellis Sturm on February 5, 1915, in Kitchener, Ontario, Canada, to Henry William Sturm, who served as mayor of Kitchener, and Lavinia Ferrier Sturm. Attended Kitchener-Waterloo Collegiate Institute, where she studied music, graduated at the top of her class, and first made passing acquaintance with Kenneth Millar, participating with him on the debate team and publishing work in the same issue of the *KCI Grumbler*, but they did not remember this acquaintance. Attended the university of Toronto, majoring in classics. Encountered Kenneth once more in the university library, where she was reading Thucydides in the original Greek, and they began dating shortly thereafter. Married Millar in 1938, the day after his graduation from University of Toronto; she did not graduate. Had a daughter, Linda, in 1939. Upon being ordered to rest in bed due to cardiac problems immediately after Linda's birth, Millar read mysteries for the next two weeks and decided to try her hand at a novel. Published first novel, *The Invisible Worm*, in 1941 with Doubleday, featuring Paul Prye, a psychiatric detective, who later appeared in *The Weak-Eyed Bat* and *The Devil Loves Me* (both 1942). Moved to Ann Arbor, Michigan, in 1943 when Kenneth accepted an academic fellowship with the University of Michigan and quit his Toronto teaching job. Published *Wall of Eyes* (1943), featuring Toronto Police Inspector Sands, and a follow-up, *The Iron Gates* (1945), as well as a stand-alone novel, *Fire Will Freeze* (1944). Moved with her family to California, where Kenneth enlisted and served as an ensign in the Naval Reserves. Millar found work as a screenwriter, adapting *The Iron Gates* for Warner Brothers. The screenplay sale enabled Kenneth to quit his job as a teacher upon his return from the navy, and both husband and wife became full-time writers. (He would become celebrated for his Lew Archer novels, published under the pseudonym Ross Macdonald.) Bought a bungalow in Santa Barbara while Kenneth returned to Ann Arbor to finish his doctorate at the University of Michigan. Millar published three non-mystery novels, *Experiment in Springtime* (1947), *It's All in the Family* (1948), and *The Cannibal Heart* (1949), some of which were based on her childhood as well as her daughter Linda's. From then on, with the exception of the novel *Wives and Lovers* (1954) and the memoir *The Birds and the Beasts Were There* (1968), Millar published psychological suspense novels, all published by Random House and largely edited by the publisher's crime fiction editor Lee Wright. Published *Do Evil in Return* (1950), *Rose's Last Summer* (1952), and *Vanish in an Instant* (1952). Moved to Santa Barbara, California, where Millar would live for the rest of her life. Published *Beast in View* (1955), winner of the Edgar Award for Best Novel. Linda was involved in a fatal hit-and-run car accident in 1956, killing a thirteen-year-old boy and seriously injuring two others, but was given probation after a trial. Published *An Air That Kills* (1957), *The Listening Walls* (1959), and *A Stranger in My Grave* (1960), nominated for a Best Novel Edgar Award. *Rose's Last Summer* was adapted for *Boris Karloff's Thriller* in 1960, and *Beast in View* was adapted for *Alfred Hitchcock Presents* (1964). Published *How Like an Angel* (1962) and *The Fiend* (1964), a sympathetic portrait of a pedophile that was nominated for the Edgar Award. Linda died in her sleep on November 4, 1970, at the age of thirty-one. Published *Beyond This Point Are Monsters* (1970), dedicated to John Westwick, who as a young lawyer had represented Linda in the fatal car accident case. After a six-year hiatus, published three mystery novels featuring Hispanic lawyer Tom Aragon: *Ask for Me Tomorrow* (1976), *The Murder of Miranda* (1979), and *Mermaid* (1982). Published *Banshee* (1983); in the same year, Millar was named Grand Master of the Mystery Writers of America and Kenneth died of Alzheimer's disease. Published *Spider Webs* (1986). Beginning in the late 1970s Millar suffered from macular degeneration, which destroyed her eyesight except for peripheral vision. Died March 26, 1994, age seventy-nine, in her Santa Barbara home. *The Couple Next Door*, a short story collection, was published by Crippen & Landru in 2004.

Note on the Texts

This volume contains four crime novels published in the 1950s by American women: *Mischief* (1950) by Charlotte Armstrong, *The Blunderer* (1954) by Patricia Highsmith, *Beast in View* (1955) by Margaret Millar, and *Fools' Gold* (1958) by Dolores Hitchens.

Mischief was published in New York in 1950 by Coward-McCann, Inc. An English edition was published in 1951 by P. Davies.

The Blunderer was published in New York in 1954 by Coward-McCann, Inc. A paperback edition, retitled *Lament for a Lover*, was published the same year by Popular Library. An English edition was published in 1956 by the Cresset Press.

Beast in View was published in New York in 1955 by Random House. An English edition was published the same year by Gollancz.

Fools' Gold was published in Garden City, New York, in 1958 by Doubleday & Company, Inc., as a selection of the Crime Club. An English edition was published the same year by T. V. Boardman as part of the American Bloodhound Mystery series.

Each of the texts published here is that of the first American edition.

This volume presents the text of the original printings chosen for inclusion here, but it does not attempt to reproduce non-textual features of their typographic design. The texts are presented without change, except for the correction of typographical errors. Spelling, punctuation, and capitalization are often expressive features and are not altered, even when inconsistent or regular. The following is a list of typographical errors corrected, cited by page and line number: 16.20, humor.; 35.40, O.K?; 36.28, quickly.; 62.2, in negligee; 70.20, Jones."; 76.5, corridor.; 96.13, was hint; 97.37, apprehended.; 100.22, her."; 103.31, got.; 112.27, believe."; 118.32, get to her; 130.38, your; 153.29, Osyter; 215.40, self-consciousnes.; 221.33, scriptwritten; 310.33, glases,; 324.31, Deartment,; 332.10, her,; 359.29, eath; 364.13, cervalat; 387.16, jams; 399.27; pouring; 406.7, women; 420.28, is,"; 453.19, can, Verna; 462.13, Mabel was; 490.28, waist; 500.28, she; 517.32, cab her; 520.38, father.; 522.13, beside; 525.7, *Helen*,; 547.3, into in.; 547.21, next the; 549.17, recognittion; 569.7, insufficent; 573.7, met; 589.7, godamn; 589.35, thinks; 599.25, sqawk; 626.1, you call; 660.28, shoulders; 679.5, showings; 692.35, some some.

Notes

In the notes below, the reference numbers denote page and line of this volume (the line count includes headings). No note is made for material included in standard desk-reference books. Biblical quotations are keyed to the King James Version. For more biographical information than is contained in the Chronology, see Sarah Weinman, ed., *Troubled Daughters, Twisted Wives: Stories from the Trailblazers of Domestic Suspense* (New York: Penguin Books, 2013); Jeffrey Marks, *Atomic Renaissance: Women Mystery Writers in the 1940s and 1950s* (Delphi Books, 2003); John Connolly and Declan Burke, *Books to Die For* (New York: Atria/Emily Bestler Books, 2012); Rick Cypert, *The Virtue of Suspense: The Life and Works of Charlotte Armstrong* (Susquehanna University Press, 2008); Charlotte Armstrong, "Razzle-Dazzle," *The Writer* 66, 1 (January 1953); Joan Schenkar, *The Talented Miss Highsmith: The Secret Life and Serious Art of Patricia Highsmith* (New York: St. Martin's Press, 2009); Andrew Wilson, *Beautiful Shadow: A Life of Patricia Highsmith* (London: Bloomsbury, 2003); Marijane Meaker, *Highsmith: A Romance of the 1950's* (Cleis Press, 2003); Kathleen Sharp, "The Dangerous Housewife: Santa Barbara's Margaret Millar," *Los Angeles Review of Books*, November 28, 2013.

MISCHIEF

6.24   "Oh, dem golden slippers . . ."] Title of the 1879 song by James A. Bland (1854–1911).

12.2   Groucho Marx] Comedian (1890–1977), star with the Marx Brothers of *Horse Feathers* (1932), *Duck Soup* (1933), *A Night at the Opera* (1935), and other films.

59.2   "The time, the place, and the girl,"] Title of a 1946 film musical starring Dennis Morgan and Martha Vickers; the title had been used previously for an unrelated 1929 film musical.

THE BLUNDERER

136.1   *L.*] Lynn Roth, Highsmith's lover during the time she was writing *The Blunderer*.

136.2   *C'est plus qu'un crime, c'est une faute*] "It is worse than a crime, it is a blunder": remark attributed to Antoine Boulay de la Meurthe (1761–1840), on the occasion of Napoleon's execution of the Duc d'Enghien for his involvement in a royalist plot. (The original form is more generally cited as *C'est pire qu'un crime, c'est une faute.*)

137.7 "MARKED WOMAN,"] Film (1937), directed by Lloyd Bacon and starring Bette Davis and Humphrey Bogart, about a prosecutor's efforts to convict a mob boss who runs a prostitution racket.

156.20 White-Russian refugees] Russian subjects who emigrated during or after the Russian Revolution and Civil War (1917–22).

171.22 Boadicea] Early British ruler (died c. 60 C.E.), queen of the Celtic Iceni tribe who led an uprising against Roman occupying forces.

184.16 Medusa] In Greek mythology, a monster, one of the three Gorgons; her hair consisted of venomous snakes, and anyone who gazed into her eyes was turned to stone.

195.34 Blackstone's *Commentaries*] *Commentaries on the Laws of England* (1765–69) by Sir William Blackstone, four-volume treatise on English common law, widely used in America before the Revolution.

195.36–37 Moore's *Weight of Evidence*] *A Treatise on Facts, or the Weight and Value of Evidence* (1908) by C. C. Moore.

201.20 Scarlatti] Italian composer Domenico Scarlatti (1685–1757), best known for his keyboard sonatas.

215.8 34th Street terminal] Greyhound bus terminal built in 1935 in Art Deco style and demolished in 1972.

218.30 *World-Telegram*] The *New York World-Telegram*, founded in 1931 following the purchase of the *New York Telegram* by the *Evening Herald*; it became the *New York World-Telegram and Sun* in 1950, and ceased publication in 1966.

219.31 *Jonah*] Someone who brings bad luck to others; see Jonah 1:12: "And he said unto them, Take me up, and cast me forth into the sea; so shall the sea be calm unto you: for I know that for my sake this great tempest is upon you."

225.7 *Raffaele Gagliano*] Gagliano (1790–1857) was a member of the celebrated family of Neapolitan luthiers.

253.36–37 *Reich Mir die Hand, Mein Leben*] German translation of the duet "Là ci darem la mano" ("There we will give each other our hands") from the opera *Don Giovanni* (1787) by Wolfgang Amadeus Mozart and Lorenzo da Ponte.

274.11 "The Tennessee Waltz."] "Tennessee Waltz" (1946), song by Pee Wee King and Redd Stewart and a major hit for Patti Page in 1950.

275.29–30 Marquis de Sade's memoirs] The many surviving writings of Donatien Alphonse François de Sade (1740–1814) do not include memoirs.

288.4 Hotel Commodore] The Commodore Hotel, built in 1919, located on 42nd Street near Grand Central Station. It was entirely remodeled in 1980 and is currently known as the Grand Hyatt.

290.24 Penn Station] The original Pennsylvania Station, built in 1910, occupied two city blocks between 7th and 8th Avenues and 31st and 33rd Streets. The Beaux-Arts building was torn down in 1963 and replaced in 1969 by the current station, beneath Madison Square Garden.

308.9 *perron*] Stone block used as a step.

308.10 Vienna's Belvedere Palace] Baroque complex of palaces, built by the Hapsburgs in the early eighteenth century.

313.28 Encyclopædia Britannica] Originally published in three volumes in Edinburgh, 1768–71, the *Britannica* expanded to twenty-nine volumes by its final British edition, the eleventh (1910–11); subsequently production of the work moved to the United States, and the final print edition was published in 2010.

358.35 *Corpus Juris*] Multivolume legal encyclopedia, published by the American Law Book Company, 1914–37.

BEAST IN VIEW

381.1 BEAST IN VIEW] See the title poem from Muriel Rukeyser's collection *Beast in View* (New York: Doubleday, 1944). It reads in part (lines 9–16): "At last seeing / I came here by obscure preparing, / In vigils and encounters being / Both running hunter and fierce prey waring. / I hunted and became the followed, / Through many lives fleeing the last me, / And changing fought down a far road / Through time to myself as I will be."

382.2 *BETTY AND JOHN MERSEREAU*] Friends of Margaret and Kenneth Millar from Santa Barbara, California.

391.2 Down by the Old Mill Stream. Harvest Moon. Daisy, Daisy.] "Down by the Old Mill Stream" (1908), song written by Frank Logan Carlton and sung by Tell Taylor; "Shine On, Harvest Moon" (1908), song made popular by Nora Bayes and Jack Norworth; "Daisy Bell (A Bicycle Built for Two)" (1892), song by Harry Dacre.

392.26–27 at Scandia or the Brown Derby or the Roosevelt] Scandia, a restaurant on Sunset Boulevard that opened in 1947 and closed in 1989; the Brown Derby, chain of Los Angeles restaurants of which the first opened on 3427 Wilshire Boulevard in 1926; the Roosevelt, historic Hollywood hotel that opened in 1927.

403.39–40 *The mountain labored . . . a mouse.*] The figure is derived from a fable of Aesop.

409.19   Ava Gardner] Screen actress (1922–1990), star of *The Killers* (1946), *One Touch of Venus* (1948), *Mogambo* (1953), and other films.

428.18   Vine Street Derby] Hollywood branch of the Brown Derby restaurant chain, located at 1628 North Vine Street; largely destroyed by fire in 1987, the restaurant closed.

428.22   *Tempus fugit*] Latin: Time flies.

430.4   Dylan Thomas] Welsh poet (1914–1953) famous for his public readings of his work and his poem "Do not go gentle into that good night" (1951).

442.10   Princeton colors] Orange and black, official colors of Princeton University.

487.22–23   Biltmore Bowl] Dining room and nightclub in the Biltmore Hotel, located on Pershing Square in Los Angeles, built in 1923; the room was the site of early Academy Awards ceremonies.

492.6   Mecca] Club Mecca, on S. Normandie Avenue.

496.5   Camarillo] Camarillo State Mental Hospital in Camarillo, California, founded in 1932 and closed in 1997.

517.18   yellow jackets] Slang name for Nembutal capsules.

517.19   Nembutal] A commercial brand name for the barbiturate Pentobarbital.

FOOLS' GOLD

541.3   Sousa] American composer John Philip Sousa (1854–1932), whose marches included "The Liberty Bell" (1893) and "The Stars and Stripes Forever" (1897).

558.32–34   the Sands, the Sahara, the Flamingo, Desert Inn, the Dunes, Thunderbird] Las Vegas hotels: the Sands operated 1952–96; the Sahara opened in 1952 and closed in 2011, before reopening in 2014 as SLS Hotel & Casino; the Flamingo opened in 1946 and is currently operated by Caesars Entertainment; the Desert Inn opened in 1950 and closed in 2000; the Dunes opened in 1955 and closed in 1993, and after its demolition the Bellagio was built in its place; the Thunderbird opened in 1948, changed its name to the Silverbird in 1977 and El Rancho Casino in 1982, and closed in 1992.

606.16–17   old-fashioned Packard limousine] The Packard Motor Car Company of Detroit, Michigan, which began operations in 1899 and went out of business in 1958, the year of *Fools' Gold*'s publication.

677.20   Donner Pass] Mountain pass near Truckee, California; it is named for the party of westward emigrants who in 1846 were snowed in and suffered starvation and heavy loss of life, some allegedly resorting to cannibalism.

*This book is set in 10 point ITC Galliard Pro, a
face designed for digital composition by Matthew Carter
and based on the sixteenth-century face Granjon. The paper
is acid-free lightweight opaque and meets the requirements
for permanence of the American National Standards Institute.
The binding material is Brillianta, a woven rayon cloth made
by Van Heek–Scholco Textielfabrieken, Holland.
Composition by Dedicated Book Services. Printing and
binding by Edwards Brothers Malloy, Ann Arbor.
Designed by Bruce Campbell.*

THE LIBRARY OF AMERICA SERIES

The Library of America fosters appreciation and pride in America's literary heritage by publishing, and keeping permanently in print, authoritative editions of America's best and most significant writing. An independent nonprofit organization, it was founded in 1979 with seed funding from the National Endowment for the Humanities and the Ford Foundation.

To subscribe to the series or to order individual copies, please visit www.loa.org or call (800) 964-5778.

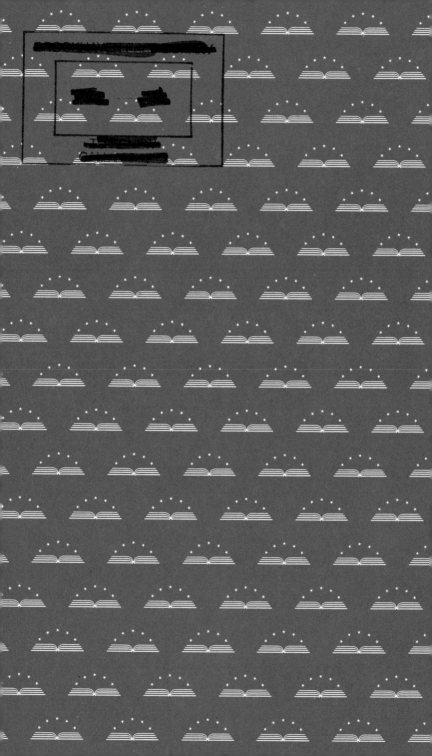